His hand glided down her elegant throat, paving the way for his lips. He wanted to kiss all of her, to taste her inch by inch, taking her between his lips, his teeth, nibbling and feeding his appetite for her.

Her nightgown parted beneath his fingers; he pushed it aside, baring the hollow of her neck and the soft roundness of her shoulder. He felt her tremble beneath his touch, heard a faint moaning sound and knew that she was as close to the edge of the great abyss as he was. He meant to carry her up and over with him, falling, falling, into a place where the hungers of the body would be met.

He was pleased to know he was affecting her with his caresses, drawing her into the swift currents of passion . . .

Also by Fern Michaels
Published by Ballantine Books:

CAPTIVE EMBRACES

CAPTIVE PASSIONS

CAPTIVE SPLENDORS

CAPTIVE INNOCENCE

VALENTINA

VIXEN IN VELVET

TENDER WARRIOR

ALL SHE CAN BE

FREE SPIRIT

Cinders to Satin

Fern Michaels

BALLANTINE BOOKS • NEW YORK

 Published in the United States by Ballantine Books, a division of Random House, Inc., New York, and simultaneously in Canada by Random House of Canada Limited, Toronto.

Library of Congress Catalog Card Number: 83-91133

ISBN 0-345-30359-8

Manufactured in the United States of America

First Edition: January 1984

CINDERS TO SATIN

Book One

Chapter One

It was a peculiar dark that fell over Dublin that night during the long hours before dawn. Damp mists, like the wraiths of souls tormented, hung low over the narrow, cobbled streets, their specter fingers stretching into doorways and rising to dissipate vaporously near the flame of the gas lights. There was a chill in the air, but it wasn't the kind of raw cold that was usual for early March. Tonight there was a promise of the coming spring.

A small figure dodged in and out of the shadows, running as though the night were reaching out to clutch at her. She carried an ungainly grocer's basket close to her thin body, struggling against the weight of it as she searched for a particular alley, praying to find it quickly so she could scurry into its obliterating darkness.

Callie James held her breath, not daring to make a sound, choking back the need to take in great gulps of air as she crouched behind an abandoned cart whose iron-rimmed wheels had long ago been removed.

The space between the cart and the back wall of a local pub was narrow and more cramped than she had anticipated, yet she dared not make a move to reposition herself. She listened intently and could hear them, her pursuers, running along the cobbled street, calling in muted shouts to one another, questioning for signs of the "filthy little robber."

The voices came closer, almost to the entrance of the alley, and Callie's heart beat a wild tattoo. If they came up the alley, she would be trapped, something she had not considered when choosing her hidey-hole. Fear gripped her. She felt her hair standing on end, and her eyes squeezed shut against her fate.

Even as she prayed, she cursed herself for her impetuosity. How had she dared to steal the grocer's basket that had stood outside the market awaiting delivery? In these poor times here in Ireland only the rich could enjoy such luxuries as this basket held. Even through her terror Callie could smell the sweet salty perfume of the smoked ham and the ripe aroma of oranges. And the bread. Dear God, the blessed bread! Huge loaves of round, crusty dough still warm from the oven. The temptation had been too great—the hunger too painful.

The penalty for stealing was death by hanging, a justice meted out under an English martial law whose tenuous grasp on law and order was maintained by making examples of felons. That's what she was now, Callie realized with shame—a felon. And if caught, no amount of pleading or claiming extenuating circumstances would save her. The grocer was an Englishman, that hated breed of men who sucked life from Ireland with their laws and edicts. While the Irish starved because of the potato blight, the English dressed in their finery and ate their fill each and every day. There would be no pity for her, no forgiveness from those who had full bellies and who possessed no understanding of starvation. Others had died at the end of the rope—men, women, and children. Only in punishment could the Irish find equality in the eyes of the English.

Boots scraped upon the cobbles, the sounds coming closer and closer. Now someone was actually entering the alley! She squeezed her eyes tighter, not daring to open them to face her horror. Oh, Mother of Jesus, why had she taken the basket? Callie thought of leaving it and making a run for it. Unencumbered by its weight, she might have a chance to save herself. Moving to put her burden aside, she heard the rustle of tissue paper, betraying the fact that there were eggs within. Eggs for the little ones. Food. That was why the unguarded basket had been such a temptation. Eight in the house and only her own poor pittance of a salary from the textile mill to support them.

Thomas James, Callie's father, had lain in bed for nearly two years complaining of back pains, malingering and defeated, refusing to seek even the lightest employment. Her grandfather, old Mack James, was too old to work, and no one would hire him.

Only her mother, Peggy James, had any backbone—in Callie's opinion—but her work at the mill had been interrupted by the birth of the twins. Owing to the lack of food and an unclean birthing, Peggy was a sick woman. Bridget and Billy, the two-year-old twins, and Hallie and Georgie, now eight and nine, and still another babe on the way, Callie thought in disgust for her father's lusty inclinations. Too sick to work but not dead enough to hinder him from putting another babe in Peggy's belly. And him strutting about like a cock o' the walk, with no thought as to how this new mouth was to be fed!

The heavy tread of boots brought Callie back to her immediate terror. They approached closer still; someone was indeed in the alley. She held her breath, her hands covering her face against the dread of seeing the grocer's plump, well-fed face when he reached through the shadows to seize her. One step and then another, the beat of a purposeful march. He finally reached the dilapidated wagon and stubbed his foot against it. With a mighty heave he tilted the cart, and Callie anticipated those heavy butcher's hands capturing her, holding her like a trapped bird, threatening to crush out her existence.

She heard the cart topple, and her hands flew away from her eyes in wide-eyed panic. Blinded by the sudden light of the flare he carried, she couldn't see beyond it to the face of the man who had discovered her hiding place.

A shout came from the street, calling into the alley. "Have you found the little barstard, sir?" It was the voice of the grocer, harsh and out of breath, yet Callie could not mistake his tone of respect when he spoke to the man with the flare.

The sound of his voice jolted her, so near, booming down at her, and it was a moment before she could grasp his answer to the grocer. "Nothing in here, man! Just an overturned dogcart!"

"Well, thank ye for your assistance, Mr. Kenyon. I wouldn't want to trouble you further on my account. The little thief must've run the other way. I'll get me goods back, don't you worry, sir. No guttersnipe is going to get away with six pounds of me best wares. There ain't another ham the likes of that one in all Dublin. It was brought in special for his Lordship, Magistrate Rawlings."

"Good luck to you then," her savior's voice replied. It was the most wonderful sound she'd ever heard.

Now that the flare wasn't being held directly in front of her, Callie was able to make a quick appraisal. His boots were knee high and polished to a shine. A gentleman's boots. The light buff of his trousers clung to his long, lean legs, and the whiteness of his shirt showed in stark relief against the dark of his hair and the rich cranberry of his coat. But it was his face that held her attention: the lean jaw, the smooth wide brow. The kindness in his light-colored eyes. His finely drawn lips twisted into a wry smile, lending a suggestion of cruelty that contradicted the expression in his eyes. No, not cruelty, Callie amended. Rather a strength of character, a type of righteousness, a possession of authority. "Mr. Kenyon" the grocer had called him, she now remembered. He lifted the flare higher, drawing it away from her.

Byrch Kenyon stood transfixed by the sight of Callie crouching against the tavern wall, defending her stolen basket. He had expected to find a dirty-faced street urchin with hard, defiant eyes. Anything but this terrorized young girl with her bright clean face and much-mended shawl. She huddled like an animal who has heard the snap of the trap shut behind her.

The glow from the flare caught the red glints in her chestnut hair and lit her pale, unblemished skin. A pretty Irish colleen. Large, luminous eyes; a firm, softly rounded chin; cheeks a bit sunken as were all of Ireland's children. It was her expression which struck him. Her full, child's mouth was set in a pout, her sky-colored eyes meeting his in a wide, unblinking stare. He felt himself smiling, no, laughing at her spunk. Here she hid, a thief, and yet she was flashing her defiance, daring him to present her to the Englishman's justice.

"Don't try to appeal to me with your sweet expression, colleen," he said sarcastically. "Regardless of how you plead, I'll not turn you into the law."

"If you think I'll be thanking you, you're sadly mistaken," Callie sniped in her soft brogue. She wished her voice were more steady and that her body would quit its trembling.

"Oh, I can see that," he told her, reaching to help her to her feet. "Gratitude would be too much to expect." Despite her shrinking away from him, he grasped her by the elbow and raised her up. He was struck by the thinness of her arm and her diminutive height. "How old are you? Twelve? Thirteen?"

Callie bristled at this affront to her womanliness. "I'm no child thank you, sir. I'll be sixteen in a month's time."

"Oh, that old, are you? Pardon, madame. And where, may I ask, are you off to with your pilfered goods? Or do you plan to stay here and devour that entire basket here and now?"

Callie looked at him suspiciously. "And why would you be asking? So you could turn me in along with my entire family?"

"I merely asked because you're not the only thief skulking around in the shadows of Dublin. You'll be lucky to carry that basket two streets without it being stolen from you!" His hand still cupped her elbow, and he could feel the tremors running through her. "You're shaking like a leaf in a storm."

"Does that surprise you, sir?" She jerked her arm out of his grasp. "I've just gotten away with my life!"

"Your bravado isn't the mark of someone who has just escaped with her life. Not the way your eyes flash and your tongue bites. You're a feisty young miss, do you know that?" He scowled, clearly annoyed.

"And what's it to you?" Immediately she regretted her words. He had helped her, and here she was giving him lip. Her mouth always got her into trouble. What if she angered him into calling the grocer? Or worse, what if he dragged her to the patrolling constable? As usual, words of apology did not come easily to Callie James. To show him her regret, she smiled up at him.

"Feisty and charming." He laughed easily, amending his earlier statement.

Callie could see his strong white teeth when he laughed, and she liked the way he threw back his head. He was tall, very tall, and his clothes were fine and well-tailored. He was a gentleman, no doubt about it. She understood why the grocer had spoken to him with respect.

"Will you tell me your name and what you're doing about the streets at this hour?"

"No, I don't think so," Callie answered, bending to retrieve her basket. "How am I to know you won't change your mind and turn me in?"

That seemed to strike him funny. "It's evident we're strangers. If you knew me better, you'd have no doubt of my opinions concerning the English Law we suffer. You'll never make it through the streets with that heavy booty, you know. You may as well leave it here and get home with you."

Callie drew herself up to her full five feet one inch, facing him brazenly. This was no time to back down. "I dragged it all the way here from the grocer's, didn't I? And at a full run, I might add. I'll make it home, all right, or die trying. I've a family to consider."

"A little thing like yourself with a family?" he questioned.

"Well, I do too! They're my own brothers and sisters."

"Come along, then. I'll walk with you. Just to be certain the grocer and his boy don't come back this way."

Callie hesitated and saw his logic. He was right. She wouldn't have to let him come all the way with her, just far enough to get out of this neighborhood. And if he tried anything with her, he'd be sorry. Her shoes were stout and their soles thick. He'd feel them where they'd hurt the most if he got any funny ideas in his head. "All right, I accept your offer. Seeing as how it means so much to you." He laughed again, and she scowled. Callie ignored him and picked up her basket, falling into step beside him.

They'd not gone a block when she was panting with effort. The basket must have weighed thirty pounds. Breaking the silence between them, he said, "If I tell you my name, will you let me help you carry your hard-earned goods?"

"I already know your name. It's Kenyon. Mr. Kenyon. However," she turned and dumped the basket unceremoniously into his arms, "I'd be obliged if you carried it a bit of the way, Mr. Kenyon."

"Byrch. Byrch Kenyon." He looked for recognition of his name but none was forthcoming.

"Any man willing to tell his name under these circumstances can't be all bad," Callie said. "Kenyon is a fine old Dublin handle. But Byrch! Why would anyone pin a moniker like that on a fine Christian lad? Hadn't your mother heard of good saintly names like Patrick or Sean?"

"And who says I'm a fine Christian lad?" This little piece of baggage had a mouth on her!

"You're Irish, aren't you? Or are you?" Callie turned and eyed him quizzically. "You speak with a fair lilt of the auld sod, but there's something else besides."

"I'm here in Dublin visiting friends," he answered smoothly.

"Here!" Callie drew up short, swaying her shoulder into his tall frame. "You're not English, are you?" she demanded. Not for anything would she associate with an Englishman.

"No. American. My father is Irish. I'm here in Dublin waiting passage back to Liverpool. Then I'm bound back to America."

"Well, at least I know you're not lying to me. No one in this world would admit to family and friends in Ireland during these hard times if it weren't so." And then she smiled, and Byrch Kenyon thought the fair sun of summer had lit the dark streets.

"If you won't tell me your name, at least tell me something about yourself," he said, hefting the basket onto his hip as though it were ho heavier than a lady's handkerchief.

"Callie."

"Callie what?"

"That's all you'll get from me, Mr. Kenyon. Why don't you tell me about yourself instead? Then I can tell my mother all about you."

"So, you have a mother. Back there in the alley I thought you were responsible for your brothers and sisters all alone."

"I didn't mean to make you think that, but you never asked about my mother. Hey! Watch where you walk! You've spattered mud on my dress!"

They were under a gaslight near the corner, and Byrch turned to look down at her. "You're a lovely child, Callie. Do you know that?"

She shrugged. "So I've been told. But listen here, you try any funny stuff, and you'll feel the toe of my boot crack your shins!"

Byrch smiled and made a courtly, mocking bow. She was a tough little scrapper, but he was beginning to suspect it was all a show. Probably she really was afraid he'd try something with her. As though his tastes ran to children! As though this little mite would stand a chance against him!

"Are you going to tell me what you do in America? We've only a little ways to go now." Callie deliberately softened her tone. Perhaps she shouldn't have said anything about him trying something. She was sensitive enough to know she'd hurt his feelings and upbraided his gallantry.

"I run a newspaper in New York City," Byrch told her, "and I'm trying to make my mark in politics there. So many Irish have come to America, and most of them have settled around New York. I intend to help them, to be their voice in government."

Callie stopped dead in her tracks and turned to face him. If he expected to see admiration in her eyes, he was mistaken. She had turned on him with a temper so fierce he felt as though an icy wind had blown him down.

"So, a voice of the people, is it? And what of the Irish here in Ireland, starvin' and sweatin' to earn a day's wages to buy bread for the table? The English know we're hungry for any kind of wage, and so it's not even a fair pay they offer us to slave in their mills and dig for their coal. To my mind, those Irish who left their country have no need of a voice in the land of milk and honey where the streets are paved with gold!"

"Times are hard for the Irish over there too, Callie. There's no milk and no honey and no gold for the Irishman. It isn't what it's cocked up to be, believe me. I'm doing what I know best and where I think I can help the most."

"Are you now?" Callie said hotly. "Don't be wasting your time and energy on me, Mr. Kenyon. Go back to your Irish in America and help them!"

She snatched the basket from his arms and ran off, leaving him standing there with an incredulous expression on his face. What had he said to make her take off like that? Then he realized they must have come close to where she lived, and it was the easiest and simplest way to rid herself of him. A smile broke on his face, and he laughed. "You're a fine girl, Callie. I hope we meet again."

Darting down an alley, taking the shortest route home, Callie hefted her basket and giggled. That was a stroke of genius, she congratulated herself. She'd gotten rid of Byrch Kenyon fast and easy. Confident now that she was safe from the hands of the law, she walked jauntily, and somehow the basket seemed lighter and lighter the closer she came to home.

Just as dawn was beginning to crack the sky, Callie turned down a pathway and could see the doorway to her home. A twinge of conscience panged her, knowing that Peggy would most certainly be lying on her bed, worrying about her. Peggy never liked the fact that Callie preferred to work in the mill from five in the afternoon to three in the morning instead of working the day shift, which ran from three in the morning to five in the afternoon. But she understood when Callie complained of slaving on the day shift and never seeing the light of day. Leaving before the sun was up and returning as it was going down made her feel like a night creature who never felt the warmth of the sun upon its face.

For the first time since seeing the unattended basket outside the market, Callie began to think of what her mother would say. Peggy James prided herself on doing the best she could for her children, raising them to have a decent sense of values. No matter how welcome the basket would be in the James's household, Callie knew Peggy would cast a dark frown her way when she questioned her about this magnificent windfall.

Callie tried to formulate a likely story of where she'd come by her goods, but soon gave up. Mum may be trying to raise us the right way, she thought, but it won't do her any good if the babies die from hunger before she has the chance to teach them to be fine and upstanding. Holding her head high, a twinge of shame and misery buried in her heart, Callie carried her basket into the damp chill of the two-room shack that housed her family.

"Mum, I'm home," she called softly, hoping to awaken her

mother and get the scolding over with in some degree of privacy. If she was going to get her ears boxed, she didn't want it done under the confused eyes of the younger children or the sympathetic gaze of her grandfather.

"Mum!" she called again, tiptoeing to the meager bed beside the woodstove in the front room. Looking down with distaste at Peggy and Thomas entangled in one another's arms, she nudged her mother's shoulder, bringing her awake.

Peggy James wrested herself from her husband's arm and rose from the bed with difficulty. Glancing down at Thomas to be certain she hadn't disturbed him, she tucked the thin coverlet closer to his chin with loving hands.

"Where have you been, Callie? Do you see what time it is? The sun's already come up." Peggy rubbed the small of her back. Her time was coming close now, and sleeping was often difficult.

"I've brought you something, Mum. But you've got to promise me it won't be tossed out!" It had only just occurred to her that Peggy might refuse her ill-gotten luxuries.

"Tossed out?" Peggy whispered. "Now what have you brought home this time? Puppy? Kitten? Good Lord, child, we've all we can do to manage as it is."

"No, Mum, nothing like that. I haven't brought home a stray since the blight began. It's on the kitchen table, but you've got to promise me you'll keep it!"

Peggy looked at her oldest surviving child and saw the tension and fright in her face. It was the same look that found the child in trouble at school or in the mill or just dealing with the neighbors. Some called it pugnacious, and others called it defiant, but Peggy knew it was just the way the good Lord had fashioned the child's face. Callie got that look when she was frightened of a scolding or worse. Peggy decided to make the promise. At least Callie would be able to lie down and get a few hours sleep before the little ones were up and making a ruckus. "All right, Callie, I promise. Now what have you brought?"

Callie led the way into the kitchen and pushed the basket over to Peggy, her eyes downcast. "Why, that looks like a grocer's basket . . . Callie James! Where did you come by this?"

"I took it, Mum. I just plain up and took it." Before the words could sink into Peggy's mind, Callie began emptying the basket's contents onto the table. "Look, Mum, bread! And oranges! Jelly and sweet rolls! Here, a chicken for soup and an onion and a carrot! But wait, Mum, wait till you see this!" She pulled out the smoked ham; its sweet tang filled the room.

"Callie . . . I asked you once, now you tell me the truth. Where did you get this?" Peggy's eyes surveyed the tabletop, already counting the number of meals she could serve. Her housewife's inventory went to the cupboard where she hoarded the last of the flour that would make dumplings for the chicken soup. One egg, two at the most, along with the flour and they could all eat their fill. The handful of dried peas would make a good porridge when the ham bone was picked clean. Her eyes scoured each item as it was presented from the basket. Sugar, tea, bread. God blessed bread!

"I told you where I got it, Mum. It's the truth. Now you promised not to toss it out, remember?"

"Yes . . . but, Callie! I thought I taught you better. I've never known you to take what wasn't your own. And now . . . now this!" Peggy sank down onto a straight-backed chair. "It's wrong, child. And you've got to take it back. This minute!"

"No, Mum, I won't. And you can't make me. I risked my neck for this basket, and I'll be damned if I'll turn it back now."

"This is a Godly house, Callie! Shame for your language."

"Mum, can you stop being a mother long enough to think? Think what this will mean to the little ones and to the one in your belly. It's not like anyone else is starving because I took it. It was packaged to be delivered to Magistrate Rawlings, and you know he's got more money than God, and he's an Englishman besides. And the grocer will just raise his prices to those who can pay. Mum, your babies are starving under your very eyes!"

"Near to it, I'll grant you, Callie, but we've managed to fill their bellies somehow."

"You and I, Mum. We're the ones who fill their bellies. You with your washing and ironing for the English officers' wives and me working in the mill. Well, the axe fell tonight, Mum. My hours have been cut and so have my wages. What will we do now? We barely managed before, and now we'll starve for certain."

"Something will turn up." Peggy ran her fingers through her rust-colored curls. There was a time when her hair had been her pride, thick and glossy, the color of the sun in its setting. Now it hung loose, already streaked with gray although she was barely thirty-two. "We're God-fearing people, Callie, and the Lord looks out for His own."

"Those aren't your words, Mum, they're Da's! He's always going around touting how the Lord will provide. It just ain't so and you know it! And where does Da do his touting? Down at the corner pub after laying abed half the day and eating more than his share."

"Callie, Callie." Peggy hung her head, her hand massaging her swollen belly. "I won't have you talking about your Da that way! Stop it this minute, please, for my sake."

Once having begun her tirade, Callie was beyond stopping. Even pity for her mother could not still her tongue. "The one who is provided for is Da. And who does the providing? Not the good Lord, I'll venture. It's me down at the mill and you leanin' over the washboard. At least Granda tries to do what he can with that little garden of his."

"It's your Da's back, Callie. Some mornings he can barely walk and you know it!" Peggy tried truthfully. "He's a man, and a man's got his pride. He doesn't want his children to think of him as a cripple. It's his own torment that he's unable to work and feed his family." Peggy wrung her hands in distress. She couldn't bear it when Callie took on about Thom's not supporting his family. Times were hard, and jobs impossible to come by. Was there no pity in the girl's soul? Didn't she see her father dandle the babes on his knee and sing the songs of old Ireland in the sweetest voice the angels ever heard? Couldn't she feel the love the man held for his family?

"How can you keep making excuses for him, Mum? Much less sleep with him. You no sooner give up nursing one babe and he puts another in your belly? Why, Mum? Why? How can you still love him?" Callie hated herself for treating Peggy this way—the one person she loved more than any other.

Peggy pushed her hair off her strong-boned face. Tears streamed down her cheeks. She realized Callie's anger toward Thom was born out of the fear of losing her mother while birthing another child.

In the dimness of the early morning light that filtered through the tiny kitchen window, Peggy walked over to her daughter and touched her face. In a soft voice, the voice she always used when speaking about Thomas, Peggy said, "When your time comes, Callie girl, you'll understand. There's something that brings a man and a woman together, and not heaven, hell, nor even a baby's hunger can change it. Makes no matter what he does, nor even if he betrays you. You'll love him, and he'll be your man till the day you die."

Callie's eyes strayed about the damp, chill room and fell on the two little ones sleeping just past the doorway in the next room, their noses always snotting, their deep-set eyes cavernlike in their thin faces. "Well, I'll not be like you, Mum. You can be sure of that. My head will never be turned by a handsome face and a strong back, even if he does sing with the voice of an angel! It's my head that'll rule my life, not my heart!"

Peggy watched her best-loved daughter's pretty face flush with the heat of her words. With a deep sigh, Peggy reached out to touch the girl and gazed somberly into her Irish blue eyes. "Well spoken, darlin', and well meant. But sometimes one must listen to the heart, for not to would be to miss the best life has to offer. Oh, it may be mingled with tears, but I'll vouch you, it's still the best."

Callie looked up into her mother's face and then buried her head against the round belly. Throughout her life Callie would think of this moment and bitterly yearn for that headstrong, willful young girl, and wish she had heeded her own words.

Chapter Two

The sound of voices awakened seven-year-old Hallie. The little girl came out to the kitchen, sleep-heavy eyes immediately brightening when she saw Callie. "Hullo, Callie. Are you going to take us for a walk later? Are you, Callie? You promised."

"Come here, sweet." Callie smiled fondly at the child whose rumpled nightdress was growing so small that her thin legs were bare from the knee down. "Give us a kiss." The child hurried over to her older sister, smiling shyly with delight.

"Are you, Callie? Can the twins and Georgie come, too?"

Picking Hallie up onto her lap, Callie nuzzled the softness under the child's chin. Tousling Hallie's bright golden curls, she hugged and kissed her soundly. Poor little thing, Callie thought, half-starved all the time and still with a disposition sweet as sugar. "Sure, love, I'll take you for a walk. But you'll have to wait till later. Hurry up now and go wake up the twins and Georgie; I've brought you a special surprise. Go on, now." She put Hallie back on the floor. "And wake Granda and Da. This surprise is for them, too."

Avoiding Peggy's angry stare, Callie directed her attention to Hallie as the child asked, "A surprise, Callie? What kind of surprise? Did you buy me a candy? I love candy. Did you bring one for Georgie, too?" Hallie's little girl's voice tugged at Callie's heart. Candy! When it was all they could do to buy the making for thin gruel and now and then a piece of fatback.

"No candy this morning, darlin'. But you'll like this much more. Hush now, no more questions. Go and get everyone up."

Hallie rushed into the next room, and Callie lifted her eyes to Peggy. She went and put her arms around the woman's thin shoulders. "What's done is done, Mum. No use thinking about it now. Come now, they'll all be in here in a minute. Best get the kettle on the hob and help me slice this ham. If I'm not mistaken, there are eggs at the bottom of the basket. I only hope there's enough for the little ones."

"Callie, don't be thinkin' me ungrateful. I'm not. I know how you try for the family. I only worry for you."

"I know, Mum. And I promise to resist temptation in the future. I doubt we'll have a windfall the likes of this again. So let's enjoy it, right?"

Peggy broke out into a grin. "Well, I guess there's no help for it, is there?" She went to the hearth and stoked the fire in the grate, hanging a kettle of water onto the hob. "I declare your Da's eyes will bug right out of his head when he sees this fare. Callie, do you think there's an extra egg for him?"

Opening the tissue paper that protected the eggs, Callie found there were half a dozen. For herself, she didn't care if she had an egg or not, but she sighed and resigned herself to the fact that although Peggy needed the nourishment more than anyone, the twins included, she would without a doubt forego the egg and give it to Thom. Well, the ham was plenty big enough, and hadn't the grocer said there wasn't another like it in all Dublin?

"What'll we tell Da and Granda where I came by this?" Callie asked as she unpacked the oranges and bread.

"It's your deed, Callie girl, so I guess it must be your lie. Tell as close to the truth as you can." Peggy's face pinched with worry. Hungry as she was and as much as she realized her children needed the food, she wondered if she would be able to swallow it. Callie had risked her life, literally, to help her family. The girl's heart had been in the right place. Still, punishment for stealing was met at the end of a rope.

Callie whispered, "Don't worry, Mum. It'll be all right, I promise you. Later I'll tell you about this man who helped me."

"A man?" Peggy's eyebrows shot up with worry.

"He'll keep the secret, Mum. It's Aunt Sara I'm worried about. Don't whisper a word of this to her," Callie warned. "Not that she'll do without anything, not the way Uncle Jack consorts with the English. I wouldn't want her turnin' me in just to put herself in good stead with her fancy English friends."

"Callie," Peggy said, "where's the love I've taught you for your family? Aunt Sara won't know a thing about this. When she brings her ironing this afternoon, you'll have taken the children for their walk. I wouldn't want her to know my own girl took to thievery to put food on the table. I'm that ashamed." Not for anything would Peggy admit that Callie's suspicions concerning her own sister had their foundations in truth.

Granda shuffled into the kitchen, his rheumy gray eyes falling immediately to the rough table where Callie, his favorite grandchild, was unloading the basket. "And what's this? Have you found the Little People's pot o' gold, child? Never have I seen such wondrous goods. Not even the time when me own Da came home from selling the cow to market and brought us a feast meant for kings!" Granda moved about the table, smelling the oranges and lifting his gaze heavenward to express his delight. He continued with his story of his own father and his brothers and sisters, his words falling on deaf ears. Granda was getting on in his years, and his mind sometimes wandered. They'd all heard the story before.

Georgie and the twins, along with Hallie, stood near the table in hungry anticipation. "Now you children keep your hands to yourselves until I've found time to prepare a proper meal," Peggy scolded.

"Aw, Mum. Just a bite of bread won't hurt," Callie defended, tearing off a chunk of bread for each of them. Bridget and Billy, the twins, stuffed the whole of it into their mouths, their eyes rolling in delight. Hallie and Georgie, following suit, resembled two golden-haired chipmunks.

Thomas James strolled into the kitchen, both arms behind him, rubbing the small of his back. His tall, lean frame was stooped over at the waist, and a wince of pain dissolved suddenly as little Bridget ran up to him, demanding to be lifted into his arms. Callie saw the streaks of white at her Da's temples and wondered if they had appeared overnight. Or was she suddenly seeing him as if for the first time? Mum was right, he did look ill.

Upon Thom's entrance, Peggy immediately brightened. "How are you this mornin', love? Look what Callie's brought us. A nice boiled egg will lift your spirits, I'll grant you."

Thomas's blue eyes, so much like Callie's, twinkled. "You're a lift to my spirits, love." He wrapped his arms around Peggy and kissed her soundly on the cheek.

"Put me aside, man. Can't you see I've got cooking to do?" Peggy's eyes went to Callie, knowing the moment had come for the girl to explain her offering.

"Where did you come by it, girl?" Thomas asked. "Have you been rolling bones outside McDonough's Pub with the rest of the fools who gamble a week's wages on the throw of the dice?" Thomas was teasing, knowing Callie was much too thrifty to risk her money in a game of chance. Still, his eyes found hers and would not release them until she answered.

"It was a shameful thing I did, Da. There was this basket, all stuffed with the best groceries in all Dublin, and no one was near it. No one! A basket, filled with food during these hard times, and no one to watch it. It was just begging for me to bring it home. So I did." Thomas looked at his oldest daughter. He'd never known her to lie, but her tale was close to unbelievable.

"I ask you, Da. Would you have left a basket such as this without a care as to who might pick it up and bring it home to their poor little brothers and sisters?"

"Enough, Callie. I don't want to hear any more. If you say the basket was left, then it was, and I'll not doubt you. The James' family is certain to come into a little luck every now and then. It's the law of averages, I'd say." Still, Thomas's gaze did not leave her until one of the children begged to sit on his lap. Sitting down and lifting Billy onto his knee, Thomas turned to Peggy. "I think it's best, love, that we not tell your sweet sister Sara about our good fortune." There was a knowing look about him as he spoke. "I wouldn't want the poor deprived woman to be jealous of the likes of us Jameses."

Hallie giggled. "Oh, Da, how could Aunt Sara be jealous of us? She lives in that fine house, and look at the pretty clothes she wears. And Uncle Jack is always jingling pennies in his pocket . . ."

"And why shouldn't she be jealous of us?" Thom pretended to scold. "We've got our own little Hallie, named for the beauteous Helen of Troy herself. And we've got Bridget, sweet as the saint in flesh." He chucked the babe under the chin and made her giggle. "Oh, and of course we've got Billy. Now I ask you, does your Aunt Sara have a fine big boy like our Billy? And Georgie. Named him for Granda, your mum and me did. And ain't he a fine, strapping lad? Smart with numbers and letters, too." Thomas rose from the chair and went to take Callie into his arms. "And none in all of Ireland, or elsewhere for that matter, has our Callie.

Named her for a great lady I once knew when I traveled to London. A great lady. Kind and lovin' and forgivin'. Callandre was her proper name. Aw, but you were such a wee one it seemed too large a name to fit you."

Callie turned in her father's arms, laying her head against his chest. Tears swam in her eyes. She did love her Da. She did. If only he hadn't put another babe in her mum's belly. If only he would try harder to find work.

Resting his chin on Callie's head, he began to croon to her, a sweet, lilting melody she remembered from when she was a little girl. "Ah, Callie, no matter how old you get and no matter what you think of your old Da, you're still my girl and I love you."

A shudder went through Callie as she leaned against Thom, burying her face into his shirtfront. God help her, she was as weak as her mother when it came to loving him. And God save her from ever loving another man just like him!

Callie bustled the children out of the tiny row house on McIver Street, grasping the twins, Bridget and Billy, by the hands. It seemed to Callie that for the first time in months the children were bright-eyed and rosy-cheeked. She knew it was impossible that hunger and privation could be assuaged by one meal, yet it gave her a kind of peace, temporary though it might be, to know that the little ones were free from the hollow cramps of hunger.

Georgie and Hallie walked together, excited about this rare outing with their older sister. They should be in school, Callie thought bitterly. Peggy's effort to teach them their letters was squeezed between cleaning the house and laundering the fancy clothes the English officers' wives sent to her, not to mention Aunt Sara's frilly petticoats and bloomers, done for half price seeing as how she was family.

Most of the public schools in Ireland had closed as a direct result of the potato blight. Towns and cities suffered for taxes, and there was no money to pay teachers. The usual education of Ireland's working class children had been sketchy and of short duration. When a child reached the age of ten, he was sent to work in the mills or a related industry. Callie herself had enjoyed the benefits of an education until she was nearly fourteen. Times had been better then; Thomas had held a regular position at the mill, and Granda had been a steady contributor to the family from his job as all-around man for several shops along Blakling Street. It wasn't until just before the twins were born, in 1845, that the first potato crop had failed. The crops had failed ever since, and that was three years now. Lord only knew what the next crop would bring. English and Irish newspapers were already calling it the Great Famine, but naming it and living it were two different things, as Callie well knew. What she didn't know were the reasons.

Ireland's population had risen sharply during the sixty or so years prior to the potato failure. Land, which had always been scarce, had become almost impossible to obtain. Even the smallest plots that would hardly yield a living were unavailable to the common man. Irish peasants led a hand-to-mouth existence. It was common to see beggars on country lanes and city streets. Employment was so scarce and so poorly paid in Ireland that enterprising men left the country to find labor jobs in England after planting their potato crop, returning only after the harvest.

The introduction of the Corn Laws in 1846 further reduced the small number of land holdings. These laws prompted landlords to turn into pasture much of the land that had been used to produce grain, and in so doing, forced numbers of Irish peasants off their rented land into utter destitution.

Because so many Irish had so little land, there was urgent need for a staple crop whose seed was cheap and simple to plant, whose harvest was easy and would feed them for months afterward. The potato, only minimally nutritious, met most of these requirements. Supplemented with buttermilk, it became the dominant crop and staple diet of the Irish. But there was great danger in being totally reliant upon the potato.

Because it was subject to spoilage and because almost no one had land enough to harvest a year's supply of food, peasants were often compelled to go into debt to live at the barest level of subsistence. There was no substitute for the potato in the event of a harvest failure, and most Irish would be unable to buy food if such a disaster should happen. When the insect that brought the potato blight struck with its full force in 1845, tragedy was the result.

But some people never seemed to have to do without, Callie thought as she hurried the children along McIver Street. Some like Aunt Sara and Uncle Jack and their precious only child, Colleen. That was why she had had to take the children out this afternoon—to avoid their telling Aunt Sara about the grocer's basket. Aunt Sara would naturally draw her own conclusions about the windfall's origins. Much as Mum refused to admit it, Aunt Sara was quite comfortable with the hard luck of the James's family, and even took haughty pleasure in Peggy's tribulations.

If only Peggy hadn't knocked out so many children, Aunt Sara was fond of saying in mild rebuke. If only she'd chosen a smart, enterprising man like Uncle Jack instead of a handsome rogue like Thom James. If only they'd learned to put enough by to see them through the hard times. If only, if only!

Callie pulled the twins along beside her at a pace that was almost too fast for their little legs. What would Aunt Sara know about it? She who had married that mewling Jack O'Brien just because he owned a dry goods store. And Colleen, that prissy-arsed twit! Her, with her fancy lace drawers and nose-in-the-air manner. What would Colleen know about going to sleep hungry and hearing her stomach growl all the night through? Not Colleen with her handsome English soldier who led her about on his arm as though she were a grand duchess while Aunt Sara glowed with pride.

Things hadn't always been rosy for the O'Briens. There was a time when they were no better off than the Jameses. But since hard times fell on the land and droves of English soldiers and their families poured into Ireland to "guard the order of the land," Uncle Jack's business had soared. The English had money to spend, and Aunt Sara and Uncle Jack waited with palms open. That the English were a hated reminder of Ireland's subservience to Great Britain and in turn dealt with the Irish with a harsh type of justice meant nothing at all to the O'Briens. As long as their shop was frequented by those who had money, they would have served the devil himself. And as far as Callie was concerned, they did.

Rounding off McIver Street onto Bayard, Callie gripped the twins' hands tightly to her sides. Horse-drawn wagons and push-carts crowded the street, adding their noise to the calls of the peddlers and the general commotion of shoppers and workers and the men lingering outside Melrose's Tavern. Women with dark shawls pulled over their heads bustled along, guarding their baskets of goods and keeping a watchful eye for roving bands of street arabs who were quick of hand and fleet of foot in their intent to separate a woman from her hard-earned purchases, her purse, or even the very shoes from her feet.

Bridget tugged at the skirt of Callie's brown linsey-woolsey dress, a castoff from cousin Colleen. "Walk slower, Callie, I can't keep up!"

"All right, then. Just a little slower until we get over onto Florham Way." Callie was eager to cross Bayard Street onto the relative quiet of Florham Way where just a few streets down there was a park where the children could play. This was the way she had run home earlier that morning, after snatching her basket out of the arms of Mr. Kenyon.

Florham Way was a double-wide street that made traffic for the carts and carriages more orderly. Trees, still skeletal in these early weeks of March, nevertheless held a hint of green, a promise of spring. Hallie and Georgie followed close on their sister's heels past rag shops and cobblers. Callie could remember when flower shops and glove shops and milliners lined the street, but in these hard times a body couldn't eat flowers, and there was no money for gloves and hats. She'd heard stories of poor folk out in the countryside who had taken to eating roots and grasses, only to die for their efforts. Callie shivered at the thought. It seemed to her that she never thought of anything else these days except food and where it would come from. Seeing her little brothers and sisters with their scrubbed and shining faces walking beside her, their heads lifted and happily teasing one another, she was glad she'd stolen the groceries. At least their bellies were full and they could laugh and play. Callie was glad she had taken the basket, and if the opportunity presented itself, she'd not hesitate to take another.

Georgie and Hallie ran across the brown, stubby grass to play along a cindered path atop a bulkhead on the waterfront. The waters of the Irish Sea were wind-chafed, rolling endlessly toward shore, pushed by the salty breezes. The sun shone warm, dancing in diamond reflections off the sea, and out in the distance there were freighters and schooners, making their way to Dublin's wharves. This was Georgie's favorite place. He always claimed, with the intensity of a seven year old, that one day he would become a sailor and be off to see the world.

Bridget and Billy searched the mottled turf for an elusive four-leaf clover. Granda had convinced the children that if they found a four-leaf clover, it would point the way to the hiding place of leprechauns, and there they would find the pot of gold.

Callie frowned, her finely drawn brows wrinkling over the bridge of her saucily tilted nose. Georgie wanting to see the world, the twins searching for a pot of gold. It was all the same to her. There was no pot of gold, and she'd never see any more of the world than Dublin and the long, austere rows of houses on McIver Street.

Bridget's light golden curls lifted on the brisk March wind. Her drab green woolen dress needed patching at the sleeve. Billy would be needing his shoes resoled before long. There was no escaping the worry, the everlasting sense of responsibility she felt toward them. Yet at the same time there was an anger, a hostility that she should have to take on such a burden.

The sun shone down on the mud flats exposed by low tide. The overripe smell of rotting vegetation and decaying fish caught in the swing of tide wrinkled Callie's nose. Huge gray boulders, exposed now, stood starkly against the dark waters of the Irish Sea. Georgie would dearly love to race across the mud flats the way he could in summer. Summer, only months away, and yet no nearer than a lifetime. Summer would come, and with it, Peggy's new babe. A new James child, a new responsibility. And what hope was there for it? Could Billy or Georgie grow to be fine, educated gentlemen like her savior from the night before, Mr. Byrch Kenyon? Would their shoulders ever be as broad, and would they wear fine cranberry velvet coats? No, she thought not.

Callie had been trying to forget Byrch Kenyon ever since she'd run away from him on the dark corner of Bayard Street, but the memory of his smile and the way he had lifted his dark brows when he laughed drew her thoughts to him again and again.

Somehow, Callie felt that meeting Mr. Kenyon was an important event in her life, even though she almost laughed at herself for thinking it. She was never likely to see him again. He had told her he was returning to America and his newspaper.

Squinting into the late afternoon sun, Callie saw Hallie and Georgie walking toward her, the freshness of the air staining their cheeks rosy. Immediately her eyes went to little Bridget who had given up the game of clover hunting to cuddle her little rag doll and sing softly to it. Swinging about, Callie searched for Billy's bright blond head.

"Bridget darlin', where's your twin?" The little girl looked about, shrugging her thin shoulders.

"Georgie, have you seen Billy?" Even before his answer, Callie knew he had not.

Going to Bridget, Callie knelt down beside her. "Tell Callie, darlin', where was Billy when you saw him last?" She tried to keep the edge of panic from creeping into her voice.

Bridget stuck her finger into her mouth as she always did when she became frightened. Her pansy blue eyes were widened. "Billy? Billy?" she called for her twin.

"Where was he when you were playing?" Callie purposely softened her tone. "Did you see where he went?"

"Billy found a clover, and he's gone to find the pot of gold!" Bridget said, pleased that she remembered.

"Yes, darlin', but which way did he go?" Bridget pulled her

finger out of her mouth and pointed back in the direction of Bayard Street.

"Oh, my God! The traffic!" Appointing Georgie to mind the children and not to leave this spot, Callie ran to where Bridget had pointed. Wild imaginings taunted her. Billy was such a little boy, too little to know the dangers of the carts and horses. She could imagine him, small and helpless, being trampled beneath the wheels of a wagon or stomped beneath the flinty hooves of a ragman's team. Looking for the pot of gold, indeed!

Pulling her shawl tight around her shoulders, Callie ran the length of Florham Way back to the noise and confusion of Bayard Street, searching for a bright blond head. There was a break in the traffic, and across the cobbled street she caught sight of a little figure scooting between the dust bins outside the wheelwright's shop. Billy! Already her hands itched to smack that little bottom for the worry he'd caused her.

Callie went after him, calling his name. "Billy James, take yourself out of there this minute! Billy James, do you hear me?"

A tall figure dressed in a cranberry coat and buff-colored breeches stood near the corner. The sound of Callie's calls caught his attention, and he turned in her direction. A sudden smile lit his clean, handsome features when he recognized her. Byrch Kenyon had spent most of his day walking up and down Bayard Street, looking for her. Since she had left him in this neighborhood, he had rightly assumed she lived nearby. His hope was that she would come out either on her way to work or on an errand.

He hadn't been able to get her out of his mind. To him, Callie was all that was Ireland during these hard times—young, desperate, and yet with that certain quality of determination and a willingness to defend herself. He laughed when he remembered her biting remarks and felt humbled when he thought of her desperation. Would he, given the same circumstances, have found the courage to risk the rope to feed his family?

Unaware that she was observed, Callie ran to where she had last seen Billy squirm between the dust bins. "Billy James, come out of there!" When she moved one of the heavy tin drums aside, expecting to find her little brother crouched behind it, she found herself peering into a narrow cellar window, Billy's skinny little legs sticking out onto the sidewalk. Before she could gather her wits to grab him by the ankles and pull him out, he slipped forward, head first, into the blackness. "Billy! Billy!"

Byrch Kenyon heard the alarm in Callie's voice, saw her bending over from the waist, heard the rumble of the tin dust bins as she hoisted them aside.

Callie was down on her knees, stretching, reaching, probing the darkness with her hand. Suddenly she felt herself being lifted aside and was vaguely aware, through her panic, of a tall man leaning through the window while he voiced calming and reassuring words to the howling child.

"Hold on there, boy. I've got you. Just let me pull you up. That's a boy!"

Within the space of a moment, Billy was dragged through the opening and out into the sunlight. It wasn't until she actually held Billy in her arms that Callie lifted her head and saw that Byrch Kenyon had come to her rescue once again.

"You!" The utterance was a combination of shock and accusation.

"Yes, regrettably so. Knowing how fiercely independent you are, I'm afraid I've interfered yet again." The mockery was there in his voice as it had been before, and Callie could see the humor in his light eyes and the wry smile that played around his mouth. His height, his leanness, his handsomeness, all came in a series of impressions. And Billy was crying with abandon.

"Hush, Billy," she soothed, "all's right now. But you should never never go off on your own like that. Think what could've happened!"

"I . . . I . . . was lookin' for the pot o' gold, Callie," the child sobbed. "I almost had it. I did!"

Seizing him by the shoulders, Callie succumbed to her frustrations. "There's nothing in the way of a pot of gold, Billy, and the sooner you know it, the better."

"There is! There is! Granda says there is!" Billy protested through his tears. His little boy's fists pounded at Callie.

"Here, here," Byrch pulled Billy away. "You shouldn't be hitting your sister that way, young man. Now tell me, what's this about a pot of gold? Did you think you'd find it in the cartwright's cellar?"

Billy nodded his head shyly. He was too young to verbalize his reasons, but in his little heart he believed in Granda's stories.

Byrch smiled down at the child and quickly lifted him onto his broad shoulders. "Well now, Billy, when I was a boy about your age, I too heard tales abut the wee people and their gold. And I once heard that if you were smart enough to find a four-leaf clover and follow the way it was pointing, a handsome prize of gold you'd find." Reaching into his pocket, Byrch withdrew a gold coin and pressed it into Billy's hand. "Here's your prize, boyo."

Billy opened his hand and looked with amazement at the shiny coin. Then his features screwed into a frown. "But it's not a whole pot o' gold the way Granda said!"

"That's because you went off without telling your sister," Byrch reasoned. "The pot of gold is only for the most worthy and the best. You mustn't frighten the ones who love you by taking risks, understand, Billy?"

Billy nodded in agreement. It was Callie who offered her protests. "Mr. Kenyon, I'll thank you not to be filling my brother's head with tales of wee people and the like. There's enough of that from Granda. And as for the coin, you're much too generous and have done quite enough already." Her clear blue eyes held his. "After all you've done we couldn't accept it, could we, Billy?"

"No! Mine!" Billy cried. "I gonna give it to Mum and Da!"

"Let him have it, won't you?" Byrch interceded. "After all, it's such a little coin for such a little boy." His smile was warm and genuine and said that she mustn't interpret the coin as charity. That, Byrch knew, Callie could never accept.

Chapter Three

Callie studied him for a long moment. "As long as it's understood it's not charity, Mr. Kenyon. I'm a girl who can take care of herself and her own."

"Without a doubt," he quickly agreed with a slightly lopsided grin.

"As I said, as long as it's understood. If you'll please put Billy down now, I've got to get back to the other children."

"I'll go with you. Which way are you heading?" It was casually asked, and his tone was friendly, but Callie was still skeptical. After all, it still wasn't too late for him to have a twinge of conscience and turn her into the authorities.

"There's no need. I'll not let this one out of my sight again." She indicated Billy with her glance.

"I insist." The simple statement stifled further argument. "Billy and I are going to be friends, aren't we, boyo?" He gripped the child's ankles hanging down from his perch atop Byrch's shoulders.

Callie led the way back to the park where the other children waited. "So, at last I know your full name," he told her, watching for her reaction. "It's James, isn't it?"

Stopping dead in her tracks, she faced him, irritated and again suspicious. "And how would you be knowing that?"

"Billy's your brother and I heard you calling him Billy James. Not an amazing piece of deduction, I assure you."

"You're quick with your mind, you are. Or at least you'd have me believe. Are you sure you weren't snooping around asking questions? You seemed overly curious about me when you walked me part way home." She tried to pretend indifference, but inside her heart was racing.

"A newspaper man should be quick and clever. I've done my share of hunting down stories and getting to the truth." He was thinking that when he got back to the States he'd like to do a story on Callie James. People were hungry for news of their homeland, and aside from politics, Byrch liked nothing better than a human interest story. Of course, he dared not mention this to her. Her fear of being betrayed was almost tangible. His hands gripping Billy's ankles could feel the small, delicate bones in the boy's legs. An occasional basket of food would never be enough to put meat on this thin, growing body. What Billy needed, what all children needed, was a proper diet each and every day.

Breaking into his thoughts, Callie asked, "What were you doing down on Bayard Street? It isn't exactly the kind of place a gentleman like you does his business."

"I'm not the only quick mind, it would seem," he complimented. "Actually I was looking for you. I had no idea how far you still had to go after you ran away, and I was worried. I thought if anything had happened, it would be talked about and I'd hear it." The hard truth was that he hadn't been able to get her out of his mind. Throughout the morning he'd been unable to complete the smallest task without wondering if she'd made it home safely. He knew he couldn't leave Ireland without knowing she was secure from the law.

Callie was surprised to find herself grateful. Perhaps she had been too hard on him. Glancing up, looking into his smiling face, she knew she had found a friend, and she returned his smile.

Byrch felt as though the sun had warmed his bones. She was lovely, this woman-child, and he suspected that there was a gaiety about her just beneath the surface of her powerful determination to surmount the hardships life had tossed her way. He liked the way her clear blue eyes met his steadily, and how her slim, delicately shaped nose turned up at the very tip, lending a saucy air to the structure and planes of her face. It was still a child's face, rounded near the chin and pink at the cheeks from the March winds, but some day, Byrch knew instinctively, Callie James would be a beautiful woman if disease and privation didn't alter the course of her future.

Georgie, Hallie, and Bridget waited near the edge of the park, anxious for Callie's return. They were surprised to see the tall man carrying Billy on his shoulders and watched with a combination of shyness and curiosity.

Seeing his siblings, Billy began shouting, "I found it! I found it! Look!" He held out the gold coin Byrch had given him.

Georgie looked with amazement from his baby brother to Callie and then back at the coin. "You . . . you found the pot o' gold?"

"No, him gave it to me," Billy explained seriously. "Next time I find the pot!"

Byrch hoisted Billy back to the ground where the others could get a closer look at the coin. "I *almost* found it," Billy said.

Callie rolled her eyes. Now she would never convince the children that the wee people were only make-believe. "You've made a hard job harder, Mr. Kenyon. There's no room in our lives for believing in leprechauns and the like. Nothing save good luck and hard work will save us." But the child in Callie rose victorious. "Still, I suppose there's no real harm in believing, is there? I grew up on Granda's tales, and they never hurt me, did they? I know what needs doing when it needs to be done." She sighed resignedly. "And they are only children, aren't they?"

"Sometimes, Callie, we all pretend to believe in something that we know couldn't possibly be true. It's the child within us. And there's no harm in it, I assure you. I'd like you to tell me about your Granda. He seems a lot like my own."

The children ran off to play, and Callie sank down onto the bench beside Byrch. She found the words tumbling out of her, telling him about Granda and Thomas and Peggy. It was good to talk, and she found herself reminiscing about happier times as she painted the canvas of her life with bold strokes of color and held it up for him to see. She'd never talked this way to anyone before, and because he seemed genuinely interested, she found herself imparting deep-seated feelings and secret thoughts she never considered sharing with another living soul. She told him of her ambivalent feelings toward her father, the love she felt for Peggy as well as her almost overwhelming need to protect her, and the frustrations of living with Granda's tales and his encroaching senility. Talking to Byrch clarified many things she had never had either the time or inclination to discover about herself.

Byrch sat listening, enthralled. Her speech was peppered with local colloquialisms, adding richness to her descriptions. He wished he had a notepad and pencil to take it all down. He wanted to remember every word. Callie James saw the world with a child's clear vision. Petty jealousies and self-centeredness were not a part of her world. She was as guileless as Billy and Bridget, even though the world and the times were bent on teaching her bitter lessons.

He realized with a start that Callie was staring at him, her words halted in mid-sentence. "What are you looking at, Callie? Have I a wart on the end of my nose?"

Callie blushed, her cheeks suffusing with color, making her eyes seem bluer and the burnished highlights in her hair appear more golden amidst the strands of deep, warm brown. "I was just thinking I've never seen eyes the likes of yours, Mr. Kenyon. Cat's eyes is what they are. Gray and green at the same time and circled in black. Mum would call them tiger eyes." Callie bit her lower lip. She was afraid she'd insulted him.

Byrch laughed, the sound reassuring her. "Tiger's eyes, eh? Do you know what they say about a cat's eyes? That he can look into your soul. Is that what you think, Callie?"

"That you can look into my soul? Hardly," she scoffed, still embarrassed by her impudent remark but quick to rally against possible ridicule. "Only the angels can see through to the soul, and you, Mr. Kenyon, are no angel, I suspect."

But you are an angel, Callie James, Byrch was thinking, and the blue of your eyes is heaven's own. He almost laughed at himself for his poetic bent of thought. Ireland and it's blarney was getting to him, he supposed. Quickly he looked away from Callie to where the children were playing. It was disconcerting to find himself thinking of this girl as more a woman than a child. It was just as well he was leaving for America in the morning. Otherwise he knew he would find himself seeking out Callie James again and again, becoming more and more involved in her life. And each time he saw her it would become increasingly difficult to remind himself that she was only a bit more than half his age.

"I really must be getting home, Mr. Kenyon," Callie told him. "Bridget and Billy did without their naps this afternoon, and I'm soon to get ready for work at the mill." Calling the children to her, she straightened Bridget's bonnet and adjusted Hallie's shoelace. She brushed the dried bits of grass from their clothes and smoothed their hair. "Like Mum always says, we may be poor and shabby, but there's no reason not to take pride in ourselves. Say goodbye to Mr. Kenyon, he's leaving for America tomorrow."

Georgie's eyes widened with interest. "Really, Mr. Kenyon? Are you gonna sail or go by steamer? What ship is taking you? Do you live in America? Are the streets paved in gold?"

Byrch answered the boy's questions. "Seems to me, young man, you've a great interest in travel."

"Oh, yes," Georgie told him. "When I'm a man, I'm going to become a merchant marine and work for the Cunard Line. My Da was a merchant marine!" he said proudly.

"Come now, children, say goodbye to Mr. Kenyon and wish him a safe voyage."

Byrch leaned over to Billy. "Have you still the coin I gave you?"

Billy extended his hand, the shiny coin resting on his grimy palm. "Just to be a fair man, what would you think if your brother and sisters had a coin just like it?"

Callie was aghast. "No, really, you mustn't..."

"It's for the children. Surely you wouldn't deprive me of the pleasure as well as them? Say it's all right, Callie."

She looked at the children's eager faces. She knew how the generous offering would alleviate some of their problems. Standing straight, stiffening her back, she lifted her chin. "Seeing as how it would please you, Mr. Kenyon," she said softly, lowering her gaze, unable to look at him.

"It does please me, Callie," he told her, making his voice light and playful. Not for anything would he want to humiliate her, but the need was obviously great. "It pleases me greatly."

Callie turned away, reluctant to observe this display of charity, for that's what it was, she knew. She wanted to protest, to refuse, but she'd often heard Peggy quote that "pride goeth before the fall." Callie wasn't exactly certain she understood or that it even applied, but she wasn't about to take chances. The James family could not fall much further without disastrous results.

Throughout Dublin posters from the emigration commissioners and advertisements from ticket brokers were stuck on building facades and eagerly read by the populace. "Flee the Famine" became a much heard cry, and entire families and groups of families were emigrating to America, giving one another moral support and solace. Where most of them found the money for their passage was a mystery, but many of them had family members who had already emigrated and who sent either the ticket or the money.

In some instances the posters appeared in rural Irish villages, though many of the Irish could not speak or read English. Often the parish priest would translate for them and explain in detail the difficulties and hardships of leaving their homeland. Many were undaunted, believing it better to learn a new language from their native Gaelic and live with the hope of saving themselves and the ones they loved from certain starvation.

In Dublin, the people were better acquainted with the English language than with Gaelic. When they read the posters, they needed no priest to translate for them; however, it was to their religious leaders that they turned for the last blessing before leaving the home soil. They cried as they boarded the boats that would take them across the Irish Sea to Liverpool, England, where packet steamers and sailing schooners were crossing the Atlantic to America. Survival was their hope, but it was without joy. They were severing themselves from the places of their birth, their homeland, from all they knew and loved. It would have been easier to tear an oak from its roots than to separate an Irishman from his country.

"The Tynans left early this mornin' on the D & L. That's the last we'll see of them." Peggy sighed, telling Callie of the emigration of their neighbors and friends. "It's as though they dropped off the face of the earth, for it's certain we'll never see them again."

Peggy busied herself near the stove, stopping in her preparation of tea to adjust the blanket on the baby who was sleeping in the old cradle near the fire's warmth. Joseph Aloysius James was now nearly three months old, and he was robust and alert. All the children had improved in health, thanks to what Callie liked to think of as her resourcefulness.

It had been a long time since Peggy last asked her oldest daughter where this bit of tea had come from, or that string of sausage, although she now looked at her first born with a deep sadness in her eyes. Ever since they'd seen the last of the money Byrch Kenyon had given the children, Callie had seen to it that there was food on the table when the need was the greatest. How she came by her windfalls Peggy could not bring herself to ask. Her admonitions to Callie were strong; she had even begged, fearing for her child's very life. Whenever she'd hear of someone being sent to prison or in many cases hanged by the neck, she took great pains to relate the news to Callie. It seemed to make no impression on the girl. Whenever she'd bring home a bit of this or a piece of that, it was with a deadly calm, as though she'd just found the parcels on the doorstep. Peggy's worry and concern grew deeper.

From time to time Thomas would look at Callie with questions in his eyes, but he never put them into words. Whatever he thought she was doing to ease the cook pot, he dared not ask.

"Your Aunt Sara is coming this morning to bring her ironing," Peggy said matter-of-factly, averting her eyes from Callie.

"So? She comes every Thursday morning, doesn't she? I swear, Mum, it sets my insides churning when I think of you mending her drawers and pressing her fine linens. You should have those things, too! There's lots of things we Jameses should have." Her tone was bitter; there was a flash in her clear blue eyes. "I suppose now that cousin Colleen is keeping company with that English corporal things are looking up for the O'Briens."

"Hmmm. So one would think," Peggy said distractedly, smoothing her hair before nestling the worn iron kettle onto the hob. "Somehow, though, I've a feeling something's preying on my sister's mind."

"Perhaps it's guilt," Callie offered snidely. "With all the comforts and security she enjoys she doesn't seem disposed to share even a crumb with you, her own flesh and blood."

"So, is it charity you'll be wanting?" Peggy retorted. "Sara pays me well for the bit of laundry I do for her."

"According to what standards? She's familiar, I'm certain, with the prices of things. In better times, Mum, what she pays you would be enough and fair. Not in these times, though, and well you know it."

Peggy met her daughter with flinty eyes. "I'm asking you, child, what is it you want Sara to do? Bestow charity?"

Callie looked away, ashamed, her argument quelled. Peggy knew her child well. Charity had a bitter taste for her. "I was talking to Mrs. Tynan the other day," Peggy reintroduced the subject of the neighbors who had emigrated to America. "She told me that they've distant relatives over there and that will make all the difference. Already Kevin has expectations of a job and so does their oldest son. Did I ever tell you I've a cousin who lives in New York? Cousin Owen and a fine upstanding man he is, or so I've heard. Do you remember him, Callie? You were only a little girl when he left Ireland."

"And if I did remember him? What's he going to do, tear up some of the pavement from those streets of gold and send it to us? Listen, Mum, I've got it on good authority that America isn't what it's cracked up to be. Things are hard for the Irish over there, too."

"Oh, yes, this good authority would be Mr. Kenyon, wouldn't it?" Peggy's tone implied that she not only remembered who Mr.

Kenyon was, but she also disapproved of the circumstances under which Callie had met him.

"Now, Mum, no more scolding. Must you relate everything I say to something else?"

"If that 'something else' can put a rope around your neck or send you to prison." Peggy's tone was hard, her eyes accusing.

There was a sound at the door and then a knock. "Hurry and put out the cups, Callie, that'll be Sara now. Oh, I hope she doesn't wake the children." Peggy tugged her apron into place and hurried to admit her sister.

Aunt Sara bustled into the James's kitchen on a breeze of perfumed air and flying flounces. A plump woman, small of stature, with light golden hair styled into dozens of sausage curls at the back of her head, she was a younger, prettier, better fed version of Peggy.

"Margaret, you do look well," Sara complimented. "I don't know, childbirth and mothering seem to do you the world of good." She moved over to the cradle beside the stove to coo down at the baby. "How I envy the ease with which you can bear children. Having Colleen nearly took my life, as you well know. I don't believe I'll ever recover! It's because my bones are so small, don't you know?"

Callie appraised Aunt Sara's wide expanse of buttocks as she bent over the cradle and almost laughed aloud. Small bones, indeed! Always making herself out to be so delicate, just like the ladies she enjoyed reading about in those penny novels. It was Peggy who possessed that slim, elegant length of bone that made each movement so graceful. "Like a dancer," Thomas liked to say.

"Callandre, child, how are you?" Aunt Sara bestowed a perfunctory kiss. "You've grown since the last I saw you. How is your position at the mill?"

"It's not a position, Aunt Sara, it's a job! And you know they've cut hours as well as wages. Those who don't like it are invited to leave. There's plenty of cheap labor coming into Dublin from the countryside."

"Tsk, tsk. That's what your Uncle Jack was saying just the other night." Sara settled herself at the table and allowed Peggy to pour tea for her. "Of course, we wouldn't think of hiring anyone and not paying them fairly. You know that, don't you, Margaret? We've taken on a new man, came here from Cork with his family."

Peggy and Callie exchanged glances over the top of Sara's head. The O'Briens had hired another hand for their dry goods business and had never given a thought to Thomas. Heartless, Callie thought nastily.

"How is Colleen?" Peggy managed to change the subject.

"Feeling much as you'd expect." Sara's ringed fingers dug into her reticule, extracting several little parcels of sugar. Passing one to Callie and one to Peggy, she liberally added the light brown granules to her own cup. "Callandre, did you know that Colleen is to be married in a week's time? There's so much to do, so little time. I'll be imposing myself on you, Margaret. There's table linens to be laundered and ironed, and I was wondering, if you've the time, would you mind coming over to the house to measure the hem on Colleen's new gown? Wait till you see it, the palest shade of blue—"

"Blue?" Callie asked. "Don't you mean white?"

Sara looked at her sister. "It seems that your mother hasn't told you . . . er . . . my darling, Colleen, seems to be . . . er . . . in the family way. But in truth, she and her young corporal couldn't be more delighted. Your Uncle Jack says the sooner they bless themselves with children the better . . ." Sara's words seemed to accelerate with her embarrassment. Suddenly she stopped in mid-sentence. "Margaret, don't tell me you've not told Callandre."

Peggy shook her head warningly.

"Tell me what?" Callie demanded, looking from her aunt to her mother.

"Margaret, you really should have told her! It's just not the kind of thing to spring on a person, especially someone as young as Callandre. And I told you before, you should have arranged for her to go with the Tynans. At least she'd be protected until she landed in America."

Callie gasped. The table seemed to swim before her eyes.

"Mum! What's she talking about?" Callie stood on wobbling feet, knocking her chair backwards. Her teacup rattled in its saucer. "Mum! What does she mean?"

Words would not come to Peggy. This was not the way she meant to break the news. "You're going to America, Callie."

Once Peggy's mind had been set, no power on earth could change it. Not Granda's intercession, not Thomas's disapproval heartily voiced, not the cries of the younger children, nor the anguish of Callie's tears. Through her fear that Callie should be caught in some misdeed and suffer the justice of the law, she had seized upon an opportunity that had suddenly presented itself.

Young, impetuous Colleen, at the end of a previous and unsuccessful romance before meeting her young English corporal, had taken to writing cousin Owen in America, telling him of her desire to emigrate. Owen had presumed to send her a passage ticket on a packet boat leaving from Liverpool. When learning of her pregnancy and being assured of the affability of the unborn child's father, Colleen had confided in Sara who, in turn, confided in Peggy. To Peggy, the passage ticket was heaven sent, a sign from God Himself.

"The girl's only sixteen!" Thomas pleaded to Peggy, finding her for once impervious to his charm. "Surely that's too young an age to be sent away from home, much less to America. Have ye no heart, Peg me love? Wasn't Callie always your best loved?"

"Aye, and that's the reason she's to go! You may be able to close your eyes to what's been going on these past months, but not me, Thomas. Would you rather see her off to cousin Owen or finding her just rewards at the hands of the law?" This was the closest Peggy could come to admitting to Thomas that he'd often filled his belly with the proceeds from Callie's thievery. "She's a good girl, love," her tone softened, "and she'll find her way, no doubt about it."

"But so far away! And what do we really know of Owen? It's been years since ye've seen him."

"Enough to know that he could afford to send a ticket to Colleen. The man must have some sort of employment. Besides, darlin', the man is family."

Thomas's shoulders slumped. There would be no changing Peg's mind. During these past days there had been a renewal of closeness between Callie and himself. She was depending on him to talk sense to her mother. Again he had failed her. He would spend the next fortnight listening to the girl's anguished tears all through the long nights.

September 19 arrived in a flood of rain. It was as though heaven itself was crying against tearing Callie away from all she knew and loved. The children were out of bed before the crack of dawn, rubbing at their red noses and hanging onto Peg's apron, wailing that Callie should not leave. Choking back tears, Peggy brushed the children away from her skirts, dutifully attending to the baby Joseph. How much like her firstborn this babe was. The same curling brown hair, and already his eyes were that clear, bright blue fringed with thick, curling lashes. Joseph, more than any of the children, was like Callie, and each day she held him in her arms or gazed into his sleeping face, Peggy would remember her first child.

Granda went about the small house shuffling, shoulders stooped, repeatedly blowing into his handkerchief. "Ah, Peg, yer takin' the heart right out of me," he moaned. "Have heart, girl."

"If you're goin' down to the D & L dock with us, Granda, you'd better get ready. And dress warm. That's a punishing rain outside." Peggy tried to keep the grief out of her voice. Callie's one hope, she constantly assured herself, was for her to be strong and not waiver. How simple it would be to tell the child that she needn't go, that her family needed her here. But that would be an act of selfishness and went against her every instinct. If Callie were to have a chance, she would not find it here in Ireland. No, America was the place for opportunity.

Callie appeared in the tiny kitchen, dressed in several layers of clothing that gave an unnatural bulk to her slim figure. Her face was deathly white, and her huge blue eyes were red-rimmed from crying. Peggy pretended not to notice. "Here's your tea, darlin'. Drink it down while it's hot. It's a terrible morning."

Callie sat obediently, blowing on the steaming brew before bringing it to her lips. Her words to Peggy these past ten days had been few and far between. This strange silence was breaking Peggy's heart. She knew she might never see her child again in this lifetime, and there was so much to say, so much love to express.

"Have you everything packed in that oilskin bag your Uncle Jack was nice enough to give you? Not to mention the ten-shillings fare on the steamboat to Liverpool. Where is it, child? Have you kept it handy?"

"Yes, Mum." That was all she would say. She was being sent away, and in many ways it was sadder and harder to bear than if the grocer had caught her that first night when she stole the basket.

"When you've finished your tea, then we'll be leaving. Sara says the lines at the D & L are longer than Moses' staff. If we get there early, we'll be able to stand beneath the tarpaulin out of the rain. Fortunate that Uncle Jack saw to it that you'd have advance booking. You'll go straight to the head of the line."

Dodging in and out of doorways, suffering the pelting of a drenching rain, the James family formed a caravan through the streets and down to the dock. Peggy carried little Joseph, and Thomas held the twins' hands. Hallie and Georgie ran ahead, waiting beneath awnings and trees still thick with summer leaves.

There was no gaiety in their running, no sense of frolic on their little faces. They were losing Callie.

Granda walked as fast as he could, tears streaming down his weathered cheeks. He knew without a doubt that he would never again hold Callie in his arms or hear her soft, tuneful humming about the house. She would be gone, out of his life, and the pain of it was not for the bearing.

Peggy kept her eyes straight ahead. Joseph wriggled in her arms. The family walked in a line, heads down against the rain and the tears, like a funeral cortege, until they reached the end of Bayard Street and could see the mottled green tarpaulin. A milling throng lined the rickety wooden fence along the wharf. A long line of people: women, men, families snaked back and forth upon itself. It would appear that all of Dublin had turned out either to leave or say goodbye. Emigrants held their numbered passes aloft, lining up numerically.

Under the tarpaulin the Jameses had relative shelter, the rain teeming into splashing puddles near their feet. "I've promised to stop my wickedness, Mum," Callie pleaded. "I've a fear I'll never see you again. Don't do this to me, Mum. Don't do this."

Peggy stiffened her back; her arms ached to hold her daughter. "It's a fine thing that you know your letters, Callie. I'll be expectin' you to write as often as you can. I'll do my best to answer." Her voice was low, almost harsh, with the force of holding back her emotions. It would be so easy to tell Callie not to go. But she knew her child, knew her devotion to her family, even at the risk of her own neck. "You be a good girl, Callie. Remember what you've been taught. I'll expect you to go to church on Sundays, circumstances allowin'. Now kiss your Da and the children."

The next moments were a blur, a confusion of motion and a struggle for air. Callie tried to commit to memory the exact shade of her father's eyes; the sweet, clean, milky smell of the baby; the strength in Granda's arms; the outpouring of love from the twins and Hallie and Georgie. But most of all she wanted to remember forever the sound of her mother's voice when she called her name.

A voice called the number on her card, "Number one-oh-seven! One-oh-seven! Please to the back of the deck!"

Peg's hand on her shoulder, pushing her forward. A last kiss from Da. Then she was in the mainstream of passengers boarding the crowded steamer, prodded like cattle to the rear decks. There was no shelter from the weather, and Callie wasn't able to distinguish her tears from the rain.

Chapter Four

Elizabeth Erin Kelly Thatcher was her name. Elizabeth for her grandmother, Erin for her great-grandmother, and Kelly was her maiden name. The Thatcher was from her husband of four years. A weary smile played around the corners of her soft mouth. Patrick Willard Thatcher, and he had become her world. Pat and little Paddy were her reasons for living. As tired as she was, ailing though she may be, her heart could still flutter wildly when Pat looked at her as he was doing now. She knew without doubt that he wanted to be off exploring this seething, overcrowded city of Liverpool. His exuberance to fill each moment of this, the greatest adventure of his life, was evident in his energy and the excitement in his eyes. Beth was the one who saw the rubble, felt the crush of milling hordes, smelled the stench of their leavings. She saw the desperate eyes, the thin, wasted bodies, and the carefully guarded pokes that contained all of life's possessions, while Pat saw only hope, determination, and a splendid future that he would carve out for Beth and Paddy. He wanted to experience all there was to see and do and know, but he realized Beth needed him here with her. He would remain at her side, the dutiful, loving husband. They were sitting in a relatively sheltered corner of Albert Docks Commonhouse. The Albert Dock was the largest and most opulent of all the Liverpool docks, with its cast-iron Doric pillars and polished marble floors, muddy and wet now from the tread of thousands of people. Pulling the rolled blankets fastened with leather straps that contained all they were taking to America, Beth smiled with forced vitality. "Go along, Patrick. See what it is that makes this place bubble as it does. Paddy and I will be just fine."

Patrick Thatcher needed no urging. His Beth never said anything unless she meant it. She was giving him free rein to search out this cauldron of humanity, and the temptation was too great to refuse. This was a part of his future, and he didn't want to miss a moment of it. He failed to notice the thin, white line of exhaustion around Beth's mouth or the dark smudges beneath her frightened eyes. His bright gaze passed over the six month's protrusion under the dark, ugly cape she wore to disguise her pregnancy. Beth would be fine, he assured himself. She had Paddy, and at three years of age the little tad would discourage any bounder from flirting with his mum. Patrick dropped a light kiss on Beth's head and tousled Paddy's coppery curls. "Be back in a shake, darlin'," he told her happily as he tugged his worn cap more securely on his head.

Beth watched her husband stride away, admiring his tall, straight back and the way he maneuvered his slim, agile body through the crowd of people. Everything will be fine, she told herself for what seemed like the thousandth time since arriving in Liverpool the day before. Pat will take care of us and see to everything. If only she could sleep. Really sleep. Without feeling as though all the world were watching for her to let down her guard. Beth was a very private person, and living and eating and performing necessary functions amidst a world of strangers was agony. Being pregnant accentuated her instinctive nesting habits, as Pat liked to call her devotion to home and family. She should be home, in her own little house, cooking and cleaning and making a comfortable life for the ones she loved. Only there was nothing left to cook and no house to clean. They had lost everything they held dear in Killaugh, a country town sixty miles from Dublin. The crops had failed and so had their livelihood.

Beth had become so lost in her thoughts, she hadn't noticed Paddy wander off. It wasn't until she heard his croupy cough at some distance from her that she became alert. Heaving herself up from the floor, she rushed to him, calling his name, warning him not to go another step.

By the time she reached Paddy his face was flushed red from

his attack of congestion, and he was having difficulty catching his breath. She gathered him close to her knee, rubbing his curls and patting his back. She should stoop down to pick him up into her arms, but she was so cumbersome that she might fall off balance. She crooned softly to her son until the coughing stopped. These attacks always left Paddy exhausted. She herself felt light-headed and weak—if only everyone wouldn't stand so close, if only they'd give her room to move, air to breathe . . . She felt herself sway, felt Paddy clutching her leg more fiercely. She couldn't give in, she couldn't. Everything was tilting, fading in and out of focus, and she was distantly aware of a firm grip holding her arm. Startled, she raised frightened eyes, expecting to see some roughneck hoping to sell her something she didn't need, or one of those ragged skalpeens looking to pick her pocket or steal her wedding ring. Paddy was whimpering, his hold on her leg a death grip, but he released his frantic hold to stare wide-eyed at the young girl who was holding his mum steady. "Where are your things?" Callie asked, tilting her head. "Where can you sit down with the boy? Can you walk?"

"Over there," Beth indicated with a lift of her chin. Callie kept her clasp on the young woman secure as she reached down to take the little boy's hand. Paddy raised trusting chestnut eyes, and it was all she could do not to burst into tears. Paddy was no older than the twins she had left behind.

"What about your baggage?" Beth asked in a voice that was barely above a whisper.

"It will take but a second to get you comfortable. If anyone even thinks of helping himself to my goods, he'll have me to deal with," Callie said fiercely. Beth believed her.

Guiding Beth and Paddy over the the sheltered corner that was indicated, Callie was quick to catch the movements of two youths curiously poking about the unguarded baggage. Beth saw them too. "That's Patrick's satchel!" she cried helplessly.

Spurred into motion, Callie steadied Beth on her feet and pushed through the edge of the crowd, shouting at the top of her voice. "You there! Leave that be! Get away from there!" In the space of a moment, she was flying at the culprits, struggling for possession of the satchel, fighting them off with coltish kicks and pounding fists. A string of epithets spewed forth, taking the youths by surprise. She wrenched Patrick's bag from the taller of the two, kicking out with all the force she could muster. The adolescent clutched his groin and doubled over. "You come one step closer," Callie warned, "and you'll get more of the same!"

Grabbing the hem of her skirts, Callie displayed the length of her knitted-stockinged leg. Strapped to the calf was a bone-handled knife. The weapon shone bright and lethal, and the look in the girl's eyes said she would not hesitate to use it.

There were grunts of approval from several men who had witnessed Callie's show of bravery before they turned around, intent on their own affairs. She had been in Liverpool two days now, and it always amazed her how, by turning their thoughts inward, people could attain a kind of precious privacy amidst a throng of thousands.

Beth's gratitude embarrassed Callie. "I don't know how to thank you," she said softly. "I know Patrick will want to thank you also." Beth's hand was pushed against the swell of her belly, and her complexion was still white.

Callie took charge. "Here, you sit right here while I get my own poke. I'll come and sit with you and the boy." Obediently Beth sank to the floor, leaning on one of the blanket rolls. Quickly, leaving Paddy with his mother, Callie retrieved her own poke. She stacked the baggage neatly against the wall, away from the temptation of any other thieves, and sat down beside Beth. Introductions were made. "I've lived in Dublin my entire life," Callie said. "My family still lives there."

"Are you going to America all by yourself?" Beth asked in amazement.

"Yes. The streets are paved in gold, don't you know?"

Beth missed the sarcasm in the girl's voice. "You sound just like Patrick," she told her, a false excitement ringing in her tone. Then allowing the guise to slip, she said wearily, "We had nothing left in Ireland. Nothing. And the failure of it was eating away at Patrick like a worm in an apple. I'm frightened, Callie. So very frightened. But I mustn't stand in Patrick's way. He's a good man. He wants so much for us. We'll find it in America, he knows we will."

"And so you will," Callie assured her. "Look about you. All these people can't be wrong, can they?" Even to her own ears her confidence struck a false note. "Sit back and rest, Mrs. Thatcher."

"Please, call me Beth. That's Patrick's name for me."

Callie smiled; whenever Patrick Thatcher's name was spoken a soft, loving glow came over Beth's face. It reminded her of the way Peggy's face and tone softened whenever she thought of Thomas. She fervently hoped that Patrick Thatcher was more of a doer than a dreamer. Thinking about Peggy and Thomas made Callie homesick. For distraction, she looked to little Paddy.

"Would you like to sit up on one of these barrels?" she asked.

Paddy nodded, and Callie slipped down and lifted the child onto the barrel beside hers. She was stunned at how thin and frail he felt in her arms. The layers of clothes he wore made him seem more robust than he was. She didn't need a doctor or the child's mother to tell her he was consumptive. Poor tyke. The wet, damp sea journey would do him no good, and from the looks of Beth, it wouldn't do her any good either. Her pregnancy was advanced, and if she could hold it that long, the babe would be born in America. If there was one thing Callie knew about, it was pregnancy. Hadn't she watched her own mother through five of them?

Callie settled Paddy and then propped up several pieces of the soft baggage beneath Beth's head. "It was wise of your husband to limit the baggage," Callie said approvingly. "I've only been in Liverpool two days, but I can tell you it pays to travel light. I've seen those with too much baggage who cannot move about without the aid of carts and wagons, and I've seen those who were as good as nailed to the spot because they had to sit guard on their boxes and trunks."

"My Patrick is as smart as men come," Beth agreed. Not for anything did she want to think about all the household goods Patrick had sold to buy passage across the Atlantic. Not for anything did she want to remember the huge family Bible that had been passed down to her from her mother's mother, or the fine linen tablecloths, or Paddy's first pair of shoes, and the low, wooden cradle into which generations of Kellys had placed their newborn babes. Gone, all of it. Never to be seen again.

"Why don't you take a short nap until your husband comes back? I'll care for the boy. I'll tell him a story the way I used to do for my own little brothers. You can trust me, Beth."

It never occurred to Beth that Callie couldn't be trusted. Her eyes were already half-closed, and it was a great relief to leave Paddy to another's care. She knew this pregnancy was a terrible drain on her. She should have convinced Patrick to wait until after the baby was born. But his arguments had made so much sense. "A babe in the arms is more difficult and more vulnerable than one in the belly," he told her. And what of washing dirty nappies? And where would they find milk if hers gave out as it had with little Paddy? "And besides, think of it, Beth. The first Thatcher born an American citizen!"

Beth had wanted to argue, to find some other answer, but she couldn't destroy Patrick's dream. She would never deprive him of anything he wanted or needed. Whatever was best for Patrick was best for her and Paddy. Patrick loved them, so it had to be right.

Paddy cuddled against Callie, and soon he too was asleep. Glancing down at him, she was touched by the delicate blue lines in his eyelids and the unhealthy bright spots in his cheeks. She was certain he was feverish. Tenderly she cradled him closer, remembering tiny Joseph and his lusty, demanding cries. Surely Mrs. Thatcher realized her son was ailing. Or did she, like so many others, attribute her child's puniness to the hard times they'd suffered?

The day was becoming colder, the wind whipping the relentless rain into wet and clinging curtains. The steamer trip from Dublin to Liverpool had been a trial of endurance. There was no shelter for the passengers; the hogs and poultry between decks enjoyed better accommodations. The inner layers of Callie's garments were still damp, and the waistband of her drawers and petticoats chafed her slender body.

Leaning back against the cold masonry wall, Callie sighed. She knew she should be down at the *Black Ball* offices seeing to her own passage instead of playing sentry for Beth and Paddy Thatcher. In the two days she had been in Liverpool, she had learned the hard facts of being an emigré. First, no ship sailed until its hold was filled with cargo. In the case of the *Yorkshire*, the ship on which cousin Owen had booked her, it would be at least another day till sailing. The agent in the ticket office where she had to confirm her passage had pointed out the tall, masted ship as she lay at anchor in the Mersey River, her furled sails hanging like shrouds in the bleak light, her hull lolling in the muddy waters like a huge, black sea bird. Callie had never seen such a preponderance of ships and steamers of all description. The muddy Mersey was trafficked by an endless line of steamers plying up and down the river to various landing places. Steam tugs and small boats with familiar dark red or tan-colored sails that were oiled to resist the wet darted in and out of the larger ships like scurrying insects. Yachts and pleasure boats rode at anchor, the commercial packet boats having precedence for dock space. Most common of all were the small black steamers whizzing industriously along, many of them crowded with passengers.

Resisting the impulse to close her eyes in sleep, Callie decided the ticket agent and the validating of her passage could wait. She was needed here to watch over her charges, to protect them should a cutthroat approach them demanding money or worse. If only there was somewhere to go to eat a proper meal and sleep in a proper bed. Such a thing was impossible, Callie knew. Thousands of people were stranded in the city, many of them seeking nonexistent employment or living the best way they could. Too often a man would find himself the victim of robbery or a poorly dealt game of cards, stripping him of the money he would have used to purchase packet tickets, leaving him and his family with nowhere to go.

The dark and dingy streets were peopled by the poorer than poor. Women openly nursed children at their breasts; men, haggard and often drunk, wandered the roads and byways, sleeping in doorways. Sick and dirty children begged on street corners. It seemed that every few steps there were taverns, and the buildings were plastered with placards advertising strong drink and food. It seemed to Callie that the entire city was geared to the business of emigration—Ship brokers, provision merchants, eating places, and public houses. And everywhere were signs advertising the Cunard Line, the Black Ball Line, and various ships. Public-service posters were squeezed in every available space. One especially chilled Callie to the bone:

TO EMIGRANTS

CHOLERA!

CHOLERA having made its appearance on board several Passenger Ships proceeding from the United Kingdom to the United States of America, and having, in some instances, been very fatal, Her Majesty's Colonial Land and Emigrations Commissioners feel it their duty to recommend to the Parents of Families in which there are many young children, and to all persons in weak health who may be contemplating Emigration, to postpone their departure until a milder season. There can be no doubt that the seasickness consequent on the rough weather, which Ships must encounter at this Season, joined to the cold and damp of a sea voyage, will render persons who are not strong more susceptible to the attacks of this disease.

To those who may Emigrate at this season the Commissioners strongly recommend that they should provide themselves with as much warm clothing as they can, and especially with flannel, to be worn next to the Skin; that they should have both their clothes and their persons quite clean before embarking, and should be careful to keep them so during the voyage, and that they should provide themselves with as much solid and wholesome food as they can procure, in addition to the Ship's allowance to be used on the voyage. It would, of course, be desirable, if they can arrange it, that such persons should not go in a Ship that is much crowded, or that is not provided with a Medical Man.

By Order of the Board
S. WALCOTT,
Secretary (sic)

Someone was making a bad joke, Callie frowned. Clean clothing, extra food, uncrowded ships! Whoever S. Walcott was, he evidently had no idea of the circumstances of the people in Liverpool. Take poverty, add cholera, and you've got disaster.

Closing her eyes momentarily, Callie fought back the rush of terror that had been picking at her bones ever since she'd left Dublin. In her thoughts, she could see Peggy at the stove, lifting the kettle onto the hob, little Joseph asleep in his cradle. The golden heads of Hallie and Georgie and the clever child-play of the twins. And it was her father's sweet tenor voice she heard singing a gay tune while he stropped his razor before shaving.

A tear of loneliness coursed down the side of her nose, and she quickly brushed it away. What's done is done, she told herself firmly. There's nothing to do but get on with it. God willing, she'd be able to send money home to Peggy and Thomas very soon. Cousin Owen, they said, was an accomplished man who would help her find work and look after her.

Paddy squirmed, whimpered in his sleep and then quieted. Callie smoothed his hair tenderly. His head had cooled to the touch and a fine beading of perspiration dampened his hairline. "Dear God," she murmured, raising her clear, bright gaze heavenward, "help this little child." Unaware, she was mimicking Peggy's intonations whenever one of the children was sick. "And help me too, Lord, I'm so scared. I suppose You think this is just punishment for what I did, but You should have known I was only trying to help the little ones." The heaviness in her chest blossomed to a throbbing ache. She was angry, angry at the injustice of it all. "And don't think you're foolin' me, Lord. This is hell. Liverpool is the real hell."

Strong white teeth bit into her full lower lip. The salty taste of her own blood did nothing to appease her fright or her anger.

Early twilight gave way to darkness and still her two charges slept. There was no sign of Patrick Thatcher and Callie knew a thrill of apprehension. She'd been out on the streets and knew the dangers. What if someone had slit his gullet and stolen his wallet? Worse, what if Mr. Thatcher decided he didn't want the responsibility of a wife and child? It would be so easy for a man to board ship and sail away. It had been done, she knew from gossip she'd overheard outside the common house where posters were hung inquiring as to the whereabouts of this man or that.

Not six yards away a card game started up with five men. Callie tried not to watch. Just this very morning she had witnessed a card game, and when money ran out, so did tempers. There were accusations of cheating, and all that remained of that particular game was a sticky pool of blood. It was the winner's blood that soaked the planks on the wharf. It was obvious to Callie that there were no winners in Liverpool. That was where she had come by the knife. It had been lying off to the side, still stained with the dead man's blood, unnoticed by the gaping crowd. It had been so easy to pick it up and hide it under her shawl. She hadn't known why she had wanted it except that she felt so defenseless in this lawless city. Now she was glad she'd taken it and tied it to her leg. It had given her authority when those two louts had tried to steal the Thatcher's baggage.

The sounds from the card game awakened Beth, and she struggled to a sitting position. Her eyes looked about wildly and calmed immediately when she saw her son nestled in Callie's arms. The sweetest of smiles touched her lips, and her eyes regarded her new little friend warmly. "Paddy slipped off just after you. I wouldn't be surprised if he doesn't sleep most of the night."

Smoothing her thick, dark hair and pushing it into a coil at the back of her head, Beth asked anxiously, "Did my husband return?"

Callie shook her head. "There's so much to see, and everywhere you go the crowds are so thick. And if Mr. Thatcher has gone to the ticket broker's, there's no telling how long it will be. People are in line there from early morning through most of the day. Mr. Thatcher wouldn't have gotten there till late in the afternoon, would he?"

"No. He'd only just left before you came to help us." Beth's tired eyes thanked Callie. She knew there was nothing she could do but wait. "I'll take Paddy now. Why don't you try to get some sleep?"

Carefully, so as not to disturb him, Callie lifted the child and placed him in his mother's arms. "If I'm to sleep, perhaps you'd better keep this handy," she whispered. She reached for the knife strapped to her leg. Beth's eyes widened in shock. Now she knew why the two ruffians hadn't pursued the baggage.

Reaching for the knife with trembling fingers, Beth asked, "You don't think anything has happened to Patrick, do you?"

Callie forced conviction into her voice. "Of course not. He'll be here soon, you'll see."

That she should rely so completely on this young girl's opinion was a puzzlement to Beth. Yet Callie seemed so able to take care of herself. She was younger than Beth by at least five years, yet she seemed to know so much and seemed so in control.

"You're right, Callie," Beth said with forced brightness. "I'm just being silly. It's just that Patrick means the world to me. I'm certain nothing's happened to him. Pat is so smart and so strong."

Callie wondered if the word "selfish" also applied to Mr. Thatcher. It was unforgivable of him to be gone so long. What if she hadn't been there to help Beth and Paddy? What then?

"He's so good, Callie," Beth said with undisguised adoration. "I can't wait for you to meet him. He'll like you, Callie, and he'll be forever grateful for what you've done for us."

This talk about the absent Mr. Thatcher was making Callie uneasy. Beth was so much like Peggy extolling Thomas's virtues. Attempting to change the subject, she asked, "What ship are you sailing?"

"The *Yorkshire*. Patrick says she's the fastest ship in the Black Ball fleet, and her commander, Captain Bailey, has a reputation for kindness and attention to his passengers. He's taken the *Yorkshire* across the Atlantic in sixteen days!"

"I'm sailing the *Yorkshire*, too," Callie told her. It would be good to know someone aboard ship. The knowledge calmed some of her fears, and she smiled at Beth with genuine cheer.

"You're frightened too, aren't you." It was a statement rather than a question.

"Mum says we're always frightened of the unknown," Callie soothed.

"Patrick says we should look upon this as an adventure." Beth said this with more confidence than she felt. "Going to America is his dream. For years, even before we were married, he's been talking about it. Now, with the way things are in Ireland, the choice was made for us. It's all he ever talks about, a new life, a new beginning for us. He'll make it happen, Callie, I know he will. It wasn't his fault that we lost the farm. You can't stop Patrick Thatcher. If he says he's going to do something, he does it."

It seemed to Callie that the only time life sparkled in Beth's eyes was when she spoke of her husband. She prayed she wasn't a fool about the man as so many women were, her mum included. "He sounds wonderful. A loving man," Callie said, hoping her voice didn't sound as skeptical as she felt.

Patrick Willard Thatcher arrived with the dawn, his eyes shining like newly minted copper. The relief on Beth's face wounded him. He shouldn't have stayed away so long, but there had been so much to see, so many people to talk to. His glance went to Paddy sleeping in the arms of a strange young girl. Beth nodded to show that it was all right.

Sitting down beside his wife, Patrick spoke in a rush, trying to tell her everything he'd seen and done since leaving her. "We've our tickets confirmed for the *Yorkshire*," he told her. "That took half the night; the lines at the broker's office were that long. Beth, I tell you, Liverpool is beyond imagining. It's a carnival; something is happening every minute. Aren't you excited, Beth?"

Callie woke at the sound of his voice. Just like a man to ask such a stupid question. Did he really expect her to dance a jig after sleeping on the floor all night? Not to mention worrying about Paddy's health and being with child to boot! Callie had no illusions about a woman's role in life, nor about her worries or her heartbreaks. Her lessons were learned early at Peggy's knee.

Callie sat up, rubbing the sleep from her eyes. Quickly Beth introduced Patrick, relating to him the help Callie had been to her. Patrick gravely thanked her and upon learning that Callie was also to sail on the *Yorkshire*, quickly offered his protection.

Paddy woke, stretching his thin arms. Spying his father, he squealed his delight and immediately said he had to pee. Patrick laughed, calling him a big boy to keep his pants clean and swung the child onto his shoulders to take him outside.

"We'll meet you back here, Patrick," Beth was saying. "I think Callie and I need a wash and a comb oursleves."

"There's a public outbuilding through those doors," Callie pointed to the rear of the warehouse they were in. She looked from Patrick to the stacked baggage, but he didn't seem to be aware that if he didn't take a few bundles with him, she and Beth would have to carry it all themselves.

"I'll meet you back here, then," Patrick told them. "C'mon, Paddy boy, hold on for another minute, won't you?" Off he strode with Paddy riding high on his shoulders, all the baggage left to Beth and Callie.

Slinging two pokes over her shoulder and carrying another in each hand, Callie left the lightest ones for Beth. "I'm afraid Patrick isn't the most practical of men," Beth apologized. "I'm certain he never gave a second thought to the baggage."

The rain had ceased, leaving huge lakes of muddy water along the paths and walkways. The lines outside the public privy were long, and Callie knew Beth was becoming increasingly uncomfortable. At last their turn came, but to their dismay there was no pump for clean water with which to wash. The stench of sewage from the cesspool was an abomination. Quickly they skipped over the puddles, trying to keep their shoes dry, and went back to the corner of the warehouse where they'd spent the night.

Callie settled down and removed a comb from the drawstring bag she carried. "I'll comb your hair, Beth, and you comb mine." Beth took the pins out of her long dark hair, allowing it to fall freely down her back, the bright auburn glints highlighting it like the sleek flanks of a roan pony. Callie, too, pulled the combs and pins from her hair, running her fingers through her chestnut tresses. She would have Beth braid it for her; it would stay neater that way and be less of a problem.

"Patrick says he loves my hair," Beth told her shyly. "Men," she said impishly, "love to run their fingers through a woman's hair. I suppose it's because their own is kept so short." Callie laughed aloud as Beth braided her hair into a long thick rope that hung down her back. "The Lord alone knows how ugly I'd be without my hair," Beth confided. "I do believe it's what made Patrick notice me out of all the girls in the village who were smitten with him. Even when we were children he loved to pull it. He's even said it was the reason he married me," she laughed happily. Callie thought about it and decided the man she would marry had better want her for more than her hair.

When Patrick returned he brought them each a large, round biscuit and a paper filled with bits of ham trimmings. He offered the food to Beth as if he were offering a gift to a queen. "Look! One of the spirit vaults, that's what they call taverns here in Liverpool, is handing out food for the hungry," he said. "The barmaid took a liking to Paddy and handed him an extra biscuit! Isn't that right, son?"

Paddy beamed, shyly handing his biscuit to Beth. "No, you eat it, dear," she told him lovingly. "That's a good boy."

"Yesterday I had the opportunity to talk with a ticket broker," Patrick told them between mouthfuls. "Weather permitting, the *Yorkshire* should make the journey in under three weeks. Think of it, Beth, in less than a month we'll be in New York!" Paddy clapped his hands in glee, infected with his father's excitement. "The agent also told me that each passenger on the *Yorkshire* is allotted two pounds of fatback and five pounds of biscuit flour each week. There are stoves for the passengers." Patrick sounded confident and pleased with what he'd learned. It was as though he were going on a pleasure cruise, Callie thought.

"Two pounds of fatback, Patrick. It hardly seems enough," Beth said hesitantly.

"It's more than enough! Two pounds each for me and you and Paddy. Added with Callie's two pounds, that makes for eight pounds altogether. Whenever did we eat eight pounds of fatback in a week?"

Beth shrugged, still doubtful. "Did the agent tell you anything else?"

"Oh, just some nonense about taking along some stomach medicine and herb teas. And he mentioned peppermint for the digestion. And, of course, we all have to go to the medical examiner to have our tickets stamped." This last he said hurriedly, rushing through his words, trying not to make his concern for Paddy's health obvious. They must go to America. They *must*! Instinctively, his hand went to his breast pocket where his father's silver watch was hidden. It was all he had, and he had been holding onto it for an extreme emergency. Bribing one of the doctors might just be that crisis.

As Patrick's hand went to his breast pocket so did Callie's hand go to the little pouch pinned to the inside of her bodice. In it rested eight shillings, given to her by Aunt Sara. With it she was to purchase coffee beans, dried peas, and tea to fortify her during the crossing. Along with the ship's allotment, it would be more than ample, Aunt Sara had told her. She had come by her knowledge first hand from a customer at their dry goods store who had made the voyage several times.

"When does the *Yorkshire* sail?" Callie asked.

"Any time now. You know she won't sail until she carries a full load of cargo. We're to watch the posters outside the broker's exchange."

Callie repeated what Aunt Sara told her about bringing extra provisions. "I've eight shillings," she told Patrick, "and since my cousin Owen will be meeting me when I land, I won't be needing to put anything by for when I reach the other side. Have you seen a place where I can buy what I need at cheap prices?"

"Eight shillings! That's a princely sum!" Patrick whistled. "I've less than that, and there's three of us! We can't afford to indulge ourselves now, we've got to save what we have for New York."

"Patrick," Beth said softly, "perhaps just a pound of coffee or just some tea. Think of Paddy, won't you?" Worry lines creased Beth's fair brow.

"Beth, my darlin', I am thinking of Paddy. Now, don't worry. The ship's allotment will be more than enough."

Once their simple meal was finished, Patrick settled himself with Paddy in his arms. The child was almost instantly asleep, the alarming spots of red flushing his cheekbones. "He'll be fine once we get to America, Beth. Trust me, won't you? It's going to be the answer to our prayers. We'll thrive, and Paddy will grow fat and jolly. We'll have to work hard, but we aren't afraid of hard work, are we, Beth?"

Callie looked away from them. She had never seen such naked devotion in anyone's eyes as when Beth smiled at Patrick.

Chapter Five

The lines seemed endless to Callie as she and the Thatchers waited their turn to move one step nearer the government health offices. Hundreds of emigrants, thousands it seemed, waited, the close press of unwashed bodies and mildewed clothing making it difficult to breathe. Patience had never been one of Callie's virtues, and she shifted from one foot to the other and then danced a little jig, much to Paddy's delight.

How like the twins he was when a smile could be coaxed from him. Poor tyke, so quiet, staring out from behind his wide, solemn eyes. He should be running and chasing with the other children who were playing a rough game of tag. The slight blue tinge around his mouth, along with the spots of vermilion on his cheeks, made Callie say a prayer that the little boy would pass the physical examination.

All about them was talk and gossip of what America was going to be like. The family ahead of them was talking about relatives who had sailed more than a year ago. Patrick strained to hear the glorious details. Callie could catch only brief snatches of the conversation. "My brother and his seven children . . . land of opportunity . . . back-breaking work . . . they do have stoves on board for cooking, but so many have to share them . . . cramped . . .

dysentery . . . typhus . . . cholera . . . not to worry, we have our health . . . warm weather will greet us.

"Another hour at the most," Patrick assured them. "We should be allowed to board the *Yorkshire* before evening. She came in from anchor and is docked at the Albert pier; they're loading her now."

Callie tried to smile appreciatively. She could never be as enthusiastic about leaving, not when it meant being thousands of miles away from Peggy and the children. A pervading sense of loneliness that she had been fighting since boarding that wretched steamer in Dublin threatened to erupt in a spring of tears. Damn Patrick Thatcher and his adventure! Callie bit into her bottom lip. No, that wasn't fair. She'd never confided why she was emigrating to America; Patrick and Beth could have no idea that she'd been all but exiled by her own mother. They seemed to trust her so; she couldn't tell them that she'd become a thief and that was why she was being sent away. If they were to know the truth and decide they didn't want her companionship, she'd be alone again. Alone and frightened.

Paddy continued to sleep against Callie's shoulder. If Patrick was right, the child would awaken just as it was their turn with the doctor. Poor little thing, he always coughed and hacked when he awoke. Maybe because he was sleeping upright against Callie, he wouldn't be so congested. She had her own views on Paddy's condition; still, he wasn't her child, and it wasn't her place to voice her beliefs. Surely Beth and Patrick couldn't really believe Paddy had nothing more than a cold.

The line at the back pressed forward, pushing Callie into almost direct contact with the family just ahead of them. She narrowed her eyes, really noticing them for the first time. Each was more dirty than the next. Callie's eyes widened still further when she saw a body louse half the size of her little fingernail crawl up the neck of the man in front of her. She backed off a step and bumped into Patrick. She motioned to him to look at the man's neck. Patrick seemed as disgusted as she and took her back another step. Callie watched in horror as another louse joined the first, crawling between the oily strands of the man's hair. The man's wife turned to say something to her husband, and Callie drew a deep breath. She was what mum would call a slattern—filthy and unkempt, dark scabs from where she had picked sores dotted her face. Abhorred by her first real contact with filth, Callie squeezed her eyes shut. Thank the good Lord *they* wouldn't be sailing on the *Yorkshire*. The physician would take one look at them and send them somewhere to clean themselves and get well.

In dumbfounded amazement Callie watched as first one child

then the next held out his ticket and the doctor stamped it perfunctorily while asking to see his or her tongue. Obediently each child stuck out his tongue and then laughed and scampered away, waving his ticket for all to see. Callie was aghast. What manner of doctor was this? In Dublin the kindly doctor wore a spotless white apron and had clean hands, unlike this disheveled man whose smock was gray with grime and food stains.

Noticing Callie's amazement, Beth whispered in her ear, "There's so many like them." She indicated the family in question. "By the time we set foot in America, no doubt we'll be just like them, scratching the lice till our skin bleeds." Her tone was so resigned, so listless and forlorn. Callie turned to reassure Beth that as long as there was water and she had a bit of soap, she'd never be that way, but the doctor was calling "next," and Patrick was jostling Callie ahead of him.

"Stick out your tongue." Callie obediently did as she was told and watched as her ticket was stamped. This was a certification that she was fit and healthy, carrying no communicable diseases. She jostled the sleeping Paddy a bit and had to resort to pinching his cheek so he would stick out his tongue for the doctor. His ticket was stamped, and Patrick had it back in his pocket when the examiner called, "Next!" and Beth stepped forward.

Outside the crowded offices, Patrick put his arms about the three of them, smiling broadly. "I told you we'd pass with flying colors, didn't I? Now all we have to do is wait for the captain of the *Yorkshire* to admit passengers. But first we'll see about getting Callie's extra provisions, and we're all going to make a visit to the privy."

Where did the man get his energy? How could he remain so excited and enthusiastic after all they'd been through? Callie herself felt flattened, deflated, her usual ebullience gone. Beth was feeling the same way, she knew. Callie reached out and took Beth by the arm, helping her skip across wide, muddy puddles. She wondered at this feeling of guardianship, protectorship, she felt for Paddy and his mother. Was it because Patrick was like Thomas in so many ways?

A raw, wet wind was whipping up again, portentous of another storm, sending up cloudy sprays of mist. It was colder than before, a damp cold that went straight through the bones. Callie longed for home and her faded, warm quilt where she would snuggle between the warm, soft bodies of the twins. She noticed the dark circles of exhaustion beneath Beth's eyes, the drawn lines around her gentle mouth. Only Patrick, with his ruddy cheeks and zest for life, looked hale and hearty.

Several hours later, just as the lamplighters came with their long sticks and lanterns to touch spark to the tall gaslamps lining the wharf, they watched as the longshoremen loading the cargo into the *Yorkshire*'s great, dark hull began closing hatches and removing empty casks and barrels from the boarding area.

Callie could feel her stomach churn with anxiety. Soon now she would be aboard the *Yorkshire*, sailing among hundreds, perhaps a thousand strangers. So far from Ireland, a world away from her mother and family. Would she ever see them again? Even amidst the growing commotion, she imagined she could hear Peggy's voice calling her name. Her feet felt leaden, the weight of the moment crushed down upon her. A prickling of tears burned the back of her eyelids. Her child's heart cried for her mother and the security of family. "Oh, Mum, you should never have sent me away," she moaned inwardly, feeling the undeniable need to bury her head in Peggy's lap and feel the comforting touch of her mother's hand brush back her hair.

It was not to be, if it was ever to be again. Callie James was about to board the packet ship *Yorkshire*, her face turned to the west, an autumn storm wind drying her tears upon her cheeks.

Callie sat in the oily glow of the gimbaled lanterns, which were hung from the inner ribs of the *Yorkshire*'s hull. It was very late, according to the call from the crew's watchman who patrolled the decks. In the relative silence that was broken only by muffled snores and the occasional whimpering of a child, his voice rang true. "Three bells! Three bells!"

Paddy slept at the far end of her own bunk, the warmth of his feverish little body pressed against her stockinged feet. In another berth, erected against the bulkhead beneath a porthole as Beth had requested, Patrick slept with his wife, his arm thrown over her swollen body. Even in sleep he wedged against her, attempting to steady her from the rolling pitch of the ship, which caused her such misery.

Touching the pen nib to her tongue, Callie smoothed the thin white sheet of paper that Patrick had given her and continued with her letter:

> Mum, I'm that happy to be with the Thatchers. They're fine people and have taken me into their family. It is Mrs. Thatcher, Beth, who worries me. This whole business of

emigrating has been very hard on her and her condition. When it was time to board the *Yorkshire*, the blue flag was raised from the mast. Never in your life have you seen such a wild scramble! People pushing and shoving to get aboard. When the gangplank was stuffed up, many tried to climb over the side only to fall into a rushing crowd. One man was trampled, and this minute he lies nursing wounds to his head and limbs. It was terrible, Mum, so terrible. We are so much cattle without decency. I'm awful scared, Mum. I can't think what will happen to me. If all the people in America are like the ones I wrote you about in Liverpool and some of those on this ship, it must be the closest place to hell anyone could know.

I managed to find a place for the Thatchers and me by running ahead. Being as I am so small, I was able to squeeze through the crowd. Good thing, since many families are sharing the smallest of quarters together with others. Mr. Thatcher almost had to beat off those who wanted to shove us out of our place. Mum, you never heard such fighting and arguing in your whole life. It was worse than Bayard Street when the good Church was handing out bread and soup.

But this is our second day out, and things are quiet now. So far the seas are calm, but you'd never know it from how many people are down with the seasickness. It mostly hits the grown people; children seem to do well.

Oh, Mum, the people, say a prayer for the people. Never have I seen such suffering. Women with swollen eyes cry for the ones they left behind. Men have a scared look about them, and their voices are rough. Mothers try to comfort their wailing babes. In one place there is an old woman who was separated from her family. She just sits, Mum, so quiet, living in a world of her own. One of the sailors said she is German, and she cannot talk to anyone or understand them.

Above us on this ship are the cabins, and they are all filled. It costs dear to travel in such luxury. Twenty-five pounds! Why would anyone who had that much money want to go to America?

Mr. Thatcher says there was a search for stowaways yesterday, just before we left the Mersey River for the open sea. First there was a roll call, and each ticket had to be presented as the name was called. I did not hear my name called because I was below deck (that is what the sailors call the steerage area where I am) taking care of Mrs. Thatcher. But Mr. Thatcher answered for me with my ticket. Afterward, he told us, the sailors and the ticket broker's clerk went below with lanterns and long poles to search for stowaways. They turned barrels in case someone was hiding inside. With long poles they poked in dark corners and the piles of bedclothes. Three stowaways were found! Mr. Thatcher said they took a terrible beating from the crew and were thrown overboard into small boats to be taken back to the docks. Mum, what am I doing here?

Your everloving daughter,
Callandre

Ten days later Callie had a neat stack of letters ready to be posted to Peggy when she arrived in New York. She had just written that she didn't know which was worse—the crowded conditions or the constant wetness. Since leaving Liverpool, they had enjoyed few hours of sunshine or clear weather. Clouds hung close over the *Yorkshire*, seeming to settle in an eternal pall over the tall masts. Drizzle and fog penetrated even the warmest clothing and made the decks so slippery that Captain Bailey posted sailors at the entrance to the hatches and companionways to prevent passengers from coming above to escape the stench of vomit and excrement below. Dysentery was becoming epidemic aboard ship, and there were whispered fears of an outbreak of cholera.

Paddy was tolerating the journey better than Callie had expected. Beth was the one plagued by the constant motion of the ship. It seemed to Callie that the young woman lived on the peppermint that Patrick had purchased from a fellow passenger at an appalling price. Everything aboard ship was dear, and Callie was glad she had followed Uncle Jack's instructions to buy coffee and beans and tea and dried peas. The ship's staples, which every passenger was promised, were dispensed the first day of the crossing and again on the seventh. Most of the food was inedible—worms and vermin had nested in the flour, and the fatback was thick with mold and on the verge of being spoiled. Before the voyage was over, the meat would have to be thrown overboard and the damp flour sifted and sifted again until barely enough remained to keep a man for a week.

Through the long days Callie took Paddy into her charge, telling him stories and encouraging him to nibble on the hard biscuit and to drink enough water. She was touched by Patrick's gentle ministrations to Beth. He was at once tender and solicitous, seeing to her every comfort. Several times in the past few days Beth had experienced alarming cramps in her lower back, and some of the women looked at her with piteous understanding. All expected Beth would come due before her time and that it would be a hard birth. Even Patrick seemed subdued, his sense of adventure dulled by worry for his wife.

Yet even between ships, as the sailors called steerage class, the Irish spirit opposed hardship. After the first few nights, revelry and song relieved the monotony. Beth was even able to smile when a fiddler began playing melancholy ballads and Patrick Thatcher lifted his voice in song. His sweet tenor when he sang the "Maid of Killee'" brought tears to the toughest of men, and Callie cried, remembering it was the song Thomas always sang to Peggy.

Dearest Mother,

It is now eighteen days into this hellish voyage. Mrs. Thatcher seems much improved and is able to sip tea and a peas porridge I made with a precious bit of fatback. Little Paddy is my concern. His cheeks are ever flushed with fever, and his eyes burn brighter than coals. Three days, it is said, until we reach New York.

The weather is much improved, and there is sunshine and fair breezes. Today the ship's doctor came below and cursed the stink and blamed the filth for the eleven passengers who died of the dysentery. Sailors brought down barrels of sea water and lye, and we were ordered to scrub and scrape and air the bedding. There was a great hullaballoo when the men were ordered to go on deck to air their clothes and wash themselves. The women attended these duties while the men were above. Grateful we are for this bit of good weather. It was the first I had heard of quarantine, and we must all be prepared for the doctor and the government inspector. Our first stop will be a place called Tompkinsville on Staten Island where we must pass inspection for disease. No amount of scrubbing will ever rid this ship of its stink!

Captain Bailey was preparing the *Yorkshire* to pass muster. Ships were generally cleaned for the first and only time just before entering port. Emigrants were made to scrub the steerage with sand, rinse it down, and then dry the timbers with pans of hot coals from the galley in an attempt to fool government officials into thinking that a clean and prosperous voyage had been made.

New York was fearful of ship fever, smallpox, and cholera, and the city was lucky to have escaped with no great epidemic such as had struck Quebec, Canada. Harking back to quarantine laws passed in colonial times, health officials set up a marine hospital on Staten Island, and all vessels coming into New York were required to anchor in the quarantine area and await inspection.

The quarantine ground was a stretch of bay marked by two buoys approximately one mile to the north and to the south. Those who died in quarantine were buried on the shore in trenches. The ground was soapstone rock, which was dug out by pick and shovel and broken into pieces to cover the coffins. This porous covering allowed the stink of rotting bodies to surface.

The *Yorkshire*'s captain had every reason to allay the suspicions of the government doctors. If disease was found aboard his ship, the passengers were sent into the hospital and the ship would be quarantined for thirty days. From Captain Bailey's experience, those could be thirty days of hell. Twice before the *Yorkshire* had been grounded in quarantine; he knew what conditions loomed before him.

He also knew that the quarantine was a farce. Twice a week friends and family could visit those being detained at the hospital, and hundreds came and went on ferry boats between the island and the city. Rags and discarded bedding from Tompkinsville were sold to ragpickers and peddlers and found their way into the city before nightfall. Hundreds of emigrants awaiting clearance dug hovels for themselves on the thirty acres of hospital grounds rather than risk being contaminated within the filthy, overcrowded buildings where health care was at a minimum. Many ships failed inspection for unsanitary conditions only to have their passengers held "for their good as well as native Americans" in conditions far worse.

An old salt as well as an experienced businessman, Captain Bailey realized all too well the economic reasons for holding a thousand people at a time in relative captivity. While detained at Tompkinsville, emigrants needed to purchase the necessities of life: coffee, tea, and food stuffs. Cook pots, blankets, medicines, preventatives, and the like were offered at outrageous prices by the bands of peddlers and hawkers who paid the health officers a generous stipend to be "allowed" to ply their trade in Tompkinsville.

* * *

Callie craned her neck to see over Patrick's shoulder as the *Yorkshire* sailed through the narrows. To the right was the low, flat land of New York City, buildings and wharves clearly visible along the harbor where ships' masts on South Street stood like a never-ending forest. To the right were the ancient, crumbling walls of Fort Wadsworth, and beyond that, hundreds of ships lying at anchor. She heard the order to weigh anchor, and the sails reefed. The *Yorkshire* bobbed in the choppy waters of Upper Bay like a cork on a string. All eyes were turned to the Island of Manhattan, the place of their future, the hope of their new beginning. Tears brimmed, and all wondered if the great city of the western world would swallow them in one greedy gulp. Or would they find the promised land?

Hardly a spit away from Manhattan at the narrows was the shore of Staten Island, a narrow beachfront from which rocky ledges rose into shallow cliffs. Beyond the cliffs Callie could see the greens and golds of trees in full autumn array. She could smell God's good earth and hear the sounds of voices carrying over the water. Small boats and steamers scooted back and forth between the anchored ships. Peddlers and merchants manned these small rivercraft, selling their goods to the passengers. Ready-made clothes, fresh bread, God blessed milk!

"Tis the American way!" Patrick beamed. "Free enterprise! And wonderful it is!"

Callie didn't think it wonderful that half-starved people should be charged prices they could scarcely afford. Nine shillings for a pint of milk, she had heard, seven for a loaf of bread. More than a month's salary for her labors at the mill in Dublin.

A pilot boat putted toward the *Yorkshire*, several officious looking gentlemen with stern expressions on their faces standing in the stern—the doctor and the government health officials. As expected, a line was thrown to the pilot boat, and a Jacob's ladder thrown over the side of the *Yorkshire*. Everyone watched dourly, silently; their futures depended upon these men.

Within minutes word spread that the *Yorkshire* was to be held in quarantine. Loud curses and hopeless wails went up among the people. They had traveled thousands of miles and were within sight of their destination only to be held back and denied entrance. They were to complete an orderly disembarkation to the beach where they were to await further medical examination. Typhus was said to be aboard the *Yorkshire*..

As ordered, pokes and baggage were brought from below.

Patrick carried Paddy and steadied Beth through the crowd. Shouts and cries filled the air; defeat and havoc prevailed. "Don't become separated!" Patrick shouted above the din, warning Callie.

Even as Patrick warned her, rough hands seized Callie's shoulders, propelling her toward the *Yorkshire*'s rail, wresting her baggage from her and tossing it to a boat below. "Over the side, girlie," the shipmate growled. Callie was half-lifted, half-thrown over the rail to grab hold of one of the many rope ladders leading down to the skiffs that hugged the *Yorkshire*'s side. She hung there, like a spider in a web, too terrified to move, too muddled with confusion and the horror of the murky waters far below. "Go on with you! First your feet, then your hands!" the shipmate instructed, already tossing someone else's poke down to the boat.

The ladder swayed, the skiff seemed miles below her, but move she must, for a man was climbing down the same ladder as she. She felt first with one foot and then the other, holding on for dear life. Hands were reaching up for her, steadying her last few steps. Even when she sat in the bobbing skiff, Callie's panic would not subside. All around her were shouts and terrified cries. Children and babies were lowered by ropes; many fell into the water to be picked up at the point of drowning by small boats that circled the area. Like rats chased from their hidey-holes, the passengers left ship. Callie worried for Beth in her bulky condition. Above, the seamen were shouting and pushing, forcing people over the side.

It was only minutes, but to Callie it was a lifetime before the skiff in which she sat was filled to capacity and made its way to shore. She held tightly to her poke, clasping it to her. It was all she had in this world: a few changes of clothes, a small bit of food, and her letters to Peggy.

There were piers built out into the water at the foot of the cliff where the large brick hospital building stood, but none of the skiffs docked there. Instead they pulled up on the beach, and their passengers had to step out into knee-deep water and wade to dry land.

Callie collapsed on the hard-packed, rock-strewn beach. She sat like a broken puppet, repelled by the sights and sounds and the experience of climbing down the rope ladder into an unsteady boat. She was terrified to the core, weak and shaken.

It was an eternity later when Patrick found her, huddled and shivering. "Callie! Callie! Beth sent me to find you . . ." Patrick sank down onto the beach, hard pebbles biting into his knees. He was astounded at finding Callie like this. Bright, tough little Callie James was stiff with fear, shaking and trembling as though the fires of hell had revealed themselves to her. The sight overwhelmed him.

"Callie! Callie! Pull yourself together!" He gathered her into his arms, held her while she burrowed against his chest. "Callie, Beth needs you. You've been the strength for all of us." He soothed her, patting her back, smoothing her long chestnut hair back from her whitened face.

"That's a girl," he said when he felt the tremblings soften. "That's our Callie. You'll be fine, won't you? You don't want them to take you to the hospital, do you? There's a shelter down the beach a ways where I've left Beth and the boy. Come along with me, Callie. Please?"

Callie nodded her head. No, she didn't want them to take her to the hospital. All she wanted was to see her mother, play with the children . . . but that was impossible. Patrick led her along the beach to find Beth. The light October breezes lifted the strands of hair that had escaped their braid and freshened her cheeks. She would be strong, she told herself over and over. She must be strong.

People milled up and down the beach. Entire families seemed to have set up camp on the beaches and along the sloping cliff. Men, women, children, most of them dressed in little more than rags, littered the beach. The hospital sat high on the hill, various out buildings lining the road down to the water's edge. Out in the bay more than twenty ships rested at anchor, their passengers within sight of New York City but prevented from going there.

When Beth saw Callie, she threw her arms around her. "Oh, I thought we'd never find you! Someone said a woman drowned before a boat could fish her out of the water . . . Oh, Callie, I thought it might have been you!"

"Hush, Beth," Callie said, "I'm here now."

Beth was staring beyond Callie to a section of the cliff where families had pitched camp. Their meager cookfires smoked from the damp tinder they were burning along with rags and anything else that would feed the flames. Her body was rigid; her eyes wide and staring. "Beth, what is it?" Patrick asked alarmed. "We're all here together and safe—"

"No! We're not safe!" Beth wailed, the terror in her voice sending chills up Callie's spine. Little Paddy began to wail in sympathy. "Don't you see?" Beth attacked Patrick in her distress. "Have you no eyes? These people are living out here in holes dug by their hands or in gullies and hovels someone else has left behind. Patrick! I don't want to have this baby in a hole in the ground!

Promise me! Promise me!" She collapsed into her husband's arms, weeping with great heaving sobs against his chest.

"Easy, darlin', easy. I promise you, I swear. We'll go to the hospital shelter; we'll be safe there. Paddy can't live outdoors with his chest. I promise you, Beth." Patrick's optimism was failing him. His beautiful, approving Beth was near the edge of madness, and he worried that even God could not save them from the ordeal they faced. Steeling his resolve, Patrick forced a smile. "Come now, love. We'll walk up the hill to see what can be done." Paddy stuck his thumb into his mouth, hanging onto his father's pants legs, demanding to be picked up. "Here now, darlin', look how you're frightening the boy."

Beth looked down at her son. "There, there, sweet, Mummy's just being silly." She touched his wayward curls in a soothing caress.

Callie looked away from the naked emotion displayed by her friends. The thought came out of nowhere: Where are you, Byrch Kenyon? *This* is something you should see so you can put it in your newspaper! Mr. Kenyon had warned her that it was no easy road for the emigrant, but did he know the inhumanity of it all?

From long habit, Callie lifted her eyes heavenward. "Lord, I know these people are praying just as hard as I am, and You aren't listening. How can You allow this? Sweet Jesus, it's time to do something!"

The walk up the hill to the Tompkinsville Hospital and its annexes was a long, hard trek, and Beth was near total exhaustion. Officials wearing red armbands imprinted with white crosses policed the crowd, herding Callie and Beth along with Paddy into a line. "Women and children for a preliminary examination," the official repeated gruffly. "Men to the other side."

"If we can just find a place to rest," Patrick said. "My wife is very near her time, and she's dead out on her feet . . ."

As though he hadn't heard, or didn't care, the official pushed Callie and Beth into line, repeating, "Women and children for a preliminary examination. Men to the other side."

"Perhaps you didn't hear me," Patrick said, his tone polite and in direct contrast to the fierce grip he had taken on the man's coat front. "My wife! She needs help!" There was desperation in Patrick's voice, a white line of hatred circling his mouth.

"Patrick! Patrick!" Beth screamed, tugging on her husband's arms, attempting to break his deathlike grip on the official.

Almost instantly two other men wearing armbands seized Patrick, throwing him roughly to the ground. "Behavior like that will get you a stint in jail," the men warned. "Keep your hands to yourself, man, if you know what's good for you. We don't like troublemakers here."

Regaining control, Patrick shrugged off the men's hands with a violent motion. Beth fell tearfully into his arms. "Patrick, please. We must do as they say." Her voice was soft, a sobbing entreaty.

"Yer little missus is right, man," said one of the men. "Yer so close now, don't ruin it for yourself. Go on over and get in line with the other men. We'll look after your wife."

Patrick responded to the man' suggestion, but when he left Beth's side, his shoulders were slumped in weariness and defeat.

Beth watched her husband, her heart breaking for him. This was supposed to be the most wonderful experience of his life! The great adventure! And because of her and Paddy it was draining the life right out of him. She'd known and loved Patrick Thatcher too long and too well not to know that his enthusiasm was fast on the wane, that worry and concern for his family were dragging him down. Patrick, her Patrick, so filled with life and eagerness for America, was beginning to realize the burden he carried. And Beth's gentle heart cried for him.

Nearly an hour later Beth and Callie were near the head of the line. Paddy slept with his head on Callie's shoulder, his thumb pushed firmly into his mouth. Pressing her cheek against his forehead, she could feel the dry heat of a fever. She looked over at Beth who was sitting on a bedroll and wondered if she realized how ill her son was, or was she just too weary to notice? Surely this would not be an indifferent examination such as they'd had back in Liverpool. Would Paddy pass? Callie hugged the child protectively, assuring herself that this was why they'd built the hospital—to care for the sick and ailing. Paddy would be fine in the competent hands of the American doctors.

When they were ushered into the low, flat, tin-roofed building, they realized why they hadn't seen any of the hundreds of women leaving. At the far end of the stark interior was an exit door. There were the women, holding their children by the hands, crying, expressions of humiliation and utter defeat on their ravaged faces. It seemed to Callie that everywhere she looked, pain and suffering were the order of the day.

Beth, along with Paddy and Callie, was hustled into a small side room by a man wearing a rubber apron. One window, grimy with dirt, shed the only light into the interior. Beth and Callie glanced around uneasily as the man was joined by a slattern of a woman carrying sharp-tipped scissors. "Sit down, girlie," the woman commanded Callie, attempting a smile that revealed her toothless gums.

"Why? Who are you? You aren't a doctor!"

"Sit!" It was an iron command. Hesitantly Callie gave Paddy over to his mother.

"If the boy is too heavy for you, you can put him down there," the woman indicated a pile of burlap sacks whose soft fullness made them appear to be stuffed with rags.

"We'll just take these pins from your hair," the man said in false friendliness. "What do you say, Sally, shall we leave her hair in the braid?"

"Aye, 'twill make it easier at that," the woman answered.

Callie anticipated their motives. "No! No, I won't let you cut my hair! Why?"

"Don't give us any of yer lip, girlie. We're told to cut your hair because it drains yer strength. And for reasons of hygiene," she added as a last word of authority. "The lice in this place is terrible from you dirty Irish. Now shut your mouth and sit still."

"I'll be damned to hell if I'll let you lay one hand on me!" Eyes wide, face white, Callie leaped from the chair. "You aren't cutting my hair! Never!" Warily she backed toward the door, her arms in front of her to ward off the expected attack.

"You have lice! Bugs, lassie. We can't be letting you mingle with the others when you've vermin crawlin' through that lovely hair, now can we? Now, be a good girl and sit down. Don't make Sally tie you up. We have to do that sometime, eh, Jake?" She winked at the burly man who seemed to be observing the scene with great amusement.

"I don't have lice and you know it!" She looked over to Beth for assistance only to see her fling her hands up before her face as though shutting out the scene would make it untrue. Paddy turned, awakened by the commotion, arms outstretched for his mother. With his movements, several of the burlap sacks fell over, revealing that they were stuffed with hanks of hair.

Paddy began to wail. "Look what you're doin' to the child," Sally said. "Now sit down and it'll be over one, two, three."

The man, Jake, yanked Callie away from the door, forcing her into the chair, holding her arms behind her back. Sally wielded the scissors, hacking away at Callie's long thick braid. Tears of humiliation stung her cheeks; her teeth bit into her full underlip. Quicker than two shakes of a lamb's tail it was over, and Sally held up the mutilated braid to Jake who stuffed it into a sack.

Beth was led without protest to the chair. Sally and Jake helped themselves to the tortoise-shell combs Beth wore in her hair and the long pins she used to fasten the gleaming, auburn tresses to the back of her head. "Put this one's hair into that separate sack, Jake. It'll bring a nice price, considering the color of it."

Callie heard the words and turned with a vengeance. "Price? What price?"

"This is America, darlin'," toothless Sally explained."Waste not, want not, just like the Bible says."

Jake and Sally pushed Beth, Paddy, and Callie out of the small room. Pulling her shawl up over her head to hide the ugliness, Callie now understood the weeping women they had seen when they first entered the building. Women who had nothing before coming to Tompkinsville and who had even less now.

Beth began to sob, touching the short, blunt ends of her hair. "Beth, it'll grow back, you'll see," Callie tried to reason. "There's nothing to do but live with it. Maybe we can fix it up a bit. Just to even it out . . ."

"Patrick loved my hair. He said it was my glory." Beth moaned. "Everything is wrong. Everything!"

Paddy whimpered and wined. Callie picked him up and cradled him to her.

"Pull your shawl up over your head, Beth," Callie instructed. "We've got to find Patrick. Don't let him see you crying like this, Beth. The worst has been done."

Lifting her head and looking her young friend directly in the eyes, Beth whispered, "Has it, Callie? Somehow, I don't think it has." The sound of Beth's tone and the expression of complete hopelessness and resignation in her red-rimmed eyes made Callie shudder. As though a goose had walked on her grave, as Peggy used to say.

Dear Mum,

I have stepped my foot on these new shores of America. I wish with all my heart you had not sent your daughter to the gates of hell. We are not allowed to go into New York as yet, although I can see the city and its wharves from this place across the bay called Staten Island. Here the waterway is very narrow, and a man can row across the bay without working up a sweat.

We are being held at a place called Tompkinsville, facing quarantine because Typhus was found aboard the *Yorkshire*. Like the doctors in Liverpool, this place too is a shame in the face of God. While they hold the poor back from their lives, the captain and his crew are free to enter the city. Were they not aboard the same ship as we? Do they have some magic against disease?

I wrote you how Beth and me had our hair cut. It doesn't look so bad now, since Beth had some little scissors and she evened it out. But it's short, Mum, shorter than Bridget's, and it's all topsy-turvy curls about my head. Mr. Thatcher tells me I look about twelve years old. If my haircut makes me look twelve, it makes Beth look about a hundred. Hers doesn't curl like mine, and it's unmercifully short and lopsided. When I told her I would try to fix hers like she did mine, she just pulled her shawl over her head and cried.

They say it was a hair-cutting ring, Mum, and they just rowed out to the island and set up shop. They caught them, Mum. Policemen came and took them away because it's a crime to cut someone's hair and sell it for profit. Mr. Thatcher says whoever buys Beth's hair and mine will make the finest wigs for some rich lady.

We are all sleeping in a shelter just outside the hospital gates, and there must be over a hundred people in here with us. I used the last bit of my tea yesterday. I did what you told me and used the same tea leaves three times before tossing them away.

I have still not seen or heard from cousin Owen.

Your daughter in America,
Callandre

It was the twenty-seventh day of the *Yorkshire*'s quarantine. While the ship stood at anchor in the bay, her passengers mingled among the thousand or more who had sailed to America in her sister ships.

The month of October had been dry, the last traces of summer warming the days until All Hallows' Eve. Then November struck with vengeance. The waters of the bay were whipped by foul winds, the ground became hard and frozen during the cold nights, warming again beneath the day's sun to become muddy trenches from the abuse of too many feet.

A roll was called, and the passengers from the *Yorkshire* were told to climb the long hill to the hospital for the medical examination before receiving the stamped passes that would allow them access to the City of New York and beyond.

Callie was dismayed to discover that she was expected to undress and submit to a thorough evaluation by a harried doctor and his even more harried nurse assistant. She was standing outside the hospital long before the Thatchers made their exit. One look at their faces told her something was terribly wrong. Beth was ashen, and Patrick's usual bright gaze was dulled and pained. Only Paddy remained the same, whimpering and listless.

Jostled by the incoming and outgoing patients, Patrick quickly led them to the bottom of the hill. For just an instant Callie saw him looking out over the river toward New York City, squinting past the sun, a yearning and longing in his face, a searching in his eyes. He looked like a man lost, without home or family, a man whose dreams must be abandoned. It wasn't until they had made the long walk down the hill to the shelter where they'd spent the last month that Beth turned to her. "It's Paddy," she said, a pitiful sob caught in her voice. "He has consumption. Tuberculosis they call it here. He won't be allowed to come into the country." This last was said in defeat.

"Beth tells you truth, Callie," Patrick said tonelessly. "They want us to send him back to Ireland. Beth and I have had our passes stamped. It's the boy."

Callie thought Beth would crumble from the pain and sorrow on Patrick's face. Tears of frustration and humiliation coursed in rivulets down her cheeks. "We can't send him back! There's no one there to take care of him!" Hysteria was rising in her voice, making it shrill, so different from her usual modulated tones.

"Hush, Beth. Paddy will always have us to care for him. Don't worry so. We'll go back to Ireland. *All* of us," Patrick said, stroking Beth's back. But over the top of her head, his eyes again reached across the river to the city beyond, the place where his dreams told him his future began. He fell silent, locked in his misery.

Late that night, tucked in between Paddy and their assorted baggage, Callie lay awake pondering the dilemma that faced the Thatchers. She was angry, inflamed by the injustice of it all. Back in Ireland and Liverpool the only thing that mattered was selling packet tickets to America. The physical examination there had been a farce. Even she had known that Paddy was a very sick little boy. The Thatchers should never have been allowed to board ship, to undergo the hardships only to be refused entry on the other side after thirty days of living in subhuman conditions.

Callie blessed herself, raised her eyes to heaven, and called on her God. The bad is outnumbering the good, she complained. And Lord help me, but I'm about to give up on You. I was taught

You're our Savior, and I'd appreciate it if You'd start saving us! No bolt of lightning ripped across the sky; no roll of thunder sounded in the heavens. Had He heard? Or was He too busy with the prayers and pleas of others more important than she?

When sleep finally came to Callie, it was light and fitful. She was aware of Beth, just the other side of their rolled pokes, lying very still, small trembling sobs shaking her shoulders. Sympathy stirred her to sit up and touch Beth's shoulder in commiseration. It was then she noticed Patrick was gone.

"Beth," Callie whispered, putting her mouth very close to Beth's ear, "where's Patrick?"

A choked response, so unbearably pained and desolate—"He's out, walking his disappointment. Oh, Callie, Paddy and I are such a burden to him. Such a terrible burden."

"Hush. It was a shock to him, Beth. Surely you understand that. He had such wonderful plans for all of you. You'll all go back to Ireland, and when Paddy is well again, he'll see his dreams realized. Patrick loves you, Beth, and he'll make it right."

"That love is killing him, Callie." There was no emotion in her voice, no tears on her cheeks. This dearth of emotion, of anger, of anything, frightened Callie. "Patrick can't be making this right. It's me and Paddy and the new babe that's holding Patrick back. We've ruined his dream, Callie. And I'll lose him because of it, just as I'll lose Paddy up to his sickness."

Words of comfort would not come to Callie. There was nothing she could say to ease Beth's pain. All that had happened was beyond the realm of her own understanding. Peggy would know what to say, what to do. She'd set Beth's head clear and thinking again. Mum could rebuild Patrick's dead dreams.

"Callie," Beth whispered, "would you change places with me? I want to be near my son. I want to hold him in my arms."

Silently Callie helped Beth to her feet. The woman placed a hand protectively on her belly. "Patrick wanted this babe to be born in America. And as it turns out, 'twould be better if it's not born at all." Bumps broke out on Callie's arms. The goose had stepped on her grave again. She'd always realized Beth Thatcher's vulnerability, her insecurity; perhaps that was why she'd always felt protective toward her. But a new resolve had crept into Beth's voice, and in the dim light of the lanterns that hung from the rafters in the bleak and overcrowded shelter, there was a new light in her eyes. It was a fervor, a determination, a grim decision to see things through to the end. Callie settled down against the bedroll, watching Beth through the darkness as she gathered her son close to her, folding him against her body as though he were the babe who lived in her womb.

Hours later, just as the dawn was breaking, Callie rolled over on the hard floor, pulling the blanket over her shoulders for warmth. She missed Paddy's warm little body tucked against her own and awakened. Glancing around her, she realized Patrick had not returned, and the place she had given to Beth was empty. Callie sat up to look across the room; not a soul in the half-lit shelter was stirring.

It was unlike Beth to leave with Paddy without saying a word. No, it was foolish to worry, Callie comforted herself. Putting her head back down on the bedroll, she closed her eyes. But sleep would not come. She remembered Beth's face and the way her eyes had burned. Could it be that the light that fevered Beth's dark eyes was madness?

Callie rose from her hard place on the floor, her eyes once again searching out the dim corners of the shelter for a sign of Beth and Paddy. The hairs on the back of her neck prickled, and there was a heaviness in the pit of her stomach. Something was warning her, telling her, she must find Beth.

Stepping over sleeping bodies, picking her way through the assorted bedrolls and baggage, she finally made her way to the door, pushing against its flimsiness until it opened into the gray-pink dawn. She looked to the left, up the hill towards the hospital. All was dark there except for the yellow glow from gaslights left on for the night. No, Beth wouldn't go there. She feared the hospital and all it represented: rejection, denial. To the right was the steep path leading down to the beach and the docks. The night air was frigid; frost crackled on the ground beneath her feet. Where was Beth? Where was Paddy?

Her heart beating wildly, Callie stepped onto the path to the dock. She peered through the dim light to the water of the bay where the packet ships lay at anchor. Her shawl was pulled tight around her shoulders, the light morning wind off the water ruffled the new freedom of her short curls.

Halfway down the path she heard the mournful humming of a familiar tune, "Sweet Maid from Killee," Patrick's favorite tune. "Patrick! Patrick!" A form, barely discernible in the light, straightened and began rushing toward her. "Patrick!" Her voice was a harsh cry; she had not known how desperate she was or how terribly frightened until she heard that cry break from her throat. "Patrick! It's Beth! Where's Beth?" Quickly she told him how she'd awakened to find Beth and Paddy gone.

"She's probably taken herself off to the privy," Patrick said logically. "Grab hold of yourself, Callie. I've never seen you this way."

"No! Beth would never have taken Paddy to the privy. You know how she loathes the filth in there. Listen to me, Patrick, something is wrong, very wrong! I don't know, there was something about Beth early this morning when I talked with her. Something desperate in the way she talked and what she said!"

Patrick responded to Callie's distress. "Where do you think she might have gone? Beth! Beth!" he called at the top of his voice. The answering silence seemed to spur his growing alarm. "Beth! For the love of God, where are you?"

"Patrick. She won't answer if she doesn't want to. We have to find her. I'll take the path down to the dock; you skirt around through the shelters and back to the privies and meet me down on the beach."

Callie turned and tore off down the path, slipping and sliding over the loose rocks and pebbles underfoot. The wind from the river was rising with the dawn. Today would be another bleak day, harsh with the promise of the coming winter.

At the end of the path were the piers and docks, the longest of these a jetty of black and slippery rocks that snaked far out into the dark waters of the bay. At the head of the jetty Callie discerned a bulky shape—a woman holding a child, her face turned to meet the dawn. Beth!

At the sound of Callie's footfalls on the pier, Beth turned, clutching little Paddy to her. "No! Don't come any closer," she warned, and to Callie's ears it was the voice of a stranger. This was not Beth's voice, soft and endearing—this was the sound an animal makes when he is cornered.

"Beth! Come back! Please, Beth! Patrick is looking for you; he sent me to find you." Tentatively Callie approached, watching, listening for the slightest sound or movement. Paddy squirmed in his mother's arms. "Callie, pick me up!" She heard his voice clearly as she moved closer to the end of the jetty.

"Hush, love," Beth crooned. "Hush. It will all be over soon, so soon."

The singsong quality of Beth's voice frightened Callie more than anything else. It was the same voice Mrs. Collier used when her little Bobby had died of the influenza and she had rocked his dead body until they came and forcibly took him from her. Beth was rocking and crooning to Paddy in that same way, as though he were already dead.

"Don't come any closer, Callie. You've been a good friend, but there's nothing you can do for us now. There's nothing anyone can do."

"Beth, come away from the edge. There's something I must tell you!" Desperately Callie searched for something to say, something that would give Beth hope, something, anything. "Beth, remember I told you and Patrick about my friend who owns a newspaper? He's a very important man, Beth. I'll send word to him about Paddy. He'll help, I know he will. You remember his name, don't you, Beth?" Cautiously Callie stepped closer and closer as she spoke, hoping she could divert Beth's attention. "Mr. Byrch Kenyon. You said it was such a fine name, remember, Beth?"

As though Callie had never uttered a word, Beth lifted her head. Her voice was a harsh whisper; the madness in her eyes shone. "Tell Patrick I'm so sorry. Tell him the only thing I can give him now is his dream."

Even as Callie watched, Beth stepped backwards, tumbling off the jetty, hardly making a splash in the cold black water, into the greedy current. Callie heard Patrick's shout of denial from somewhere behind her. She heard his feet thundering along the pier, heard him cry his wife's name. And that was all she knew until she found herself shivering in the arms of a stranger. At the end of the jetty there was a crowd of people, like buyers at a market stall. That was her first thought.

She looked down at the black and oily waters of the bay. This was a day she would never forget, didn't want to forget. Tears streaming down her cheeks, Callie walked away from the crowd, away from Patrick, away from the knowledge of what Beth had done for love. All for love.

This was America.

This was the land of hopes and dreams.

This was the day Callie James grew up.

Chapter Six

Callie pulled her shawl closer about the shoulders of her brown woolen dress, careful not to disturb the hand-crocheted lace collar that had been a gift from Peggy. The dainty white cotton lace contrasted sharply with her wind-pink cheeks and the delicate paleness of her throat. It was her best dress, although it was now a bit short and swung just above the ankles of her high-topped, black-buttoned shoes.

She had risen very early that morning to have access to the privy where she washed herself all over, including her hair which now tumbled in thick chestnut curls about her head. Her shoes, a bit run-down at the heels, were wiped and polished with spit the night before. Everything she owned was rolled and packed into two pokes which were secured with laces from an ancient pair of Thomas's shoes. She had to look her best, as Peggy had instructed, when she met cousin Owen for the first time. Only Mum couldn't know that soaking in a tub for three days couldn't remove the Tompkinsville stink that soiled not only the body but the soul as well.

Yesterday afternoon they had found the bodies of Beth and Paddy, snagged on rocks and tree stumps nearly half a mile from the pier where she had taken that final leap. It amazed Callie that hardly any thought was given to the living here in Tompkinsville but huge efforts were made to find a dead woman and child and bring them back for proper burial. Even in death, Beth could not escape Tompkinsville. The current in the river had carried her downstream but never across to the city of New York.

The last time Callie had seen Patrick was at the funeral. Patrick, thinking clearly for the moment, had instructed Callie not to utter a word that Beth's plunge had not been purely accidental. Callie understood. Beth had died an unholy death by committing suicide and would not be allowed to rest in sanctified ground. The unbidden thought that Beth had also committed murder by taking little Paddy with her left Callie breathless and shaken. No one would understand that Beth had been out of her mind with grief and disappointment. Patrick was right. The less said the better. Everyone believed that Beth had had an unfortunate accident; no woman intent on suicide would take her unborn child and her young son with her.

On the flat of land behind the hospital, long deep trenches were dug in the soft and porous soapstone. Here the reek of death was all around, filling the air, even in the cold of November. The dead were buried in trenches nine feet deep, and the rustic coffins were placed in three tiers. The ground was dug out by pick, and broken pieces were scattered to cover the graves. The rain penetrated through the strewn rocks and thin earth, and the stink rose. Here, in an unmarked place, Beth and Paddy were laid. Patrick had stood woodenly at the grave site, head bowed, eyes dry, but in them an expression of grief and defeat that had never been there even during the hardest of times. Callie grieved for Beth and Paddy, placing on the lonely grave a bouquet of thistle and bittersweet she had picked in the bramble hedges along the road to the cemetery. But when the prayers were over, she looked at Patrick and realized, somewhat to her shame, that he would now have a chance to fulfill his dream. It was a gift from Beth, given with her heart. And the cost was her life.

Callie sat on a crate, poke baggage at her feet, riding the ferry across Upper Bay to the city. The November wind lashed at her cheeks on this sunless, dismal day as she looked back at Staten Island and the hospital facilities that stood high on the hill. She raised her eyes to heaven. "I pray it'll be the last I ever see of that place," she said softly. Then she turned to look at the nearing shoreline of the island of Manhattan. And even as I live and work here, she told herself with resolve, I'll never look across the water again! Callie did not seem to be alone in her thinking. As she looked about at the other passengers, not a single head was turned back towards Tompkinsville; all eyes were searching the city before them, looking to the future, determined to forget the past.

The open ferry slid soundlessly into its berth. The engine belched steam, and its whistle blew with an asthmatic groan to herald its arrival at the South Street port. Falling into step with the other passengers, Callie walked the cobbled slope into the busy terminal. Hustled and jostled, she found a relatively quiet corner against a window looking out onto the streets of New York. Byrch Kenyon had told her the truth; the street was not paved in gold nor did anyone here seem especially prosperous. New York City seemed to hold the same ragged masses as did Dublin. Long lines of travelers and peddlers waited to be taken across on the returning ferry to Tompkinsville. Vendors selling hot chestnuts and peculiar twists of bread plied their wares. Men pushed wooden-wheeled carts filled with rags or vegetables; others sold apples at three cents apiece. That was something she'd have to learn, American dollars and cents. She'd had a taste of it during the quarantine, and it seemed simple enough. Patrick had shown her a silvered coin and told her it was called a nickel. Callie had decided it was her favorite. Still, all manner of money was acceptable to these Americans. The lead-colored shilling she had saved from Uncle Jack's generosity, the copper penny, and the little round ha'penny were all safely stowed away in a little drawstring pouch pinned to her chemise.

Callie huddled into her corner, waiting for the appearance of cousin Owen. Most of her fellow passengers from the ferry had left the terminal, having been met by family or friends or wandered into the city on their own. Porters, or runners, as Callie had heard them called, wrestled with crates and baggage, checking names against tags and extending their hands for gratuities reluctantly given. As she waited, apprehension was churning in Callie's breast. She had no way of knowing who, among these men loitering about the terminal, might be Peggy's cousin. For that matter, he had no way of knowing her either. Colleen had sent him a description of herself as he had asked, stating her height and weight and bright auburn hair. But where Callie was diminuative, Colleen was tall and buxom; where Colleen was bright-haired and freckled, Callie felt as brown and dim as a backyard wren. Also, there was the difference in their ages: Colleen was almost nineteen and already a woman; Callie was just sixteen but looked even younger. Would Cousin Owen be terribly disappointed?

A small man, wearing what Callie could only think of as a horse blanket tailored into a jacket and trousers, was staring at her across the nearly empty terminal. She could feel his eyes boring into her even though she looked away. Was this the way Americans dressed? Bright tweeds and boxy plaids, walking sticks and jaunty caps? A shiny stickpin was prominently displayed in the fold of his cravat. A diamond? Glass? Whatever, it was big enough to choke the horse who'd lost the blanket. As she had feared, the flamboyantly attired man approached her, a lopsided grin breaking across his narrow face. "Beggin' yer pardon, Miss, but you wouldn't be Colleen O'Brien, would you?"

It was clear to Callie that the man truly hoped she wasn't. "Allow me to introduce myself," he said importantly, "Owen Gallagher, Miss. I was awaiting the arrival of my cousin from Dublin, Colleen O'Brien."

She searched for her voice, knowing how disappointed he would be when she told him. "I'm Callie James, your cousin Peg's oldest girl. Colleen couldn't come because she's getting married. She gave me the ticket you sent, instead." There, it was out. Let him make of it what he would. If he didn't want her, couldn't help her, then let him send her back, and pray God he did.

Owen Gallagher tipped his cap back, revealing a high forehead and thin, tight blond curls. Hands on hips, he looked up and down the length of her, his features tightening with disapproval. Callie spoke up. "I'm young and I'm strong, and I can give a good day's work!" She realized that if Peggy and the family were to survive, she must make her way here in America.

Owen Gallagher continued to look her up and down. He was thinking he had bought himself a pig in a poke. What good was this child to him? Thirteen, if she was a day, and her hair was an abomination. Men like to run their fingers through a woman's hair. True, her hair was thick and glossy and tumbled around her head in wicked little curls, but she'd been shorn like a sheep in springtime. For sure, this little lamb wouldn't get him a return on his investment of a ticket from Ireland. She looked as though a good wind would blow her over, and he didn't like the sound of the cough she tried to hide. On the other hand, she was the picture of an Irish lass: fair skin, pink cheeks, clear blue eyes fringed with long black lashes, and a pert little nose that pointed straight up to heaven. There were men who had appetites for the very young—the younger and smaller the more they paid. No, all wasn't lost, Gallagher told himself, suddenly pleased. Especially considering that this little one had no one to depend upon but himself. She'd be putty in his hands. The older, more independent Colleen might have taken it into her head that she didn't need nor want cousin Owen's protection.

Thrusting his hands into his trouser pockets, he walked around Callie, appraising her carefully. She squirmed beneath his inspection. She didn't like cousin Owen; he was as slick as a greased pig at the fair.

"How old are ya? How much do you weigh?"

"What's it to you, sir?" The title of respect was said with sarcasm. "You paid for my ticket and here I am." No, she didn't like cousin Owen, and though there were no snakes in Ireland, she'd seen pictures of them in the Bible, their black reptilian eyes staring out from the page, the soul behind them hidden from view. Owen Gallagher had such eyes.

"A sharp tongue won't serve you here, girlie. Be nice and polite," he admonished, a hard edge in his voice raising the hackles on the back of Callie's neck.

Something in Callie shrank from this man who was supposed to be her protector. As she had since she was a wee child, to save herself the shame and embarrassment of showing weakness, Callie stared at him levelly, pursing her full lips and tilting her chin upwards, steeling herself, holding back her fear.

"Feisty little thing, ain't cha?" Gallagher sneered. "Don't be getting hoity-toity with me, Miss. The way I sees it, you owe me the price of a ticket from Ireland to New York. You cheated me by showin' up instead of Colleen, and the law won't look too kindly on that, I can tell you." He leaned so close to her that she could smell the liquor on his breath. "And don't be thinkin' I won't go to the law just because you're family. A deal's a deal, and the honest business man is treated fairly here in America." His words had the impact he intended. She shrank back against the wall; he could hear her breathing, sharp and erratic, but damn it all, she still had that look of defiance about her. Instinct told him this piece of fluff was going to make trouble. He should just forget the loss of her fare from Ireland and let her go her own way. After all, what was a few pounds to a man who always had the jingle of a coin in his pocket and still more hidden under the floorboards in his basement flat? But studying her more closely, he recognized a good deal of potential in this girl. She was young and small, and if he was any judge, her hips would be slim as a boy's and her chest not much more developed. She would be a good one to add to his stable, allowing him to cater to some men's specialized preferences.

Owen backed off a step or two, giving Callie breathing room. "Since you're here, you can come along with me. But don't forget, I won't put up with any shenanigans." It was a threat; it was a promise.

"I'm a hard worker; I'll give a good day's work for a day's pay. I can read and write and do numbers—"

"Oh! A real educated Miss, I see. Well, you won't get nowhere unless you know when to keep your mouth shut. What I have in mind for you don't require no readin' nor writin'. You might say I won't mind you layin' down on the job!" This struck Owen as hilariously funny, and he broke into raucous laughter. "All right, Miss James, is it? Get your things and come along. Is this all you have in the way of baggage?" He smiled at her. The attempt at friendliness was almost an obscenity, and Callie bristled.

"My trunks and hat boxes, not to mention the royal jewels, will be arriving on the Cunard line!" she drawled insolently. "Of course this is all I have. If I had more, do you think I'd be dependent on *your* good will?"

Quicker than a striking snake, cousin Owen had her by the arm, squeezing it unmercifully. "I told you to watch that sharp tongue of yours," he warned, his soft, lilting tone in direct contrast to the threat in his eyes and the force on her arm. "Men . . . people don't like to hear a young girl being fresh. I take back what I said about you being educated. You're smart, all right, alley smart. Now pick up your things and come along."

His release on her arm was as sudden as his grip, leaving her shaken and afraid, aware of his potential for violence and making her feel more alone than ever. She might be young and inexperienced, but she was no fool. Cousin Owen was not going to use her fairly. Callie raised her eyes heavenward. "Good Lord, what have You gotten me into? It's clear my interests aren't at the top of Your list."

"Did you say somethin'?" Owen asked over his shoulder.

"I talk to myself sometimes," Callie answered.

Owen rolled his eyes. A cuckoo in the bargain. He led the way out of the terminal into the harsh November wind. Callie, burdened by her blanket pokes, followed close behind. As he walked, Owen swung his brass-handled walking stick, moving along at a jaunty pace. The trousers of his suit were tight-fitting and strapped beneath the boots—hugging his bowed legs which probably were the reason for his unusual toe-out gait—as though he were squashing bugs under his heels.

They walked several blocks along the cobbled streets. Buildings and tenement houses rose up from the sidewalks to an astonishing four or five stories, their red brick facades decorated by slate lintels over the windows and doorways. Every house, it seemed, was fronted by a porch, or stoop as they called it in Dublin, and all were attached to one another just like the row houses back home. Home, Callie thought. This was home now.

Shops and eating houses and taverns spilled their sounds and smells onto the street; delivery carts and beer wagons clattered over the cobbles, their horses slat-ribbed and plodding. She heard the sounds of her own Ireland in the brogue and lilt of voices, and there were other sounds too: the harsh, guttural tones of Germans, the melodious language of black men and women, and even, to her surprise, a small yellow man dressed in black with a round hat perched on his head and a long black pigtail hanging down his back. He turned to look at her, his flat features breaking into a smile, his slanted eyes dancing with amusement.

"What kind of man is that?" Callie asked, tugging at Owen's sleeve.

"Him? He's a Chinee. You'll see people from all over the world here. Eyetalians, Germans, Portugee, but thank yer stars it's mostly the fine folk of Ireland you'll find yourself with. Course, there's them what calls themselves Americans. They was born here and think they don't stink because of it!" Owen spit down on the sidewalk. "Those are the kind to stay away from, take my advice. They don't think much of the Irish, and I'm pleased to say the Irish don't think much of them. Think they're better than the rest of us." Owen loved it when he could display his worldliness and thought of himself as a man about town.

"Where are we going?" Callie ventured to ask, lugging her pokes and shifting them from one arm to the other. She could feel her stomach rumble. She'd not even had a cup of tea this morning and couldn't remember the last time she'd had a piece of bread.

"It's not far. Just uptowns a ways. We'll take the trolley at the next corner."

He saw her struggling with her belongings but didn't offer to help. She'd lugged them all the way from Dublin, she could lug them a ways farther. "See them tracks set in the street?" he pointed. "Those is trolley tracks. Makes for a nice, easy ride over the cobbles. Hurry up now, don't fall behind. I've got business to take care of."

Callie quickened her pace, almost falling into step beside him but not quite. "There are no streets paved with gold . . . are there?"

"Now don't you be tellin' me you believed that fairy tale. Tis a land of opportunity, but only for those who work at it. And me, cousin deary, I work at it."

"What kind of work? What'll I be doing here? I need money to send my mum back in Dublin. You know what's going on there, don't you? Sometimes there's hardly enough for the little one's supper."

"Now ain't that a shame!" Owen sneered. "Listen, girlie, I don't care what's happening in Ireland or anywhere else for that matter. Owen Gallagher only concerns himself with himself and his own pockets. If you want to take everything you've got and throw it away, that's your business, not mine. I said you were smart; it won't take long before you think of yourself first and leave the rest to the devil."

"Why did you bring me over here?" Callie demanded, her voice a hiss. "We all thought you were trying to help out some. I came to work, to send money to the family—"

"Listen," Owen said nastily, "I didn't bring you over here. T'was Colleen I sent for. I could tell from her letters that she's an enterprising young lady and wanted more than anythin' to get herself away from Ireland. She seemed to know what life was all about. You said she's gettin' married. No doubt she's already got a cake in the oven, right?"

Callie looked at him quizzically. Then it dawned on her. "Yes, Colleen's going to have a baby . . ."

"That's what I said, right? She knows what life's all about. Trouble is, she didn't know enough. Now, my girls know how to take care of themselves, they do. Or out they go! I don't keep no charity cases, and when a girl can't work, she's got no place with me. Just you remember that." This was all wrong. She should be grateful. Instead he found himself with a hellcat. There would be no fooling this one for long. He thought of the handsome prices she could earn for him, and he had recently lost Trisha because of a botched-up abortion. An empty bed in his house brought no revenue, and he was eager to fill it.

A horse-drawn conveyance pulled up the street at a clip. The car was open-sided with benches all in a row, some of them facing outward to the street. Cousin Owen instructed Callie to get aboard while he dug in his pocket for two coins, which he dropped into a little change box held out by the conductor. Callie sank down on the hard, painted seat, tucking her pokes alongside her.

"Don't get too comfortable, it's not that far."

"Then why didn't we walk?"

"Owen Gallagher never walks when he can ride."

Callie hung out over the side, looking up at buildings and down at the people passing by. A group of children tossed a ball back and forth, and she heard their shouts and calls at play. The sound was somehow comforting.

"We get off here," Owen told her. "Come along and don't leave anything behind."

"Hardly, when this is all I own in the world," Callie muttered. She was liking her situation and Cousin Owen less and less by the moment. She didn't like the way he tugged at her arm and practically pushed her off the high step of the trolley. When her feet touched the street, she dropped her pokes and stood facing him, hands on hips. "I'm not moving another step unless you tell me where you're taking me and what I'll be doing when I get there!"

"Just shut that mouth of yours and quit attracting attention. I'm known in this town and I have a reputation to consider, and I don't want you spoiling it for me. Now keep quiet and talk when I tell you." He picked up her pokes and was pushing them into her arms.

"Why?" Callie demanded bluntly, dropping her pokes for the second time. "I want to know *now*!"

A brat! A big mouth! He certainly didn't need this skinny piece of baggage. "You'll be livin' in that fine house across the street there. You'll be with other girls, and they'll tell you what t'do. They like it!" he said defensively.

"And exactly what do you get out of all this? You said you were a business man and only concerned with your own pockets. You tell me now, or I don't go one step further."

Owen glanced around in desperation. His quick eye caught a glimpse of a blue uniform down on the next corner. He didn't need the police poking into his business; he paid enough in graft as it was. And what if one of his rivals saw one of his girls giving him trouble? "You'll just do what the girls tell you, and I get a piece of your wages. Er . . . for room and board and, of course, my protection."

Callie didn't miss the desperate look in Owen's eyes as he looked up and down the street, and she was becoming more suspicious by the minute. "What kind of house do you have? Is it anything like that whorehouse at the end of Bayard Street back in Dublin?" She purposely made her voice loud.

Owen was sweating under his collar, keeping a quick eye on the policeman strolling up the street, swinging his billy club. "Now where would a little thing like you ever learn about whorehouses?

For shame!" Then an idea hit him, one that had worked before with reluctant employees. "Turn around, cousin, look to the end of the street to that blue uniform swaggering up the block. D'ya know who that is? Well, I'll tell ya. T'is the law, a copper, a blue jacket, a policeman. Understand? I don't plan on standing out here freezing. Either you come with me now or I'll turn you over to him. Remember how fine things were over to Tompkinsville? He knows a right fine place for girls the likes of you who don't want to work. A place that'll make Tompkinsville seem like paradise. Then how'll you send money to your mum?"

Owen saw doubt creep into Callie's eyes. He'd scared her just the way he had scared all the rest when they'd given him trouble. But there was something behind her rebellious blue stare that made him think she'd cut his heart out if given the chance. This one was going to give him headaches, he knew it.

Without a word, Callie picked up her pokes and followed Owen across the thoroughfare to 16 Cortlandt Street, a four-story tenement. She climbed the nine steps of the front stoop and waited while he jingled the assortment of keys on his ring and unlocked the front door. Perhaps she was wrong. Owen Gallagher must be a well-to-do businessman if he possessed the keys to the front door! To the entire house! In Dublin, six or seven families might live in a house much smaller than this. Inside the house, Callie was assailed by the stench of cooked cabbage and dirt. The hallway was dark and narrow, the stairs leading to the floors above worn and rickety and much in need of repair. The floor needed a good sweeping and scrubbing, and there was a lingering odor of old cigar smoke and something that reminded her of urine.

She was ushered into a room at the front, which Owen called a parlor. It was meagerly furnished with a dilapidated sofa, a chair, and several small tables. Callie sniffed and sneezed from its close atmosphere and the balls of dust that hid in the corners.

"You wait here and I'll be right back," Owen grumbled. "Now sit!"

Owen returned to the front hall and ran up the flight of dark, narrow stairs to the next floor. He rapped smartly on one of the six panel doors that led off the center hall. "Go 'way!" came a muffled complaint.

"Madge, get your tail out of that bed and come to the door. We've got a problem."

A frowzy woman of questionable age with ponderous breasts struggled up from her sagging mattress. She loved her bed and spent every spare minute in it. It was a joke that once Madge got a man in the bellied-out hollow of that mattress he'd yell for mercy. She pushed back long kinky hair from her face to which the ravages of last night's lip rouge and powder still clung. She opened the door, leaning against the jamb, looking out at Owen. "Why is it 'we' have a problem when you get yourself into a mess and 'I' have a problem when the money doesn't come in fast enough?"

"Never mind, never mind." Owen pushed his way into the heavily curtained room that did not allow even a glimmer of light from the window. "Fer God's sake, why do ya keep this room so dark?"

"'Cause I like it that way! Now what's your problem? O'Shaughnessy refuse to deliver the liquor till you've paid your bill?"

"Nah! I've got a cousin downstairs—"

"A cousin now, is it? Well, don't ever count me as one of your family, you snake." Madge scratched her rump; the narrow gray straps of her chemise fell off her fleshy shoulder. "You said yesterday you'd be bringing in a girl to replace Trisha, rest her soul. I said it before and I say it again, that business with Trisha was your fault, Gallagher. If you'd been a little more careful and a bit more generous, she could've had the job done at the usual place instead of with the butcher you set her to."

"That's water under the bridge." Owen scowled, pulling open one of the drapes, wishing he hadn't when he turned to face Madge again. All traces of prettiness were lost to the aging harlot, lost to sin and liquor. But she ran a decent house and kept the girls in line and paid off the law and anyone else who nosed around more than was good for them. Madge was all right. "Fer Jesus sake, put some clothes on!"

Madge took the order as a compliment. "Why, Owen sweet, I didn't think anything could rouse you. Whatever you say," she said, pulling on a beribboned scarlet wrapper over her chemise.

"The problem is," Owen asserted, "she's just over from Ireland, and they cut her hair out to Tompkinsville. Almost as short as my own, blast their souls. She looks more a lad than me own brother. She can't be more than thirteen, and she's so little and skinny the wind would blow her over. On top of that, she's a tongue that would make the devil himself wish for sainthood. That's the straight of it, and I don't know what to do with her."

"Send her back. I don't want no part of a kid. If you're smart, you won't have nothin' to do with her either. I'm in this business for money, not to wet-nurse some kid."

"You ain't too smart, are ye, Madge? This kid ain't got nobody here in America but me. Only me. Who's she gonna run to? Besides, you know yourself, there's those men who have a taste for little girls. She'd even be appealing to them what have a hankering for boys. There's money in her, Madge, I can smell it. And since this is my house and my business, I don't want no lip from you. You'll do as I say."

Madge arched her thin, pencilled brows. "And who says so, Mr. Gallagher? There's plenty of pimps who'd want me to run their houses for them and keep the girls in line, and don't you forget it!"

Owen knew this to be true and tried a different tack. "Ain't you ever had the urge to be a mother? She'll steal your heart, this one will. Be nice to her, Madge, take her under your wing and teach her the business."

"Steal my heart? What heart? And if she's kin to you, that's not all she'll be stealing. If you've got any more bright ideas, save them. You're a slick weasel, is what you are, Owen Gallagher. Why I put up with the likes of you is more than I know."

Owen dreaded the look he saw on Madge's face. Looks like that always emptied his purse. Later he would worry about dealing with Madge; right now he had a little investment down in the parlor that, if handled the right way, would make him a rich man. "I have business up on Broadway that needs my attention," he said, "so I'll leave the girl up to you. Her name is Callie. Don't let her mouth worry you none."

"How hard can it be to deal with a kid?" Madge snorted, missing the way Owen's eyes rolled. "Go on and see to your business, and I'll handle things here. But I'm warning you, Gallagher, I'll try her for two days, that's all. I've got better things to do with my time. After that, if she doesn't work out, you get her out of here and off my hands. Agreed?"

Owen Gallagher would have agreed to selling his soul at that moment. He nodded briskly and slid through the open doorway like the snake he was.

Madge sighed lustily. She did everything lustily. She wondered if she should take the time for a quick wash and decided against it. She'd better see to the kid. She'd try a bit of the mothering Gallagher suggested.

Callie had just completed her ninth circle of the small parlor and was becoming impatient. Where was Owen? All manner of doubts were creeping into her head when she looked up and saw a woman dressed in the most magnificent wrapper she'd ever seen. She was conscious of the buxom shelf of breasts and then of the darkest, dancingest eyes smiling down at her. She couldn't help herself, and she reached out to touch the gaudy dressing gown. "It's beautiful," she murmured with awe. "Some day I'd like to send my mum one just like it."

Madge eyed Callie suspiciously but found no hint of mockery in her face. Her youth and innocence almost brought tears to Madge's eyes. Oh, no you don't, Madge Collins, she scolded herself, there's no such thing as a whore with a heart of gold and you know it! She looked down into Callie's sweet face and saw the clear blue eyes fringed with thick black lashes. The kid's gonna be a beauty, her experienced eye told her. "A gentleman friend brought me this from Paris. That's Paris, France," she clarified. "Once it had feathers up here, but they all molted like the bird they came from."

"Even without the feathers, it's beautiful! My mum would look like a stage actress in that. I know it must have cost a fortune, and your gentleman friend must have thought very highly of you to bring it all the way from France. I know I'll never see Paris, France."

"Don't say never," Madge said. "I used to say things like 'never' and 'ever' and 'forever' and look at me. I got me this dressing gown fit for a queen and who'd 've thought it? Not me, I'll tell ya! Say, you look hungry and so'm I. When's the last time you had something to eat?"

"Yesterday. I didn't even have time for tea this morning, thank you, Mrs. . . ."

"Collins. But you call me Madge, you hear? A little thing like you needs to eat regular. Come with me." Madge ushered Callie down the dark hallway to the kitchen. "Let's have some bacon, potatoes, and eggs. How's that sound? Do you like buttermilk? I think there's some in the window box, and it should be nice and cold, considering the weather we've had recently. I've got some fresh bread, and we can have some of that wild strawberry jam I made last summer," she said proudly. "Why'nt you get the buttermilk? It's right outside that window."

Callie lifted the grimy window to fetch the milk out of the little window box. The aroma of frying bacon and potatoes was ambrosia to her senses, and the sizzle of the eggs frying in the fat was music to her ears. When Madge put her plate down in front of her, Callie felt light-headed just looking at it. "I'm almost afraid to eat it. It's been so long I'm afraid I'll get sick."

"Eat slow and chew it well and your stomach won't object." Jesus, now where had she heard that? Madge wondered with a start. She sounded like her own mother. The feeling was nice. "After we eat, you're gonna have a bubble bath. Did you ever have a bubble bath?"

"Ma'am, my mum kept us real clean. I got a bath once or twice a week, whenever we could afford the peat for the fire to heat water. Lately its been cold water for all of us. We were poor," she said quietly.

"Kid, I've been poor myself. I know what it's all about. You sit there and eat while I heat some water. I'm gonna scrub you down myself and wash your hair. What happened to it, anyways?"

"They cut it off because they said I had lice."

Madge held her fork poised in mid-air. "Do you?" She hated vermin of any kind.

"No. They just said that so they could cut my hair and sell it to wigmakers. It was a . . ." She searched for the right word. "Scam."

"Now where would a kid like you hear a word like that?"

"A kid like me had it done to her. I have eyes and ears, and that's what I heard them say it was. But I don't have lice and never did. You can look in my hair if you don't believe me."

"I believe you, I believe you," Madge declined the offer. "I hate cooties, hate 'em more than anything. Only thing to do for them is to wash your hair with kerosene and that burns like hell." Madge studied her young guest and felt her heart swell as Callie popped a potato into her mouth. How young she was, and how alone, with no one but that pimp Owen to thank for her living. Madge sighed heavily.

"Mrs. Collins . . . Madge. What will you do with me after the bath? What kind of work will I do here?"

"I have to give it some thought. But you can believe one thing and it ain't two. I'll do what's best for you. I promise you that. Here, have another slice of bread and more jam. Put some meat on those bones." Madge herself reached for the jam jar and spread it thickly on the bread.

"Do you work for my cousin Owen?"

"In a manner of speaking. I think it'd be more truthful to say we're sort of partners."

"What do you do?"

"I guess you could say I deal in services. Yeah, I sell my services."

"Does that mean you're a lady of the evening?" Callie asked quietly.

Madge suppressed a chuckle. Owen was right. This kid was

no dummy. "Of the evening and the morning and afternoon. Whatever, whenever."

"And my cousin thinks I'm going to learn the trade from you. Is that why he brought me here?"

"No, kid, no. He brought you here because he had nowhere else to take you. You're so young. The other girls . . . well, the other girls are older. Twenty, and even as old as twenty-five. Good girls, all of them, they do what they're told and don't make trouble. That's how we all make out."

Callie worked on her plate of eggs and drained her glass of buttermilk dry. "You just sit there, give your stomach a rest. The water isn't hot enough yet for your bath. You'll have to do some fancy soaking, and we've got to air out those clothes of yours. And wash your drawers and things. Maybe we've got some things around here that'll fit you."

"What will you do with me?"

"The Lord only knows. Just trust me, kid. Can you do that?"

"How many girls work here?"

"You're the nosey one, ain't you. There's nine girls, including me and a woman who works in the kitchen. None of us are much at cooking and cleaning."

"You are, Madge. That was the best plate of eggs I ever ate!"

The compliment endeared Callie to Madge forever. "Come along now," she instructed, "you can help me carry the tub in here, and we'll put it in front of the stove where it's warm. You fill it, and I'll get some towels and clean clothes for you. Where's your baggage?"

"In the parlor. I don't have anything much, and everything smells just the same as I do." Callie's back stiffened against the shame of it. She knew she sounded defensive, but she couldn't help it. "I am what I am," she told Madge. "Take me or leave me, it's your choice."

"Couldn't have said it better myself. We'll get along just fine. You do what I say and we won't have any problems."

"Is that the same thing as saying, 'If I want your opinion, I'll tell you what it is'?"

Madge roared with laughter. Callie noticed she didn't answer, though.

By the time the final rinse water was carted off and Callie was wrapped in a large towel, the house began to take on life. The cook arrived and was busy getting dinner ready for "her girls." The gentlemen would start arriving when darkness fell. Madge wrapped a smaller towel around Callie's head and headed her in the direction of the stairs, but first she stopped in the front parlor to introduce Callie to what she called her constituents. It was hard to guess their ages with all the makeup the women had on their faces. None of them seemed as old as Madge, but neither were any of them as young as Callie. Seasoned was what Madge called them. Callie made a note to figure all of that out later.

"Listen, ladies, I have an announcement to make. I won't be working this evening." If Madge had dropped a bomb, she couldn't have gotten a better reaction. It was obvious that Madge never took time off. The second bomb dropped when she announced that she had to make a dress for Callie.

"But you don't know how to sew," Shirley said in a squeaky voice. Shirley pretended to be seventeen, but everyone knew she'd never see twenty-seven again.

"I know, but I'm going to do the best I can. The kid has nothing to wear," Madge said.

"Where are you going to get the material? You had Bessie make you a dress out of that yellow silk a month ago," said a young woman named Dorothy. "I suppose you'll be wanting that length of blue wool that Mr. Warner gave me."

"It never crossed my mind," Madge said.

"And what about button holes? I'm the only one who knows how to make button holes," Sara said haughtily. "If you go trying to make button holes, you'll botch up the whole dress."

"I know, but I'm going to try. We can't have this kid going around looking like a ricky-ticky immigrant."

"I could give you that yard of lace Mr. Johns gave me last year," a plump woman named Elsie offered.

"Never! For shame. I know how you treasure that lace," Madge responded.

"Tell me you aren't going to ask for my muslin!" said a tall, overly made up woman who had the same kind of cough as Paddy.

"Bite your tongue, Fanny Mae. I'd never ask for your muslin. If the kid has to go without a petticoat, why should you care?"

"Does she have bloomers?" a tiny girl named Hester demanded.

"I don't know. Callie, do you have bloomers?"

"No, ma'am."

"You see! You see, this tyke has nothing."

"Mr. Owen Gallagher is going to be throwing a fancy fit if we close down tonight," Sara giggled.

"Who cares?" Bessie laughed. "Come on, girls, let's get this waif started. No disrespect, Madge, but you just sit and watch."

"Girls, you are too generous. Too generous. Aren't they generous, Callie?"

"Very generous," Callie said, enjoying the way Madge had set up her little scam. Women, Callie decided, could do just about anything they set their minds to.

Madge gave the cook the night off and told her to lock all the doors. "Hang a sign on the front door saying we're closed . . . for repairs." The girls doubled over laughing. Madge joined in and almost fell off the parlor sofa.

"Now, you girls go get your sewing things, and I'll just sit here and try to figure out a way for Mr. Owen Gallagher to be paying us recompense for the night off. Be prepared to rebel if the going gets sticky. That man is a weasel, and we all know it!"

The women in Madge's employ were impressed with the boss's sudden display of concern for young Callie. Theirs was a world devoid of children, for the most part, and the generous feeling quickly spread among them. For the night, at least, they would all be honorary mothers, and they could forget the tawdrier side of their lives. In Callie, they had a common goal, not to mention a rare night off with pay.

"Rosey," Madge directed the cook, "get a couple of pitchers of beer before you leave. And on your way home have O'Shaughnessy bring over a keg. We'll use those fancy beer mugs we save for our best customers." She garnered appreciation and smiles from the other women. "I'm certain Mr. Gallagher would want us to enjoy only the best." There was more than one way to skin a cat; you just had to know which way to yank the hide.

It was a night to remember as far as Callie was concerned. They all laughed and sang and told jokes that she didn't quite understand, but she laughed anyway. It was so long since she had laughed and had been around happy people. It was good to feel like a child again—without responsibility, with someone looking out for her for a change. By midnight she was the proud possessor of a new light-blue wool dress, two petticoats, and three pairs of bloomers, all exquisitely hand-stitched. Her other clothing had been aired and washed and ironed, and her shoes were polished to a respectable shine.

In the wee hours of the morning, when the keg of beer was nearly empty, Madge hit upon the solution to Callie's dilemma. "Now we're all agreed this is no life for the kid. And we all know how those female societies keep banging on our door and demanding this house and others like it be shut down by the blue jackets. They want to save us from this life of sin, they say, so who better to save little Callie here? Fine upstanding women of the community, they call themselves. Pains in the ass, I calls them. But they just may be the answer to our kid's problem."

Fanny lifted her head from her sewing. She was putting a patch on a tear in Callie's old dress. "A nasty patch is better than a pretty hole, my mother always said," she repeated several times as she worked, receiving praise from the others on the fine quality of her handiwork. Now she questioned Madge, "And how do you suppose we'll get our kid over to them? Just walk up, bang on their door, and leave Callie on their doorstep?"

Madge took another swallow of frothy beer. "Nah! That's too risky, too much chance of our kindhearted Mr. Gallagher finding out. No, what we've got to do is arrange to have Callie kidnapped."

"Kidnapped!" the gasps filled the room.

"Right, kidnapped. I heard there was a place over to five corners that didn't pay protection to the blue jackets, and those fancy ladies just marched in and had the girls taken away. That's the closest thing to kidnapping I ever heard. So, what I'm thinkin' is we'll get in touch with that Magdalene Female Society, the ones who have a place out on Bleecker Street. Callie'll be safe there, and that weasel Gallagher will never find her. Even if he does, he'll have some tall explaining to do." Madge was toasted by clinking beer mugs and pronounced the smartest woman in New York.

Callie listened and frowned. Everything was still so uncertain. Where would she find work? When would she be able to send money home to Peggy? And who or what was this Magdalene Female Society anyway?

Callie slept in Madge's hammock-shaped bed, warm against her protector's fleshy body. By noon the next day everyone was enjoying Madge's famous fried eggs, done to a turn in hot bacon fat and sizzled with brown lace around the edges. From her place by the stove, Madge lectured importantly.

"Now, ladies, if we want this kidnapping to come off on schedule, we have to plan it. As you all know, Bessie took herself off to Bleecker Street this morning posing as a do-gooder from the swell end of town. She described Callie and told them she'd be outside just after three o'clock this afternoon. Now, Callie, put on all the bloomers, the two petticoats, and your new dress. Anything else you'll want to take, put in your poke, and I'll see it gets sent on to you later, but you'll have enough to keep you meantime. And since you took such a fancy to my wrapper, I'll be sending it on to your mum if you give me the address. I'll have it washed and ironed first, of course," Madge added hastily.

Callie was wide-eyed and astonished. "You'd do that for me?" she asked with awe as she tried to picture Peggy's face when she opened the parcel.

Madge shrugged. "I never did like the man who gave it to me. I just took it to be polite. In this business you don't look a gift horse in the mouth." She turned back to her frying eggs before the glisten of tears in her dark eyes could be noticed.

Promptly at three o'clock Callie rushed around kissing and hugging everyone who'd made it possible for her to leave. She lingered with Madge, a shyness suddenly coming over her. She didn't quite know what to say to this woman who had taken charge of her for so short a time. "If I didn't already have a mother, I know I'd want one just like you. I won't forget what you did for me, Madge. I hope you don't get into trouble with Owen."

Madge hugged the girl close. "Let's just pretend I was standin' in for your mum for a day or so. Go along with you now. You know where we are in case you need us. You'll be safe with those fancy ladies looking after you."

"Fancy or not, they can't be as good as you, Madge!"

"We'll be watching out the windows, Callie. Everything will work out, you'll see. Remember to take the broom out of the kitchen, so's it looks like you were sent out to sweep the stoop."

Callie tried to concentrate on sweeping the debris and cigar butts from the steps. She felt heavy and lopsided wearing three pairs of bloomers, two petticoats, and the warm woolen stockings Bessie had given her. The comb and brush and few coins Madge had pressed on her at the last minute were safely tucked away in a reticule worn about her waist under the new blue dress. Callie worked her way down the steps, forcing herself to keep from looking up and down the street for the people who were to come and kidnap her. She was nearing the bottom step when two men and a woman approached and asked her name.

"Callie James," she told the woman, looking into a square, plain face that was topped by a black hat worn at a tilt over the brow and festooned with quivering feathers.

"Don't make a scene and come along quietly," the woman told her. "We mean you no harm. We've come to save you from a life of sin and the reward of hell. You're a Christian, we take it?"

Callie nodded her head, reminding herself not to look back toward the house to see if anyone was watching from the windows.

"It matters little if you've already fallen from God's grace," the woman told her. "We cast no stones. We want to save your soul, Callie James. Do you love the Lord? Do you believe in His Word?" she held up a black book, pushing it under Callie's nose, letting her recognize the Bible.

Callie nodded. Yes, she'd been taught to love the Lord. Yes, Peggy had taught her to believe His Word.

"Then come along, Callie James, to save your life and your soul."

Callie fell into step between the two men. She prayed this was the right thing to do. Madge said it was, so it must be.

Behind the heavy drapes of 16 Cortlandt Street, Madge and her girls clung together watching Callie being escorted away. They clung to one another, wiping at their eyes, until Madge blew her nose lustily and said they would break out Owen's last bottle of corn whiskey.

"Fanny, I want you to take my red wrapper to the Chinee on the corner and have him clean it. I have to make arrangements to post it off tomorrow. A promise is a promise. All right, ladies, we have things to do, and we've got to get our stories straight for Gallagher, so let's get to it."

The women settled themselves in the parlor and listened to Madge. "We all know the best lie is the one closest to the truth. Here's what we'll say. Too hoodlums broke in here last night just before opening. We'll say they looked like part of that gang from over in Hoboken that Gallagher's so afraid of. Anyways, they broke in and stole Gallagher's corn whiskey and beer and had their way with each of us. First they hung out the sign that said the house was closed for repairs, only they had me print it 'cause they can't write. Then we say they took Callie off with them because they liked little girls, and they said they'd kill anyone who tried to get her back."

When Owen Gallagher heard Madge's story, he shook his head, his face whitening in fear of the Hoboken gang that was pushing its way into the neighborhood. His fear squelched any sympathy or regret over losing Callie. He didn't even squawk when Madge demanded "a night's pay for all we went through when we could've been killed!"

"If you weren't so cheap, you'd pay for some protection around here, Gallagher. My girls and me won't work another night until you get us some bodyguards!"

It seemed to Madge that Owen couldn't peel off the bills fast enough before making tracks down the street.

Chapter Seven

If Madge and the others had known what they were sending Callie to, they might have reconsidered and judged that their little "refugee" was better off in their own care and under the auspices of Owen Gallagher. As it was, the female societies enjoyed good public relations, and because they were supported by generous patronesses who lived at the best addresses in New York, they were looked upon as estimable organizations for the protection and moral refinement of their wards. In some instances this might be true, but in most cases the opposite was the reality.

Callie was escorted to a plain brick building on Bleecker Street, which was designated by a polished brass shield over the door, Bleecker Street Magdalene Female Society. This, Callie thought, was appropriate. Wasn't Mary Magdalene the prostitute in the Bible who was saved by the love of Jesus? Wasn't she herself only just rescued from the same profession?

The well-dressed woman who had accompanied the two men to Madge's house introduced herself as Mrs. van Nostram and seemed delighted to have rescued this bright-looking child from the clutches of sin. She took Callie by the hand and led her up the front steps, nodding a farewell to the two silent men.

"This is a day you'll remember the rest of your life, child," she told Callie. "This is the day of your salvation! You'll be meeting Mrs. Slater, who is the wardress here. She's a fine, upstanding woman who has dedicated her life to the society. She may seem a little difficult at first, but rest assured, she knows what's best for you."

Callie was a little sick of everyone thinking they knew what was best for her. First, her mum sending her off to America, then the emigration officials keeping her in quarantine, then Madge, and now this Mrs. Slater.

Mrs. van Nostram pulled the bell chain and turned to face the child she'd redeemed. Good clear skin, bright blue eyes, a tumble of glossy ringlets bobbing on her head. But there was something about the girl that denied her apparent youth. There was a knowledge in her eyes, a shadow of suffering that bespoke maturity. So many children in New York had this same look in their eyes, and it was born out of suffering and hardship. Lately, since the throng of Irish immigrants had landed, that look was becoming the natural order of things.

Callie heard the sound of brass hittting against brass as several bolts were thrown before the door swung open. A drab woman wearing a dark dress, her hair falling in strings about her gaunt face, recognized Mrs. van Nostram immediately and stepped aside to admit them. In the hallway stood a pail of soapy water and the scrub brush the woman had been using to wash the stairs leading to the second floor. She showed the guests into the front parlor, which was nicely appointed with horsehair furniture and green-velvet draperies. A low fire burned in the marble hearth, lending its warmth to the room. "Tell Mrs. Slater I've brought her someone," Mrs. van Nostram instructed. The woman's eyes went to Callie, seeing her youth, and there was an instant of pity there.

"No need for that," said a deep voice, slightly gravelly. With a swish of taffeta petticoats, a tall, square-shouldered woman entered the room. The grim line of her mouth lifted slightly at the corners in welcome to Mrs. van Nostram, but her glance was centered on Callie.

"I've brought you another girl, Mrs. Slater. We rescued her from a bawdy house and only just in time, I understand. Poor little thing. Naturally I brought her here to you."

"Naturally." Mrs. Slater's brows lifted, and she crossed her hands over her bosom. "You realize, Mrs. van Nostram, our dormitory is already full, and we'll be hard pressed to feed another mouth."

"Oh, of course, I didn't mean . . ." Mrs. van Nostram took a deep breath and seemed to shrink beneath Mrs. Slater's scrutiny. "Of course, I'll speak to the board about raising the price for another bed." Charity, in the form of orphanages and homes for wayward woman, was very fashionable these days, and she hadn't a doubt that her contemporaries would dig a little deeper into their purses when she told them of this lovely child.

"That will be most kind of you, Mrs. van Nostram. Without that assurance I would be forced to turn this girl away." Mrs. Slater's eyes went once again to Callie, seeming to measure her for some future purpose.

"You understand, girl, you will stay here only on the condition that you lend your services to the keeping of this establishment. We keep no lazy women here." Her heavy voice filled the room with its volume, and Callie felt herself shrinking backward. She knew she didn't like this Mrs. Slater with her button eyes and her slash for a mouth. There was something hard and mercenary in the way she appraised her new boarder. Almost like the way Owen had looked at Callie in the ferry terminal.

"If you will see about raising the money this child needs, Mrs. van Nostram, I'll let you be on your way." It was more a command than permission to leave. "I will personally see to this child." The corners of her mouth lifted again in a charade of a smile. "I can see how you've come to take such an interest in her."

Mrs. Slater looked on as Mrs. van Nostram offered a few words of encouragement to Callie before bustling out of the room. When the doors closed behind her and Callie was left alone with Mrs. Slater, the atmosphere in the room dropped to a chill.

"Very well, you'll come along with me now to the dormitory upstairs. We'll get you proper clothing to wear," she said, eyeing Callie's dress with interest. "You can't go about in that."

"Beggin' your pardon, Mrs. Slater, but it's a new dress—"

"Did I give you permission to speak? We don't like trouble-makers here. You will turn in that dress and your other belongings."

"But it's new! I've had it for less than a day!"

"I can see myself that the garment is hardly used. Elsewise why would I want it? It will be sold to help defray your expenses while you're here." This time there was no broaching an argument as Mrs. Slater stepped close, looming over her like a great black crow. "Come with me!"

Callie followed her into the hallway where the woman who had opened the door was on her knees, scrubbing the floor. The woman's eyes followed Callie, and there was again a glimmer of pity for the young girl.

"Don't gawk, Ellen, get about your work!" Lifting the hem of her skirt like a grand lady, Mrs. Slater started up the stairs, Callie close at her heels.

"The kitchen is in the basement," Mrs. Slater stated. "After you've changed, you can go down there and see what help is needed. It's only temporary until we find you employment. The second floor is prohibited to you and the others, except for cleaning. Those are my private quarters and offices. The third and fourth floors are the dormitories where you will spend your time when you are not at work. No one lives here for nothing, you will soon learn. You, like the others, will be trained for employment."

They had just reached the second floor, and Mrs. Slater pointed to the right. "Down the end of this hallway is our work room. Sewing is brought in from the outside for the women who are unable at this time to go outside for employment."

Callie could hear the murmur of voices as she followed the wardress down the hall. Mrs. Slater opened the door, and immediately all conversation stopped. Inside no fewer than twenty women, most of them in various stages of pregnancy, stitched away at button holes and collars from a huge stack of men's shirts. The light was dim; only one flickering lamp illuminated the interior, aside from the feeble daylight coming in through the tall, narrow windows, which were blocked by stacks and boxes of work to be done. The women bent their heads over their work, sewing industriously, nervous fingers working and turning collars, all of them pretending Mrs. Slater was not standing in the doorway; all of them dressed in the same shabby black dresses with dark gray aprons.

"Who dared to light this lamp against my wishes?" Mrs. Slater demanded. "Oil is expensive. Am I to take it that you're all willing to give over to support your luxury?"

"It's a gray day outside, Mrs. Slater," a woman sitting in a far corner spoke up, "and Tillie's eyes ain't what they should be."

"Let her sit near the window," was Mrs. Slater's solution.

"Aw, stay where you are, Tillie," said a woman with frowzy blond hair, awkward in the last stages of pregnancy. "How much more can she take from our wages that she ain't taken already?"

"Mrs. Slater?" a soft girlish voice called. She was hardly older than Callie herself. "When can I see my baby? Last time I was with him, he had such a bad cold—"

"You'll see him when you're able to repay me the cost of the doctor," came the harsh reply. "Get back to work, all of you, and stop your sniveling. All this talk about babies. If you were all good Christian women, you wouldn't be having these problems. Open your legs for any man and then cry when you've got to pay for your sins."

The silence in the room was oppressive, and Callie hung her head, unable to meet anyone's eyes. If this was Christian charity, she wanted no part of it; if this was mercy and goodness, she'd rather be back with Madge and the others.

The dormitories on the third and fourth floors were large and expansive, walls having been removed to create a single area. Beds, low and narrow but clean, were arranged around the perimeters creating a crowded impression. In each end of of the rooms stood a wash stand. It was spare and austere without a trace of anyone's personal belongings. As she was instructed, Callie removed her new blue dress, and when Mrs. Slater noticed the fresh, clean muslin of her petticoats, she was told to give those over as well. Callie hoped Mrs. Slater wouldn't notice the new drawers she was wearing.

"Here, put this on, it looks as though it should fit." A black dress, the same as the others had been wearing, was tossed to her. As she slipped it on, she noticed Mrs. Slater fingering the light-blue wool. "Will I get my dress back?" Callie asked meekly.

"Hrmph! The same as the rest, expecting to be given clean living quarters and a good meal each day for nothing. No, you'll not be getting your dress back. It will be sold to pay for your first week's lodgings until you receive your first pay. Then your expenses will automatically be deducted from your salary, which will be sent directly to me."

Callie looked at Mrs. Slater blankly. Hadn't she heard her tell Mrs. van Nostram to raise the price for another bed and lodging from the board, whatever that was? Callie's lips puckered, her chin lifted. Trembling inside, intimidated by this woman who held her future in her hands, Callie faced her bravely. "I've always given a good day's work for a day's wages. I won't be needing charity, nor do I need someone to manage my wages for me. I pay my debts, Mrs. Slater, and I'll be thanking you to leave me my dress. You needn't bother to sell it. Mrs. van Nostram will get my week's lodgings from the board."

"You little snit!" Mrs. Slater's hand cracked across Callie's face. "I knew you were trouble the first time I laid eyes on you! Listen to me, girl. You'll do as I say and live by the rules of this house or you'll regret it!"

"I don't want to stay here! I want to go back to Madge's. I'd rather take my chances with a whore than the likes of you!" The words were out before she could stop them, but instead of Mrs. Slater being properly shocked at being judged beneath a whore, she merely laughed. The sound was a witch's cackle to Callie.

"Oh, you would, would you? Well, let me tell you a few things, my girl. This is the end of the road for you. You won't be going anywhere unless it's to prison!" She was satisfied by the look of horror in Callie's eyes. "That's right—to prison!" Her words were sharp and short like gunfire. "We know what to do with girls like you here in America."

Apparently Mrs. Slater was satisfied by Callie's astonished silence, for she took the blue dress and petticoats and left the dormitory.

Prison! Callie was just unsophisticated enough to believe Mrs. Slater's threat. After Tompkinsville and Owen Gallagher anything was possible. Prison! The very thing Peggy had sent her away to avoid now loomed on Callie's horizon. Callie reluctantly donned the black dress Mrs. Slater had given her, finding it much too big and too long. She hiked up the waistband and secured it by tying the gray apron over it, then looked down to see the uneven hemline and the spots and stains marring its front. She mourned the loss of her blue dress.

Walking softly through the house, Callie found her way to the basement and the kitchens. Here three women, including the one who had just finished scrubbing the front hall, went about their tasks of readying the evening meal. From the ovens came the mouth-watering aroma of a roast and the scent of fresh bread. At a long table, bread dough was being kneaded.

"So you're the new girl Lizzie told us about," a stout woman with a kind face addressed her. "Do you have a name?"

"Callie . . . Callie James."

"Well, come over here, Callie James, and put yourself to good use. There's pots and pans that need washing. I'm Sadie, and this here is Ellen; she's the one who saw you come in with Mrs. van Nostram. I see Mrs. Slater took that fine blue dress Ellen said you were wearing. I hope you bid it a fond farewell, for 'tis the last you'll be seein' of it. Ain't that right, Flora?" Sadie said to the third woman.

"The very last," Flora agreed sourly. On closer inspection Callie saw that Flora wasn't much past the age of eighteen or twenty, but her face was thin and haggard, and her stooped shoulders and slow movements gave her the appearance of a woman in her forties.

While Callie did the pots and pans, they asked her questions about where she'd come from. Ellen, in particular, was interested when she learned Callie was only recently from Dublin. "I hauled over on the *Meridian* two years ago; that was before things got so bad in Ireland. Came over with my brother and sister, I did. They're both gone now. Eileen came down with sickness, and Lester was hit over the head in a card game. I hail from Cork myself, but I been to Dublin once. My husband, though, he was born right here in New York."

Callie turned a questioning eye to Ellen. If she had a husband, what was she doing here in the Magdalene House. "My Nathaniel was taken sick last winter," Ellen explained. "He died on the sixth of January, leaving me up to my neck in debt and a baby on the way. Things got bad for me, and before I knew it, I was out on the street. Couple or three months ago somebody told me I could come here to have my baby. Nathaniel, I calls him because his father was a good man, just unlucky. I work for the babe's support as well as my own, but I don't get to see much of it so's I could save and get myself out of here. Last week I was feelin' poorly and couldn't work; now they say I can't see the babe till I've paid what's owed."

"Who won't let you see your baby? Where is he?" The questions bubbled out of Callie. She couldn't imagine a mother being separated from her child. "Who feeds him?"

"Herself, Mrs. Slater and Mr. Hatterchain. They run this place and take good money to do it. Themselves, so high and mighty, takin' a woman's wages when they've already gotten what was due us from those do-gooders up on Fifth Avenue. Lots of us here have kids; they keep them in a house near here, under lock and key. If they didn't, you'd better believe most of us would take our chances out on the street, but we gotta do what they say or we don't never see our kids again. As for feedin' them, the poor little tykes live for the most part on sugar tits and they get some wet nurses in otherwise."

Callie remembered the tiny pieces of sugar wrapped in clean linen that Peg had comforted the babies with during better times.

"Did Mrs. Slater say where you'd be working?" Sadie asked. "She didn't say nothin' to me about your working in the kitchen full-time."

"No, she only said I'd help out here for the day."

"Most likely send you over to Cullen's, that a button factory.

Sortin' and countin' more than likely. It wouldn't be such a bad place to work if a girl could keep her wages, but Mr. Hatterchain has a deal with Cullen and your wages will come right here and you'll never see it in your hand, I can vouch. Here, Flora, put those pans over here for the bread to rise. Better get busy gettin' those turnips mashed if they're to be ready in time for supper."

The scents of cooking and good food filled the kitchen, but when Sadie pulled the roast out of the oven, Callie wondered how such a small piece of meat could feed everyone.

"Why, child, this here meat ain't for the likes of us, you can believe. No, it's for Mrs. Slater and Mr. Hatterchain's supper. The girls are having bread and lard and mashed turnip. But since you're such a good girl, I'll dip a piece of bread into the juices, and if you gobble it up quick before Mrs. Slater comes in here, I'll be grateful."

That night Callie lay in her bed, the rough cover tucked under her chin. It was cold in the dormitory. Sounds of sleeping women surrounded her, punctuated from time to time by what sounded like a sob. The Magdalene Female Society was hardly more than a work house and a place for collective misery. That night at supper, when the women from the sewing room and those who worked outside came into the dining hall, she saw that they all had the same bleak, desolate expressions on their faces. Mrs. Slater told her she'd go to work the next morning with Irene who also worked in the Cullen Button Factory.

Callie turned over, bringing the thin blanket with her. She had never posted the letters she'd written to Peggy, and she didn't know when she'd find the time to write again. A tear slipped down her cheek; she missed home so much. So very much. But mostly she missed her mother's voice and her loving touch. Letters would have to wait until there was something happy to write home about.

Callie's eyes closed in sleep. She was one day older and a lifetime smarter.

Byrch Kenyon gave his pearl-gray cravat a vicious yank, nearly succeeding in strangling himself. He disliked these obligatory dinner parties almost as much as he disliked his host and hostess for the evening. He could write a story on the dinner his cousin Kevin Darcy and his wife Bridget were giving, could script their moves, cue their dialogue, and predict the meal right down to the pattern of the china and the value of the silverware.

While Byrch disliked his cousin Kevin, he came closer to loathing Bridget Darcy, and their children were self-important little brats. Tonight, no doubt, they would be called down from the nursery to recite a newly learned rhyme or to sing along while Bridget manhandled the pianoforte.

Byrch fastened his pocket watch and fob to his cobalt-blue waistcoat, the satiny fabric delineating the steely, rock-ribbed planes of his torso. The main reason he abhorred attending social functions held by the Darcys was their pretentious attitude and their obvious shame in being Irish. Bridget was forever telling anyone within earshot that their surname was of English origin.

Byrch shrugged into his frockcoat, smoothing the velvet lapels over his broad shoulders. A last touch to the cravat, a tug on the indigo-blue coat, and a hitch at the waist of the slim, matching trousers, and he felt ready to sally forth. He checked to be certain he had enough tobacco; how Bridget did fuss about the manly aroma of pipe tobacco in her dining room. He added some loose change to his trouser pocket and secreted his billfold in the inside pocket of his coat. He wondered who the Darcys had selected as his dinner partner this evening. Kevin and Bridget were of the opinion that if Byrch were married to a presentable female with the social conscience befitting her class, he would cease being a renegade in his editorial opinions concerning the working masses.

Byrch hoped the evening would pass quickly, that he could refrain from introducing the subject of politics, and that his cousin Kevin would keep his psuedo-aristocratic nose out of the *Clarion*'s viewpoint. He knew it was too much to hope for, but hope always did spring eternal for an Irishman.

The dinner was exactly as Byrch had predicted. The courses were too numerous, the sauces too heavy, the chicken overdone to the point of being burnt. "Crisp," Bridget called it, mimicking her new French cook. The potatoes were boiled and parsleyed and would have met his satisfaction if not for the thick white wine sauce slathered over them.

The china was the Cabbage Rose pattern so popular these days, and the silver so ostentatious Byrch longed for a plain every-day utensil that a man could hold and still manage to feed himself. The dessert, fresh fruit in a clear, light white wine, was the only redeeming feature.

His dinner partner was also exactly what he'd expected—a patrician from one of the best families on Park Avenue, Miss Flanna Beauchamp, in attendance with her stout, simpering mother with a keen eye to a "good match" and her overstuffed father, a financier whom she referred to as Papa, with the French inflection. The girl was a beauty, Byrch would give Bridget that, with an elegant long neck and smooth white shoulders. But he had no idea whether there was anything resembling a working brain beneath that wealth of raven hair, for Mrs. Beauchamp and Bridget monopolized the idle conversation.

Bridget presided over her table like a reigning queen. Kevin was clearly enraptured by his confection of a wife and hung on her every meaningless word. Byrch was not averse to light conversation and was known to engage in it himself, but Bridget's superficiality and Kevin's posturing rubbed him the wrong way.

"Byrch, why don't you explain to Flanna the way the *Clarion* operates? I know she would be most interested, wouldn't you, Flanna?"

Byrch could have cheerfully choked Bridget. Flanna's dark eyes were turned on his expectantly, her fork poised in mid-air, as though explaining how a major New York newspaper conducted its business could be told between bites. "It really is so boring I can't put it into words." Promptly Flanna Beauchamp bit into another piece of fruit torte. "By the way, Kevin," Byrch said, turning back to his cousin, "Father is delighted with my editorials. What do you think of them, Kevin? You're usually so free with your views?"

Kevin Darcy sucked in his plump cheeks and stared across the table at his cousin. He knew he would never be the man Byrch was. At twenty-nine Kevin's hair was becoming thinner by the day. He envied Byrch's thick mane of mahogany hair and his strong jaw. Kevin would partner with the devil if it would guarantee he could look like Byrch. Tall, broad of shoulder, slim of hip, long of leg. But it wasn't only the physical attributes that gave Byrch his dash; there was something hard and worldly about him, something that Bridget had said was like a "modern-day pirate." Yes, that was what he envied most, Byrch's sense of purpose, his dash and flair. Kevin's rotund figure did nothing for his own self-image. There were days when he wondered how he had managed to snag the lovely, butter-gold Bridget for his wife.

Now, looking across at Byrch, seeing Mr. and Mrs. Beauchamp heap attention upon a likely match for their elegant daughter, Kevin secretly thought he hated his own life, along with Bridget and the children. He would much prefer to be like Byrch, footloose and carefree, a single man of good repute welcome at the tables in the best of homes, sought after as a prospective son-in-law. Of course, after a rowdy night between the sheets with Bridget, Kevin's opinion changed, but that was another thing that was falling apart. Bridget was rejecting his ardor, waiting to dole out her favors only when she wanted something. Like tonight. She had promised if he didn't get into a spat with Byrch, she would let him cuddle with her for as long as he wished. All day Kevin had walked about in a state of excitement, waiting for the time when the lights went out. Now Byrch was spoiling it, the way he always spoiled everything. Bridget and Byrch were waiting for him to respond as to what he thought of the editorials. He had to be careful or he would spoil his hopes for a long, ardent night. Any way he looked at it, he was caught in the middle. And, damn it, this was the night he was going to dare suggest they leave the lamp burning for just a little while. Damn Byrch, he always spoiled things.

"Well," Byrch prompted, "what do you say, Kevin?" The perverse side of Byrch was enjoying Kevin's misery. He stifled a grin, and Kevin noticed. He was being baited, teased, dared. Bastard! Bridget was staring at him in a way he hated. It was going to be a long, cold, lonely winter. Damn Byrch Kenyon! How smug he'd be if he knew he was controlling my sex life! That's another thing. I know, I just know Byrch has a woman every night of the week. A *different* woman every night!

Everyone was waiting for Kevin's answer. "Now, Byrch," he said, "can't we just once have a nice, pleasant dinner without going into business?"

"Yes, that's right, Byrch," Bridget interceded. "You know you always rile Kevin up and then Kevin riles me up. It simply isn't fair to our other guests."

Byrch wanted to tell her that her dinner parties were so boring they were near to being deadly, and the only way he knew anyone was alive was to start a lively discussion. Bridget's tone verged on childishness, but there was a hard center to her words that broached no opposition. Poor Kevin, he'd probably pay the piper if Bridget was made unhappy.

Leaning his elbows on the table because he knew it would irritate Bridget, Byrch stared across at her. "It's your party, Bridget, what would you like to discuss?"

Disconcerted by his intense gaze, Bridget found herself stuttering, "Why . . . why we . . . we could discuss something that would interest the ladies. Yes, yes, that would certainly be a welcome change, wouldn't it, Flanna?" She felt Byrch's heated stare drop to the smoothness of her shoulders and then to the exposed cleavage above the deep neckline of her jade-green gown. The others were also aware of his intense scrutiny, especially Kevin. Now for certain he would demand time alone later. Already she could feel a backache coming on, and her head had been pounding from the moment Byrch had arrived. She should have worn another gown. Something less revealing—Byrch was a womanizer, everyone knew that. Yet the heat in his penetrating cat-green eyes was warming her flesh, creating a flush of pink to her bosom.

"And what would that be, Bridget?" His tone was insolently intimate.

Squaring her shoulders, Bridget repelled this latest attempt to unnerve her. She cleared her throat. "Actually, Byrch, you may even find yourself interested and want to write a column in the *Clarion* about this Magdalene Female Society. All of us here, including the Beauchamps, contribute generously. If the society garnered some favorable publicity, it might even stir the public to open its pockets and make donations. It's a shelter for wayward women and their children. They have so little, and we who enjoy so much must be charitable, don't you agree, ladies?"

Mrs. Beauchamp agreed so exuberantly that one of her haircombs fell onto her plate when she nodded. Flanna dipped her head, her long, elegant neck arching like a swan's.

"Tell me something," Byrch said, addressing himself to Mr. Beauchamp and Kevin, "did you investigate this society before you allowed your wives to make contributions? There have been rumors about these societies, as I'm certain you're well-aware."

"Now just a minute, Byrch!" Bridget sputtered. "This is a fine Christian group, sponsored by the best people. It isn't some soup kitchen down in Hell's Kitchen. It has a rather smart address, 23 Bleecker Street."

"How impressive," Byrch answered snidely. "Somehow, Bridget, I didn't think you would contribute money to where it was needed the most."

Mrs. Beauchamp gasped. "Mr. Kenyon, do you know something about this society that we don't?"

"No, I don't have any particulars. That's why I'm inquiring as to what kind of investigation Kevin made."

Kevin's tone was apologetic. "Certainly I looked into it . . . that is, as far as it was possible. Some of our friends made a trip to the house on Bleecker Street and saw for themselves what those good people are doing for homeless and wayward women."

Bridget assumed a lofty attitude. "Information came on the best authority, Byrch. Mr. and Mrs. van Nostram are supporters of the society, and Mrs. van Nostram actually visits the house." She was pleased to introduce the van Nostram name in front of the Beauchamps, smiling at them, gratified that they were impressed.

"An announced visit, I'm certain," Byrch continued cynically, "so that preparations were made, and your friends were shown exactly what they wished to see. Haven't you learned anything being associated with a newspaper, Kevin? You should have made an unexpected visit so you could have received a more accurate impression, find out the real story. I'm glad to say your main concern with the *Clarion* is advertising accounts."

"I am not in the custom of performing sneak attacks, Byrch," Kevin said. Secretly he agreed with Byrch, but Bridget had overridden him, saying all her friends were donating considerable sums, and she didn't want to be left out or seem ignorant of her social duty. Now here was Byrch reinforcing Kevin's doubts. Still, he wouldn't give his cousin the satisfaction of agreeing with him verbally.

"That may be true, Kevin," Byrch continued, "but how would you feel if you were to learn that all of these charitable donations were not being used in good faith? I wouldn't be much of a reporter if I didn't get to the bottom of things, and to be honest, I'd not hesitate to list the names of the poor pigeons who were taken in by a scam. Perhaps it would serve to warn others to be more selective as to where they offer assistance."

Bridget bristled and then paled. "Byrch! You aren't saying you know something about this Magdalene Society, are you?" Good Lord, if she'd been duped along with her friends, they would never be able to hold up their heads in public again!

"What Mr. Kenyon says makes a good deal of sense," Mr. Beauchamp agreed. "Will you be conducting an investigation for us, Mr. Kenyon?"

"I think I might. If I find it to be honest, a feature article in the *Clarion* might induce others to contribute. If, on the other hand, it isn't what it should be, donors will be prevented from making fools of themselves."

"Oh, come now, Byrch, I hardly think we're fools. We merely acted on the report the committee members submitted," Bridget said. "If you're bent on discussing fools, I think you should first look to yourself and some of those hot-headed editorials you're responsible for. If it were up to you, you'd feed and clothe every filthy immigrant who lands on these shores. Admit it!" Bridget demanded spitefully.

"For the deserving, Bridget. Someone has to help them. These new organizations springing up all over the city need monitoring.

The Irish especially seem to be the victims; of course, just the sheer numbers of them coming to America throws the balance in that direction. But I won't forget that they're my people, Bridget, just as much as they're yours and Kevin's. I didn't say this Bleecker Street establishment was corrupt. I said I had my suspicions, and I agreed to check it out."

"And publish our names if we've been duped?"

Byrch cocked an unruly brow at Bridget. "Do I take it you also have your suspicions? Besides, what better way to prevent you and others like you from making the same mistake twice? If donations were made intelligently, these scam artists would not assume that money was out there for the taking, and the interests of the poor would be better served. Surely you wouldn't expect me to suppress my findings just so you won't lose face among your friends?"

"Of course not," Bridget replied.

"Then again," Byrch added, "think what a heroine you could be if your name was linked with the exposure, if it proves necessary."

Bridget thought for an instant. Yes, she would like it very much. She'd never thought of herself as a heroine, but she had to admit it, it was a very appealing notion.

Chapter Eight

Byrch Kenyon stepped out of the offices of the *Clarion-Observer* in the nine-hundred block of West Broadway exactly one week after his dinner engagement with Kevin and Bridget. He left behind the busy, paper-strewn front desk and the thrum and clack of the presses. During this week, he had nearly completed a cursory investigation into some of the more prominent houses for the needy. These included the public work house just west of Market Street and several orphanages. This afternoon, he was going to the Magdalene Female Society at 23 Bleecker Street.

Some of his findings had been extraordinary, revealing that while one particular organization could be a haven for the needy, others could be closer to hell. He'd already outlined his first two articles and had enlisted the aid of Bennington Brown, a reporter, to do some of the footwork.

It was the opinion of many officers and officials connected with the Metropolitan Police Force that all efforts at reforming the fallen and indigent of the city were useless or nearly so. Byrch found it dourly amusing that the word "poor" was interchanged with "wayward" or "fallen." Regardless of what these officials believed, social reformers founded and maintained numerous benevolent institutions throughout the city.

The largest and best-known of these societies was the Midnight Mission at 23 Amity Street. It was a large, four-story brick house, two short blocks from Broadway. Byrch considered the mission a success.

Every Thursday and Friday evening meetings were held at the mission. Advertisements of these meetings were distributed among the houses of prostitution, which abounded in the neighborhood. Missionaries, clergymen, and church elders would walk the streets at night and give the cards to those women who would accept them. The meetings were very successful, attendance was popular. Plain, simple refreshments were served, and there was a religious service. The women were persuaded to tell their stories, unfolding the troubles of their lives, receiving advice, direction, and comfort.

Of all the charities Byrch had investigated, the Midnight Mission seemed to be the best. The committee readily opened their books to him, and Byrch found them to be in order. He was impressed with the dedication the members of the society possessed. While they tried to help those who sought it, they did not labor under the belief that they would bring a halt to all prostitution and crime in the city.

Of the worst of the institutions, Byrch was already mapping out his article. The Home of the Merciful near the foot of Seventy-fifth Street was solely for the reformation of fallen women. It was headed by a zealous woman who called herself Mrs. Harper and claimed to be the widow of a Reverend Joseph Harper from Cincinnati. In Byrch's opinion, the woman had come from the midwest for the sole purpose of lining her pockets with the contributions donated to her organization. Mrs. Harper was reluctant to discuss the workings of her institution, and she refused to open her ledgers. While she herself seemed to be particularly well-fed, there were several girls, hardly more than children, who were in advanced stages of malnutrition. Upon inquiring, Byrch discovered they'd been living at the House of the Merciful for almost a year. Captain Gordon of the Eighth Precinct was now in the process of investigating Mrs. Harper's origins and reputation as a favor to Byrch.

Byrch knew he had his work cut out for him. Although he had already visited nine or ten organizations for the needy, he knew he hadn't even scratched the surface. So it was with grave suspicions that he now went to 23 Bleecker Street to learn about Kevin and Bridget's favorite charity.

He took a hansom cab to the corner of Broadway and Bleecker, walking down the street to get his bearings and a feel for the neighborhood. The windows in the brick houses were dark for the most part, except for an occasional halo of lamplight. Dusk was fast approaching, and pedestrian traffic was increasing with the flow of the masses returning home from work. Minuscule front courtyards surrounded by pretentious iron fencing broke the monotony of the identical brick houses, as did several sapling trees flanking the street.

Byrch crossed Bleecker Street and stood in front of number 23. The yard and walk were clean of debris; the narrow slate stones leading around to the back of the four-story house were swept and tended. Warm yellow lamplight peeped from between cracks in the drawn draperies. The house itself was like any other on Bleecker Street, except for the shield near the front door that read MAGDALENE FEMALE SOCIETY.

Byrch decided on the spur of the moment to follow the walk around to the back of the house. A kitchen could tell an entire story about the people who lived there and how well they were cared for, especially near dinnertime.

He rapped smartly on the worn back door and waited. When there was no response, he knocked again. He hadn't formulated what he expected in the way of a greeting, but it certainly wasn't the woman who stood almost as tall as he and outweighed him by at least forty pounds. Her pale white face was in direct contrast to the raven blackness of her hair, which was pulled back into a severe knot making her angular features even less attractive.

Byrch found himself forcing a smile. "I'm Byrch Kenyon from the *Clarion-Observer*. I'd like to do a story on your organization. It might help you get additional funding," he added as bait.

"You would, would you? Why didn't you knock on the front door like a gentleman? Back doors are for tradesmen, or didn't you know?" Byrch was taken aback by the depth and volume of the woman's voice.

"I did go to the front door," Byrch lied. "No one answered."

"I find that hard to believe. I have excellent hearing, and I was in the front parlor."

Byrch smiled what he hoped was an enchanting smile. "I'm afraid I haven't had the pleasure of an introduction."

"Mrs. Slater to you! And don't try your charm on me. That smile will get you nowhere. Go around to the front door, and I'll speak to Mr. Hatterchain about admitting you. We don't just let anyone in, you understand. This is a decent house for unfortunate women."

"I understand that, Mrs. Slater. Mr. and Mrs. Kevin Darcy, who are so enthusiastic about the work you're doing here, convinced me to do a story." He tried to peer into the kitchen beyond her, aware of the aroma of roast pork and fried potatoes. This doubled his suspicions. Even the Midnight Mission couldn't afford such quality food, and they were the most generous he'd found yet.

"That's very nice, Mr.....Kenyon was it? Well, don't just stand there, go around the front."

Byrch smiled again, this time a wide, boyish grin. "Hmmm! Sure smells good in there." He tried to pass her into the kitchen, but she moved her bulk, blocking his view. "Couldn't I just come through this way?"

"Impossible. And if you continue to be impertinent, I will not ask Mr. Hatterchain to see you." There was a finality to her words, and stepping backward into the kitchen, she slammed the door between them.

He didn't fail to hear the snick of the bolt and the hook into the screw-eye. It was the second shot of a bolt being sent home against its brass housing that puzzled him. Three locks on one door! Did the Magdalene have so much to protect within its walls? Were they keeping people in—or keeping them out? Perhaps Mr. Hatterchain would give him a clue.

When the front door was finally opened to admit Byrch, he was face-to-face with a small, benign-looking gentleman wearing spectacles. He greeted Byrch warmly, extending his hand in welcome, his peculiar high-pitched yet raspy voice bidding him to "Come in, come in!" Mr. Hatterchain was unduly jovial to the point of Byrch's irritation.

Once settled into the opulent front parlor, Byrch explained that he was with the *Clarion-Observer*, doing a feature article that could speak well of the Magdalene Society, and also hinted at a windfall of new and generous donations.

Matthew Hatterchain leaned forward, elbows on knees, rubbing his hands together in anticipation. The man's small eyes danced with glee, and he was so free and open with information and the names of their present patrons that his very innocence made Byrch suspicious.

"I wish you had arranged for an appointment, Mr. Kenyon, so we could have prepared for your visit. I would gladly give you a tour of this establishment if you would come back again tomorrow.

Say just after noon? It is the end of the day, and the women are tired..." He shrugged and threw up his hands. "You know how women are, Mr. Kenyon, so protective of their privacy." This last he said in a conspiratorial tone as though he, along with Byrch, were all too familiar with the female psyche.

"It wouldn't take long, Mr. Hatterchain. I merely want to see what accommodations you offer. I'm afraid I have an early morning deadline, and I can't include the Magdalene Society in my article if I don't see for myself what I write about. Of course, I would like to speak to several of the women—for direct quotes, you understand. However, since you say it's impossible, I'm sorry to have taken your time. Perhaps we'll be doing a feature article on these charitable institutions at a later date. Your organization could be included then."

Matthew Hatterchain thought about the missed opportunity. "Please, don't misunderstand. I'm certain the committee will be most delighted with your interest in us. We do have some very prestigious sponsors, as I'm certain you must know. Why, two weeks from this very day they are sponsoring a charity ball, and all the proceeds come to the Magdalene Female Society." Hatterchain's voice rose in pitch. "Please excuse my bad manners. You want to see what we offer here and, of course, you must. We have women waiting to come here, but we simply don't have the accommodations necessary. With additional funding we could possibly extend to other buildings. Ah," he sighed, "it always comes down to money."

Byrch nodded appropriately. "Yes, it would be a shame not to be included in the feature."

Mr. Hatterchain was suddenly very accommodating. "This, as you can see, is our parlor. After dinner the women will be sewing or visiting here. There's a box of toys behind the door for the children."

The room was very comfortable to the point of opulence. The good Samaritans would need a respectable front parlor to have tea when they came to call. Mr. Hatterchain signaled Byrch to follow him.

"This is the dining room. As you can see, we've incorporated another room to make it as spacious as possible. Right now, there are nearly fifty women in residence, and meals are somewhat hectic. But we all do our share, Mr. Kenyon, we all do our share!"

Here, in the dining hall, so close to the kitchen, Byrch detected the delicious aromas of fresh bread and meat roasting. It was reassuring to know that the occupants of 23 Bleecker Street ate well.

"If you'll follow me to the dormitories," Hatterchain offered. "We wish we didn't have to crowd the women into this type of accommodation, but it's the best we can do for now. Of course, most of them come from very deprived conditions, and we don't hear any complaints. We're all pulling together, Mr. Kenyon, making the best of the situation. A roof over the head, food in the belly, and work. It's the stuff of life!" he offered philosophically.

They went up the front hall stairs to the second floor, and Byrch was surprised when Hatterchain continued to the third floor. "Mrs. Slater and myself keep rooms on this floor, and our offices, of course. The dormitories are on the third and fourth floors." A mischievous smile played around Hatterchain's mouth when he rapped on the door and called out that a visitor was here for an inspection. "You understand, we have to give them time in the event they are are not decently garbed."

Byrch was perturbed about something, and he realized it was the silence of the house. Fifty odd women living here and not a single voice to be heard.

"How much do you know about our organization?" Hatterchain asked, lounging against the door frame.

"Not too much. I've picked up dribs and drabs, but I've nothing first-hand. Is it true you find employment for the women and help them become established so they're able to move out on their own? What about those who have children? Who tends to them? Are the women paid a decent wage? Do they get to keep what they earn? Where do they work? I'll need the details and perhaps an interview with several of the women."

Hatterchain's eyes clouded, contradicting his words. "I don't see why not. Of course, you understand that will be impossible today. I'll have to take the matter up with the committee. You see, Mr. Kenyon, we do all we can to protect individual privacy." While seeming perfectly at ease speaking with Byrch, a thin film of perspiration beaded on Mr. Hatterchain's upper lip, and his fingers kept going to his waistcoat to finger his pocket watch.

"Where do you find these women?"

Hatterchain shrugged. "Anywhere, everywhere. Some are brought here by concerned patrons of the society. From all walks of life, Mr. Kenyon, all befallen on hard times." He allowed a mournful note to creep into his voice. "We have some who, having no other choice, found themselves in prostitution. We're here to heal the body and save the soul, Mr. Kenyon. Er . . . you might put that little quotation in your article. Not very long ago a young girl was brought to us from a nearby house of prostitution. We hope to enrich her life and set her feet on the path of righteousness. Er . . ."

"I know, I can quote that." Byrch smiled agreeably, disliking Mr. Hatterchain more by the minute. The man's pretentiousness could only be equaled by Bridget's. "You were telling me about a young girl from a brothel?"

"Yes. She's fresh from Ireland, an immigrant. I'm sorry to say we're seeing more and more of those these days," he sighed. "At the moment, she's recovering from a fever. Nothing more than a cold. However, she insists on working and is putting in as many hours as she's able in a button factory. I have to say I admire her ambition to reform."

Hatterchain rapped on the door again, voicing the warning, "We're coming in!" Suddenly the door was opened by a haggard woman with large, solemn eyes. She looked first at Hatterchain and then at Byrch, moving aside to allow them to enter. There was sorrow in her eyes and a bitterness about her mouth, and the drab of her dress accentuated the sallowness of her complexion.

All the rooms on the third floor had been opened to form one large area. Beds of every description lined the walls and were put in rows down the middle. Small cots and blankets filled every available space. Several women sat on the edge of their beds. A maudlin, suspicious silence surrounded him. The perspiration on Hatterchain's upper lip seemed to have increased.

Questions bounded through Byrch's brain. Where were the children? His attention was caught by a startled gasp, and he turned to find its source. His eyes widened when he saw a slender young girl with a tousle of cropped chestnut hair and eyes as blue as the clear skies of Ireland. He would never forget those eyes and the defiance on that young face. How had Callie James come to be in the Magdalene Society? He was about to speak when she turned her eyes away and shook her head. A worried frown drew her brows together. She didn't want Byrch to admit recognition of her. Uncertain of his next move, he made several comments and asked unimportant questions of the residents. His attention kept returning to Callie. He could feel Hatterchain's intensity and noticed that the women all kept their eyes averted from him. Before he turned to leave, Byrch made a pretense of offering his handkerchief to Callie, who was racked with a seizure of coughing. He took the opportunity to whisper, "Is this place what it seems?"

Callie turned her glance to Byrch, looking up at him through an intense blue stare. He watched her lips quiver and heard the strangled one-word reply: "No."

So his suspicions had been right. So much for the outward appearances of a charitable organization. Quickly, without advance warning, Byrch pointed his finger at several of the women and then at Callie. "Where do you work? You? You?" It was only Callie's reply that interested him.

"The Cullen Button Factory."

It was enough, it was all he needed. How in the name of all that was holy had that child found her way here from Ireland? "We'll meet again, and we'll talk about your stay here at the Magdalene Society," he said expansively. "I'm certain you have Mr. Hatterchain to thank for your present circumstances!" He wasn't certain, but he thought he saw relief on Callie's face. How many times, whenever he thought of Ireland, had he remembered Callie and her spirit and her devotion to her family. To him, she was the spirit of Ireland, and her young pretty face and wide, defiant eyes had haunted him.

The following morning Byrch awakened to the sudden thrumming of the presses in the basement of the *Clarion-Observer* building. He stretched his arms, rubbed the back of his neck, and felt the chill penetrate to his bones. He'd spent the night in his office, rifling through old files and working on his editorial. The ancient leather sofa he'd taken from his study at home had been his bed, and since it would not accommodate the length of him, his knees were stiff and sore.

Byrch added more coal to the cast-iron parlor stove in the corner of his office and then opened the door and called to the front desk for coffee. A few moments later young James Riley brought a cup of the steaming brew and placed it on Byrch's desk.

"I see you've spent the night," Jimmy stated. "Have trouble putting the paper to bed last night?"

"No trouble. The late edition came out on schedule. No, it's something else I'm working on—those charitable societies for the needy. Do you know anything about them?"

"Not much. But when I was a newsboy, before you brought me into the offices," Jimmy smiled his gratitude, "I heard that some of those places have their fingers in a lot of pies."

This struck Byrch. "Say, Jim, d'you know anything about a

Cullen Button Factory? See what you can get me on that, will you? Another thing—think you can manage to get me one of those knit caps, you know, like the longshoremen wear, and one of those pea jackets too?"

"Sure, boss. There's a place down at the docks that sells them. Anything else?"

"Yes," Byrch said distractedly. "More coffee!" Sitting down at his desk, he reviewed the notations he'd made the night before. First thing was to get a quick shave; second, he intended to call on the Beauchamps. Through them he would form a list of donors to the Magdalene Society. By speaking to those people, he would gather information, and the picture would come together. Something was wrong, very wrong, at 23 Bleecker Street.

From that moment on Byrch devoted every waking hour to his investigation. It was six and a half days before he had what he thought was the entire picture.

The house on Bleecker Street was a society supposedly operating as a non-profit organization whose committee consisted of several known businessmen as well as the duo of Mrs. Jeanette Slater and Mr. Matthew Hatterchain. It had become fashionable to be among its contributors. Most of the women it claimed to care for either worked for no pay or their wages were turned over to the society for payment of room and board. If a child was involved, a women had to work extra hours to pay for his keep. Jimmy Riley had been instrumental in locating a woman who was once a resident of 23 Bleecker Street. She attested to the poor food, the wresting of her wages, and the sorrowful fact that she'd been separated from her child and denied the privilege of seeing him unless she worked double shifts. Another astounding fact was that Matthew Hatterchain's brother-in-law, John Cullen, owned and operated the Cullen Button Factory where most of the women were sent to work. Those who were pregnant were sent to work in a sewing room where they accomplished piece work for slave's wages.

A thorough search of the records gave Byrch the names of the society's wealthy backers. Again he was staggered by the prominence of the names. In the end, thousands of dollars were being raked in in the name of charity, and most of it found its way into the already lined pockets of the committee.

Byrch leaned his head onto his arms. Lord, he was tired. He tried to remember the last time he'd had more than a two-hour catnap or something other than a sandwich washed down with a cold beer. Too long.

A second thought struck him. Would he have delved into the internal workings of the Magdalene Society if he hadn't seen Callie James there? He knew it wasn't just an exposé or an editorial any longer—it was an obsession. The waif from Dublin had wormed her way into his life, and he felt responsible for her. He had already formulated a rescue for Callie.

He was also determined to save Callie's reputation. The *Clarion* wasn't the only newspaper in the city, and he wanted her out of that terrible place before the story broke. Being connected with known prostitutes and a scandal would stigmatize her for years to come. She had already borne enough hardship. Byrch made his plans carefully.

Today was a Friday, and his sources told him it was pay day. Jimmy Riley had discovered that the women were escorted home by burly employees of the button factory, no doubt a concession by Cullen to his brother-in-law, Matthew Hatterchain.

It was a gray, dark afternoon and was nearing four o'clock when Byrch stationed himself within sight of the factory entrance. Soon the women would be exiting, escorted home by several men. In the dark peacoat and knit hat Byrch looked like a dock worker waiting for someone.

Within the hour a pelting rain began to fall, and Byrch could feel it penetrating his clothing. The rain would work to his advantage, he decided, pulling his collar farther up against his chin. He still didn't know what he was going to do with his "damsel in distress" once he rescued her. He wasn't exactly the white knight, and there was no such thing as happy ever after. Callie was so young, and on top of that, she didn't seem to be in good health. He remembered the hacking cough and had noticed the weight loss and the dark hollows under her eyes. He knew he'd have his hands full.

The door of the button factory opened. The women filed out, heads bent against the rain. Alongside, two men accompanied them. Byrch clenched his hands into fists. If it was a fight he was in for, he was ready for it. Shoulders hunched, head down, he crossed the street, sidestepping a passing dray. Moving at a fast pace, he came abreast of the women, having already picked Callie out of the group. The smallest and slightest, she had her shawl pulled over her head. Her hand covered her mouth as she coughed. Thank you, sweetheart, Byrch thought, now I know for certain which one you are.

Byrch swallowed hard and reached out an arm, literally dragging Callie off the ground, and for one crazy moment he thought they would both topple over backwards. Regaining his balance, he pulled the frightened Callie toward him. "Shut up! If you know how to run, now's the time to do it!"

Callie was taken by surprise, and it was only at the last instant that she recognized this stranger with the knit seaman's cap and coat. She saw his cat-green eyes. Mr. Kenyon! He gave her a not-too-gentle push to send her streaking off ahead of him.

"Hey! What's going on there?" a man's voice shouted, reaching out to capture Callie as she ran past him.

Byrch blocked the effort with a solid blow from his shoulder, knocking the man to the sidewalk. He heard the shrieks of the women behind him, heard the first tentative footfalls of the second man giving chase. Byrch followed Callie's small figure as she darted into an alleyway and out the other end onto Prince Street. When the running figure ahead of him slipped and fell, sprawling into a puddle, he caught up with her, picked her up, and kept running. On the corner of Wooster and Spring Streets he was successful in hailing a hansom, and he pushed Callie inside. She heard him instruct the oilskin-garbed driver, "St. Luke's Place." Shivering with the cold, teeth rattling, Callie cuddled against the warmth Byrch offered. Arms wrapped around her, aware of her fragility, he murmured over and over, "It's all right, Callie James. You're with me now, and I'll take care of you."

Callie closed her eyes, nestling her face against the wet of his peacoat, hearing his promise, feeling safe for the first time in what seemed like a lifetime.

Within thirty minutes the hansom pulled onto St. Luke's Place, and Byrch stirred to tap upward on the canvas roof to give the driver directions. Jumping down onto the wet cobbled street, he turned and lifted Callie into his arms, carrying her across the walk to his front door. He used his booted foot to pound on the polished brass kickplate, cursing aloud for Edward, his manservant, to hurry.

The door swung open to reveal a tall black man with an astonished expression on his face. "Mr. Kenyon!" he exclaimed in the clipped accent of the British West Indies. Stepping aside, he admitted his employer and his burden.

"Go out there and pay the driver, Edward, and put in extra for him. Another hansom driver probably wouldn't have stopped for us, considering the way we look."

"Yes, sir." Edward peered at the space between his employer's neck and his shoulder, seeing the pale little face and the tiny upturned nose. He was too well-trained to display his astonishment or curiosity.

"Then put on your oilskins and go down the street for Dr. Jameson. We've got a sick little girl on our hands."

Byrch carried Callie up the stairs to the second floor and took her into a bed-sitting room where a fire was burning with a cheery glow. He rushed around like a doting mother bringing towels and an assortment of dry clothes. "I'm going down to brew us some hot tea," he told her, wincing inwardly as she coughed. "Can you get yourself out of those wet things and into dry clothes? Don't worry if they don't fit, this isn't a fashion parade. Dry your head before you catch your death. Do it now!" he commanded before closing the door.

Callie was exhausted, wet, and too disoriented to notice her surroundings. She followed Byrch's orders as best she could, stripping out of her dress and petticoat and undergarments, standing before the fire, and allowing its warmth to penetrate her skin. The soft cambric shirt fell past her knees; warm knitted stockings came up to fill the gap. A warm, fleecy robe trailed along the floor, but it was a fine wool and so warm and clean. She rubbed briskly at her curls, and knew if she sat before the fire, her hair would be dry within minutes.

Byrch came back to the room, knocking before entering, carrying a tray bearing a teapot, cups, and a tall, brown bottle of whiskey. He placed it on the small pie-crust table to one side of the hearth and poured, lacing the tea liberally with the whiskey. "Drink this while I change into something dry," he ordered. "Where the hell is Edward and Dr. Jameson?" he wondered aloud, wishing for reinforcements. The sudden responsibility for this girl was weighing heavily on him, and when she choked on the strong brew and continued hacking, he watched her in misery and helplessness.

Changing hurriedly into dry trousers and a fresh shirt, Byrch stepped into house slippers and quickly returned to the bed-sitting room where he'd left Callie. Questions flooded through his brain: How had she come to America? Why had she left Ireland? Had she finally gotten herself into serious trouble with the law? When had she arrived? How long had she been here? How did she come to be in the Magdalene Female Society? What did that bastard Hatterchain mean when he'd said Callie had been rescued from a brothel? And most of all, where in hell were Edward and Dr. Jameson?

"Are you hungry?" Byrch asked. Callie nodded her head, the

chestnut curls almost dry now, wispy tendrils still clinging to the sides of her face, giving her the look of a gamin. It was then that he saw the huge eyes fill with tears, welling glassily before tumbling down onto her softly curving cheeks. Poor little thing.

He went to her, putting the teacup to her lips, encouraging her to drink. He saw that she was shivering with cold, her full, pouting underlip faintly blue. Yanking a blanket from the bed, he wrapped it tightly around her and thought about putting her to bed, but it was so much warmer here by the fire. Lifting her into his arms, he settled himself with his bundle into the Windsor chair beside the hearth, holding her close to him, imparting his warmth.

The dampness of her curls was pressed against his cheek; his hands felt the smallness of her beneath the bundling of the blanket. She rested quietly against him, taking his comfort. Her body trembled, quaking, and he couldn't be certain if it was from the cold or from the tears she choked down. "I don't know how you came to New York, little one, or how it is that you're back in my life, and I don't even know what I'm going to do with you, but you must know you can trust me, Callie."

His voice was warm, soothing, and deep; she could hear it rumbling up from his chest. "Do you remember the last time we met?" he asked softly. "I thought we became friends that day. You found out my name, even that I own a newspaper. I wouldn't have been too difficult to find. Why didn't you come to me, Callie? You could've avoided so much suffering." At that moment he would have cheerfully killed any man who touched this girl-child. She was so young, so vulnerable, and there was such innocence in those great, soulful eyes. His protective instincts rose. In some way Callie James belonged to him, but he preferred to think of his instincts as paternal.

After a long moment he heard her sigh, felt her relax herself against him, heard her sniffle. "Everything happened so fast," she whispered. "I didn't know how ugly things could be." A shuddering sob shook her.

Holding her close, his lips against her heated brow, Byrch felt such tenderness well up within him that it left him nearly speechless. "Hush now, sweet, don't think about it. You're here with me now."

They sat together before the fire, Callie nestled on his lap, his arms holding her close. The silence held for such a long time until, bending his head to see if she'd fallen asleep, Byrch found she was staring wide-eyed into the fire. "What are you thinking, little one?" he asked softly.

The reply was hardly more than a whisper. "I'm thinking that if my mum could see me now, she'd go up in smoke!"

Book Two

Chapter Nine

Callie felt like a fairy-tale princess in her own bed in Byrch's guest bedroom. The sheets were the smoothest, softest muslin; the comforter the silkiest satin; her nightdress and bed jacket the frothiest, frilliest lace bedecked with pink ribbons and silk rosettes. Across the pale green and gold room a fire sizzled cheerily in the hearth, and Edward, Byrch's manservant, seemed to take it upon himself to be sure she had every delicacy New York had to offer. Oxtail soup, fresh oranges, sweet butter, vanilla custard, fluffy yellow muffins, and pots and pots of tea and jars of jellies and jams. Chocolates, something she had never tasted until now, were packaged in lovely tins and ornate boxes and were forever within her reach.

Callie smacked her lips and patted her tummy. She was going to grow absolutely fat! Kindly Dr. Jameson had been to see her three times, and on each of his visits he was more pleased with her, encouraging Edward to continue his good care and suggesting that Callie seemed well enough to partake of heartier fare such as beef stew and fish chowder. Edward was the one who had thought to bring her several night shifts and the exquisite bed jacket, his startling white smile spreading across his ebony face when he perceived her pleasure. Byrch came to see her several times each day and always for a few moments before leaving for the newspaper. He doted on her like a mother hen, forever touching her brow for signs of her fever returning. Only last night he had told her that Dr. Jameson was certain she could leave her bed for a few hours each day, and Byrch had promised to take his supper with her in her room to celebrate.

Exactly as promised, Byrch followed Edward into Callie's room that evening, directing him to serve the meal in front of the fire. Callie eyed the roast chicken greedily, smelling the pungent aroma of baked fruit torte and fresh bread dripping with creamery butter. It had been nearly three hours since she'd finished her last box of chocolates, and she was famished!

Byrch laughed when he saw Callie dig into the tender white meat of the chicken. "I'm glad to see your appetite has returned," he teased. "Edward tells me he has to force those chocolates down your throat!"

Callie blushed. "It's just that everything tastes so good! I feel as though I've been empty for so long I just can't seem to fill up!"

Byrch laughed again, and Callie liked the sound, although it seemed to her that almost everything she said he found to be funny. Sometimes it irked her, but she was feeling so pleasantly satisfied, she decided not to argue. Let him tease her. He had saved her, hadn't he?

After the meal, Edward came to clear away the plates, bringing Byrch a snifter of brandy along with his pipe and tobacco. Callie walked to the far end of the room, liking the feel of her little house slippers sliding over the Oriental carpet. Her dressing gown was the palest shade of pink and fell in a straight line from just over the bosom, ending in a little flare near the hem. It was by far the loveliest thing she'd ever owned.

"Sit down, Callie. It's high time we had a talk," Byrch said quietly. He found himself completely captivated by this girl whose cheeks were once again taking on the bloom of Ireland and whose rose-petal lips always seemed moist and tender. Even the unruly tumble of her glossy chestnut curls seemed coquettishly feminine.

Something in the tone of his voice caused Callie alarm. It was the same tone Thomas James would use when he had something dire to announce to the family, something that would disappoint or injure. She'd heard herself use that same somber tone when she would tell the younger children not to believe in Granda's stories. Was Byrch going to tell her this was all a dream and she had to go back to the Magdalene Society?

Callie crossed the carpet on whisper-quiet feet and sat down on the edge of the tapestry-upholstered Queen Anne armchair opposite her benefactor.

Her eyes were downcast and her expression so grim that Byrch smiled. "Perk up, Callie, it isn't as serious as all that. It's simply . . . simply that I don't know what to do with you. What's best for you, that is."

Inwardly Callie bristled, her temper flaring. So he didn't know what to do with her. After he'd interfered in her life for the second time, taken her into his home, he'd decided she wasn't worth the trouble! Forcing herself into a show of bravado, Callie lifted her chin; her clear blue eyes looked levelly into his. "I wondered when you were going to tell me what's to become of me!" She heard the edge of temper in her voice and said, in a more indifferent tone, "Since you've been poking your nose in my business, I thought you'd have something in mind for me. But since you don't, I'll be thankin' you to take me back to Madge's on Cortlandt Street. No doubt, she'll think of something."

Byrch stared at her incredulously. "Are you talking about that prostitute who sent you off to the house on Bleecker Street?" He attempted to keep his voice light, took the time to puff on his pipe, but he was shaken to the quick. "Suppose you tell me the whole story, Callie. Start from the beginning, from when I left you in Dublin."

"Why? What difference does it make?" She felt she'd become a terrible burden on him and was ashamed of it. Her words crackled like the logs in the hearth; her voice piped high and brittle.

"Because I said so, that's why, dammit!" Byrch watched her shrink beneath his command. He felt he understood her. She was like a boxer he'd seen once, throwing fists and battling his opponent, jabbing and thrusting long after the bell sounded to end the round. The man had been nearly dead on his feet, and still he continued to fight. Byrch supposed Callie had been fighting and struggling for so long and so desperately that, like a boxer, she didn't know when the round had ended, when she could retreat to her corner.

Callie curled up in the chair, obediently and quietly, and told him about the events that had led to his finding her on Bleecker Street. When she mentioned her cousin, Owen Gallagher, Byrch choked on the pipe smoke.

"Owen Gallagher? That pimp? You say he's your cousin? For Christ's sake!"

"Now look here, Mr. Kenyon," Callie defended, family loyalty rising, "I know just what you're thinking! That my family is filled with thieves and whoremasters. Well, it's just not true. We're decent people, we are! Owen is only my mother's second cousin through marriage—"

"Shut up, Callie," he scolded, finding her excuses tiresome.

"Get on with what happened at the Magdalene. I'm doing a story on that society and others like them."

"You are?" Callie perked up. "And you want me to tell you what goes on there, and you'll be printing it in the paper?" She suddenly felt very important and began to give him a first-hand account of the inner workings of the Magdalene. "I don't want to go back there," she told him. "I'd rather take my chances with Madge!"

"You won't be going back to either place. I'll think of something." He was angry that Callie had no conception of her own worth. Each time she mentioned Madge, Byrch wanted to gnash his teeth. His irritation was communicated to Callie, doubling her shame and increasing her defenses. Only through anger could she maintain her pride.

"You should have had all this thought out before you snatched me," Callie said, feeling more and more unwanted by the moment. She hadn't asked him to rescue her, and she hadn't asked him to help her escape the grocer in Dublin the first time she'd met him. If he didn't want her here, then she didn't want to be here!

"Whatever you think of, I hope it'll include me earning a wage. I've been gone from home since September 19, and I've yet to send a farthing home to my Mum! Which brings me to another matter, Mr. Kenyon. Everything I owned in this world is at that house on Bleecker Street, including letters to my mother that I never had the chance nor the postage to send her. Can you do anything about that, Mr. Kenyon? I'd really like to have my own things!"

"Quit wailing like a banshee!" he ordered. "If you want those things, I'll see about getting them for you. For the time being, though, I want you to tell me everything, everything that's happened to you since you left Dublin. I want to smell the smells, hear the sounds—understand?" He stood up from his chair and went over to the little desk in the corner, taking out paper and quill. "Begin!" he commanded.

Long into the night Callie told him her story and the stories of so many others like her. She mentioned Beth and Patrick Thatcher, telling him that she'd made the crossing with them but omitting Beth's death. Somehow that was too personal, too painful to recount, even to Byrch. She relived how they'd cut her hair and what a devastating effect it had had on Beth. "She was never the same after that, poor love," Callie mourned.

Byrch was stricken by Callie's description of events. He'd traveled by steamship, cabin class, and the number of immigrants sailing with him had been few, owing to the price of the tickets. He'd known about quarantine, but like other Americans, he had thought it to be a necessary evil, dealt out humanely. Others must know about these atrocities, and if they didn't, they would soon find out when they read the *Clarion*.

Callie's eyes were heavy with drowsiness, and Byrch could see the delicate blue lines that hemmed her lashes. "Go to bed, Callie. We'll finish this discussion another time."

"Have you made up your mind what to do with me?"

Byrch sighed wearily. "What do you want me to do with you, Callie? I'll be damned if I have the solution."

Callie was exasperated, humiliated. This wasn't what she wanted to hear. She hated to be a burden to him. He'd been good and kind to her, and she had nothing to offer him in return. Lifting her chin obstinately, she said, "I can't be hanging about here, regaling you with stories of my life, Mr. Kenyon. I'm grateful for what you've done for me, but it's time for me to get on with my business, if you don't mind. I'll be leaving in the morning."

Byrch was agitated with Callie's impatience and angry with himself for not having a solution to the problem. He was bone tired, exhausted from listening to the profound tragedies Callie had recounted. His mind was already directed to the task of putting it all down on paper. He hoped he could capture the essence of her bravery and the pathos of her tale.

Misunderstanding, thinking Byrch's weariness and frown were a direct result of his not knowing what to do with her, Callie insisted, "You're supposed to be a smart man. You're supposed to have all the answers. Oh, why can't you leave me alone, just let me be on my way? I'm not addlewitted, and I'm used to hard work; I'll make my own way here in America!"

"If you don't shut that mouth of yours, I'm going to whack you where it'll do the most good! Perhaps I was a busybody back in Dublin, but I like to think I saved that neck of yours. I didn't like the idea of a child being hanged for stealing!" He ran a finger under his chin and then made a loud cracking sound that made Callie shiver. "One snap and it's all over. Your mum would've cried for at least two days."

"A child, is it!" Callie challenged, fully awake now. "And I suppose you're older than Moses!" The expression in her eyes changed to inquiry. "Just how old are you anyway, Mr. Kenyon?"

"Twenty-eight and ten times smarter than you are! At least I know when to shut my mouth!" He stood up from the desk suddenly, his green eyes flaring with anger, advancing on her one step at a time, rolling up his shirt sleeves in a manner that suggested she had gone too far and was going to get a spanking for it.

Yelping like a scalded puppy, Callie ran for the bed, leaping under the mound of feather comforters and pulling them over her head.

Long after the lights were out and Byrch had left the room, Callie lay awake pondering her predicament. It was only right that she leave. Byrch Kenyon didn't owe her anything. The scales were thrown to the other side; she owed him her safety and her life. Still, she sighed, turning her face into the pillow, it would be nice to be a little girl again and climb into his lap as she'd done that first night and feel him wrap her in tenderness and security.

Byrch sat in his bed-sitting room into the long hours before dawn, outlining and composing the articles for the *Clarion*. He would leave other news to his staff of reporters; this he would handle himself. It felt good to get back to writing again, finding the words to express himself and his beliefs. Too long he'd been working the business end of the *Clarion-Observer*; telling a story was like a breath of fresh air. Editorials were something else entirely; they were points of view, opinions. This was something he could get his teeth into; it was about people, life.

He thought about the girl in the room across the hall. She'd lived a lifetime in the short span of a few years. She'd watched her family come to ruin because of the Potato Blight, had felt the responsibility for them weigh heavily on her. She'd seen the intolerable and inhumane conditions at Tompkinsville, been thrown into a brothel, and been saved by a greed-ridden society that garnished her wages. And still there was spirit in her, something that would not be vanquished. He admired her resiliency. But now, what to do with her?

Byrch considered several alternatives, discarding them all as unfeasible. He had to be careful not to overstep his bounds or else she'd become resentful, and then Lord only knew what she'd do. What Callie needed, he decided at last, was to be in a family situation, preferably in a household where there were young people. He considered asking Kevin and Bridget to employ her but disregarded the notion. Bridget wouldn't hear of it, he knew; her standards for household help were most rigid. And she would never consider Callie as a companion for the children, nor would she want a constant reminder of her faux pas with the Magdalene Society. Callie couldn't remain here with him; she needed a woman's guidance. What to do with her?

His eyes ached and his temples throbbed, but he put pen to paper and began to write a list of his friends and acquaintances, evaluating each name as a possible place for Callie. The list was long and tiresome, and each name, except one, was vetoed for being unsuitable. Jasper Powers was the only name he could consider. Jasper himself would pose no problem; he was a soft-hearted man with great empathy for his fellow Irishmen. It was his wife, Anne, who would be the problem. He knew he shouldn't allow his personal dislike for Anne Powers to influence his decision; even though Anne was a self-righteous, social-climbing bitch like Bridget, she was nevertheless a fine mother and ran a good Christian household. Callie could learn the duties of a domestic servant under her eye. He would have liked to do so much more for Callie but was afraid to injure that raw, yet delicate, pride of hers.

Byrch rubbed his fist against his chin, feeling the stubble of beard. He thought about what he knew of the Powerses. Anne Powers was what her own husband called Lace Curtain Irish, with aspirations to have her origins forgotten and to be thought of as a regal Bostonian. Once Jasper had grumbled in a rare moment of confidence that his wife's one ambition was to marry the children off "well." After another drink of whiskey Jasper said that Anne didn't care for bedroom antics and suffered silently, occasionally being known to mutter, "Just do it and get it over with!" Yet Jasper loved his wife, regardless of the fact that he was constantly being reminded that she had married beneath herself.

At the time the Powerses were married, Jasper was a clerk in the Manhattan City Bank, and in spite of the fact that he was now president, Anne never let him forget his humble beginnings. In retaliation, or perhaps just for the warmth and caring of a woman, Jasper had taken a mistress, although he continued to live at home and pay the bills. Jasper was essentially a family man, and he loved his children. Rossiter, his only son and the eldest, had the same tall, golden, handsome looks of his mother's family. Little Annie, as he called his oldest daughter, was the mirror image of his wife, and although he knew her to be selfish and demanding, he was so beguiled by her slender elegance and quick mind that he usually acceded to her wishes. But it was Mary he adored. Her freckled face and auburn hair reminded him of his own sister back in Ireland. She was a child close to his heart, and she returned his love.

How would Callie fare in this household? Byrch's mind drifted back to the Powers children. It was because of the youngest child, Mary, that he decided to ask Jasper to hire Callie. Perhaps Callie could be Mary's companion. The Powerses lived out on Staten Island, away from the city and all its evils.

In a very few hours it would be dawn—Saturday and the banks were closed. Jasper would be enjoying a late morning at home. Never one to drag his feet once his mind had been made up, Byrch decided to catch a few hours' sleep before taking the ferry out to the island.

Before nine o'clock that morning Byrch took the ferry, along with his rented hackney cab and driver, across the Upper Bay to the town of St. George, which was just north of Tompkinsville and the quarantine station. In the cold of mid-December he looked out over the gray waters at the sailing ships and small boats either at anchor or sailing to and from the city. He'd seen this sight many times before, but now, after Callie's account of her experiences, he saw the whole scene from a different point of view. Quarantine, while necessary to the health of the city at large, was nonetheless a scourge on those subjected to it, he realized.

He traveled over the part of Staten Island he was familiar with: rolling hills, sandy beaches, good farm land, and rich top soil. Many of the city's élite kept summer homes out here, and Staten Island also harbored a society all its own in the section of the island where the Powerses lived—Todt Hill, almost three miles inland. Here on the craggy redstone rock, the wealthy erected their homes which, from this vantage, had a magnificent view of the Narrows and both bays. Tompkinsville, nestled beneath the shelter of the bluffs, was obscured from their view.

The hackney turned off Todt Hill Road onto a cinder-paved drive leading to the Powers's house, which perched on the highest outcropping of land. The house was impressive—three stories high, of clapboard and brick. A wide porch skirted three sides of the first floor, and several of the upstairs rooms opened onto balconies with ornamental railings and cone-shaped shingled roofs. Here the wind was a mighty adversary, rushing down upon the hilltop in cold, blustery breaths. Anne Powers's artistic hand could be seen in the careful placement of shrubs and trees, and Byrch knew that from early spring to late autumn a myriad of bright and fragrant flowers grew in gay abundance. Now, with the onset of winter, the grass was that sleeping shade of brown and the trees, except for the evergreens, were bare, reaching to scrape the sky with bony fingers.

Alighting from the hackney, Byrch said to the driver, "Go around back and tell them you drove Mr. Kenyon out. You'll warm yourself and have one of the best cups of coffee you've ever tasted."

Byrch bounded up the front porch, using the brass clapper to knock on the door. There was a shuffling from within, and Jasper Powers himself opened the door. "Byrch, you son-of-a-gun! Come in, come in!"

Jasper was a tall, heavily built, white-haired Irishman with intelligent blue eyes that twinkled merrily. He was the stuff leprechauns were made of, Byrch had thought on many occasions. He greeted Jasper with enthusiasm and warmth, feeling himself pulled into a bear hug.

"What brings you out to the island?" Jasper asked. "Don't tell me you had a hankering for a ferry ride on this miserable day. You didn't receive bad news from Ireland, did you?"

"No." Byrch put Jasper's mind at rest. "Da is doing fine, or so he said in his last letter. He's talking about making a trip out this summer, but we both know he says that every year. Why don't you write and encourage him? He mentioned a letter from you not too long ago."

"There's nothing I'd like better than to see my old friend Seamus. But I fear he's far too happy over there on the 'auld sod.' He complains that when he's here in the States he's only a displaced Irishman."

"Like so many others these days," Byrch said sourly, thinking of Callie and following Jasper into his library, which he liked to refer to as his "inner sanctum." Here Anne Powers was forbidden to enter with either dust cloth or broom. The room had the aroma of Jasper's cigars and aged leather. The long, multipaned windows looked out over the side lawn and beyond into the valley leading to the bay. It was a good, manly room, where a body could put his feet up and undo his cravat and engage in lengthy conversation about politics while sipping Jasper's finest Irish whiskey.

"If you'd been an hour later, Byrch, you would have missed me. I intended to go out to Kreischerville to check on the summerhouse and farm. But I'd rather spend the day with you, if you're amicable?"

"Sorry, Jasper. I must get back to the city." It suddenly seemed to Byrch that almost every moment's thought was devoted to the girl; it was exhausting.

"Pity. Anne is having a shoulder of pork for dinner, complete with applesauce from our own trees. Can't I tempt you?" Jasper moved over to a large, impressively carved desk and a silver coffee service from which he poured Byrch a mug of brew. None of Anne's delicate porcelain for his study; these mugs were thick-handled and large. "Then you've come here for a reason, and I take it it's rather important, considering I'll be back in the city on Monday morning." Jasper settled himself in a cracked leather chair behind his desk, propping his feet up on the newspapers and journals that littered its top. "Talk to me, Byrch, and don't leave anything out. Details, the kind you put in your newspaper. Makes for a good story."

"All in good time. First, appease my curiosity. Tell me about the children. How's Rossiter? The girls are all but young ladies by now—I wonder if I'll know them when I see them next."

"You'd know them," Jasper said sourly. "It's the same old story. Anne dotes on Rossiter as though he's the second coming of Christ! Although, to the boy's credit, he does balk under her influence. I suppose there's hope for him yet. And Little Anne is the picture of her mother, growing prettier and more elegant by the day."

"And Mary? How's Mary doing?" Byrch asked softly, watching the expression on his friend's face soften to a paternal glow.

"Mary's becoming a handful," Jasper broke into a wide grin. "She's giving Anne a difficult time of it. That one takes after my side of the family, a renegade, sure and delightful! Anne is giving some thought to sending her off to boarding school where they'll teach her to become a lady. Do you know what that little rascal did last week? She took her mother's best petticoat and made a kite!" Jasper guffawed with amusement. "If that wasn't bad enough, she was caught flying the damn thing in the churchyard and some of Anne's friends happened to be there. When Little Annie squealed to their mother, Mary retaliated by putting burrs in Annie's bloomers. Needless to say, Mary is confined to her room. That little one is too bright and intelligent for the namby-pamby rules Anne sets. She needs to use her mind, to be creative."

Byrch roared with laughter, more at the imagined expression on haughty Anne Powers's face than at what Mary had done. He also saw this as the perfect opportunity to introduce the subject of Callie.

"Jasper, I think I may have the answer to your problems with Mary." Quickly Byrch related Callie's story. All the while he watched Jasper's face, praying the man would agree to take Callie into his household.

"An Irish lass, you say. Sounds as though she's had a tough time of it."

"Tougher than you'd imagine, but to her credit, her spirit isn't broken. And she's young. But she's got a good head on her shoulders. I neglected to say I had the occasion to make her acquaintance in Dublin; I've seen her first-hand with her little brothers and sisters, and she's very conscientious. She'd be good for Mary, and Mary would be good for her. What do you say, Jasper? It would be a great favor to me and one to yourself as well."

"She sounds perfect to me. I suppose I should talk it over with Anne, but if I do, I run the risk of her refusal. Our best bet would be for you to bring the girl out here when she's fully recovered from her cold. When I tell Anne how fashionable it would be for Mary to have her own companion, she'll see the light."

Callie was curled up in the Queen Anne chair near the fireplace. Edward had just finished clearing away the lunch tray and had brought her several copies of the *Clarion-Observer* to peruse. He had told her how impressed he was that she could read and write, and Callie preened beneath his compliments. "Aunt Sara and my mother went to formal school," she informed him. "I went too, for a few years, before things got so bad and we moved to Dublin. Then I had to work in the mill, but Mum made me keep up with my studies. Then I was able to help her with Georgie and Hallie. The twins were still too little."

Edward listened to Callie's animated account and then saw the sorrow in her eyes. The child was homesick. That was something Edward knew about. Especially on gray, dreary days of winter, like this one, he longed for his island paradise in the West Indies. Placing a huge black hand on Callie's shoulder, Edward commiserated. "I do know how you feel, Missy, and there's no way in God's world to hurry the healing. But I promise you, in time the hurt is less, but you'll never stop longing for home and those you left behind."

Callie covered Edward's hand with her own; it looked small and very pale on top of his. "You miss home too, don't you, Edward?"

"That I do, Missy. But not every moment. There's much to be said for three meals a day and a clean bed. And I've made friends here. Mr. Kenyon, for one."

"And me too?" Callie inquired, looking up from her chair into his dusky black eyes.

"Yes, Missy. You too."

Edward carried the tray out of the room, taking one last glance at the young girl who seemed to be swallowed up by the large chair. He had no idea what plans Mr. Kenyon was going to make for her, but Edward had one wish: that the world would deal kindly with Callie James.

That was how Byrch found Callie when he returned. He moved across the room and dropped her own blanket poke at her feet. "Here's your things, rescued as promised from Bleecker Street. I didn't have any trouble getting them; Mr. Hatterchain was most eager to help and also to bend my ear in defense of himself and the Magdalene Society."

Callie dove for her belongings, opening the straps and searching through the odd assortment of clothes. The blue dress! The blue dress Madge had made her and the petticoats! Digging deeper, she brought out a packet of folded papers. "They're here!" she clapped in glee. "The blue dress and petticoats Madge made me are here and my letters to Mum!"

Byrch found himself smiling down at her. She was like a kitten under a Christmas tree, all life and curiosity and joy. How young and defenseless she was. He knew there were others like her in this vast city, but Callie had grown on him ever since that black night in a Dublin alley. This girl was special, and he couldn't allow her to drift off on her own with the hope that maybe she'd be all right. Maybe wasn't good enough. Byrch needed to *know* Callie was safe and cared for. He cleared his throat and saw her shining blue eyes snap to attention. "It's all settled. I've found a position for you. Tomorrow, after breakfast, I'll take you to my friend Jasper Powers. You'll learn domestic duties and the way ladies like things to be done, but you'll also be a companion to their youngest child, Mary. She's eight years old and quite high-spirited, something like you, Callie. Perhaps in teaching her, you'll learn yourself." He didn't know where the words were coming from; they just kept rushing out of him. "You'll be paid a fair and decent wage, and you'll save most of it if you're wise. You'll be given room and board and an allowance for clothing. If you want to send part of your wages home to your mother, Mr. Powers will arrange it for you. He's a good and decent man, Callie, otherwise I would never send you to him."

Callie nodded her head, refusing to allow her eyes to meet his. She was aware of a sense of loss. Was she really hoping to stay here? She tried to smile to show her appreciation for his efforts and felt it came off lamely.

"I have to go to the office, Callie. You don't mind, do you? Edward will be here with you, and I'll be back in time for supper." Byrch turned and strode out the door. Well, what had he expected? That she would throw herself at his feet in gratitude? Or perhaps that she would resist, telling him she preferred to stay with him? "Ridiculous!" Byrch muttered scornfully. Why would Callie want to put herself under a bachelor's care? What would he do with her? All the alternatives he'd pondered earlier that morning came coursing back. No, he told himself firmly. He'd done what was right for Callie. But somehow there was little satisfaction in the knowledge. Already she'd gotten under his skin, and he'd found himself running home from the *Clarion* this past week just to have supper with her and to watch her prance around the room in her little pink housecoat. This is ridiculous, he chided himself. He'd been house-bound for too long and was working too hard. He'd been neglecting his personal life; he'd been without a woman for too long. Before he did another thing, he was going to send a note off to Flanna Beauchamp of the elegant swan neck. If he wasn't mistaken, she was eager and ripe for the picking; he wondered how that slender long torso of hers would bend in his arms.

For the remainder of the afternoon, Callie pored through copies of the *Clarion-Observer*, searching for articles with the byline of Byrch Kenyon or simply, Editor. Through those articles, she learned a lot about her benefactor, admiring him for his search for truth and justice. She learned about the newsboys' strike and about the competition between volunteer and city-paid firemen. But mostly she learned about Byrch, the man.

Dropping the last paper onto the floor, Callie leaned back, gazing into the flames. Lord, Lord, to think that a man like him would jump to help a little nobody like me. Lord, Lord, if only I were as pretty and as old as Colleen. Callie didn't even dare to complete the wish or its consequences. She was too realistic to believe that she, an ugly duckling, could become a swan, or that a little Irish girl could become a fairy princess loved by the handsome prince. Those were stories Granda liked to tell the children. And she, Callie James, was no longer a child.

Last night at supper, Byrch had presented her with a paper-wrapped parcel. Inside was a navy serge jumper and two white blouses with long sleeves and wide, round collars. Three pairs of black cotton stockings and two camisoles and britches. At least that's what he called them. Drawers, Mum always said. But most luxurious of all was the coat, warm gray wool that buttoned down the front. The black, beaver shawl collar that draped over her shoulders added additional warmth.

"I would have liked to get you bright colors, Callie," Byrch apologized, "but they wouldn't have been befitting your station as a domestic, I'm afraid." Even now he scowled at the drab, although well-made, goods.

"Where did you get them?" Callie asked excitedly, holding the jumper in front of her, not at all concerned about the dark colors.

"Over on Hester Street. There's a factory there for ready-made clothing. It's run by Jews, and this being their Sabbath, I had myself quite a time of it."

Callie looked up at him blankly, clearly not understanding.

"Jewish people don't conduct business on their Sabbath, Callie. Sidney even refused my money. I'll have to send it over to him on Monday. And since you'll need something to put everything in, I've brought you a little satchel."

Callie took the small black suitcase from him. "Open it," he instructed. Inside was another package containing a hairbrush, a comb, a toothbrush, and a sparkling bottle of rosewater.

Byrch laughed over Callie's clowning antics as she tried on one of the white blouses over her housedress, but inwardly he frowned. He would have liked to take credit for his generosity, but he knew it was Anne Powers's opinion that had prompted him to make the purchases. Her acceptance of Callie would be made upon first impression, and he was determined that it be a good one. That's why he had chosen dark, utilitarian garments, presentable yet far from ostentatious—just the sort of garb a domestic would wear.

Now, dressed in her new clothes, Callie sat beside Byrch in the hackney, heading south. Her new satchel, containing her old clothes and some of the new ones, as well as the pretty pink nightdresses, bed jacket, and housecoat that were gifts from him also, was by her side. She looked out through the cab window into the quiet streets of the city. When they reached the end of Broadway, some of the buildings became familiar, and when the hackney entered the line for the St. George's Ferry, Callie realized where she was and panicked.

"You didn't tell me we were going on a boat!" she whispered hoarsely.

"You didn't ask. Besides, it's not a boat, it's a ferry. Take a look, here it comes into dock. We'll be across in no time; you won't have a chance to get seasick."

"Isn't there some other way to go?" Callie asked, her voice desperate.

Byrch looked down at his young charge, saw that the color had left her face. "What's the matter, sweeting? Are you afraid of the water? Tell me," he demanded, cupping her face between his hands.

Unshed tears burned Callie's eyes. She wouldn't cry in front of him no matter how much she remembered, no matter how much she suffered. "I don't like this place, that's all!" was her heart-torn answer.

"I know a lie when I hear one," Byrch growled when Callie pulled away from him, cringing against the seat in the hackney. "If you aren't afraid of the water, and I believe you aren't, there's another reason. Staten Island is only across the bay; it isn't the other side of the world!" Even as he uttered the name of the island, he realized the basis for Callie's fear: "Callie, the quarantine hospital is only one small place on a good-sized island. I promise you, you'll not even have to look in that direction, and the Powers's house sits high up on a hill, miles away from Tompkinsville. I hadn't thought about the memories Staten Island would bring you."

Callie cowered against the seat, and Byrch could see his plans for her future and her security flying out the window unless he could get her to face her fears and accept reality. "Let's talk about it," he began, only to have her turn her face away. "Talk! Dammit! I want to know what's going on in that head of yours! I can't help if I don't know!" His patience was at an end, and he seized her by the shoulders and shook her until she thought her teeth would rattle.

Callie moved her lips to protest, to fight him back. Instead, the rush of words that poured out began the story of Beth and Patrick. Byrch had to ask her to slow down while he tried to absorb all that she was telling him. He stared at her, hardly believing what she was saying.

"And she jumped! She just jumped with little Paddy still in her arms! She didn't want to have her baby in a hole in the ground! I didn't know! I swear I didn't know she was going to do it until the end. I tried to stop her, to talk to her, but she killed herself and the baby and Paddy, and Patrick was at the end of the dock and he saw her do it. I know he saw her!" Callie collapsed in a hysteria of tears, burrowing her face against Byrch's topcoat.

Byrch stroked the chestnut curls, trying to give comfort. "Patrick saw her, but he didn't save her. Why? Why?" she moaned, and the sound tore at Byrch's heart. "She loved him so much that she killed herself to give him his dream. Now she's buried out there behind the hospital and Patrick has his dream . . ."

Byrch swallowed past the lump in his throat. Good God! What a monstrous thing to have witnessed. And now she wanted answers from him; she kept sobbing over and over, "Why?"

"Callie, your friend Beth was a foolish but very unselfish woman . . ." he began.

Callie raised her face from his breast, looking him squarely in the eye, her lower lip jutting out in anger. "Don't talk to me about unselfish love and what it all means. I know all about it! I watched my mother with my father. Then I watched Beth with Patrick. I suppose what I can't accept is that I know Patrick wouldn't have done that for her. I wanted him to love her as much as she loved him and to be worthy of that love. I wanted them to have a life together. Patrick loved Beth, but I know he wouldn't have done the same for her."

"Callie, love is such a fragile thing. Women sometimes think they have a monopoly on it. I never met Patrick, but I'm certain that given enough time he would have come up with a solution to their problem. You don't know for certain that Patrick wouldn't have done the same for Beth, that he didn't love her unselfishly."

Callie backed away, staring at him through tear-filled eyes. "Well, that explanation isn't good enough for me! I said those same things to myself while I watched them bury her. Don't you be handing me any malarkey about Patrick finding a solution. He'd never find a solution because he believed Beth was a burden to him. When his dream was dashed, or he thought it was, he was broken. In the end, it would have been Beth who solved the problem. And . . . and I suppose that's just what she did, just so the man she loved could have his dream. Why are women always falling in love with the wrong man? I never will, that's for sure! I never want to love any man!" Byrch handed her his handkerchief, and she blew her nose lustily. "I see you have no answer for that one, do you?" she challenged.

Byrch scowled. On that point she was correct.

The hackney cab moved along in line, boarding the ferry. When the horse was tethered and blocks thrown under the wheels, Byrch assisted Callie out to the rail. The thin sunshine of December shone down on his ruffled dark hair, and he gazed out at the water with a grim expression. Callie stood beside him, small and vulnerable, her hands gripping the rail as the ferry began to steam across the bay.

"I don't have the answers you're looking for, sweeting," Byrch said softly. "It's the system of things. Laws are made for the good of the majority. Quarantine is necessary. You don't understand it all takes time to—"

"Understand? I understand, all right!" Callie answered. "Beth didn't have time. Little Paddy was on borrowed time. You," she said, jamming a finger into his midsection, "have the power to change things. Why aren't you doing it? You didn't even know what's going on in your country, even though it's happening less than five miles away, over there"—she pointed an accusatory finger across the bay—"there in Tompkinsville!"

Byrch was so startled by her outburst that he was temporarily at a loss for words.

"You should be out there beating the bushes, as my mum would say. You have that newspaper of yours, and you should use it to make things right! Make it so women like Beth don't have to live in a hole in the ground just to avoid the filth and disease in the hospital! She was so afraid, Beth was, of having that baby like an animal." Spent with her outburst, Callie stared in defiant outrage at Byrch.

"I'll try, Callie. I promise, I'll try." Byrch's cat-green eyes had deepened to a murky sage as he guided Callie away from the rail to a polished plank bench and then sat beside her. She was a spitfire, a hellcat of the first order. But then, he'd known that from their first meeting. Callie James was not ordinary, she would never be ordinary. This little girl from Ireland had given him plenty to think about. He did have the power as she put it. Now if he could figure out the best way to use it, he might be able to help others like Callie James.

The ferry was midway across the channel, and in the nearby distance ships weighed at anchor and small boats volleyed around the harbor. "Look over there, Callie. See that? It's the entrance to the channel leading to Tompkinsville. See how it looks from here? Harmless. That's what most New Yorkers see, and there's nothing that would distress them. Don't blame me, Callie. Don't blame others like me. I promised to try to help change things, and I will. Do you believe me?"

Callie nodded her head, her short curls ruffling in the wind. "I suppose I'll have to," she murmured, but she knew in her heart that Byrch Kenyon was a man who cared, and she lowered her eyes so he wouldn't see the shining adoration she felt for him.

Just as they entered the hackney again before disembarking from the ferry, Callie turned to Byrch and asked one last favor. "I've got these letters to my mother. Lord only knows when I'll be able to post them. She'll be worried not to hear from me for so long. Last night I told her about going to work for the Powers family, but I couldn't break her heart by telling her about Owen Gallagher and what a toad he is. Would you send them for me?"

Quickly she opened her little satchel and brought out the packet of letters. The top sheet of folded paper held the address.

Byrch took the packet and stuffed it into his inside coat pocket, patting it into place. He felt as though he held her life against his heart.

Chapter Ten

As their hackney pulled up the Powers's drive, Callie looked ahead, wide-eyed and open-mouthed. "Am I to live here?" she asked weakly. "Surely I'm not to live here! Oooh! 'Tis grand as a castle!"

Byrch smiled, liking the way Callie's brogue thickened when she became excited or terribly pleased. "Yes, that's where you'll live. And it is a grand place," he agreed. "It sits upon the highest hill. Look out there," he pointed, "you can see the narrows and just across, that's Brooklyn. That way," he said, pointing to the left, "is where we've just come from. So you see, I'll be a little more than a stone's throw away." It was almost on the tip of his tongue to tell her that she wasn't alone, that he'd always be there for her. No, he never wanted her to be alone. Instead he helped her from the hackney as though she were a grand lady and led her across the yard to the front porch.

He watched her out of the corner of his eye, saw the way she tilted her chin upward, held herself erect. Poor little thing, she must be scared to death, and yet here she was with that certain brand of bravado that was hers alone.

Callie liked Jasper Powers immediately. Byrch was astounded at the expression of sheer ecstasy on both their faces as Jasper foled her into a bear-hug embrace. His friend held the girl at a distance, staring deeply into her eyes. "Forgive me for doing that, child, it's just that you've the look of Ireland all about you, and for a moment I held the old country close."

Callie smiled, nearly breaking into a giggle. Jasper didn't know what Byrch had seen in the depths of Callie's eyes, but he himself read loyalty, determination, and strength. She might be slight, but this girl held an iron power. He could feel it. Callie James would become a force to be reckoned with. Somehow she reminded him of his own mother with her iron will, indefatigable energy, and unfailing sense of justice.

Callie found herself speechless when Jasper guided her into his house. Never in all her dreams had she imagined such elegance. Mrs. Powers looked like a queen in her brocade afternoon dress. Her blue-black hair was as dark and vibrant as Byrch's. Callie curtsied politely and lowered her eyes, afraid of what might be disapproval in the regal woman's grim expression. Jasper's indulgent tone to his wife was not lost on Callie.

Mrs. Powers sniffed haughtily at her husband's introduction and reached out to lift Callie's chin, tilting her face this way and that. "You've the look of trouble about you, girl," Anne Powers said. "I'll have you know right from the beginning that it won't be tolerated." Callie inwardly shrank from the woman's inhospitable words, but as the fates would have it, her eyes met the woman's levally, her chin lifted, her lower lip pouted impudently, creating the mask of defiance that was the bane of her life.

"Jasper, look at this child! Look at this impudence! I won't have it, I tell you. I won't!"

"Now, Anne, I don't see anything wrong," Jasper insisted. "You've simply scared her half to death with your poking and prodding. Leave her be, won't you?"

"Hrmph!" Anne Powers sniffed, chancing a glance at Byrch, who was glaring in her direction. She was quick to remember the scandal he told Jasper he'd uncovered at the Magdalene Society, to which she was a very generous donor, and Byrch's promise to keep her name out of the paper if she took this girl into her employ.

Anne nodded curtly to her husband. "Very well, then. I don't usually employ anyone without proper references, you understand," she addressed Callie, who was bewildered by the term, "but since this is a special case," she smiled at Byrch, "I suppose you'll do." Satisfied that she'd properly set both her husband and his young friend in their places, she clasped a hand on Callie's shoulder. "Come with me, girl. I'll take you upstairs to Mary.

Today is Sunday, so it's no time for you to learn what your household duties will be. Tomorrow will be time enough." Feeling the touch of fine wool under her hand, she openly admired Callie's new coat. "I must say, you're properly dressed, at least. We won't have to be ashamed of you at any rate." She glanced pointedly at Byrch, certain that he was responsible for Callie's fine coat and no doubt for everything else she had in that little satchel.

"Come along, come along," Mrs. Powers commanded as she started up the wide staircase in the front hall. "I'll take you up to Mary now. My youngest daughter is not the best behaved child," she explained as Callie followed her up the stairs. Callie looked back for one parting glance at Byrch, who forced a smile as if to say everything would be fine. Something told her nothing could be further from the truth.

"The child needs a firm hand," Mrs. Powers was saying, "and a slap or two if the deed warrants. You're to remember you are a companion to Mary, not a playmate! Is that understood? You're to keep her in hand. She's a constant embarrassment to all of us. We never know what she'll say or do from one minute to the next. You will monitor her every move and her every word."

Callie nodded in understanding. Mrs. Powers was tired of Mary's disobedience but unable to control it; she would content herself with having someone else to blame for her daughter's conduct. Any child of Anne Powers was not allowed to be anything less than perfect.

"Do you understand?" Mrs. Powers turned abruptly when she reached the second-floor landing.

"Yes, mum."

"No, no, don't refer to me as 'mum.' I am 'Ma'am' or 'Mrs. Powers.' My husband, of course is 'Mr. Powers' or 'Sir.' The children, of course, address us as '*Mamán*' and '*Papá*,' with the French inflection."

Of course! Callie thought to herself, with the French inflection, whatever that was. Silently, she mouthed, *Mamán* and *Papá*, trying the new syllables for use.

"And I'll expect you do so something about that terrible Irish brogue! I simply cannot have it in my home, and God forbid Mary picks it up from you. I'll expect you to improve yourself under my tutelage, Callie. You'll discover I haven't Mr. Powers's affection for all things Irish. My family," she drawled, "are Bostonians and have been wise enough to separate themselves from Ireland for many generations now. I, like them, am an American!"

"Yes, Ma'am." Callie snapped her lips shut. She wanted to

ask why Mrs. Powers thought being an American was something of distinction. Beth's and Patrick's new baby would have been an American just because it would have been born here. Wisely Callie kept her silence and tagged along behind her new employer.

On the third floor, Mrs. Powers drew up before a door, opening it onto a light and sunny room.

"This is Mary's nursery. She's being punished and has to stay in here for the balance of the day. She will not be permitted to eat at the dinner table with us because she refuses to eat with the silver. She chooses to use her fingers. Distasteful! Until she learns proper manners she will stay in this room. I will tolerate no excuses where Mary is concerned. She is your job, your responsibility, and you will straighten her out. How I ever had a child like this is beyond me. Anne is such a joy, such a lady. She takes after my side of the family. Rossiter is a brilliant young man and also takes after my side. It's obvious that Mary favors my husband's side of the family. They all have rebellious streaks in them. If only we could do something with that hideous red hair she has, but we can't. It's nothing but a rat's nest of snarls and tangles. She won't let anyone within an inch of her. *You* will make her presentable!"

A miracle worker was what they needed here, not a companion, Callie thought sourly. She could barely wait to set eyes on the hell raiser that was to be her charge.

"Mary, *Mamán* is here with your new nursemaid. Come, dear, and say hello, and let's mind our manners. Mary, where are your clothes? Why are you in your underwear?"

A child, small for her years, was sitting in the middle of the floor, building a tower with some brightly colored blocks. She ignored her mother and concentrated on what she was doing. Callie watched her as she maneuvered the blocks to achieve the height she wanted. It wasn't until Mrs. Powers walked over to the stack of colored blocks that the child looked up and acknowledged her mother. She stared up at the two women. There was a question in her eyes.

"Mary, why are you in your underwear? Where are your clothes? Get dressed immediately. This is your companion. Her name is Callie James. Now say 'hello' and do what you're told."

Mary looked up at her mother and then at Callie. She said nothing, and instead of obeying her mother's orders, she sat down and began to build onto her tower. Callie wasn't certain if Mrs. Powers did it deliberately or it was an accident, but the tower crumbled to the floor. The hem of Mrs. Powers's afternoon dress must have brushed against the teetering blocks. But if that were true, why did the woman seem so pleased?

Callie waited to see if Mary would throw a tantrum. Instead she calmly began to rebuild, ignoring her mother completely.

Mrs. Powers threw her hands into the air and turned to leave the room. "She's impossible! If you can't do something with her, we'll be forced to send her to a proper school where they'll take her in hand. And that," Mrs. Powers turned, seizing Callie in her gaze, "means you will not be needed here!" It was a threat and well taken by Callie. Either Mary would come up to her mother's standards or Callie would be out on her ear.

Removing her new gray coat and placing it at the foot of Mary's frilly pink and white bedspread, Callie crossed the room to sit down on the floor next to the little girl. They took turns adding block on top of block. When it appeared that another addition would make the structure topple, Mary sat back and stared at her vibrant creation. "My Papá would say this is beautiful, but he can't come to the nursery because I'm being punished."

"Then let's get dressed and get started doing things so that your moth . . . *Mamán*," Callie tried the new word with the French inflection for the first time aloud, "your *Mamán* will allow you to go downstairs. I'll brush your hair and turn you into a beautiful little girl that will please your *Papá* and *Mamán*. Won't that be nice?"

Mary frowned at Callie, tilting her head to the side, watching her new companion's face. Then ignoring her, she began to rebuild the blocks. Knowing she had to show this little one that she meant what she said, Callie touched Mary's shoulder and held out her hand for the child to grasp and pulled her to her feet. The smile Mary offered Callie was dazzling, her sherry-colored eyes dancing with delight. This apparent swing of moods puzzled Callie. How could the child be so oblivious to her one moment and then bestow the friendliest of smiles upon her the next?

Settling Mary on a small chair, Callie reached for the brush on the dressing table and held it aloft, the child watching her every movement. "We'll make a game of this, and before you can say 'leprechaun,' your hair will be done." Callie crouched low and advanced slowly, a wide smile on her face, teasing and playing with Mary as she had with Georgie and Hallie and the twins. But would this peculiar child respond in play?

Mary shrieked with laughter as Callie made wide, sweeping motions with the brush. She worked on one hank of brilliant red-gold hair at a time, beginning at the ends and working toward the scalp until it was entirely free of tangles. It fell nearly to Mary's waist like a rippling, molten waterfall. Callie viewed her handiwork and marched the child to the mirror. "You're beautiful, Mary. Now show me where your dresses are, and we'll make you look like a princess." Mary turned and gave Callie a grateful hug.

"You didn't pull my hair and hurt me." Then backing away to look into her face, the child said, "I don't know your name."

"Callie. Callie James." Something uneasy moved in Callie, so intent was the child's gaze.

Then breaking away and going back to her toys, Mary said, "Come build a castle with me, Callie."

"Mary! I told you to show me where your dresses are!" The little girl looked at her questioningly, and Callie frowned.

"Come build a castle with me," Mary repeated.

Callie turned her back to Mary. "I can't build a castle with you, Mary Powers, because I've got to tend to the little monkey who's hiding in my satchel." She turned abruptly and saw that Mary continued to arrange the blocks. "Yes, I've a little monkey in there, and he likes to eat apples, and he's just waiting for some little girl to take him out and hug him." Again she turned. This time Mary was frowning, but when she saw Callie's inquiring gaze, she quickly looked away. Something was wrong. If she'd said the same to the kids back home, they'd be running and crawling all over the satchel, looking for a way to release the monkey, squealing at the top of their lungs.

"My monkey has a long, curling tail and little, little hands, and he can climb along roof tops, and he loves little girls."

"Hmmm? Come play with me, Callie!"

Callie dropped to her knees. She recognized that inquiring expression now. It was Granda's. She touched Mary's shoulder again. "You've trouble hearing, haven't you?" Mary shrunk backwards, suspicion and apprehension clouding those bright sherry eyes, her lower lip beginning to tremble.

"I can hear when you're facing me and you're close to me." The child hung her head in shame. "How did you know? Even *Mamán* and *Papá* don't know." Then as though touched with the flat of a hot iron, Mary became very animated. "Don't tell, Callie, please don't tell. It's a secret. *Mamán* will send me away if she knows. *Mamán* doesn't like for anything to go wrong. Anne can hear and so can Rossiter. I don't want to be different. You won't tell? Please don't tell!"

Callie was dumbfounded by the heart-rending plea and the expression of sheer helplessness on Mary's face. How could she refuse this child, betray her trust? Yet how could she neglect to tell the Powers's something as important as this? It was easy to understand how Mary's impairment made her parents think she was ignoring their orders and disobeying their wishes. This child had obviously become expert at hiding her infirmity. Knowing Mrs. Powers, Callie could understand why. If Mary was correct, and Callie suspected she was, Anne Powers could not tolerate such a defect in her child. She would send her away somewhere, and that would leave Callie without a position, out on her ear, and dependent once more on Byrch Kenyon.

Mary saw the indecision on Callie's face, and it frightened her. She threw her arms around Callie's neck, hugging her tightly. "Please don't tell. Please." Her small body trembled and quaked, and Callie's child's heart went out to her new little friend. "I wasn't always this way, only since I had the measles last spring. I caught a fever. Then when Anne boxed my ears for doing something naughty and *Mamán* boxed them again because we were fighting, it got worse."

"Why didn't you tell your *Mamán*, Mary?"

"Because I was afraid she'd send me away. She's always saying she'll send me away. I'd never see *Papá* again; he'd say *Mamán* knows best! Please, Callie, please."

The two children held each other, pledging themselves to their conspiracy. Callie knew she was wrong in not telling the Powerses, but Mary was so frightened, as frightened as Beth Thatcher had been when she thought Patrick's dream was being destroyed. Life had not dealt kindly with Beth then, and Callie's mistrust in the fates gave her no reason to think they would deal any more kindly with Mary.

It was a cold, gray morning, and Callie was loath to leave her bed in the tiny room adjacent to Mary's nursery. Here the ceiling was merely the naked rafter that lay just beneath the shingles and eight inches of snow. The only warmth in the room came from a grate in the central chimney, which ran up the center of the house from the fireplace in the parlor on the first floor. Since the fire was never lit before ten in the morning, Callie woke each day shivering beneath her blanket.

She'd been employed at the Powers's house for nearly two weeks, and several days ago she'd been instructed to get Mary and her clothes ready for the Christmas trip to Boston, which was less than a week away.

Jumping from her bed, Callie was quick to dress, taking pleasure in the long, dark stockings that covered her legs and grateful for the warmth of her blouse and jumper. Stoically, she splashed water on her face and dipped her finger in a small pot of salt, rubbing it over her teeth the way Peggy had taught her. She rinsed her mouth with water from a cracked ironstone pitcher and spat into the chamber pot. That was another of her duties aside from being companion to Mary—chamber pots and bed linens and laundering her own clothing as well as Mary's. Last night she'd added another paragraph in her letter to Peggy, telling her how she'd learned to polish silver in the wood ashes from the kitchen stove and was learning to be a proper hand at the dining-room table. She did not recount for Peggy, however, the vast amounts of sumptuous foods served at the Powers's house nor the fact that no one ever seemed to clean his plate, thinking it would be cruel in the face of her family's poverty.

Callie was waiting until the end of next month to post her letters when she could include a bank draft secured by Jasper Powers. Out of the glorious fourteen dollars she would earn each month, she would send Peggy twelve. She would have gladly sent it all home, but Mr. Powers thought it unwise. Twelve American dollars he told her, converted to English pounds, would go far in Dublin.

> . . . Little Mary Powers is the sweetest of girls, Mum. I already feel as though she might be my own little sister, even though no one could ever take the place of Hallie or Bridget in my heart. But, Mum, you should just see this one. She has bright red hair, the color of fire in the sky, and dancing brown eyes that have the gold of berry tea in them and that are quick as a deer's and do not miss a trick. She is a smart one, is our little Mary, and good with her letters and figures and can remember long rhymes and ditty songs.
>
> Mary has her own teacher who comes to the house twice a week to hear her lessons. His name is Mr. Harrison Reader, and Mrs. Powers says he is a fine young man of exceptional virtue. He has a clear, fine voice that can be heard throughout the house, and when he reads poetry or plays, he stands with one hand on his heart and the book at arm's length in the other and recites as though he were an actor on the stage. Mary likes Mr. Reader and so do I. I am allowed to sit in on Mary's lessons because Mrs. Powers hopes Mr. Reader will teach me to talk without my brogue. I am trying. Mr. Reader says I have a fine mind and I am good and quick

with numbers. He likes to teach history and government best. He says that politics is close to the heart of every Irishman, and he must be right because I like to hear about Mr. George Washington and Mr. Thomas Jefferson and the Kings and Queens of Europe.

Mary's sister is seventeen years old, and she goes into New York City to attend school three days a week. On Tuesday, Wednesday, and Thursday she lives in the City at Miss Rose Northrup's School of Quality and Ladyship. Those three days are the most peaceful here at the house. I have already written what a hoity-toity she is, and I do not like her very much. But she is pretty with hair blacker than coal and eyes darker than shoe polish and skin whiter than little baby Joseph's bottom. Miss Anne is much involved with her friends and spends most of her day doing needlework or sitting before her mirror.

When Mr. and Mrs. Powers take the family to Boston—that's a city far north of New York—I will stay here on Staten Island with Mr. MacDuff, the handyman, and Lena, the cook. They are both very nice to me and teach me how to do things the way Mrs. Powers likes them done.

In the spring, Mr. MacDuff is going to teach me how to grow pansies and Scotch roses. He is a Scotsman and talks with a funny burr. I wonder why Mrs. Powers does not seem to mind a Scottish burr, but the sound of an Irish brogue raises her hackles.

Callie tripped lightly down the back stairs and entered the kitchen where Lena, a stout, red-cheeked widow woman, was standing at the stove. Hugh MacDuff was sitting at the table, sipping scalding coffee from a mug. "Good morning!" Callie greeted them cheerfully. "Is the water hot for Mary's tea?"

"It's already poured," Lena said, busy with the raisin scones and spattering bacon. "You're a bit late this morning, girl. Didn't you sleep well last night?"

"Well enough." Callie accepted a strip of crisp fried bacon. "I just had a hard time finding the courage to put my feet on the floor."

"What did I tell you, MacDuff? That room of Callie's is smaller than a rabbit hutch and colder than a well-digger's backside in winter. Do you think you'll find a spare piece of carpet somewhere to lay next to her bed?"

"Aye. That I will," Hugh growled as was his way in the early morning. Callie suspected he romanced an occasional bottle in his room over the carriage house. But she genuinely liked this tall, bony man whose face was square and sharp with an everpresent growth of grizzled stubble on his chin. "As soon as her highness takes off for Boston, I'll poke around in the attic and find you something." Hugh always referred to Mrs. Powers as "her highness" when she was out of earshot, and it never failed to make Callie giggle.

"Sit down, child, Mary's eggs will take a minute yet. Have you done everything Mrs. Powers told you? Did you be certain to pack only Mary's very best dresses? She'll be wanting to make the best impression on her famous family, I can tell you." Lena talked as she buttered several hot scones. "You've made such a change in that little one in the short time you've been here. I don't think Mrs. Powers has had to take the hairbrush to her once!"

"Aye!" Hugh smiled. "She's a good lassie and only needed a bit of loving, I says. I'd like to see how they make out with her without you along, lass."

Callie, too, was worried about Mary. What if someone noticed that she was hard of hearing?

"It will be a well-deserved holiday for us, though, the family going to Boston." Hugh took a swallow of coffee and wiped his mouth on the sleeve of his heavy workshirt. "I've even got a little tree in the woods picked out for us. And through the goodness of Mr. Powers's heart, there's a goose to cook for Christmas Day."

"Another Christmas," Lena sighed. Callie knew she was thinking of her daughters who lived with their families somewhere in New Jersey.

"Can't you go to see your grandchildren, Lena? I know how much you'd like to."

"Argh! Much as I would, it won't happen this year. I've postponed my Christmas holiday for sometime in March when my youngest girl has her first child. I'll be going out there to help out." Lena brightened, patted Callie's hand, and smiled. "Don't you worry, girl, we'll make Christmas right here, just the three of us. And maybe you can talk that grumpy old man over there into going to church with us. It couldn't hurt his black soul to pray to his Maker for once."

"And what do you know of my black soul? Have ye seen it?"

"Lena," Callie interrupted before they got started on one of their arguments, "can you hurry with Mary's breakfast? There's still so much to do to get her ready."

"Aye, Lena, get on with the child's breakfast. For certain that good for nothing Tilly won't be giving our Callie a hand with what needs to be done!" Tilly was the day worker who came in each morning to do housework and laundry. Possessing an inflated opinion of herself and her station in the Powers's household, she was resentful of the fact that Callie had been appointed to the more important position of Mary's companion. Tilly had said to Hugh that if it was a playmate for their brat the Powerses were looking for, they'd have done better to pick a guttersnipe from the streets than an Irish girl and a greenhorn at that! Tilly had forgotten for the moment that Hugh himself had been born outside the country and hated the term 'greenhorn.' Since that day, Hugh had become Callie's staunch defender.

"Finish up that coffee, MacDuff. Mrs. Powers has those trunks ready to take down to the wagon. And don't forget to dress warm," Lena added. "It's a long, cold ride to the ferry and colder even going across."

Hugh MacDuff was to drive the Powerses to the ferry and take them across to South Street where they would meet Mr. Powers, who had stayed in the city the night before. From there, they were taking a steamship up the coast to Boston Harbor.

"Callie," Lena directed, placing another sweel roll on Mary's tray, "you can take this up to Miss Mary now. There's an extra sweet roll for you, and since you haven't time for a proper breakfast this morning, you'll take your lunch down here with MacDuff and me."

Callie carried the tray up the backstairs to Mary's nursery on the third floor. Her shoes were soundless on the carpeted stairs and hallway. As she passed the second floor where Mrs. Powers's bedroom was, she heard Miss Anne speaking with her mother.

"*Mamán*! How can you be so cruel? I'm seventeen, nearly eighteen, and I don't see why I must share a cabin with that little monster! Really, *Mamán*," she continued to whine, "that little brat is always poking into my things, and she has such dirty little habits. *Mamán*! You're not listening to me!"

"Anne," Mrs. Powers said crisply, "I am listening and I don't care for what I hear. The arrangements have already been made for our accommodations aboard the steamship, and you will share a cabin with your sister whether you like it or not! Cabin space is at a premium this time of year with the holidays upon us, and it was the best we could do."

"*Mamán*!" came another whine.

"If you will please attend to your packing, Anne, I will be most grateful. Don't forget to pack your new dancing slippers to go with your ball gown. And I don't want to hear another word about Mary. You will just have to make do."

"Ugh! It just makes me ill the way everyone fawns over that little brat. And I suppose when Rossiter joins us at Grandfather's house, he'll just dote on her and spoil her even more than she already is."

"Hmmm? Yes, I suppose. But what harm can it do? And Rossiter always was such a generous-natured boy." There was a softening of Mrs. Powers's tone when she mentioned her son.

"You always favor Ross over me," Anne continued to whine.

Callie continued up to the third floor, deciding she had heard enough. Usually Mrs. Powers cossetted her oldest daughter, but this morning she evidently had little patience for her whining and wheedling. And Callie believed she knew the reason. Rossiter. Mrs. Powers had been talking about this trip to Boston and her eagerness to be reunited with her son ever since Callie had come to work.

Sometimes it seemed to Callie that the world loved Rossiter Powers. Faces seemed to brighten whenever his name was mentioned, and his exploits and virtues were common discussion. Over the mantle in the parlor was an artist's rendering of him standing beside his favorite horse. Callie had peered deeply into that handsome young face, and she thought him to be the most beautiful young man she had ever seen. His eyes were a soft gray, or so Mary had told her, and Callie could see from the portrait that his hair was the stuff of spun gold. He was possessed of an engaging smile that made you want to smile back at him. If asked to describe him, Callie would have said he looked exactly like the golden-haired guardian angel in the sacristy of St. John's Church in Dublin.

"Hurry up now, Mary," Callie said as she put the tray down on the little table near the high window. "We've got to be quicker than two greased pigs to get you ready in time."

Mary was sitting on the edge of her bed, and from the expression on her face, she was sulking. "I want you to come with us," she pouted.

Callie went to sit beside her, touching her gently. "I can't come with you, little one, I'm to stay here. I know you're thinking you'll get yourself into some kind of trouble if I'm not there with you—"

"No!" Mary threw herself into Callie's arms. "That's not it at all. I'll . . . I'll miss you!"

Burying her face into the sweet warmth at the back of Mary's neck, Callie clucked just the way Peggy used to do. "But I'll be here when you come back. You know I will. Think of it, you'll be celebrating Christmas in Boston the way you've done every year since you were born. And you'll see Rossiter after all these months. You've been telling me how special he is and how he pays you special attention. Come on, be a good girl now. Let's get ready so we don't make your *Mamán* angry."

Mary released herself from Callie's embrace and moved to the little table to eat her breakfast. "I'm going to tell Rossiter all about you, Callie. I'm going to tell him how pretty you are and how you take such good care of me, and how *Papá* thinks you're the best thing to happen to this house since gas lighting."

Callie laughed. "And if you tell him all that, do you think you'll have breath enough left to tell him how pleased Mr. Reader is with your lessons? Or whisper to him how you used your *Mamán*'s petticoat for a kite in the churchyard?"

Mary giggled, nibbling on her scone. "Rossiter is so much fun, Callie. He likes to dance and sing, and he knows the funniest stories you'll ever hear. And he's so-ooo pretty," Mary sighed, rolling her eyes. "Callie, can I tell him that your real name is Callandre and that you're named for a lovely lady your Da knew in London?"

"My *father*, not *Da*. Don't let your *Mamán* catch you talking like an Irishman. She'd banish me from the house forever! And if you spend all your time with Rossiter talking about me, you'll find he's soon bored!" Callie was folding Mary's nightdress and putting it in the basket of laundry she would wash later that day.

"You never get bored hearing about Rossiter, do you, Callie?"

"No, I enjoy listening about him. But most of all, I like to see the way your eyes dance with pleasure every time you think of him."

"You know what, Callie?" Mary asked between bites of crisp bacon. "I think Rossiter's eyes are going to dance too when he finally meets you this summer."

"Don't be a goose! Hurry, finish your breakfast." Callie felt a surge of excitement that stirred her blood and freshened her cheeks. It was silly, of course. Why should a young man as wonderful as Rossiter Powers even give a thought to a skinny little girl from Ireland who cleaned his mother's house and played with his little sister. Still, the tingle would not leave her.

Callie was standing on the wide porch that ran along three sides of the house, watching MacDuff toss the last of the baggage into the wagon. In the hackney cab that Mr. Powers had sent for his wife and daughters, Mary was leaning far out the window, waving to Callie.

"Callie!" MacDuff called. "Miss Anne wants to tell you something!"

Callie skipped out to the hackney and around to the opposite side. Miss Anne was leaning out the door. "I nearly forgot to tell you; there's a packet for you on my dressing table. *Papá* gave it to me several days ago to bring home to you. It's from Mr. Kenyon," she turned to explain to her mother whose finely drawn brows were raised in surprise.

A package! From Byrch Kenyon! Callie's curiosity made her feet itch to run up the stairs to see what it was.

The Powers family was on their way, and they would not return until after the New Year. Callie stood on the porch waving until the hackney was out of sight. She saw Mrs. Powers pull Mary away from the window, shaking a scolding finger under the child's nose. "Mary, Mary," Callie whispered, "please be a good child and don't cause trouble or sorrow for yourself."

"Well, they're gone at last," Lena breathed with relief, taking Callie back indoors with her. "Every year it's the same thing! Rush, rush, rush. You'd think by now Mrs. Powers would have the sense to get everything ready days ahead of time to avoid this last minute lunacy. Where're you going, Callie? Won't you come have a cuppa tea with me? We'll toast our feet near the stove."

Callie was already half way up the front stairs. "In a minute, Lena. Miss Anne said there was a package for me from Mr. Kenyon!"

"And so I heard," Lena muttered. "What *I'd* like to know is why she didn't give it to you right away?"

When Callie came back down to the kitchen, eyes bright with tears and a solmen expression around her pouting mouth, she carried brown wrapping paper and several newspapers, copies of the *Clarion-Observer*.

"What's the trouble, girl? Did you get a Christmas present you don't care for?" Lena asked quietly, seeing Callie's lower lip tremble with emotion. "Come here now, it can't be that bad, can it?"

"Bad, no, it's not bad," Callie whispered, laying the papers on the table for Lena to see. There, on the front page of each of them were long columns, feature articles, complete with drawings of the hospital at Tompkinsville. Reading the columns, Callie recognized the words as her own. There was a note included from Byrch.

Dear Sweeting,
Before I posted the letters you gave me, I took the liberty of reading them. I felt I could not say it better myself, and I hope you forgive me for using them in the *Clarion*. I've kept your name a secret, but your story is here, Callie, all the pain, the suffering. I only had the power, Sweeting, you had the words. There have already been several inquiries, and an investigation of the quarantine practices is planned. Because of you, I am certain conditions will improve for others coming so far from their homes to find their futures in America.

Your friend,
Byrch Kenyon

"What a grand man he is, your Mr. Kenyon," Lena told her, wiping a tear from her eyes after she read the articles, "and it's a grand girl you are, Callie James!"

Chapter Eleven

The weeks passed quickly, racing into months, and one day Callie realized she had been in service to the Powerses for more than a year. It was April, and in two weeks she would have a birthday, her eighteenth.

The friendship between Mary and Callie had deepened into devotion. Because of Callie's patient understanding and love, Mary was coping very well with her hearing problem, which miraculously was still undetected by the family. Nearly ten years old, Mary had learned to be alert and aware, becoming quite adept at watching their lips to augment her diminishing hearing. Under Callie's undivided attention, she had grown from a frustrated little hellion into a long-legged, graceful child, both watchful and reserved.

Mr. Harrison Reader still came in twice a week to teach Mary. And Callie, in constant attendance at these lessons, benefited from them. Her own speech patterns had been refined, her vocabulary broadened, and her instinctive gift for mimicry and natural intelligence placed her in the good graces of Mrs. Powers, who was glad to hear that Callie's heavy brogue and predilection for homilies and colloquialisms had all but vanished. She was a good example for Mary with her quiet, thrifty ways, and Anne Powers was forced to admit that Byrch Kenyon and Jasper had done her a real service by bringing her Callie James.

While social conditions as well as the potato crop had not improved in Ireland, the James family was faring pretty well, thanks to Callie's prompt letters and the monthly bank draft, which had increased from twelve to fourteen dollars because of Jasper's insistence that Callie had proved herself invaluable.

That past Christmas, the second spent away from home, Callie had received a letter from Ireland. Peggy's handwriting leaped out from the thin paper.

Our Own Callie,

It has been a year and several months since you left us, and we sorely miss you, especially at this time of year. The twins have sent along drawings they made for you. Billy drew one of our little Joseph, but don't be thinking your sweet baby brother is as hairless as Billy shows him to be. Our Joseph's hair is as fine and as gold as Georgie's at the same age.

Our Georgie is attending school full-time, thanks to your generous help each month. He still works as a delivery boy for the shops on Bayard Street. He'll be twelve soon, and a fine strapping lad he is, tall and serious and gifted with numbers and letters. Father Brisard at the Holy Mother Church says our Georgie is a bright lad. Your brother still talks about going off to sea, but your Da tells him to stick to his studies and wait until he can go as a midshipman rather than a common swabbie. So far Georgie is listening to your Da. Oftentimes the lad speaks of going off to America as you did. We are all so proud of you, Callie, you are such a good daughter. I know Georgie admires you and would like to do as much for the family as you are.

Bridget and Billy are looking fat and sassy, thanks to the money you send. They will be six on their next birthday. Granda is as fit as a fiddle, but his eyesight is going, and our Hallie has taken it upon herself to walk him about. You should see them, Hallie young and tender as a new sapling and Granda old and bent as an oak, wandering down McIver Street and onto Bayard to pick up a bit of news and watch the passersby.

Your Da sends his love to you. He misses you and never a day goes by that he doesn't speak of you or ask if a letter came. You would be so proud of your Da. He works regular in the tinsmith shop, and though the pay is not much, it keeps him busy and he feels like he is doing something for his family. I would be lying if I said he never went near the Melrose Tavern, but more often he sends Georgie out for a growler of ale and tosses it down here at home. Your Aunt Sara says the man is finally getting some sense about him. It was hard for others to see, but I always knew he was a good man, and I have loved him for it.

Your cousin Colleen is expecting another babe in a few months' time, but her gentleman officer husband was recalled to England. Something fishy is going on there because my sister breaks into tears every time she mentions Colleen, and your Uncle Jack has a look in his eye that's harder than a loan shark's, and you know how Jack was always laughing and merry. Da said he heard at Melrose's Tavern that Colleen's husband already had a wife in England when he married your cousin. Sara sometimes says she wishes she'd never given away Owen Gallagher's ticket to America, and I know she's thinking that her own daughter could be doing as well as you are. I've told her about those letters you sent telling us about the hardships to be suffered in getting to America, but Sara just sighs. Even if she doesn't know that Colleen isn't half as strong and smart as you are, I know it. Colleen could never have gotten as far as you have, Callie.

The Bailey family from down the street left for America two weeks ago along with the Dooleys. They wanted me to give them your address so they could look you up, but your Da told them what a fine family you work for and that they wouldn't want the likes of them hanging about for a handout. Your Da does not want anyone to spoil things for you.

We are getting ready for Christmas, and there seems too much to do and too little time to do it. Hallie helps me about the house, and we are scrubbing from top to bottom. Our landlord, Mr. Halloran, sent for Moonshine Eddie to come by and clean out the privy house out back. Our own Granda gave the poor man that name years and years ago because of the moon-shaped hole cut out in privy doors. All of Dublin calls him by that horrid name, and I think the man has all but forgotten what his Baptism name was. It cost half a quid for Moonshine Eddie's services, and your Da says it's cheap at twice the price. I honestly don't know how Mrs. Moonshine lets that man in the house after a day's work digging out privies.

Little Joseph is crying for his supper. I will write again. Say hello and Merry Christmas to your little Mary. We all feel as though she is part of our family. We all love you, Callie, especially your mother.

For days Callie walked about with Peggy's letter stuffed in her apron pocket. Whenever she felt homesick for the holiday season at home, she would touch her apron and hear the crackle of the paper, and it was almost as good as hearing Peggy's voice. She'd hung the pictures Billy and Bridget sent on the wall in her attic room, and they were the first thing she would see upon rising and the last before she went to bed.

Shortly after she received that letter, another came, this time from Georgie and Hallie. Georgie sent along a little Christmas poem he and Hallie had composed and printed in red ink borrowed from Father Brisard. Although she was half a world away from them, Callie never ceased to feel a part of the spirit and the daily lives of those she had left behind. Ireland, Dublin, and the Jameses were always in her thoughts. How easy life could be for some and how hard for others, Callie thought, comparing her family to the Powerses.

Miss Anne had spent the entire summer past with cousins in Boston and had chosen to abandon Miss Rose Northrup's School for a more prestigious one in Lowell, Massachusetts, coming home only occasionally for holidays. It was expected that the Powers's eldest daughter would make a good match for the son of a socially prominent Boston family.

Rossiter, who had been expected home for the summer, had instead joined a school friend on a tour of Italy and France, writing home of his fascination with the art galleries and museums. Rossiter had always been interested in the arts, and had even been judged to have talent himself. This was something Mrs. Powers bridled against. Her son would not spend his life as a penniless artist living in a loft, praying for the northern light. She had her sights set much higher for her beloved son and had decided upon the world of finance for him.

During Callie's first summer with the Powerses she had moved with them from the house on Todt Hill to the farmhouse in Kreischerville at the southern tip of the island. This was an idyllic time for her as her duties were few and she was able to spend her time reading and playing with Mary in the meadows surrounding the house. Mr. and Mrs. Powers had traveled to Boston for the month of August, and she had been left behind with Mary, Lena, and Hugh MacDuff. Like a small family, the four spent a great deal of time together. Sunshine, exercise, and a healthy diet had worked their magic for Callie, and she no longer felt like an ugly duckling. Now, when she looked into her mirror, she saw a girl on the brink of womanhood. Her rail-thin body had filled out in all the right places, and although she was still diminutive, she'd grown nearly three inches and had to discard her jumper for the two uniforms Mrs. Powers had given her along with several castoffs from Anne.

While the women in the household took Callie's growing up for granted, it was Hugh MacDuff and Jasper who were amazed and approving of the change in her. The girl was a delight to both eye and ear. The bloom of the rose was on her cheeks, which had lost their girlish roundness. Her hair had grown, and the glossy chestnut curls captured the gold of the sun, twining in heavy burnished coils at the nape of her neck. There was a long, graceful sweep of back from shoulder to hip, and her eyes seemed to be always filled with laughter, their clear blue brilliance shining with an undeniable zest for life. But it was her laugh, low and throaty with the barest hint of something sensual in it, that fell in such pleasing notes upon the ear. Hugh MacDuff particularly found his ear tuned for that merry sound, thinking to himself more than once that it held the same magic as the gurgling of a Scottish brook in the highlands of his homeland.

While Hugh appreciated the physical changes in Callie, it was Jasper who took pleasure in the development of her mind. Byrch Kenyon always sent her copies of the *Clarion-Observer*, and often he would underscore a column, article, or advertisement that he thought would be of special interest to his little protégé. Jasper had opened the doors of his library to her, encouraging her in her selections, and began subscribing to various periodicals of the day as well as the *Criterion*, which was sent to him from Dublin. Over the breakfast table Jasper would elicit Callie's sometimes startling opinions concerning topical events.

Just after the turn of the New Year 1849, Jasper received a letter from Byrch Kenyon, who had been in Ireland for the past six months, writing and sending his articles across the ocean to the *Clarion*. In the letter Byrch asked Jasper to take Callie to Tompkinsville for the laying of the cornerstone for the Bailey Hospital. This had been a very important day for Callie. As she stood at the top of the bluff looking across at the city of New York, she could appreciate the changes that had taken place. The area had been cleaned and tended, additional shelters had been built, and for the most part, people were processed through quarantine in a quicker and more orderly way. Out in the bay, on Wade's Island, a hospice had been established for those immigrants who were not sick. While all wasn't heaven, it was far from the hell it had been when she arrived on these shores.

After the ceremonies Callie had visited the graves of Beth and Paddy. She still grieved for Beth and the little boy who lay in her arms beneath the soapstone rock. As she placed her bouquet of holly leaves and berries on the frozen earth, Callie had a recollection of herself and her mother in the quiet kitchen back home. She had vowed that her head would never be turned by a handsome face and a strong back. It was her head that would rule her life, she had vowed, not her heart.

Even as she remembered her resolution, a chill seized her in its grip, and she felt as though a goose had stepped on her grave.

"*Papá*," Mary said brightly, climbing onto Jasper's lap as he sat reading in his library. She settled herself against his plump, soft belly and looked into his face. Jasper felt his heart squeeze for this loving child of his. He loved the way she watched him through round, sherry-colored eyes with what he believed was adoring attention, little realizing that Mary was ever watchful of his lips, and that she nestled close to him in order to hear him better.

"What is it, dear? You look like the cat that swallowed the canary," he said fondly.

"I have a secret, *Papá*, and I need your help. Say you'll help me!"

"First, I must know your secret." Jasper's hand found the sausage curls hanging long on Mary's shoulders, feeling the crisp red locks beneath his fingers.

"It's about Callie," Mary confided seriously. "Did you know it will be her birthday and she will be eighteen years old? She was born on April eleventh at four-thirty in the morning, 1831."

"You seem to know quite a bit about it. Were you there by any chance?" Jasper laughed, teasing this beloved daughter.

"No-oo, *Papá*, but I'll be here for this one, and I want to do something very special for her."

"I see. And did you have something in mind?"

"Yes. I want to have a party for Callie, and I want all her friends to come! Imagine how surprised she'll be! She's never had a party, did you know that, *Papá*? Do you think we can invite

Mr. Kenyon? Callie thinks he's a fine man, *Papá*, almost as fine as you are!"

Jasper smiled indulgently, considering whether this was Callie's opinion or his daughter's. "I see no harm in it. Have you spoken to your mother?"

Mary's head bent, and she played with the ribbons on the front of her dress. "No, *Papá*. I thought you would do it for me," she said meekly. "*Mamán* never listens to anything I say. She thinks I'm still a baby, and I'm not. I'm a grown girl now, and I want to have a grown-up party for Callie."

Anne Powers's mouth formed a round O. "What! It's unthinkable!" she complained. Jasper was always one for wild schemes, and she disapproved of his familiarity and fondness for an employee. "Absolutely not! Why, it goes against the grain! Wherever did you come up with such a fool idea, Jasper? A birthday party for a housemaid."

"Anne, you know Callie is much more than a housemaid. Think of what she's done for our Mary. And it was Mary's idea, you know. Not my own."

"What would my friends think if it got out? It's absolutely unheard of!"

"Why should your friends know? It's only a simple party to celebrate the girl's eighteenth birthday. You needn't even attend, although it would disappoint Mary sorely. You know she idolizes you." This last seemed to smooth Anne's ruffled feathers. "We could have a very informal affair on the back porch. Mary has asked me to invite Byrch Kenyon. Think of his esteem when he sees the miracle your example has accomplished in the little waif he brought to us."

Anne studied her husband's face and saw nothing there to alarm her. "Do you really think so, Jasper?"

"Yes. And I should think that your garden club and church group would envy you your poise and charm and your wisdom and, of course, kindness to bend a little to an employee for services well-given. Did you know that it was once the fashion, and still is in many places, for the master and mistress to mingle with tenants and domestics during a harvest celebration? It was once quite the rage. Why, you could be responsible for bringing back the fashion."

Once in a while Jasper did come up with a good idea, Anne thought. Particularly the time when he prodded her to take Callie into their employ. "Perhaps you're right, Jasper. I have an idea," she said, becoming caught up in the plans. "You will invite Byrch

Kenyon for tea in the afternoon for Callie, and then afterwards we can have a dinner party for some friends of mine. This way I can casually mention that we had this little affair and possibly introduce her to them. I must say you're right, that girl certainly has come a long way."

Jasper smiled, listening to Anne plan the day. It had been a stroke of genius to flatter her into believing that she alone was responsible for Callie's maturity and poise. "It's perfect, Anne. I could never have thought of it myself."

"You never were a thinker, Jasper," Anne said haughtily. "It's my side of the family who think. Your side only pretends."

Jasper continued to smile. "Is it to remain a surprise as Mary wants?"

"But of course. With a present," Anne said absentmindedly.

"Not a present. Lots of presents. One from everyone."

"You're right, Jasper. We must be generous. Several presents. Callie will be so happy. How lucky for her that I took her in."

"I'm certain she's eternally grateful," Jasper answered in a snide tone that was lost on his wife.

When the door closed behind Anne, Jasper went to his cellarette and poured himself a healthy shot of whiskey. That should keep Anne busy for the next two weeks. Now what to give Callie for her birthday? He must get her something special, something to show his appreciation for the wonderful care she gave his favorite daughter. In the end, he decided on a locket with her name engraved on the back. Anne was going to have plenty to say about it later, but once the engraving was done, there would be nothing she could do. His daughter was certainly worth a gold locket.

Byrch Kenyon whistled in surprise when he received the handwritten invitation to celebrate Callie's eighteenth birthday. He penned his acceptance and gave it to Jimmy Riley at the front desk to post for him.

Leaning back in his swivel chair, he propped his long legs up on his desk. Byrch wondered how Callie had fared these past months. In the beginning, he'd somewhat kept in touch with her by speaking with Jasper and by sending her a subscription to the *Clarion-Observer* in her own name. A few notes had passed between them, but none since he left for Ireland and had returned, and all of them had been polite little missives concerning articles or editorials in the newspaper.

The first series of stories Byrch had written and published about the plight of the immigrants were told very personally from Callie's point of view. Then he had launched his crusade against the unscrupulous charities that preyed upon the poor. At present, he was investigating labor unions and the opposition they were facing. In his own circles he was known either as a troublemaker or a social reformer, and he didn't know which label pleased or suited him best. In any case, the increased circulation of the *Clarion*, as well as his own burgeoning reputation, was influenced by Callie James. She had told him during that emotional ride on the St. George Ferry that the power was in his hands, and the challenge in her eyes had demanded he use that power to the best of his ability.

Callie was a remarkable child; he had known it from the first. She had invaded his thoughts time and again during this past year, and always afterward he found that he was cross and irritable. He could never explain it to himself, this dissatisfaction, as though he'd left something undone, let a precious opportunity slip through his fingers. He also felt guilty that he hadn't found the time to go out to Todt Hill to see her and offer her some encouragement.

Dammit! Callie hadn't needed any encouragement, not if the Powerses were having a birthday celebration for her. She must have charmed her way into their lives the way she had into his. Byrch bristled irrationally at the fact that the girl hadn't come to him for anything since the last time he'd seen her and that she'd managed to do well enough on her own without any further help from him.

That was what he'd wanted, wasn't it? To pass her off on someone else, ridding himself of the responsibility? Why then, Byrch asked himself, did he think so often of that day when he'd spirited her away from the button factory? He remembered sitting before the fire in the bed-sitting room, waiting for Edward to return with the doctor. She had nestled her shivering body close to him as he'd held her on his lap. She was so tiny, so defenseless, such a light burden in his arms. He could still feel the damp of her curls against his cheek as she'd nestled her head against his shoulder.

Byrch slammed his feet down on the floor, leaning over his desk to face his work. He must be insane! The girl was hardly more than a child. He had a newspaper to manage and work to do.

It was three days before Callie's surprise birthday party, and Mary was brimming over with excitement. When Callie questioned the child, all she would say was that Callie was going to receive a wonderful, simply wonderful, present. *Papá* had picked it out himself, and no one has one like it in the entire world! Try as she might, she could get no further information.

Callie never ceased to be amazed at Jasper Powers's kindness and generosity. Just the other day he had told her she was growing into a beautiful young woman. Mary had been close enough to hear. When they were alone in the nursery, Mary motioned for Callie to stand back so she could observe her. "*Papá* is right. You are beautiful. You're even prettier than Anne. I think that's why she doesn't like you. She doesn't want anyone to be prettier than she is. Even Hugh MacDuff says you're a bonnie lass!" Mary giggled. "And we all know Mr. MacDuff doesn't pass off compliments easily, does he? Wait till Rossiter sees you. He likes pretty girls. And wait till you meet him, Callie! You'll love him, I know you will. Everyone loves Rossiter!"

"Stop talking nonsense," Callie scolded. "You seem to forget I am not the fairy princess waiting for Prince Charming to awaken me with a kiss." She would never admit it, but Mary's words pleased her. She had gazed so often at the portrait in the parlor that she was beginning to imagine she knew Rossiter Powers. And if ever there was a Prince Charming, it certainly must be he. Or perhaps he was like one of those Greek or Roman gods Mr. Harrison Reader was always telling them about. Adonis was said to have golden hair and a smile that could charm the angels.

Callie caught a glimpse of herself in Mary's dresser mirror. Sometimes even she was startled by the change in herself. She'd grown, filled out, and her hair, which had been so cruelly cropped, now curled in soft waves below her shoulders. There was color in her cheeks, and she had nice clothes to wear. She was happy here, happy with Mary and Lena and Hugh MacDuff, who had turned over a patch of garden for Callie to cultivate. She sent most of her wages home to Ireland, but she always had a bit left over for herself. Each night before she fell asleep she said her God-blesses and thanked Him and Byrch Kenyon for giving her the opportunity to come to the Powers's house. Then she asked God to forgive her for the deception about Mary's hearing.

She tried to learn as much as she could about Mary's problem. Jasper himself had given her the most information, telling her that surgery was something they were just beginning to experiment with in Europe, and most of the time it was unsuccessful. He brought out a book from his library that depicted the intricacies of the ear and then asked why she wanted to know. She gave him a vague answer about one of her cousins suffering from such an affliction following a fever. Jasper read through the text and shook his head, saying in a solemn voice that the best one could do was to live with it and develop other senses, and that there was a school in Switzerland that taught the deaf.

Callie was worrying more and more about Mary. Mr. Harrison Reader had noticed that Mary couldn't follow along in the tunes he tried to teach her, and he would shake his head, muttering something about a "tin ear." It seemed that what hearing Mary had was fading. Mary herself awakened one morning and saw the rain beating aginst her window. She ran to Callie, terror contorting her face, clapping her hands over her ears. "I can't hear it, Callie! I can't hear the rain!"

As the day wore on, Mary's hearing returned to its previous level. Callie begged the child to release her from her promise. Mary was adamant. No one was to know. She didn't want to be different, and she didn't want to be sent away to a school for the deaf. As long as she had Callie, she didn't need to hear.

From that moment on, Callie doubled her efforts to help Mary practice reading lips. They would sit face to face on the carpeted floor while Callie read from school books or just engaged in conversation. Mary knew it wasn't a game they were playing and paid rapt attention to her young instructor. "Always remember, Mary, don't turn your back to people. And you must learn not to stare so intently at their mouths. That will give you away. Try to watch the whole face." Her fear of being sent away was all the incentive the little girl needed. "We have to work on your speech also. You're beginning to talk too loud. I'll work out a signal for you."

There were times Callie would have sworn that Mary's hearing was normal, she was so adept at lip-reading. "I have the advantage, Callie," Mary laughed. "I can 'hear' what people are saying across a room just by watching them. Rossiter better watch out or I'll know all his secrets! He's my most favorite brother!"

"He's your only brother," Callie teased.

"What will you do if when Rossiter comes home he falls in love with you?" Mary asked bluntly. Ever since Mr. Reader had assigned them passages from *Romeo and Juliet*, Mary was preoccupied with love and romance.

"I'll tell him quite honestly that I've no time for romance because I have this little girl who takes all my time and my love. I'll tell him there's none left for tall, golden-haired young men, and if he persists in loving me, I shall beat him off with a stick!"

Mary loved the game and giggled delightedly. Rossiter *would* love Callie. *Papá* loved Callie. She loved Callie.

* * *

There was a secret smile playing around Mary's mouth as she watched Callie dress for the day. Mary had arisen early, earlier even than Callie, and had burst in upon Callie even before her eyes were opened for the day. Today was Callie's birthday, and if the surprise of the party weren't enough, Mary had learned something wonderful that very monring. Rossiter was coming home! Today! She had seen the hall gas lamp lit on the second floor and saw *Mamán* walking across the landing to *Papá*'s room. Curious, she had gone to the open bedroom door and saw that *Mamán*'s face was wreathed in smiles. The kind of smile that was reserved for Rossiter alone.

"Come in, chick," *Papá* had called, lifting her onto his huge, high bed. "Your *Mamán* has just received a message from Rossiter saying he's coming in on the afternoon ferry."

Yes, Rossiter was coming home, and she would be with the two people she loved best in the world besides *Papá*—Callie and her brother.

"You aren't going to wear that old thing, are you?" Mary frowned as Callie went to her wardrobe and withdrew one of her two black bombazine uniforms. She didn't want to mention the birthday, so she answered Callie's questioning look offhandedly. "It's only that it promises to be such a beautiful day. The sun is already so nice and warm, and don't you remember? Mr. MacDuff is taking us into St. George so I can buy some new watercolors."

Callie watched Mary's dancing eyes with suspicion. "No, I haven't forgotten. Well, what should I wear then? My jumper? I warn you, it's much too short on me and squeezes me in the most alarming places."

"Wear the white muslin with the blue dimity print that Anne gave you. It looks so nice on you, Callie, and goes so well with the knitted shawl Lena made for you."

"Such a fancy dress just to go shopping in St. George? You'd think we were going across the river to New York."

"Please, Callie? I'll wear my new yellow eyelet if you do."

"All right, seeing as it means so much to you." Callie sighed. She hadn't forgotten that today was her eighteenth birthday, and she liked the idea of dressing like a grown woman for a change. Mary was so filled with herself, dancing about the room and making every pretense of not mentioning the birthday that Callie suspected there was some sort of conspiracy underway.

"You're all grown up today," Mary blurted, quickly covering her mouth before more of the secret spilled out. "I mean, you look so grown up in that dress. Don't you think you should put your hair up like Anne and her friends do? I'll let you borrow my hair pins, and I think I've got a blue ribbon just the shade of your sash."

"All right," Callie giggled. "If it will make you happy."

The white muslin dress with delicate blue cornflowers flattered Callie's coloring, enhancing the pink of her cheeks and the azure in her eyes. The high-necked, ruffled collar delineated the elegant length of her neck and rested softly beneath the rebellious curls at her nape. "Now, wear those high-heeled slippers Anne didn't want anymore, and you'll be gorgeous!"

"You imp! Come here and I'll fix your hair. With me being so gorgeous, we can't have you looking like a little urchin. Perhaps on the way home from St. George, Mr. MacDuff will let us stop in the meadow behind the church. The cherry blossoms and dogwood should be in bloom. We can pick armfuls for your *Mamán*. Don't forget your bonnet, darling; an hour in the sun and you'll be a summer full of freckles.

The outing was a delight. Hugh MacDuff drove them into St. George in the buggy, waiting outside the little shop where Mary purchased her new watercolors. Spring was in the air, and they could smell the sunshine turning the grasses a brighter shade of green. In the meadow behind the church, they gathered fragile pink and white dogwood blossoms and fragrant, blush-colored cherry flowers.

MacDuff sat atop the buggy, smoking his pipe, watching Mary and Callie chase each other across the field. He was a taciturn man with a love of nature and children, and he always went out of his way to make whatever time Mary and Callie spent with him enjoyable. He had helped gather the blossoms with them, his pipe clenched firmly between his teeth. Callie liked him, and so did Mary. Hugh was never one to say two words when one would do, and the girls' frolicking and laughter brought a smile to his weather-beaten face.

The lass was a comely one, Hugh thought watching Callie run lithely after Mary. He'd watched her change before his very eyes this past year. She'd come to the Powerses a frightened child, and here she was, eighteen today and a young woman with a promise of enormous beauty. His gaze darkened as he recalled that this very afternoon young Rossiter was to come home. What changes would he see in the young man? Two years away from his domineering *Mamán* would surely have changed the young buck. Hugh had always liked the young man with his wild, rebellious ways.

Rossiter was a good lad, but he had a dangerous flaw as far as Hugh was concerned. He was weak. Too tied to his *Mamán*'s apron strings. Two years away *must* have made the difference, but Hugh worried that these changes would only be external. The young man's character had been formed years ago. Rossiter had once confided to Hugh that he had an ambition to become a painter, and remembering that Rossiter had always had an eye for beauty, the man's eye turned to Callie.

A new wrinkle formed on Hugh's weathered brow. Rossiter was known and loved for his charm and his astounding good looks. The boy could have his pick of any beautiful young girl, and Callie, so young and inexperienced, would fall easy prey to that dashing rogue. A sour look crossed his face. If Rossiter's *Mamán* got wind of any flirtatious interest on her son's part, Callie would find herself out on the street, bag and baggage. It must be hard to be young, he decided. He didn't think he'd ever been young. He was born old and crotchety.

There were times, like now, when the world was young with spring, that Hugh wished he'd found himself a good woman to marry and raise children. Now it was too late. More than half his life was gone. Keeping his snoot in a bottle every chance he got wasn't something a woman would put up with, not if there were children to be fed and clothed. Did he really have regrets? Probably not, he thought as he drew on his pipe. He was carefully tamping fresh tobacco when Mary ran back to the buggy with a bunch of wild bluebells. "For you, Mr. MacDuff, for having the patience to wait for us. I'll never forget today." She smiled brightly. "Here, let me stick some in your hatband. You'll look so handsome, Lena will want to catch you and kiss you. What would you do if a woman caught you?" Mary teased as she worked stems of the delicate flowers into the handyman's hatband.

"Why, I'll just let her catch me. That's what any self-respecting man would do, right, lassie?" he asked, directing his question to Callie, who was blushing furiously. A pity one like her hadn't crossed his path in his younger days.

When Callie and Mary returned to the house, the atmosphere was so quiet and still for this particular time of day, Callie assumed everyone had succumbed to the lazy sunshine and had retreated for afternoon naps.

"Let's take these flowers out onto the back porch; they'll look so pretty with all the sunshine coming through the windows," Mary said, her eyes sparkling with mischief. "You go first, Callie, so you can open the door for me."

"Hush, I think everyone's taking a nap; we don't want to wake them." Quietly Callie and Mary crossed through the dining room and out through the side door to the glass-enclosed sun porch.

It was Byrch Callie saw first, but it was Jasper's voice that thundered, "Surprise! Happy Birthday!" For a long moment Callie stood poised like a cat, ready to spring, uncomprehending that the gathering was for her, to celebrate her birthday. Her cheeks pinked to the color of the cherry blossoms in her arms as everyone offered their congratulations. Mary and Mr. Powers, Lena and Hugh, Miss Anne, Mrs. Powers, and last but never least, Byrch Kenyon.

Byrch stood off at a distance watching. Was it the warmth of the sun coming through the gleaming windows or was it the astonishing change in Callie that bubbled through his blood? Gone was the little urchin from the alleyway in Dublin and the drenched little kitten from the button factory. Here stood Callie on the beautiful brink of womanhood, and she was a sight to behold.

She'd grown inches since he'd last seen her, and the graceful sweep of her back and neck, combined with the delightful swell of her high, firm breasts, hinted at an elegant length of leg beneath her sweeping muslin skirt. Callie was the image of the summer to come, cheeks flushed, eyes clear and bright, bluer than an August sky, chestnut hair shot with gold. He had never seen her hair this way—soft and loose, confettied with cherry-blossom petals—and he realized his hand itched to touch it. His tiger eyes narrowed as he surveyed the tiny waist and the feminine curve of hip below. And most amazing of all, Byrch found himself thinking, was that these changes only presaged the promise of her full beauty yet to come. Already the turned up nose had taken on a new balance and a slimness in her adult face. The planes and hollows of her features had elongated from childish roundness to a nearly perfect oval, the high cheekbones adding an obliqueness to her eyes, slanting them slightly at the corners.

Shyly, Callie reached out her hand to Byrch, winding her fingers between his. She lowered her eyes demurely. "Your being here means so much to me," she said in her deeper woman's voice that held only a hint of Ireland. The rich, lyrical tone was music to his ears.

Jasper Powers watched the little scene between Callie and her friend. She was indeed a beautiful girl, and apparently Byrch thought so as well. Jasper was quick to note a certain tenseness in Byrch's neck and could see a stiffening of his broad shoulders. Surely he hadn't expected Callie to remain a child. Girls did have a way of growing into women.

The back porch had been decorated with pink and green streamers and the table set with a lace cloth and Anne Powers's best crystal punch bowl. The silver tea service was waiting on the sideboard. Lena had outdone herself with a wonder of a confection: a three-layered cake with pure white frosting under pale pink rosebuds and green jelly stems. Plates of delicate sandwiches of watercress and ham salad stood beside a sparkling pitcher of lemonade. Callie presided at the table as though to the manner born. She was aware of Byrch's eyes upon her, and she struggled to retain her poise and grace although it seemed that tiny bubbles were bursting within her. He was so handsome in his dark green coat, quilted satin waistcoat, and tan trousers. The whiteness of his shirt and high cravat was accentuated by the bronze of his skin and the black of his hair. But it was his eyes that filled her awareness: a tiger's eyes watching, watching her.

It seemed he could not take his gaze from her. The tiny pink petals still clung to her hair, and he found the soft gold-flinted curls that rested against her cheek adorable. Her lips, that in childhood had seemed a bit full and pouty, were now balanced amid her other features, and he admired their soft, petulant curve. The girl was beautiful! The year and more that she'd been employed by Anne Powers had added decades to her education. She presided at the table, deftly pouring lemonade and tea as though she'd been doing it all her life. She was able to maintain a charming conversation with Anne and Jasper and still direct fond glances at young Mary, who obviously worshipped her. Yes, Callie had become a woman; more, she was a lady, yet there was still a girlish exuberance that added to her charm, making her positively bewitching.

Apparently Callie's charm was not admired only by himself, Byrch thought as he accepted a steaming cup of tea. Old MacDuff was clearly besotted with the girl, and Jasper treated her as though she was his third daughter. Even Anne Powers, formidable and forbidding, seemed to accept Callie's grace and gentility as a matter of course. It was only Miss Anne, the oldest daughter, who seemed emphatically bored by the whole idea of all this fuss for a servant's birthday. If anything, she was even offended by it and had only condescended to attend because of her mother's demands. The girl lounged insolently against the back of her chair, a sour expression on her young face, which in time would be an exact replica of her mother's. Several times Byrch caught Anne glancing at him out of the corner of her eye, and he knew that her pretense of complete boredom was for his sake, and that she hoped he would think her too mature and sophisticated for children's birthdays.

"Won't you have a sandwich, Mr. Kenyon?" Callie extended the plate in his direction, and for just a moment their eyes met and held. Her clear blue gaze smiled into his, and he was hypnotized by the effect. At that moment, Byrch wanted nothing more than to carry her off, to have her to himself, to be free to touch that soft, downy skin and to smell the sunshine in her hair. Her body was so slim, so supple, he knew it would bend in his embrace, fitting itself to him. . . .

It was Jasper who broke the awkward moment by clearing his throat. "There seems to be a carriage coming up the drive," he announced, steeling himself against the effect it would have upon his wife and daughter.

"A carriage?" Anne questioned. Then, "Rossiter! It must be Rossiter!"

Callie quickly glanced at Mary, who was already jumping up from her chair. "I kept it as a surprise!" she explained. "I wanted to surprise you!"

"Come, everyone," Anne Powers directed. "Everyone come and give my son a proper welcome!"

As the family rushed to the front door, Callie and Byrch lagged behind. At the doorway to the dining room, Byrch allowed Callie to pass in front of him, touching the flat of his hand to the small of her back. It was a touch he never wanted to withdraw. He was close enough now to see the thick fringe of lashes and the delicate, finely textured skin and to smell the heady scent of sunshine and wild flowers that forever he would associate with Callie James.

The family gathered around the newcomer; Hugh and Lena stood aside with Byrch and Callie. Callie caught only a glimpse of a cranberry-red shoulder, a black, shining boot, and the sun glinting off the soft, vagabond curls of gold.

"Rossiter! Ross!" Mary was squealing with delight. "You're the best present for Callie's birthday party!"

Chapter Twelve

"*Callie's birthday*!" *he* exclaimed. "Where is this wonder you've written me about?" He laughed at his little sister. "Am I at last to meet your wonderful Callie?"

Mary seized her brother by the hand, pulling him to where Callie stood beside Byrch. Callie's first impression was of dark, laughing eyes beneath thick, ashy brows, a square jaw, and a star-bright smile. Callie was instantly drawn to his magnetic charm as he took her hand and pressed the fingers to his lips. She was aware of the shocked gasp emitted by Miss Anne and of the disapproval in Mrs. Powers's face. Everyone else seemed to take it for granted that Rossiter should kiss a pretty girl's hand for the amusement of his little sister. Callie pulled her hand away, blushing prettily, not wishing to offend either Rossiter or his mother and sister.

Byrch witnessed Callie's interest in Rossiter. He frowned as he recalled Jasper confiding that his son had been embroiled in several misalliances, one of which had irreparably damaged a young woman's reputation. "Miss James," Rossiter was murmuring as though for Callie's ears alone, "Mary has written volumes about you, but nothing she could have said would have prepared me for this moment." He looked down at her, gratified by her smile and the demure lowering of her eyes.

"Rossiter, you of course remember Byrch Kenyon. He's come to help us celebrate Callie's birthday," Jasper said heartily.

"Yes, of course. How do you do, Mr. Kenyon?" Rossiter replied, hardly taking his eyes from Callie.

"*Mamán*, isn't it time to serve the cake?" Anne asked her mother. "The sooner this charade is done with, the better," she complained, not liking Callie's attraction either for her brother or for the dashing Byrch Kenyon.

"Yes, certainly," Anne Powers agreed. She glanced at Jasper to see if he was disapproving of Rossiter's attention to a servant. Her husband's smiling face set her teeth on edge. This entire idea of a birthday for a domestic was a mistake, a huge error of judgment. At the first opportunity she must take Rossiter aside and explain that this celebration for Callie's birthday was merely an indulgence for Mary.

Rossiter stepped away from Callie and Mary as though noticing Hugh MacDuff and Lena for the first time. He greeted them cheerfully and mentioned to Hugh that as soon as possible he'd like to go out to Kreischerville to see his horse. "I feel as though it's been years since I've ridden. Really ridden," he emphasized, "in the woods and over meadows. In Boston, riding down the village green to meet and converse is considered exercising one's mount. Except for hunts, of course, but then proper dress is demanded. I want to get on Pirate's back and taken him for a real run. Have you been taking care of him for me, MacDuff?"

"Sure and certain, Master Rossiter. There's a boy at the farm who sees to his exercise. You'll find him fit and in good fettle for you, sir."

"Good man!" Ross clapped MacDuff on the shoulder. "And you, Lena? Are those my favorite cookies I smell?"

"They are, Master Rossiter," Lena grinned. "Soon's I heard you were coming home, I began chopping the walnuts."

Out on the sun-filled porch once again, Callie felt Rossiter's gaze upon her, and how she managed to cut and serve slabs of Lena's perfect cake with any amount of poise and assurance was a mystery to her. She felt absolutely giddy beneath his attention and wondered at Byrch's sulky frown. Surely Byrch didn't dislike this golden young man with the face of an archangel?

"Open your presents, Callie. It's time, isn't it, *Mamán*?" Mary cried excitedly.

"Of course, by all means," Anne Powers said. She was more than eager to end this little celebration. It had all been a dreadful mistake.

"Sit here, Callie. You're the guest of honor, so you get to sit in *Papá*'s chair. It's all right, isn't it *Papá*?"

Jasper's grin broadened. "I wouldn't have it otherwise." He was overjoyed to have his son home after all this time and to be in the midst of this family gathering. He was oblivious to his wife's pointed stares and his oldest daughter's sullenness. "Sit here and open your presents, Callie, before Mary crawls out of her skin."

With trembling hands, Callie undid the ribbon on a small box. It was a gift of face powder from Miss Anne. From Mrs. Powers there was a yellow silk scarf, from Jasper a pair of white kid gloves. From Lena and Hugh McDuff, a bright red umbrella.

"Now mine, open mine next!"

It was a small package, and Callie's nervousness made it barely possible for her to untie the knot in the ribbon. Nestled in a bed of purple velvet lay a gold locket. Tears gathered in Callie's eyes as she hugged the little girl. "You can put my picture in it. See, I found a daguerreotype of Rossiter and me in *Mamán*'s album. I thought you might like it, although I was such a baby when it was taken. Besides, it's the only one that will fit. You don't mind having Rossiter's picture with mine, do you, Callie? Say you don't mind!"

"Of course, I don't mind." Callie looked at the picture Mary had enclosed with the locket. It had been taken nearly two years ago, and Mary's face was rounder and younger, but Rossiter looked very much the same.

From Byrch there was lovely onionskin stationery, imprinted with a delicate green shamrock, done on the *Clarion*'s presses, he told her. Also there was a pewter ink jar, feather quill, and a sharpener.

"For your letters home, Callie," he told her softly, nearly bursting with pleasure at her apparent joy. She tried to thank him, but the words wouldn't come.

Rossiter, who had left the gathering for a moment, returned. He held his hand behind his back, smiling mischievously. "I won't allow it that Callie not receive a gift from me," he explained. "Since I was unaware today was your birthday, Callie, I was unprepared, but perhaps you'll accept something of my own." He brought forward a little blue book covered in the softest leather with gilt-edged pages. "It's a book of my favorite poems," he explained.

Callie took the book from him, looking at the title. It was *Don Juan* by Lord Byron.

"Do you know his work, Callie?" Rossiter asked. "I'm afraid he's unabashedly romantic, but *Don Juan* is considered his masterpiece. The man himself was more romantic and tragic than anything he's written, isn't that so, Byrch?"

"It is true," Byrch said simply, not endeavoring to continue the conversation. The puritan in him regarded the works of the dissipated and controversial Byron as an unsuitable gift for an innocent young lady. Considering this, Byrch almost laughed aloud. When had he ascribed to puritanical mores? Or was it simply that he hesitated to think of Callie as the recipient of a lusty, romantic gift if it did not come from himself? Hypocrite! He chided himself.

"Now you can read them to me at night before I fall asleep," Mary prompted Callie, admiring the luxurious binding on the book.

"Oh, no you don't, little one," Rossiter warned. "The contents are hardly suitable for one your age. It takes an older, more sophisticated mind to appreciate it. A woman's heart to understand it."

Callie felt herself flushing beneath Rossiter's flattery. It was nice to be thought of as a woman, especially by someone so handsome and whose eyes searched hers.

"Were you surprised, Callie? Really surprised? I thought I'd go mad keeping the secret. *Papá* said he'd give me a nickel if I kept the secret. You have to pay me a nickel, *Papá*," Mary quipped, going to Jasper to put her arms around his neck.

"Of course, I was surprised. You truly did keep the secret. I shall trust you will all my secrets from now on."

"And what kind of secrets would they be?" Byrch asked in a cool voice, studying her face as he waited for her answer.

Callie blinked. His tone was as strange as his forbidding look, and she mourned the ease they had always had between them. Something had happened in their relationship, she could feel it, she could see it in those tiger eyes. "I don't have any secrets. Not yet anyway." She smiled, hoping for a return of her affability. Byrch sat there, silently observing her. In an effort to break the silence, she turned to Mrs. Powers. "I can't thank you enough for this party. It was most generous of you. I've never had a birthday party, not a real one like this, and I'll never forget the day I turned eighteen." She turned, beaming her smile on Hugh and Lena and the others. Byrch felt his heart turn over in his chest.

"*Mamán* is the most generous woman in the world, aren't you, *Mamán*?" Rossiter praised, bending to kiss his mother's dry cheek.

Anne Powers preened and beamed at her son. "Mr. Powers

and I were only too glad to do it. It's our way of showing our appreciation for what you've done for Mary."

"And *Mamán* is a most gracious woman, also," Rossiter teased easily. "*Mamán* is one in a million, isn't that so, Father?"

"Absolutely, one in a million," Jasper echoed his son. "Well now, since this party seems to be at an end, let's you and I go into my study," he said, turning to Byrch. "I want to hear more about these labor unions. You say the printers are making noises about unionizing? How will that affect the *Clarion*?"

Before following after Jasper, Byrch took Callie's hand. "Happy Birthday, Callie. It's been too long since we've seen one another. I'm happy you're doing so well here at the Powers's."

"Thank you, Mr. Kenyon. It was grand of you to give me such a wonderful present. I'll always treasure the inkpot and quill because they came from you. And Mum will be so suprised when she receives my next letter to find our own shamrock printed in the corner."

It was on the tip of Byrch's tongue to ask if she would treasure his gift as much as the book of poetry. Instead, he held his tongue and followed Jasper into his study.

"Rossiter, Callie and I are going upstairs. Will you come up to the nursery to see us?" Mary piped.

"But of course! How could I not?"

Anne Powers overheard this exchange. "Rossiter will have no time for you today, Mary. He's arrived home just in time for my dinner party this evening, and I'm certain he'll want to rest from his trip."

"We'll be waiting for you, Ross," Mary said, never taking her eyes from her adored brother.

"Mary Powers! You haven't heard a word I've said!" Anne Powers scolded. Her statement made Callie's blood run cold. Quickly she reached out to touch her little friend's shoulder, making a small indication toward her mother.

Stiffening slightly, realizing she'd made a faux pas, Mary quickly turned to her mother. "Excuse me, *Mamán*?"

"That's better," Anne Powers smiled stiffly. "Don't let all this excitement rush to your head, Mary. I said Rossiter will have no time for you today. He must rest and ready himself for my dinner party this evening. And you, Callie, I believe there are preparations you must make and lend a hand to Lena in the kitchen. You will be serving at table this evening." Anne shot a meaningful glance at her son, reminding him exactly what Callie's position was in the Powers's household. A domestic, nothing more, in spite of the little party this afternoon.

"Isn't Mr. Kenyon a handsome man?" Mary asked as she helped Callie carry her presents up to her room. "I wish I were as old as Anne so I could have him come court me," she chatted.

Rossiter stood in the doorway, watching his sister and her companion head for the front stairs. He noticed that Callie didn't respond to Mary's impetuous statement. He was no fool; he knew that a man like Kenyon could never be attracted to a sour-faced, self-important chit like his sister Anne. He'd seen for himself the way the man had stared at Callie, witnessed the interest and admiration he held for her.

For years Rossiter had been envious of Jasper's friendship with Byrch. The camaraderie and genuine affection they shared was something he'd never known. Many a time he'd approached his father in a manner he thought similar to Byrch's but it was to no avail. He should be sitting in his father's study instead of Byrch Kenyon. At the very least, he should have been included in the invitation to share in a snifter of brandy, talking about business and current events. There weren't that many years' difference between Kenyon and himself. Kenyon was the kind of man Jasper would want for his son, and for the life of him, Rossiter would never understand it. He only knew that somehow he'd been a disappointment to his father, and he could still feel it when he and Jasper were together.

It was nearly an hour after the birthday party disbanded when the sound of carriage wheels on the gravel drive indicated that Byrch Kenyon had left to return to the city. That was when Mary, standing near the window in the nursery, remembered the wild flowers and cherry blossoms she and Callie had picked earlier. She ran down to the kitchen to beg vases and jugs from Lena and deftly arranged her precious hoard with a child's sense of artfulness. Jasper's study was transformed by the festoon of blossoms. A special arrangement was meant for Mary's mother. Proud of her handiwork, Mary marched up the stairs to her mother's room to present her flowers.

"It was very nice of you to think of me, Mary," Anne Powers smiled absently, her mind on the coming dinner party. "Just place them on my washstand."

"Is Anne in her room?"

"Yes, I think so. How sweet of you, Mary, to want to give your sister flowers. I'm certain she'll be pleased."

Anne wasn't in her room. Since there was no vase to hold the delicate pink blossoms, Mary filled a waterglass from the pitcher on Anne's washstand and gently untangled the flower stems. Callie was struck by the way she handled the fragile offering. Laughing delightedly, Mary skipped ahead of Callie toward the nursery.

Later when Jasper and Anne Powers questioned her, Callie was at a loss to explain exactly what had happened. One minute Mary was happy as a lark and the next she was rolling and tousling with Anne on the floor, shrieking her head off. The wild flowers that had been so precious just moments before were crushed and matted on the floor from their furious activity. Upon questioning by her father, Mary said that Anne had destroyed some drawings that she'd made for Rossiter. Anne said Mary was a baby and drew pictures like a baby, and she was only trying to prevent her sister from making a fool of herself in front of her brother. So she took it upon herself to destroy the colorful pictures that Mary had labored over.

It was all Callie could do to separate the screaming sisters. With all the strength she could muster, Callie yanked at the snarling Anne and pulled her off Mary's prone body. Anne turned and with a vicious swing socked Callie in the left eye. Smarting with the blow, Callie dropped to her knees as Anne fled from the room, only to return moments later with the glass of cherry blossoms. She hurled the dainty flowers, glass and all, into the fireplace. Glass shattered, and the flowers flew in all directions. Anne shrieked and shouted curses at her younger sister. "You just wait till I tell *Mamán* how you attacked me you . . . you lunatic!" Anne screeched as she fled from the room.

Mary was sitting in the middle of the floor, sobbing. "Why did she do that to me? Why does she hate me so much, Callie?"

"I don't know, Mary," Callie said, gathering the little girl close to her. She crooned soft words to the child and wiped at her cheeks. Gently she brushed back the hair from the little girl's forehead. "You can't let it bother you, Mary."

Callie did nothing to ease the burning on her eye and cheek. It was more important now to comfort Mary. She sat on the carpet amidst the shattered petals in a pool of sunlight from the window, rocking Mary in her arms, cradling and crooning to her.

Rossiter Powers stood transfixed in the nursery doorway, his artist's eye mesmerized by the sight of swirling summer skirts, tumbles of dark and auburn hair haloed to gold by the incoming light, the pathos of the scene before him. He was unaware of the fracas between his sisters, but Mary was in obvious distress, her lips swollen with misery, her cheeks wet with tears. He felt like an interloper, bursting into a very intimate moment, and he felt foolish standing there with the gaily wrapped coming-home present for his youngest sister. He made a sound, and Callie turned around.

Gently Callie prodded Mary and half-turned her about, administering pressure to the upper part of her arm, telling her someone was in the room. Mary sniffed and looked up, her tiny face lighting like a thousand candles. "Rossiter! You came! You came after all!"

Mary clung to Rossiter's midsection. "Didn't I tell you Callie was the most wonderful person in the world? She saved me from Anne. She saved me."

"That's all over now," Rossiter soothed. "Look, I've brought you a present all the way from Italy. Callie, what happened to your eye?"

"Anne hit her in the eye. Oh, Ross, she's so mean. She ripped up all the pictures I made for you. She hates me, Rossiter. Why does she hate me?"

Rossiter frowned, his perfect brow knitting in his concern for Mary. His dark eyes fell on Callie to seek confirmation of what he was hearing. "Here, Puss, open your present while I put a cool compress on Callie's eye." Moving over to Mary's washstand, Rossiter poured water from the pitcher into the basin, dipping in the washcloth and squeezing it out. He applied the cool cloth to Callie's cheek and eye, his fingers gently touching her as though they were feathers, sending little unexpected ripples through her veins.

"Listen to me, Mary," Rossiter spoke as his sister worked the ribbons on the package, "Anne doesn't hate you. She's only jealous that you're the youngest and get so much attention. And she could be jealous that you have such a wonderful friend as Callie." His voice was soft, soothing, and when he said her name, it brought a flush to Callie's cheek. How beautiful he was, golden as summer, tall and lithe like a sapling ready to burst into bud.

Mary squealed in delight over the porcelain doll with eyes that opened and closed. "Oh, Ross, she's beautiful! Just beautiful! Almost as beautiful as my Callie. That's what I'll call her," Mary clutched the doll to her chest, "Callandre. That's her name."

Ross pressed the compress into Callie's hand. "I'll be leaving you ladies now. If I were you, Puss," he addressed Mary, "I'd get this room cleaned up before *Mamán* makes a surprise visit." His attention lingered a moment longer on Callie. If anyone asked his opinion, he would disagree with Mary. Callie was twice as beautiful as the porcelain doll with the real eyelashes.

The summons was not unexpected. Callie and Mary were to appear in the downstairs drawing room—promptly. Callie's stomach churned and fluttered. She was frightened out of her wits at the order to appear before both Mr. and Mrs. Powers. Would they dismiss her? She didn't want to leave here. She couldn't leave now that she had met Rossiter. She could still feel his touch on her face where he'd held the compress.

Mary saw the agitation in Callie's face and her rapidly swelling eye. It was all Anne's fault. *Mamán* would never listen. Anne would blame Mary, and Callie would be discharged. *Mamán* never listened to excuses. Her spine stiffened. If Callie was to go, then she would go with her. No one would stop her.

"We best tidy up here before we go down," Callie said as she bent over to pick up the crushed flowers. How her head ached. Her thoughts were fuzzy. She had to gather her wits about her and try to do her best for her young charge.

Anne Powers sat in a high-backed chair that made her appear taller and more forbidding. Jasper Powers stood near the mantle with a scowl on his pleasant features. Anne sat on a footstool at her mother's feet with her hands folded. She looked demure and yet pitiful at the same time. Jasper wasn't fooled for a minute. He hated scenes.

Callie ushered Mary into the room. She didn't like the closed half-circle that appeared before her. She could only hope Jasper Powers would spring to her defense. She could sense Mary's stiff back. It amazed her that the child wasn't ranting and raving and trying to defend herself against her sister's blatant attack. Callie advanced a step and placed her hands gently on Mary's shoulders.

"Mother of God, what happened to your eye!" Jasper said, walking over to Callie and grasping her face in his large hand. Callie swallowed hard. To lie or not to lie?

"I walked into a right hook, sir," she said honestly.

"Anne socked her, *Papá*, for no reason. We were tousling on the floor, and she tried to separate us," Mary said in a calm, even voice.

"You don't really expect us to believe that, do you?" Anne Powers asked. "Anne does not tousle on the floor like a street urchin. Anne is a lady. I thought we were making a lady out of you, Mary."

"Did you do this to Callie?" Jasper said, hauling Anne to her feet.

Anne squealed and cried, "*Mamán*!"

"Jasper, unhand that child. You only have to look at her to know she did nothing. Now, young lady, I want the straight facts this minute. Callie, how did you allow this to happen? I'm shocked. You are in charge of Mary, and I thought you had the situation well in hand. Obviously I was wrong. I don't see how I can do anything but dis—"

"*Mamán*, don't be hasty," Rossiter said, coming into the room. "Now if you had a witness to this deed, would you back down like the wonderful woman I know you to be?" He put his arms around his mother's shoulders and bent to kiss the top of her head. Anne Powers smiled, the first genuine smile Callie had ever seen on her dry, bony face.

"But, of course, dear boy. Have you ever known me to be anything but fair where you children are concerned?" Above his mother's head, he stared at his father. Jasper sucked in his cheeks and turned his head slightly. Callie held her breath. Mary remained stiff as a board beneath her hands.

"Miss Goody-Two-Shoes there took it upon herself to tear up some drawings Mary made as a gift for me on my return. Mary didn't like it and said so. Later your darling daughter returned with a glass of flowers and threw them into the fireplace. I saw it all!" Rossiter lied.

"Rossiter, you wretch!" Anne screamed as she fled the room. "I hate you! I hate you, Rossiter!"

Callie's breath came out in a whoosh. Mary slumped against her and would have fallen if Callie had not gripped her shoulders tightly. Gentle pressure told the little girl it wasn't over yet. No matter what, a reprimand was in order. Someone must suffer for the favorite daughter's humiliation.

"Let the girls go, *Mamán*, so I can begin to regale you with tales of my too-long holiday." Rossiter tightened his hands on his mother's shoulders and once again kissed her, this time on the temple.

"Jasper, you handle the girls. Mary isn't to come to the table tonight. Callie, you keep something cold on that cheek and apply some of that face powder before you serve at dinner this evening."

"What about Anne?" Jasper asked quietly.

Callie could see Rossiter's grip on his mother's shoulders tighten. "Anne is hardly a child, Jasper, and can't be dismissed from the dinner table. How would I explain her absence? We'll think of something, won't we, Anne?"

Out in the front hall, Jasper picked Mary up and sat her on his shoulder. "*Papá*! I'm too big for this!" Mary cried. She couldn't see what he was saying if she sat perched on his shoulder. Callie would have to keep the conversation going.

"Both of you handled yourselves very well. Did Rossiter tell the straight of it?" he asked Callie.

"Yes, sir, but we told him that was what had happened. He didn't actually see it."

"Oh, well, hearing is almost the same as seeing. We won't mention this again. I'll have a few words with Anne and see if I can make her see the light. She's getting too old for such nonsense."

At the nursery door, Jasper hugged Mary and then on impulse gathered Callie into his embrace. What a sweet girl she was. He wished she were one of his own. "Which one of you two do I have to thank for the flowers on my desk?"

"Me, *Papá*. Do you really like them, really? Hugh took us to the meadow behind the church. It was so beautiful, *Papá*. Callie and I picked as many as we could."

"I'm thanking you personally for thinking of me, darling. Many was the time I picked wild flowers in my youth for the girl I was courting."

"For *Mamán*?" Mary asked in surprise.

Jasper eyes took on a faraway gleam. "No, you rascal, it wasn't your *Mamán*. It was a girl no older than Callie, back in Ireland. Her name was Sheila, and she did love wild flowers. She used to make garlands of them, and once she made me a crown. She said I was the king and she was my queen."

"What happened to her?" Mary asked.

"She died of a fever the year I came to America."

"Did you put wild flowers on her grave?" Callie asked.

"Yes. Yes, I did. Run along, you two, and no more nonsense. Be sure to thank your brother for the fib he told to keep you out of hot water."

Now how did the girl know he put wild flowers on Sheila's grave? Lord, that was so long ago. He often wondered what his life would have been like if he had married Sheila Flannery. If she hadn't died, would he have found a way to bring her to America? It was strange how he could remember the anniversary of Sheila's death but not his wife's birthday. Sheila was his first love. No matter how old he got, he would never forget those wild, exhilarating times.

After Jasper left them, Mary kept up a running conversation about Rossiter and what a wonderful brother he was and how he always came to her rescue when she needed him. "He's like a good angel, Callie, my own personal good angel. Nothing bad ever happens to me when Rossiter is around. Don't you just adore him. One time I heard *Mamán* tell that to *Papá*. She was upset, and *Papá* just laughed. If he gets married, then I'll have a new sister. Can you imagine that, Callie? Callie, did you hear me?"

"Of course I heard you. You love your brother. You should love him. He's your own flesh and blood. Both of us must remember to thank him for getting us out of our problem." She was safe, thanks to Rossiter. She wasn't to be dismissed for neglecting her duties. Rossiter had come to her defense even if it meant telling a white lie.

"You didn't answer me, Callie. Do you think Rossiter is the most handsome man you ever saw, and what do you think about me getting a new sister if he marries?"

He wasn't handsome—he was beautiful. He was young. He was noble and had come to their defense like a knight in shining armor. He was younger than Byrch Kenyon. Now why was she thinking about Byrch Kenyon at a time like this? Married? Mary said something about Rossiter getting married and his wife becoming her sister. She felt her mouth pucker into sour lines. "I thought you said I was like a sister to you," Callie said childishly.

The remainder of the afternoon went by swiftly with Callie helping Lena in the kitchen. When Lena and MacDuff saw what had happened to her eye, they sympathized. "Looks like you've got the beginnings of a real mouse there, Callie," MacDuff said. "I hope you gave her double for that."

"No, Mr. MacDuff, I like to think it was an accident." She was conscious of her eye and could hardly bear the thought of serving at the table tonight looking like a street arab in front of Mrs. Powers's guests and Rossiter.

"Lena, make up a poultice for the girl. Use some of that stewing beef and lay it in the vinegar for a minute or two. That'll take the swelling down. And hand over that bread dough, woman," he said, rolling up his sleeves. "Our Callie can't hold the poultice and knead the dough at the same time."

Lena looked at MacDuff for a long moment, her hands poised in the flour. Since when did MacDuff offer to help around the kitchen? She turned to glance at Callie and then back at the handyman. Was something going on here? Lena turned back to her bread dough, slamming her fist into it. "If it's a poultice you want for 'our Callie,' get it yourself, man. Can't you see I'm busy?" She stole another glance at Callie. All these years Lena had been trying to light a fire under MacDuff, and it seems Callie was the one to set the spark.

Callie's eye was much improved by dinnertime. The face powder Anne had given her hid the explosive redness. Dressed in her black bombazine dress with a clean, frilly apron, Callie managed to serve dinner that evening. Rossiter regaled everyone with descriptions of the museums and churches he'd visited in France and Italy. He was so animated, so engaging that Callie wondered how life had gone on at all at the Powers's house before Rossiter came home.

Chapter Thirteen

"*Callie, wait till* you hear!" Mary was sitting up in Callie's bed waiting for the dinner party to end so she could share her news. It was very late, and Callie was exhausted. Cleaning the kitchen with Lena seemed to take forever. Finally Hugh MacDuff had come in for a late cup of coffee and offered to scrub the last of the pots and pans.

"Wait till I hear what? Why aren't you in your own bed, Miss? Do you know what time it is?"

"I just had to wait for you, Callie, I had to! I have such exciting news!"

"I don't think I can handle any more excitement for one day, darling. But you won't sleep unless you tell me."

"Rossiter said he'd take us for a buggy ride tomorrow. Not Anne, no one else but us! *Mamán* said it was all right since she'd be wanting to sleep late in the morning. We can have a picnic lunch and everything. Two wonderful days in one week!" Mary hugged the pillow, rolling over onto her tummy. "I do so love Rossiter. I think I'll take my new doll along for the ride. I'll have two Callandres with me. Aren't you excited, Callie? Rossiter said you were pretty. He said you were the prettiest girl he'd ever seen!"

"That I doubt, Mary. No doubt you prompted him to say that. Now are you going off to bed by yourself, or do I have to drag you? Get along, darling, I'll come and tuck you in as soon as I've changed."

Mary leaped out of Callie's bed and hugged her soundly. "I don't think I've ever been this happy. Never in my entire life!" Then she scampered off to the nursery to wait for Callie to hear her prayers.

Rossiter Powers woke from a dreamless sleep ready to start the day. Bright, golden sunshine danced across the bedroom floor. He stretched and yawned. He liked this time of morning best of all. To wake when things were serene and quiet allowed him to think pleasant thoughts, to remember wonderful times in the past and to project his longings for the future.

Lacing his hands behind his head, he closed his eyes. The smile that played around his full, sensuous mouth was wicked as he let his mind travel back to his last encounter with a vibrant young lady before returning home. His active mind searched for a name to place with the vivacious young woman who had literally devoured him. Jane . . . Janet . . . Janelle! That was it—Janelle. He didn't like to think of himself as a callous youth like some of his friends. He took his affairs seriously and always parted company with fond words and an empty purse. He detested emotional scenes, preferring to say he would return one day and pick up where he left off. In a way it salved his conscience and allowed the young woman a few more dreams. He didn't consider himself a lover who hopped from one bed to another. He liked to seek and choose a woman who pleased him and then build their hours together into something lovely that could be remembered and thought about in the early hours of the morning. Like now. One had to take the bull by the horns and live life to the fullest. One walked away from every incident and encounter with dignity. Rossiter Powers was a young gentleman. A gentle, considerate man. A young man his mother could be proud of. A young man his father wished he could have been at his age. It was hard sometimes to live up to such expectations, but he tried.

Take little Mary, for instance. She adored him. The child would laugh and smile all day in his presence. Mary always reminded him of a tadpole for some reason. Not a pretty child like her sister, she was up against it in more ways than he could count. But now that she had her own companion, it looked as though the tadpole could swim at last with expert guidance in the presence of Callie James. Beautiful, gentle Callie James.

Rossiter swung his long, muscular legs over the side of the bed. He smoothed back his rich, golden hair and laughed aloud. He did love life. He was home in the bosom of his family, loved by all. The sun was shining, and he was taking his favorite little sister and her companion for an outing. A day long outing. The tadpole was going to have a day to remember with her big brother.

He whistled softly to himself as he shaved and combed his hair. He dressed carefully but casually. He knew he looked good in almost anything he chose to wear. Janelle had told him he had more style than all the men she had ever known. Janelle hadn't been all *that* young, so there must have been many men parading through her life.

Satisfied with his image, Rossiter headed for the dining room and his breakfast. He couldn't start the day and offer a day to remember without being fortified.

Callie drew Mary to her and spoke slowly. "You're going to be careful today, Mary. Remember, you must face your brother whenever possible." The little girl nodded happily, her round eyes full of excitement. More and more as time passed, Callie wished she had told Mr. Powers about Mary's hearing problem. To be denied the sounds of life was almost unbearable. Why had she promised the child? Because she was a child herself at the time and didn't know any better. Not to hear the birds at first light, not to hear the wind whisper in the trees at eventide. Yet the child was happy. She had her own world, and Callie could tell that Mary was more aware than she was of things going on around her. Her other senses were honed to a fine degree and served her well. But these were all excuses, and Callie knew it. Each day she prayed that her guilt would subside, but it didn't. If anything, it intensified as the days passed. What if an operation a year ago could have restored Mary's hearing? Now that time had passed, the child was hearing less and less, it could be too late.

Mary's thin arms went around Callie's neck. "I do love you, Callie James. I love you more than Anne, but not as much as Rossiter. Well, maybe as much as Rossiter. Yes, I love you the same." Callie laughed. She did love this winsome little one. "If I didn't have these wretched freckles on my face, I would be truly happy," Mary complained.

"Nonsense," Callie smiled. "Think of them as small copper pennies, and you'll never be poor. They're . . ." Callie sought the right word. "Fashionable. They make you different. I wish I had freckles."

"Do you really, Callie?" Mary squealed, hugging her companion again. "Do you really wish you had freckles?"

"Of course. I would think of them as tiny badges of honor. I wouldn't care if no one else had them. They would make me different, make people look at me a second time. People would point me out and say, 'Look at that young lady with freckles.' I should love the attention."

"Oh, Callie, whatever would I do without you? You always make me feel so much better. Promise me you'll never leave here."

"I'll do my best, Mary. But remember that talk we had not too long ago. I told you that forever is a long, long time. I can't make a promise like that to you. I'll stay as long as your *Mamán* and *Papá* feel you need me. Now, if you're ready, I think we should be getting downstairs. Tardiness is not a virtue."

"You're right, Callie. You're always right. Rossiter detests women who tarry and primp and preen. He says if God wanted you stuck to a looking glass, He would have glued you there in the first place. Isn't that funny, Callie?" Not waiting for a reply, she rushed on, "Do you think this dress is acceptable? Does it make me look like a little girl. Does it, Callie, does it?"

Callie tried to hide her smile. "What did I tell you about trying to be something you aren't? You would look silly trying to pretend to be Anne in her ruffles and ribbons. You look very nice. The green in that dress is just the right shade for your hair. And, yes, you do look like a little girl. A beautiful little girl. Now, mind your manners and let's be on our way."

"You look fine, too! That face powder did the trick with your eye. Rossiter is going to love you, Callie. I just know he's going to love you as much as I do."

It was an unusually warm day with the sun shining brightly. To Callie, nothing could be more perfect.

Rossiter kept up a running conversation with Mary but was careful to include Callie in everything. He would ask her opinion or explain something she questioned him on. Mary was scrooched sideways on her seat so that she was half on Callie's lap. This way she didn't miss one word her adored brother said. He liked Callie, she could tell. And Callie liked Rossiter. Callie kept blushing and smiling the whole time. It was wonderful. Just wonderful. Her two favorite people in the whole world liking one another.

Rossiter was at a loss to explain the wonderful time he was having. Was it the look of wide-eyed wonder on Callie's face when he pointed out something to her and Mary? Was it the warm color that flooded her cheeks when he spoke to her? Was it her shyness and her protection of his little sister that tugged at his heart? Whatever it was, he was having the time of his life. He threw back his head and roared with laughter when the two girls giggled about something. It was such a contagious sound, he couldn't help laughing. At his suggestion they took a break from sightseeing around St. George and had tea and cakes. Rossiter himself served each of them with a flourish and bowed elaborately after the waitress left their table. While they dallied over tea and cakes, Mary begged for an ice cream cone. "I don't think Callie's ever had one. Please, Rossiter."

"For you, tadpole, anything. Chocolate or vanilla?"

"Vanilla," Mary chirped.

"I . . . I don't know," Callie stuttered.

"When in doubt, chocolate. Besides, it's my favorite."

"Rossiter lets it drip down his chin and then tries to make his tongue stretch to lick it off," Mary gurgled happily.

They sauntered down the tree-lined street, licking their ice cream. Callie thought she had never been so happy when Rossiter said he would walk between his "two girls." Conversation wasn't necessary as they made their way through the busy shoppers and sightseers.

The day ended on a glad note for both girls. Rossiter bought each of them a red balloon to tie on their wrists. Mary was ecstatic when Rossiter, seeing how tired she was, picked her up and carried her on his broad shoulders. Was it Callie's imagination, or was Rossiter walking closer to her than necessary? When she felt him reach over to take her hand, she almost fainted with happiness and dread. Quickly she looked up at Mary on her high perch and was regarded with a roguish wink from the little girl.

The buggy ride back to the house was a blur for Callie. Mary dozed against Rossiter's chest, while she sat nestled beside him as he drove. If she had died and gone to heaven, she couldn't have been happier.

Callie was jolted to awareness when Rossiter looked at her and spoke quietly. "Do you have any free time to yourself? I don't suppose the tadpole sleeps during the day or takes a nap." At Callie's negative nod, he pretended to think. "What do you do after she goes to sleep at night?"

"I go to sleep," Callie said honestly.

Rossiter chuckled. "If you didn't go to sleep, what would you do?"

"Read a book from your father's library or make a lesson for Mary."

"You're a beautiful young lady. Has anyone ever told you that?"

"So are you. Beautiful, I mean," Callie said in a flustered tone. "No, no, no one has ever told me that before."

The buggy rode easily over the hard-packed road through the countryside. The only sound was the rhythmic clopping of the horses' hooves, which sent up little spirals of dust, and the croaking of the frogs in the rushes that stood tall along the ditches. The last vestiges of the sun burned the sky a radiant red and gold. The air had become cooler, and Callie pulled the rug up over the sleeping Mary, tucking it under the little girl's chin. Her own cheeks were freshened by the evening air, but she felt warm sitting beside Rossiter. He had said she was beautiful, and she felt it was so each time he turned to look at her. His eyes seemed to linger on her face, touching it from brow to lips, but it was always to her eyes that his gaze returned, seeming to sear and penetrate her very soul.

"Have you looked at the book I gave you yesterday, Callie?" he asked, the timbre of his voice warming her. "No, I thought not, when would you have had the time? Do you know anything about the poet?"

Callie shook her head.

"Shall I tell you about him then? He really is my favorite. His own life was more flamboyant than his poetry. Lord Byron was just thirty-six years old when he died fighting for Greek independence against the Turks. He was born with a club foot, but his deformity went unnoticed by the loves in his life because of the beauty of his mind. He was quite a figure in the English and Italian courts and was so beloved by all that his . . . er . . . transgressions were overlooked. Indeed, they were forgiven. Byron was capable of deep love, and his poetry reflects his own life. His most famous affair was with Lady Caroline Lamb, who was a married woman, but the great love of his life was his own half-sister. His life was a scandal, I'm afraid, but he did live it to the fullest."

Callie listened as Rossiter quoted lines from Byron's poems; she blushed when he related some of the more scandalous and lusty achievements of the poet, embellishing where he might, watching the color suffuse her features. When he began to recount tales of Byron's homosexual trysts, Callie threw her hands over her face and turned away.

Rossiter drew the buggy to the side of the road, reaching across Mary to put his arms around Callie. "Lovey, I didn't mean to upset you," he murmured. "I only supposed that a girl your age . . . that is . . . I never thought you'd be offended by adult conversation. I'm sorry, Callie, do you forgive me? I had no idea you were such a baby."

"I'm not a baby, Rossiter," Callie protested. "It's just that no one ever told me about things like that . . ."

"I know, lovely, I know. Show me you forgive me, Callie." He lifted her chin, looking deep into her eyes, moving closer. His lips touched hers in a caress so soft, so gentle. His hand was cupped against her throat, and he could feel her pulses beating there, stirring him to deepen the kiss. He inhaled the fresh scent of her cheek, felt her mouth yield beneath his, opening slightly, offering invitation. "Callie, you're so beautiful!" he gasped before capturing her lips once again. His hand left her throat, following a downward path to brush against her breast. He felt her spine stiffen, but he was also keenly aware of the tautening of the soft flesh beneath his hand and of the nubbin tip aroused against his palm. He was amazed when she didn't pull back. He supposed it was true that if a girl allowed you to talk about sex, she'd allow you to do it! He was almost instantly contrite for his roguish thoughts when Callie squirmed beneath his touch and pulled her mouth away to gasp for air. His hand that was cupping the ripe fullness of her breast fell innocently into his own lap.

Callie's flesh tingled, as though having a life of its own, independent of her. She felt her breasts pushing against the thin fabric of her chemise, their coral-pink crests erect and hard, rubbing pleasantly against her garment. She was certain Rossiter's hand upon her bosom was most accidental; otherwise, she would never be able to face him again. Her lips were warm, moist, full from his kiss, and she felt as though she'd stepped through a doorway, leaving childhood behind, embarking upon womanhood. She wondered at this odd sensation at her center, pulsing and rigid yet at the same time soft and yielding. A new awareness of herself pulsed through her veins, and she kept her eyes lowered as Rossiter picked up the reins and turned the buggy down the road toward home. She was certain if he looked into her eyes, he would see the naked enthrallment he had instilled in her.

Mary shifted in her seat, turning so that her head fell against Callie's breast. She placed her arm around the little girl's shoulders and rested her cheek on top of those fiery red curls. On the day of her eighteenth birthday Rossiter had come into her life. And on the next day, he had shown her what had been missing from that life.

* * *

Sleep was impossible. Callie tossed and turned in her narrow bed, tangling the sheets and blankets around her legs. One minute she felt warm, the next a chill. Her thoughts churned and churned, reliving that moment in the buggy when Rossiter had kissed her until it seemed she had had no past before that kiss and could not contemplate the future until the next one. There would be another kiss, she was certain of it. She remembered the way his lips had lingered upon hers, the way the tip of his tongue had barely penetrated the soft yielding she had offered.

Jumping from her bed, Callie lit the lamp on her washstand, peering at her face in the mirror hanging above. She stared at her image, trying to discern a difference there. Surely there must be a difference! Something had happened to her, something she had no name for. Her blood rushed faster, and the imprint of Rossiter's lips on hers was so vivid—surely it must be seen. Slowly Callie opened the ties of her nightdress, pulling the fabric aside to bare her breasts. She had never looked at herself this way before, had merely accepted the changes in her body. But now, she gazed at her smooth, creamy breast, saw the pink nipples rising, felt the heaviness in her hips and a strange emptiness in that place between her legs, making her thighs grip together in an effort to relieve it. He had said she was beautiful and that was the way he made her feel. Was it possible to love someone in so short a time? Or had she really fallen in love with him the first time she'd studied his portrait in the downstairs parlor?

Callie lifted the little gold locket from between her breasts, opened it, and looked inside. Mary's dear little face looked out at her, but it was the image of Rossiter that really held her gaze. He said she was beautiful. Did that mean he could love her, this golden young man whose laugh could lighten her heart? Peggy would know. Madge and her girls would know. Even Byrch Kenyon would know. Why then didn't she?

She closed the locket and climbed into bed. The velvety lashes fell against her cheeks as Callie gave herself up to sleep, nuzzling her face against the pillow, pretending it was Rossiter's shoulder.

The next morning after breakfast, Callie settled Mary down with her lessons and the promise of a walk when she was done. "We can take your balloon and perhaps Mr. MacDuff will tie a longer string on it for you. He's also promised I can plant some seeds in the little patch of garden he's tilled for me." Mary diligently worked the sums and composition Mr. Reader had assigned her while Callie sat near the window, reading the latest copy of the *Clarion-Observer*. She was so engrossed in an account of the little theatre groups cropping up on lower Broadway that she almost missed seeing Rossiter walk down the hall. Her eyes widened, and her heart began to patter. Surely he would stop in to say good morning. She waited, hardly daring to breathe. He didn't return. Perhaps he didn't want to disturb Mary at her lessons.

It was impossible to concentrate on the newspaper now. The words were running together and held no meaning. Callie almost cried with relief when Mary finished her work and asked, "Can we go out now, Callie?"

Where had Rossiter been going? What did he do during the day? Callie had to know. The kitchen. She would take Mary through the kitchen and pick up a few cookies to take outside. Lena always knew everything. Surely she would know something, or Hugh would tell her if Rossiter had taken the buggy into town.

At the last moment her nerve failed her. She turned Mary to face her and mouthed the words silently. "Ask Lena if she knows where your brother is."

Mary skipped ahead and pounced on the buxom cook. "Lena, do you know where Rossiter is? Did you see him this morning? Can I have some cookies? How do you like my balloon? Rossiter bought it for me? Isn't it beautiful?"

Lena's doughy features creased into a wide smile. Hands on her ample hips, she beamed down at the little girl. "One question at a time. Yes, you may have a sackful of cookies. I made them just for you yesterday. Raisin-filled. I saw your brother when I served him his breakfast. He was in here mooching my cookies just the way you are, a few minutes ago. Your *Papá* is looking for him too. He wants to take him to the office with him this afternoon. Best you tell him that when you see him. Your balloon is a beauty. Don't go popping it and scaring me out of my wits now, you hear me?"

"I won't, I promise." Mary giggled. "Is Mr. MacDuff about? Callie wants to see him so he can help her plant some seeds."

"MacDuff is out to the stable," Lena answered. "He's diddlin' with those seedlings he started last February. I think it's his intention to put out the sugar peas in that cold frame of his."

When the screen door slammed behind the girls and the floating balloon, Lena frowned. Now, why would Callie be looking so relieved? She went back to paring her vegetables for lunch. She stopped, the knife poised in mid-air. She wiped her hands on her apron and went to the back door. MacDuff was coming out of the carriage house, waving brightly to Callie. Then he was laughing, his weathered face lifting into a wreath of smiles. There was something different about MacDuff when Callie was around, Lena noticed. There seemed to be a softening of his rough edges, a softer burr to his voice, a merriness about the eyes. Lately he'd even taken to getting regular haircuts, and he kept his grizzled gray hair brushed and combed. And wasn't that a new shirt he was wearing?

Lena's eyes went to Callie. The girl's face seemed to light up the countryside. The sight made Lena frown. It was none of her business, after all. She went back to paring her vegetables with a vengeance. Callie was hardly more than a child! Eighteen years old didn't make a girl a woman, only life and experience did that. She would have to speak to MacDuff about this.

The winds that played about the crest of Todt Hill that day were gentle, bringing the tang from the harbor with them. Callie worked beside Hugh MacDuff in the garden, following his instruction, liking the way his large, calloused hands handled the young plants as he lovingly placed them into the hard, brown earth. She liked the aroma of pipe tobacco that clung to his clothes and the way his eyes crinkled at the corners when he smiled, which he did often that young spring day when he had Callie's attentions all to himself.

Mary was running with her balloon in the front yard, watching the wind lift it, the bright red color dazzling against the sky. "We'll have rain before the afternoon is out," MacDuff said as he stood to stretch his back, looking off into the distance.

"How can you tell, Mr. MacDuff? It seems to me the sun will shine forever."

MacDuff drew on his pipe. "C'mere, lass." He brought her to her feet, placing her in front of him. "Look there, over the bay. See those clouds drifting this way? Rain for certain. Not a storm, mind you, but rain nonetheless." Callie lifted her chin, looking out over the bay, unaware that MacDuff was looking down at her, grazing his eyes over the soft chestnut of her hair and the pink of her cheeks, lingering about the new softness that touched her lips. Something had happened to Callie, Hugh found himself thinking. She was almost a grown woman. Did a girl's eighteenth birthday bring about such a subtle yet sudden change?

Callie was the focus of someone else's attention also. Unseen, Rossiter was peering out the back attic window where he sat with pencils and pad, sketching the yard and the way it fell off steeply from the hill toward the patchwork green of the valley and the fall of land onto the beach. But he had tired of sketching the landscape, and now his artist's eye was tempted by Callie's slim form bending over her garden patch and the graceful arch her arms made when she reached to pat the earth over her tiny seeds. The wind played through her hair, lifting it from the purity of her neck and the width of her brow. How tiny she seemed standing beside MacDuff's rangy height. How vulnerable she looked. He put his pencil to a clean sheet from the pad and began to sketch her, finding her much more challenging than the landscape, more tempting to the eye. He shouldn't have kissed her the evening before—Rossiter frowned as he worked. She was obviously inexperienced with men, and worse, he knew that the first rule for a young man of his class and station was not to dally with the servants. Yet knowing Callie was forbidden to him heightened his sense of adventure and excitement. He remembered the way Byrch Kenyon had stared at Callie at the birthday celebration. He too had seen her blossoming beauty, the promise of the woman she was yet to become. Rossiter scowled, feeling the familiar pang of envy he held for the tall, lean Irishman. If Kenyon could entertain thoughts about a domestic, then so could he. In fact, Rossiter considered himself at a distinct advantage where Callie was concerned. He remembered with a thrill the excitement of touching her breast, feeling the softness tauten and harden against his palm. He would touch those breasts again, he knew without doubt, and he would feel those tempting crests pressed beneath his lips.

The rain began after lunch, a soft spring rain that splattered into shallow puddles. The house seemed too quiet to Mary—everyone seemed to have something to do except her. She wandered out onto the back sunporch. She tried to listen very hard but could only imagine the sound of the raindrops against the windows. For some reason, when she was alone, she felt her affliction more. She knew the birds were hiding beneath the rhododendron bush, seeking shelter from the rain, chirping as they huddled together. If only she could hear them. Her world of near silence could be terrifying to her, but as long as she had Callie, she would feel safe and loved. When she grew up, like Anne, she wouldn't be able to hear the music. Sooner or later, Mary knew with certainty, her secret would be out. She flinched at what she had imagined would happen, how *Mamán* would send her away. She imagined the loathing in her mother's face and the tears in *Papá*'s eyes. Rossiter would love her anyway, just the way Callie did. But Rossiter would go away again. He never stayed long when he came home to visit.

Thin little fingers with nails chewed to the nub pulled at her earlobes. Feeling the wind was almost as good as hearing it. Seeing the sparks fly and the logs burst into flame in the fireplace was every bit as good as hearing the snap and crackle of the flames. It was. A single tear trickled from the corner of Mary's sherry-colored eyes. So what if I can't hear, she thought defiantly. I can see, I can smell, and best of all, I can feel.

"Tadpole, what's the trouble?" Rossiter demanded. "Look at me, Mary—what's wrong? I spoke to you twice. Don't tell me instead of the cat getting your tongue he took your ears instead!" he said jokingly.

Feeling the touch to her shoulder, Mary turned quickly, startled from her thoughts. She wiped at the lone tear and faced her brother. "I guess I was thinking of something else. It always seems so lonely when everyone has something to do and I have nothing. *Papá* is busy in his study, *Mamán* is taking a nap, and Anne is at Miss Rose's school."

"So that's what's bothering you? I wondered if something terrible had happened. I spoke twice before you heard me. Where's Callie?" he asked casually.

"She's in the kitchen ironing my dresses. I don't know why *Mamán* insists that Callie do my laundry. Why can't she send everything to the laundress in town? Why does she have to keep Callie so busy she hardly has time to play with me?"

"It's far too nice a day to be ironing," Rossiter said, making Mary look at him questioningly and then out at the rain. "Why don't you go get her and that new umbrella she got for her birthday. We'll all take a walk in the rain, and if we see any fat worms, we'll stuff them in my pockets to put under Anne's pillow. Won't that be a surprise for Miss Goody-Two-Shoes?" He smiled devilishly.

"Oh, Rossiter!" Mary squealed with mischief. "Would you really do that? Truly?"

"No. On second thought, it would be most unfair to the worm, wouldn't it? But it would be fun. You'd hear her screams all the way up to your nursery." The slight stiffening of Mary's shoulders puzzled him. "Go on, go get Callie and that bright red umbrella."

An hour before tea, Mrs. Powers summoned Lena into the dining room. "I wish to speak to you about a dinner I'm planning for next week. I've invited the Tottens, and you realize they're the most important family on the island. I do want things to go smoothly. I've been thinking about sending Mr. MacDuff into the city for a large ham. How many jars of applesauce are left in the pantry? And of course, I'll be expecting your famous blueberry torte—what is that racket?" she asked, annoyed by the sounds coming from outside the window. She left her seat near the table and lifted the curtain to look outside.

Lena drew in her breath. She knew what the racket was and wished she were somewhere else.

"Would you look at that! Would you just look at that! Where's my husband, Lena?"

"In his study, Mrs. Powers. Is something wrong?"

"Just look! Just look!" Anne Powers sputtered.

Lena craned her neck to look through the window. Master Rossiter was carrying his shoes in one hand and the red umbrella in the other, holding it over Callie's head, and they were both dancing barefoot through the puddles. Mary danced beside them, squealing for Callie to hold her skirts higher and not to drop her shoes. Callie was giggling, laughing, holding fast to Rossiter's arm and smiling adoringly up into his face.

"I can't believe what I'm seeing! Send my husband to me immediately!"

Jasper Powers threw his papers onto the floor, lifting his spectacles off his nose. "Now what!" he groaned. A man couldn't get a moment's peace in this house.

In the dining room, his wife was still leaning against the window. "I won't tolerate this behavior, Jasper. Do you hear me? I simply won't tolerate it! Why, she's acting like a little trollop. Bare feet indeed! And holding to my son's arm so . . . so . . . intimately! In the rain, Jasper. In the rain! Are you listening to me?"

"Of course, dear, I always listen to you," Jasper said wearily.

"Yes, you listen, but you don't do anything. Callie is definitely overstepping her bounds, and her responsibility to Mary is sadly lacking. Imagine taking that child out into the rain! That girl is becoming a problem, Jasper, and I think it's time we considered sending Mary off to school and discharging Callie. I have enough problems without having my servant frolic in the rain with my son! And in broad daylight!"

"Would you rather they frolic at night?" Jasper quipped, hoping to lighten a situation that he clearly did not consider serious.

"You are impossible. I dislike saying this, Jasper, but your lack of breeding is becoming quite evident. Can't you see what's going on under your very nose?"

"I don't see anything," Jasper growled. "Callie is a good girl, and Mary adores her. And why is it you never place any blame on Rossiter? He's old enough to know proper behavior."

"I will not have Rossiter cavorting around with a servant. I won't have it."

"Anne, what is the harm in a little fun?"

"Fun! I expect Callie to set a good example for Mary. Do you call that a good example?"

"I see no harm in it. It's time there was a little fun and life in this house. And I think you're overlooking something. I'd wager it was Rossiter who suggested this little venture into the puddles."

"My son! Never! Rossiter has class and breeding—"

"Apparently not, dear. Is that or is it not Rossiter whom I see out there? I will call the children in, but that is all. I will have something to say about what goes on in my own house, and I forbid you to mention this to them. I will have a little talk with Rossiter about his responsibilities to his sister. That is the end of it, Anne."

Anne Powers's mouth formed a round O. Was it her imagination or was her husband all too willing to leap to the defense of Callie and Mary? She sniffed. If this was to be the lay of the land, she would handle any future matters concerning the children herself!

She turned to glance out the window, watching Rossiter and Callie run back toward the house when Jasper called. Her eyes narrowed as she saw her son's hand steadying the girl over the lawn, and she gasped when he threw his arm around her shoulder to pull her beneath the shelter of the umbrella. Callie's dress was lifted almost to her knees, displaying a gracefully turned leg and delicate ankles. The rain had soaked through the bodice of her dress, the thin material clinging to her recently formed curves. Anne Powers's eyebrows lifted in surprise. How had the chit grown beneath her own eyes and she never noticed? She dropped the lace curtain and turned from the window.

Chapter Fourteen

Long after the clock in the hall struck eleven, Rossiter still paced the confines of his room, which was directly under the nursery. It seemed to him that every one of his senses was trained upon the room above, next to the nursery, where Callie slept. He imagined her snuggled in her bed, eyelids and lips moist with sleep, her lithe body curled beneath the sheets, her breasts rising and falling with each breath.

Earlier that afternoon, when little Mary had been sent inside to rest after lunch, he and Callie had slipped out of the house into the light drizzle of rain. He'd wanted to show her his secret hiding place under the front porch, he'd told her. There, hidden beneath the floor boards, behind the lattices, they'd crouched on the pungent, damp earth. There, with the sound of the rain all about them, excited by the danger of discovery, he had kissed her again. And again. Until it seemed he could never have enough of those soft, full lips, the tender tip of her tongue captured by his own, the shudders of her breathing as she came into his arms, so young, so pliant, as he laid siege to the temptation of her throat and shoulders, pulling aside her bodice to taste the freshness of her breasts.

She was so innocent, protesting against the liberties he was taking with her, but he also sensed an awakening of the woman inside the girl, and her defenses were washed away by the insistence of his passion and the discovery of her own.

Now, as he paced his room, he battled with unrequited hungers, his arousal biting deep in the pit of his belly. He wanted Callie James, perhaps more than he'd ever wanted any girl. A shred of decency warned him that she was good, pure, inexperienced, and that to take advantage of her could bring about her ruin. But Rossiter was adept at turning a deaf ear to his conscience, and he wanted nothing as much as to climb the stairs to her room and take her for his own.

Common sense and logic told him it could also be his own ruination if they were caught by the family. Jasper held Callie in high regard, and he would never forgive his son for bringing about her downfall. But the risk seemed only to heighten his desire, bringing a sense of adventure with it. Rossiter was not in the habit of being denied, by himself or by anyone else for that matter. Callie was off limits by any bounds of decency and he should conduct himself like the gentleman he was supposed to be. Yet there she was, one floor above him, and instinct told him she would not deny him what he craved.

Rossiter picked up his sketch pad, thumbing through the pages until he found the one he'd done of Callie in her little patch of garden. In the lower right hand corner of the page he'd done a small drawing of her head and shoulders, the wayward tendrils of her hair blown by the wind, falling against her face. He had done her eyes from memory: clear, level, staring out from the page in what seemed to him a declaration of her goodness and purity. He tossed the pad onto his dresser and slumped down onto his bed, bending his head into his hands, his fingers ravaging his thick, golden hair. There was a fire in his loins and an aching need in his chest. No! No! He told himself over and over, and yet he could not find the courage of his convictions at his core, could not find the sacrifice of his own hungers in his character. He knew himself to be weak and hated himself for it. Spoiled and indulged, he was used to having his way for the price of an engaging smile or a charming compliment. His handsome face and splendid body won acceptance for him wherever he went, and yet he knew that the man within was undeserving of such approval. Callie was good, truthful, and pure, and *because he was not*, it added to his torment.

Rossiter rose from the bed, stepping over to the dresser to pick up the sketch pad once again. There was talent here: he had been told that by teachers and artists alike. He wanted to pursue that talent but doubted he possessed the necessary discipline the art required. It was easier to believe that being a painter was unsuitable for a Boston aristocrat whose father was a success in the world of finance. Frustrated, angry, he stared at Callie's image, perceiving in the face he had drawn a challenge and a mockery, as though she knew that he would never be more than he already was.

He ripped the page to shreds, tearing it with shaking hands, unable to complete the deed quickly enough to erase the imagined derision in those carefully drawn features. He was bad, underserving, a worthless rogue! There was only one way to achieve an equality between himself and Callie, one way to place them on the same level. His own innocence was long gone, and the road to self-sacrifice and virtue was too long and too hard. He envied Callie's honor, wished it for himself, but at the same time it shamed him, and a perversity in his nature compelled him to destroy it. Rossiter pulled open his door and climbed the stairs to the room beside the nursery.

Callie tossed restlessly on her bed, unable to find sleep. Her body trembled and shivered as she recalled those moments with Rossiter beneath the front porch. She could still feel the sweetness of his mouth drawing upon her own, could still hear the soft sounds of pleasure he made when he found her breasts with his lips. It had given her a sense of power to know that this beautiful young man desired her, had begged for her favors. His hands had been so gentle, and her heart had fluttered like the wings of a butterfly when he reclaimed her lips again and again. Even now there was an ache at the center of her, an empty longing that only Rossiter could fill.

The soft glow of her lamp created shadows and light in her spare attic room. She could not bring herself to put it out, feeling she could not bear the pang of isolation that the darkness would bring. Her eyes fell upon the book Rossiter had given her for her birthday; the gilt-edged pages gleamed in the lamplight. Under the book lay the box of stationery Byrch Kenyon had given her. The pale green sheets of onionskin paper were a sharp rebuke that she had not written to her mother in over a week. But how could she write without mentioning Rossiter? How, when there didn't seem to be anything or anyone else in her life except Rossiter? Callie knew she couldn't mention him to Peggy, not yet, at any rate. Her feelings were still too new, too fragile to share with anyone, her unformulated hopes for the future too delicate to bear examination.

She heard a step in the hall outside her room, and before she could consider its source, Rossiter opened the door and loomed in the doorway. The feeble flickering of the lamp barely reached his face, but she could feel his eyes upon her, touching her face, moving downward to her breasts beneath the thin cambric of her nightdress.

She watched him close the door behind him, unable to speak or find the words to ask why he had come. A primal instinct gave her the answer when she watched him silently cross the floor towards her bed, his slender hips moving against the rhythm of his broad shoulders, like a lion stalking the night. His shirt was unbuttoned to the waist; she could see his hard, muscular chest, could detect the fine golden hairs that streaked below his navel and downward. Her eyes moved upward to his face, saw how his mouth was set in a firm, grim line, perceived the shadow of pain in the depths of that dark gaze.

Alarmed, she sat up in bed, the covers falling away. Her heart ached with loving him. Her finely attuned senses told her that he was deeply troubled, that he was embittered with anger and bristling with hostility. Toward her? What had she done? He sank to his knees beside her bed, roughly pulling her into his arms. She could feel the tight muscles in his neck, the rigidity of his spine. He spoke her name—it was more a sob—and the suddenness of his appearance here in her room and the way he held her fast, devouring her mouth with his own, frightened her.

Callie struggled to free herself from his hurting hands, making little sounds of protest, always aware that Mary slept on just the other side of the wall.

Rossiter resisted her struggles, heard her protests, felt her hands pushing against his shoulders, and realized how vulnerable she was. But he only knew he wanted her, must have her, and was glad for this raging anger he was feeling that insulated him against her complaints as well as the order of decency. "I want you, Callie," he whispered hoarsely, hardly recognizing the voice as his own. "I need you. God, how I need you! Please, Callie, please," his words came in a rush, his lips traced the sweet hollows of her throat, his hands held an iron grip on her soft upper arms. "Please, Callie, please, I need you," he pleaded, feeling her resolve melt, knowing that her struggles had ceased, that her arms were taking him into her embrace. He buried his face against her beating heart.

Because she loved him, because of his puzzling anger and heart-rending pain, Callie took him into her arms, issuing soft, soothing sounds. There were no words to comfort him; she had no magic to ease his anger and assuage his misery. She had only herself and her love to fill that need.

He felt her resistance cease, exerted pressure to pull her forward, and before his lips claimed hers, he inhaled the fresh, clean, soapy scent of her. When his mouth took hers again, her lips moved beneath his, reciting the lessons she had learned in the damp beneath the porch. He moved over their softness, seeking her response and finding it.

Callie offered a sweet kiss, tentatively parting her lips, allowing his tongue entrance to hers. She was aware of that fullness and the curling sensation it created within her. His thumb traced circular patterns in the sensitive hollow below her ear, arousing senses that had lain hidden from her. He made her warm, he made her tingle and shiver with expectation.

The eagerness of Callie's response brought an instant and demanding reaction from Rossiter. She felt as though she were being devoured, consumed by his ravishing hunger for her. The sweet yielding of her lips, the enticing touch of her tongue burned Rossiter with a raw, primal need. His hand glided down her elegant throat, paving the way for his lips. He wanted to kiss all of her, to taste her inch by inch, taking her between his lips, his teeth, nibbling and feeding his appetite for her. Her nightgown parted beneath his fingers; he pushed it aside, baring the hollow of her neck and the soft roundness of her shoulder. He felt her tremble beneath his touch, heard a faint moaning sound and knew that she was as close to the edge of this great yawning abyss as himself. He meant to carry her up and over with him, falling, falling into a place where the hungers of the body would be met. He knew he was affecting her with his caresses, drawing her into swift currents of passion. Encouraged by the heated throb of her body, he took her hand, lifting it and placing it between his open shirt front. He guided it to the expanse of bare chest, and even though the touch was anticipated and expected, he gasped as her fingers splayed over the heat of his skin.

Callie thought she was drifting into a world beyond reason. Nothing existed to her but this moment and Rossiter. He encouraged her to explore his body, and she felt his muscles contract beneath her touch. Soft, almost invisible golden chest hairs rubbed against her palm as she caressed his breasts and grazed her fingers over sensitive nipples that, to her amazement, became rigid and puckered with excitement, just like her own. His mouth returned to take hers in a driving possession, pushing her backwards onto her pillow, following with his body. His breathing came in gasps as he murmured his delight in her, sending new thrills through Callie that this beautiful, powerful man could find pleasure in her.

He was impatient with the boundaries set by her chaste nightgown, and he rucked it up from her legs and over her hips, pulling it over her head, leaving her naked and exposed to his hands and lips. Callie made a movement to prevent him, but he murmured, "Don't be frightened, Callie, don't be frightened! I'll never hurt you, don't you know that? Don't you know?"

Her small hands wound around his shoulders, smoothing over his skin, holding him close against her, wordlessly assuring him that she wasn't afraid. She could never be afraid as long as he held her, kissing her as he was, loving her. When he lowered his head to claim her breasts, her fingers burrowed into the thick golden hair at the base of his neck, holding him there while his lips opened upon the soft, tender flesh to take the taut, rosy pink between his teeth. Callie writhed beneath this new assault, clenching her thighs together in an effort to assuage the building pressure she was experiencing there.

Rossiter let his hand travel downward while his lips continued their attention to her breasts. On the slow, teasing descent, his fingers caressed the slimness of her waist, the swell of her hip, and the flatness of her belly. At the instant her hips arched against his hand, he slid his fingers into the silky patch between her thighs, roaming there in soft, barely traceable patterns.

Instinctively Callie's hips began to move with the rhythm he set, her thighs parting beneath his pressure to allow him a more intimate search for the warm moistness of her center. Soft, panting sounds of pleasure emanated from her throat as he dared to claim her entry. She experienced a separateness from her body; her mind and heart were filled with Rossiter, tenderly loving him, wanting to impart to him something of herself, imprinting him with her devotion. All the while her body was answering his demands, instinctively moving beneath him to excite and stir his passions, inflaming him with her innate provocativeness.

Fire licked his veins at her uninhibited response to his caress. Tearing himself away from her breasts, he reclaimed her mouth, bruising her lips, driving them apart to invade the warm recesses within. His own fevered need was throbbing urgently, driving him to satisfy the screaming need within him. His clothing was a barrier between his flesh and hers, a separation that could not be tolerated.

Fast, ruthless fingers tore away his garments, removing his shirt and trousers before she even realized he had left her. He stretched out full length beside her, fitting the gentle curves of her body against his. She opened herself to his touch, arched her hips to bring herself closer to the lean length of him. He wedged his leg between her thighs, pulling her under him as he mounted her. A hot eagerness pulsed through him as he probed between the incredibly soft folds of her sex, riding into her with slow deliberation. When he reached the tremulous barrier of her virginity, he thrust forward, piercing it, prepared for her cry of pain by muffling her mouth against his own.

Callie twisted, turned, pushing against his chest, knowing only the searing heat from inside her, trying to escape his further invasion of her, expecting a repeat of the pain. Rossiter lay quiet, grinding his hips against hers to still her movements. He soothed her by stroking her hair back from her fevered brow, his lips continuing to demand and evoke an answer from hers. The weight of him pressed her into the thin mattress, forcing her to accept his presence inside her. After what seemed an eternity, he felt her struggles cease; his satisfaction and reward was so close now, just over the edge, and he would not be denied. He continued kissing her, moving his lips over her throat and down to her breasts, his hand sliding over her hips and between their bodies in an effort to revive the passions that had fled in the face of her pain. When he moved against her again, he felt her stiffen, but she didn't struggle; it was when his own fever inflamed his loins that her nails dug into his shoulders and she uttered a choked sound of pain at this deeper penetration that seemed to be carving an opening within her, sculpting her tender flesh to accommodate his rigid maleness.

He shuddered with the force of his passion as he spent himself within her, holding her fast, burying his face into the hollow of her neck. His breath came in mournful little gasps, and she wondered if he shared her pain. Her love for him prompted her soothing fingers in his hair and tender little kisses to his ear.

"Oh, Callie," she heard him whisper, still trembling with the force of his passion, "you're just what I need. You're all that I need."

And because she loved him, and because he needed her, she forgave.

Rossiter lay beside her, holding her close, his breathing returning from the shallow, heaving intake of air to deeper, longer breaths. Without a word, he rose from the bed, pulling the blanket up over her nakedness. Silently he dressed, carefully fastening each and every button. She watched him in the yellow glow of the lamp, adoring the lines of his body, thrilling to the knowledge that this beautiful, passionate man had taken her for his own. Bending over her, he planted a fond kiss on her brow and quietly closed the door behind him.

Callie lay for what seemed an eternity before rising from the bed. Seeing a tiny red stain on the sheet, her fingers dipped downward, feeling the warm stickiness of blood. Quickly she washed away all traces of her lost virginity and donned a clean nightdress. As she was about to gutter the lamp, her eyes fell on the packet of letters from Ireland. Her mother's letters. Tentatively her fingers touched the crisp sheaf of papers. Tears glistened in her eyes as she cried in a hoarse whisper, "Mum, what have I done?" Callie was suddenly afraid. Afraid her deed would be discovered, and she would be sent away. Afraid of the woman within her. But most of all, she was afraid she would never have the strength to refuse Rossiter if he ever came to her again.

Rossiter threw himself across his bed, still fully clothed, his arm thrown over his eyes as if to hide from himself. Emotions welled within him, regret that could not be solaced by the comfort in his loins. Turning his face into the pillow, he sobbed his grief for Callie's lost innocence, for what he'd done. But through his torrent of self-indulgent tears there was a rainbow. He had seen himself reflected in Callie's eyes, and he was good—as good and pure as Callie James.

Callie stood over the wash tub on the back service porch, watching Mary follow Mr. MacDuff across the yard to the chicken coop. The pail of feed the child insisted on carrying was far too cumbersome, making her list to the opposite side as she walked. Callie smiled. If Mary realized that the chickens that graced the dining table once a week came from the flock out in back, she'd never eat again.

She was soaking the laundry in a solution of hot water and Kirkman's soap powder. Afterward, she would hang it on the line in the backyard where it would dry before she ironed it. Was it only last week that she'd stood over this same tub, scrubbing at the blood stain on her bed sheet, worrying that it would be a permanent sign revealing that she was no longer a girl but a woman? A woman in love with Rossiter Powers.

The various household duties she had always gladly accomplished now seemed too numerous, requiring so much of her time—

time that she would have liked to spend with Rossiter. He was in the habit of taking paints and canvas to the other side of the hill where he could look down upon a wide expanse of fields dotted with trees and shrubs and the river beyond. Yesterday he'd gone into the city to purchase a particular shade of paint he wanted, and he'd brought her back a shell comb for her hair from the Four and Nine Cent's store on lower Broadway. He'd presented her gift late last night when everyone was asleep, and he'd crept up to her room as he had done every night since the first.

Callie's every waking moment was filled with awareness of Rossiter. Even when he was away from the house, gone across the hill, she followed him in her thoughts, imagining what he was doing, what he was thinking. Although she knew that sharing Rossiter's love outside of marriage contradicted every morality she'd ever been taught, she could not help herself. What they were doing might be wrong in the eyes of the world, but there were no eyes in the dark of her room when her golden god came to her, loving her, making her his own. At times, Callie was so filled with love for him she hardly believed she could draw breath. Nothing existed for her except the touch of his mouth on hers and the feel of his hands on her flesh. He had encouraged her to become familiar with his body, and she had done so, worshipping it with her hands, adoring it with her lips, and always, always loving him. There was no past, no future, only the here and now, and Rossiter—beautiful, golden Rossiter.

Using the pale green stationery Byrch had given her, she wrote to Peggy, unable to keep herself from mentioning Rossiter, but careful not to confide the full extent of their relationship. Rossiter had become a part of her life, and she wanted the world to know it. He loved her, there was no doubt about it, but until the day she became his wife, she must keep her secret. So she must content herself with telling Peggy simple, ordinary things about him: how he loved to paint, how sweet he was to Mary, how he was the object of his mother's adoration. In her last letter she had written about the gift of the shell comb; she was so happy with his attention and thoughtfulness that she could not keep it to herself. Now, after dropping the letter in the mail box, knowing that the postman had already taken it, Callie regretted her hastiness. Peggy was too wise, too knowledgeable about her oldest daughter, and the risk was too great that she might read between the lines. The thought of anyone, even Peggy, dashing cold water on her love affair was not to be borne.

Lena popped her head in the door. "Lands, child! Are you still at that laundry? The day'll be over before you hang it out, and it'll never dry! You know how Mrs. Powers deplores wash hanging out so late in the day. You'd better get on with it." The cook's sharp glance took in Callie's wistful expression. "What have we here? Looks to me like you've got a case of spring fever. Suppose I should get out the molasses and vinegar tonic and give you a dose?" Lena smiled, but Callie's lack of energy annoyed her. Usually the girl was so good about lending a hand, and she'd come to depend on her. "I'm taking the last of the pickled cabbage today, and I'll need help scrubbing the crocks. And there's potatoes to be peeled for dinner . . ."

Callie heard, but she kept her gaze out the window, watching Mary return with Mr. MacDuff, her thoughts on Rossiter and how she'd like to be with him on the other side of the hill, all alone, feeling his lips against her own.

Lena's glance narrowed as she observed Callie; having raised two daughters, she recognized that lovesick expression when she saw it. Peering over the girl's shoulder and out the window, she saw MacDuff and little Mary coming around the carriage house. When she looked back at Callie, the friendliness was gone from her eyes. Something inside her seemed to go dead. What had MacDuff and this girl been up to? She herself had seen the way his eyes followed after Callie. He never looked at her that way, the way she *wanted* him to see her.

MacDuff went in to the carriage house, and Mary came through the back door, slamming the screen behind her. Lena went back to the kitchen, leaving Callie over the washboard. "I fed the chickens, Callie, and one of the brood hens had a new clutch of eggs. Will you come out and see them?"

"Not now, darling," Callie said. "There's too much to do today."

"Not even for a minute?" Mary watched Callie's face, waiting for her answer. She was unused to having Callie ignore her, and she was bewildered by it.

"Not today." Callie kept her eyes averted to the washtub, wringing out a petticoat. She knew how cutting her lack of interest was, how hurt Mary must be, yet she couldn't muster any enthusiasm for anything or anyone save Rossiter. Every waking moment, it seemed, was spent devising ways to be with him, to see him, to hear his voice. She spent hours dreaming about him, far more time than she actually spent with him. She disliked and resented the secretiveness, the hurried loving, how quickly he always left her afterward when she wished that he would hold her in his arms and share her deepest thoughts.

When he would leave her room at night, she would curl into her blankets, seeking the sleep that would not come. At these times she always felt on the brink of something wonderful that was just out of her reach, a dissatisfaction she could not name. She wondered why, after the loving, Rossiter seemed so content and sleepy while she herself felt she could climb the walls. Was there something she didn't know, something she was doing wrong? She loved being with him, feeling his nakedness against her own. She delighted in the way he touched her, the way he would whisper, telling her how she pleased him, how pretty she was. It didn't hurt when he entered her the way it had the first time, and her body seemed to relish his presence inside her, driving toward some mysterious end. But just as she could feel she was about to topple over the edge, to float out of herself, Rossiter would suddenly stiffen, becoming very still, squeezing his eyes shut in an exquisite agony. Then he would lie beside her, very quietly, and soon after would leave her.

"Callie, you're not even hearing me!" Mary interrupted her thoughts. "Why can't you come out to see the eggs? Mr. MacDuff said that in about a month's time we'll have new little chicks and he's hoping for a rooster. He says the one we have now is getting too old."

"I can't today, that's all. There's this laundry and potatoes to peel and cabbage crocks to scrub . . ." When Callie turned about, Mary was gone.

Late that afternoon, Callie went out into the yard to take down the laundry. Lena had scolded that it was nearly evening, and everything would get damp again from the night air. And it didn't look like it was going to get ironed today, after all, and Mrs. Powers better not be the wiser. Callie let the door close on Lena's parting statements. It seemed she couldn't do anything right these days.

The fresh evening wind billowed the ruffled petticoats, and Callie struggled to fold them and place them in the wicker basket. Suddenly two arms came around from behind, lifting her off her feet. A warm kiss was planted on the nape of her neck. "Rossiter!" she squealed.

"Shhh! Don't let anyone hear you! Come here," he commanded, pulling her by the hand across the yard, taking a quick, nervous glance back at the house. He took her through the wide doors of the carriage house into the deeper shadows behind the buggy. The air was pungent with the smell of horseflesh and earth, and he took her into his arms, kissing her deeply. His hands were on her back, holding her close, pressing her length against him, feeling the fullness of her breasts against his chest.

Callie clung to him, smelling the sunshine in his hair and tasting the salty perspiration on his lips. Her heart beat a wild rhythm, and she knew she had just pretended to be alive all day while she waited for this moment in his arms.

His fingers began playing with the buttons on the front of her black bombazine dress, hurriedly opening them, following their path with hot, searing kisses. Callie leaned back, affording him access to her body, her hips tilted forward pressing upon the swelling of his desire. He rucked up her skirts, groping between her legs, searching for the moist warmth he knew he would find there. Just as he was about to press her down to the ground, they heard the clatter of metal against metal and Hugh MacDuff's heavy footsteps.

Rossiter uttered an oath, quickly placing Callie away from him, adjusting his trousers. Callie gasped her disappointment, fussing with her hair and the opening of her dress front.

"Miss Callie?" Hugh called. "Callie, lass, are you in here?"

She struggled for her voice. "Yes, I'm here, Mr. MacDuff."

"I thought so. You left your laundry basket here by the door . . ." Stepping further into the carriage house, Hugh came upon them, immediately sensing their embarrassment, conscious of the fact that Master Rossiter avoided his eyes.

"Yes, well, I'd better take it into the house. Thank you, Mr. MacDuff." Gathering her skirts, Callie moved quickly to escape the questioning look on MacDuff's face.

"I . . . I was just showing Callie . . ." Rossiter began when she was gone.

MacDuff tilted his head back, arms crossed in front of him, drawing on his cold pipe. "What did you say you were showing Callie?" he challenged.

Rossiter laughed uneasily. "It doesn't matter." Then, assuming his authority over an employee, he said dryly, "Don't you have something to do, MacDuff? Why aren't you down to the ferry to carry *Papá* home?"

"Your father is staying in the city tonight, lad." Insolently he maintained his position, staring Rossiter down.

"Yes. Well, I'll be getting back to the house. Get on with what you were doing." Quickly Rossiter made his exit, escaping MacDuff's all-too-knowing eyes.

* * *

"Stick out your tongue, Rossiter," Anne Powers said sharply.

"*Mamán*, there's nothing wrong with me. Seeing my tongue isn't going to cure my headache. Stop fussing."

"Don't tell me there's nothing wrong with you. I'm your mother, and I know my children. You should see yourself, Rossiter. Your eyes are glassy, you're flushed, and your lips are a queer color. Now I want you upstairs and into bed this minute. I'll have Lena boil up some peppermint tea. A plaster on your chest and back won't do any harm either." She clucked like a mother hen, keeping up a running monologue as she walked Rossiter to his room.

God, did he feel rotten. He hadn't felt this terrible since he'd had pneumonia as a child. He wondered when his mother would discover how high his fever was.

"I wouldn't be surprised to know you've a fever, and it will only be worse come nightfall," she scolded, as though reading his mind. "It was all that slopping around in the rain, going barefoot in puddles."

He knew his mother well enough to know what she was not saying—that she suspected there was something between himself and Callie. He had not failed to notice her curious eyes as she watched Callie serve him at the dining table, and he was all too aware of her reasons for refusing to allow him to take Mary and her companion to the other side of the hill while he spent the afternoon painting. If he wasn't feeling so ill, he would have taken his mother to task for what she was thinking and would have charmed her right out of her suspicions.

"*Mamán*, my slopping around in the rain, as you call it, was two weeks ago. I hardly think it is the reason for the way I feel today."

"Nonsense! Regardless of when it was done, you did it, and I'm afraid you're going to pay for it!" She glared at him, clearly communicating to Rossiter that his illness was going to be a severe imposition on her, since she must nurse him back to health. "I intend to isolate you, Rossiter. We cannot have the rest of the family suffering because of your foolishness. You concentrate on getting well. When you've recovered, we can all go to Boston. I was going to surprise you with my plans, but they must be postponed until you're better."

Anne Powers bustled around the room, turning down Rossiter's bed and fluffing the pillows. "Here," she said, tossing him a clean nightshirt, "put this on and get under the covers immediately!"

Rossiter stepped into the tiny dressing room off his bedroom to comply with his mother's orders. Anne's taffeta skirt rustled as she moved about her son's room, straightening and fussing, moving his hairbrushes and shaving equipment into order on his dresser, picking up discarded shirts and adjusting the window shades. Her eyes fell upon his paints and canvases, and a sour expression lined her face. She liked to call it Rossiter's little hobby, but she was well aware of her son's ambitions to become an artist. Thankfully she was also well aware that Rossiter was without any driving motivation. He was still pliant and malleable to her notion that he follow his uncle and father into the world of finance. The boy simply needed a bit more maturing under her careful eye, and she believed he would not disappoint her.

Pushing aside the canvases and paint box, she noticed his sketch pad and his interpretation of the valley on the other side of the hill. It was quite good, really, she thought with a measure of pride, but then Rossiter could be successful at almost anything—with the right direction, of course. Direction she herself intended to bestow. Flipping over to the next page, Anne Powers's eyes narrowed, and she felt as though her air was being choked off. There was a drawing of Callie, done in pen and ink, the clear, level eyes staring out at her. But it was the style in which the drawing was done that alarmed her. Callie was reclining on a bed of flowers, one arm thrown over her head in a languishing pose that revealed the rounded contours of her body, one knee bent and lifted beneath the thin fabric of her skirt. Rossiter's sketch portrayed the image of a seductress, of a woman whose lover had just left her side. Sexuality was evident in the pouting mouth, the arch of the back, the swell of the breasts straining against an indecently low neckline. Anne Powers was stunned with revelation. Her mind's eyes still saw Callie as a skinny little girl with short, cropped hair and a child's pug nose. Where had she been looking when Callie grew into womanhood? And was this the way Rossiter saw her? Half-clothed, erotic, reeking with sensuality?

Quickly she shoved the sketch pad behind the canvases stacked on the floor. This would bear thinking about. Her mind went back to the day she'd witnessed Mary, Rossiter, and Callie romping in the rain, stomping through the puddles. Theirs had been the play of children, but even then she'd detected something between her son and the servant. It was in the way Callie had held onto Rossiter's arm, the way she smiled up into his face. It had all been there to see, but that fool Jasper had convinced her of their innocence!

Rossiter came out of his dressing room and climbed into bed, falling back against the pillows, too sick to notice the questioning appraisal in his mother's eyes. He was really sick. His head pounded, and every bone in his body ached.

Down in the kitchen, Anne Powers herself put on the kettle for Rossiter's tea. "Mix the plasters for Rossiter's chest, Lena," she directed, tying a white baker's apron over her dark blue afternoon dress. "I think I will have to send MacDuff into St. George for Dr. Margolis. Rossiter is ill, and we'll be fortunate if it doesn't prove to be pneumonia."

Lena was wordless as she gathered the ingredients for the mustard plasters. There was something about Mrs. Powers that forbade conversation. The woman seemed preoccupied with her thoughts, and there was a definite scowl about her mouth that lent to her severity.

"Lena," Mrs. Powers said, turning suddenly. "I've decided that my son needs complete rest. Complete and total, without any disturbances. I will tend to him myself, and he will be confined to his room. For all intents and purposes, I don't wish to have his presence known for a few days at least. That means, Lena, you will not inform the children or Mary's companion that Rossiter is confined to his room. Since it is at the back of the house, I don't anticipate any difficulty. Mary and her companion will be told to confine their activities to the nursery. Not a word, Lena. If Master Rossiter is inquired about, you know nothing. Am I understood?"

Lena dropped her eyes to the bowl she was mixing and nodded. She understood the words, but she understood the threat better. Ever since MacDuff had confided to her how he'd come upon Callie and Master Rossiter in the carriage house, her jealousy of the young girl had disappeared. It wasn't MacDuff who had the girl lovesick, it was the young master. Poor Callie. How unfair life could be, especially with Mrs. Powers calling the plays.

"You'll pass the word to MacDuff. I don't want him giving out any secrets once he gets a few drinks in him. I'll hold you responsible, Lena. Do we understand each other?"

"Yes, Mrs. Powers," Lena agreed, stirring briskly. She understood all right, better than anyone else.

"Rossiter is quite ill. Brave boy that he is, he tried to deny it. We'll do our best today, and if there's no improvement by tomorrow, then we'll send for a doctor."

Lena frowned. It was "we," as though Mrs. Powers had found a co-conspirator. "I'll bring up the plaster as soon as it's finished."

"Be certain to warm the flannel first," Anne Powers directed, picking up the tea tray. Lena grimaced. As if she didn't know enough to warm the flannel. If memory served her right, she had been the one who made plasters for Mr. Powers years ago and had shown Mrs. Powers how to do it. She was out of sorts today, and this encounter with Mrs. Powers wasn't helping. Lena liked to think of herself as being a straightforward person, and she didn't care for trickery or deceit. Maybe Mrs. Powers was Rossiter's mother and Callie's employer, but that didn't give her the right to— Lena clamped down on the thought. There she was again, poking her nose in where it didn't belong. At her age a new position would be hard to find and without excellent references, damn near impossible. Things would work out in their own good time, she was sure of it.

Callie was called down to the parlor by Mrs. Powers herself. Outside the weather promised rain, and she expected to see Rossiter about the house after Mary's lessons with Mr. Reader, but he was nowhere in sight.

"Callie," Mrs. Powers began, "Mary is looking a little peaked to me these days. I think, perhaps, she's overtired from running about the countryside. Also, I believe she's been neglecting her lessons. Therefore, I would prefer that she keep to her room for the next several days. You, of course, are to stay with her. I believe there are hems on several of her dresses that need altering. Since I'm not entertaining and Miss Anne will be staying in the city with friends, you will not be needed to serve at table."

Anne Powers's eyes burned into Callie. Yes, it was there if one looked for it. A certain maturing, a blossoming, if one cared to call it that. Callie James was hardly a child any longer. She resolved she was doing the right thing by enforcing this separation from the all-too-vulnerable Rossiter. Men never knew what was best for them. As soon as he was well, she would spirit him off to Boston and then rid this family of his temptation—namely, Callie James.

Callie squirmed beneath Anne Powers's glare. Was she mistaken or was there a definite hostility there and an increased coldness in her tone? It was clear that she was being banished to the nursery along with Mary, but the question was why? A sound from the dining room made her lift her head expectantly. It was only Lena. Where was Rossiter? Had he gone into town? He hadn't mentioned anything last night when he'd come up to her room.

"You are excused," Mrs. Powers said imperiously. "See that you follow my instructions."

"Yes, Mrs. Powers . . ." A great sneeze suddenly tore out of Callie, and she groped in her pocket for her handkerchief.

Mrs. Powers's eyes widened, then narrowed. "It seems you're coming down with a cold, Callie," she said smoothly. "Now where in the world would you have caught that? Perhaps it will be necessary to confine you to your room. We can't have Mary catching it, can we? I will let you know."

Long after Callie left the parlor, Anne Powers's face held a bitter sneer. *Yes, I'll let you know, Callie James. And when I do, you'll be out on your ear and good riddance to bad rubbish!*

Late that night Callie lay awake in her bed, listening for the sound of Rossiter's footstep outside her door. It never came.

Chapter Fifteen

The following day Rossiter's condition was not improved, and Anne Powers sent MacDuff into St. George for Dr. Margolis, a dark, romantic figure of a man who was new to Staten Island. She had met him on one other occasion at a dinner given by mutual friends, and she was much impressed with the middle-aged bachelor. Today she dressed in a royal-blue afternoon dress shot with silver thread in a pattern of delicate leaves. The cut of the dress with its dropped waistline gave her slenderness a willowy appearance that added to her height. She had dressed her jet hair into a severe coil, which she believed added drama to her angular features.

Dr. Margolis arrived just after lunch, and Anne was certain Mary and Callie were up on the third floor. Jasper was still at the office, having remained in the city overnight. It had occurred to her from time to time to wonder if her husband had a woman somewhere in the city, but the idea was so repulsive to her that she had banished the thought.

After examining Rossiter, the physician came to the same conclusion as Anne. A summer cold. Nasty and miserable, but only a cold. "Still," he said, aware of Anne's disappointment that Rossiter's illness was so terribly ordinary, "it bears watching. Perhaps

I'll come out tomorrow and check on the young man." Anne seemed pleased with this and smiled her approval.

Evan Margolis was a tall, swarthy man, just a shade too dark and a shade too thin. Yet he dressed in the height of fashion, and his grooming was impeccable. The fact that he was an eligible bachelor added to his acceptance in the Staten Island community of social matrons. An extra man at a party was so valuable. His attention to this thin, severe, angular woman was wholly based on the fact that she carried a good deal of weight in the community, and her approval and friendship would place him in good stead with the best people.

Following him down the stairs to the front hall, Anne wrung her hands together. "Do you really think he'll be all right, doctor?"

"Yes, of course. It's the change in the weather, I believe. So many others are bothered with the same complaints. Keep him quiet, change the plaster tomorrow, and force liquids on him. Keep him warm, close all the windows, and don't let this miserable damp air into the room. He'll mend, Mrs. Powers. He's a strapping young man." He turned at the door, facing her, concern evident in his expression. "I don't want you overtaxing yourself. Get the servants to spell you in the sick room. We don't want you coming down with the same illness, do we?"

Anne smiled shyly, playing the coquette. What a nice man the doctor was, so considerate. And so handsome and distinguished with just the barest touch of silver near the temples. "I do want to thank you for coming so promptly, Dr. Margolis. Do you know, doctor," she blurted in a sudden burst of confidence, "if I hadn't married, I think I would have become a nurse. As it was, I wanted so much to offer my services down at the hospital in Tompkinsville, but Mr. Powers wouldn't hear of it. He said a woman of my class and breeding just doesn't do things like that."

Evan Margolis's dark blue eyes widened. He knew he was supposed to say something flattering, but it was difficult to think about such trivial matters when he knew the next patient he was to visit was terminally ill. Still, Mrs. Powers's influence would be valuable to a physician starting a new practice. "May I say, Mrs. Powers, that it is our loss you didn't go into nursing. We need dedication in that honorable profession. Most women are afraid of the sight of blood and hard work. So often I believe women are only interested in wearing a little white cap and brewing tea. There's so much more to the profession, as I am certain you know."

Anne Powers blanched slightly. How did he know she only

had a hankering for that small, starched white hat? Blood always made her gag. Especially her own.

"If you would like to call upon me at my office, I can direct you to ways you can help the sick. Perhaps you'd like to work in the clinic I've a notion of starting. But," he held up a warning finger, "only if you're serious."

"I am, Dr. Margolis. I'll be certain to do as you suggest when I return from Boston. I plan to take the children as soon as Rossiter is well enough to travel."

"Whatever suits you, madame. Angels of mercy are in short supply. Bedpans, it seems, are always disagreeable, and one must be terribly dedicated." A soft white hand, which Anne thought of as a pianist's hand, was laid gently upon her shoulder. "Think about it, Mrs. Powers, Anne, and come to me when you feel you can give of yourself."

Bedpans! Good God, she hadn't thought about those! She swallowed hard. Anne, he'd called her Anne. "Certainly. Although, I may be gone for some time, and then there's my other charities to be considered."

"Any time," Evan Margolis said as he pushed his hat down over his thick, wavy hair.

How distinguished he appeared wearing his fedora. Good God, she was feeling like a school girl with a crush on her teacher.

She schooled her face to impassivity. "I'll be in touch. But, of course, I'll expect to see you tomorrow." What was this sudden rush she felt going to her head? Evan Margolis was so tall, so dangerously handsome. Logical answers darted through her brain. She was only feeling this attraction, this desire to swoon into his arms because of what was going on between Rossiter and the Irish girl. But his hand felt so warm in hers, so strong. She felt herself being to sway. His arms came around to capture her, holding her firmly against himself. Anne Powers's face tilted upwards; his lips were so near, so devastatingly close. Impulsively her arms slid around his neck, her lips found his, and she kissed him, feeling as though her feet had left the floor, that her foundations had been swept away.

Evan Margolis responded passively, alarmed by this sudden display of emotion from a woman whom he had considered cool and poised, if not frigid. He was used to having his women patients entertain romantic thoughts about him, but he'd never quite encountered this kind of surprising advance. It was quite possible the woman was mad! But to risk offending her was to jeopardize the inroads he was making in the community.

Pulling away from him, Anne Powers was aghast at what she had done. "I'm . . . I'm so terribly . . ." she stuttered.

Dr. Margolis recognized the opportunity to place himself forever in the lady's good graces. "No, no, dear lady," he soothed, "it is my place to beg your forgiveness. I'm afraid I was quite overcome by your charms."

Anne Powers stared at him, grateful for his valor, flattered by his admission that he was powerless to resist her charms.

"A bachelor like myself is quite vulnerable to a woman like you. Say you will forgive me."

"Tomorrow, then," she tried for a lightness in her tone. She held the door for him, watching him hurry to his big buggy. Already she was planning what to wear for his next visit. A dab of cologne wouldn't hurt. Men did like a touch of scent. Perhaps she would ask him to stay for tea.

Callie stared anxiously out the nursery window. The raindrops against the pane were like tears falling. She had stayed awake until early morning and still Rossiter had not come to her. Why? She asked herself over and over. Was he tiring of her? All day yesterday she had not seen him, and since she and Mary had been confined to the third floor, she had not seen him at dinner either. She was half-crazy.

Careful questioning of Mary had produced no results. She hadn't seen her brother either and had heard nothing from her *Mamán* nor anyone else. Callie knew her neglect of Mary these past weeks was unforgivable, and she deeply regretted it, but it seemed she couldn't gain control of herself or her emotions. Nothing and no one existed, except him.

"Mary, would you like to try on your green gingham so I can measure the hem. Then perhaps we can read a story . . ." Turning, Callie realized Mary was no longer in the nursery. Puzzled, she went out into the hall and into her own room, thinking the child might have gone in there, but with no results. Going back into the nursery, she noticed for the first time that the lunch tray was missing. Mary must have taken it downstairs to the kitchen with the hope of begging cookies from Lena. "Mary Powers," Callie muttered, "you'd better hope your mother doesn't catch you. When she says we're to stay upstairs, that's exactly what she means!"

Callie headed for the stairs, carefully tiptoeing past Mrs. Powers's room on the second floor. She debated using the back stairs but thought she'd have a better chance of encountering

Mary in the front of the house. She went quietly along the hallway to the main stairs, alert for the slightest sound. Halfway down, with a clear view of the front door, she stood in shock. Mrs. Powers was hard in the embrace of a tall, dark man, and she was kissing him! "Tomorrow then," she heard the familiar voice say to the man before she held the door open for him and watched him leave. All instincts told Callie she had just witnessed something she wasn't supposed to have seen. Just as she was about to turn around and go back upstairs, Mrs. Powers suddenly looked up. The shock that leaped from her eyes dissolved into an open hatred. For a long, long moment Mrs. Powers held Callie in her stare, as though challenging her to utter a word. Then silently the woman turned and went into the front parlor, closing the door behind her.

Unknown to either Mrs. Powers or Callie, Mary was just coming down the hall from the dining room, carrying a pitcher of milk and a plate of cookies. She had hidden behind the door when she saw her mother and a tall man walk to the front hall. She hadn't known *Mamán* had guests. What she saw next shook her to the foundations. *Mamán* was kissing the strange man. Mary's mouth dropped open, her cinnamon eyes widened. *Mamán* never kissed anybody except Rossiter! *Mamán* never even kissed *Papá*!

Mary saw her mother show the man out of the house, and then something very curious happened. *Mamán* glanced upward. A bitter expression, like the one when she scolded, passed over her face. Then she quietly went into the parlor and closed the doors behind her.

Mary thought better of using the front stairs to go back to the nursery, so she turned and went through the kitchen again, heading for the back staircase.

Anne Powers lay quietly musing on the chair beside Rossiter's bed, a cup of cold tea at her elbow. Neither food nor drink appealed to her. Her active mind would not allow anything but thoughts of Evan Margolis. What a fool she'd been! A kiss meant nothing to him, of that she was certain. Yet he didn't seem to be the kind of man Anne herself would call a womanizer. Surely, if he were, it would be the source of gossip. Evan Margolis had an impeccable reputation as far as she knew. So, she thought egotistically, the man must be smitten with her. Now whatever might have come of it was ruined because of that little Irish bitch sneaking around the stairs. Just as soon as Anne Powers returned from Boston,

Callie James would find herself without a position. Damn Jasper and his protectiveness toward the girl. As soon as she told him what had been going on between her and his son, Jasper would sing a different tune! It was time for Mary to go to boarding school. Children from the best families attended. Besides, it was time, Anne thought to herself, that she found a way to escape the rigors of motherhood. She was still a young woman! Still attractive! It was her time, after all these years of child-rearing, to think of herself for a change.

As Anne Powers mused, a terrible thought occurred to her. She couldn't tell Jasper what she suspected was going on between her son and his little Irish girl. What if Callie were to retaliate by informing Jasper how she'd seen his wife in the arms of a strange man? The thought that someone could point a finger at her, especially someone as far beneath her as a servant, made Anne's veins turn to ice, feeding the hatred she was already feeling.

No, she told herself. Don't be hasty. The time will come. For the time being, it will be enough to separate Rossiter from that girl. There would be time later to dismiss her, when she returned from Boston, without Rossiter.

Her mind switched to the preparations she would make for the trip—clothes to pack, letters to be written, Jasper to be dealt with. Her brother Stephen was embarking on a new business venture. With a little prodding, she knew she could elicit his help to entice Jasper to Boston. There was nothing Jasper liked more than to put his finger in a new pie, especially if it promised to be profitable. Her eyes fell on Rossiter, sleeping heavily in the bed beside her. Boston was just what Rossiter needed. Boston with its social life, with all the world's culture, with lovely, rich, suitable girls. Perhaps it was time for her son to take a wife. Anne leaned back, resting her head, her thoughts whirling as she counted her Bostonian friends who had eligible daughters. Rossiter would make a dazzling match, she was certain of it.

The late spring rains continued for nearly ten days, and Callie was fraught with depression. In all this time she'd not seen nor heard a word of Rossiter. He had not come to her room at night, and when she peered out the window down the drive hoping for sight of him, none came. No one came or went from the Powers's house except Mary's tutor and the tall, dark stranger she had seen kissing Mrs. Powers.

Callie didn't try to fool herself. She knew that because of what she'd accidentally seen, she had made a terrible enemy in the woman. No reminders were needed to encourage her to stay up on the third floor with her young charge who was becoming more restless by the hour. Even Mary wondered where Rossiter was, and several times she had the occasion to ask her mother. Anne Powers answered in an offhanded way that Rossiter was not at home.

"I've never seen you so jittery, Callie. Is there anything I can do? Do you think you're still sick from your cold? Lena has all kinds of remedies for colds. Do you want me to ask her?"

"No, darling. I guess I'm just thinking about home and my mother. I miss her and my family very much."

Mary's small face turned downward in a frown. "I'm sorry you miss your mother, Callie. I would just die if I was sent away from my family. Especially *Papá*." Clearly Mary was thinking of the secret about her hearing.

Callie fingered the locket around her neck. She'd lost track of the times she'd opened it to look at Rossiter's picture. Where was he? Why didn't he come to see her? What had she done?

The rain beat against the window relentlessly. If only it would stop! Then perhaps she and Mary would be allowed to go downstairs; then perhaps she could learn something about Rossiter. She was staring out the window with her nose pressed against the steamy glass when Jasper Powers knocked on the door and called her name. Callie turned in a rush, certain he was going to tell her something about Rossiter.

"Callie, Mrs. Powers and I will be taking Rossiter and Anne to Boston tomorrow. We're leaving you in charge of Mary."

Callie's heart missed a beat. "How long will you be gone, Mr. Powers?"

"It's hard to tell. Several weeks at least. Possibly a month."

"Why is Rossiter going?" Mary squealed. "Rossiter is all grown up and doesn't need any more culture. Why can't Callie and I go? Why don't I ever get to go anywhere, *Papá*?"

"Because you're too little," Jasper said fondly as he rumpled her curls. "It won't be too much for you, will it, Callie? You won't want for anything. Lena will be here, of course, and MacDuff. I'll tell him to take you and Mary into town for ice cream."

Mary pouted, angry that she was always left behind. "I still don't see why Rossiter is going. I haven't seen him for a week. Where is he, *Papá*?"

"Rossiter has been under the weather with the worst sort of summer cold. It settled in his chest, and your *Mamán* has been nursing him round the clock. He's on the mend, and your mother feels that this trip is just what he needs to get him back on his feet."

He was alive. He hadn't deserted her. He was sick. The world was once again right side up. The sun was shining in her heart. Pray. She had to remember to pray this evening. For what? a niggling voice asked. He's going away. His mother is taking him with her tomorrow. You won't see him. But he hasn't deserted me. He was sick, her heart sang. He'll come back and . . . he'll come back.

The smile she favored Jasper Powers with was dazzling. Jasper was so fond of this girl with her bright blue eyes and spirited disposition. Whatever Anne was hinting at between Callie and Rossiter was ridiculous. Callie was hardly more than a child, and Jasper knew his son's tastes ran toward more sophisticated girls from extremely wealthy families.

The first light of a new day pierced the dimness of Callie's attic room. She could hear birds singing and smell the fragrance of new grasses and budding flowers through her open window. At last the rain had stopped. The world was alive. But she was dead, had died during the night as she lay awake listening and waiting for Rossiter. He was leaving today, leaving her. Surely somehow, some way, he could have come to her. He'd been ill, but now he was well enough to travel. How could he just leave this way? Why? Tears burned her eyes, and she fought to keep them from slipping down her cheeks.

Last evening Mary had been called downstairs to bid her good-byes to the family. Because of their early departure, they explained to their youngest daughter, there would be little time in the morning. As far as Callie knew, Mary was still asleep in the nursery next door.

Callie stretched, her body stiff and unyielding. More than anything she wanted to go downstairs for a glimpse of Rossiter. More than anything she wanted to hear him tell her he'd soon return and look into her eyes with unspoken promises. But he had not come to her, he was keeping himself from her, and her pride would not allow her to beg his favors now. Far below, on the first floor, she could hear the distant booming of Jasper's voice and Mrs. Powers's shrill directives. Finally, unable to stop herself, she went to the window, looking down into the drive, praying for and dreading a last glimpse of Rossiter.

Below, Rossiter sat at the dining-room table with his sister and parents. He was becoming exceedingly angry with his mother's undue attention. It was as though she were reluctant to let him out of her sight! "Perhaps I'll go upstairs and give the tadpole a last kiss," he said offhandedly. "I really can't see why we don't bring Mary with us. She loves going to Boston, and things can get a bit dull around here during the summer."

"You will do no such thing!" Anne Powers hissed. "I will not have you waking that child and subject me to a last-minute fit of hysteria just before we leave. It's better that she sleeps and we leave quietly. Any goodbyes that are necessary were said last evening."

"Yes, perhaps you're right, *Mamán*. You're always right, *Mamán*," Rossiter murmured, not trying to hide the derision in his tone. Jasper caught it, though, and peered at his son over the rim of his cup. Rossiter's inclination to go upstairs for a moment with Callie dissolved. He was angry and offended that during his illness she had not once come to his room to inquire after him or to help him while away the lonely hours. Several times during the past few days, when he was feeling more like himself, he had been tempted to go upstairs after everyone was asleep, but his pride would not allow it, however great his need. With the disappearance of his fever, his baser needs had returned, and the satisfaction for those hungers lay just a floor above him. But it had become obvious to him that Callie neither sought nor welcomed his attentions.

"Your mother is right, Rossiter. Although I quite agree with you, I can't see the sense in leaving Mary here."

"Jasper!" Anne turned on her husband. "If you think I want to spend my holiday chasing after that child, you're sadly mistaken. Am I not entitled to a lessening of my responsibilities?"

Clattering his cup back into its saucer, Jasper said, "Dammit! Why don't we bring Callie with us? She'll look after Mary for you, she always does. And the apartments in Boston are certainly large enough to accommodate one small girl and her companion."

"No. Absolutely not! Think of it, Jasper. Mary would be confined to the apartment; the city streets are no place for a child. At least here she has the run of the yard, and MacDuff will take them into Richmond or St. George for a bit of diversion."

"That's not what you said two weeks ago! You said Mary was becoming a little savage and needed to be subdued. That was why you ordered Mary and Callie confined to the nursery, or am I mistaken?"

"No, you're not mistaken. And it accomplished just what I set out to do. Now, I'll not hear another word."

Rossiter pretended interest in the scone he was buttering. His ears were pricked when Jasper mentioned Mary and Callie being confined to the nursery. *That* was why Callie hadn't come to see him as he lay in bed recovering. She was under orders from his mother!

"I must admit, *Papá*," said Anne, "It will be quite a relief not to have that little brat underfoot along with her companion!" The imperious tilting of her sharp little chin set her glossy dark curls bobbing. "Perhaps now that Rossiter is well again, *Mamán* can turn her attention to me for a change. *Mamán* was positively encamped in Rossiter's room for practically the entire time he was unwell. It's a wonder to me how she didn't catch whatever it was he had." She turned to her brother. "Did you know that when she wasn't sleeping in your room, she slept in the guest room just across the hall from you so she could hear your every breath!"

Rossiter's eyes went from his sister to his mother. His brows shot up in surprise when he recognized triumph in his mother's face. She knew! Or if she didn't exactly know, then she suspected, which with a woman like his mother was almost as deadly. He must get upstairs to see Callie before he left. Wiping his mouth on the fine linen napkin, Rossiter pushed away from the table.

"Where are you going? You've hardly touched your breakfast." Anne challenged.

"I'm going upstairs to my room. I think I've forgotten to pack some of my paints—"

"No, absolutely not! Whatever you've forgotten you can purchase in Boston."

"*Mamán*, I am going upstairs."

Anne Powers fixed her son with an authoritative gaze, her mouth set in a tight, grim line. "Sit down, Rossiter," she ordered. "Sit and finish your breakfast." Her tone was quiet, almost devoid of emotion, but the message was clear. And the boy in Rossiter complied, obeying his mother as he had since he was a child, too much in awe of her authority to argue.

Picking up his fork, Rossiter began to nibble at the coddled eggs on his plate. If only, if only she weren't so strong . . . if only he weren't so weak. He wasn't certain exactly what his feelings for Callie meant; he only knew he wanted to see her, to tell her goodbye for now, that before summer's end he would return.

The thought brought him comfort. There was no need to go against his mother. In a few short weeks' time he would return, and he and Callie could pick up where they'd left off. He felt his appetite returning and his annoyance at being treated like a child begin to fade. Before summer's end, he promised himself again.

* * *

Lessons, games, long walks over the hill, rides into town with Hugh MacDuff all became deadly chores for Callie as the days wore on and she missed Rossiter more every minute. One week passed, then two and then three with no word from him. Letters came for Mary from her parents, but any mention of Rossiter or what he was doing or when he was expected back home was vague. Week four and then five slipped into six. The hot days of August were upon them, and the breezes that blew in from the bay were heavy with humidity. Callie became dull-eyed and gaunt; violet smudges stained her eyelids. There was a chilling kind of beauty to her as she imagined she struggled with her sanity. A letter arrived from Ireland and remained on her dresser unopened. She didn't want to hear from Peggy nor read any rebukes concerning the scarcity of her own letters home. All she could think about, all she wanted to think about, was Rossiter.

What could she have done to make him leave without a parting word? Why hadn't he at least written her? If only she didn't feel so tired and ill all the time. If only she could keep more than tea and broth in her stomach. The mirror told her she was looking as she had when she first came to America. Her reflection alarmed her. There in her own eyes she could see the image of Beth Thatcher—the same desperation burning, the same helplessness. As she stared at her reflection, she thought at least she knew what Beth had felt for Patrick and why she'd done what she'd done. Callie herself would have turned the world inside out if it would mean Rossiter's happiness and that he'd come back to her.

Hugh MacDuff took a paternal interest in his young friend, helping her with her little patch of garden and making suggestions of activities that might break her lethargy. He discussed Callie with Lena, who tried her best to mother the girl without seeming to interfere. Both she and MacDuff were becoming alarmed by her appearance and her loss of spirit. Mary was not oblivious to Callie's lack of interest in everything. She sorely missed Callie's attention and company, but quietly went about her activities, silent and subdued. She contented herself with having the run of the house and doing as she pleased for long hours at a time.

"The postman! The postman is here," Mary shouted as she ran to the door to greet him. "Look, Lena, there's a letter for Mr. MacDuff from *Papá*! Fetch him quick so he can tell us what it says. Hurry, Lena, while I get Callie!"

Lena ran to call MacDuff into the kitchen so he could read his letter. Callie followed Mary downstairs, eagerly anticipating any news of Rossiter.

Hugh MacDuff slit the envelope with the point of his pocket-knife, making great ceremony over the event. By the time he ran his work-calloused hand through his hair and perched his spectacles on the bridge of his nose, Callie was ready to scream. Surely there would be news of Rossiter. Some small bit concerning him. MacDuff cleared his throat and read, his Scottish burr lending its note to Jasper's written words.

Dear Mr. MacDuff,

Please be at the ferry in St. George to meet Mrs. Powers and Miss Anne on the afternoon of the 7th September approximately three o'clock. I will not be returning with them as I have business here that has not been completed. I am trusting you are overseeing the farm in Kreischerville. Master Rossiter will remain here with me, and I trust you to look after my family in my absence. A letter will follow to dear Mary.

Regards,
Jasper Powers

MacDuff extended the letter to Callie, his light gray eyes watching her sorrowfully. Callie shook her head and put out her hand as though to push the letter away. She felt so choked she thought she would faint. Lena led her to a chair and rushed to get her a cup of tea. MacDuff watched Callie's pain, twisting the letter in his huge hands. He felt so useless. Poor Callie. What would happen to her? Who would watch after her?

"Mary, darlin'," Lena said, "don't you think you should check on those new chicks? It's terribly hot, and they might need cool water." Mary ran outside, and Lena indicated to Hugh that he should follow.

Alone with Callie, Lena sat opposite her. The time had come for some straight talk. "Callie, girl, there's no use you pining after Master Rossiter. I think his mother got wind of what was going on between the two of you, just as MacDuff and myself did. Mrs. Powers isn't about to allow her son to come back here to you. I've a good idea she's plotting how to rid herself of you this very minute. You'd best accept that fact, child, right here and now and start worrying what you're going to do with the baby."

Callie raised startled eyes, her lower lip quivering, "What baby?"

"Good God, girl, the child you're carrying. Master Rossiter's baby. That's what I'm talking about."

"How . . . how do you know?"

"I've had two girls of my own and both of them mothers. All I have to do is look at you and I can see. Mrs. Powers will know too, soon as she sets eyes on you. You'd best be thinking of what you'll do."

Callie looked at Lena blankly, too startled for tears, knowing the truth although she'd been denying it even to herself. How stupid she felt. A baby. Quickly she let her mind calculate, and when she fixed her mind on the right date, she paled. Merciful God! No, no, it couldn't be true, but it was and she knew it.

"You can't be far along, child. Think, how long has it been?"

"Since just before my birthday."

Lena counted on her fingers. "Your birthday was April eleventh and now it's . . . Lord, Callie, you're nearly four months along! I . . . I don't know what to say," she fretted. "What I do know is that life here in the house will be unbearable when Mrs. Powers discovers what you've been up to!"

Callie hung her head in shame. It was all too ugly. Something so beautiful between Rossiter and herself had suddenly become very ugly. And the shame of it was carried in her belly.

"Don't be thinking Mr. Powers will intervene in your behalf, Callie. There's a difference between rich people and folks like us. They never mix, you can count on it. We've got to think of what you can do. Do you have any friends or relatives here who might be willing to help?"

Callie thought of her cousin Owen Gallagher and Madge. She shook her head. Not for the world would she even consider Byrch Kenyon. He had done enough for her, given her a chance, and she couldn't go crying to him now.

"Don't be dreaming and fooling yourself that you'll be allowed to stay here. This won't be the first time a rich woman's son got a servant with child. It's simply not tolerated, and somehow if you're rich, you don't have to struggle with your conscience. We've got to start planning for you, but I have to admit, I don't know where to start. MacDuff might have some ideas. He's got friends in the city, not that you'd ever know, the way he keeps his lip buttoned. You drink this tea now, it's cooled enough. Better yet, take it to your room, and I'll keep my eye on Mary. She'll be busy for a while yet with the new chicks. Don't be despairing now, we've still got time before Mrs. Powers comes home."

Callie hated to say it, and the words almost stuck in her throat, but she had to say it nevertheless. "Rossiter," she managed to croak, "I've got to tell Rossiter."

"I understand that, child, but I doubt you'll be getting the chance to say anything to young Master Rossiter. You have to start thinking for yourself now because he isn't here to help you. Master Rossiter has a way to go before he becomes a man." The child had to know. Had to believe. He was a boy still with his mama pampering him. He was probably off somewhere painting his pictures that no one wanted to buy or chasing another skirt. She snorted at the unworthy occupation.

"No, Lena. Rossiter told me he loved me. If he knew about this, he would rush home to me. I know it. He said he loved me, Lena."

"All men say that," Lena said. "All they want from a young girl like yourself is one thing. No man likes to take responsibility. Master Rossiter has a good many oats to sow yet, and he won't be tying himself down with a wife and baby, even if his mama would allow it, which she won't. I'm not trying to be cruel, Callie," Lena added kindly. "I don't want to see you get hurt more than you are now."

"I'll write a letter to him and tell him," Callie said. "As soon as he knows, he'll come home. He said he loved me, Lena, and I believed him."

"I'm sure, lass, that he did mean it when he said it, but now that he isn't here and he's in Boston where his mama is jamming society down his throat . . ." What was the use, the child didn't need more misery. She would have to find out the hard way, the way all women found out. "Go along, Callie, and rest a bit. I have some tall thinking to do. We'll watch out for Miss Mary."

Callie dragged herself back to her rooms. A baby. Rossiter's baby. Her hand went to the round of her stomach and stayed there for a moment.

I won't feel ashamed. I won't. Anything as wonderful as their love couldn't be shameful. It just couldn't. Rossiter *did* mean everything he said. He wouldn't lie to her. Rossiter wasn't like that. Callie buried her head in her pillow as sobs racked her body. Small, clenched fists pounded the pillows. He did love her. He did!

Chapter Sixteen

Mrs. Powers and Anne returned on a glorious September day, full of the wild colors of summer and sunshine. Callie ached as she stood by the nursery window watching Mary run to her mother, holding out her arms. Anne Powers swooped down and folded the child against her, but not before she let her eyes travel to the third-floor window where Callie was watching. Callie wished she could run into Peggy's arms just that way, to be held and mothered and clucked over and made to believe that nothing was so important as what was making Callie unhappy. But Callie couldn't even unburden herself by confiding in Peggy. It would break her mother's heart to know she had disgraced herself. Also, one of Peggy's letters stood clearly in Callie's mind.

It was the letter in answer to the one Callie had sent that was filled with descriptions of Rossiter. Callie had been so overwhelmed by his trifling gift of the shell comb that she just had to share it with someone she loved. Peggy's returning letter was filled with news of the family and local gossip that would interest Callie. But midway through, giving it a place of little importance, wise Peggy had issued her warning. "You have always been such a good girl, my Callie, and your mother's treasure. I miss those long talks we used to have over a cuppa tea. Often you'd make me angry when you'd talk down your own Da, and I used to tell you that only in giving your heart completely to the one you loved, if it was deserved or not, could you find real happiness. I still believe a woman should give her heart over to her husband. It takes a world of trust to do that, I know, but if a man speaks for a girl and marries her, it is the least she can give him."

That had been the turning phrase, the warning—"To her husband," Peggy had said. Callie had cried when she'd read the letter. She'd called her Mum a fool for loving Thom the way she did, for defending him and overlooking his lack of responsibility. But if Da had done nothing else in his entire life for Mum, he had married her, and the children, however sorry their state, carried his name. But what saddened Callie most of all was the faith Peggy had in her, a trust that had been betrayed almost from the moment Callie had set eyes upon Rossiter.

It seemed hours before Mary returned to the nursery with two gaily wrapped presents. "From *Papá*, Callie," Mary squealed happily. "Isn't it wonderful that we're a family again? Well, almost a family. *Papá* isn't back yet, and neither is Rossiter. At least I think Rossiter will come home with *Papá*. *Mamán* didn't say for sure." If only Mary knew how Callie held her breath, hoping for more news of Rossiter.

"Why . . . why didn't your brother come home with your mother?" Callie finally mustered the courage to ask.

"You know why." Mary looked at her friend, puzzled. "It was there in *Papá*'s letter to Mr. MacDuff. He's staying in Boston with *Papá*. Maybe *Papá* is teaching him how to do business. And *Mamán* told me a secret." Mary lowered her voice conspiratorially. "He's found a girl in Boston, and *Mamán* thinks it's a perfect match. Anne said it was. Anne said that all the young ladies in Boston had their caps set for Rossiter because he's so handsome. Isn't that wonderful, Callie? Just think, Rossiter might get married. *Mamán* will be so happy." Mary was tearing through the wrapping paper. "Look, Callie, *Papá* sent a doll almost like the one Rossiter gave me. Now I can pretend they're sisters. No, I'll pretend one is you and one is me. What's your present, Callie?"

Callie opened her box and withdrew a lavender lace shawl. She hardly noticed the fine lace, her thoughts were so filled with Rossiter and unanswered questions.

"It's beautiful," Mary sighed. "Almost beautiful enough to get married in, but you're supposed to wear white, aren't you?" Mary poked beneath the doll's dress to see what she was wearing underneath.

"I think so. I'll put this away. Why don't you play with your dolls? I want to write a letter and post it tomorrow."

"You'll have to post it after you see *Mamán*. She said to tell you to come to her directly after breakfast. Just you, Callie. She told me to stay here in the nursery."

Callie's heart thumped wildly. She had been expecting the summons, so it came as no surprise. Later, she would worry about it later, but not now. Now she was going to write a letter to Rossiter.

Settling herself on the edge of the bed, she selected a sheet of the stationery Byrch Kenyon had given her for her birthday. Her birthday, the day she had first met Rossiter. She would never have another birthday without thinking of him. She stared at the blank page for a long time. How should she tell him? What were the words? In the end, it was a simple little letter:

Dear Rossiter,

I am truly sorry you did not return with your mother and sister. I miss you very much. I am writing to tell you some news, and I know when you learn it, you will come home. I will be waiting. I am going to have your baby. I love you, Rossiter, and I know that you love me. You said you loved me, and I believed you.

Please hurry home so that we can be together again. I forgive you for not writing to me and for not saying goodbye before you left. I need to know what to do. Should I tell your mother, or should I wait till you return?

Your devoted love,
Callie

Callie read and reread the letter. It said everything she had to say. Now she would have to wait for Rossiter to answer. Maybe he would rush home to her instead of writing. A prayer filled her heart.

It was impossible to sleep. Rossiter's face kept stealing into her dreams. Rossiter had said he loved her, and she believed him. Something kept niggling at her brain, like a little fish nibbling at the bait. *Had* Rossiter told her he loved her? Or had he said he liked loving her? Was there really a difference? Her mind denied it.

She simply hadn't heard from Rossiter because he was a man and he didn't like to write letters. Her excuses for him became legion. He hadn't come to say goodbye because it was a sad business and he was sparing her the misery. Rossiter just didn't realize how important he was to her; men just didn't understand things like that.

Lordy, her head ached. If she didn't get some sleep, she was going to look as if someone had taken a club to her in the morning. It was important to be at her best when she saw Mrs. Powers after breakfast.

Dawn was creeping into day when Callie finally closed her eyes. She woke a short time later feeling sluggish and sick to her stomach. She hated this queasiness that was almost constantly with her, but she was bright enough to realize it was accentuated by her mental suffering. Today, when she posted the letter to Rossiter, she would be taking the first step in the right direction. It was time she took charge of her life. She was actually feeling somewhat better when she remembered she had to see Mrs. Powers. She washed her face and dressed for the day, taking particular care with her appearance. Mary was awake for the day, rambling on about Mr. Reader coming in for her lessons next week and complaining of hunger and what she wanted for breakfast. The thought of food almost made Callie gag.

Anne Powers sat at the breakfast table as though she were holding court. She was up and dressed for the day in a lightweight linen dress of pale green trimmed with accents of a darker shade of the same color. Her hair, worn simply in this damnable heat, was brought to the back of her head and secured in a thick roll. She dabbed her mouth with a snowy white napkin. Breakfast was one of her favorite meals, although she enjoyed lunch and thought of dinner as a social event. But now her thoughts were centered upon Callie James, and a bitter expression came over her face. Now she could handle the situation without fear of Callie running off to Jasper to tell him what she'd seen in the front hall the day Dr. Margolis came to call.

How best to manage it? There was no rush, really. Rossiter wouldn't be returning home for some time. She herself had arranged for Rossiter to accompany his uncle to Chicago to learn the foundations of a new enterprise in which the two families were investing. Jasper would be gone at least until the end of the month.

Some instinct told her it would be unwise to discharge Callie now, so soon after her return. Jasper would not see just cause to the dismissal. Mary was well and had thrived during their absence. The child certainly had a mind of her own and would be quick to tell her father there was nothing amiss. It would be best to wait a while, perhaps a week or so, to give herself time to manufacture something that would discredit the girl. Still, there was no harm in baiting her, letting Callie know that she wasn't fooling her for one minute. If there was one thing she had learned from her husband, it was how to play a waiting game, and wasn't it Byrch Kenyon who was forever saying there was more than one way to skin a cat?

And she had another problem weighing on her mind. She had promised Evan Margolis that she would stop by his offices. A warm flush crept up her neck and lodged in her cheeks, making them throb. As far as Callie was concerned with that little matter, the best way to handle the situation was to say and do nothing. To protest, to defend, would make the situation more than it was. Callie knew her place. But to have been caught by the little slut was almost more than Anne could bear. Did she really want to see the good doctor again? Of course she did, but there was no way she was going to offer her services as a nurse. She would plead headaches and ask for something in the way of medicine, saying there were days when the headaches were so bad she couldn't get out of bed. From that point on she would wait and see what developed.

It was strange, but her ears felt warm. She felt warm all over, deliciously so. Her mind rambled as she tried to think what she would do if Evan felt the same as she did. Was she capable of carrying on an affair? Absurd! Of course not. She was a good woman. A respectable woman. A faithful wife!

What harm could come from a little hand-holding or a few discreet kisses? Her ears became warmer as she remembered how wanton she had felt standing in the alcove by the front door, kissing her son's doctor. She knew she had never kissed Jasper like that. Jasper had never kissed her like that, either. Rossiter would have kissed Callie like that. Her lips started to quiver at the thought. Callie James was a slut.

When Callie knocked on the parlor door, Anne Powers composed herself. Or so she thought. She knew what Callie looked like, but she wasn't prepared for this slim, hollow-eyed young woman who stared at her with what Anne could only describe later as defiance.

"How did things go while we were away, Callie?"

"Very well, Mrs. Powers." Oh, if only she dared ask all the questions she needed answers to.

"You don't look well, Callie. Haven't you been sleeping? Is Mary too much for you to handle? She is a growing girl, and if you feel that you can't handle so much responsibility, I can relieve you of your duties."

"No, Mrs. Powers, everything is fine. If my appearance offends you, I'll stay out of your sight," Callie said bluntly. What was she supposed to say? Was it going to come down to her begging for her job? Mrs. Powers was playing a cat-and-mouse game with her. Of this she was certain. It was cruel and unnecessary. Her shoulders stiffened imperceptibly, and her head inched a shade higher on her slim shoulders. The clear blue eyes were defiant, almost insolent, Anne Powers thought. She could feel her stomach churn when she thought of what her son and this slut had been doing together.

She tossed Callie a bone to see what she would do. "I plan to invite Dr. Margolis to tea one day this week and would like Mary to attend. Just Mary."

Callie thought her heart would leap out of her chest. Dr. Margolis might detect Mary's problem! When Mary was alone, she had a tendency to become careless. The defiant eyes became frightened, and Callie backed off a step. She didn't like the way her legs trembled or the way her stomach was heaving. "Yes, Mrs. Powers," she managed to mutter.

"Are you going somewhere, Callie? Why are you backing away from me like that?" Anne Powers demanded harshly. This little slut was judging her, Anne thought, believing Callie knew that the man she'd seen her employer kissing was the same Dr. Margolis.

"I wasn't. Was there something else, Mrs. Powers?" Callie asked in a choked voice. Now she was in for it. Mary would never make it through an entire tea with a doctor watching and listening to her shrill voice. Never! What would the child do when she found out! Oh, Mum, if only you were here to tell me what to do.

"Don't you want to hear about our trip to Boston, Callie?" Not waiting for the girl to reply, she rushed on. "My dear, I had to screen, I mean really screen the young men who flocked after Anne. The girl had such a dizzying array of parties and luncheons that she never slept. Rossiter was so in demand by all the young ladies, I almost went out of my mind. I'll tell you something in confidence, Callie, and you mustn't whisper a word of it to Mary. I want your promise now." Callie nodded. "Rossiter has proposed to a beautiful young woman," Anne Powers lied. "An heiress. Isn't that simply wonderful? She accepted, of course. You must be happy for him the way we all are. Tell me, are you happy for my son, Callie? I want to hear you say the words," she said spitefully.

Callie swallowed hard, feeling as though the floor was about to heave under her feet.

She stared levelly at her employer and spoke quietly. "I'm very happy for your son, Mrs. Powers. I'm happy for you also." Callie fixed her gaze, shoulders squared, chin tilted upward. The world was shattering around her, but she held to her pride. Her steadiness seemed to upset Mrs. Powers. It was as though the woman expected her to grovel on hands and knees, begging to hear that what she'd told her about Rossiter wasn't true. Callie's fingers touched the crisp envelope in her apron pocket. Rossiter would answer. Rossiter would come back.

Anne Powers's eyes narrowed on Callie, flashing hatred at this little chit who had assumed herself to be good enough for Rossiter. "Enough!" she exclaimed. "Go and tend to your chores!" She turned away, listening for Callie to leave. The nerve, the colossal nerve of the girl! How dare she mock her? A deep bone-crunching hatred overcame her. For one brief instant she wondered if the hatred was for Callie or herself. It had been her duty to keep a vigilant eye on the comings and goings of her children. She should have suspected earlier that something was happening between Rossiter and the little slut. She never should have allowed herself to be caught in a compromising situation. Then this whole business could have been dealt with cleanly and swiftly. As it was, she almost felt as though she was at Callie's mercy.

Pondering her next move, Anne paced the parlor, swiftly kicking her long skirts out in front of her. The sun was streaming in the parlor windows, making lacy patterns on the carpet through the curtains. A movement at the end of the drive caught her attention. Callie, closing the mailbox, lifting the red flag to alert the postman. Curiosity prickled the back of her neck. Perhaps it was just another letter to that Irish tribe back in Dublin. But something about the way Callie glanced to the left and then to the right alarmed her and sharpened her instincts. She watched the girl run back up the drive, heard the front door close quietly, the latch catching. After a good, long moment, Anne Powers left the house and walked to the mailbox. Inside rested a letter addressed to Rossiter. Quickly, leaving the red flag up, she pocketed the crisp, white envelope. Her conscience gave her no qualms. She was simply saving her son from being harassed by a lovesick servant girl's letter of adoring worship. Back in the parlor, it occurred to Anne to open the letter and read it, but the idea was abhorrent to her. She had no wish to sully herself with the deed nor to know first-hand exactly what relationship existed between Rossiter and Callie. It was enough to know she had successfully nipped it in the bud. Striking a sulphur match to flame, she held it to the envelope, watching it catch and burn. She dropped the ash into the hearth and dusted her hands with finality.

Callie went into the kitchen, knowing Mary would be out on the service porch with the calico kittens she'd named One, Two, and Three. Lena was nowhere about. A large kettle simmered on the stove, and the everpresent scent of fresh coffee assailed her.

Hugh MacDuff came into the kitchen to pour himself a cup. Seeing Callie sitting in Lena's chair, dabbing at her eyes, made him want to reach out to comfort her. "I saw the postman stop at the end of the drive and open the box."

"I mailed a letter to Rossiter," Callie whispered. Hugh nodded his head, adding thick yellow cream to his cup and a few grains of sugar. "Do you know where Lena is?"

"Root cellar, I expect. I'm going up to the attic with her later to lay out the apple slices to dry. They'll come in handy this winter. They always do. I could make you a cuppa tea, lass, if you've a mind to put somethin' in your stomach."

"No thank you, Mr. MacDuff. I'll just wait for Lena. Is Mary on the service porch?"

"Aye, and she's just fine. Happy as a lark with them kittens."

Mrs. Powers's words swarmed around Callie's brain like angry bees. Rossiter proposed to an heiress, and she accepted him. Rossiter was going to marry someone else. Rossiter loved someone else? How could that be? Rossiter had loved *her*. He told her he loved her. The heiress was beautiful and wealthy; she was a servant and as poor as a church mouse. Rossiter was in love with someone else. How could he forget her so soon? How could he do this to her? Would Mrs. Powers lie to her about her son? A mother wouldn't lie about her son. Peggy never told a lie in her life. A mother didn't lie. God would punish a woman who would do such a terrible thing. No, it had to be the truth, but knowing it was the truth didn't make it easier to bear.

The letter! When Rossiter got her letter, he would change his mind and realize how much he loved her. He'd know that their love had made a child, his and hers. She would be able to accept his straying from her love if he returned to her now that she was going to have a baby. She would work so hard, she would make life so easy for her beloved if only he gave her the chance. She would cook and clean and iron his beautiful shirts. She would love him twenty-four hours out of every day. It had to be Mrs. Powers's fault. Rossiter would never have deserted her on his own. Mrs. Powers wanted someone more suitable for Rossiter than a mere servant girl. Callie felt so confused. Mothers didn't lie. They didn't.

Lena dumped her vegetables on the work table and wiped her hands on a clean cloth. There was no need for words. She gathered the girl into her arms and held her close. Poor thing. Her world was crashing down about her, and this was just the beginning.

Callie choked out the words and watched Lena's round, pink face. She was stunned to see the deep hatred in the woman's eyes. "Don't fret so, child. You sent your letter, and you have to wait for Master Rossiter to reply. All you can do now is wait. Listen to me, child," Lena said, cupping the young face in both hands. "I want you to stay out of sight of Mrs. Powers as much as you can. We don't want her getting ideas before it's time. She'll send you packing without so much as a minute's notice. We have to plan, MacDuff and me. We need time, Callie. This isn't going to be easy. We have to do what's best for you. Make up your mind, child, that you're going to have to leave here."

"Oh, Lena, I can't leave here. Mary . . . I can't leave Mary . . . you don't understand. Rossiter . . . what if Rossiter comes back and I'm not here?"

"I'll tell him where you are, and he can go to wherever that is. Mary will be all right. Right now, you have to start thinking about yourself, Callie."

"Lena, you don't understand about Mary . . . I can't leave Mary because . . . I can't leave Mary."

"You have no other choice. What will you be doing if Mrs. Powers takes it into her head to toss you out on your ear before we can find some place for you to go? What will you do about Mary then? Nothing. There won't be a thing you can do. Try and understand, child, what it is I'm telling you."

Oh, Mum, I need you so. If you were here, what would you be telling me to do? Her thoughts flitted to Byrch Kenyon. He would know exactly what to do and how to do it. He would understand about Mary too. No, even if she was dying with the world crashing down about her ears, she wouldn't go to Byrch Kenyon for help. Lena was right; it was she and Hugh MacDuff who would help her. There wasn't another soul in the whole world who cared a thing about her. You said you loved me, Rossiter. I believed you. I loved you. He would come back. As soon as he received her letter, he would return. She had to believe that! She had to!

Callie walked the basket of laundry out to the service porch. Pumping the water into the washtub and lifting the heavy kettle to add the hot water nearly exhausted her. She looked down at the little white pinafores and underwear and sighed. Let them soak for a while; she was feeling dizzy and light-headed and wanted nothing more than to just sit.

When she went back into the kitchen, Lena took one look at her and indicated her own chair near the work table. "I'll get you a cuppa tea," the cook bustled. Mary was scooting around the floor, playing with the kittens. Little bells had been tied about their fuzzy necks, thanks to Mr. MacDuff. "So Mary can hear them and not have to chase all over hell and creation to find them," he had said tersely. Bells so Mary could hear. It would almost be ludicrous to Callie, if it weren't so sad.

"Callie," Lena said, lowering her voice so Mary wouldn't overhear, "Mrs. Powers sent Miss Anne here a while ago to say she wanted to see Mary in her parlor. I told the child, but she's being obstinate today. She won't even look at me, much less listen to what I'm saying. I think she might be coming down with something. She looks peaked to me. I don't know what's got into her. When I speak to her, she just ignores me. She sits and plays with the kittens well enough. Have you noticed her being under the weather?"

"No," Callie said shortly. Her stomach fluttered wildly at what she imagined Mrs. Powers was going to do. She bent down and shook Mary by the shoulders. "Mary, Lena seems to think you're not well. She said she's been talking to you, and you aren't answering her. That's very poor manners. Your *Mamán* is going to think I haven't been teaching you properly. Remember I told you that your *Mamán* wanted you to have tea one day soon with Dr. Margolis? I think today might be the day. Your sister said your *Mamán* wants to see you in her parlor. But first you must apologize to Lena." Callie exerted some gentle pressure on the child's thin shoulder. A stricken look settled on Mary's face. By turning her back to Lena, she had closed out the world, and now she would have to pay for it.

"Lena, Lena, I'm sorry. I was being contrary because... because my stomach is upset." She threw her arms around Lena and looked up at her, knowing the woman would hug her and immediately think of something to make her feel better. Mary felt only a small pang of remorse at the trick she was playing on Lena. But for Callie she would do anything. It was Callie who was sick. Poor Callie, being so brave and pretending everything was all right. No one knew how Callie suffered but herself, and she would never tell, under pain of death. Poor, poor Callie. Each night now for a long time she had cried herself to sleep. It was Mary who crept in and turned the sodden pillow over after Callie fell asleep. What would she ever do without Callie? She couldn't manage without Callie's help. Today was a perfect example.

"I have just the thing," Lena said bending over to hug Mary. "Strong peppermint tea. You'll be right as rain in minutes. You don't want your *Mamán* ordering you to bed now, do you?" Mary shook her head and settled herself on a stool to wait for the tea.

"I'll just take this on up to my room, and when I'm finished, I'll stop in the parlor to see *Mamán*," Mary said holding the heavy mug carefully. "Are you coming, Callie?"

For the first time in days Callie had something to occupy her mind besides thoughts of Rossiter and the baby she carried. How was Mary going to manage? Mary's tendency to carelessness when in the company of her parents and her dependency on Callie to see her through her "ordeals," as she called them, could cause problems. Her shrill voice of late was another concern for Callie. The doctor was sure to wonder why the child spoke in such a manner. It was the one thing Callie couldn't control. She wouldn't draw an easy breath until the child was back safe next to her.

"Lena made this peppermint tea for me, but I think you need it more than I do. I'm sorry, Callie, for being so careless. I was having such a wonderful time with the kittens, I wasn't paying attention to Lena. I thought she was busy with her baking. I'm so sorry, Callie. I won't do it again. I promise to be more careful from now on."

"All right. I know you didn't do it on purpose. Come here, let me freshen your face a little, and a quick brush to those curls won't hurt. We don't want your *Mamán* to think you're a raga-muffin now, do we?" Callie dabbed at Mary's face with a clean, wet cloth and then brushed the tangled curls gently. "Just to be on the safe side, let's put on a fresh pinafore. I see cat hairs all over the one you're wearing. You're ready, Mary. Now be careful and please behave."

Mary hugged Callie and pointed to the teacup before she scamp-ered out of the room. Callie sighed deeply.

Anne Powers stared at her daughter for a full moment, uncertain of how to proceed. Mary was always such a difficult child. Not a child who was easy to love for some strange reason, considering Anne and Rossiter. Perhaps it was Mary's unruly red hair and the freckles. If only she looked more like Anne. And that shrill voice of hers grated on her nerves. Always in trouble of one kind or another. Why couldn't she be more like Anne? Rossiter and Jasper seemed to adore her. She wished she felt more maternal where Mary was concerned. "Come here, Mary. I don't think you look well. I think we better have Dr. Margolis take a look at you."

"There's nothing wrong with me, *Mamán*. I'm fine. I don't hurt anywhere. I don't have a fever, and my throat doesn't hurt." She didn't want to see Dr. Margolis. Doctors poked and jabbed and always came up with some reason why you had to stay in bed. She brightened for a minute. If she had to be put to bed that meant she wouldn't have to go to the tea and Callie could stop being nervous. Now she was sorry she had spoken so rashly. Better to be sent to bed and let everyone fuss over her.

"I think I know best. Let me feel your forehead. It does feel a little warm. We don't want you getting as sick as Rossiter was, now do we?"

"No, *Mamán*," Mary said in her high-pitched voice.

"Mary, could you please lower your voice. You're positively shrill at times. It is not pleasant. Especially for when Dr. Margolis is here. The truth now—what hurts you?"

Mary grimaced. She would get sick for Callie. Anything to take the look of worry off her face. It seemed fair to her. It was only a small lie, and no one need know about it. Lena would lend credence to the lie with the peppermint tea. "It's my stomach. Sometimes I can't stand up straight. Sometimes I roll on the floor."

"I knew it!" Anne Powers said triumphantly. "It's perfect . . . what I mean is, it's perfect timing for you to get sick because Dr. Margolis will be able to check you over this afternoon. Why didn't Callie tell me about this? Mary, how long have you been feeling like this?"

"Callie doesn't know. I didn't tell her I was sick. If I was sick, she wouldn't let me go outdoors or play with the new kittens. I didn't let her see me . . . roll on the floor or double over. Callie doesn't know, *Mamán*."

Mary shrilled so loudly, Anne Powers clapped her hands over her ears. It was no wonder Mr. Reader declared the child possessed no ear for music. Her voice was nasal and flat and too loud! "We'll just see about that. You go back to the nursery and get into bed.

I'll send Hugh MacDuff for the doctor. I'll be up shortly to see Callie. Not another word, Mary. Mind me and get along."

Mary raced back to the nursery. She shouted and shrilled at Callie to make her aware of what was going on. The look of dismay on Callie's face was enough to make Mary burst into tears. "Every time I try to do the right thing for *Mamán*, I make trouble. If only *Papá* were here. He'd take care of this. Callie, I'm not sick! I don't want to be sick and be in bed, but I'll do it. *Mamán* is so angry. Quick, help me get this dress and pinafore off. *Mamán* expects me to be in bed."

Callie thought her heart would leap out of her chest. God must be displeased with her to be making her suffer so. What she didn't need was another meeting with Mrs. Powers. Poor Mary, she was beside herself through no fault of her own.

"She didn't believe a word I said, Callie! She *wants* to believe that it's all your fault! If only *Papá* were here."

"Hush. It's all right, Mary. Your *Mamán* will understand. She's just worried. All mothers worry about their children. It will be all right, I'm sure of it. Together we'll talk to your mother and make things right."

Mary's movements were frantic and feverish. Callie didn't doubt for a minute that the child would work herself into such a pitch she really would be sick when the doctor arrived. Poor thing.

Anne Powers came up to the nursery a short while later, carrying a small tray with bottles on it. "Just in case," she said to Callie as she set it down next to Mary's bed. "Lena is sending up some tea and toast. Hugh MacDuff went off to ask the doctor to stop by. You rest now," she said, wagging a finger at Mary.

The minute her mother's back was turned, Mary stuck out her tongue and then dove under the covers. She quickly surfaced when she realized her mother was turning on Callie in an attack that was vicious and uncalled for. Mary saw the contortion of her mother's face, the bitterness in her eyes, and watched the movements of her mouth.

"I won't tolerate such behavior from you, Callie. My husband saw to it that your duties were so light as to be almost inconsequential. He wanted you to devote all your time to Mary, and I agreed. How could you not know this child was sick? How could you? What is it you're mooning over? Look at the poor child. Where is your brain? Mary is your first concern, and you've failed her. I've had to call the doctor. Mr. Powers is going to be most unhappy when he hears about this situation on his return."

Callie suffered Mrs. Powers's verbal abuse with her head high.

Never in her life had she been more miserable. "Well, young woman, what do you have to say for yourself?"

"I'm sorry, Mrs. Powers. It is my fault. I was lax in my duties. It won't happen again, I promise you that."

Mary leaped out of bed and raced to her mother. With flailing fists she lashed out, "I told you it wasn't Callie's fault! I told you that! Why are you blaming her? I'm going to tell *Papá* when he comes back!"

The child's voice was high-pitched, deafening in its shrillness, as Callie struggled to pull her away from her mother. At Callie's firm touch the hysterical girl screamed all the louder.

Anne Powers suffered her daughter's attack in stunned disbelief. Her eyes were venomous as she watched Callie try to calm Mary. "Enough!" she shouted to be heard above Mary's screams. "Enough, Mary! I refuse to tolerate this inexcusable behavior another second." With a quick, violent motion she shook the frantic child from her skirts and stepped backward.

Callie's grip on Mary's thin arm remained firm as she, too, backed off several steps. Mary's breathing was harsh and raspy as she struggled against Callie's iron grip on her upper arms. Frightened almost out of her wits at the scene being played out in front of her, Callie continued to back away from Anne Powers, dragging a screaming, kicking Mary with her.

Mary had never behaved in such a manner before. Callie's mind raced as she tried to figure out if there was something between the child and her mother of which she was unaware. How could she have neglected Mary these past weeks? She adored the child and considered her a younger sister. She was her responsibility, and one she didn't take lightly.

Mary in her frenzy whirled around and was about to lash out at Callie with her foot until she saw the warning and misery in Callie's eyes. Her own eyes widened as she realized what she had done. She calmed immediately. Callie led the limp little girl to the bed and helped her into it. All the while her dark gaze warned the child that she should say nothing more. "I'll handle this," she mouthed the words for Mary's benefit as she pulled the light coverlet up to the little girl's chin.

And just how was she to handle this, she wondered? Poor Mary. With all the dignity she could muster she advanced within a few feet of her employer. "I'm sorry, Mrs. Powers. I don't know what got into Mary. I think she misses her *Papá* and brother. She didn't say anything to me about not feeling well this morning. She was fine when she went to sleep last evening. I apologize for her distressing behavior and assure you she won't misbehave in such a fashion again. When she's feeling better, she'll apologize herself. Please forgive both of us, Mrs. Powers."

Anne Powers's lips curled distastefully. Where had the little snip come by such dignity? How haughty she looked standing there, apologizing for her laxness. "We'll discuss this later, Callie," she said.

"Yes, Mrs. Powers," Callie answered weakly. Surely, when the doctor arrived he would confirm that Mary wasn't ill. Surely things would right themselves at that time.

Mary lay in her bed, her slim body rigid. Her eyes were closed in feigned sleep. Callie wouldn't disturb her if she thought she was asleep. Something was wrong. It was wrong with Callie, and it was wrong with her mother, too. Whatever "it" was. Even Hugh and Lena had been acting peculiar as though they knew a secret and promised not to tell. That's what it was, a secret of some kind, and everyone knew about it but her. Callie was jittery and looked peaked. Even Lena said she looked peaked. Her mother looked flushed, and her eyes were too bright. Both signs of sickness. If they were sick, why was she the one in bed waiting for a doctor to come? Everyone thought because she was a little girl she was dumb and didn't know what was going on. Children should be seen and not heard. But she had seen, and she had heard. Was that why her mother was treating her so . . . so . . . meanly?

Her mother *wanted* her to be sick, and she had gone along with the idea to prevent Callie from being blamed. Callie had been different lately. Her smiles were weak, and her eyes watery from time to time. Lena kept a sharp eye on her, as did Mr. MacDuff. Why? What did they know that she didn't know? If only she could hear. Why did her mother want her to be sick? Mothers always wanted their children to be well so they wouldn't have to worry.

The doctor was coming to see her. She hated doctors. She didn't want him touching her and sticking his stick down her throat. She didn't want him to thump on her chest and listen to her heart beat, but most of all she didn't want him looking in her ears or even talking to her. Callie was scared of the doctor's visit. If Callie was scared, then so was she.

Mamán had something up her sleeve, as *Papá* would say. And whatever it was that was up her sleeve, besides her arm, it had to do with Callie. Mary was certain of it. She was also just as certain that no one was going to tell her what it was. If only Rossiter or *Papá* were here. She had no one to talk to, no one to confide in. Callie wasn't the same anymore.

What would she ever do without Callie? How would she manage? Callie had promised she would never leave her. She had to believe that. She did believe it—as long as *Papá* was around. She remembered other things her mother had done against her father's wishes while he was away. Would she do something to Callie? Mary's hand flew to her mouth. Of course, she could. If it pleased her, she would do anything, regardless of how hurt anyone might be!

She had to warn Callie. She had to warn Callie to be as good as she was going to be before her mother got it into her head to do something terrible. She didn't feel disloyal toward her mother at all. Instead she felt protective of Callie, so much so that she realized she would lie, cheat or steal to make things right for her friend. Callie came first. Callie, next to *Papá* and Rossiter, was the only one who cared about her at all.

Chapter Seventeen

Anne Powers peered closely at her reflection in the mirror. There was no need for rouge on her flushed cheeks. She liked the brightness in her eyes and the excitement that was coursing through her. The bright gaze in the mirror ignored the dry, prematurely aged skin and the excess flesh hanging at her neck. Her thoughts were those of a much younger woman as she primped at her hair and patted the sleeves of her burgundy afternoon dress. A delicious shiver of excitement raced up her arms when she remembered how she was drawn to Evan Margolis's hands and the way those same hands felt on her back when he held her in his arms. She gave herself a little shake and started from the room. She had to see to tea and make certain Lena understood that she wasn't to be disturbed after the doctor made his examination of Mary and handed over his little packet of pills for her stomach ailment. Surely the doctor would take the time for tea and a few words. She wondered if he had thought of her in the past weeks as much as she had thought of him. She hoped he wouldn't bring up her impulsive confession of wanting to nurse the sick. If he did, she would go along with whatever he said and make decisions later.

Carefully worded inquiries among her closest friends concerning Dr. Margolis had produced only positive replies. He was regarded as a "wonderful catch" and well-off in the bargain. Surely the man had income other than his medical fees. Otherwise how could he live in such a pretentious house and have so many servants? Ellen Macaffey, her closest friend, whispered behind her hand that Dr. Margolis was a bachelor by choice. Women flocked after the man, and he had to literally beat them off with a stick. The woman, she continued to whisper, who could lure the good doctor into her arms would indeed be a lucky woman. It had been all Anne could do to remain silent about her brief encounter in the hallway. Ellen would positively shrivel up and die if she so much as suspected anything going on with her good friend. Only "other women" did things like that. Sexual encounters were duties or something to be endured. Of course, if one wanted children, one put on a good face about it. *Good* women never enjoyed sexual relations or even pretended to enjoy them; they simply endured.

How many nights had she lain in bed letting her imagination run away with her? So many she lost track of the count. Always, however, she stopped her runaway imagination when it was time to shed her clothes and get in bed with the dashing doctor. Sagging breasts and loose skin dismayed her and would certainly startle him. And what if he found out that she had trouble with her skin cracking and peeling on her feet? She would be so humiliated. What she needed, she told herself, was a magic potion to restore some semblance of youth.

Darkness was the answer. Her mouth stretched into a thin line. Feeling was almost the same as seeing. She must remember to order a new supply of glycerin and rose water.

They would be discreet. They would meet in carefully chosen places for tea or a light lunch and pretend they met by accident. Mary would probably need a series of house calls till she was back on her feet. She herself could pretend to be under the weather with one or another female complaint. There were unlimited possibilities, she told herself, if she wanted to take advantage of them.

For the thousandth time she wished she knew what the good doctor felt after they had embraced so wickedly in the hall that day last spring. Her first impression was that she had startled him with her aggression. Then, when she had time to think about it a little more, she realized he was as overcome with passion as she was. There was no doubt about it, kissing was a dangerous business. Kissing led to all manner of wicked things. Children were often the result of kissing, in an indirect way, she told herself.

When was the last time Jasper kissed her? Jasper's kisses had always been safe, chaste. Dry, she told herself. There had never been any tongue touching, no moistness. Jasper was a dry man in more ways than one. A nice man but a dry man. Jasper had never excited her, never thrilled her to the core of her being. A pity she had to wait to be this old to want more. But did she want more? Did she hunger for wild, passionate kisses and a little wanton behavior with all her clothes on? Did she yearn for clandestine luncheons and secretive meetings? If she ever did manage to get into bed with the doctor, would she reach fulfillment as she never had with Jasper?

She was getting a headache, her best and favorite excuse when Jasper wanted into her bed. Something told her she would never plead a headache where the doctor was concerned.

Her movements were hurried as she made her way to the library to check out the tea setting. The doctor would enjoy tea in the library, she told herself, since it was a man's room. It would be awkward in the main parlor with the servants going past and gawking. Besides, she wanted to be able to shut the door and have him all to herself. Should they have tea first and then have him check on Mary, or have him check on Mary first? Mary first, she told herself. The doctor would recognize her concern and not even think that she had concocted this little charade for her own benefit. Men were so naive.

When the front-door bell rang, Anne almost jumped a foot. She inhaled slowly and deeply to regain control of her feelings, then rose from her chair and walked languidly into the foyer to greet the doctor. Why wasn't he smiling at her as she offered her hand? He looked tired, poor man. Wary. The man was tired. It wasn't wariness at all, but desire. The thought made her bold. "I've missed you," she said, leaning closer to the doctor.

"I was wondering when you were returning," Margolis said in a harried tone. "Tell me, how is the child? Can she hold food in her stomach? Is she plagued with nausea like so many of the children I've seen in the past few days."

"A little," Anne said vaguely. Up close he looked so much younger than she remembered. He wasn't making any move to kiss her or even touch her. Surely he couldn't be *that* tired. He seemed to like her boldness the last time he visited the house. How old was he? In his early forties or late thirties. Did he guess she was a hateful fifty-five years old? Men never thought of things like that, she told herself. Right now, this very minute, she didn't feel any older than her daughter Anne. "Come along, doctor," she said, briskly leading the way to the nursery. "I've taken the liberty of ordering tea. Now I'm glad that I did. You look positively wrung out, doctor. I won't take no for an answer. You busy men, you never take the time to eat properly. You could get sick too, you know," she said, wagging a playful finger under the doctor's nose. "Consider it a brief respite from your busy rounds." He should have touched her arm by now. Laid a hand on her shoulder. Those beautiful hands. Her heart took on a furious beat as her step slowed. Was she going to have to do it all? Evidently. Taking a deep breath, she purposely stopped in mid-stride and allowed the doctor to brush against her. He moved as though touched by fire. "I'm not sorry I did that. I meant for you to—"

"Dear lady, I realize exactly what you did. However, this is not the time or the place for a romantic interlude. About the last time I was here . . . I think I . . ."

"There's no need for you to apologize. I enjoyed the kiss. My heavens, doctor, I'm a wordly woman, not some stuffy school teacher who is oblivious to the outside world. You move in the same sophisticated social circles as myself. I don't think either of us should apologize." There, she had said it. It was out. Now he would think of her the way he thought of the other women he was rumored to squire around town. The only difference would be that he would have to squire her in secrecy. After all, she was a married woman with no intention of disrupting her tidy, humdrum life. Her reputation was not to be a subject for gossip.

The wary look was back in the doctor's eyes. He had to say something to this foolish woman who was so bent on seducing him. Good God, she must be old enough to be his mother, or if not his mother, his aging aunt. He didn't want to humiliate her, and yet he didn't want her to pester him by calling him to the house for unnecessary house calls. He took his medical practice seriously and would continue to do so. If there was one thing he would never do, it was to dally around with a married woman. Especially *this* woman. His tastes ran more to the lush, the soft, and the mature younger woman. A woman like the beautiful stage actress Fallon Michels. The tea, he had to get out of the tea; but first he had to see the child who was ill. Perhaps an idea would come to him while he was practicing his profession. A little help from the Almighty wouldn't hurt either.

"I know you want to kiss me as much as I want you to, but you're right. This is neither the time or the place. While we have tea, we can discuss it," Anne said coyly. The doctor winced as he watched the woman open the door to the nursery.

Good God, what had he gotten himself into? He couldn't think about that now. He had a patient to consider and an examination to perform. He looked around the pleasant room and knew that if he ever had children, he would have a nursery just like it. Bright and vibrant colors were everywhere. His eyes went to the young woman with the wide eyes. He stared at her for a moment, letting his eyes take in her entire being. She was beautiful. When he realized his stare was becoming obvious to her as well as to Mrs. Powers, he walked over to the bed and smiled down at the tousled-haired child.

"Your mother tells me your name is Mary. Mary is a very pretty name for such a pretty little girl. I do adore red curls." Turning around, he motioned for Mrs. Powers and Callie to leave the room. "I'll call you if I have need of your help. For now I want to be alone with my patient."

"But I—" Callie said hoarsely.

"Didn't you hear the doctor, Callie? He wants us to wait outside. We must do as he wishes. You of all people should want what's best for Mary since you're responsible for her illness. Now come along and let the doctor examine Mary."

Callie stepped into the hall with Mrs. Powers. She was confused and worried. Worried that the doctor would immediately discover Mary's deafness, confused that Mrs. Powers would again entertain the dark stranger Callie had seen her kissing. And then there was the surprised recognition on Mary's face when the doctor stepped into the nursery. What did it mean?

Dr. Margolis stared at Mary. It wasn't his imagination. She was frightened out of her wits. The little girl in the bed was taking her cue from her companion who was just as frightened. What had he stumbled upon here? He would have wagered his entire medical career that the child had nothing more than a stomach ache if she had anything at all. This particular house call was nothing more than a way for the amorous Mrs. Powers to—he had to do something to wipe the fright from the child's eyes.

"I'm not going to hurt you," he said softly. "Your friend—she is your friend, isn't she?—will be right back." Mary nodded. "Good, now tell me where you have pain." Mary pointed to her stomach and pulled the bed clothes higher. Her gaze was so intent the doctor felt unnerved. Good Lord, how could she stare at him like that and not even blink? He felt nonplussed as the child tried to burrow deeper into the mound of pillows behind her back.

"Let's take a look at your throat. Stick out your tongue and say, aaah." Mary did as ordered and waited with wide eyes for the doctor's next words. "Your throat seems clear enough. Let's take a look at your ears, and then we'll work our way down to your stomach." At the doctor's words Mary jerked back so violently the doctor lost his tongue depressor in the bed covers and had to rummage for it. He was stunned at the child's reaction. So far, she had not uttered a word. There was more here than met the eye. "Would you rather I checked your stomach? You don't want me looking in your ears, do you?" Purposely he turned his back and kept a running conversation with the child. "Well, do you agree with what I said or not?" he asked casually.

Mary's eyes went from puzzled to frightened. She shrugged.

"You can do better than that. You're a big girl, and big girls answer when they're spoken to. I cannot help you get well if you won't talk to me and tell me what's wrong. I have to check everything when someone is sick. I promised I wouldn't hurt you, and I'll keep that promise."

Mary's flat, toneless voice startled the doctor. "My stomach hurts, not my ears."

"But you didn't object when I wanted to look at your throat. Your throat doesn't have anything to do with your stomach, either. Do you have an ear ache and didn't tell your mother?"

Mary shook her head. She watched as the doctor leaned over the side of the bed to remove something from his medical bag. He spoke loudly, almost shouting, and then swiveled quickly in time to catch the child trying to regain her position in the bed. He sighed loudly.

"I feel better," Mary said, drawing away from him.

"I believe you," Dr. Margolis said softly. "You don't like doctors, is that it?"

Mary said nothing, her gaze blunt and direct.

"All right, let's take a look at your stomach. Tell me as I touch it if you have any pain or if it just feels tender. Can you do that?"

The relief in Mary's defiant eyes was all the doctor needed to confirm his diagnosis. He was at a loss to understand why Mrs. Powers hadn't mentioned the child's hearing problem. Was it possible that she was unaware of Mary's problem? What to do, how to proceed? What to say aloud, what to keep to himself? "Everything seems all right. I think, little lady, that you just had a mild upset stomach. Stay in bed the rest of the day and look at your picture books. Tomorrow you'll be good as new. Now," he said jovially, "that wasn't all that bad, was it?"

Mary shook her head and again pulled the covers up to her chin. Her intense gaze never wavered. Clearly this was something he should discuss with Mr. Powers, and he would do so the first chance he got. Of course, he was going to have to mention it and question Mrs. Powers. Tea then was essential.

Mary watched the doctor close his medical bag with a loud snap. His casual words didn't fool her for a minute. He knew or at least suspected that she had a problem with her ears, and it was her fault. If only Callie had been permitted to stay in the room, things might be different.

"Is your *Papá* away on business or at his office?" A spark of hope flared in Mary's small chest. Did that mean he would talk to her father instead of her mother? Her hope was short-lived. She had no idea when her father would return. She was forced to shrug her shoulders. Callie said she read in Mr. Kenyon's newspaper that tests were given to people with hearing problems at a clinic on the other side of town. Eye examinations too, for spectacles. It had been a wild idea on Callie's part to enlist the aid of Hugh MacDuff to drive them to the clinic for Mary to be examined secretly. That had been her plan, and Mary had willingly agreed until the following day when Callie reported on the sequel to the story that said minor children had to be accompanied by their parents.

Callie was becoming more and more worried about her problem, she could tell. She was regretting the decision she had made not to tell her parents. Over and over she kept saying, "What if a doctor can fix your ears?" Four separate times Callie had asked to be released from her promise. Each time Mary had been adamant. Lately Callie hadn't asked. Lately Callie appeared to have problems of her own.

"You lie there and rest now for the rest of the day. Tomorrow you'll be up and everything will be fine," Dr. Margolis whispered. Again Mary nodded.

Living in a soundless world must be hell, the doctor thought as he rolled down his shirt sleeves. No sounds of laughter, no birds singing. Never to hear beautiful music. He knew that with hearing loss the other senses were honed to a sharpness almost beyond belief. What he wanted to know, needed to know, was whether Mrs. Powers knew of the child's problem. If so, why hadn't she mentioned it? True, she had other things on her mind, like finding ways to seduce him in the middle of the afternoon. He struggled with his conscience as he slipped into his coat and smiled down at the anxious child. Much too anxious. Too frightened. The companion was frightened too. Was she protecting the little one? If so, why? He hated questions with no answers. The best and only thing he could do was try to find out from Mrs. Powers what was wrong with Mary. He felt no guilt about his decision not to speak out to the child's mother. The problem wasn't an emergency from the looks of things. Since he hadn't actually physically examined the child's ears, there was no need to mention it at all. But he couldn't leave this house without knowing. Later, when the time was right, he could decide what to do about it.

Dr. Margolis was tempted to bend over the bed and reassure the child somehow, but his bedside manner failed him when he noticed the look of misery in the child's eyes. Were they pleading or simply frightened? He didn't know. He patted her head gently and turned to leave.

Mary's miserable, pinched face told Callie all she needed to know. She gathered the child closely to her and crooned soft words as she stroked the tangled red curls. They would wait. Both of them would wait. There was nothing else to do.

With three chairs and a love seat to choose from, Dr. Margolis chose a comfortable-looking chair as far from the love seat as he could get. The look of disappointment on Anne Powers's face was almost laughable. He had to get to the point as quickly as possible and pretend to enjoy this small feast. And it was a feast. Never had he seen such an elaborate tea. The array of cakes and tiny sandwiches would feed ten immigrants.

Anne Powers poured tea from a silver pot. Margolis noted the unattractive brown spots and large veins standing out on the backs on her hands. It must be a burden for women to grow old, he thought. The things he found unattractive in women wouldn't bother him in the least if he saw them in a man. Wrinkles, thinning hair, and brown spots on the flesh added character to a man. In a woman they were signs of age. Time and age were a woman's enemy. He couldn't get off the track here. He had to accept the tea, make a pretense of nibbling the decorative sandwiches, ask his questions, and leave this house, preferably without another amorous encounter.

"Tell me, doctor, how did you find Mary?" Anne hoped her voice had the proper mixture of maternal concern and worldliness.

"A minor stomach ache. She'll be fine tomorrow. Let her stay in bed for the balance of the day. Tea and toast."

"I thought so myself, but I did want to be sure. Children come down with any assortment of things from time to time. When she contracted the measles, I was terrified by her high fever." Anne gave a delicate shudder to make her point. "You see, Dr. Margolis," she said, quietly leaning across the small tea table, "Mary is the apple of her father's eye, and if she came down with something and I didn't call a doctor, I shudder to think what he might say or do."

"Where is Mr. Powers?"

"In Boston. I don't expect him back for some time. Possibly a month, even longer," she said coyly over the rim of her teacup.

"That long?"

"Business. We all know what that's like. Take yourself, Dr. Margolis. You look very tired. Yet you keep making house calls because you're dedicated. My husband is dedicated to his business too. Why do you ask?"

"No reason, Mrs. Powers, no reason at all."

"Call me Anne. We've been most fortunate with our children. They're rarely sick. Rossiter never got ill until this last time when you treated him. Very, foolishly, I admit, he wandered about in the rain with his sister. Anne is subject to headaches. Even as a small child she was never ill. Mary is as strong as an ox. I've never had to call the doctor for her." Goodness, how easy it was to talk to this wonderful man. The interest he was taking in her children was simply . . . wonderful. Everything was wonderful.

"That's amazing, simply amazing. You're most fortunate, Mrs. . . . Anne, that your children are so healthy. Other parents would envy you. Mary seems a very happy child."

"Oh, she is. She's even happier now that my husband engaged her companion." She lowered her voice to a conspiratorial tone and rushed on. "We were having a bit of a problem with Mary. Why, for a short period of time she was willful, disrespectful, and almost beyond our control. She shrieked and wailed and carried on like you wouldn't believe. Why, she even went so far as to ignore us when we spoke to her. My husband was at his wit's end. I knew it was a stage she was going through. Then Callie, that's the companion, came to us and from that day on Mary has been a wonderful little girl, just like before. She still shrieks a bit and has a high-pitched voice, but we've all come to live with it." She could tell this man anything. Imagine confiding her child's personal problems to a doctor. How understanding he was. There should be no secrets between them.

"Amazing. Are you telling me Mary never had sore throats and ear aches?"

"Good heavens, yes. She's had her share of sore throats but never an ear ache. My older daughter never had ear aches, either. Now that I think about it, Rossiter never had ear aches, either."

"Remarkable. How long has Mary had her companion? I find

that a bit unusual at her age." He hoped his tone was as complimentary as he could make it.

"Almost two years. My husband insisted. Actually she does have other duties here, light ones, but mainly she takes care of Mary."

"I don't mean to be inquisitive, but what happens when the baby arrives?"

The small bite-sized sandwich stopped in mid-air. Evan Margolis had never seen a flesh and blood still life before. A warning bell sounded somewhere in the deep recesses of his brain. Was it possible Anne Powers was unaware of the companion's condition as well as her daughter's hearing? Good God, what did the woman do, live in a cocoon? Her face was chalk white, her reddened lips a crimson slash in her face. Margolis remembered the handsome young son he'd treated last spring. Rossiter. The warning bell pealed louder. Surely he'd put his foot in it this time. At least he wouldn't have to worry about a clutching, groping attack in the hallway again. Anne Powers was somewhere else at the moment. He would have wagered a year's medical fees that she had forgotten his very existence. No sense compounding the problem of the child's hearing at the moment. Besides, he wanted to think about it a little longer and perhaps get in touch with a colleague who specialized in ear treatment before he spoke to Jasper Powers. Now he must smooth things over.

"I do want to thank you for a lovely tea. You're not to concern yourself with your little girl. She's going to be fine. You look tired, Mrs. Powers. I'll leave a sedative here on the table. Take it if you feel the need. Thank you again for the tea. Don't get up. I'll see myself out."

"What?" Anne Powers said blankly.

"I said I can let myself out."

"Yes, yes, you do that. Thank you for coming."

The sound of the front door closing shook Anne from her deep thoughts. With a wild, angry motion she lashed out at the tea table and swept china, food, and silverware to the floor. He was gone. Mary was all right. Callie was pregnant! The little slut, Rossiter's child. How dare she! Evan hadn't said anything about coming back, of seeing her again. Of course not, and it was all Callie's fault. He had such a knowing look in his eyes as though he knew that Rossiter was the father of the girl's child. Now what was she to do? She'd be the laughing stock among her friends. She would get no help from Jasper when he returned. Get rid of her. That was the answer. Now. The sooner the better. Mary would survive.

What did she care what Jasper thought! She had the family to consider. The fact that she herself had been willing to sully that same family just minutes ago didn't occur to her.

She had to think, make some plan of action. Mary would throw a tantrum and behave like a wild banshee. She would have to put up with it or slap her a time or two to quiet her. Mary was just a child.

Looking at the debris on the floor, her best china, her best silver, did nothing for her frame of mind. She had never liked Callie from the day she entered the house. She was honest enough with herself to admit that the main reason she didn't care for the girl was because Jasper hadn't consulted with her before agreeing to take her off Byrch Kenyon's hands. As far as Jasper was concerned, Callie could do no wrong. Jasper never fooled her for a minute. He was disappointed in Rossiter, and his older daughter left him with a feeling that he was around merely to provide for her. Mary, with her wild, willful ways, was the apple of his eye.

The nursery was middle-of-the-night quiet when Anne Powers thrust open the door. The movement caught Mary's eye, and she burrowed deeper into the crook of Callie's arm.

Caught like a thief, that was how Callie James looked, Anne thought smugly. How far along was she? Two months, three? It was hard to tell.

"I want to talk to you. Now," she said, addressing the companion, "come with me into your room. Leave Mary here."

Callie disengaged the stranglehold the child had on her and gently laid her back against the pillows. "Your *Mamán* wants to talk to me," she whispered. Mary's frightened eyes pleaded with Callie not to leave her. Callie smiled and let her eyes convey the message that Mary wanted. Everything would be all right.

The moment the door closed behind her mother and Callie, Mary bounded out of bed and flew to the door of Callie's room. She peeked through the keyhole, hoping she could watch the discussion and find out exactly what was going on. Whatever it was, it wasn't going to be good for Callie. Too often she had seen that look on her mother's face.

Callie sat on the edge of her bed, her hands folded primly in front of her; Mrs. Powers took a chair opposite. Her gaze was respectful when she stared straight at her employer. She had to think about Mary and her hearing problem. She would take her punishment and plead . . . what would she plead? Ignorance? Say that a childish promise to a little girl made by another girl should be honored? But she wasn't a little girl any longer. Childish promises no longer held. Honor? Stand tall and take whatever verbal abuse the lady of the house handed out. Jasper Powers, when he found out, would understand. She had to remember that. She had to hold fast to that thought.

"Dr. Margolis tells me you're pregnant," Mrs. Powers said. Callie didn't know what she had expected, but this opening statement wasn't it. A wave of nausea washed over her as she tried to return Mrs. Powers's penetrating stare. She was forced to lower her eyes. She couldn't bear the look of disgust she saw on the older woman's face.

"You thought you hoodwinked me, didn't you? Well, you didn't. I was wise to your shenanagins from the moment you set eyes on Rossiter's portrait. You didn't know I saw you mooning about, staring at his picture in the parlor, did you? Rossiter is a handsome young man, and women fall in love with him at the drop of a hat. You're unsuitable for my son. I cannot allow you even to think there could be something between the two of you. I don't want to hear any self-righteous talk about you carrying my son's child. How do I know it's Rossiter's child? Because you say so? Any girl who would do what you did would do it with any man. You can't stay here any longer. I have my family to consider. I don't want Mary to know anything of this. You're to pack your bags and be gone within the hour. I never want to see you again." At Callie's stricken look she rushed on, "Don't hold out any grand hopes that my son is going to rush to your side. He isn't. He's marrying someone else in Boston. He fell in love while we were there with a wonderful, young lady. There is no room in Rossiter's life for you. Be sure you understand that fact."

Callie raised miserable eyes to Mrs. Powers. Thank God there was nothing mentioned about Mary and her hearing problem. Leave. She had to leave this house. She was never to see Rossiter again. How could she live without Rossiter? All her dreams, all her hopes for the future were dashed. Where could she go? What could she do? How was it possible that Rossiter didn't love her? How could he marry someone else? She was unsuitable. What an awful, hateful word. She was the same person she always was. But now she was unsuitable for Rossiter Powers. She wasn't an heiress. Money, then, made the difference.

"I don't know where to go," Callie said miserably.

"That's your problem. You should have thought about that before you enticed my son into your bed. Surely you weren't stupid enough to think he would actually marry the likes of you. Yes. I guess you were. Call on your friend, Byrch Kenyon. After all, he was the one who foisted you off on my husband. I'm sure he can find some place for you to go. I don't want you in this house one minute longer than necessary. Get your things together and be out of here as soon as possible."

"Mrs. Powers, what about Mary? Who will take care of Mary?"

"That's no longer your concern. Mary will have to get along without you. Don't even speak the child's name to me, you have no right. Do you think I want her seeing what you are? Knowing what you've done with her brother?"

Callie dabbed at her eyes with the hem of her apron. "I loved Rossiter, Mrs. Powers. Truly I did. This baby is Rossiter's child. It's your flesh and blood."

"I don't know that. I only have your word for it. There's no point in discussing any of this any further. I want you to start packing immediately. Love!" Anne Powers snorted. "What do you know about love?"

The screeching, shrieking whirlwind that flew through the room to tear at her mother showed no mercy as she beat at the woman with clenched fists. "I hate you. You're a mean, nasty, terrible person, and I hate you. I'll always hate you if you send Callie away. I want to go with Callie. I'll tell *Papá*. *Papá* will let Callie stay." Small feet kicked out at Anne Powers's legs, forcing the woman to yelp in pain. Clenched fists and nails raked at her. Pushing and shoving, Mary forced the woman back against the wall with her extraordinary strength, strength Callie never would have believed the child possessed. She should do something, try to pull the shrieking child off her mother. Anger poured out of Callie. She was no longer in Anne Powers's employ. She didn't have to do a thing. Mary needed to do what she was doing, even though it wasn't right. She made the instant decision not to interfere.

Anne Powers was now shrieking as loud as her daughter as she tried to get away from her. Her efforts only incensed Mary all the more. "I saw you. I saw you kissing that doctor. I'm going to tell *Papá* when he comes home. I don't care if Callie kissed Rossiter. I don't care! If you can kiss Dr. Margolis, why can't Callie kiss Rossiter?" Mary shrieked. "I'm going to tell. I'm going to tell everyone. I hate you. I never want to see you again." Mary then turned her venom and frustration on Callie. "I hate you, too. You broke your promise to me."

Callie sat down on the bed and wept. There was nothing she could do. She had to make the effort for Mary. Wiping at her eyes with the sleeve of her dress, she got to her feet again and held out her arms to Mary. "Please, Mary, you don't understand. Come here and let—"

"No," Mary shrieked. "You'll just lie to me again. I don't want to listen to you anymore. Get away from me. Don't come near me." Sobbing hysterically, Mary ran from the room. Out to the corridor and down the stairs to the kitchen. Without looking at a startled Lena, she banged through the screen door and raced past Hugh MacDuff. On and on she ran, down the slope of the backyard and up the steep incline to what was called the high bluff. Tripping and falling, she picked herself up only to fall again. Angry tears, hurtful tears, ran down her cheeks, making her gasp for breath. Unable to hear Hugh's and Lena's cries for her to come back, she ran on and on. Her only friend was leaving her. Her mother was sending Callie away. The doctor would tell everyone about her hearing, and then they'd send her away too. As she fought for breath, she wondered why her mother never mentioned her hearing to Callie. Because, she told herself, they were waiting for Callie to leave before they sent her away. Callie would have tried to stop them. No, she wouldn't. Callie lied. Callie said everything was going to be all right.

On and on the little girl ran, up and onward to the top of the bluff. With the tears burning her eyes, she paid no mind to what or where she was going. All she knew was that it was getting harder and harder to breathe, harder and harder to make her feet work. Lena's shrill cries and Hugh MacDuff's hoarse shouts went unheeded as the child finally fell in exhaustion against a gnarled oak tree. Her trembling feet poked at a pile of leaves, working them into a small mound. Satisfied with her temporary nest, she climbed into the leaves and cried.

Her humiliation complete, Anne Powers struggled to her feet. Her gaze was stony and hateful as she watched Callie close the satchel with her belongings. Venom poured out of her eyes as the girl made her way to the door. She didn't look back or acknowledge Anne Powers in any way. "You could have stopped her. You could have controlled the little monster. Why didn't you?" God, Mary in her rage said she had seen her mother kissing Evan Margolis. She pooh-poohed the idea that either her daughter or Callie would tell her husband. And if they did, Jasper would never believe it. Mary was a hysterical, backward child. Callie was a slut. No one would believe either of them. "Well, answer me!" Anne Powers commanded in a strangled voice.

Callie turned slowly to stare at the ravaged woman. "I'm no

longer in your employ, Mrs. Powers." Without another word Callie was through the door and in the hallway. Once she was clear of the room, she ran as fast as she could with her heavy satchel down the stairs and into the kitchen. It was empty. She had to find Mary. Explain to the child somehow that she wasn't deserting her, that she hadn't lied to her. Would she understand? She was such a child. A sweet, wonderful, lovable child. She owed the little girl so much. Without her, Callie's first months in this country would have been unbearable. She had to find Mary. Mary must have run through the kitchen to go outdoors. Lena's absence must mean that she and Hugh were chasing after her. Mary knew every inch of the Powers's property, so she couldn't get lost. But if the troubled child ran to the top of the bluff, she could have a serious accident.

Callie set her satchel on the back porch and stepped down to the yard. Good Lord, she could have gone in any direction. Instead of going after the child, she should be thinking about where she was going to spend the night now that she was cast out of the Powers's household.

Callie struck off to the right of the house behind Hugh MacDuff's potting shed. She was halfway up a small incline when she saw the handyman coming toward her. Quickly she explained what happened and wanted to cry at the miserable look on the older man's face. "We have to find Mary, Mr. MacDuff. Where's Lena?"

"She went that way," he pointed to his right. "We knew something was wrong when the girl raced through the kitchen, screaming like a banshee. Lena will find her. She's been calling her all the while."

"But she won't hear, Mr. MacDuff. Mary can't hear! Anything could happen to her if she goes up to the bluff. It's a sheer dropoff. She's tired and upset. She doesn't have her wits about her. We have to find her! Please, Mr. MacDuff, help me find her."

"You can't be climbing in your condition. Don't worry, lass. Lena told me, and my mouth is clamped tight. Lena told me the missus would be tossing you out if she found out. Right she was. That confounded woman is always right. Here she comes now."

Callie fell into the cook's arms and sobbed. "What if something happens to Mary, Lena? I'll never forgive myself. I don't know where to go or what to do? Mrs. Powers said I had to be out of here in an hour."

"When the missus says something like that, you best do as she says. If she sees you hanging about, she'll set the law on you.

Have you deported. She would do it too, isn't that a fact, Lena?" Lena nodded her head, the gray corkscrew curls bobbing in her agitation.

The stout cook clapped both hands over her head. "Let me think a minute. Both of you be quiet and let me see if an idea pops into my head." Hugh and Callie watched Lena with anxious faces. Lena could always be counted on to come up with the best solution to a problem.

Moments later Lena removed her hands from her head. "The only thing I can come up with is for Callie to remove herself immediately from here. Hugh, send her down to the rooming house in St. George and let her stay there for the time being until we can figure something better. We have a good two hours to look for the child. Hugh, you go down the street and see if you can't get some of the other men to help you."

MacDuff agreed, giving Callie directions to the rooming house. "Don't you be worrying now. We'll find the lass before dark."

Callie didn't like it, but Lena was right. For now it was the best solution. She could not call Byrch Kenyon. She wouldn't call him, no matter what. From here on in she would manage her own problems.

"Go along now, child. MacDuff and I will go after Mary and bring her back." Lena wrapped her arms around the trembling girl and kissed her on the cheek. "Don't you be thinking dark thoughts now. Everything is going to turn out right."

Blinking back her tears, Callie started down Todt Hill and began her trek into St. George to what Hugh called a clean and orderly rooming house.

All through the night Hugh MacDuff and the men on the hill searched for Mary Powers. They shouted and called her name to no avail. It was Hugh's decision not to tell the others about Mary's hearing problem. Best not to make known the Powers's personal business, Lena warned.

It was past three in the morning when the men returned to the Powers's kitchen with their lanterns swinging in the darkness like oversized fireflies. Lena poured coffee and drew Hugh aside out of the others' hearing. "I spoke to Mrs. Powers around midnight, and she shouted at me through the door that she didn't want to hear a word about Mary. Not a word, she said. I tried to talk to her through the door, but she refused to listen. I don't even know if she heard me or not. She was screaming at me just the way the child used to. If only Mr. Powers were here. He would know what to do. Are you and the men going back out again?"

"I don't think there's much use. The child must be hiding, and if she can't hear us call her name, there isn't much point to a search now in the darkness. If the moon stayed out, I would consider it, but it's dark as Hades out there. The men gave me their word they'd be here at sunrise to start out again," Hugh said wearily. "I'm not as young as I used to be. Tramping and climbing that bluff is for the likes of someone a lot younger than me."

"MacDuff, you don't think . . . she wouldn't . . . what I mean . . ."

"Did she go over the bluff? Is that what you're trying to say? I don't know. We won't know till morning. Maybe you better have another try at the missus."

"At three o'clock in the morning?" Lena's tone was incredulous. "You didn't hear her the last time I spoke to her. She meant it when she said she didn't want to hear another word about Mary."

"Then Miss Anne? Wake her and tell her about her little sister?"

"They should be told, but you know as well as I do that the Powerses aren't like other people. All right, all right, I'll wake Mrs. Powers," Lena said. "But she isn't going to speak to me, I just want you to know that." Lena marched up the stairs to Anne Powers's suite of rooms. She rapped sharply and waited. When there was no response, she rapped again. And then a third time. When there was still no response, she kicked angrily at the door with her foot. The loud sound was enough to wake the dead. "What is it?" came the muffled reply.

"It's Lena, Mrs. Powers. It's about Mary. I have to talk to you."

"Tomorrow, Lena. Not one more word about that . . . that child. I will not be disturbed at this hour of the night. Handle the matter, whatever it is, and don't bother me again. This is the second time I've had to speak to you, Lena. One more time is grounds for dismissal."

Lena sighed wearily. She had come this far, she might as well go all the way. She was a good cook, and good cooks who knew their business could always get a job. "Mrs. Powers, Mary has been missing since this afternoon. Hugh and the other men on the hill have been looking for her, but we can't find her."

"That's utter nonsense. The child is hiding. She does it all the time. She loves it when she's the center of attention and is making trouble for everyone. Go to sleep and don't bother me again. Go back to bed before you wake Miss Anne."

Lena felt the urge to put her fist through the heavy door. Instead she turned on her heel and headed back to the kitchen. Hugh sat at the wooden table, his untouched cup of coffee in front of him.

Lena's tone was cool, almost mocking, when she made her statement. "Mrs. Powers doesn't wish to be bothered. She said Mary was hiding and liked to cause trouble. She doesn't want to be disturbed again until morning. She told me to be quiet before I woke Miss Anne. I kicked the door."

"Did you now. I always said you were a woman with her own mind," Hugh said tiredly. "I probably would have knocked the door down myself."

"I wanted to put my fist through it," Lena admitted. "Hugh, do you think anything happened to the tyke? I've always had a special kind of feeling for little Mary. I can hardly believe she can't hear, but it does explain so many things. I used to talk to her till I was blue in the face and she would just turn and smile at me. The times I wanted to take a stick to her. Now I'm glad I didn't. You should have married, Hugh, and had children of your own. I know how you love Mary and Callie. I also know they are the children you never had. You didn't fool me for one minute."

Hugh swallowed his coffee. "Who would be wanting to marry the likes of a man like myself? Someone else's children are less wearying and less trouble than one's own. But right now I feel like Mary is my own. Callie too. We have to put our heads together and figure out what to do for the lass now that a baby is coming."

"You'll be acting like a grandfather next thing you know," Lena said, trying for a light tone.

"'Spect you're right. Time will tell. I'll be getting some shut-eye. The coffee was good, Lena. The men said their thanks to me. Get some sleep, and we'll give it another round at sunup."

Lena washed and rinsed the cups and then dried them. She washed out the coffee pot and readied it for morning. Her kitchen set to rights, she went to her room and lay down fully clothed. Sunup would arrive shortly.

Hugh rubbed at his aching knee joints and leaned back in his bed. The moonlight was gone, and before long it was going to rain. His knees said so. If the poor child didn't find some protection, she would get soaking wet. She must be cold and hungry by now. If there was only something he could do. He was realistic enough to know that dead of night was no time to search the woods and the bluff. A body could go right off without even knowing it until it was too late. Little girls who were upset and couldn't hear could lose their bearings and plummet down to the bottom. The thought was so horrible Hugh dragged out his pipe and pretended to stuff it with tobacco. When he realized he was just fingering the pipe, he stuck it back into his pocket in disgust.

Callie was now another worry. Lord, what had he done wrong to have these problems foisted on him? He cared, he told himself, and the Almighty also chose those who cared to carry out his wishes. He believed this implicitly. What would become of the young girl from Ireland? Someone had to take care of her now that she was expecting a child. It wouldn't be easy to find her any kind of job in her condition. What employer would put up with a servant who was sick half the time? Lena had told him on more than one occasion that she caught Callie vomiting and holding her stomach. He had to come up with some kind of solution and come up with it quick. Poor lass, she would have been better off to stay in Ireland. America wasn't treating her too well, and now with a baby coming God alone knew what would happen to her.

What he needed was a couple of dollops of whiskey, for the ache in his knee. He'd long ago given up liniments and salve in favor of the whiskey bottle. Several mouthfuls later he was tempted to make the trek into St. George to tell Callie they hadn't found Mary. Now what good would that do? It would only make her more anxious, more fretful. No, he would wait till he had something to report.

She was a bonny lass, Callie James was. A fitting bride and wife for young Rossiter Powers. A pity the boy wasn't man enough to realize what he was losing. Tied to his *Mamán*'s apron strings with a knot in the middle of the string, Hugh thought sourly. The whole damn kit and kaboodle of the Powers family, with the exception of Mary, weren't worth Callie's little finger. He snorted angrily as he tried to shift to a more comfortable position on his narrow bed over the carriage house.

The minute the first drop of rain hit the roof Hugh was up like a streak of lightning. A few more minutes and it would be dawn. He felt damp and chilled. If he knew Lena, she would have a fire going in the kitchen and a pot of coffee bubbling on the stove.

As soon as Lena saw him, she wrung her hands and cried, "She didn't come back at all during the night. I lay awake with my door open. I swear I didn't get a wink of sleep. She's lost to us, MacDuff, I can feel it in my bones."

"The others will be here soon to start the search. Did you make plenty of coffee?"

"A whole pot. There's plenty. Hugh, it's raining hard, and it's so damp and miserable out there. The child can get deathly ill from such a damp chill. Drink your coffee now. I can see Josh and Ian coming up the path." Quickly she set out two more cups and poured the dark, fragrant brew. The men drank it gratefully and helped themselves to some of Lena's homemade muffins that were full of wild blueberries she and Mary had picked the summer before. Her eyes filled with tears as she looked from face to face. How grim they looked. They must know as I do that something has happened, she thought. Poor child, to be so upset she ran away like that with no thought about anything. The screen door slammed a second time as Carl, Henry, and a man named Jack, along with his fourteen-year-old son Seth walked into the kitchen. They drank their coffee quickly and set out single file. Within seconds they were lost to Lena's view with the low-lying mist and steady rain shrouding them. Never one to leave anything to chance, Lena blessed herself, not once but twice.

Chapter Eighteen

Mary awakened into her world of silence. At first she was frightened not to find herself home, safe, in her own bed. But then she remembered where she was and why. Her small face pinched with the pain of her insecurity, and she tried to snuggle back down into her nest of leaves and scrub. The wet, chilly air made her shiver miserably. She had to go home. Home to face her angry mother and accept her punishment. Mary still wasn't quite certain of the details of yesterday afternoon. She only knew she'd attacked her mother and that she was losing Callie. She didn't care about the punishment, she even believed she deserved it. She didn't care about anything except Callie and being warm again.

Feeling small and frightened by the whipping of the wind and the rain that was beginning to fall in slanting sheets, Mary took cover beneath the protection of an oak tree, trying to orient herself, uncertain of which way was home. She'd never wandered so far from the house before, and everything appeared unfamiliar in the rain. She held out her arm and spun in a circle. When she stopped, she would go in the direction she pointed. Sooner or later she would find her way.

She must have slept the night. It was today, not yesterday. She didn't remember what time she'd run from the house, but it must have been before dinner—her stomach was rumbling. Her thoughts were chaotic as she attempted to piece together yesterday's events. "I didn't say my prayers last night!" Since Callie's arrival she and Mary made a practice of kneeling beside their beds and saying their prayers. Quickly Mary dropped to the ground, the wet seeping through her lisle stockings and the hem of her dress. "Please, God, take care of Callie. Let her miss me the way I miss her. I'm sorry I screamed at her. Please, let her love me again. Bless *Papá* and Rossiter and Lena and Mr. MacDuff. Bless the kittens, especially the littlest one because his legs aren't so strong. Some day make me hear again if it isn't too much trouble." She was about to ask for her own blessing when she grudgingly added two additional requests. "Bless Anne and *Mamán*. Don't forget what I said about Callie. Oh, yes, bless me and help me get back home, and I'd be obliged if You didn't let me get sick. This is Mary Powers, Your loving child, God." Mary blessed herself and immediately felt better. Everything was in His hands now.

Heading off in the direction she thought was home, Mary braced herself against the wind and the rain, her thoughts on Lena's warm kitchen with the new kittens sleeping by the stove. Warm chocolate and honey buns would taste so good right now. She smacked her lips in anticipation.

The heavens opened up, and the rain came pelting down. Lightning flashed in the sky, and she could almost hear the sharp cracks of thunder. It seemed the trees were reaching out for her with bony fingers as they bent in the wind, the shadows beneath them darker and more terrifying. Was she going in the right direction? She didn't think so; it seemed she had been climbing for too long a time. All she had to do was change direction, back up, move to the left, and she'd be going downhill. She knew her house was not at the highest point of Todt Hill, it was just below the crest. She didn't hear the snap of the tree branches or the skittering of rocks and earth. She did feel the uncertainty of the ledge and the rumblings of the thunder in her stomach, like a big drum vibrating within her.

Frightened, Mary grasped at bushes and scrub, stripping their leaves, unable to get a handhold. The ledge began to crumble under her, mud sliding from beneath her feet. She felt herself slipping, sliding down the bluff. She was falling, falling . . . "Cal-llliiiieee!"

It was mid-afternoon when the somber-faced search party filed up the path to the Powers's kitchen. Hugh MacDuff carried Mary's broken, battered body. Lena took one look at his burden and felt the floor sway under her feet. Ian Flannery and Josh helped her to her chair near the stove. "Give her here to me." Lena reached out for Mary, cradling the little girl in her lap, tenderly brushing away the dirt and leaves that clung to her face and hair. She rocked back and forth, crooning, crying. MacDuff angrily brushed at the tears streaming down his craggy face. "She was such a little one," he murmured, "so frightened and lost. Aye, but she's home now. Give her over to me, Lena, I'll bring her up to her room and lay her in her bed."

This time Lena didn't bother knocking on Mrs. Powers's door. She opened it and walked into the dimness. The curtains were still drawn, and sounds of quiet breathing came from the bed. Lena touched Anne's shoulder, rousing her, speaking her name.

Anne awakened grudgingly. "How dare you come into my room?" she croaked hoarsely. Lena's eyes spied a packet of sleeping powders on the bedside table. "It's barely daylight," Anne complained. "If the house isn't on fire, you'd better have a good explanation." She struggled to a sitting position and was about to launch into further complaints when she noticed the expression on Lena's face and was stilled. Something was wrong, terribly wrong.

Lena licked dry lips. How to say it, where were the words? How to soften the blow? "It's Mary, ma'am."

"I thought I told . . ." Seeing pity in Lena's eyes, Anne straightened, locking her gaze with Lena's. "What about Mary? Did she hurt herself?" A knot of apprehension lodged itself in her throat.

Lena clenched her hands, wringing them. Best to say it right out—"Mary is dead." She waited for her words to sink in, waited for the reaction. None was forthcoming. The message was too far from the limits of comprehension. "Hugh MacDuff just brought the poor mite's body home. She . . . she fell off the bluff. MacDuff says the ground was weakened by the rain and just pulled away from under her. We . . . we have her in her room. We didn't know what to do."

"Dead! Mary can't be dead!" Anne rejected Lena's words, her mind reeling. "Why, just yesterday she was being so willful and naughty. Some other child, someone else's child, not Mary. Not *my* Mary!" How could her child be dead? She was so full of life. There must be a mistake! There was a terrible mistake! Lena's eyes told her it was no mistake.

"I'll take you up to her, Mrs. Powers. You'll want to see to things yourself."

Anne climbed from bed and tried on two attempts to fit her arms into her wrapper. Finally Lena had to help her. Supporting her mistress with a firm grip, she led her up the stairs to the nursery. Gently she pushed the stricken mother closer to the small, narrow bed. MacDuff tenderly pulled back the sheet and stood nearby with folded hands, tears glistening in his eyes.

Anne's hands flew to her mouth as she sank to her knees, her head dropping to the little chest. Harsh sobs racked her body as she took one small, bruised hand into her own. How cold her child was. The bright red hair and dotting of freckles were stark against the pale, ashen features. "Oh God, oh God!" she wailed. "A doctor, call a doctor!"

"It's too late for a doctor," MacDuff said gruffly. "The child is dead, and you've got to be thinking of her father now. How can we reach him?"

"Yes, yes. You take care of that, Hugh. You'll find the address on my desk. Send for him. Rossiter too," she added as an afterthought. Anne Powers's strength failed her. Mary's death had reduced her to a state of helplessness, dependent upon others. She reached out a trembling hand to touch Mary's face, smoothing back the tendrils of damp hair that clung to her forehead. "How could this have happened?" she asked in a small voice.

Lena's lips clamped shut, her eyes narrowed. How? How indeed?

Hugh MacDuff brought the letter to Jasper directly to a Boston-bound steamer, with payment and instructions that it be delivered immediately upon reaching port. Then he retraced his steps to St. George and the rooming house where Callie was staying. He thought it to be the saddest mission he would ever do in his life—telling Callie about Mary's death. He knew she would blame herself, and he anticipated her grief.

At first Callie could hardly believe what she was hearing. Dead? Mary dead? Her eyes widened in disbelief; she crossed the bare floorboards of her meager room, hands extended to Hugh, imploring him to tell her it was all a mistake, that Mary was fine, that she ran across the yard to the chicken coop, that she played with the kittens near the kitchen stove. That she hadn't fallen from the bluff.

Hugh stood in the center of the room, as tall and as strong as a tree, wincing from the plight of her pain not from the attack of her tiny fists beating against him, demanding he take back his words, demanding he tell her Mary was alive.

Hugh seized her wrists in his large, calloused hands, holding them still, meeting Callie's pain with tears in his own eyes. "'Tis true, lass," he murmured mournfully. "The wee one is dead, and there's naught to be done for it."

Callie fell against him, seeing the terrible truth in his face. He held her, feeling an overpowering protectiveness toward her. She was so young, so vulnerable, and in spite of her resiliency and spunk, there was a heart-rending frailty about her, as though she would fly into a thousand pieces that would never be put together again. The young could never deal with death, he told himself; it took age and maturity to face mortality and to have the faith and the certainty that life could go on.

Hugh lifted her into his arms, hardly burdened by the weight of her. She wrapped her arms around him, weeping broken-heartedly into the hollow of his neck. He placed her on the bed, sitting beside her, feeling helpless and ineffectual as he patted her back and smoothed her hair, staying with her as she cried her grief. When she quieted, he told her softly, "It's to be a simple funeral, Callie lass, only the family. There's nothing you can do for our Mary now, except pray for her soul and keeping yourself strong. I've just now sent a letter to Mr. Powers in Boston calling him and Master Rossiter home."

Callie nodded through her tears. She understood what Hugh was telling her. Rossiter would come home for Mary's funeral, and Hugh would make it his business to tell him where to find Callie. Ignorant of the fact that Anne Powers had purloined Callie's letter from the mailbox, they both assumed that Rossiter knew he was to become a father.

"All things work for the best in the end, Callie," Hugh told her. "You mustn't be thinking about Mary now. Think of yourself and the child you carry and that Rossiter will soon come to you."

Callie did not attend Mary's funeral, realizing she would be unwelcome. Jasper returned from Boston alone. Rossiter was in Chicago with his uncle and was still not aware there was a death in the family. It was only Hugh's promise that when the first wildflowers came to bloom, he would take her to visit the grave, that comforted Callie.

As the days wore on and Callie's spirits and strength returned, Hugh, on one of his daily visits to bring food from the Powers's kitchen, told her that Mrs. Powers had returned to Boston with Jasper and Anne and the house was empty. He and Lena had been given notice, and as soon as the house was closed, they were dismissed and the house put up for sale. He forced a smile when he showed Callie the generous severance pay Jasper had given him.

"The house is being sold, you say?" Callie questioned, her eyes speaking the unasked.

"Aye, lass. I asked after Master Rossiter, and all I could glean was that he was away with his uncle. Lena's been trying to find out his exact whereabouts, but the answers are always vague."

"I know what you and Lena are trying to do, and I thank you both, but surely Rossiter has received my letter by now and knows about the baby. It's obvious he doesn't care." Callie lifted her chin as she murmured this last, having come face to face with the reality over the long days. She was amazed that she could say it aloud, that the hopes and dreams she had held so close were as cold and dead as little Mary.

Hugh led Callie over to a hard-backed chair, kneeling before her, cap in hand, looking up into her sweet face. "Callie, lass, I want to help you, and I've an offer to make. I'm not a young man, Callie, and I should have married years ago and raised a family of my own. This past year I've given a good deal of thought to what I've missed in my life and, well . . . I want to marry you, Callie," he blurted. Then once the words were out, he seemed to gather courage. "Your bairn will be needing a name, Callie, and I want to give you my protection for as long as you need it. I can't offer much, but I can put a roof over your head and food in your stomach, that much I can promise you."

Callie stared at MacDuff in disbelief. "You would do that for me?"

"And more if I could. You've come to mean so much to me, lass. I can give you a good life. You and the bairn." Hugh looked into Callie's face, feeling his heart swell with tenderness and loving. He cast his eyes downward, unwilling for her to see the emotion there. His motives were not entirely unselfish; this child, who had come into his life and heart with her short-cropped hair and snub nose, had become a woman before his very eyes. His hand wanted to reach out, to touch the softness of her skin and the silkiness of her hair. She was like a gift that had come so late into his life, soft and shining, singing and laughing, and he loved her. But she was so young, so lovely, and she deserved more in life than to be married to a hard-lipped old codger like himself. Callie deserved youth to match her own, beauty to enhance her own . . . no, he promised, he would never force himself upon her.

He could only hope that one day she would accept him as a man and bring herself to him, just as she had given herself to Rossiter.

Sensing her hesitancy to answer, he patted her hand lightly, rising to his feet. "Don't decide this minute. Think about it, and I'll come back tomorrow. There's still work to be done at the house."

Long after Hugh had left, Callie pondered the fairness of accepting his offer of marriage. She paced the confines of her rented room, knowing that this shelter too would soon be gone. She had some savings, but not enough to keep her until after the baby was born. It was not her own needs for food and shelter that troubled her. It was only the baby's. Only the baby mattered.

How could she marry Hugh MacDuff when it was Rossiter she loved? She, who had nowhere to turn, had been offered a solution. She must force herself to admit that Rossiter was lost to her forever. He did not want her, nor did he want their child. Hugh must know this too, otherwise he never would have offered marriage.

Callie's only other choice seemed to be Byrch Kenyon, but her shame was so great she couldn't bear the thought of facing him, disappointing him, going to him with shattered pride. She had to make her own way in this life; she could not depend upon the charity of others. Hugh said he wanted a wife, a family. He said there was a place in his life she could fill. Marrying him would be an answer, not one to her liking, but an answer nevertheless.

Callie curled up on the bed, her temples throbbing with apprehension. How could she ever repay Hugh's generosity? She would try to be a good wife. She would cook and clean and make life as pleasant as she could for the lonely man. She would do her best for him. But she would never love him.

She turned her face into her pillow, weeping for the girl she had once been, so full of spirit and determination, the girl Byrch had met in the alley the night she'd stolen the basket of groceries. Where had that girl gone? What had happened to her? She thought of Beth and her unswerving adoration of Patrick and of her sacrifice. She thought of her mother, defending Thom, having one child after another, and living in poverty. Then there was herself, falling in love with Rossiter, giving herself to him because she believed she could make him happy. Why? She pounded her fists into the pillow, her body heaving with racking sobs. Why were women always falling in love with the wrong men?

She remembered standing in the kitchen with her mother, the early morning light coming through the window, everyone else in the house asleep. "I'll not be like you, Mum!" she had protested

Peggy's defense of her worthless husband. "It's my head that'll rule my life. Not my heart!" Tears washed onto the pillow, tears for the baby, for Rossiter, for the girl she had once been.

Five days later the house on Todt Hill was closed. Lena covered all the furniture and closed the drapes. It was never what one would have called a happy home. It had always been a house of intrigues and secrets and jealousies. It had been more than Lena had expected when Mrs. Powers told her that she'd found employment for her with the Schuyller family in Richmondtown, a town just to the south on Staten Island. Mr. Powers had been generous with her severance pay, and the small wad of bills was sewn into the hem of her best nightgown.

Lena would miss working in this house, in the kitchen she'd come to call her own over the past eighteen years. She sighed; she would have one last cup of coffee and then wash out the pot. The larder and pantry and root cellar were empty. The apples she'd peeled and sliced and spread on clean sheets in the attic to dry had been lifted, removed, and disposed of. The carrots and potatoes that still grew in the carefully tilled earth in the kitchen garden would go to rot. The hams and corned beef and crocks of sauerkraut and preserved jams and jellies were all donated to the church, as were the sacks of flour and rice and barley wheat. The chickens and Mary's kittens were given to the Flannery family; the carriage and buggy and the team of horses were also given to the church. Nothing was left to show a family had once lived here—nothing except used furniture and unwanted clothing left behind.

Lena would miss the gruff, taciturn Hugh MacDuff. A pity she'd been unable to woo him. The Lord knew she'd tried hard enough. He certainly wasn't the best catch in the world, but she was getting up in years herself. A tear glistened in the corner of her eye. It would be nice to grow old with someone, even if it was someone as cantankerous as MacDuff. Her dreams of carrying him a hot toddy on cold winter evenings and having him rub her back were over. Now she'd have to come up with something else to put her to sleep. Some other dream. MacDuff wasn't the marrying kind, never was and never would be. Too set in his ways. He liked to sit in the tavern with his cronies over a dollop or two. With her luck, on the night she wanted her back rubbed, he would be swapping stories with his cronies and not give her aching back a thought. He'd probably spend all her small savings on whiskey, and then where would she be? Out in the cold, that's where. She would carry a warm spot in her heart for a long time for the Scotsman.

Hugh was sitting at the kitchen table, waiting for her when Lena walked through the wide doorway. Just like a man, he wouldn't dream of making the coffee or pouring for the both of them. Wait for her to wait on him hand and foot. A lot he cared about her aching back. As she set about rinsing the pot for fresh brew, she watched him out of the corner of her eye. "Have you had any luck with getting a job, Hugh?"

"I haven't been doing much looking. The two leads Mr. Powers gave me were filled when I got there. I got time. Don't get cocky with me now just because you're stepping into a new fine position."

"Hrmph," Lena snorted as she measured coffee into the pot. "I'm not going to worry about an old codger like you. I have myself to think about."

"You should worry, you aren't getting any younger," Hugh snapped.

Hands on hips, Lena bristled. "What's that supposed to mean?"

"It means that you're going to have to find a family that will take care of you in your old years, that's what it means. You should have gotten remarried a long time ago," Hugh mumbled.

"I would have if someone asked me. I would have married you if you asked me. What do you think of that, Hugh MacDuff?"

"Not much. I'm not near good enough for you, Lena. I'm not saying I'm not honored by your devotion, but what would you be wanting with the likes of me?"

"I thought you might rub my back on cold winter nights," Lena said sourly. Hugh made a sound that Lena supposed was a laugh. With Hugh it was hard to tell. "I'm going to miss you, you miserable old man."

"I'll miss you too, Lena. You make the best coffee and apple pie I ever tasted."

"Hold up your cup now and drink hearty. What do you say we add a few dollops of that 'medicine' you carry about in your hip pocket?"

"That's one of your better suggestions, Lena. You see, you're getting the hang of things. That's what a man likes."

Two coffee pots later, the flask from Hugh's pocket was empty. He rocked back on his chair, staring at Lena. "You're not an ugly woman. In fact, I think you're one hell of a woman, and the man who finally lands you is going to get a fine wife," Hugh said, his tongue loosened by the whiskey.

"The problem is, if I do find him, will he rub my back for me?"

"Well, if he doesn't, you call me, and I'll come and do it for you. I won't marry you, but I'll rub your back. It's the least I can do for all the coffee and pie."

Lena felt as though her eyes were crossed. She wondered what would happen if she stood up. Not liking what she thought might be the answer, she stayed glued to her chair, her hands around her coffeecup. She decided she was as drunk as Hugh, maybe more so. Hugh didn't have a twin brother sitting next to him. "You're tipsy," she hiccoughed.

"I know. So are you. Shame too, you being such a fine woman and all."

"If I'm such a damn fine woman, why won't you marry me, you old goat?"

Hugh leaned across the table and leered at her. "Because I'm marrying someone else. Out of . . . necessity."

Lena thought she would swallow her tongue. "You old lecher, are you telling me you got some woman into a spot, and now you're marrying her to make an honest woman of her? If that's true, you're a dis . . . disgusting, dirty old man. Who would climb beneath the covers with the likes of you? Who is it?" Lena asked, slamming her coffee cup down on the table with a loud bang. She watched as the coffee sloshed over the clean table and dripped onto the floor. She wasn't cleaning it up. By God, she might not even clean out the coffee pot. She should get up off her chair and push that crazy old fool right off his chair and them stomp him to death. Here she was, pouring out her heart, confiding about her bad back, and drinking with the old coot in the bargain, and what does he do? Tell's her he's marrying someone else.

"Why do you want to know?" MacDuff asked craftily. "You wouldn't be having ideas about objecting to the nuptials now, would you?"

"Not likely, Hugh MacDuff. Not likely at all. Anyone fool enough to marry the likes of you deserves everything she gets. You should be ashamed of yourself. Who are you marrying?" Lena demanded.

"Callie James," Hugh blustered.

Lena sat and stared at Hugh for a long time. Her gaze was wide and unblinking. Tears filled her eyes and ran down her cheeks. "Hugh MacDuff, I take back everything I said about you. That's the nicest thing I ever heard of. Is Callie happy?"

"I don't know. There wasn't any other choice for her. What

could she do, where could she go? I'll take care of her and give the bairn my name. It's a sin for a child to be born out of wedlock. Callie thanked me for my offer. I'll be good to her and the bairn. Stop your crying now, or I swear I'll never rub your back. If the lass wasn't in such dire straits, I might have given you a second thought. I know I'm drunk and so are you, but I know what I'm saying. You're a fine woman, and don't you ever let anyone tell you different."

Lena wiped her eyes and sniffed loudly. "You wouldn't be lying to me now, would you?"

"Not to a fine woman like yourself. I best be getting back. If I was you, Lena, I'd take a small snooze. People here on the hill won't take kindly to a drunken housekeeper wobbling down the road. Don't wash the pot, just throw it and the cups out in the trash. Can you get in bed by yourself?"

"I'm just drunk, not feeble," Lena grumbled as she staggered to her room off the kitchen.

"Mind to set the latch when you leave," Hugh warned.

Loud, lusty snores wafted through the doorway. He had to admit it, she was one hell of a woman. Rubbing her back on a cold winter night wouldn't have been all that bad. Lena would be all right. He fixed the latch and left the Powers's house for the last time. He didn't look back.

The day Callie James married Hugh MacDuff was damp and cold with an October wind that chilled the bones. Early that morning, Hugh had come for her at the rooming house in St. George. The mist had hung close to the ground, obscuring the pavement and the heavens alike. They had taken the ferry across to New York City, hiring a porter to take their belongings in his cart to the apartment on Fulton Street that Hugh had rented.

The best that could be said for the three squalid rooms was that they were mean-looking. Only the parlor had two windows that faced onto the street; the other two room were interior compartments without any windows at all. The stove in the kitchen was thick with grease and burnt-on food; a table and two chairs, one of them broken, stood in the middle of the spare room. There was only a dry sink; water would have to be brought from the pump two floors down, outside the back door. In the front parlor was a heavy horsehair sofa and one chair, both dirty and shabby, upholstered in what once must have been a dark cranberry red. Scarred tables of assorted sizes and shapes were grouped around the peeling walls, and there was one oil lamp. The bedroom was a narrow cell containing an iron bedstead with a gray, lumpy mattress and an odd hard-backed chair. A bedspread and a rag rug would help. Soap and elbow grease, combined with determination, would work wonders, but they couldn't produce miracles.

"You're deserving of so much more than this," Hugh told her somberly, "but rents being what they are, this was the best I could do."

Callie touched the sleeve of Hugh's tweed jacket, her voice warmed by gratitude. "I'll make it a home for you, Mr. Mac . . . Hugh. If it weren't for you, I'd have much less than this." Unwillingly her eyes went to the iron bedstead. Hugh shuffled from one foot to the other, cap held between nervous, fumbling fingers.

"I know you don't think of me that way, lass, and I won't be forcing myself on you. I'll be sleeping out on the sofa until you tell me otherwise."

Callie's hands flew to her face to hide the sudden flush of color; her breath came in small, desperate gasps. "No, no, it's all wrong! You're a good man, you deserve a woman who'll be a real wife to you," she wept.

"Here, here, don't be cryin' like that, it breaks my heart, lass. I only want to be your friend and only ask that you be here when I come home in the evening. It's more than a man like me has a right to expect, having a pretty young lass like yourself for my wife and having you share the bairn with me. Don't cry, Callie, please don't cry!" His voice rose in alarm; his experience with women was limited. He was a hard-bitten man, unused to expressing his feelings. He knew there were times he came across as stiff and unbending, but it was only his way. He didn't know much about being a husband, less about being a lover, but he did know that he loved Callie James and would wait for the day when she would come unbidden into his arms, the Good Lord willing. And if that day never came, he would be satisfied to have her share her life with him, share her child, and allow him to worship her from afar.

These very emotions, if he'd been able to express them, might have softened Callie's heart, might have touched her sympathy and innate sense of fairness. But she was overwhelmed by her gratitude, and that blinded her to Hugh's real desires. She was simply grateful that his demands on her were so few; that loving Rossiter as she did and knowing what it meant for a woman to give herself to a man, Hugh would not demand this of her.

Together they dashed through the wet mists to City Hall where they pronounced their vows before a court justice. Callie had to be asked to raise her voice, to repeat the vows twice before the justice nodded, smiling at this shy young girl who was marrying this fine Scotsman. Callie was nearly paralyzed by the import of what she was doing. She was marrying a man she didn't love while her hands were clasped over her belly to hide the babe another man had put there. Her guilt made her feel helpless, her helplessness angered her, and her anger brought a wave of remorse. She tried to remember her gratitude to Hugh, but instead she felt only anger—at herself and at Rossiter. Granda used to say that no matter how hard the bed, if you made it, you must sleep in it. Callie gritted her teeth and swore to honor and obey.

Busy days followed for Callie as she scrubbed and cleaned the tiny apartment from top to bottom. She made an agreement with the landlord's wife that if whitewash was provided she would paint the rooms. She let out the seams of her dresses, glad that she'd taken the uniforms Mrs. Powers had provided. The heavy black bombazine was warm on a winter's day and disguised her burgeoning belly.

Each day Hugh would set out to find work, only to return each evening in defeat. He was always too late or too old or something. Work was hard to find, he would say, trying to keep the bitterness out of his tone. So many times he'd bitten back the words that because of the influx of Irish immigrants, labor was plentiful and cheap, making it difficult for an unskilled worker to find employment.

Almost guiltily Hugh told Callie he'd heard of a woman who wanted ironing done. He would pick up and deliver if Callie was willing. His young bride nodded enthusiastically. She would have scrubbed floors or returned to the button factory if it would help Hugh. She owed him so much—for the roof over her head and the food in her stomach. He had dug into his small savings to purchase a frypan and a decent cookpot, clean pillows and warm blankets for her bed. The stove was never without coal, warming them through the dark November days, and fresh cream and butter and slabs of bacon were in the box hanging outside the parlor windows. Each morning he brought a fresh pail of water from the pump downstairs and had bought Callie a thick-lined cloak that was wide and flowing to cover her swollen body and keep out the wind.

One ironing job turned into two and then three. She spent long hours standing near the stove to heat her flatirons, perspiration dripping down her face. Her back ached and her legs throbbed, but she never complained. Dutifully she would hand over the payment to her husband, never keeping any for herself. He provided for her, she reasoned, he was her husband, and all she ever had to do was to ask for what she wanted. But Callie never asked.

Callie did her best as the weeks dragged into months. She cooked hot, substantial meals for Hugh, who was becoming more discouraged by the day with no permanent offers of work coming his way. He had taken to bringing home a bottle of whiskey, bought with her ironing money. He began coming home later and later, she noticed. Twice in one week she'd had to trudge across town, lugging a heavy basket, because he hadn't come home to deliver it. When she had finally made her way back home, she had collapsed on the bed, her legs throbbing with cramps, her back near to breaking. She wished she believed in miracles. This was to be her life, the same as her mother's. With one difference—Peggy loved Thomas.

Once the baby was born, things would be different, she promised herself. She wondered if her mother had ever had the same hope. Things would never be different unless Hugh found a steady job. Now that he was drinking more and more, she wasn't sure of anything. All she knew was that she was a burden to him, and perhaps she was being unfair because she felt so helpless in these late stages of her pregnancy. Maybe Hugh *was* doing his best. It wasn't his fault he couldn't find steady work. Another ironing job would help, and perhaps they could put enough by to pay the midwife when she was needed. Tears of frustration and confusion trickled down her cheeks. She was so sick of feeling helpless, of not taking charge of her life. She was thinking of Beth more and more these days, and visions of Mary would intrude at the oddest moments. Then she would stand over her ironing board and cry for her mother and the little ones back home. Things must get better, she prayed. They must!

Callie was wrong. It was a snowy January, a month before the baby was due, when the landlord knocked on the apartment door, demanding not one but two months' back rent.

"We just owe you for this month," Callie said in a frightened voice.

"If that's what your man's been telling you, he lied. Get his snoot out of the bottle and pay up or out you go. You have to the end of the week."

Hugh came home a bit after sundown, carrying a basket of ironing to be done. He wore a pleased expression as he told her he picked up two days' wages doing yard work for the woman who asked to have the ironing back by morning. "That's why I got the job, Callie. I hated to take it, and I know how tired you are. But it was the only edge I had over three others who came for the same job."

"I'm not that tired that I can't iron out a few things. But you look tired, Hugh. Sit here while I fix you some supper." While she heated butter in the cast-iron frypan, she told him about the landlord's ultimatum that morning. She tried to keep her tone light, as though she wasn't worried, but Hugh's shoulders slumped in defeat.

"With the two days' wages and your ironing it still won't be enough. There's hardly any food left for the rest of the week, and then Lord knows what'll happen."

Callie's heart went out to him, and she rushed to his side, putting her arms around his neck, pressing her cheek against his grizzled hair. "We'll manage. We have so far. We could look for a cheaper place to live. Anything is all right with me. Don't be blaming yourself. We're both doing all we can. Oh, Hugh," she cried in a sudden rush of emotion, "I don't ever want you to be sorry you married me."

"I could never be sorry," Hugh said, gripping her arms in his hands, overwhelmed by this display of affection. How long he'd prayed, how many nights he'd slept out on the sofa listening for her slightest whisper! "It's you I'm concerned about, Callie. I painted you such a bright picture of how I'd take care of you, and this is so bleak, it'd make a convict cry. I'm fifty-odd years old, Callie, and look every day of it. It's young, strong backs they want when they hire, not defeated old men."

"You're not old! You're not! And they don't know how strong you are; I've seen you work, Hugh. I've watched you carry those heavy sacks of feed for the Powers's horses and lift and move furniture as though they were sticks of matches. You'll get your chance; I know you will!"

"Thank you for your vote of confidence, lass. You're a dear one to say it. But you're right about one thing—we do have to find cheaper lodgings. At least until things get better for us. I know I haven't been much help with my snoot in the bottle, spending good money on whiskey. I won't do it anymore, my solemn promise."

Callie nodded, hiding the despair in her eyes. How often she'd heard her father, Thomas, say those same words to Peggy, make those same promises. How often she'd seen the spark of hope in her mother's eyes. Some things never changed. Like mother, like daughter.

Chapter Nineteen

The next morning Hugh was up before dawn. Callie folded the last freshly ironed pillow slip and laid it on top of the basket. She ached so violently that she actually felt numb. Hugh led her to a chair and pulled her shoes off, gently massaging her feet and swollen legs. "You stay here. When I get back, I'll pack everything that needs taking. When I went out last night, I found us a place; it's not to our liking, but it'll have to do. When I've finished work, I'll hire a wagon for us and our things. Let's have a smile now, and say you forgive this old man for making things so hard on you."

Callie smiled weakly. "Everything will be fine, Hugh. You take that ironing back, and I'll sleep for a while. I'll help you pack. I'm all right, really I am."

He waited for her to ask where he was taking her, but she didn't. It was best she not know until the last. The Irish called it Shantytown, and it was a miserable place of hovels at the far end of a field uptown past Seventy-second Street. A crony from the tavern down the street told him there was a vacancy just near his sister-in-law's place, and if he grabbed it before anyone else, it would be his. Hugh had followed the man's instructions, taking the endlessly long walk uptown. The poverty of the slum he found made his heart turn over, but just as his friend had said, there was a vacant shack. It had been picked clean, not even the cast-iron stove remained, but it had a roof and walls and would keep out the wind if not the cold. And Callie would be among her own people.

Callie was an angel from heaven for not blaming him, Hugh told himself. His conscience pricked him all the way to the house where he delivered the ironing. He worked half the day, clearing out the woman's basement and repairing the coal bin. With the money in his hand from an honest day's labor he felt almost rich. The woman told him she would recommend him to her friends and that he should come by next week to see if she had any more work for him. Hugh was heartened. Callie couldn't do any more ironing. He had wanted to cry earlier that morning when he massaged her swollen feet. He wasn't doing right by her, and he knew it. All he had to do was stay away from that devil whiskey and things would look up. Once *their* baby was born, things would be better for sure.

Hugh found himself thinking of Callie's child as his own. As he came to know Callie better, came to love her more, it was increasingly difficult for him to admit that she had been with another man. He refused to think about Rossiter, even to speak his name. Callie's child would be his own, and one day, with heaven's help, Callie would come to him as a real wife, inviting him to share her bed. She had so much love to give, she needed to be loved, and Hugh was determined to be the man to give it to her.

Callie didn't like skipping out without paying the rent, but she knew there was no other way. There simply wasn't the money, and by the end of the week they would have been thrown out on the street anyway, with the landlord more than likely confiscating all their worldly possessions. The wagon Hugh hired rolled through the streets, lurching and bouncing in and out of the ruts, shuddering over the cobbles. On the edge of the city the driver took them to what must have once been an open field. Now it was a rabbit warren of little hovels, their stove pipes sticking through the patchwork roofs like indignant little fingers pointing to the sky. Trash and litter abounded between the huts, and Callie knew that when it rained, Shantytown would become a sea of mud and refuse. The little one-room shacks reminded Callie of the skalpeens in Ireland, constructed entirely from bits of timber and thatch salvaged from tumbled cottages and pilfered from fences. She caught the sound of someone speaking Gaelic and then voices thick with brogue. Had she sounded like that when she'd first come to America?

Hugh, sitting beside her, broke into her thoughts. "Did you hear that, Callie? You'll be among your own here. Irishmen, just like you."

Callie scowled, dropping her head so Hugh wouldn't see. Her own indeed. This wasn't where she belonged, Irish or not. Not this shanty town, not these filthy little hovels overcrowded with people and children and disease. This was what she wanted herself and her family to escape!

"It isn't much, Callie lass, but it's just for a while, I promise you. Just until the baby comes and we get a little money put aside. You won't be doing any ironing and standing on your feet either. I'll make sure you've got food in your belly if I have to steal it. I know skipping out on the rent wasn't right, nor helping ourselves to the poor furniture. But when we get on our feet, I'll make it right."

Callie turned on her seat beside the driver and looked over her shoulder. Under a tarpaulin she could just see the outline of the iron bedstead and the kitchen table and chairs. "When did you take down the bed, Hugh? I didn't see you do it."

"Aye, I know that, lass. I kept you busy washing out the pots down at the pump. I know you wouldn't have liked it, but you'll be glad I took them. The cottage is empty, lass, not a stick in it. Don't you worry now." He patted her hand. "I said I'll make it right some day, and I will."

Callie believed him. Peggy always believed Thom.

It was nearly dark when Hugh took her to the hut, but it wasn't too dark to see where the tarpaper roof and walls had been patched with odd boards and rusted tin. They'd had to walk the last bit of the way because the dirt lane did not go past their door; their hut was squeezed in between hundreds of others just like it.

When Hugh pushed open the door, Callie gasped in shock as a burly man wielding a cudgel made a threatening advance. Suddenly recognition dawned. "Oh, it's you, MacDuff. Well, I did what you told me, and I beat off anybody who thought to take over the place."

"Little wonder with that club you carry," Hugh grumbled, digging into his pocket for a coin to pay the man. He noticed Callie's questioning glance. "I have to pay the man, lass. Were it not for hiring him, somebody else would've grabbed the place and we'd have nowhere to go."

Callie glanced around the interior, seeing the small, one-room area with the chimney flue coming down from the roof and ending impotently in midair. Someone had taken the stove. The floor was partially built of boards; the rest was just dirt. How could she live here? How could Hugh have brought her here? She'd known poverty in her life, God knew, but nothing like this. Her father would never expect Peggy to live in a place like this. She squinted at her unshaven husband. He said it would be all right; she had to believe that.

Hugh and the driver brought in their pitiful belongings. Hugh was right; she was glad that he'd taken the bed and table and chairs. There wasn't room for much else besides a stove, which they didn't have, but Hugh, resourceful as he was, constructed a crude hearth from a rubble of stones, and by leaving the door open a crack, the small fire's smoke found its way up the flue. When they were alone, Hugh pointed to the double bed that stood at the far end of the room. "I'll have to share it with you, lass." He placed his hands on her shoulders expectantly, waiting for her to say something. Instead Callie just nodded, holding back the tears. Was her baby to be born here, in this hovel? Rossiter's child, born here?

That night Callie slept beside her husband for the first time. While she slept, Hugh lay awake, turned on his side, watching her, longing for her. The small light from the dying fire illuminated her profile, and he could feel the warmth emanating from her. It was a long time before he closed his eyes.

In the days that followed, Hugh managed to find a few odd jobs to keep them in food and to purchase a second-hand stove. It was only a pot-belly contraption, but it was sufficient for stoking with wood and coals and was usable for cooking. Callie fought to keep a cheerful countenance, but she had never been more miserable. Because of her misery she went out of her way to be extra kind and patient with Hugh. None of this was his fault, really. It was her own doing that had brought her to this. She knew it was wrong to sleep with Rossiter; it went against everything Peggy had taught her. Mum had a way of saying, "Bad things happen to bad children." But she was no longer a child, and had loving Rossiter been bad? Her hand covered the swelling of her belly as though shielding the child within. How could a baby be bad? If anyone had been bad, it was Rossiter. Callie vacillated between loving Rossiter and damning him. There would always be, she supposed, a tenderness within her for the man who had initiated her into womanhood, but also a deep resentment.

She and the baby should have been Rossiter's responsibility, not Hugh's. Rossiter should be paying the bills and worrying after her and his child. Instead he had probably married his lovely, young Boston heiress and had never given Callie a passing thought.

The cold winter wind howled through the shanty, although Hugh, taking a cue from his neighbors, had stuffed newspapers and mud chinking between the open boards. It was little consolation to Callie that most of her neighbors were Irish immigrants like herself. She felt removed from them, isolated amidst the crowd. While she was pleasant and made acquaintance with many of them, she realized that they were worlds apart. Living on Staten Island with the Powers family had educated Callie. She knew about the finer things in life, about the culture of the upper classes. That time with the Powerses had acquainted her with fine china and sparkling crystal and made her greedy for a real home and clean clothes and a decent life. Living in Shantytown was like being reduced to an animal. It was almost impossible to do laundry when you had to carry water from the public pump, and coal and wood were so scarce and costly that to heat water would have been a waste of fuel, to say nothing of the cost of soap. Still Callie did her best to keep the shack as clean as possible, washing clothes and sheets in icy water and hanging them to dry inside. Hanging laundry outside was impossible. If everything wasn't stolen within a matter of minutes, the black smoke from chimney flues and the everpresent mud would destroy all efforts. When she thought of the prospect of the baby's laundry and all the diapers, she nearly cried.

Callie was no stranger to the care and keeping of a baby. Ever since she was a little girl, she had helped her mum care for the other children. She knew about sickness and sleepless nights and clothes so quickly outgrown. What must her family in Dublin be thinking? she wondered. It had been so long since she'd written and even longer since she'd sent money. The last time she'd written to Peggy she'd told her that she was married and had moved from the Powers's house and that a child was on the way. If Peggy had answered, Callie would never know. The last address she'd given was the one on Fulton Street; there were no addresses in Shantytown. This lack of communication between her mother and herself depressed Callie, but she refused to lie to her mum, and she would never tell her under what conditions she was now living. Later, after the babe was born, when things were better, Callie would sit down and write a long, long letter. God willing, she would have the money to post it.

It was dark when MacDuff staggered home, a half-empty bottle under the crook of his arm. The temptation had been more than he could resist. It was cold, and a wee nip wouldn't hurt a thing. There was food in the larder for the rest of the week. He wasn't depriving Callie of food for her and the young one as yet unborn. That was what made him buy the bottle. The birth was almost here. It was almost time. A man needed a little fortification for something as important as his wife giving birth. No, the lass wouldn't begrudge him this one bottle. He had after all worked for four hours scavenging down by the docks. Never once had the lass complained, and she wasn't likely to do so now.

Hugh walked slowly, his gait lopsided as he tried not to step in the squalid, filthy puddles that were everywhere. A mangy stray dog came up to him, sniffed, backed up a step, and then sprang forward, sinking his teeth into Hugh's bony leg. The bottle dropped to the ground and shattered. Sharp curses and a well-aimed kick sent the slat-ribbed dog scurrying. The sight of the whiskey laying in a puddle made Hugh want to cry. It wasn't fair. Goddamn it, it wasn't fair. It was so long since things had gone right for him. Ever since the day he married Callie James, things had gone wrong. Wiping at his eyes, he staggered on down the rat-infested road. How could doing something good for someone turn out so miserable? Where had it all gone wrong? Was it his fault that the rich folk only wanted to hire younger men? Was it his fault the lass was pregnant? Was it his fault that Miss Mary died and the Powerses moved out? None of it was his fault. He'd never told anyone, even Callie, that he heard the whispers on Todt Hill that maybe he had something to do with the little girl's death because he was the one who called off the search in the middle of the night and he was alone when he found the still, little body. The gossips didn't know about Mary's hearing loss, and he wouldn't give the hateful people anything more to talk about. Jasper Powers didn't blame him, he was sure of it. Lena knew the truth, Callie knew the truth. Jealous, spiteful people with nothing better to do than blacken a man's good name were the ones responsible for such vicious rumors. That was all behind him. St. George was a long way from here, and he felt in his gut that he would never go back. He hated the thought that he would continue to live, and maybe die, in the squalor of Shantytown.

Hugh kicked out at a tin can as he tried to see where he was going. It was dark as hell, and each damned shack looked like the other. Which one was his? There was no number, for Christ's sake. There was nothing to say where he lived. Down one crooked road into another, like a maze. A maze for rats. He was a rat like all the others. Only the rats could find their way home, and he couldn't. He was drunk. Drunk as sin. He wished he knew what time it was. Why were the damn hovels so dark?

The mangy dog was back, sniffing at his leg. Hugh kicked out again and slipped in the slimy mud. Cursing and yelling at the dog, he picked himself up and continued down the maze. He wasn't getting anywhere. Like a child, he leaned against one of the buildings and shouted Callie's name. Over and over till he was hoarse, he called her name.

Callie woke, listless and light-headed. She hadn't eaten today at all. It was so dark. Where was Hugh? He should have been home a long time ago. Fear knotted in her throat. What if something happened to him? What would become of her? Quickly she lit the lamp to see if there were any signs of her husband having come home and gone out again. The hovel was the same as before she fell asleep. And then she heard it. Someone was calling her name. Over and over she heard her name being called. She hated to open the door and go out into the night, but she had to do it. It must be Hugh. Maybe he was hurt. She stood still listening to the calls. Gingerly she made her way through the litter that lined the lane, careful to hold her hems high.

He was so pitiful. Her voice was soft and gentle when she spoke to him. She struggled to get him to his feet. With her arm around his shoulder, she led him down the darkened lane. The moment she got him through the door, he slid from her grasp and fell to the floor. Callie stood looking down at her drunken husband. In no way, shape, or form was this a dream. It was her reality. Would it be better to die than to have only this, with nothing to look forward to? Beth. Was this how Beth felt before she stepped off the dock? Dear God, don't let me think such dark, terrible thoughts. I have a baby to think of. If I can't make it with Hugh, I'll have to do it on my own. If it means I have to go to Byrch Kenyon, then I'll go to Byrch Kenyon. Not for myself but for my baby.

Callie grabbed the quilt from the bed and covered her husband. She pulled her cloak from the nail on the wall and drew it close about her. The end of another miserable, wasteful day.

Hugh MacDuff woke slowly. He was aware of the sour taste in his mouth and the stench of his unwashed body. He looked around the mean, little one-room shanty, his eyes went to the rusty brass bed and his wife. She lay curled in a tight, little ball with her cloak for a blanket.

It took a minute or so before Hugh could make his bleary eyes focus on the quilt that covered him. All his wonderful plans and grand promises had been reduced to cinders. His gaze went to Callie again. How was he to face her when she awakened? Not by look or word would she condemn him, he knew. He wished he had a drink. He had to get hold of himself before he began whizzing in his pants during his drunken stupors. The horrible thought forced him to sit upright. A thin dawn was prying its way into the shanty. Rubbing at his stiff joints, Hugh struggled to his feet, careful to make no sound. The lass needed her sleep. It was almost her time.

Another wave of guilt washed over him. Almost her time and no midwife, much less a doctor, and no money to pay for one. He was certain the neighbor women would help; all of them had had children of their own. But he wanted so much more for Callie, had promised her a better life than this. Maybe it wasn't too late. Maybe he could turn over a new leaf. First, he would go outside and get some water from the rain barrel and wash himself. He would change into the clean clothes Callie had laundered and ironed for him. He would shave, clean up his shoes, and slick down his hair.

Hugh felt much better when he finished washing and dressing. He crept about the shanty, stoking the fire, brewing coffee, and taking the cold ashes from the stove outside. He'd eat a little of the soup she had made from beef bones and potatoes and brace himself to go out and earn the money for the midwife. If there was no work to be had, then he'd steal. He was going to keep his promise to his angel wife, come hell or high water!

The soup didn't sit well in his sour stomach, but he took deep breaths and swallowed hard. The strong, bitter coffee helped. He wished with all his soul that he had some oranges for Callie. Some long forgotten memory from boyhood rose to the surface of his mind. He could see his mother, big and swollen, sucking on an orange, pure rapture on her face. That would be his goal for the day. An orange for Callie. An orange and a mid-wife—in that order.

Callie stirred and woke instantly. Her eyes went immediately to where she had left Hugh the night before. She was surprised to see him sitting at the table, clean-shaven and looking like the old Hugh from the Powers's house. Had something happened? She said nothing but watched him as she tried to move her cumbersome body from the dip in the middle of the smelly mattress.

"Sit there a moment, Callie," Hugh said, pouring coffee into a cracked cup. Callie was startled to see that his hands were steady. Something must have happened. Something good. She could feel it.

"Where are your dirty clothes, Hugh? I'll wash them right away. You look nice and clean," she said shyly.

"I'm sorry about last night, girl. You just saw the end of my drinking days. You won't be finding my snoot in the bottle again." There it was again. The rash promise. Callie understood. He was going to try.

Callie smiled at her husband. How many times had she heard her Da say the same thing? How often had she seen her Mum smile just the way she was doing? The bottle was part of him. His good intentions would last a while and then something would happen and he'd be swigging away. For now it was all right. A man had to do what he had to do. It didn't matter if she liked it or if her Mum liked it. That's the way it was.

"Did you eat anything?" she asked with concern. "It was nice of you to make the coffee. You should have woken me up. I would have done it for you."

"I know that, lass. It didn't hurt me to do it, now did it? Yes, I ate the soup, and right good it was," he lied. "You sit here and drink your coffee. I have to go out for a minute. I'll be right back. Don't be washing clothes now or anything else. I want your promise, Callie."

"All right." She smiled as she promised. How could she not smile at this repentant man? The long day stretching in front of her made her jittery. After she washed Hugh's clothes, tidied up the shack, and thinned out the soup what would she do? Write to her mum. Maybe, she told herself. Take a nap. Eat a little. The day and early evening yawned ahead of her. How she wished she had a friend. What she should do was go to church. Perhaps talk to the priest. If it wasn't so far, she would have seriously considered it. Her legs would never hold up. The unborn child moved within her. Quickly Callie set her coffeecup down and placed both hands over her stomach. She loved to feel the child move and to see her stomach ripple with its movements. Again, as she did every day, she said a silent prayer that the child would be a boy and that he would be healthy.

Callie was rinsing out the coffee cups when Hugh returned, a beaming smile on his face. "Now don't be asking questions so I don't have to give you answers. Look what I fetched for you." Proudly he pulled his hands from behind his back, held out a stack of newspapers, and handed them to Callie. "Every paper is there for the whole week. I'll stoke up the fire for you and stack some wood. You sit here on the chair and read every word in all them papers. Tonight when I get home you can tell me what they said."

"Oh, Hugh, how wonderful. Where . . . thank you." Impulsively she threw her arms around his neck and kissed him soundly on the cheek. Her protruding stomach pressed against Hugh. The baby made a quick movement, and Callie laughed aloud as she pulled at Hugh's hand to place it on her stomach. She laughed again in pure delight at the stunned look on his face.

Hugh had trouble regaining his composure. If she had given him moonbeams and stars, he would have ignored them for that one touch. He had things to do, an orange to find, and a job so he could pay a good midwife. He felt like cock-of-the-walk as he whistled his way up the filthy alley that led to the main street. But before he did that, he had to go by the corner carry-all store and clean up for the man who gave him the week-old newspapers and had generously tossed in today's copy. He would make that store cleaner than it had ever been before. The man trusted him to come back. He had to honor that promise. What was three hours out of a whole day? Maybe he could make a deal for an orange. He was sure going to give it one hell of a try.

Hugh swept, cleaned, and dusted the store till it sparkled. He set shelves to rights, stacked cartons, and cleaned the bakery glass. When he was finished, he whistled with satisfaction. Old Mr. McGovern would be hard pressed to find fault with his work. "Tell me, Mr. McGovern, what would I have to do for you to give me one of those big oranges. My wife is pregnant, and that orange would taste mighty good to her. I'd be most obliged if you'd let me work it off."

Dillis McGovern knew a man in need when he saw one. He liked this hard-working man. "Pregnant wife, eh? I'll be making the orange a gift to you if that's all right by you?" Seeing the look of indecision on Hugh's face, he added hastily. "You're not to be considering it charity now. It's a gift. A gift is different than charity. Me wife would agree."

Hugh stared at the cherry-cheeked Irishman and knew he meant everything he said. "I'll be accepting the orange, Mr. McGovern. You have my thanks. You wouldn't be knowing any of the shopkeepers needing help, now would you?"

The old man shook his head. "I could be giving you an hour or two of work a day if you have a mind to accept. My wife is ailing, and it would give me some time to spend with her. We live in the back of the store. Can ye be making change?" Hugh nodded. He would do anything, say anything. "Ye got an honest look in your eye, Hugh MacDuff." They settled on a fair amount for wages. Hugh's nimble brain quickly calculated what he thought the cost of a midwife would be and how long he'd have to work. Now if the baby didn't arrive early, he could manage to keep his promise to Callie.

His hat in his hand, Hugh reached out to grasp the older man's hand. "I can't be thanking you enough, Mr. McGovern. Not nearly enough."

Bright blue eyes twinkled. "The Good Book says to help those in need. It's bad times we're seeing. One day ye might be helping me. Only the good Lord knows what the future holds."

Hugh fondled the orange in his hand before slipping it into his pocket. "What time would you want me tomorrow? Hugh asked.

"Early afternoon," the storekeeper replied. Hugh tipped his cap and left the store, his step jaunty.

He felt good. Damn good. He'd done two really wonderful things for Callie today. He would go down to the fish market and see if they could use an extra hand for an hour or two. Fresh fish came in early, and if there was any day that would be best, this was it. His luck held, and he worked for four hours. He would never be rich, but he felt like King Midas as he walked back to Shantytown with his meager earnings. The orange meant more to him than the seven hard hours of work he'd put in. Hell, he would have worked ten hours for the orange. But no one besides himself needed to know that. Callie was going to be pleased and proud of him. He could feel it, see the look on her face. Damn, he felt good.

Hugh could barely contain himself as he told Callie about his day. He told her about Dillis McGovern and his gift to her, careful not to mention what it was until the right moment. He handed over his wages and watched as her eyes widened and then settled into relief. Lord, she was beautiful.

"McGovern told me he could give me a few hours work every day, at least for a while. The Lord was watching over me today, Callie, that's for sure."

"Hugh, what's the gift? Tell me," she cried excitedly.

Hugh made a pretense of rummaging in his coat pocket. His hand closed around the orange. Was she going to think him a fool? An orange, what if she laughed at him? Just because his mother liked oranges and McGovern's wife likes oranges didn't mean Callie was going to like it. Well, she was waiting, he had to give it to her now. For one brief moment he was tempted to squeeze the luscious fruit between his fingers. He pulled the orange out of his pocket and handed it to Callie.

Callie stared at the orange in her husband's hand. How did he know that she loved oranges? On Christmas she always got an orange in her stocking. Her eyes were filled with wonder at the marvelous gift. "Why?" she whispered. "It's not Christmas. It's wonderful. You must tell Mr. McGovern how much I appreciate his thoughtfulness. And you, Hugh, how wonderful of you to think of me and for you to want me to have this." For the second time in one day she threw her arms around his neck and kissed him soundly on the cheek. Hugh drew back and pretended to be busy at the table. "Sit down here and I'll peel and slice it for you. I want you to savor every mouthful." Why was he feeling so strange? He should be happy as a lark at the look of delight on Callie's face. He hadn't made a fool of himself after all, and his worrying had been for nought.

"Sit down yourself. I'll be eating some of it, and you'll be eating some too. We're going to share. I don't want to hear a word, Hugh MacDuff. We share the orange, or we don't eat it at all."

They sat together, smiling at one another, one with eyes full of gratitude and the other with eyes full of wondrous puzzlement.

Callie and Hugh settled down into something akin to contentment. Each day he went out to work for Dillis McGovern and managed to pick up an odd job.

On the night of February 6, Callie went into labor. Outside a new snow had fallen, and it covered the shabbiness of Shantytown with its purity. The wind had quieted and did not howl through the cracks. It was still, as still as a church, Hugh had said when Callie first complained of pains, and thank the Lord the McInty funeral was over and the fiddler had fallen down dead drunk.

Hugh raced to Dillis McGovern's apartment behind the store as planned, waiting impatiently for Dillis's frail wife to give him directions to the midwife. Hugh took off on a dead run, his heart pumping furiously. He wanted to get back to Callie, and Molly Riordan's calm attitude and slow pace annoyed and frustrated him to the point of wanting to pick her up and bodily carry her back to the shanty.

It was a long, hard labor that went through the night and the better part of the following day. Hugh never left Callie's side. He walked with her, offering his arm for support. He wiped her brow and offered her sips of water. It was his hands that massaged her back and rubbed her feet and held her hands when the contractions came. He talked softly and gently while Molly sipped tea at the meager table. Every so often, between pains, Callie would doze, but Hugh remained alert, never taking his eyes from her. Poor thing, how she was suffering, but so far she hadn't uttered more than a moan.

Callie opened her eyes, turning her head toward Hugh. She managed a weak smile, but to Hugh it was the smile of an angel, radiant and pure. She reached for his hand, holding tight, drawing on its strength through her pain. When the contraction passed, Hugh wiped her brow. "Hugh, you can't know how much it means to me for you to be here," she whispered her gratitude.

"I'm here, and here I'll stay," he told her, wishing his voice didn't sound so gruff; so labored. In his heart he knew that sharing the birth of the babe would bring Callie closer to him. He loved her, but for the life of him he couldn't find the words to tell her so. He had cursed himself many times during the past months because he was so unimaginative, so unspontaneous, that he was unable to express his feelings. He couldn't bring himself to tell her what she meant to him, that the sun and the moon rose on her, that he was willing and prepared to love the child she carried as his own just because it was there inside her, part of her. He hoped she knew he loved her and appreciated her. She'd been so kind to him, and since he'd kept a hold of himself working for McGovern, she'd even displayed her affection. Why couldn't he respond? Why was he so stiff and unbending, just like his own father had been? He was trapped in the prison of his own inhibitions, his own shyness. He wasn't an ugly man, he knew. In his day he'd been considered quite handsome. Had he changed that much? He didn't think so. He was a bit soft in the middle, but these past months on short rations had toughened him again. His hair was no longer black, but it was thick and wavy. Could someone as beautiful as Callie ever come to love a man like himself, or would he be forever bound by her gratitude?

Molly Riordan stood by Callie's bed, grateful for the daylight. This girl would have a hard time of it, she knew. This shanty, although remarkably clean, was no better than the gutter as far as she was concerned. And Mr. MacDuff, for all his care and solicitousness, didn't seem to be much of a provider. Those were the things a woman depended upon, Molly reminded herself. Sobriety and ambition. Everything else was just window dressing.

Callie's contractions were coming closer together; her back arched in agony. She felt the compulsion to bear down, to grit her teeth, to curse the heavens and bear down, to be done with it, rid of it, this stranger invading her body. Perspiration beaded on her forehead as she sank her head back down into the pillow. All the while, Hugh murmured words of encouragement, talking to her softly, seeing her through the pain.

"It's almost time now," Molly said. "It won't be long."

Callie turned to Hugh, saw the worry in his eyes, heard the concern in his voice. "Hugh, go away. Go away now!" Another pain ripped down the small of her back, gripping her thighs, forcing her to arch against it.

"I'll stay, Callie. I want to stay, lass."

Callie shook her head, gritting her teeth. She didn't want him here to see the last of her pain, to see what she was going through to bring another man's child into the world. Her tone was sharp, pained. "Hugh, please, go! I don't want you here!"

Tears stung his eyes. He didn't understand. "I'll be right outside then, Callie. I'll be right outside the door . . ."

Callie brought herself up on her elbows. Her eyes were wild with pain, with fear. She'd seen childbirth before, knew what was to come. She wanted to be free to shout, to call for her mother, to plead with God. But most of all she was afraid she would scream Rossiter's name and that would be the cruelest blow of all. "No! I don't want you here! I want you to leave! Go sit with Mr. McGovern—"

"You'd better go," Molly interceded. "She shouldn't be upset this way. This is woman's work, and you'll only clutter up the place. Get on with you now!"

Hugh stood by the bed, smoothing Callie's hair back from her face, bending to kiss her cheek. "All right, lass, if it's what you want."

Hugh shrugged into his coat and stepped out the door. Once outside, he bent his head into his hard, calloused hands and wept. She didn't want him; even now when her need was the greatest, she didn't want him. Head hung low, shoulders stooped, he walked off in the direction of Malone's Tavern.

The hours bore down on Callie during her long labor with the same incessant need that caused her body to bear down in an effort to expel this child. With each pain she seemed to be losing more of herself, her conscious mind retreating to a place of sunshine and safety, away from the black pit that threatened to engulf her, away from the fear that held her in its grip with evil fingers, seeming to squeeze the life from her. The shadows of the valley of death, she'd once heard childbirth called, and now she believed.

How could a child that was so dearly wanted, loved even before its birth, punish her this way? How could her body, which had warmed with welcome for the seed that had planted this child, now be stiff with cold fear, rigid and unyielding?

Between the pains Callie threw herself back against the pillow. Molly fanned her perspiring face with yesterday's newspaper, but to Callie it was the cool breezes of Ireland, fresh from the sea. The fire in the stove became the warm summer sun, bright and golden. And in that precious golden light, her dress billowing in the sea breeze, was Peggy. Mother. Safety. Love. Peggy's arms opened to her, gentle eyes sending comfort, a small secret smile playing about her mouth. "That's my good girl," the wind seemed to bring her voice with it, "that's my own Callie. Go with it child, let the babe come. Sweetly now, Callie," Peggy called. "Soon you'll have him in your arms, and it'll all be worth the pain."

Callie felt herself filled with her mother's presence, taking strength from it, smiling through her pain just the way Peggy had smiled away Callie's worry when the twins were born. As Callie's child came into the world, it was Peggy's voice she listened to, Peggy's smile she saw, her mother's love reaching halfway around the world.

Less than an hour later, Rory James MacDuff came into the world. Callie looked down at the pink cherub in her arms. Golden curls framed the perfectly round head. Tiny pink lips groped for her breast.

Molly stood back to admire the infant. She'd delivered so many over the past years; they all looked alike. Except this one. Pink and white and golden, an angel of a child. The mother was pretty, true enough, and in better times might be called beautiful. But of all the children she'd brought into the world, this child was exceptional.

"He's going to be a real heartbreaker," Molly said.

Callie stared down at the babe in her arms, touching the damp, golden curls, lifting the tiny star-shaped hand to her lips.

Rory James McDuff looked just like his father.

Chapter Twenty

Hugh sat alone in Malone's, drinking steadily. There were so many things he didn't understand. Maybe he should go to church. Maybe his luck would turn. Women, he knew, were a mystery. Ever sine he'd turned over his new leaf almost three weeks ago and took his snoot out of the bottle, he and Callie had been, if not quite happy, at least content. There was nothing he liked better than coming home to her and the supper she'd prepared for him. Afterwards, she'd sit near the one lamp on the kitchen table and read to him from those newspapers he'd brought her. He loved the way she seemed to understand things, and he loved her smile when he would walk through the door, carrying last night's paper from McGovern's, waving it like a flag.

Sitting quietly, head hanging, he ignored the rough men's talk going on about him. He had too much thinking to do. All the while Callie had been in labor he'd sat by her side, wiping at her brow, holding her hand and offering kind words when the pains got bad. And just when she needed him the most, she had turned on him, chasing him away like a stray dog from a back door. Told him to leave, not just to move from her side, but to leave the shanty. How could she have done it? In his drunkenness, Hugh decided it was because giving birth to Rossiter Powers's child had nothing to do with him. He was good enough to feed her and put a roof over her head, but not good enough to share the birth of her child. Her child and Rossiter's. For months now, he'd deluded himself, made himself believe that the baby would be more his own than any other man's. As he gulped at the fiery drink, he felt confusion settle over him.

The bottle was almost finished when the men started to leave the tavern. Instead of following them, he ordered another. He ignored the angry-eyed proprietor and kept up with his steady drinking. He was drunk as a loon on a warm September night, and he didn't care. When it came right down to it, he didn't care about a hell of a lot this day. He should be home with Callie, he told himself. Callie didn't need him. The baby didn't need him. The midwife didn't need him. His drunken mind tried to focus on something tangible in the tavern, but his eyes were too clouded with mist.

"I'll be closing now, MacDuff. Best be on your way to that beautiful wife of yours," the bartender said, not unkindly. "Come along, man, I'll help you outside. I'll cork the bottle for you, and you can carry it with you." Hugh didn't object to the man's helping him outside. When he heard the snick of the bolt being shot home, he knew he had no place else to go. MacDuff tried to keep his balance as he staggered down the rabbit warren of crooked streets. When he finally came to the shanty, only a dim light burned within. He fell against the door and lurched inside.

"Close the door, Hugh, so the baby doesn't get a draft. Come here and take a look at my son."

Not our son, *her* son. He supposed it was true. Why would he want to look at another man's son? Maybe he would be interested in looking at another man's daughter. He was so sure it was going to be a girl.

"Oh, Hugh, you're drunk. Why?" Callie asked anxiously. Hugh shuffled on his feet as he dutifully leaned over to peer at the tiny bundle in Callie's arms. She looked so different with her hair pulled back from her face. The thin nightgown was buttoned to her neck, making her look as angelic as her new born baby. He frowned when he looked down at the pink-faced child whose head was crowned with golden ringlets. Just like his father, he thought sourly.

"Sit here, Hugh, and tell me why you got drunk. You were doing so well, Hugh. We had a little money put aside and things were beginning to look up for both of us. I want to thank you for being here with me and making it easier for me. I owe you so much, Hugh. You have been good to me. Whatever would I have done without you?"

Hugh heard the words she was saying, but they seemed to be floating about him. The most important day of his life and she had sent him away. Didn't she know how that hurt him? Didn't she care?

"He's a fine-looking boy," Hugh mumbled as he bent down to take off his shoes. As drunk as he was, he was careful to walk straight and even more careful when he sat down on the bed and pulled the cover up to his chin. Truth was truth. It was a fine-looking boy child. With Callie for his mother, how could the child be anything but perfect? Normally he would be asleep in seconds with as much whiskey as he had in him. Instead he lay for a long time, listening to Callie as she softly hummed an Irish tune to the baby. He lay rigid, wanting to reach out to her beneath the covers, to hold her hand. He wanted to say so many things to her, to apologize for breaking his promise. Did she know that he wasn't sleeping? Something told him she wasn't even aware that he was in the same bed. He felt like blubbering. He squeezed his eyes shut and prayed silently for sleep to come.

Callie stared at her newborn child. The baby's head seemed to be as golden as the lamplight. A smile played around her mouth. This child, her child, was more beautiful than any of the cherubs painted in the church. This was indeed an angel. Her own angel. If only her mum could see him. She knew she would never tire of looking at this exquisite child who was as beautiful as the beginning of a summer day. This child was going to grow up into a bonny lad, knowing only love and devotion from his mother. She made a vow to herself that she would work day and night to give him every advantage in this new world. She would make it up to him that he didn't have his own father. She was young, healthy, and strong. She could make a life for the both of them. For *all* of them!

In the weeks and months that followed Rory and Callie both bloomed like flowers in early spring. Hugh MacDuff watched his wife change from a young, frightened girl into a strong woman who juggled the care of her son with minding the shack and taking in ironing. No longer did she hand him her money, but instead put it in her writing box. Now, when Hugh managed to work for Dillis McGovern, Callie would hold out her hand when he walked in the front door. She added his money to the fund in the box. Each Saturday night she would count out enough for him to go to the tavern. Fair was fair, she decided. Any extra money Hugh managed to pick up, he kept for a game of cards or a bottle during the middle of the week. Callie said nothing about this, allowing him his own measure of freedom. As long as a bit was put by for medicine or a doctor for Rory, should the need arise, Callie was content. She barely noticed Hugh's late return each evening. She learned to prepare foods that were easily reheated, and he said nothing about the fact that he often ate alone.

Sometimes when she sat near the stove nursing Rory, she would catch a certain look in Hugh's eyes as he studied mother and child. She would look up at him and smile, but rarely did he return it, and if he did, it seemed begrudged. He would watch Rory pulling on Callie's breast, hungry little mouth working the nipple, star-shaped hands continually plucking at her flesh or the bodice of her dress. Something naked and crude in Hugh's eyes would cause Callie to cover her breast, shielding her body from his view. Never guessing the depths of her husband's emotions, Callie couldn't know that it wasn't her breast that fascinated him but Rory, greedily sucking. Hugh was resentful and jealous that Rossiter's child meant the world to Callie while he, her husband, counted for nothing.

As Rory grew, and the spring lazed into summer, it was a usual sight to see Callie delivering ironing to the women outside of Shantytown. At first Rory would lie amidst his swaddling of blankets in the used wagon Hugh had found for her, and later Callie propped him up in his own little basket, riding along with the clean laundry and taking his first look at the world.

It brought Callie no end of pleasure and pride when men and women would stop to admire her son. Pink and golden, bright blue eyes smiling, Rory accepted their appreciation as his due, cooing and gurgling his delight. "That's a fine boy you've got there, Mrs. MacDuff," her neighbors would compliment. "He's got the face of an angel and a disposition to match." Callie's heart would swell with pride.

Rory was indeed a beautiful child, and Callie was beguiled by him. A strong, sturdy boy, Rory could pull himself up on his feet before he was nine months old; he'd been sitting erect since the age of five months.

Callie literally glowed from within; she loved her child with such devotion and passion that at times she had to force herself to put him down in his bed. Every minute she could spare from her ironing was spent with Rory: playing, cooing, rocking, just feeling his soft warmth against her. The only thing that could equal her love for Rory was her pride in him.

When Callie made her rounds delivering the ironing, she always brought Rory with her, weather permitting. Her customers quickly became admirers of her son, and there was always an extra penny "to buy the lad something" or a freshly baked cookie, and on several occasions, Rory became the recipient of hand-me-downs from their nephews or grandsons. Mrs. Coen was particularly enthralled with the child, and for Christmas she had knitted him a pale blue sweater and hat. Callie was appreciative of this generosity and repaid it by doing extra mending or replacing lost buttons. While Rory's popularity grew, her own reputation for her work did also, and there was almost more than she could handle. But she never refused work, and being of an enterprising mind, she engaged the help of Maggie Crenshaw, who lived several shacks down from her, to iron the flat pieces, such as sheets and pillow slips, extracting a small commission, while she herself continued doing the frilly petticoats and delicate laces and pleatings.

Dillis McGovern's wife, Fanny, was a particular admirer of Rory. Never having had children of her own, Fanny was completely enthralled with Callie's son. Little gifts from the store, such as stockings and tiny soft slippers and fleecy warm blankets, were bestowed with generosity. Almost every day that Hugh worked for Dillis he returned home with a sugar tidbit or a spare pint of milk or a cookie. Every so often a stranger on the street would pause to admire the child who rode in the rickety wagon beside the clean laundry and would press a penny into the baby's hand. These pennies Callie would never refuse, taking them and hiding them away, saving for Rory's future.

Although Callie's prosperity seemed to grow, there simply wasn't enough money to send back to Ireland. To her great relief, Peggy assured her that her help wasn't needed. Things were looking up in Ireland; people were adjusting to shortages, and with so many people having left the country, there was more to go around. Prices were dropping slowly but steadily. Thom continued to work for the tinsmith, and there was always the washing that Peggy took in, and besides, Georgie had won himself a position at the mill as junior clerk, thanks to the help Callie had given during those first years so the lad could get an education. Everyone was fine, although Granda was almost completely blind now. Little Joseph was the terror of the neighborhood, petted and favored by his entire family.

Callie read between the lines and knew that although her family wasn't going hungry, they were barely making ends meet. Georgie's job at the mill indicated that he was no longer studying with Father Brisard, and there was no mention of Hallie attending a proper school. Peggy's letters were infrequent, an indication that the pennies for postage could be better spent elsewhere. But whatever the circumstances, their love came through to her, and Peggy expressed that her greatest wish was someday to hold her grandson in her arms.

Callie's life seemed to have fallen into the same pattern as Peggy's, and she felt closer to her mother than ever before. Perhaps it was because she was now a mother herself, experiencing the same frustrated ambitions and worries for her child.

Time passed quickly for Callie. Almost before she knew it, Rory's first birthday came and went. Hugh was drinking heavily, and Dillis McGovern had been forced to let him go in favor of more dependable help. Hugh took his dismissal in stride; it was almost as if he had expected it, Callie judged. Instead of chastising him or making mention of the lost income, Callie took on more work for herself and Maggie Crenshaw. At times it was even necessary to ask Maggie's oldest daughter to give a hand.

Maggie's daughter, Trisha, was fourteen years old and positively doted on little Rory. Because the girl was so reliable and trustworthy, Callie looked outside the shanty for employment. She found it only blocks away in the Tea Room, working as a waitress for Sylvia Levy, a buxom woman who was impressed with Callie's refined manners and easy grace. The wages were small, but they added to the income from her ironing. More than anything, Callie wanted to save enough money to have a steady income so that she could take Rory out of Shantytown. Her one great fear the entire winter past was of fire. Earlier that December, fire broke out in the northernmost section of the field, and several people were burned in their beds or in the alleyways as they tried to escape through the narrow, twisted passages between the shacks. She knew Hugh didn't approve of her hiring herself out, as he called it, but when she went purposefully about her business and threw an extra coin his way for an evening at Malone's his protests were silenced.

If Hugh noticed his wife's labors and business sense, he did not mention it. He only knew that she no longer held out her hand for his day's wages if he should manage to find work, and she never said a word about him spending his time at Malone's Tavern. To Hugh's chagrin, Callie never seemed to notice him at all except for the fact that his clothes were always clean, should he take the time to wash and change, and there was always a pot of soup or stew on the stove for his supper.

Callie tried to ignore Hugh's drinking. When he came home from Malone's, he would reek with whiskey and stale sweat. Rather than climb into bed beside him, Callie preferred to work long into the night, sleeping when exhaustion overcame her. Rory had his own small bed, and she had managed to put enough money aside to purchase a second-hand rocking chair that Hugh fixed for her in one of his more sober periods. Many a night Callie rocked herself to sleep in the chair, only to wake sore and stiff the next morning.

As Rory progressed from baby to toddler, Hugh became sullen and withdrawn. It seemed to him that Callie's every thought, every action, was geared to the golden-haired child. It angered him, and his tone sharpened, and his moods went from dark to black when he watched Callie pick up the boy to rock him in her chair. He was sick of seeing her bending over the washtub to do Rory's diapers and tiny clothes with such inordinate care, of seeing her straining her eyes near the lamp while she embroidered a pillowcase for his bed or hemmed and fixed the hand-me-downs so that they fit to perfection. Rory lived in Shantytown, but he never looked like the rest of the children. The others wore clothes that never fit and were gray and faded from either dirt or too many washings; Rory wore clothes fit for a prince. Just once Hugh would have liked to see the tyke with bare feet, dirty from the grime of Shantytown; just once he would have been satisfied to have Callie let the boy cry the way every baby should. But no, Callie was too devoted a mother for that. Rory was washed and scrubbed to a pink; he never was without stockings and little felt slippers, and he never cried. He simply had to make his wishes known, and Callie would stop what she was doing to fulfill them. It never occurred to Hugh that if Rory had been his own child, he would have been delighted with the love and patience shown him. But what infuriated Hugh more than anything else was when Rory would climb out of his bed and creep beneath it to sleep. Callie only shook her head in amusement and began keeping a folded blanket under the bed to cushion Rory from the hard floor. Hugh didn't know why Rory's antic annoyed him, but it did. Perhaps it was the way Callie would smile. She never smiled at him that way. Now that Hugh thought about it, Callie never smiled at him at all anymore. Once when he hadn't found work for more than a week and his pockets were empty, he went to her writing box and took out enough money for a bottle of whiskey. He had watched out of the corner of his eye when Callie wiped her hands on her apron, hands that were red and chapped from scrubbing Rory's clothes and bed linens, and started toward him. Seeing the expression on Hugh's face, she had backed off and refused to meet his eyes. Tears of frustration burned her as she went back to the laundry in the round, wooden tub. Hugh had never gone near the box again.

Night after night, Hugh lay in bed, tormenting himself by watching her through half-closed eyes. His entire body, his soul, felt like one gaping sore that refused to heal, festering with a disease that had no name, a sickness that could only be cured by his wife's loving touch.

Callie was aware of Hugh's eyes always upon her, and it frightened her. She was perversely relieved when he took to the bottle, drinking himself into a stupor. She found it easier simply to give him the money when he needed it and have him out of the shanty. Hugh's bitterness and heavy hand were something she never thought she would have to endure from him. How often she'd seen the same fate befall her mother. "I made my bed, and I'll be lying in it, thank you, Callie James," Peggy had said often enough. And then the exhausting list of excuses she'd make for Thomas. Callie tried to make the best of her situation. Without Rory, she told herself, it would have been unbearable. She never allowed the thought to go to the next step. Without Rory, it would have been unnecessary.

Rossiter Powers returned to New York City on a cold dreary day in late March. Unknown to him, his son had celebrated his first birthday just the month before less than three miles away in the field of despair and devastation called Shantytown.

Walking away from the pier where the steamship had brought him from Boston, he tipped his brown beaver hat at several well-dressed ladies who eyed his impeccable tailoring and his tall, broad-shouldered figure. He hailed a cab and instructed his driver to take him to the Midtown Bank on Third Avenue where Jasper still kept a suite of offices. He was eager to see his father again, especially since his rift with his mother. He was certain he would find an enthusiastic welcome from Jasper, whom he had not seen in almost two years. Two years! Mary would be dead two years late this summer. Where had the time flown?

Jasper Powers seemed even taller and broader to his son, his cheeks ruddier, his hair whiter. And there was a kind of contentment around the button blue eyes that hadn't been there before, Rossiter thought. He supposed it was due to the fact that his parents had abandoned their marriage, and since his sister had made a fine marriage, there was little need for pretense between them. Anne Powers had taken up household in her widowed brother's home in Boston, while Jasper had taken a house with Loretta Cummings, his lady love for more than fifteen years. Mary's death had created a total separation; the family would never be restored.

Jasper's welcome of his son was cool and distant, almost wary. They spoke in quiet tones, measuring one another. He saw a young man who looked no different from the last time he had seen him. There were the same good looks, the same square chin, the abundance of thick, golden hair that waved about his head. There didn't seem to be a trace of the maturity he had always hoped Rossiter would achieve. The kind of sobriety and seriousness with which Byrch Kenyon seemed to have been born. Jasper was pleased to see his son, but he wondered at Rossiter's sudden appearance. Since Mary's death and the rift between Anne and himself, Jasper had little or no contact with his surviving children.

"We were all saddened that you couldn't get home for Mary's funeral," Jasper found himself saying. His tone was so flat, so devoid of emotion, that Rossiter felt close to cringing.

"I want to explain about that, *Papá*. As you know, I traveled to Chicago with Uncle William." Rossiter took a deep breath and then blurted, "Papá, you and I both know that I'm not cut out for business. I want to paint! I have talent, I know I do. I've even sold a few things." Even Rossiter heard the whine in his voice. He cleared his throat and went on more calmly. "I went north, into Minnesota. That's why I didn't hear about the tadpole until it was too late. I'll never forgive myself for not being there. I find it so difficult to believe she isn't with us anymore."

Jasper softened toward his son. There was genuine grief there, of that he was certain. Rossiter always was kind and loving to Mary. He had been quick to spot the intensity in Rossiter's eyes when he spoke of his painting. Maybe Rossiter had talent, but Jasper didn't believe he possessed the discipline necessary to bring it to fruition. Rossiter had never possessed ambition and dedication; he always looked for the easy way out and refused to accept responsibility for his actions. Like with young Callie. Anne had told Jasper after the funeral that she had sent Callie away because of the girl's unabashed and embarrassing fascination towards Rossiter. Jasper doubted that Rossiter was completely innocent, as Anne had claimed. His son's past deeds and scandalous behavior with comely young women were well-known to Jasper and to his purse as well. God, how he wished he knew what had become of the girl. He was genuinely fond of her and missed her, especially now since his little Mary was gone. Her dismissal was something Byrch Kenyon would never forgive. How well he remembered the steely glint in his friend's eyes and his harsh words. "Dammit, Jasper, I trusted that girl to your keeping!" Byrch had been like a madman the next few days as he tried to discover Callie's whereabouts. "She can't just have fallen from the face of the earth!" He had attacked anyone within hearing, even Lena, who claimed to know nothing. They had to accept that Callie was lost to them just as Mary was.

"Have you seen your mother?" Jasper asked, turning a sharp glance toward his son. He found it remarkable that Rossiter had come to see him this way. What could the boy want that Anne would refuse him?

Rossiter hung his head, finding it difficult to face his father. "I'm afraid *Mamán* is very upset with me. In her opinion, I'm guilty of an unforgivable faux pas. I found it necessary to break my engagement to Dorothy Lyons. Of course, my actions are unforgivable, and I quite understand *Mamán*'s disappointment."

Jasper exhaled in a loud whoosh. "I should say your action is beneath a gentleman. You know, of course, the embarrassment you've caused Miss Lyons; a broken engagement when not initiated by the woman can ruin her reputation. And if I know Dorothy's father, and I think I do, Anthony Lyons will not stop at any extreme to discredit you and undoubtedly make things quite unbearable for your mother, who still lives and socializes in Boston. You've created a scandal, Rossiter, and that alone is unforgivable in your mother's eyes."

"Yes, but I insisted that Dorothy feel free to take credit for the broken engagement. I would never say otherwise!"

"That was most generous of you, Rossiter," Jasper sneered. "However, truth has a way of surfacing. Every servant in the Lyons household knows the truth, and the servants in your Uncle William's house, and the entire family. You've made the girl a laughing stock, although I am quite of the opinion that she is better off without you. Little wonder your mother will have nothing to do with you. So now you've come crawling to me, is that it?"

"I'm not crawling. You're my father—"

"What do you want, Rossiter?" Jasper cut him off, wanting only to be rid of him. He decided at that moment that there was nothing to be salvaged in their relationship. He stood up from his desk, indicating that their time together was at an end. Rossiter held out his hand; Jasper pretended not to see. "I ask you again, why have you come here? Money?"

Rossiter choked back his answer. Although money had been the primary reason for coming to Jasper, it would be beneath him to admit it now. Where had everything gone wrong? First *Mamán* and now *Papá*. He felt lost, without roots, floating adrift in a sea of unfriendly faces. He missed his mother's strength, her abject approval and devotion. It had been months now since she would even have him outside her door. She had cut off his allowance. And now Jasper too had withdrawn his support. Rossiter needed someone who would accept him for exactly who he was. Someone who wouldn't keep insisting he prove himself. Someone who loved him blindly, just as *Mamán* once had.

"I know you've sold the house on Todt Hill, *Papá*, but I wonder if you know where . . . where Lena or MacDuff are? Are they managing the farm in Kreischerville?" He wanted to ask Jasper directly if he knew of Callie's whereabouts, but the sudden piercing glance from Jasper's bright blue eyes made him hesitate.

"No, the farm in Kreischerville is up for sale. I've no idea where MacDuff took himself off to, but Lena is working in Richmondtown. Give my regards to your mother if you should see her."

Rossiter swallowed past the bitter lump in his throat. He had told his father that he intended to remain in New York indefinitely, but this abrupt dismissal indicated Jasper's disinclination to meet with his son again. He shuffled from one foot to the other. How could he just walk off this way? Surely there was more to be said between father and son than this. There were so many things he wanted to say to his father, things he would have liked to confide. He would have liked to tell him about Callie. Rossiter felt less than ten years old when he left Jasper's presence. A ten-year-old who had just been punished for something that was none of his own doing.

Outside in the bracing air, Rossiter walked down Third Avenue. The biting wind tore at him, making him clench his teeth. If it remained this cold for even several days, the buds would freeze. All the color and life of spring would be destroyed. It saddened him. Life should be full of vibrant colors, beautiful words, and wonderful music. That's what his life should be, but he'd been stripped of everything that mattered. Home, family, parents, and most of all, his self-respect. Somehow he must regain it. Somehow he must find someone he could mean something to, someone to love him. Someone like Callie.

The chilling wind sent shivers up Rossiter's back when he disembarked from the ferry at St. George and hired a hansom to bring him up the hill across Staten Island to Richmondtown, the island's oldest community. It would be good to see Lena again, almost like touching home base, something Rossiter sorely needed. The Powers's former cook could usually be depended upon to have answers to questions he had never wanted to ask his parents. Questions like what had become of Callie James.

Rossiter left the hansom at the end of Aultman Avenue and walked the rest of the way. He thought about Lena and the delicious aromas that used to come from her kitchen. For some reason, he had always thought that some day Lena would marry Hugh MacDuff.

Here it was, a large, four-story house set back from a wide, sweeping lawn. Two carriage houses in the back at the end of a long, curving drive. Although it sat in the center of town, the house dominated the location and was graced by a grove of elm trees near the street. Rossiter's gaze sharpened. He'd been here before, he remembered, visiting with his mother.

As he walked around the back of the house, he was reminded of the house on Todt Hill with the ivy growing up the east wall and trailing between the diamond-shaped window panes. In summer it appeared cool and welcoming. He longed for the house on the hill and for the carefree days of youth. Rossiter nearly laughed aloud at the thought. His youth? When had he come to feel so old, so used?

Rounding the back of the house and climbing the steps to the service porch, he saw the door suddenly swing open. "Master Rossiter!" Lena's eyes registered shock as she faced him.

He smiled engagingly. "It's cold out here, Lena. Can I come in for a cup of your coffee?"

Inside the warm kitchen, Rossiter wrapped Lena in his embrace. He didn't think it possible, but she squeezed him harder than he squeezed her. She seemed so happy to see him. She fussed over him, taking his coat and brown beaver hat, hanging it on the hook behind the pantry door. Motioning for him to sit at her table, she set out a jug of cream and a server of sugar, along with a plate of freshly baked cookies. The coffee was hot and freshly brewed.

When the social amenities were over, the inquiries about everyone's health and regrets about little Mary, Rossiter leaned back, a large sugar cookie in his hand. Would Lena bring up the subject of Callie, or should he? While he debated his question, he let his eyes stray around the homey kitchen. Lena's influence in the room brought a familiar feeling of security. A cheery fire snapped and crackled, and a yellow cat dozed on Lena's own high-backed rocker. The wooden service table was polished to a high sheen and held jars of preserves and pungent carrots from the root cellar together with rough-skinned potatoes and fragrant bunches of herbs. Lena must be planning a hearty stew, he thought, his mouth watering when he remembered her tasty dish. Even though it was early in the day, she had already made a rhubarb pie. The window sills and shelves over the tabletops held pots of herbs and spices and green-leafed plants. "I see you've brought the plants from Todt Hill," Rossiter said, striving to break the silence.

"They were mine, all grown from seedlings. I brought them with me," Lena said defensively.

"I didn't mean—"

"I know you didn't, Master Rossiter, and I shouldn't have snapped like that. I do like some of my own things about me. You know the feeling, I'm sure. Something to call your own."

Rossiter nodded, sipping from his cup. When he replaced it on the tabletop, he faced her directly. "Lena, do you know where Callie is?"

There it was, the question she'd been dreading ever since Rossiter appeared at the door. There he was, sitting at her table, munching his cookie, just the way he did back on the hill. But they weren't on the hill anymore. Time had passed and so had water under the bridge. Things were changed, even Rossiter himself was different. Oh, he looked like the boy she remembered, handsome and strong and golden, but there was an emptiness in his eyes that Lena didn't like, a kind of listlessness. Or was it defeat? She didn't like the anxious expression he wore or the way he kept kneading his fists. What right did he have coming back now to find Callie? An imp of Satan perched on her shoulder and whispered in her ear. Perhaps if Callie and Rossiter found each other, old MacDuff would come back to rub her back at night. Angrily Lena shook her gray head. She didn't need the likes of MacDuff cluttering up her life at this late date. All she needed was her yellow cat who purred in her arms as she rocked with her cuppa tea and the few drops of brandy she alloted herself each evening.

"Is something wrong, Lena? It's as though I just told you the house was on fire."

"Is it now?" Lena hedged. There was no help for it; she had

to answer the young man. She might as well do it and get it over with. She couldn't lie; she wouldn't.

"You know, Master Rossiter, you should have written to the girl. It was a terrible thing you did, going off and leaving her without so much as a wave of your hand. She wrote you, I happen to know, and you should have answered."

"Lena, I never received a letter from Callie. I know I should have written, but *Mamán* had me . . . it isn't important. I'm to blame. I'll never forgive myself for not being here for Mary's funeral, but it was weeks before I learned about her death. *Mamán* and *Papá* had already separated."

How miserable the boy looked. That was the problem, he was still a boy. His long absence had only aged him in years and had nothing to do with maturity. "Well, I don't know why you didn't receive a letter. I myself saw Callie walk to the mailbox and raise the flag to hail the postman."

"I was moving around quite a lot—Boston, Chicago, and Minnesota—"

"I suppose that would explain it." Lena's tone was doubtful. She wouldn't have put it past Anne Powers to have waylaid the letter, though none of them had thought about it at the time.

Rossiter's expression brightened for the first time since entering the kitchen. "It's nice to know Callie took the time to write me. Where is she, Lena? I'd like to see her."

"What if she doesn't want to see you? Have you thought of that? Callie has made a life for herself now, and do you think it's wise for you to disturb her?"

Rossiter was stunned. "Why wouldn't she want to see me?" he asked incredulously. "What new life? Housemaids don't make new lives. They simply continue to work. Their lives belong to the people who sponsor them."

If Lena had bit into a lemon, her words couldn't have been more sour. "Is that the way you see it, Master Rossiter?"

"Yes, that's the way I see it. Callie will want to see me. I know she will. I also know you know where she is, so will you please tell me?"

Lena narrowed her eyes. "The last I heard she was living in a furnished apartment on Fulton Street in the city. I know she moved, and I don't have the address."

"Why was she living in a rooming house, and why did she move? I know you know, Lena."

"I heard it was because her husband couldn't pay the rent, and they were evicted."

"What husband?" Rossiter was stunned. Callie couldn't be married. It was a joke, a cruel joke. "Evicted? Only petty crooks and drunkards get evicted from their lodgings. Callie is none of those. Good God, you aren't telling me she married a drunken thief, are you?"

Lena said nothing.

"Who did she marry, Lena?"

"Hugh MacDuff."

Rossiter gasped. "That's impossible. Callie would never marry that old man. You were supposed to marry him. Why didn't you?" he shouted as he banged his fist on the wooden table. "Why?"

"Because your mother tossed her out on her ear when she found out she was going to have your baby. That's why, Master Rossiter."

Rossiter ran his fingers around the neck of his shirt and tie. It was hard to breathe. Surely he hadn't heard what Lena said. Surely it was all a bad dream, and he would wake any minute now in his room that was floor-to-ceiling with canvases. It had to be a bad dream. "Baby? You said Callie was going to have my baby? How do you know that it—"

"Don't be saying it, Master Rossiter, not if you want to walk out of here on your own two feet. You asked me, and I told you. If you don't like my answers, you shouldn't have come here to ask me. There's no reason for me to lie to you. What would you have the girl do? Where could she go? Your own mother tossed her out like trash on a Saturday morning. How was she to survive?"

Rossiter dropped his head into his hands. He wanted to cry. Callie couldn't have had a baby. Lord, she was little more than a child herself. Oh, God, what had he done?

"Are you sure you don't know where she is?" Rossiter asked.

"I have no idea. New York would be my guess. I think I would have heard from Callie or Hugh if they'd stayed around here. None of the men mention Hugh at all. He did the girl a favor, Master Rossiter. There was no one else to take care of her, to help her. You remember that."

"I have to find her. The baby, where was it born? How old is it?"

"The babe should be about a year old by now. I have no idea if it was a boy or a girl. I told you I lost track of them when they left the island. Best to leave things alone, Master Rossiter. Callie doesn't need your kind of trouble."

"What exactly is my kind of trouble, Lena?" Rossiter snarled.

Lena didn't lower her eyes but stared at him till he dropped his gaze.

"Thank you for the coffee and cookies," Rossiter intoned, retrieving his own hat and coat from behind the pantry door. "When I find her, I'll be sure to give her your regards."

"You do that, young man." Lena's voice was tight and clipped. She brushed fitfully at a tear that gathered in her eye. Damn Rossiter Powers. Damn him to hell. Quickly she blessed herself and began hacking at a bunch of carrots. It wasn't until she was finished that she realized what she'd done. Each time the knife had come down, she'd leaned on it, smashing the orange rounds. She stared at the mess and then brushed it into the waste pail. Men were such rotters. Just to prove the point, she stuck out her foot and gave the yellow cat a not-too-gentle kick. "Snoring and lazing all the day. Get on with catching mice for your dinner because I'm not about to feed you!"

The yellow tomcat let out a yowl and scuttled off for his secondary sleeping place. Lena's bed.

Chapter Twenty-One

Outside in the biting cold, Rossiter leaned against the newel post at the end of the drive. He felt as though he'd been kicked in the belly. Callie married. Callie with his baby. Callie with Hugh MacDuff. How was he to find her? To find his child? Byrch Kenyon might know. Like hell, he thought. It would be a cold day in hell before he asked Kenyon for anything that included the time of day. By God, he would find Callie on his own if it meant searching day and night, twenty-three hours out of every twenty-four.

Early the next morning, Rossiter left his hotel and took a hansom to Fulton Street, a shabby neighborhood by any standards. All night long he had thought of Callie, remembering the light of adoration in her eyes each time she looked at him. He needed that now, that love, that approval. He needed to be back in her life; he wanted to see his child.

Starting at the corner of Trinity Place and working his way toward South Street, Rossiter knocked on every door, inquiring after the McDuffs. It was a long, tiring day, and Rossiter had just about given up hope when he decided he would try one more tenement house before calling it a day. Knocking on the basement apartment door, Rossiter waited. A burly man answered, a grizzled beard growing on thick jowls.

"What is it? What d'you want?"

Rossiter made his explanations.

"Yeah, I know 'em, all right. Skipped out on the rent, they did, and took half the furniture with 'em. MacDuff was a drunk, and that little wife of his was big with child and worked her fingers to the bone to keep the old man in liquor. I was on the point of evicting them, hadn't paid their rent. You let one get away with it and all the others try the same thing," the landlord complained. "I'm a business man, not a charitable organization. You want charity, go to church, I always says."

"How much did they owe you?" Rossiter asked through clenched teeth.

Smelling the money in the gentleman's pocket, the sour-faced landlord turned crafty. "Twenty dollars."

"More like ten, and that's nine dollars too much for this sty." Rossiter handed over the crisp bills. "There's ten more like it if you can tell me where they went. If you're thinking of lying to me, I'll come back and beat it out of you."

The man shook his head. "They just left one evening. I wasn't home, else I'd have saved my furniture. Decent, hard-working people don't skip on their rent. I liked the wife. She was a hard worker. Doing all that ironing and him drinking up her wages. It was a sin is what it was. I ain't seen nor heard a word about 'em since. If you've a mind to part with that ten spot, I could be telling you where you might try looking. I ain't saying there's where you'll find them, mind you. But it'll give you a place to start. When you're scraping the bottom the way those two were, the only place left is Shantytown." Rossiter handed over the bill and watched it disappear as quickly as the first.

For days Rossiter walked the streets, asking questions. In the rabbit warren of Shantytown he soon gave up after his first try. If anyone did know anything of the MacDuffs, they were keeping it to themselves. This handsome lad with his fancy clothes had no business asking questions about one of their own. One old woman took a broom to his back, shouting and screaming that she would set the dogs on him if he ever showed his face again. Callie couldn't be living in this pig sty. Not his Callie. The stench made him retch as he ran up the narrow, winding lanes. It wasn't long before he was lost and unable to get his bearings. He was going to have to to throw away his fine leather boots when he got back to his hotel. God alone knew what he had been stepping in.

Eventually he made his way out of the dim labyrinth of crooked alleys. He heaved a sigh of relief. He was certain that no matter how poor Callie was, no matter how desperate, she would never consent to live in such a hovel. Somehow, some way, she would find something better than this rat trap.

Days went by as Rossiter searched out neighborhoods, describing Callie and Hugh to anyone who would listen. It wasn't until he stopped by a green grocer's shop and spoke to one Dillis McGovern that he felt he was close to finding the answer he wanted. It wasn't what the man said but what he didn't say that convinced Rossiter he was right. McGovern denied any knowledge of the MacDuffs. His eyes narrowed, and he seemed to be holding his breath, waiting for Rossiter's next question. "MacDuff's wife is my sister," Rossiter lied. "I have to find her. My mother is very ill and wants to see her." From there he concocted a story that would have made men stronger than McGovern cry. But the man held firm, denying that he knew anything about the MacDuffs.

Goddamn Irish clods. They stuck together like glue, Rossiter thought nastily. He couldn't shake the feeling that he was getting closer to Callie. If McGovern did indeed know Callie and Hugh, it might behoove him to concentrate his efforts in the immediate vicinity. Sooner or later someone would lead him in the right direction.

Another week passed with Rossiter canvassing the neighborhoods from morning to dark. He had never realized what a close-mouthed lot the Irish were. Not one of them bought his story about Callie being his sister. Eventually he discarded the myth and said he was from a lawyer's office searching for Callie in order to bestow a small inheritance. He didn't do any better with that story and soon gave it up. He then switched tactics and started asking around for Hugh MacDuff, saying he needed a handyman and he had heard that MacDuff was available. He got snorts and smirks for his efforts. So much for the Irish looking for work.

He wasn't going to give up. Sooner or later he would find Callie. Sooner or later she was going to be there when he least expected it.

It was late in the afternoon when Rossiter was walking down the street, peering into windows and generally paying no mind to anything except his deep, dark thoughts. If a group of running, laughing children hadn't forced him off the sidewalk, he wouldn't have fallen against the doorway of Sylvia Levy's Tea Room. Callie was just leaving for the day, her apron folded neatly over her arm. Her thoughts were just as dark and deep as Rossiter's as she remembered all the washing and ironing she still had to do when she got back to the shanty. If she was lucky, she might be able to spend a few minutes with little Rory before it was time to put him to bed. Lord, she was tired. She had been on her feet all day, and she still had a good seven hours to go before she could fall exhausted into a light sleep. With Rory's cough she had to remain alert so he didn't choke while sleeping. All the medicine and all the warm tea and honey didn't seem to be helping.

Callie suddenly looked up, expecting an apology from the stranger who had nearly knocked her off her feet. In that instant she felt as though the breath had been driven from her body. The neatly folded apron fell to the ground unnoticed. It couldn't be, not after all this time. But it was. "Rossiter!" was all she could manage to choke. It seemed the world had tilted sideways, leaving her dangling somewhere in space. The two years that had passed evaporated like the mists over the harbor.

His arms reached out to her, holding her steady, drawing her into his embrace. Callie felt her cheek fall against his shoulder. Her thoughts whirled, and her heart fluttered wildly. She felt as though she had finally come to a safe harbor. "Callie, Callie! You don't know how I've searched for you. How much you mean to me!" His words were fast, urgent; she could feel the pounding of his heart beneath his greatcoat. "Callie, Lena told me about the child. I didn't know, I swear it! No one knew where you'd gone, but now I've found you again."

Callie tried to speak but the words wouldn't come. He was here, at last. He was telling her things, offering explanations. All her dreams, her prayers, were answered. All the hard work, all the grief and worry would come to an end. Or would it? Callie tilted her chin, looking into Rossiter's eyes. He was the same, his eyes were the same. In his face she saw the face of her son, his son, Rory. "You have a son, Rossiter. I've christened him Rory."

Rossiter drew a deep breath, holding her tight, so tightly he thought he could make her a part of himself. He couldn't lose her again. "Callie, where have you been? How could I have lost you?"

Confusion pounded through Callie's brain. This was her dream, finding Rossiter again, telling him about his son. But somehow the script was all wrong. He was asking her questions that had plagued her for nearly two years, but they didn't seem important any longer. What was wrong with her? Was it just the shock of seeing him again? She had dreamed about finding him this way; she had thought she would fly into his arms. Instead she found herself pulling away, avoiding his eyes.

Rossiter drew her back into his embrace. He couldn't lose her again. Not again. "Callie, darling, we have to talk. There's so much to say, so many things you must forgive, understand." He moved into a doorway, taking her with him, bending to find her mouth with his own.

Callie stiffened against the contact. Was she wrong, or had she seen him glance covertly up the street as though he were ashamed of being seen with a tea-shop waitress? If anyone should be concerned about being observed, it was she. She was a married woman, and *she* was known in this neighborhood, not Rossiter. It was her reputation that would suffer. "Rossiter, let me go! Please!"

He released her, his confusion mingling with relief at having found her. It had never occurred to him that Callie might be satisfied with her life, that she might no longer want him. "Callie, what's wrong? Aren't you glad to see me?"

The hurt in his eyes was so real, so much like her own Rory's, that Callie's heart gave a little leap and her fingers reached up to touch his cheek and graze upward to the golden curls over his ear. So much like Rory. "Of course I'm happy to see you, Rossiter," she intoned softly. "It's only that I'm late and must get home to Rory."

"But I've got to talk to you, to explain! Oh, Callie, I was never so glad to see anyone. Tell me how much you've missed me," he pleaded, drawing her close again, reinforcing his embrace.

"I'm very glad to see you, Rossiter," she smiled.

He looked down into her face, his eyes lingering on the softly waved chestnut hair shimmering with golden lights, the gentle curve of her cheekbones, the newly molded hollows beneath drawing his glance to the fine structure of a perfectly sculptured jaw and chin. He would have known her anywhere, recognized her immediately. There was the same prettiness—no, he corrected—there was beauty come to fruition. The changes time had wrought were subtle but at the same time startling. Callie was a girl no longer; she was a beautiful woman. The bright blue eyes, once filled with innocence and trust, were still the color of a summer sky, but there were mysterious shadows in their depths. The slim, girlish body had been transformed into new curves, new voluptuousness. Her mouth, once full almost to the point of petulance, was now a woman's mouth: soft, full, ripe. She couldn't leave him this way. He had to see her, he had to have her again. He sensed her wish to leave, and that made him want her all the more. She said she had to get home, to her son. Their son. "Stay with me, Callie. Don't go!" He heard the desperation in his own voice.

"I can't, Rossiter. I mustn't."

"At least tell me where you live. Where I can find you?"

Callie laughed, a soft, throaty sound. "Even if I told you, you'd never find me. Rory and I live in Shantytown."

Rossiter marveled at her directness. There was no shame, no defense or explanation that she and their son lived in the most notorious slum in the city. And she was right; he would never find her in that rabbit warren of alleys and shacks.

Callie saw the disappointment cloud Rossiter's eyes. What had he expected? That she would have an apartment on Fifth Avenue? There was a roaring in her ears as confusion pounded in contra-rhythm to her pulses. The only emotion she could feel, could recognize, was anger. Anger for the life she'd been living, for the things Rory should have and didn't, for Hugh's generosity that had turned to resentment. Nothing seemed clear any longer. Nothing seemed to have purpose except Rory. Questions were exploding in her brain. Where had Rossiter been? Had he married his socialite heiress? What did he mean he'd been searching for her? He said he hadn't known about the child. Why hadn't he received her letter?

"I have to go, Rossiter! I have to get back to Rory!" She struggled away from his grasp, swallowing great gulps of air. She couldn't think straight. Everything was muddled and blurred. "I have to get back to Rory, and there's two baskets of ironing to be done before the night is out." It was the truth, and yet it was a feeble excuse. Rossiter would never understand about duty or work or obligation.

"I can't let you go. I won't," he said stubbornly.

"You must!" she saw the distress she was causing him and softened her tone. "Tomorrow. It's my day off. If you like, I can meet you right here. Three o'clock?" Her words were hesitant; she knew they stung. There was the same crestfallen expression on Rossiter's face that she'd seen so often on their son's face when she had to leave him to go to work. In many ways, Rory was as demanding as Rossiter. Or was it that Rossiter was as demanding as her infant? She didn't know, she couldn't think! In some ways she was so happy he had found her, and in others she wasn't. She'd been managing her own life for so long—hers and Rory's and even Hugh's. And she'd been doing a damn good job of it, too. What right had he to come back into her life this way and make demands on her?

"Make it in the morning, Callie," he said, trying to infuse her with his eagerness. "I won't be able to wait another whole day. Why can't I come with you now? I want to see my son."

Instantly Callie bristled. How easily those words seemed to come to him. "My son," he had said as though the biological relationship entitled him to Rory. Rory was *her* son! Hers alone! She was the one who had cared for him from the moment of his birth, who had held him through the long nights, who worked her fingers to the bone to provide for him. "You can't come home with me, Rossiter. Hugh will be there, and I won't have him upset. You can wait until tomorrow afternoon. We'll have a long talk then." She turned, not wanting to see the pleading on his face. He was so much like Rory that denying him anything tugged at her heart. "Three o'clock," she promised.

"Callie, don't go! Wait. Stay here with me. Don't leave when I've just found you."

"I must go home to Rory. He needs me. I'm all he has—"

"At least let me walk with you. I promise not to come into your house—"

"No," Callie said firmly.

Rossiter hardly recognized the word, but he knew the tone. It was one his *Mamán* used to make a point. He had to be satisfied.

He watched Callie walk away from him without a backward glance. He hadn't known exactly what to expect when he found her, but this certainly wasn't it. This wasn't the old Callie, the girl he knew back on Todt Hill. What was that nonsense about two baskets of ironing? Surely she wasn't taking in laundry! She had almost said it with pride. Rossiter shuffled his feet like a schoolboy whose selfish desires had been denied.

Rossiter spent the night vacillating between exhilaration and depression. He was a father with a son who, according to Callie, looked just like him. Rory. She had called him Rory. But Callie was different, all grown up with a woman's face and a woman's body. Where had the girl gone? She was stunningly beautiful, and just the thought of her excited him. He wanted her and meant to have her. It would be as though these past two years had never been. He needed her now, more than ever. He needed her strength to help him find his own direction.

Still, it annoyed him when he remembered the control she had exercised during their brief meeting. He had come away with the feeling that she didn't quite approve of him, and wasn't that one of the reasons he had searched for her so desperately? Since his rift with his mother, he needed a woman in his life who could give him that loving approval. A strong woman. A woman in whose eyes he could see himself reflected in the most flattering light. He needed Callie, and he wanted his son. She possessed the serenity he needed in his life, and that would enable him to paint. And always beneath that serenity there was vitality and soundess and purpose. He had sensed her strength even when she was a girl, and that, more than her sky-blue eyes looking adoringly into his, had drawn him to her. It was the kind of strength his mother possessed, but it was tempered with love and an assuring calm.

Thinking about his mother depressed him. A vision flashed before him of Callie and himself and a small son living in a cottage, attempting to eke out an existence. He almost gagged. If he could barely support himself, how could he support Callie and the child? He might make amends with his mother, but she would never come to terms with the fact that he had found Callie again, much less accept his son. Apprehension and self-doubt roiled his innards. Reconciliation with his mother might be impossible. No, he would have to depend upon Callie. Callie loved him. No thought to the contrary ever crossed his mind.

It was well past midnight when Callie folded Mrs. Rawlings's intricately pleated camisole and placed it in the basket. Her arms were stiff, and the back of her neck and shoulders ached. Callie's reputation and clientele had grown because of the exactness of her work and her knack for handling the narrow, ridged pleating iron she had trained herself to use. It was said she had the talent of a French lady's maid, and the compliment never failed to please her.

Her legs and back were practically numb, but she still had three shirts to iron before she could crawl into bed. Her eyes went to the small, low bed in the corner of the one-room shanty. Seeing it was empty didn't alarm her; Rory lay curled into a ball under his bed. She would pick him up and lay him back under his covers. She had no idea why the tyke crawled under his bed. She supposed it gave him a sense of security, being curled into the small space. He'd outgrow it, she knew with the certainty of one who had a long association with children.

Callie's eyes went to the double bed; Hugh still wasn't home. Most likely he would stagger in toward morning. She had ceased to worry about her husband and his drinking. He had become only a minor inconvenience, someone else to feed and look after. Her own life and work was going well. She was satisfied with the mall savings she had managed to put away. Soon, very soon, ne would make the move out of Shantytown into an apartment.

Callie's eyes widened, and she was brought up short. Would er plans change now that Rossiter was back? Rossiter was back. imple and declarative. How strange, uncanny really, that she hould meet him again as she had. As she tested the flatiron before pplying it to one of the shirts, she allowed Rossiter into her mind. n her daydreams she had always known exactly what she would ay, exactly how she would act if she should ever meet him again. low many times she'd rehearsed her little speech. And then, when onfronted with the reality, she had done none of the things she'd lanned. She still could not resolve the anger that was like a hidden vell inside of her. Until meeting Rossiter again she had direction n her life. She had plans and knew exactly where they would ake her and Rory.

Upon reflection, she thought she had behaved rather well. She ad quelled her questions, stifled her anger and resentments, and ontrolled the situation. She had been the one to take charge, to nake the decision. She was the one who had put him off, suggesting a meeting the next day. Her heart fluttered and then stilled. Did she love Rossiter? Or had she picked up the pieces of her fe, examined them, and found them satisfactory? What about her lans for the future—a difficult future, true—but one in which he was in charge of her own life and Rory's?

Callie slammed the iron down onto the shirt front. She recalled ow on first sight she had fallen into his arms. That had to mean omething. Relief? But what were her deeper feelings? Was there oom in her life for Rossiter? And what about Hugh? Whatever ne circumstances, she was his wife and he was her husband, not omething Callie took lightly. If she had, Hugh would have been ut on his ear long ago. No, she couldn't think about Hugh, or erself for that matter. Rory had to come first; he was the only ne who counted. There were so many feelings she had to sort ut before she met Rossiter tomorrow!

Naturally Rossiter wanted to see his son. But how would Hugh eact? Lately he had been more snarly and nasty than usual, often gnoring Rory completely. Twice during the past months he had een physically abusive to her. There wouldn't be a third time. he hoped Hugh remembered her words as she backed away from im and reached for her flatiron. No man, regardless of who he vas, would ever lay a hand on her. She wouldn't permit it. The ratitude she had felt for Hugh at first had diminished bit by bit ntil there was nothing left. This saddened her. She knew that she was in some way responsible for his change from a good frier who enjoyed a nip or two into a slovenly drunkard whose ey were filled with bitterness.

Callie glanced once again at Rory, admiring his sleep-flushe cheeks and the pink rosebud of his mouth. Maternal protectivene and love welled within her breast. Rory was the one who mattere Only Rory. Her own feelings for Rossiter weren't important. Rory chance for a decent future was not here in Shantytown or in tiny, cramped apartment with a mother who was overworked ar exhausted. If there was any hope for Rory, only Rossiter coul give it to him.

The last shirt was finished and carefully folded. She quickl washed her face and hands, changed into her nightdress, and cre between the covers. She was exhausted. She couldn't think abo Rossiter or Rory or even herself and Hugh. Tomorrow would b time enough to deal with it all. Almost before her cheek touche the pillow, Callie was asleep.

Rossiter arrived outside Sylvia Levy's Tea Room at two o'cloc eager to see Callie again. He had supposed that her eagerne matched his and that she would arrive early. Three o'clock cam and went. Rossiter paced the busy sidewalk, becoming more ap prehensive as the hands of his pocketwatch approached four.

At ten minutes to four Callie walked briskly down Columbu Avenue. While she didn't dawdle, neither did she hurry. She ha dressed carefully for her meeting with Rossiter, more out of pric than from any intention to impress or seduce. From her meag wardrobe, she had selected her best dress, a castoff from one c her customers' daughters. It fit a bit snug in the bosom and she' had to nip in the waistline, but the clear lavender blue accentuate the ivory tones of her skin and brought out the shimmering dar of her hair. White gloves and a white straw bonnet tied with ribbor to match the dress completed the outfit. Her only jewelry was th gold locket Mary had given her on her eighteenth birthday. Calli was twenty now, a woman. Girlhood, if she had indeed ever bee a girl, was left behind. The sorrow of Mary's death was als behind her, and not long ago Callie had realized she could ope the locket and gaze upon the little girl's sweet face without re crimination. Now she was going to meet the other face in th locket. Rossiter.

Rossiter recognized Callie coming up the avenue. She walke with her chin held high, shoulders squared, hips swinging light with that same gentle grace he remembered and which never faile to excite him. He was so glad to see her, he almost forgot his disappointment that she didn't break into a run or approach him breathlessly, offering excuses for her lateness. She merely smiled at him and waited for him to open the door to the Tea Room. He noted that she was greeted by name by the proprietress and several women patrons, which she acknowledged graciously. She waited for Rossiter to hold her chair. He was slightly put off his stride by this formal, grown-up Callie.

"I've been waiting around outside since two o'clock. I thought you'd be as eager to see me as I was to see you." While not actually a complaint, the message was clear. Rossiter was annoyed.

Callie smiled, waiting for him to give the waitress their order of tea and cakes. "I'm sorry to be late, Rossiter," she told him gently. "I had certain things that required my attention." It wasn't an excuse nor an apology, he realized, only the facts. "How is your family. How is your father?"

"*Papá* is fine; so is *Mamán*. Anne is married, you know. Callie, you're so beautiful. I can't quite come to terms with the fact that the lovely, simple girl I knew has become a grown-up lady."

Callie laughed, a musical trill. "Time changes all of us, Rossiter."

"I've dreamed about you, missed you! You must know, Callie, I still love you, I never stopped loving you!" There was such earnestness in his tone, such emotion in his eyes, that Callie was suddenly shaken with the memories of those nights when he had come to her room and looked at her the way he was doing now, saying her name as he had just said it. "I can't believe that after all my searching I should come upon you by the sheerest of accidents."

Callie steeled herself, keeping her control at great cost. She wanted to rant and rail and beat upon him, cursing him for leaving her alone and never thinking to inquire after her until nearly two years later. It stung to suddenly discover this anger; it hurt to know how little she had meant to him after all. Biting back the sharpness from her voice, she faced Rossiter directly, willing herself not to see her own Rory's dear face in the face of his father. "Evidently thinking and dreaming and longing were enough for you, Rossiter. You never came home to see me, you never wrote. I wrote you, Rossiter; you didn't anser."

Was this Callie, *his* Callie, speaking to him this way, with such cool control in her voice? Accusing him? "Lena said you wrote. I never received it," he defended. "If I had known, I would have returned immediately. You must believe that, Callie!"

"Do you believe it, Rossiter? Would you have gone against your *Mamán* to come back to me? Last I heard, you were busy courting a lovely young heiress. Did you ever marry her?"

Rossiter hung his head, remembering the scandal he had caused and his mother's final rejection of him. "No, I was engaged to her, but we never married. I had a change of heart." He lifted his head, looking into her eyes, willing her to believe him. "I couldn't marry another when it was you I loved."

The waitress chose that inopportune moment to bring the tea tray and cakes, forcing him to restrain his words. As he watched the delicate china pot and teacups placed upon the white cloth he had time to think. He remembered Jasper's coolness when he had made it clear that he wanted nothing to do with his son. If Lena knew about Callie's child, was it possible Jasper also knew?

As soon as the waitress left, Rossiter reached across the table grasping Callie's hand. "Does my father know about the child?"

Callie sensed his need for reassurance. "No, I didn't see any need to . . . to burden him at such a painful time. He had only come back for Mary's funeral, you know. I couldn't go to him for help; I couldn't hurt him that way. I'm married, and Rory bears the MacDuff name."

"You married Hugh MacDuff, the handyman! He's old enough to be your father. How could you, Callie, how could you?"

Callie stared across the small table at the man she once had loved. Oh, she had no doubt of that, she had loved him, more than anything or anyone. Now he asked how she could have married Hugh, the only person who had given one roaring hoot what would become of her. How indeed! Her tone was light almost musical, when she replied, "I married Hugh MacDuff because of your child, Rossiter. It was a question of survival. I'm certain you've never had to think in those terms, but I did. Hugh offered me marriage so *your* child would have a name. He was a good man. I'll always be grateful to him. He put a roof over my head and saw to it I didn't starve."

Rossiter scoffed, the corners of his mouth drawing downward in mockery. "He took such good care of you that you skipped out on the rent you owed on Fulton Street. I saw your old landlord I paid your debt."

"You're a fool, Rossiter. You shouldn't have done that. I paid that debt months ago and added a generous sum for the furniture we took. I'm not proud of running out on the rent, but Hugh had some hard luck and we had no other choice. It's been paid back—every cent."

It wasn't possible, but it seemed her head was held even higher than before. Her cool stare was causing him great agitation. He shouldn't have mentioned the rent; it made him appear petty and spiteful. "You should have gone to my family, Callie, regardless of your pride. After all, that's my child you gave the name of MacDuff. That's my child living in that abomination called Shantytown!"

"Your mother knew about the baby." She waited for the impact of her statement to sink in. "So much for turning to your family. I told you, Rossiter, it's called survival. I live where I can afford to pay the rent. I provide for my child the best way I can. If it means I have to live in Shantytown the rest of my life, I'll do it. I'm not afraid of hard work, Rossiter. Your *Mamán* saw to that."

"Callie, my poor, sweet Callie. Let's not argue. All that's important is that you're here, with me. I want you, Callie. I want our son. I love you." He took her hands in his, pretending not to see the ragged nails, the reddened, cracked skin. Callie made no motion to hide her hands from him. It wasn't supposed to be like this. She should be in his arms, telling him how often she had dreamed of being with him again, professing her love for him. Instead she was sitting across from him, wondering if Hugh was at home and if Rory was all right with Trisha. Love and survival were two different things, as she had discovered, and she would rather have a healthy dollop of the latter than the former. "Aren't you going to tell me you love me, Callie?" Rossiter asked petulantly, breaking into her thoughts.

"Is that what you expect? Yes, I can see you do. A lot of time has passed, Rossiter. I'm married. I have no intention of becoming your mistress. That was your intention, wasn't it?"

"Well, yes . . . no . . . what I mean is . . . I can take care of you, Callie. You and the boy. Divorce isn't unheard of, and I'm certain that all you have to do is tell MacDuff that I'm back now and I'll be looking after my own family."

"Why should I tell him? Why don't you tell him?"

"Come away with me, Callie. Now, today!"

"Go away where? To what? What about your parents?" Oh, God, was this her own voice speaking so indifferently, so callously? Would she ever forgive Rossiter for leaving her the way he had?

Rossiter paled and then reddened at her questions. "*Papá* will see it my way. He always thought the world of you, Callie. And now with little Rory, how could he turn us away?"

Callie stared at Rossiter for a long time; she didn't like what she was seeing, what she was hearing. Instinct told her that Rossiter needed a way back into Jasper's good graces, and Rory and herself would be just the ticket. "Tell me you'll come away with me, Callie," he was saying.

Finally Callie's resolve melted. She thought of Rory spending his life in poverty with a laundress for a mother and a drunk for a father. Her son could have all the advantages if only she would agree with Rossiter. Advantages and opportunities that were his birthright.

"Tell me, Callie. Tell me!"

"I have to think about it. I don't know just yet. It isn't right . . ." She lifted her head, clear blue eyes sparkling with unshed tears for herself, for Rory, for Rossiter, and for Hugh. What a mess it all was. An ugly mess. She never doubted for a moment her mother's words that bad things happened to bad girls. She had known she was being bad when she let Rossiter come to her in the middle of the night, but she often wondered how love could be bad. "If you want to talk with Hugh, I'll make certain he's sober and home when you arrive. The day after tomorrow will be fine. I'll meet you here at the Tea Room and take you back with me."

"The day after tomorrow!" Rossiter exclaimed. "Surely you can fit me in before that! That's what you're doing, isn't it? Fitting me in?"

Callie didn't like his snarly tone nor the expression on his face. She set her teacup down and picked up her gloves. "Yes, that's exactly what I'm doing, Rossiter. I have to leave now. I'll be here at nine-thirty in the evening day after tomorrow. You have till then to reconsider."

"Callie, don't leave until you tell me you love me. You do, don't you?"

"I'll see you on Thursday, Rossiter." Without forethought, she allowed her hand to fall on his golden hair, feeling the soft waves resist her fingers. How like Rory's. A smile illuminated her face, and Rossiter felt as though the moon and the stars were shining just for him. She must love him, she must!

Chapter Twenty-Two

Callie dragged herself home. She felt as though her entire body was boiling with turmoil. What had she done? Why had she been so harsh with him, so unbending? Hadn't he fulfilled her dreams by declaring his love for her? Callie shook her head. It was wrong, all wrong! The feelings, the emotions were all wrong. He had asked her to say she loved him, but the words would not come. How was it possible to be so in love and then two short years later to find that love had gone, burned itself out, until there was nothing but dead, cold ashes that would never burn again?

He had wanted her to go away with him, but he had not said one word about marriage. He merely wanted her, wanted their son, and the awful truth of it was that he never for one moment believed he would be refused. The blurred vision of the adolescent was clear now, and she saw him through a woman's eyes. He was still golden, still beautiful, but he was still a boy. She wondered when she had become a woman. Was it when Rory was born? When she'd had her fill of suffering and uncertainty and had begun to seek ways to support herself and her son? Is that what it would take for Rossiter to become a man? Responsibility and suffering?

She didn't look forward to telling Hugh about Rossiter. She knew Hugh would be upset when she brought him to see Rory, but she mustn't allow it to make a difference. Rory was Rossiter's son, and with God's help, he deserved some of the advantages that relationship could bring him. A vision of her son living in a big house with a big yard to play in and a room of his own flashed through her head. Her thoughts never progressed to consider herself or Rossiter or Hugh.

It was early the following morning when Callie took Rory to Maggie Crenshaw's and left him in Trisha's care. She went back to the shanty she shared with Hugh and met him at the door. "Where you been?" he slurred with the effects of last night's brew.

"I just took Rory over to Maggie Crenshaw's. I have to deliver these two baskets of ironing. I made coffee, Hugh. It might be good if you drank some. You don't look well to me. Are you ill?" Callie asked quietly, her tone patient and concerned.

Hugh sneered at his wife. He knew she disapproved of his drinking. Why couldn't she just come out and say she knew he was drunk instead of saying he looked ill? All she cared about was that boy of hers. There was no room left in her heart for an old drunk like himself.

Hugh had a moment of remorse when he watched her load the heavy baskets onto the rickety old wagon he'd fixed for her. She did work hard. There was no sense in lying to himself. She doled out his allowance for whiskey and never said a word. And why should she, Hugh defended himself. Whatever she gave him was only a pittance compared to what she stashed away under that loose floorboard. One of these days when she was out, he was going to lift that board and see for himself how much she'd saved. Callie thought he didn't know. Ha! There was very little he didn't know about Callie. He told himself that he'd have to be in pretty desperate straits and beyond caring before he touched her hoard.

He watched through the open door as Callie trundled the wagon down the mud-rutted lane. When she returned, she would have the wagon filled to overflowing with more ironing to be done. He was sick of seeing Callie leaning over the board through the wee hours of the morning. He was sick of having other people's fine clothes hanging about the shanty and even sicker of seeing Callie dress and go out to work at that fancy Tea Room. She took no pleasure in anything, Hugh scowled, only Rory. Rory alone could bring a smile to her face. Why couldn't Callie smile in his direction for once? Why couldn't he make her laugh? Why didn't she remember the orange? Why?

But what hurt the most was that Callie didn't trust him to mind little Rory. Oh, no, she paid out good money to the Crenshaws to keep an eye on the little one. She had never said he was too drunk and wasn't to be trusted, but actions spoke louder than words.

Hugh lowered himself onto the bed, his thoughts focusing on his beautiful young wife, the young wife who had never lain in his arms. He was surprised she hadn't left him by now. He didn't know why she stayed with him. Was gratitude enough, or was it possible that she cared for him?

Hugh slept fitfully. His dreams were filled with a laughing Callie romping through the meadow of wild flowers with Mary Powers fast on her heels. He could see himself standing by the buggy, his pipe clenched between his teeth as he watched them frolic. And then the young and spirited Callie seemed to change before his very eyes, losing the roundness of girlhood to the sharper, more defined curves of a young woman. Her long chestnut hair flowed behind her as she glided through the field, cherry petals falling like snow all about her. Her crystal blue eyes looked into his, her full, ripe mouth parted, inviting a kiss.

Hugh woke in a sweat from his dream. His heart pounded, and his mouth was dry as he punched his pillow and rolled over. It was a dream he hated, a vision he loved. He hated that she'd become a woman—cool and lovely, responsible and independent. The very qualities he so admired were the same ones that put such a breach between them. He wanted her to be the young girl he'd adored for so long, the girl who was within his reach, the girl he could love without expecting anything in return. But Callie's beauty did things to a man. A man could expect a woman to return his affection, to show her love. Tears of frustration dropped onto the pillow. Callie was a woman now, and he was a man. Not much of a man by some standards, but a man nonetheless.

Callie returned to the shanty with the wagonload of fancy goods to be ironed. The flat pieces and simpler garments had been left with Maggie Crenshaw. As she sprinkled the freshly laundered goods and ironed, she kept a watchful eye on Hugh, who was sleeping off his drunk in their bed. It was good that she'd left Rory with Trisha Crenshaw. Hugh was more restless than usual, and he could be nasty and surly when he awakened. His rantings and threats were not something she wanted Rory to see.

Callie didn't like Hugh MacDuff these days. The sour smell of whiskey seemed to follow him wherever he went, leaving traces where he sat and where he slept. She would have given anything for a bed of her own, not to be surrounded by the stink even as she slept. Her life was little better than her mother's, and she wondered how and when she had become such an extension of Peggy, inheriting her own mother's lot in life.

Rossiter could be her answer. But what exactly was Rossiter prepared to do for her? He'd mentioned divorcing Hugh, but he'd never said anything about marriage. Could she leave Hugh so heartlessly? Did she *want* to marry Rossiter? Now, seeing him through a woman's eyes, she realized how immature and selfish Rossiter really was. She had married Hugh out of desperation, making her vows reluctantly, but they were vows nonetheless. Could she break them? Could she just take Rory and leave? What kind of person would that make her? Her Mum wouldn't ever consider such a thing. Callie brushed back a lock of her hair with the back of her hand and spat on the flatiron to test its heat. The iron slammed down on the board, paralleling the force of her emotions. Well, she wasn't her Mum! She was herself, Callie James MacDuff, and her own wants and needs had no bearing on the situation. What was best for Rory, that's what she had to decide.

At eight o'clock the following evening, Callie began to dress for her meeting with Rossiter. It was amazing that she felt so calm. She remembered the days in the Powers's house on Staten Island when just the thought of seeing Rossiter would set her heart to pounding. Now, tonight, it was simply something she had to do. Callie had given every waking thought to the dilemma she faced, and she had finally made up her mind. She would bring Rossiter here to see his son, and she would not, in the future, prevent him from seeing Rory. But as for herself, she had made her bed, and she would sleep in it. She was a married woman, regardless of how reluctant her vows were, and she would not leave Hugh for Rossiter. It had been a simple decision actually. If Rossiter was inclined to be generous toward his son, so much the better, but she would not leave her husband for a man she no longer loved. She supposed she would always have a tender place in her heart for Rossiter, but he was from the past, and Callie could only direct her eyes to the future.

She brushed her hair to a gleaming shine and used its length to create a charming, soft puff on top of her head. Loose, unruly tendrils escaped at her nape and against her cheeks, curling around her tiny ears. She pinched her cheeks for color and used a touch of rose water and glycerine salve on her lips. She put on her lavender blue dress and adjusted her petticoats. She cast a dismal eye at her red, chafed hands. The glycerine helped somewhat, but they were work-worn and unattractive. It would be a long time, if ever, until her hands were restored to their former whiteness.

A smile tugged at her lips when she tried to imagine the expression on Rossiter's face when she brought him to the shanty. She knew he would never see the order and cleanliness she had worked so hard to achieve, nor would he notice the scent of pine water and soap. No, Rossiter would only see the drabness, the ugliness of the sagging bed, the rickety table, and the hard, wooden chairs that cried for a coat of paint. It was only a tarpaper shack, but it was a roof over their heads, and Callie was thankful for it.

She almost laughed aloud when she recalled an article that had appeared in a lady's magazine one of the patrons of the Tea Room had left behind.

> On the west side of the city above Fifty-ninth Street, on the outskirts, squatters' shanties are perched on the rocks or nestled in the hollows. The luxuriance of the vines over those small abodes is a comfort and a refreshment to the eyes; grapevine, trumpet-creepers, scarlet runners, morning glories, big posies of sunflowers subdued into almost delicacy of form and color by the green surroundings and the gray of the background.

Apparently the writer had stepped no closer than her nose would allow. Or was it that reporting hardship and squalor and misery was unfit for the fashionable magazine? There was nothing mentioned of the stink from the varnish factory or the mud and filth. It wouldn't be long before Callie could leave this shack behind and afford an apartment in a decent house. And she would require no help from anyone, not even Rossiter, to achieve her end. This thought alone brought a triumphant smile to her face. She had decided that what was best for Rory was a mother with principles and ethics and character. Just as Peggy had been the best for her, so Callie would be for Rory.

Maggie Crenshaw came to stay with Rory while Callie went out. Maggie was typical of the women in Shantytown—old before her time, worn and sour-faced. But she had an abiding loyalty to Callie, who had helped improve the Crenshaw circumstances by commissioning out the simpler ironing. She knew the fancy ladies on Columbus Avenue were impressed with Callie's neat appearance and pretty face and that she was able to secure work where

Maggie could not. Settling in the rocking chair, Maggie took Rory onto her lap, crooning to him in her native brogue.

"I won't be long, Maggie. I'm only going up to the Tea Room to meet an old friend and bring him back here." Rory held out his arms to Callie for her kiss, his bright, button blue eyes half-closed with drowsiness, his cheeks pink and soft beneath her lips. Rory wasn't upset at his mother's leaving. Maggie or her daughter always sat with him while Callie went out to work. But tonight he wrapped his sturdy arms around her neck and held fast.

"Mama won't be long, darlin'. And when I come back I'll bring a new friend for you." She buried her face in the sweet warmth of his neck, giving him an extra squeeze. "You be a good boy for Maggie."

"I won't be long, an hour at best," she repeated for Maggie, wrapping her shawl over her shoulders.

"What should I do if the 'auld blether comes home?"

"Wait till I get back, Maggie. Hugh won't be fit to take care of Rory. Promise me?"

"You've my promise, Callie. Would yer think I'd leave this angel to the likes of his father when he's in his cups? Believe me, I've enough of that at me own house, that's fer sure."

Callie arrived at the Tea House a few minutes before nine. She was surprised to find Rossiter drinking a cup of tea. Since Sylvia Levy usually closed at seven, she raised a questioning eyebrow.

"I paid Mrs. Levy to stay open. I didn't want to meet you out on the street as though you were a common working girl."

"But that's exactly what I am, Rossiter." She debated telling him now that she wasn't going anywhere with him, but decided she would wait until he'd seen Rory. She wanted Rory to have a chance to know his father, and she didn't want Rossiter petulant and stubborn the first time he met his son.

"We've no time for tea, Rossiter. The woman who's staying with Rory has her own children to care for, and I don't want to keep her waiting. I haven't said anything to Hugh about your coming. I thought it would be better if you saw your son alone for the first time."

Rossiter set his cup down precisely in the center of the saucer and left several bills on the table. He felt immense relief that he wasn't going to have to deal with Hugh MacDuff this evening. If the man wasn't home, he would have Callie all to himself, and God knew how he longed to have her in his arms once again.

Callie glanced down at the money on the table. There was enough there to feed Hugh, Rory, and herself for a week.

Callie walked briskly, her hands crossed over her chest as she held each end of her shawl. It wasn't that chilly this evening, although there was a good breeze in the air. She simply didn't want Rossiter reaching for her hand.

"Callie, I don't see why we couldn't use the hansom I hired. I don't care for walking through this neighborhood at night. God knows, it's almost impossible to see where we're going," Rossiter complained, stopping to scrape the bottom of his boot in the dust. "If it wasn't for that light in the sky, it'd be blacker than hell."

"Rossiter, I told you, the hansom cab couldn't go into Shantytown. The lanes are too narrow, and I doubt the driver would . . . what light?" Callie lifted her head, looking into the distance. A peculiar brightness lit the night sky, red and gold and fiery in its intensity. Suddenly a chill washed over her, freezing her in her tracks. Fire! "Oh, my God! It's the varnish factory! Oh, my God!" Terror and panic struck her. Her throat closed, blocking off the air. She tried to calculate where she was and how great the distance to her shanty. The varnish factory was on the east side, bordering Shantytown not far from her shack. Terribly close to Rory! A fire amidst the shacks spelled disaster, since no fire company would enter the territory of squattersville.

Without another thought except for her son, Callie took off at a dead run. Rossiter found himself hard pressed to keep up with her. On and on she ran, through the crooked, narrow alleys that were quickly becoming jammed with the panic-stricken occupants of Shantytown. People were standing, mouths agape, the fire reflected in their eyes. Others were already carrying out all their worldly possessions; mothers were gathering their children.

Callie and Rossiter forced their way through the crowd. Suddenly there was the sound of several explosions, one after another. The night sky was a backdrop for fireworks as vat after vat of highly flammable varnish exploded, sending burning debris high into the air. Rory! Rory!

The pins in her hair came loose; her hair fell about her face and shoulders. She'd lost her shawl, and her heart beat faster and faster as she pushed and fought her way through a sea of faceless people. "Please, God, not my baby! Not my Rory!" she screamed as she forced her cramped legs to run faster. The bottoms of her feet were burning through the thin leather of her shoes; she swallowed great gulps of air, crying prayers, frantically pushing her way through the exodus of inhabitants.

"Callie! Wait for me! Callie! If I lose you now, I'll never be able to find you," Rossiter shouted.

Callie ignored him. She kept running and pushing. Shouts and curses and confusion were all about her as she flew around the path. Her eyes took in the shooting flames; the tarpaper shacks were fuel for the fire; occasional bursts proclaimed the explosion of lamp oil. In the red glow of the fire she searched out her own shanty and wanted to cry with relief when she saw the fire hadn't reached it. "Thank you, God, thank you."

A group of men began a bucket brigade, trying to save the shacks still untouched, but their efforts were as yet ineffectual. Women and children were running with their belongings clutched in their arms. Where were Maggie and Rory? She had to be certain they weren't still in the shack. She had to find her baby! Shooting cinders showered in the air, cascading around Callie. She beat at the burning ashes with her hands, hardly feeling their sting. The smell of scorched yarn and singed hair, combined with the stench of the varnish, made her gag. She had to find her son.

"My God! What happened?" Rossiter demanded as he watched the men shifting buckets of water from a nearby pump down the line to douse the shacks.

"Use your eyes, Rossiter," she said shortly. "I have to find Rory. Make yourself useful for once in your life. Help the men, for God's sake!"

"Get back!" a burly Irishman was shouting to be heard above the clamor. "Everyone get back! We can't work here. Get a bucket, man, and get in line."

Callie rubbed at her burning eyes, choking on the thick, black smoke. The wind had shifted and was blowing the worst of the fumes into the squatter's field. "Do as the man says, Rossiter. Oh, God, there's Hugh. Hugh, here I am! What happened? Where's Maggie and Rory? Hugh, answer me, don't be pulling one of your drunken stupors now. Where's Rory?" Her frantic tone and wild eyes were all Hugh needed to push him to the edge of sobriety.

"I just got here, Callie. I saw the commotion from Malone's Tavern. Don't you be worrying, Callie, I'll get the little fella. Wait here for me."

"No, no, I'll come with you. I want to come with you." Callie and Hugh pushed past the men in the bucket brigade down the lane to their shanty. Thank the Lord the flames hadn't reached the shack yet. The smoke here was worse, thick and black. They fought their way past the shouting melee of people, then Callie stumbled and fell, nearly being trampled by feet. "Hugh! Hugh!"

"Trust me, lass. I'll get the boy!"

"Hurry, Hugh! Hurry!"

Cat-green eyes squinted through the smoke and cinders. A tall, lean figure heard the woman's cry, saw her fall to the ground in danger of being trampled. He had come to Shantytown on business and was about to leave when the varnish factory exploded. Handing his bucket to the next man in line, he rushed to the fallen woman to help her to her feet. Through her tears and the smoke, Callie could hardly discern the figure helping her. As she swept her hair back from her face, she heard him gasp, "Callie!"

"Byrch!" She clutched furiously at his shirt sleeves. "Byrch, my son is in there!" she choked out, pointing. Her intake of breath brought a volume of smoke into her lungs, leaving her coughing and sputtering.

"Where, Callie, where? Show me!"

"In there, the third shanty. Hugh went in after Rory, but he's drunk. My baby, my baby!"

Byrch Kenyon's eyes narrowed with pity. Good Lord, that couldn't be Rossiter Powers standing about helplessly, could it? He didn't have time to think. He shook away Callie's fierce grip on his arms and went to Rossiter. "Your coat, man! Give me your coat!"

Dumbfounded, Rossiter stood staring, filled with the shock of the bedlam surrounding him. Without explanation, Byrch literally tore the coat from him, stopping only to soak it in one of the buckets being passed down the line. Wrapping it over his head, he headed for the shack after MacDuff.

"Byrch! Maggie's in there! Byrch! Look under the little bed! Under Rory's bed!"

Byrch rushed past a man stooped just outside the shanty door, gasping for air. Inside, in the stagnant black smoke, instinct led him to the little narrow bed on the far side of the room. His hand searched for the baby. Finding no sign, he remembered Callie's words. Dropping to his knees, he felt the blanket pad beneath the bed and made contact with warm, soft flesh. Dropping the coat from his head, he shielded the baby with his own body, racing for the door, his lungs hungry for air. Outside in the light from the fire, cinders and ash falling around him, Byrch knew the life was gone from the small body in his arms. His eyes searched for Callie and found her as she bent over a man lying on the ground. He was near enough to hear them. Unashamedly he listened, all the while his heart was breaking.

"I've failed you again, lass. I couldn't find the tyke, but I brought Maggie out!"

"Shhh. I know you did, Hugh. I know you tried." Just before

Byrch had entered the shanty, Hugh had carried out Maggie, who was choking and sputtering now as others attended to her. "It's all right now," Callie told Hugh confidently, certain Byrch would find Rory and bring him out. She worried about Hugh now, who coughed and sputtered and clutched at his chest, grimacing in pain. When the seizure seemed to have passed, Callie lifted Hugh's soot-blackened head and held him to her breast.

His words were painfully spoken. "Say you forgive me, Callie. I loved you, Callie girl. First as a father and then the way a man loves a woman." The words were a strain; he kept grasping at his heart.

"Hush, hush, save your strength—"

"No, no, I've got to tell you. I can't be going to my Maker with this on my conscience. I failed you, in so many ways." He was attacked with a fit of coughing.

A sob caught in Callie's throat. She held Hugh, her tears mingling with his. His voice grew weaker as he struggled to say the words he had held so long in check. "Say you don't hate me, lass. Say you forgive."

"There's nothing to forgive, Hugh. I married you, for better or worse. I didn't know how you felt, I swear I didn't know. It's you who must forgive me."

Hugh shook his head, clenching his teeth against the pain. When he regained his breath, he looked at her. The love he'd never been able to express was shining in his eyes. "I'm that sorry, Callie m'love. I promised to put the world at your feet, and instead I've brought it down about your head. Believe me when I tell you I've loved the bairn. I wanted to think of him as me own. It's a fine laddie; he'll be good and strong . . . like his mother."

"Yes, Hugh, yes. I always knew somehow that you loved Rory." Hugh was making a supreme effort to speak; Callie leaned closer, putting his mouth to her ear.

"Callie lass, when you put the flowers on Mary's grave . . . could ye be seein' fit to put some on mine?"

"Yes, yes," Callie cried, rocking him in her arms, tears streaming down her cheeks. But Hugh couldn't hear her any longer. He was gone. Callie sobbed violently, filled with pity for Hugh and remorse that she hadn't seen his love for her, that she hadn't tried to bring out the best in this man. How could she not have known how he loved her? How? The truth that would have made Hugh free in life made Callie a prisoner of remorse in his death.

"Callie." It was Byrch calling her name. He stood a small distance away, Rory's golden head held in the crook of his arm.

Gently Callie laid Hugh's grizzled gray head onto the ground, looking about wildly for something with which to cover him.

"Callie," Byrch called again.

"Thank you, Byrch, for bringing my son out to me. Poor darling, look how he's sleeping, even in all this bedlam. Come to Mama, Rory," she said, reaching for her child.

Byrch backed off a step. "Callie."

"I'll take him now, he's not that heavy. I want to get him away from this place . . ."

There was a hoarseness Callie didn't recognize in Byrch's voice. Fear leaped into her eyes as she looked down at her beloved son. With her hands stretched out before her as though to ward off the terrible truth, she retreated backward. "Oh, no! No. No. I won't believe . . . Rooorrryyy!" A safe, black void reached up for her, and she slipped into it, gratefully.

"Rossiter! Rossiter!" Byrch barked, seeing the young man standing there, watching the scene played out before him, stricken and unmoving. "Rossiter, come take this child." Byrch thrust little Rory's body into his arms, completely unaware that the boy was Rossiter's son.

Rossiter had watched Callie's strength crumble, and he only wished for escape, but his feet were leaden, and he was incapable of movement. He longed for the familiar security of his mother and wished for Anne Powers's cool, unruffled detachment. He felt a terrible loss for the son he had never known, and he wanted to be comforted. The child was placed in his arms, his first and only contact with his son. He stared down at the tiny, peaceful face that so resembled his own. He needed someone to tell him what to do. The tiny body was such a heavy burden. A burden too heavy for him to bear.

Byrch bent over Callie, lifting her into his arms, reviving her. How had she come to Shantytown? How had she come to marry the Powers's handyman? And the babe, dear God, the babe!

When Callie opened her eyes, she came to immediate cognizance. "I thought Rory was just sleeping. It was the smoke, wasn't it?"

Byrch nodded, helping her to her feet. His face was a reflection of her misery as he watched her walk to Rossiter and take her son into her arms. Tender fingers brushed back the babe's golden curls; a mother's kiss was placed on the tiny rosebud mouth. But when she lifted her eyes, there was the fury of hell in them as she accused Rossiter. "You put this child in my body and then you deserted me. You took my innocence, my love, and you went away without so much as a wave of your hand. And then, when you needed someone to love you, to fall in worship at your feet, you came looking for me! You're a rotter, a spoiler, and the only good thing you ever did in your life was to create a son like Rory!" She turned to Hugh's lifeless form. "You tried to save me, but you couldn't. And when I saved myself, you hated me for it!"

Callie began to sway on her feet. Byrch rushed to her side. "Callie, give me the boy. I'll take care of him." Her grief was so overwhelming, she allowed Rory to be taken from her by Byrch's gentle hands. Yes, he would take care of Rory. Rossiter stood there, pathetically helpless, his soot-blackened hands covering his face. "Callie," he cried, "Callie, help me!"

"Go back to your mother, Rossiter," she said heartlessly. She had no heart—hers had died. "At least Ann Powers still has her son. Mine is lost to me."

Rossiter believed he had never heard such venom in anyone's voice. He dropped his hands, staring at her, mouth agape, misery stamped in his eyes. He mourned the loss of his beautiful son, the son he had never known. He reached tentatively for Callie, seeking her comfort, but seeing how impossible it was, he began to back away, finally turning tail and running from the disgust in Callie's eyes. He was a coward, and he hated himself for it; self-loathing was a mortal wound that he believed would never, ever heal.

Callie stood beside Byrch and her son while Shantytown burned around her. Glowing cinders showered the night sky. When she looked up at Byrch, she saw mirrored there in his tiger eyes her own devastating sorrow.

•

Book Three

Chapter Twenty-Three

Standing beside Byrch, Callie reached out a hand to caress her son's golden curls, engraving the contours of his sweet little head on her memory. Upswept lashes fell against Rory's smooth pink cheeks, and the boy looked for all the world as though he were sleeping.

"Give him to me." She reached out to take the babe in her arms. When Byrch hesitated, she looked up into his face, the agony of her loss visible in her eyes and in the grimace of her mouth. "You must give him to me," she said softly. "I've got to remember the way he feels in my arms; I must see him one more time."

Reluctantly Byrch gave Rory back to his mother, watching her cradle him into the curve of her arms, seeing the outpouring of love and devotion she held for him. Feeling as though he were witnessing a sacrament, Byrch turned his head, allowing Callie this one last moment of privacy with her child. He knew that the sight of her tearless eyes and the way her fingers brought the babe's hand to her lips would haunt him forever.

The woman Hugh had carried out of the shanty was approaching Callie. Hesitantly the woman touched Callie's shoulder, but there was no response. "Callie . . . oh, Callie!" She wept, but Callie did not hear her or notice her presence. Her every thought, her every sense, was centered upon her child. Anguished, the woman turned to Byrch. "I fell asleep in the rocker..." she told him, her voice breathless and heavy. "I never meant for this...this to happen," Maggie sobbed, wringing her hands, her tears creating pink rivulets down her soot-darkened cheeks.

Byrch reached for Maggie's hands to comfort her. "She doesn't hear you," he said softly. "This is her time with her son."

Maggie nodded, understanding. "I just don't want her to hate me, although I'd never blame her if she did. I loved the babe almost like me own."

"Hush," Byrch whispered. "Go home to your children, to your family. Callie was grateful to Hugh for bringing you out, she said so, I heard her."

"If only I hadn't fallen asleep..."

"You were overcome by the smoke, you nearly lost your own life. Go to your children, they need you now."

Maggie nodded, her eyes going again to Callie who stood with Rory in her arms, rocking him as though she were putting him to sleep. "God bless you, Callie," she whispered, putting an arm about Callie's shoulders, bending to press a last kiss to Rory's cheek, her tears mourning a mother's loss. Before she left, she took her shawl and tenderly covered the babe as though to protect him from the night air. Just as she turned to leave, she heard Callie whisper, "Thank you, Maggie. God bless."

For a long moment Callie looked into Rory's precious face before placing him down beside Hugh, laying the child in the protective crook of her husband's arm. Tenderly she covered them both with Maggie's shawl, hiding them from the view of others, leaving them to the private world of death.

Byrch went to Maggie Crenshaw's husband and withdrew several bills from his pocket, making arrangements for the Crenshaws to watch over Hugh and Rory until he could send someone for the bodies. Maggie wept openly, assuring him they would see the job was done.

Byrch led Callie away from Shantytown, resolving to himself that she would never set foot there again. Poverty and want and tragedy would never again find Callie James. As he led her to his carriage, Callie walked beside him woodenly, her face expressionless, her eyes vacant. Byrch guided her protectively, leading her through the gawking crowd, the sea of teary faces, the grim acceptance of men and women who had so little and expected no more from life.

It seemed to Byrch that he always arrived at the crises of Callie's life. In the alley in Dublin, at the Magdalene Society, and at her eighteenth birthday party, which although it appeared happy and serene, was indeed a time of crisis. That was the day she had met Rossiter. Yet this young woman beside him seemed a stranger. She who had been scrapping, even insolent, and defiantly proud was now a defeated woman, strangely quiet and dry-eyed.

Once in the carriage, he tried to draw Callie close to him. She was stiff, unyielding, closing herself off to being comforted. She was holding herself together with invisible twine and transparent paste, pretending to be made of grit and iron. But she was a woman who had lost her child, and the devastation was taking hold like the cold fingers of death. At twenty she had seen more tragedy than most people see in a lifetime.

Callie clenched her hands into fists. If she could only cry, loosen this band about her heart. She wanted to kick, to scream, to curse the fates that had robbed her of her son. Everything seemed so remote, so distant from her, as though it were all happening to someone else and she was merely a dispassionate bystander. What had she done to deserve this? What had a child, innocent and tender, done to deserve such a wicked end? Was this Divine Retribution? Was this her punishment for aspiring to a better life for her son? Didn't the heavens know that she'd already decided she wouldn't go away with Rossiter? She was only hoping that Rossiter would take an interest in his son, help Rory along somehow, give him advantages and a hope for the future. Was that so wrong, or was it what Peggy called "stepping out of place"?

Callie leaned her head back against the soft leather of the carriage seat. From the first grocery basket she'd stolen, to falling in love with Rossiter, she had stepped out of place, defied the fates. Wasn't it true that she had expected Rossiter to marry her? And hadn't she paid by being left homeless and pregnant and feeling responsible for little Mary's death? Wasn't it true that she aspired to a better life than Shantytown and Hugh? And she'd been punished, and Hugh and Rory had paid the price. "Know your place, Callie," Peggy had warned often enough. There was always a price to be paid, a lesson to be learned, dues owed.

Byrch put an arm around her shoulders, bringing her close. "It's all right to cry, Callie," he told her, wishing she would scream, cry, anything except this terrible silence.

Callie allowed herself to be taken into his arms, allowed him to place her head against his heart. "I can't feel anything," she whispered. "That's wrong. I should be crying for my son, for a husband who loved me and I was too blind to see it. I've done wrong, Byrch. Terrible wrong."

"Hush, sweeting, it's all too much for you. You can't face your grief right now, you're not ready. When it's time, you'll cry," he reassured her gently. "For now, you've got to think of yourself so you can get through the days to come. I'll help you, Callie," he told her softly as he strengthened his embrace. "We'll talk later."

"I don't ever want to talk about it." Her voice was tight, near the edge of exhaustion.

"Then we won't. We'll talk about other things. We'll look ahead into the future. You may find this difficult to believe, sweeting, but we all have a future."

Callie fell back into silence. Byrch felt himself stiffen for a moment, and there was a slight tremor in his hand as he stroked her soot-singed hair. Once before he had felt this way, and long-submerged memories rose to the surface. It seemed a lifetime ago that he'd rescued her from the button factory and had brought her home to Edward. An enormous wave of guilt washed over him. He should have remained in closer contact with her; he never should have trusted her to anyone else. He shouldn't have blown up at Jasper Powers when he was told Callie had disappeared. He should have made every effort to find her. Reason excused him, but his heart didn't believe it. By God, this time she wasn't going to get away from him! This time he wouldn't trust her to anyone, save himself. He would always be there for her—always. It never occurred to Byrch that Callie would refuse or reject his intervention.

"We're home, Callie. Look, Edward has the lights burning for us. It's as though he knew I was bringing you home."

With an effort Callie raised her head. Through narrowed lids she recognized the townhouse where she had spent ten wonderful days a lifetime ago. She was a child then. Byrch lifted her out of the carriage, carrying her easily up the front brick steps. In the yellow gaslight Callie stared up into his cat-green eyes. "You shouldn't be so good to me," she told him. "I don't deserve it. Don't you know, Byrch? I'm dead, just as dead as Rory and Hugh. It was all my fault, all of it. I should have accepted my lot in life; I should have been a real wife to Hugh. I stepped out of my place, and now the price is paid."

Byrch winced against the pain in her eyes, against the terrible sound of her voice as she choked back her sobs. "You're wrong, Callie, but I won't expect you to believe me now. You will someday. For now I'm going to get you into the house and put you to bed." Broaching no protest, Byrch held her in his arms and carried her up the front steps. Inside the small foyer he kicked the door shut behind him and bellowed for Edward, who came on the run.

The stately manservant immediately took in the scene, smelling the pungent smoke on their clothes and seeing their cinder-smudged faces. It was when Callie turned her summer-blue eyes on him that he recognized her. "Miss Callie!" He saw the shadows of grief there and reached his hand out to touch her. "Miss Callie," he intoned gently, ignorant of the facts and only sensing the deep sorrow she harbored.

"Go for Dr. Jameson, Edward. Use my carriage outside. And tell him not to spare the shoe leather."

"Yes, sir, Mr. Kenyon. The guest room is clean and ready. You'll have to get the wash basin from your room. I just put out hot water for you."

Callie sighed wearily, pushing back her tumbled hair from her eyes. Beneath the soot and ash, her face was pale and wan, her lips bloodless. "I can walk, Byrch, truly I can."

"I don't doubt it for a minute, but allow me my small pleasure. It's been a long time since I carried you into my house."

She rested her head against his shoulder with the movement of a broken doll, allowing him to carry her up the stairs.

A low groan of misery escaped Byrch. He remembered the first time he'd seen Callie in a dirty Dublin alley, full of spirit and spunk. Somewhere inside that spirited girl was still there, and whether Callie realized it or not, it was that girl who would struggle to survive. Reaching the third floor, he entered the guest bedroom and gently placed her on the bed. "I don't want you to move a muscle till I get back. I'll only be a minute." He was as good as his word, returning with a clean nightshirt and the basin of hot water with soap and a cloth. A large, fleecy towel was draped over his shoulder. She hadn't moved, he noticed; she still sat on the edge of the high tester bed, her feet almost a foot from the floor. She looked as young and small and vulnerable as she had when he'd brought her home from the button factory.

"I'm going to clean you up a bit. I've never done this before, so if I do something wrong, tell me."

Callie was silent, unresponsive, lost in her world of grief. He could not allow her to slip further away, hiding behind a wall of silence. He would talk to her, babble like an idiot if he had to, but he must force her awareness, make her hear, feel, see, or he would lose her completely.

"You smell like a sugar-cured ham. Edward would heartily disapprove if I let you get into one of his snowy clean beds all soot and cinders. He's gone to fetch Dr. Jameson, and we want you looking clean and fresh . . ." His words trailed off as she held him in her stare. Even to himself he sounded like a clucking mother hen. "I *need* to do this, Callie. I have to do something for you, and I don't think you're capable of doing it for yourself."

Callie sat still beneath his tender ministrations. She was too weary to protest, too empty to care. She kept wanting to cry, but the tears wouldn't surface. She felt him take the remaining pins from her hair, and she closed her eyes to the gentle wipes and dabs of the soft cloth on her neck and throat. When he lifted her hands to wash them, she felt like a child again. It was so good to leave the details of living to someone else. All she had to do was sit here, allow him to do this for her. With deliberate and knowledgeable fingers, he undid the buttons down the back of her dress. She felt it slide over her head and frowned when she remembered it was ruined. It didn't matter. Nothing mattered. She felt so alone, so disconnected. Only the touch of Byrch's hands reminded her she was in the world of the living. The petticoats were next, then the shoes and stockings. The camisole and bloomers were the last to be removed.

"I can't wait for the day when women give up all these clothes. It's nearly May, for God's sake. It's beyond me how you women stand being boned and tied and gussetted! And they call yours the weaker sex!"

Byrch kept up a stream of inconsequential banter to keep his mind off what he was seeing and feeling. She was so quiet, so solemn, as he patted and wiped at her silken skin. She suffered his inept attendance with stoic calm. He doubted if she were really aware of the intimate nature of the deed he was performing. Quickly he pulled the nightshirt over her head and tucked it down around her. His audible sigh of relief startled him. He hadn't realized that he'd been holding his breath.

"Into bed with you. Edward will be here soon with the doctor. I'll sit here with you. Lie back, Callie. Don't be ashamed to cry. I can't feel your pain, but I know what you must be feeling."

Callie dropped back against the fluffy pillows. How could he know what she was feeling when she didn't know herself?

"Close your eyes, Callie. Try to rest until Dr. Jameson comes. You've been through a horrendous ordeal, and right now you're tighter than a drum. Your nerves . . ." He was saying all the wrong things, doing everything wrong. If Edward were here, he'd know what Callie needed.

Callie's eyes were wide and staring. Sleep. Never again would she sleep. Sleep was for people who were at peace with themselves. Her unblinking gaze circled the room. It was familiar; there was a sense of remembered safety here. The crisp, ruffled curtains waved in the light breeze. They were the same, delicate and beautiful. The wing-backed chairs were still before the hearth, their deep tapestry cushions soft and inviting. She could almost picture herself nearly four years ago sitting in one of them, poring over copies of the *Clarion-Observer* with her feet propped up on the needlepoint-cushioned footstool. The wallpaper was still pale green sprigged, the bedspread and hangings soft gold, and the cherrywood furniture gleamed in the light from the lamp. It was a wonderful room, and once she had thought it had been created with a little girl in mind. There was a rocker in the corner, new and shiny, so different from her own rocker back in the shanty. It was the rocker that made her breath catch in an anguished sob.

Byrch was at her side instantly, taking her hand in his. She didn't resist, nor did she acknowledge his presence.

The sound of the front door opening and closing alerted Byrch to Edward's return with the doctor. Leaving Callie for the moment, he met the two men outside in the hallway, careful to close the bedroom door behind him. Quickly, somberly, he informed them of the fire and of Callie's loss. Edward's eyes widened in disbelief and then narrowed as he shook his head. "Our poor little miss has certainly had a bad time of it," he commiserated. "Poor Miss Callie, her heart must be broken."

"Well, step aside, Byrch. I liked that little girl you brought home a few years ago, and I thought you were a fool for letting her go. She was like a fine wine; all she needed was a little aging," Jameson said. "Let me in, and I'll see what I can do for her."

Daniel Jameson was a jowly bear of a man with a rich twinkle in his eyes. His faded carrot-colored hair stood out in stiff little peaks like meringue on a pie. When Byrch and Edward began to follow him into the bedroom, his attitude clearly said this was his domain, and he didn't need two fools cluttering up the place. He would make it right. A gentle talk, a shoulder to cry on, a little of his famous bedside manner, and this child would survive if he had to breathe life into her. He'd seen her kind before—a survivor.

Dr. Jameson smiled down at Callie and remembered the other time when he'd been called to tend her. His smile widened in appreciation of the transformation from that pug-nosed girl to this lovely creature. It was exactly as he'd told Byrch. All she'd needed was a little aging.

In the narrow hallway Byrch and Edward waited. "I take the liberty of placing myself at Miss Callie's disposal," Edward told his employer authoritatively, "with your permission, of course, sir. Don't worry, Mr. Kenyon, that young woman has exactly what it takes to get by in this world. She had it as a child, and I'm confident she still possesses it as a woman. I would also like to take the liberty of saying the child has become a beautiful woman. I seem to recall telling you she would. I'm so glad she didn't disappoint me."

"Is there anything you don't know?" Byrch snapped.

"Very little, Mr. Kenyon," Edward said urbanely. "Reading the *Clarion-Observer* every day does give a man an education."

Byrch smiled weakly. "I don't know what I'd do without you, Edward."

"Actually, Mr. Kenyon, neither do I. Am I correct in assuming that you're waiting for Miss Callie to fall asleep before you go out to attend to the arrangements?"

"Of course. How could I leave her here and do what I have to do if there's the slightest doubt in my mind that anything . . . that she . . . oh, hell, you know what I'm trying to say."

"It mystifies me that a man of your eloquence is having such difficulty expressing himself," Edward observed. If he remembered correctly, the last time Callie stayed at the house on St. Luke's Place, Byrch was also in a dither much of the time. Such an unnatural state for a sophisticated man!

"Dammit, Edward, stop looking so smug. I'm not having any difficulty expressing myself, it's only that Callie . . . what I mean . . . Callie is a . . ."

"A very special young woman who is suffering a very trying time. Is that what you're trying to say?"

Byrch merely growled.

"Take heart, Mr. Kenyon. Miss Callie has what you Irish call 'grit.' Time will make things right for her. Time and the right people around her."

"How you ever got so smart beats the hell out of me. You came to me barefoot and cross-eyed and look at you now." There was a fondness and deep friendship between the black man and his employer.

"Begging your pardon, I may have been barefoot when I first met you in Jamaica, but I have never been cross-eyed," Edward argued stiffly.

Daniel Jameson closed the door softly behind him. "She's dropping off to sleep, and she should sleep till noon tomorrow if you two mules can ever stop your confounded arguing. I gave her a sleeping draught." At the anxious expression in both men's eyes, the genial doctor smiled. "She's going to be fine. It will only take time."

Edward straightened; the smile on his face was smug and knowing.

"I'll send you the bill, Byrch. Edward, it was nice seeing you again. My man tells me you won three out of four chess games with him. If you've a mind to, I'd appreciate it if you'd show me one or two of those trickier moves. Anatole is in to me for half my house at this point!"

"I'd be delighted to have a game with you, Dr. Jameson," Edward said in his clipped British accent. He locked his hands behind his back and rocked back and forth on his heels. He did love a challenge, but the doctor was an abysmal player.

"Thanks for coming, Daniel," Byrch said. "Have you heard anything about the fire? Are there many casualties?"

Jameson shook his head. "It's too far uptown, for one thing. I doubt they've got adequate help up there. If you don't mind, I'd like to borrow your carriage and head up there now. Perhaps there's something I can do."

"Of course. I can walk over to St. Matthew's Missionary to see Father Muldoon. One thing, Dan. If you wouldn't mind stopping by and picking up Jimmy Riley. I want him to bring Callie's husband and baby back here. I left the poor souls in charge of the neighbors."

"Consider it done. I'll send him back with the carriage, if that's all right. Now don't worry about that young woman; she's strong. Callie will be right as rain in time. Feed her light, Edward, but insist she eat. Call me if you need me."

"What are your plans for the wake," Edward asked after the doctor had gone.

"There won't be a wake," Byrch said tightly. "I'm going to see Father Muldoon now. We're going to have a Mass said, and the burial will take place directly afterward. I hate to ask this of you, Edward, but someone has to do it. I'll ask Father Muldoon to send one of the good sisters over. Would you give a hand in preparing for the burial? Use anything of mine you need for Hugh MacDuff. I'll be back as soon as I can."

Edward swallowed hard. He would have sold his soul for Byrch

Kenyon, but preparing the dead for burial wasn't something he'd ever considered.

When Byrch returned home after his meeting with a sleepy Father Muldoon, he wasn't surprised to see the kitchen lights blazing up the stairwell. He walked downstairs and felt his lips tighten. Two Sisters of Charity were carefully tending to Hugh MacDuff, their black, flowing habits fluttering with their movements, their serene faces somber and prayerful. They had attired Hugh in Byrch's own best blue garbardine suit with a white shirt and dark blue cravat.

Byrch's eyes traveled to Edward who was standing at the wooden table where Rory's little body rested on a blanket. He couldn't bear to watch as Edward's elegant dark hands dressed the babe in a pale blue nightdress. Edward's expressive mahogany eyes shone with tears as he brushed the soft golden curls. "Such a beautiful child," Edward mourned. "Miss Callie's loss is a terrible one." With loving respect he covered the babe with a fold of the blanket.

"It's late, Mr. Kenyon," Edward said. "I've taken the liberty of running a bath for you. The water should be exactly right now." Edward was quick to notice Sister Angelica's admiring glance toward the kitchen sink. Byrch Kenyon's house was one of the few in New York equipped with a copper, tin-lined water tower on the roof. Pipes led down to the kitchen and the dressing room off the master bedroom. It worked quite well except in cold weather when the pipes had a tendency to freeze.

"Thank you, Edward. I've arranged everything with Father Muldoon for eleven o'clock in the morning. I can tell you, I'm not looking forward to it." His eyes went to the tiny bundle near Edward, and he felt a pang of misery for Callie. How could someone ever recover from losing a child? Yet people did—or they seemed to, he amended.

Byrch climbed the stairs to the third floor, feeling as old as Moses. He opened the guest-room door a crack and peeked in at Callie. She seemed to be resting peacefully, thanks to the sleeping powder. Her dark hair fanned out on the pillow, and she looked small and vulnerable in the high tester bed.

Byrch sank down gratefully into the bath water, sipping at the brandy he'd poured from the decanter in his bedroom. He leaned back, letting the liquid blaze down through his chest. God, he was tired. Exhausted. He longed for his bed, but he had already decided to sit sentinel in the wing-backed chair in Callie's room in case she needed someone during the night. Callie's bedroom. Ever since she'd stayed here what seemed an eternity ago, he had thought of the spare bedroom as hers. His mind was a jumble of thoughts, of unanswered questions. He knew that Rory was Rossiter's son from that verbal attack Callie had launched in Shantytown. What had happened? The reporter in him wanted details, facts, reasons. The man in him wanted Callie James MacDuff.

Dressed in clean trousers and his robe, Byrch sank down into the soft cushions in the chair beside the cold hearth. He drained the last of the brandy from his glass and rested his head back with a weary sigh. The lamp was shining dimly, casting shadows near the bed where Callie slept. He watched her, his heart tugging when her shoulders quivered in a silent sob. The medicine could make her sleep, but it couldn't erase the nightmare.

It was the soft chiming of the clock in the downstairs hall that awakened him. He opened his eyes with a start, seeing Callie standing beside him, looking down at him with haunted eyes. He remained motionless, afraid to startle her should she be sleepwalking. Her soft hair drifted like a dark storm cloud about her shoulders. "Byrch," she murmured his name, the edges of the sound torn and shredded with grief, her eyes dry, empty hollows.

He reached out his arms, and she came into them, curling onto his lap, soft and warm from sleep. She rested her head against his shoulder. He was struck by her fragility, just as he had been once before when he had held her this way, silently offering his companionship and compassion in the face of her misery.

They sat for a long time, Callie quietly drawing strength from Byrch. She had awakened, feeling more alone than ever before in her life. Her arms ached for her son; her heart broke for her husband. She was burying both in the morning. How was she to bear the pain? Don't think about Rory, she told herself. Don't think about him as he was and don't dream about what he would have been. But it was impossible. Not to think, not to remember, would be like denying Rory's existence. She must face losing him, and she must remember him, always. She owed it to her son and to Hugh. There was no other way to live except one day at a time, one minute after the other.

Callie curled close to Byrch. She took comfort from him, needing the closeness of another human being. She felt disconnected, half-dead, like a flower whose roots had withered while the bloom was still on the stem. Callie wrapped her arms around Byrch's neck, inhaling the fragrance of his soap, burying her face into the warmth of his shoulder. "Byrch," she whispered, a small sob catching in her throat, "I've been a daughter, a mother, and a wife. But never a woman. Never! Do you understand? I'm alive, but I don't feel anything. I need to feel. I need to be a woman. If I don't, I may not survive. I have to be strong, like you. I want you to make me strong; I want you to make me a woman."

His lips stroked her brow, but his embrace was unchanged, and neither did he answer. Tipping her head back, she looked up into his face, seeing almost for the first time that there was a new rugged leanness to his jaw, that the lines in his face had deepened. He had aged during these past four years, she realized, and the strength of his character was there in the set of his mouth and the intensity of his tiger eyes. She realized that tonight was not the first time she'd thought about Byrch Kenyon, the man. When had the girl in her given way to the woman? The decade between their ages that had been a gulf when she was sixteen was negligible now at twenty.

Byrch looked down at her, feeling a quickening of his heart. She was telling him she wanted him to make love to her, to arouse her to life, to make her a woman. All his protective instincts rebelled against the idea. She was grief-stricken, too vulnerable, unable to make a responsible decision. Her eyes were dark and shadowy in the dim light, her mouth was soft and inviting. Reflexively his hand curved around her throat, his thumb tracing intricate patterns along her jaw. "Callie, you don't know what you're asking. You're not thinking straight, and I won't take advantage of you."

"You don't want me then?" She lowered her eyes, hiding the shadows, hiding her need.

His words were a broken lament. "Not want you? My God!" he exclaimed softly, chest heaving beneath her cheek. "I don't think I can remember a day when I didn't want you! In that alley in Dublin, at the Park with your brothers and sisters, on your eighteenth birthday. The devil take my soul, Callie, but I've always wanted you!"

The intensity of his emotion startled her, frightened her a little, but her own need seemed so great, so urgent, that she nestled back against him. "Then take me, Byrch. Have me. I need you to have me." There was a throaty quality to her voice that he'd never heard before. She began tracing a sweet trail of kisses along his jaw, dipping downward into the space between collar and neck.

Byrch heard himself moan, feeling his resolve melt beneath her touch. How long he'd wanted her, how long he had tried to think of her as only a child. "Callie. Callie," he intoned hoarsely before bringing his mouth to hers.

Her moist lips opened to him, he tasted their sweetness, drawing rom them a gentle kiss that deepened with passion. When he eleased her, his cat-green eyes searched hers, looking for a re-ponse.

Somewhere in Callie an ember was growing to a spark. For ne instant she had not thought of Rory or Hugh or anything, only yrch and the way his mouth had melted onto hers. Thick, dark ashes closed; she heard her own breath come in ragged little gasps s she boldly brought her mouth once again to his, offering herself, eliberately seducing him, begging him to take her and to light he darkness in her soul, to make her forget.

Byrch felt her disengage herself from his embrace. She left his rms and stood before him, holding him in her gaze. Slowly she nbuttoned the nightshirt, allowing it to fall from her body, stand-ng naked and proud before him. Gracefully she lowered herself o her knees, crouching between his thighs, looking up into his ace.

"If you could find it in your heart to make love to me, I'd be o grateful."

Byrch leaned forward, so close he could feel her breath upon is face. His hand found the gentle curve of her throat, his fingers rushed her hair back from her face. "Callie," he groaned, "don't ver, ever be grateful!" He lifted her to her knees, holding her lose, feeling her softness against him. When his mouth claimed ers, it was a kiss given by a man to a woman—long, deep, earning.

When he withdrew, she was watching him, her mouth trembling lightly. Tenderly he kissed one eye closed and then the other, asting the salt of a tear. He nuzzled her cheek and the tip of her ose. She opened her eyes and smiled before reaching up to offer er mouth again.

Byrch picked Callie up in his arms, carrying her to the bed nd placing her down among the pillows. He sat beside her, leaning ver her adoringly. His fingers traced the smooth line of her cheeks own to the ridge of her jaw. He picked up a lock of her hair, ubbing it across his lips. He hadn't realized until now how often e had dreamed of being with her this way, allowing him to touch er, to love her.

Callie's hands drove through the thick, dark hair at his nape. he lifted her head to press her lips against the hollow of his hroat, inhaling his clean, masculine scent. She felt the stubble of is beard, rough against her face, was aware of his arms holding er, tightening around her. Impatient with the confines of his robe, he pulled it apart, exposing his chest to her caress and kiss.

Byrch's hands trembled as he smoothed the silken skin of he shoulders and breasts. No other woman had affected him this way and he knew that he had been waiting only for her—only fo Callie. And Callie was a woman now.

Standing, he shrugged off his robe and garments, feeling he eyes upon him, watching him in fascination, little flames lickin his flesh wherever her gaze touched him. She lay on her back one knee bent, hiding her womanhood from his view. Her breast were ivory globes, full and firm, delineating the slimness of he waist and the soft roundness of her belly. With no trace of th coquette, she lay perfectly still, exposed to his view, allowing hi tiger eyes to warm her flesh. She seemed to be sculpted fron marble, but he knew she would be warm and yielding under hi touch.

In the soft light from the lamp, Callie watched his movements She saw the wide, broad shoulders, his deep chest, the narrownes of his haunches and the strength of his thighs. A soft, dark furrin of chest hair swirled over his chest, narrowing to a thin line ove his belly to bloom again in a rougher coat near his manhood. Hi buttocks were firm, high, accentuating the slope of his neck an the curve of his torso.

Byrch lay down beside her, feeding on the sight of her, knowin she was waiting for him to make her feel, to make her know sh was alive, that she hadn't died. To make her a woman, she ha said, unaware that she was more woman, more alive then anyon he'd ever known. Thoughts were ricocheting around in his head Callie had been a wife, had been a mother, and yet she claime she knew nothing of being a woman. Did that mean she had neve been aroused, never had found fulfillment with a man? The ide excited him, seemed to make her more his own, yet instinct tol him to keep his passions in check, to awaken her slowly, eve watchful for any sign of her retreat.

Callie lay breathless beside him, so still, so alert to his ever move. She was like a small bird held motionless by the hypnoti stare of the hunter. She felt as though she'd been waiting a lifetim for something she could not name, something that had never show itself to her, but which only Byrch could reveal. He seemed t see within her, touching that part of her that was her soul.

Byrch kissed her again, receiving her parted lips, tentativel exploring their soft undersides with the tip of his tongue. H continued his excursion along the delicately molded ridge of h jaw to her ear, his warm breath sending shivers of delight throug her, echoing somewhere in that part of her that had never bee touched. His tender, sensitive hands explored her face, the elegance of her neck, the sweeping smoothness of her shoulder, marking a path that was followed by his lips and tongue and light, teasing bites. Following the contours of her arm, he lifted her hand to his mouth, placing an exquisitely passionate kiss on her palm that aroused excited chills.

Callie closed her eyes, yielding to the rhythmic surges that seemed to be exploding within her. His warm lips claimed the hollow at the base of her throat and explored the valley between her breasts. He fed on the smooth texture of her skin, on the soft firmness of her breasts, feeling the change beneath his lips as he approached the pouting crest. A surge of heat throbbed in his loins when he heard the intake of her breath, the slight, gasping surprise as he took it into his mouth.

Callie lay still beneath his touch. The bridled torment of holding his passion in control only seemed to excite him the more. Instinct reminded him to go slowly, to awaken her as though from a dream and become a part of that dream.

Callie's breath began to quicken, her pulses fluttered. Rossiter had never ignited these emotions within her; her body had never ached and yearned to become a part of his. With Rossiter, she had allowed him to satiate himself with her body, never becoming a part of that satisfaction. Because she had loved him, she wanted to fill a need for him. With Rossiter, it was something she gave; with Byrch, it would be something she would share. And she knew that afterwards, there would be no feeling of aloneness.

Callie's sudden response caught Byrch by surprise. She lifted herself into his arms, wrapping herself close to him, fitting the curves of her body against his, pressing close against the hard presence of his manhood. Her hands gripped his back, smoothing and feeling the musculature beneath his skin. She described patterns against his mouth, following the line of his lips with the tip of her tongue, penetrating within to seek and to find. Fingers raking through his hair, she pushed his head toward her breast, arching her back to help him in his discovery. When his lips closed over the crest, her breath came in a ragged gasp, inciting him to suckle, tempting him to find the other with his hand and to mimic the movements of his lips and tongue with his fingers.

Byrch was caught in her passions, matching them with his own. His responses were guided by hers; her needs were echoed in his. He wanted her all at once, could not have enough of her. He wanted to experience her capacity for giving and loving. She pushed herself up to him, shuddering. Her eyes were filled by him; her world had narrowed to this time and place. All that existed was her need answering his, his desire flaming hers.

He caressed her belly, her hip, her leg, and she felt herself opening to him. He cupped his hand over her woman's mound of dark curls, and she experienced a rush of damp warmth and felt the sudden jolt of his manhood pressed tight against her thigh.

The sudden tenseness in his groin caught Byrch by surprise, and willpower alone increased the struggle to contain himself. The battle was almost lost when he felt another rush of wetness against his hand. She was so lovely, so much a woman. His sensuality was heightened by the instinct that although she was not an inexperienced virgin, this was her first awareness of her sexuality. He was the first to step into that territory, the first to help her explore the realm of her womanhood. He claimed her mouth for his own, searching the moist recesses, feeling the smoothness of her palate and the softness beneath her tongue, and was drawn into the incredible appetite of her kiss-swollen lips as they answered his hungers.

She rotated her hips against the pressure of his hand with urgent, searching movements. Her sex opened to him, welcoming his touch between the velvety folds. A sensation of pressure filled her loins, stretching along the inner muscles of her thighs, bringing her focus to her center beneath the strokings of his fingers. She felt as though she were folding inward on herself, that she had diminished in awareness to only that urgency between her thighs and Byrch's knowing touch.

She became aware that he had lifted away from her, that he was watching her arch rhythmically against the caresses of his hand. She looked up into his eyes, seeing the reflection of her own passions there, unashamed to meet his hot, searing gaze, allowing it to travel down the length of her body to where he claimed her.

Brych drew in his breath, astounded by her answering pulsations to his caresses. She was the most beautiful creature he had ever seen. It seemed he was discovering something about himself also. He was aware of his own driving need to give, to be tender, never to threaten the trust she had placed in him. Every thought was of her, every motion brought pleasure from the pleasure he brought her. He heard her breathe his name; he saw her lift herself to look down to where he had captured her sex, encouraging him to continue his caress. His loins were afire, his manhood eager, ready to claim her, and he fought for control. He wanted to plunge himself into the depths of her, feel her body surround him, sheathing him in the warm wetness, drawing him into her. Just as he feared he had reached the limit of his sensibilities, she threw back her head, losing herself to the tide and the ebb of sensation coursing through her. Suddenly she arched upward and cried out as she climaxed beneath his touch.

Byrch covered her with his body, pressing his weight against her, excited to a fever by the clench of her thighs on his hand, as though she never wanted to be without his touch. Gently he smoothed back the tumble of dark hair from her face, watching the play of emotions cross her features. "You're so beautiful," he whispered, "so incredibly beautiful." He loved the way she opened herself to him, the expression in her eyes—a mingling of surprise and joy. He knew it had never been this way for her before, just as he knew he had never been with a woman he had wanted more.

"Come to me, Byrch, come to me," she murmured, urging him with her hands, sliding herself beneath him. There was naked desire in her eyes, a want for further fulfillment. He slid between her thighs as she arched up to receive him. Her arms were around him, slipping down to his haunches, pressing him forward to enter her. He was drawn into her depths, surrounded by her pulsating warmth, enfolded within her. He drew back, coming forward again, stroking and driving, feeling her legs lift to wrap around his hips, pulling him into her. He moved within her, reveling in the supreme pleasure of having her accept his full, proud manhood into her hungry warmth. She rose against him, holding him fast, aware of a sweeping tide surging within her, filling her. The sound of her name fell on her ears as he found his release and brought her to her own.

For a long, long time Byrch lay beside her, spooning her back against his chest, his arms cuddling her possessively. He found the sweetness at the nape of her neck and nuzzled it with his lips. She lay quietly, not breaking the silence between them. He wanted to tell her how deeply she had touched him, that he knew beyond a doubt that she meant more to him than any other woman ever could. But Byrch kept his counsel, afraid to burden her with his emotions, fearful that he would add to her confusion and misery. There would be other times when he could reveal himself to her, tell her that he'd found her and would never let her go. Byrch had never fancied himself in love before this. He often berated himself for being too cynical, even too arrogant, to express himself or declare love. And now he knew why. All his life he had been waiting for this woman, for this moment. Later, when Callie had learned to live with her grief, when she could open herself to a new love, a new life, he would share this joy with her and make her truly his own.

"What are you thinking, sweeting?" he asked, his voice hardly more than a murmur, reluctant to intrude on her thoughts but feeling the sorrow emanating from her in the slope of her shoulders and the drop of her head. She turned in his arms, resting her head against his shoulder, staring up at the ceiling. Her cheeks were damp with tears, and they sparkled on her lashes.

"I was thinking of Rory and how I'll miss him."

Byrch strengthened his embrace, his voice becoming a croon. "Cry, sweeting, cry it all out. I'll be here with you."

His words evoked a response, as though she'd been waiting for his permission, his empathy. He held her as the dam burst, feeling her shudders wrack through her fragile body. Her tears did not frighten him, she realized, as a woman's tears frightened some men. He shared them with her, holding her tightly, his tears mingling with her own. He had exposed her to her grief, broken down her defenses through the intensity of their union. But at the same time he had exposed her to life. Holding on to him, sharing her loss, she had found something. As Callie's grief was expressed, it began to heal her soul, and she began to soar, rising from the cinders of her past.

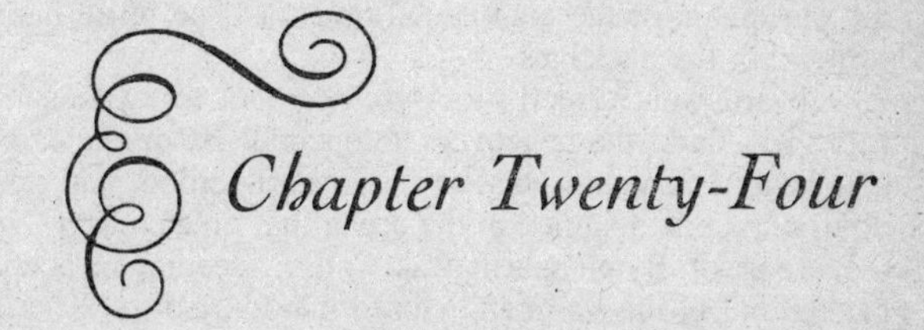

Chapter Twenty-Four

The undertaker came before six in the morning, bringing two coffin boxes, one of them terribly small. Rory and Hugh would be delivered directly to St. Matthew's Mission Church to await the Requiem Mass. It was best that Miss Callie not know any of the details, and that the bodies be gone from the house before she awakened.

Edward prepared the breakfast coffee. When he went out to buy a dress for Miss Callie, he'd stop by the bakery and purchase some sweetrolls to serve in the parlor. When the coffee began to perk, he reached up for the jar that held money for extra household expenses. He had no idea how much a lady's ready-made dress would cost. A bonnet too. He couldn't be stingy with Miss Callie. Mr. Kenyon hadn't given any thought to what Miss Callie would wear to her baby's funeral. Edward sighed wearily. It was true—whatever would Mr. Kenyon do without him?

As soon as the coffee was done, he poured himself a cup and set the pot on the back burner to keep warm. He looked at his gold pocketwatch, a Christmas gift and his most prized possession from Mr. Kenyon. He would get to the Emporium just as it opened.

Edward was back home before nine o'clock, his packages under his arm. He took a deep breath as he set the sweetrolls and coffee pot on a large tray. He added cups and a bunch of daffodils in a crystal vase and took the tray into the front parlor. He quickly lit a fire to banish the chill. Miss Callie would be cold. She was going to shiver for a good time to come. At the last minute he had added a shawl to his purchases. Satisfied with the fire and the placement of the continental breakfast, he made his way upstairs with the packages.

Edward went directly to Byrch's room to awaken him. The room was dark, the bedcovers untouched. Before he came to any conclusions, Edward went to the guest bedroom and opened the door a crack and smiled at the scene that greeted him. Nestled in the crook of Byrch's arm was Callie, sleeping peacefully. He backed out of the room and closed the door softly. Then he went back to Byrch's door and rapped sharply. "Mr. Kenyon, it's almost nine o'clock. I went to the Emporium and purchased some clothing for Miss Callie. I'll leave them outside your door. I don't have the heart to disturb her. Breakfast is ready in the front parlor. Best move smartly now, Father Muldoon appreciates promptness."

A smirk played about Edward's mouth as he went back down the stairs. Only a servant of refined sensibilities and superior quality could have carried off what might have been an embarrassing moment with such delicacy.

Byrch's eyes flew open. He knew instantly where he was and what had transpired just hours ago. He shifted slightly and looked down at Callie who was nestled against his chest. He hated to waken her. Long into the night she had held him, crying out her grief, mourning for the loss of her child and her failure as a wife. Most of her cries were barely coherent, blurted, incomplete sentences about knowing her place and paying the price. But he had held her, chasing back the night demons that haunted her, soothing her with his touch and listening to her as she told him about falling in love with Rossiter and marrying Hugh. He suffered with her when she told him about Mary Powers and pleaded with her to believe that keeping the secret of Mary's hearing was more a kindness than a sin. Now, looking at her as she slept, seeing her features soft and unguarded, he wanted her to enjoy the small peace she had found in the forgetfulness of sleep. He stroked her tumble of chestnut hair and felt her stir beneath his touch. "Time to wake up, sweeting," he murmured as she pulled herself from sleep. He felt her stiffen at the sound of his voice, saw her look up quickly as though surprised to find him there.

Callie rolled out of Byrch's embrace, unwilling to allow herself to nestle against him, to take comfort from his presence. She was assaulted by memories from the night before; she remembered her brazen request that he make love to her, recalled the long hours she had wept in his arms, telling him things that must have shocked him and diminished her in his eyes.

Byrch frowned at this rejection of him. It seemed to him that she was deliberately gripping the sheets around her to hide from him. He wanted to turn her in his arms, to renew the closeness they had shared the night before, but he considered it unwise. Callie needed time to deal with her grief. When she needed him, he would be there. "Edward said he brought you some clothes and left them outside my door," he said, hoping to break the silence and uneasiness between them.

A lump formed in Callie's throat as she silently watched Byrch pad naked to the door and come back a moment later. How could she face him after what she'd done? She hated herself. What kind of woman was she, and how could she get up from this bed, naked as the day she was born, and go to the funeral of her husband and son? Hugh wasn't even cold in his grave and she had given herself to another man. Hugh, who had loved her and who had never known her as a man should know his wife, was cheated of the very loving she had so willingly given to Byrch. Her place was with her husband and son, not here in this bed, in another man's arms. The tears rolled down her cheeks as she struggled with the sheet to wrap her nakedness.

Rubbing the stubble on his chin, Byrch turned in time to see Callie cover herself. He wanted to punch his fist into the wall when he noticed the shimmering tears on her face. She was retreating from him, closing herself off, and there seemed to be little he could do about it. If ever he knew anything, anything at all, it was that he wanted to make things right for Callie, and by God, nothing was ever going to separate them again. Not even Callie herself.

She avoided his gaze as she slipped out of the bed, the sheet still tightly wrapped around her. She took the package from him, still avoiding his eyes, and turned her back, standing frozen and still, dismissing him. He retrieved his robe and trousers from the side of the bed and turned to look at her again. She was distant from him, as though she were on the other side of the world. He left the room, knowing it was impossible to approach her. He had almost reached his own bedroom when he heard Callie's door close. The noise jarred him; he didn't believe he'd ever heard a more terminal sound. Feeling despondent, he shaved and dressed. In the end, it was Edward who pointed out that his cravat wasn't properly knotted and his shoes needed more of a shine. His cuff links didn't match. Within moments, Edward made him presentable. Byrch hardly noticed.

Callie sat on the edge of the bed for what seemed to her an eternity. Here in this package were the clothes she would wear to her son's funeral. She undid the package with trembling fingers and stared down at a plain cotton camisole, underdrawers, black stockings, petticoat, corset and garters, and a simple black dress and bonnet. Even black gloves were included. Edward must have been up all night to do this for her. Seeing to her needs while she was lying in Byrch's arms. She had asked for and received what she'd wanted, and the knowledge that it was more than she'd expected or had any right to ask did not console her. In fact, the pleasure she had taken increased her sense of guilt.

Why had she done it? Wasn't she ever going to learn? Was she doomed to make the same mistakes over and over? She had stepped out of her place again, she had dared to rise above herself, to reach out for something she never should have. What form would her punishment take this time? What trick would fate play? In Byrch's arms she had found something she had believed she would never find, and she was too cautious to put a name to it. She would only dare to admit that Byrch meant something to her; he meant too much. Would that swift sword of retribution strike him next to punish her? The lump in her throat seemed to grow, threatening to choke. "Mum, I did it again," she wept hoarsely. "But never again. I know my place, and I'll remember it. I won't have anything or anyone I can't afford to lose. I won't be hurt again."

Furiously she slapped water from the pitcher onto her face. The sudden coolness shocked her to the awareness of what she still must face. She shivered as she washed and rinsed her body. The new garments felt scratchy against her skin. She deserved this small discomfort. The shoes were a bit big, but with the strap across the instep, they would do. For a moment, Callie remembered another time when Edward had brought back a similar package. Then it had been frilly bedgowns and slippers meant for a young girl. Now it was mourning clothes to take her to the funeral of her husband and son.

She brushed at her tears. She needed strength to get through the day. More strength than she'd ever needed before. There were so many things to think about, so many decisions to be made.

One thing at a time. Her guilts and her worries would have to wait.

Dressed, except for the buttons at the back of her dress, Callie timidly went down the hall to stand outside Byrch's open door. He smelled of shaving soap, clean and fresh, and the fragrance brought back memories of the night before in a consuming wave. She held her head high, facing him for the first time since awakening, her eyes cool and forbidding. They spoke at the same time, breaking the silence, and a wide grin split Byrch's handsome features as he made a move to take her into his arms. Again Callie sidestepped and motioned for Edward to button her dress. "Is there coffee, Edward?" she asked quietly, pretending not to notice Byrch's questioning glance. His eyes were telling her that he would have buttoned her dress, that he would have *wanted* to button it. His frustration was marked by the way he raked his fingers through the dark ruffles of his hair, upsetting the careful grooming he had attained with his brush.

"There's a tray laid out in the parlor, Miss Callie," Edward intoned, nimble fingers completing the long row of tiny buttons. When Callie turned to face him, he took the opportunity to express his condolences.

"You're very kind, Edward. Everyone is extremely kind. I want to thank you for securing these clothes for me. I lost everything in the fire, you know." Callie missed the tortured expression on Byrch's face for Edward's understanding nod. Time, it seemed to say. Time healed all.

Byrch and Callie sat near the fire like two storefront mannequins. Callie had difficulty holding her cup steady while Byrch shredded and picked apart Edward's delicious breakfast rolls. The manservant hovered nearby in case his services were needed. His expert eye told him that the fire he had lit earlier would burn for another hour. Anticipating Callie's grief and low spirits, he knew she would be particularly susceptible to the damp chill on this early April morning.

Both Edward and Byrch were aware of the trembling in the slim body and the slight quivering of her voice when Callie spoke. "Did I thank you for the clothes, Edward? I'm so grateful for your thoughtfulness."

"Yes, it was considerate of you, Edward. I'm sorry I didn't think of it myself," Byrch said.

"It was understandable, Mr. Kenyon. You had other things on your mind," Edward answered. "You have fifteen minutes, sir. I took the liberty of ordering your carriage."

Byrch acknowledged Edward with a nod, but his attention was focused on Callie. She seemed so fragile and yet somehow volatile, as though she were about to shatter into a million unmendable fragments. He wished she would look at him, say something instead of sitting there white and bloodless. Byrch continued to observe Callie, his heart going out to her. When she did raise her eyes to look at him, it was to ask a question.

"Where are Rory and Hugh?"

"At St. Matthew's Mission Church, sweeting."

"Byrch, do you think . . ." she hesitated, her fingers picked at her skirt, her throat working convulsively to swallow back her cries. "Do you think I could see him? Just one last time?"

Immediately Byrch was on his knees, clasping her tortured fingers, looking up into her face. He was having difficulty with his own voice, and he cleared his throat before he could speak. "Of course you can, sweeting. Rory still belongs to you, forever. No one would deny you." He felt her fingers tremble in his hand.

"Do you think I could be alone with him? To kiss him again and just for a moment, only for a moment, pretend that he's only sleeping? Do you?"

"I promise, Callie. I swear to you." Astonishingly her summer blue eyes cleared, the smoky shadows dissipating. Her chin lifted, and the smallest smile touched the corners of her mouth.

"Then let's leave for the church now," she told him. "My son is waiting for me."

Byrch's hopes soared. Her distance had made her seem unapproachable, and he was hurt. Ever since she'd opened her eyes this morning, she had given him the impression that she was staring through him, as though she wanted to deny his existence. Now his hopes were short-lived; before they left the house, Callie seemed to remove herself again from his presence, becoming remote and inaccessible.

It was past three in the afternoon before the small entourage arrived back at the house on St. Luke's Place. Callie was white and drawn, but as Byrch later put it to Edward, she was holding her own. She'd gotten through the worst of it. There was no need to tell Edward that at every glance, every avoidance of his touch, Callie froze him with her direct, almost defiant, gaze. She refused to accept his patient understanding. There was nothing he could do but stand near her, hoping she would turn to him for comfort. When she didn't, Byrch felt as though he had lost part of his world, a very precious part.

If only she would allow him to do something for her!

Byrch's worries increased as the days wore on. Callie was too self-absorbed, too calm and withdrawn. Byrch became convinced she was bent on a course of self-destruction, barely eating enough to keep a bird alive and pacing her room for hours on end through the long, dark nights. She was totally self-absorbed, insulating herself against any reminder that she still lived and breathed, a young, vital woman who must deal with her grief and go on with her life. Her words were always soft, yet listless, and no matter how gently he tried to get close, she rejected him with her eyes. The night she had slept in his arms seemed so long ago, so far away. Was it possible that he'd only dreamed it?

Every minute Byrch wasn't concentrating on his work at the *Clarion* was spent on recrimination and regrets. His thoughts continued to circle, like whirlpools in a murky river, having no beginning or end, but seeming to draw him deeper and deeper into a despair that could only be relieved by one smile, one gesture that was never given. He tried to reassure himself that what he was seeing in Callie's eyes was grief for her loss and not resentment toward himself. His confusion disturbed his work, his every thought, and in the end one simple truth surfaced. He would not lose her again, regardless of what measures he must take, in spite of Callie herself. He would not lose her. Somehow he would get through to her, make her aware of him and his feelings.

Edward supplied Byrch with daily progress reports on Callie. Edward was having more luck with Callie than he was. At least Callie communicated with Edward, whereas she merely seemed to tolerate him. Often after dinner, when she would hastily excuse herself and go to her room, he would sit and drink more brandy than he should.

Edward could hear Byrch pacing in his room while Miss Callie walked the confines of hers. A duet, Edward would muse. It was a pity—each had so much to offer the other.

Edward had set the table, laid the meal out in the parlor, and left to play chess with Daniel Jameson's man, Anatole. Byrch and Callie would have the evening to themselves.

Edward felt he'd outdone himself in the preparation of this superb meal—the first step toward getting Byrch and Callie out of their armed truce. He'd become concerned that the relationship they'd established on the first night would never be repeated and that Callie might decide to leave the house on St. Luke's Place. Never once considering himself a romantic, preferring to think of himself as logical and pragmatic, Edward had prepared a small, plump chicken with herbs, candied yams, fresh green beans with slivers of toasted almonds, and a delectable green salad. For the appetizer, there were iced Long Island oysters. If the wine he selected failed to do the trick, Edward thought smugly, the oysters surely would. Thick, yellow butter in a leaf mold, flaky croissants, and freshly made peach torte completed the meal. The white linen tablecloth and napkins had once belonged to Mr. Kenyon's mother, along with the heavy silver and lead crystal goblets. The small bouquet of daisies, the first of the year, was laced with ferns for the centerpiece. Edward was proud of his efforts as he left the house. Who, he asked himself as he opened his umbrella against the downpour, could resist such a tempting evening?

The conversation through dinner mostly concerned Edward's expertise in the kitchen. The fire glowed softly, casting its golden light on Callie who was wearing her somber black dress.

Byrch had come to hate the unrelieved black she wore. Edward had seen to it that Callie had several dresses and undergarments to choose from, but everything was the color of mourning. Callie's coloring was too delicate to be smothered in drabness, her spirit too vital to be hidden mourning. During the last few days Byrch had come to the decision that this sorrow must not continue, that she must not be allowed to sink further into her despair. He resolved to shake her out of it, forcibly if he must, to make Callie open her eyes to life and embrace it once again. He didn't expect her not to mourn her son, but neither did he expect her to crawl into the grave with him and cease to exist.

"Edward tells me you're enjoying the little garden out back," Byrch began on a light note. Her nod frustrated him. Couldn't she even give a simple answer to a simple statement?

"I'd imagine your dresses are uncomfortably warm in this weather. Did you know they're predicting an unusually hot summer?"

Callie merely shrugged, picking at her food, the tines of her fork making clicking sounds against the china. She was wishing he didn't take such notice of her, that he would just leave her be. Her heart ached for him, her senses were finely tuned to the sight of him, the sound of his voice, the scent of his shaving soap. She must not give in to her feelings. Mustn't step out of her place again. She couldn't bear another tragedy, another disaster befalling someone she loved. Only in denying herself Byrch, Callie felt, could she protect him.

Byrch placed his fork against the edge of his plate and rested his elbows on the table, making a steeple out of his fingers. "Callie, look at me. What do you see?"

Slowly she lifted her gaze, bringing her eyes level with his. The lamplight threw a burnished glow onto his thick dark hair and reflected in those mysterious tiger eyes, lightening their green to gold. His white shirtfront contrasted with the tawny shade of his skin, and his broad shoulders were delineated perfectly in the cut of his coat.

"Tell me," Byrch insisted gently, "what do you see when you look at me?"

Unable to answer, Callie lowered her eyes again.

"I had hoped, Callie, that you would say you saw a friend. Someone who cares for you deeply." He had to restrain himself from continuing, so great was his need to declare his feelings for her. Yet he instinctively knew that she was unready for such a confession, that she would view it as a further burden, that it would add to her confusion. "Do you know I'm your friend, Callie?"

After a moment she nodded her head, still refusing to lift her gaze to him. "And do you trust me?" Again she nodded silently. "Then you know I have your interests at heart." In a more assertive manner, he made his announcement. "Then you will agree to see the dressmaker I've commissioned to come here. I realize you may not yet be quite up to going out, and this will be the best solution. You can't go about the rest of the summer in those heavy dresses."

"I don't mind. It doesn't matter what I wear," she said softly, her voice barely audible.

"It matters to me. It will be your first step toward coming back into life. To thinking of yourself." Byrch was afraid he had pushed too far and too soon. Afraid he would wake one morning and find her gone. He had nightmares about it. Why couldn't they hold a simple conversation? Why was it so difficult to tell her what she meant to him? His gut churned and answered for him. Because she doesn't feel the same way. That night in your arms meant nothing to her, simply a way of filling an immediate need. She used you that night, face it, admit it, and go on from there.

He stared across the table at the too-thin face and felt his throat constrict. He sensed that she was holding herself in check, that there was a delicate line here that was demanding he be careful, very careful. If he told her what she meant to him, she would bolt and run. Byrch simply wasn't willing to take that chance. Whatever he had to do to ensure her staying here, he would do. He would not risk losing her again.

When Callie spoke, it startled him. "I simply can't accept your offer of new dresses. I am too far in your debt as it is, and I can't live on your charity."

"Indebtedness? Charity? What debt do you owe?"

"The price of the funerals. And now the dresses. It's simply more than I can pay. I cannot accept the dresses."

Her emotionless response infuriated Byrch. Couldn't she see what she was doing to him? Didn't she care? Didn't she know what making love to her had meant to him? Such joy, such love, didn't she feel it? His voice took an arrogant tone, which he hadn't planned. He was bridling against the hurt. "You will have the dresses, and there will be no discussion about what you think you owe me. A moment ago you admitted I was your friend. Friends do not discuss debts owed or favors granted."

Callie bit her lip. His tone punished her, letting her know that he already despised her. How was it possible to feel such shame and guilt all at the same time? He was probably remembering what a wanton she'd been that first night, throwing herself into his arms, pleading with him to make love to her. No more, no more ever. She knew her place, and she was never going to step out of it again.

"Yes, I want to discuss it. Now." There, it came out right. Her tone was firm, her hands folded into a tight ball in her lap to still their trembling. "I cannot be indebted to you, Byrch. Friend or not. You've done too much for me already. I can't continue to stay here. I plan to work and repay you." Don't you see? she pleaded silently. I can't take and take and take. I know what you did for me that first night when I went to you. You . . . you serviced me! A hot flush worked its way up to her throat.

Byrch struggled with his words. The only thing he'd heard was that she was leaving. He wouldn't let her go. He couldn't. No matter what he had to do. His voice, when he answered, was cynical and hurting. "There is more than one way to repay a debt. Money isn't the answer to everything." Damn, had he really said that? At the stricken look on Callie's face, he knew he had.

"What are you saying?"

He was quick to see the spark in her eyes, hear the anger in her voice. It wasn't what he'd wanted, but it was some sign of life. Brazenly he continued along the same vein. "Simply, sweeting, that some debts are paid in currency and others can be paid in services." The hard glint in his eyes conveyed his message. He paralyzed her beneath his gaze, daring her to bolt and run.

Once his statement registered in Callie's brain, she literally froze. "Exactly what does that mean? I think you should explain it to me," she demanded.

Byrch's tiger eyes held her pinned like a butterfly to a mounting board. "I think you know exactly what I mean."

Callie's mind whirled. She had a crazy feeling that she wanted to laugh, bray like a donkey. She knew she shouldn't sit here and suffer this insult. She shouldn't allow him to proposition her. She should run, leave, never turn back, but she was frozen in her seat. Something was holding her back. She wanted to hurt him in return, shock him, throw his words back at him. She stared into those cat-green depths and spoke, each word clear and concise. "I suppose it's better to be a rich man's whore than a poor man's wife."

Byrch nearly fell off his chair. If he'd been sitting closer, he would have slapped her for such a remark. Couldn't she see what she was doing to him? Didn't she feel anything for him? Anything at all? He didn't care. It wasn't important, not now. All that was important was that she would stay because he had no intention of letting her go, now or ever. "You have it all wrong, sweeting," he said bitterly. "I am talking about marriage."

Callie was stunned. When she found her voice, she asked, "You want to marry me? Why?"

"I thought that was obvious. You want to cancel out what you feel is your debt, and I felt the arrangement would be agreeable to both of us." Sheer will kept his tone impersonal; self-contempt for what he was doing to her put a brittle edge to his voice.

"Well, it's not agreeable to me! There must be some other way." Callie felt sick. This couldn't be happening. Her head was aching, throbbing like a drum. Only now at this sudden eruption of emotions could she even guess at how much this man meant to her. And it was ruined. All of it. She was torn between wanting to belong to him and fearing that if she reached out for happiness, it would be snatched away again. Her eyes pleaded with him to help her.

Byrch felt her vulnerability as though it were a tangible thing. He watched her carefully, steadily, ready to capture her if she tried to run from him. Time, he told himself. All he needed was time to make her see what she meant to him, to make her love him. If cruelty had evoked her response, then so be it, he would not risk changing tactics now. "If marriage is not agreeable, there is always the first method you mentioned. You've already said it was better than being a poor man's wife, or anyone's wife for that matter, I take it."

Callie stood abruptly, tipping her wineglass onto the tablecloth. She saw Byrch tense. Head high and proud, eyes shooting sparks, she demanded, "How long will it take me to repay you? How great is my debt, and what am I worth to you? What is my rate of exchange?"

Byrch was stunned, unbelieving she still refused his offer of marriage, unable to think of an answer to her questions. "I'll let you know when the time comes." It was with great effort that he kept his voice steady.

"That isn't good enough. I want an answer, how long?" Her voice was as cold as an arctic wind.

Damn! Where had he gone wrong? What had he done to make her hate him this way? "Three months," he blurted, groping for an answer.

Callie's eyes were diamond bright as she locked her gaze with his. "I don't see that I have much choice. I will agree to be in your service."

Byrch's mind reeled. He wanted to lash out, to crush and destroy. "You have that all wrong, sweeting. I believe when last I shared your bed, it was I who serviced you!"

Callie was devastated. There was no comeback. That final statement said it all. She tossed down her napkin and raced from the room.

An expression of pure torture covered Byrch's face. It was a nightmare. He was going to awaken any second now, and it would all have been a dream. He had compromised the woman he loved by propositioning her, all because he was too much a coward to tell her he loved her. Gulping his wine, he admitted he would rather have her this way than no way at all.

Callie lay in her bed, hoping for, yet dreading, Byrch's appearance at her door. Persistently her thoughts roiled and returned to the night of the fire when he'd held her in his arms and cried with her for her loss. Since then she'd been more than half-dead, walking about like a ghost. Tonight Byrch had reawakened her, forced her emotions, and in spite of his cruel "arrangement," as he liked to call it, she told herself, she could have a little bit of him, regardless of the price, and never have to fear she was stepping out of her place.

She waited long into the night for the footsteps at the door that never came.

* * *

Callie went down to the kitchen late the next morning, in an effort to avoid Byrch. Edward was near the stove, reheating the morning coffee. He was quick to notice that the color seemed to be returning to Callie's cheeks.

"Good morning, Miss Callie. You're looking well this morning, I'm pleased to say."

"Good morning, Edward. Just coffee, if you please, I'm not very hungry."

"Now, Miss Callie, I've already put some sausage aside for you, and it won't take but a minute to fry some eggs. You just sit and read the morning paper, and I'll get your breakfast for you. The dressmaker is coming this morning, and I doubt you'll have time for more than a quick lunch."

Callie settled herself at the breakfast table and reached for the morning edition of the *Clarion-Observer*. Edward poured her a cup of steaming coffee, placing the delicate china cup near her elbow. "Mr. Kenyon said to express his regrets that he could not join you for breakfast, Miss Callie. He had an early morning appointment before going to the paper. It must be a rather serious one, considering the expression on his face this morning. I imagine his entering politics is a weighty matter."

"Politics? I didn't know Byrch entertained political ambitions."

"Oh, yes, miss, Mr. Kenyon has his eyes set on the mayoral seat. It's expected that by this time next year he'll be actively campaigning."

Edward put a plate before her, prompting her to eat. "Mr. Kenyon also said that he hadn't had time to mention it last night, but he's asked Mrs. Darcy, his cousin's wife, to sit in on your appointment with the dressmaker. You have an hour before Mrs. Darcy arrives."

Callie accepted the news with an inward groan. She wasn't ready to meet new people, and she mentally calculated the cost of the planned wardrobe, adding the numbers to her already long list of debts. And it rankled that Byrch didn't think she had the good sense or the proper taste to select her own clothes.

As though reading her mind, Edward added, "Since the dressmaker is one employed by Mrs. Darcy, she insisted on being included." It was obvious to Callie that Edward didn't care for Byrch's relative.

Bridget Darcy arrived on the stroke of ten, dressed in her most becoming morning dress of pale yellow silk, the white lace at the throat and cuffs fluttering as she walked. The fragrance of her expensive French scent followed in her wake and added to the picture of her total femininity. She paraded past Edward into the parlor and, finding it vacant, turned on the manservant accusingly. "Well, where is she? Callie—that's her name, isn't it? Where is she?"

"I will announce you to Miss Callie," Edward said imperiously, ignoring Bridget's rudeness.

"Yes, do that," she said, removing her gloves and dropping them on the table. "The dressmaker was told to arrive promptly at ten-thirty, and I have a tea to attend early this afternoon. I don't like to be kept waiting."

Edward met Callie on the second-floor landing. "You can do this, Miss Callie," he encouraged quietly when he noticed the stirrings of panic in her eyes. A gentle touch to her shoulder calmed her. She trusted Edward. If he said it was going to be all right, then it would be.

Head high, shoulders straight, Callie followed Edward into the parlor. He introduced her as Miss Callie James, and she wondered if he had forgotten her married name or if Byrch had instructed him to ignore it. When Edward withdrew, he kept discreetly out of sight, his ear and eye to the door. Miss Callie would not suffer insolence or get short shrift if he could help it. Too often he had heard Byrch express his opinion of Bridget Darcy and her delusions of grandeur.

Common, Bridget thought to herself as she viewed Callie. God alone knew why she was being so charitable to Byrch's little folly. Her mouth pursed in a slight grimace. The things one did for one's family when the political winds were blowing.

Callie took a deep breath and motioned for Bridget to sit down. "I appreciate what you're doing for me, Mrs. Darcy. I can see for myself that you've an instinctive flair for fashion. I know Byrch appreciates your kindness also."

Bridget settled herself on the sofa. "Byrch," she called him! Well, what did she expect? This woman was sleeping with him, and she could hardly call him "Mr. Kenyon." How guilty she looked, Bridget thought uncharitably. Little tart that this Callie James was, she should feel guilty in the presence of a decent woman. What ever prompted her to come along and dress the girl properly, just because Byrch had inquired after her own personal dressmaker, Bridget would never understand. Except, of course, that there was every chance that Byrch would be successful in his campaign to be New York's mayor, and she must make every attempt to save him embarrassment. For the family, of course.

She hoped that by the time the campaign was actually underway, he would have rid himself of this little piece of baggage. Until then, she supposed, they would all have to bear it. No one had ever had much luck in telling Byrch what he should or shouldn't do.

"Now then," Bridget began, beaming her most fradulent smile, "suppose you tell me what colors you prefer and if there is a certain style you favor. I assume from your dress that you're in mourning?"

"Yes, I've recently lost my—"

"Oh, what does it matter?" Bridget fluttered her hands impatiently. "I can imagine how eager you are to dispose of those drab, heavy dresses, and I assure you I'll make certain Agnes sets aside all else to hurry your wardrobe. Except what I've commissioned, of course."

"Of course."

Bridget scribbled on a small pad, prodding Callie for her preferences and digressing into long descriptions of the latest gowns being worn and the new additions to her own wardrobe. Callie was quick to see that Bridget Darcy was happiest and most interested when she was talking about herself.

Edward entered the parlor and placed a tray of lemonade and cookies on the server in the adjoining dining room just as the doorbell rang.

"Edward!" Bridget called stridently, "that must be Agnes. Hurry, answer the door!"

Few things in life stunned Edward, but the sight of Agnes the dressmaker, Aggie for short, was enough to make him blink. She towered over him by a good head and looked down at him with merry eyes. Spots of rouge and brilliantly pomaded lips reminded him of a particular lady who strolled by on a Sunday evening. Agnes extended her hand and gave Edward a bone crushing shake. To his credit, he didn't flinch, and he found himself wondering how Agnes held a needle in those large, mannish hands. Edward decided he would watch and wait. If he didn't like what was going on, he'd put a stop to it immediately. No one, and that included Mr. Kenyon's cousin, was going to have any kind of sport with Miss Callie.

"Sit down, Aggie, and have some lemonade. Miss James is your client. I spoke with her briefly, and this is her list of colors and preferences. Mr. Kenyon wants her dressed fashionably and suitably." Bridget spoke with her usual take charge manner.

"Stand up! Let's have a look at you!" Aggie commanded. Callie obeyed. "Beautiful. Good bones. You're a bit too thin, but that's fashionable these days. I'll make wide seams so they can be let out if you gain a pound or two. If your man will bring in my pattern books and fabric samples, we can begin with your selections and measuring."

Edward was at the door before Callie could summon him. She tried to hide her smile, but he caught it and winked. He returned minutes later, his arms full of pattern books and bolts of cloth. For the first time since she had come to the house, Edward noticed a gleam in Callie's eyes. Vanity. Pretty things. That's what women liked, and who could blame them? This was a wise move on the master's part, he decided.

Three hours later, Callie sank down into her chair. She had no idea how tiring selecting and being fitted for garments could be. Aggie wore a pleased expression as she jabbed pins back into a wrist cushion. Scissors followed, as did the tape measure. "It will be my pleasure to dress you, Miss James. You're a joy, simply a joy. Good hips, enough of a bosom. You'll show off my creations to the best possible advantage. And you've made very intelligent choices. I'll start work tomorrow, and we can have a fitting a week from today. Also, I require a deposit," she said, almost all in one breath.

Bridget enjoyed the expression of panic in Callie's eyes when Aggie mentioned money. Almost before the words were out of the seamstress's mouth, Edward was there, holding out a white envelope. Bridget felt cheated. She knew the black man would have a sneer on his face when he turned to face her. Instead she was rewarded with a blank look that was perfectably respectable. How did Byrch do it? She couldn't find help like this treasure.

"Miss Callie, you have an appointment in fifteen minutes," Edward said quietly to indicate the meeting was over. Bridget took her cue, rising and waiting impatiently while Aggie said her good-byes and then following her to the door. She accepted Callie's expression of thanks with a slight sniff and gushed with false congeniality. "Perfectly all right, Callie. I wouldn't have missed this for the world! Heaven knows you need *someone* to turn you into a silk purse!" She smiled, showing her small white teeth. "Ta! I'll pop by for tea one afternoon, and we can have a real girl talk!"

"Go along to the kitchen," Edward said softly. "I just made fresh lemonade, and there's a salad. I have to carry these bolts and books out to the carriage, and then I'll join you."

Callie nodded gratefully. How would she ever manage without

this man? When he returned to the kitchen, Callie faced him anxiously. "Edward, I need to know how much all of this is costing. It must be a fortune, and I don't think I can accept it."

"You should discuss that with Mr. Kenyon. It's not my place to discuss finances with you." His tone was gentle but firm. Callie understood perfectly when he said, "not my place." Edward was aware of his place just as she should be aware of hers. Why couldn't she remember it? Why did she always have to aspire to something more, something or someone that wasn't meant to be hers? She must remember her place, be careful of stepping out of it. She would die if Byrch ever had to suffer the consequences. She *must* remember her place!

Chapter Twenty-Five

All through another of Edward's perfect dinners of roast lamb and fresh green salad and mint jelly, Callie watched Byrch across the immaculately appointed table. Byrch usually returned from the *Clarion* rather late, staying in the office until he "put the paper to bed," as he called it. Although the approaching summer days were longer, it was necessary to light the lamps when they finally sat down to dinner at seven-thirty.

Byrch played the perfect host, slicing off the most tender bits of lamb for Callie and serving her the piquant rosé wine he knew she preferred. "Did you have fun with the dressmaker today, Callie?" he asked, looking up from his plate.

"Yes, I did," she answered. "Aggie seems to know her business, but of course, I'm hardly a judge. The little I know about dressmaking comes from my time in the Powers family. But I'm certain Aggie would please even Mrs. Powers."

"It's strange, but I've never really thought of Anne Powers as a fashionable woman," Byrch mused. "Oh, I've always known her tastes ran to the finest, but perhaps because I've never liked the woman, I've never thought of her as feminine or fashionable. Expensive, socially aspiring, yes."

"I know what you mean," Callie told him. "I've always thought of her as a kind of dowager queen, running her kingdom with an iron hand. Poor Mr. Powers," she sighed.

"Oh, don't feel too sorry for Jasper." Byrch poured the sparkling pink wine into his glass. "I'm certain you'd be hard put to find a happier man these days."

At Callie's curious glance, he continued. At least, Byrch told himself, this was a pleasant conversation, and she seemed interested. It had been so long since he'd had her friendly attention. He went into great detail about Jasper. "Jasper assures me Anne Powers is quite content living in Boston and acting as her widowed brother's hostess," he concluded. "And Jasper himself looks better and younger than he has in years since he's taken up residence with Loretta Cummings. He's still president of the bank, and he's been in love with Loretta for years. She's a wonderful woman, and she's good for him. Naturally it goes without saying, there's been no mention of divorcing Anne. She probably wouldn't allow it. It would be publicly humiliating for her."

"I'm glad for him. I always felt Mr. Powers had a great capacity for love, and I'm glad he's found a woman to return it in kind," Callie said softly, thinking of the many kindnesses Jasper had shown her and remembering how the man poured out his love to little Mary. A haunted expression came over her features, and Byrch noticed.

"Sweeting, you just said you were glad for Jasper. What's the problem?"

"Oh, I was just thinking of Mary and how much he loved her. I know now what it means to lose a child, and I don't think it's something you ever recover from."

"No, I don't suppose it is. And no one is expecting you to forget Rory. I don't want you to. I like to hear you talk about him, Callie, and it's good for you to do so. I only wish I could have known him; I think we would have become great friends."

"Yes, Byrch, I think you would have." She smiled with only the barest trace of wistfulness. He was glad to see that her eyes betrayed no hint of tears and that she was at last able to mention her son without choking with emotion. Edward was right. Time. All things in good time.

"Now tell me about the dressmaker. But first tell me what you thought of my cousin Bridget. You didn't let her intimidate you, did you?"

Throughout dinner, Callie relaxed and regaled Byrch with descriptions of Aggie and a detailed list of the proposed garments. She hardly mentioned Bridget, except to say that Mrs. Darcy was most helpful and certainly a fine example of fashion. Byrch enjoyed Callie's description of Edward's reaction to Aggie, laughing when she told him how his fastidious manservant hovered nearby and had to replenish the plate of finger sandwiches three times before the seamstress had had her fill.

"Callie, it sounds as though you had an enjoyable afternoon. Don't think for a moment, sweeting, that I expect you to cast off your grief along with those black dresses. I don't. But suffering the summer heat won't change the situation, and I simply wanted to do this for you." If he expected her to express her gratitude, he was mistaken.

"And because it's something you think I should have, I've added to my debt." Although it was a statement, there was a sharp edge to her words.

"All right, consider it part of what you *think* you owe me." Byrch raised his voice in exasperation. "You know, Callie, I never said you were indebted to me in any way. That was entirely *your* idea!"

"And whose idea was this little arrangement between us, Mr. Kenyon? Perhaps you need to be reminded!" Frustrated, Callie threw down her napkin and stood abruptly, nearly knocking her chair backward.

Following suit, Byrch did the same, picking up his wine glass and stalking into the parlor. Damn! Why was she so exasperating? Anger swelled in his chest. With a cold, cynical voice he hadn't known he was capable of, he turned to face her. "Seeing as how you're so mindful of your obligations, go upstairs. I'll be joining you shortly."

Callie stood frozen in her tracks. It was difficult to believe Byrch could speak in that cold, impersonal tone. He meant to collect on his debt and expected her to live up to the arrangement. Stubborn defiance pushed Callie's chin upwards, glazing her eyes with bitterness and stiffening her spine with outrage. Slowly, deliberately, she walked through the parlor and to the stairs.

Her silence and resignation further prompted Byrch's anger. He had prepared himself for an argument—at least that was some form of communication—and perhaps they would have been able to work out their differences. Perhaps he would have been able to unburden himself and tell her how much she meant to him. But her resentment seemed to crackle through the air, and her bitter resignation was a wound. Dammit! If she wouldn't invite him into her bed, then he would have to invite himself! At least he would have that much of her. And God alone knew how his arms ached to hold her again. His own vulnerability and hurt prompted the hateful words, "And when I get up there, I don't want to find you in that miserable black dress. You agreed to be a rich man's whore, and I expect you to act the part!"

Callie's step halted for just a moment before climbing the stairs. She didn't turn to look at him, but he knew she'd heard. Her back was stiff, her shoulders thrown back and squared. He knew he'd landed a devastating blow to her pride, and he immediately wanted to take back what he'd said. But he wasn't given the opportunity. Callie continued up the stairs slowly, almost the way Byrch imagined a man would walk to his execution. Hating himself, a part of him even hating Callie, Byrch threw his glass into the cold, empty hearth; the fine crystal glass shattered.

When Byrch climbed the stairs nearly an hour later, each foot that touched the treads was heavy, leaden. He reached the second floor of his townhouse, passing the long, narrow room he used as a library and the bedroom where Edward kept his quarters, grateful the manservant was playing chess with friends this night. He wouldn't have wanted anyone, not even Edward, to witness what he'd done or the torment it was causing him—ordering the only woman who had ever meant anything to him to act as his whore, demanding her body when it was her love he wanted.

Slowly he climbed to the third floor where his and Callie's bedrooms were almost opposite one another. He should just pass her room, go into his own with the half-bottle of brandy he'd brought with him. Even the two snifters he'd consumed downstairs hadn't dulled the sharp edges of his conscience. Her door was open, a soft light glowing from within.

Callie heard Byrch coming up the stairs. With each measured step, her tension increased. She had done as he'd ordered and removed the black dress. She sat cold and shivering in her undergarments, uncertain as to what she should do. He'd told her to act the whore, but what exactly did that mean? How, aside from being a willing partner in bed, did a whore behave?

He stepped into the room, filling the doorway with his broad shoulders and lean height. She immediately noticed the bottle he carried and frowned. Byrch was a moderate drinker, never becoming sloppy or offensive as Hugh had during those last months. She remembered the sour smell of whiskey that hung about Hugh, recalling his surliness and hostility. Did drink make all men mean?

Byrch stood looking at her for a long moment before crossing the room. She was relieved to see he walked straight and tall, apparently not suffering the effects of the brandy.

He stood over her, looking down, seeing her dark cloud of hair hanging softly about her shoulders, and he was tempted to reach out and touch it, feel it slide silkily between his fingers. The whiteness of her lacy camisole and petticoats enchanced the honeyed tones of her skin and revealed the gentle slope of her shoulders and the pretty roundness of her arms. She looked so young sitting there, so vulnerable and lovely, so frightened. The white ring of terror around her mouth brought him a pang of physical pain. To Callie, it was a cruel sneer, and she shrank back against the chair. Seeing her cower from him brought a rush of rage. He wanted to lift her out of that chair and shake her until her teeth rattled; he wanted to soften the grim line of her mouth with his kisses, to evoke a response from her, to have her welcome him, open and unafraid, to remove the terror he read in her eyes and replace it with desire.

"Callie, come here to me," he whispered, afraid that the mere sound of his voice would send her running.

Obediently she stood and advanced two steps to stand before him. Her throat worked convulsively as she choked back her tears. She would not cry; she would not!

Byrch looked down at her, angered by her fright, hating himself for being the cause of it. "Stop looking at me as though I were about to eat you up!" he scolded.

"And how is it I'm supposed to look?" she asked. "I'm not exactly experienced in this role. How do whores look, and what do they do?" She challenged him with her eyes to put an end to this charade, to release her from their arrangement, to set her free. And this Byrch could never do. His cat-green eyes narrowed, glittering fiercely in the dim lamplight, the pupils blacker than a midnight sky, the thick fringe of lashes lowering insolently.

"You're not all that inexperienced," he lashed back. "If I remember correctly, the last time you shared my bed you were quite willing and most helpful in securing my services. Now it's your services I require." Even before the words were out of his mouth, he regretted them. It was almost as though he could see her back arch, her spine stiffen, like a cat's, ready to spring and defend itself with tooth and claw. Instead she lowered her eyes, not meeting the challenge, reaching forward to undo the buttons on his shirtfront. He stood there, accessible to her hands, holding his breath for her first touch against his skin. She handled the fabric of his shirt delicately, avoiding contact with him while she pulled the tails out of his trousers. Her hands moved to his waist, struggling with the buckle on his belt, incapable of unfastening it. When his hands dropped to help her, she pulled away as though touched by fire. Her movements as she bent to remove his boots and take his shirt after he'd shrugged out of it were servile; she was performing a service for him.

Unable to tolerate it a moment longer, Byrch seized her by the shoulders, shaking her and then pulling her hard against his solid, naked chest. "Dammit! I don't you this way! Not this way! I want you greedy, hungry for my loving!"

Callie's eyes accused him. "What does a whore know about loving and being loved?"

"A good whore is also an able actress," he muttered through clenched teeth, driving his hand through the wealth of long chestnut hair at the back of her head, pulling her forward and upward. "Even if you don't feel anything for me, pretend!" He choked, too lost in his need for her to consider his pride. He only knew he must have her as he had that first night. Hungrily he brought his mouth down to hers, covering it with his own, determined to evoke a response.

The response Byrch sought was there, bubbling just beneath her surface—throbbing, pounding, demanding to be set free. While her mind cautioned and clamored, warning her that she was on the brink of disaster, Callie's womanly needs and wants rose in a counter-cry, thrumming in her pulses, closing her off to everything but the feel of his arms around her and the possession of his mouth on hers. She tried to remember Rory, her past, the pain and loss that was her fate whenever she reached out for something she wanted, whenever happiness was within her grasp. She didn't want to open herself to that kind of hurt again, that kind of loss. She mustn't let herself love Byrch, not even secretly, but the pressure of his lips had softened, moving over her mouth in a tender seduction that she was helpless to resist. Slowly, cautiously, her arms reached for him, her hands pressing into the hard muscles of his back, her lips parting beneath his in an answering kiss. The groan of need and expectancy that swelled in her own throat was uttered by Byrch as he brought her full length against him, pressing her into himself as though he would make her a part of him. The swell of his desire was hard against her belly, and she drove herself into it, forgetting the fates, defying the future, and knowing only that for this time at least she wanted to belong to this man who could break her heart with a glance and bring her to life with his touch.

Byrch was shaken by her sudden willingness, by the way her full, soft lips parted beneath his and her anxious fingers probed the flesh of his back. When he found the strength to pull his mouth from hers, his eyes searched her lovely face, chasing the shadows in her eyes, attempting to read her soul. Was this Callie's answer to his kisses and his passions, or was she acceding to his demands and playing the part of a willing whore? Thick, black lashes closed over her eyes, refusing him admittance.

She lifted herself on tiptoe to reclaim his mouth, the tip of her tongue sparring with his, and she heard her own breath come in ragged little gasps as she offered herself to him, kissing him deeply, searchingly, reaching for her forbidden happiness, totally lost to him and their shared desire.

Sensing that she would not turn away from him now, Byrch's touch became gentle and unhurried. His fingers wound through her hair, along the bone of her cheek to the ridge of her jaw and along her throat where he could feel her pulses beating against the fragile skin. He yearned to tell her how lovely she was, how beautiful to him. He wanted to hear her tell him she must belong to him, that she loved him.

Lifting her into his arms, he carried her across the room and put her on the high tester bed. He captured her mouth with his own, entering with his tongue, feeling the velvet of hers. She moved closer to him, offering herself, allowing his hands to move over her body, exciting her hungers until they matched his own. She yielded to his touch, growing languorous as he found her breasts, his mouth exploring hers, tasting and caressing with a gentleness and seduction that sent her senses reeling.

He lifted her petticoat, sliding his hand along her bare leg, rising upwards between her thighs, and she moved against his touch and heard the echo of her desires in the deepness of his voice. "You're so beautiful, Callie. I know you want me to touch you, to love you. You do, I know you do." More than his life, Byrch wanted to believe his own words. He needed to believe she wanted him, that she loved him, even a little. He hoped, prayed, she would tell him it was so, but there was no sound except for the beating of their hearts and the rustle of her body against the sheets.

Another kiss and Callie pulled herself out of his arms, kneeling beside him on the bed. In the glow of the lamp he watched her, his arms feeling empty without her to warm them. Slowly she undid the ties of her camisole, the thin fabric delineating her breasts and their hard, firm crests that pushed against their restraints.

Feeling his eyes upon her, she worked slowly, trembling fingers fussing with laces, rapidly beating heart making her pulses race. One by one, she removed her garments, revealing herself to him a little at a time, whetting his appetite for her. The lamp gave a burnished sheen to her skin, the curves of her body emphasized by deepening shadows in the valleys. Taking his cue from her, Byrch stripped off his clothes, his thoughts leaping ahead to the next touch, the next kiss, the next secret discovered. He was eager to be naked with her, wanting the heat from her body to warm that cold place in his heart. He wouldn't listen to that devil inside him, for now at least he would believe it was desire he saw in her eyes and passion he heard in those soft, mewling sounds she made.

Rolling onto his back, he took her with him, grazing his fingers down her spine and returning again and again to sample the roundness of her bottom. He took her hands and placed them on his chest, inviting her touch and inspiring her caresses. He wanted her to take pleasure in him; he wanted to stir those fragile passions.

Callie smoothed her palms over the broad expanse of his chest, pulling at the thicket of dark hair patterned there, grazing over the sensitive nubs of his nipples, feeling them tauten and rise just like her own. She bent to kiss them, taking them into her mouth, licking, tasting, widening her explorations to include the flatness of his belly and the firmness of his thighs.

Byrch pushed her backwards, following with his weight, putting her beneath him once again. He found the sweetness of her mouth, the curious moistness of her eyelids and the tender curve of her jaw. She sought him with her lips, possessed him with her hands, her own senses soaring as she realized the pleasure he was finding in her, feeling herself to be beautiful beneath his touch. The boldness of his sex seemed vulnerable to her touch, and it was not something to be feared; it was evidence of his desire for her, quivering with expectancy and need.

His hands warmed her body, following each line of her flesh, each curve and plane, seeking and exploring with tender adoration. He moved over her, pressing her thighs apart with his knee, his eyes feasting on her as she lay in tremulous expectation. Her dark hair fanned upon the pillow, curling tendrils softening the line of her cheek and creating shadows over her eyes. Her flesh was bathed in a sleek sheen that highlighted the contours of her body. Her arms reached for him, tempting him into her embrace, but this he denied her, taking her hands in his and kissing her fingertips. He sat back on his haunches, caressing her body, watching as the tip of her tongue darted between her lips, her head thrown back, giving herself over to these feelings he was creating within her. It was only when he called her name that she looked at him, sultry eyes following his every motion. He encouraged her to watch as his hands slid along her body, touching first the hollow of her throat and moving downward to the cleft between her breasts, following their curves upward to cup their fullness. Over and over in a rhythmic pattern, the cadence of his hands teased her, skimming lower and lower toward her opened thighs and to the secret of her sex. Her body arched, driving herself against his touch, willing those artful, expressive hands to possess her, to bring her the release he himself had taught her. He was her maestro; she was a finely tuned instrument created only for the sound of his music. With him she could ride the crescendo, keeping to the rhythm, beating with the drum that was her passion-stirred heart. When his hands dipped to her center, she cried out, legs parting wider to admit his touch, straining her hips to arch against his gently circling fingers.

He tamed her passions and excited her desires, feeling the heat from her invade his body, reveling in it. She cried softly as he took her to the edge of sensation, holding back, afraid to plunge over the edge, afraid of finding herself alone and without him. It was the point of no return, and the sound of her name on his lips pushed her over the edge into a maelstrom of passion's winds and love's fury. She had found her release; he had given it like a gift, but at the center of herself there was an emptiness that only he could fill. She felt as though her body was drawing inward on itself, contracting, seeking to find something to make it whole again. When he leaned forward, driving himself into her, she knew that this was what her body sought—his body, filling her with his throbbing masculinity.

She strained beneath him, sharing his long-awaited pleasure. His mouth claimed hers, kissing her deeply, and his movements were smooth and unhurried as he stroked within her, encouraging her to match his movements, stirring her responses until she knew she would find that sweet release once again.

Her hands smoothed along his back to find the firm roundness of his haunches, holding fast and driving herself against him. Her legs seemed to rise at their own volition, changing their position, allowing him deeper entry. She felt him lift her bottom, raising her up, thrusting himself into her with short, quick strokes. She heard her muffled cries at this new, exquisite sensation, and her body heated and closed around his, taking him with her to the edge of that crevasse. And locked in one another's arms, they plunged forward to find themselves lifted on the winds of sensation and flying the midnight sky to passion's reward.

The room was silent, the lamp still glowing softly, creating shadows in the far corners. Byrch lay beside Callie, holding her, her head nestled against his chest. The only sound was her soft breathing as she slept. Long into the night he held her, cherishing her closeness. Their lovemaking had been exquisite, a journey into a realm of pleasure that he'd never known. But a part of him was uneasy, unfulfilled. He wanted to talk, to share, to tell her of his love, but he was afraid to break the silence between them and end their truce. She'd obeyed his demands to act his whore, pretended to welcome his lovemaking until instinct took over. Callie was a sensual woman, awakened now to her desires and needs. His thoughts went back to that first night when she'd asked him to make her a woman. Even that first time she'd been an artful lover, listening to her instincts, acting upon her passions. She had learned her lessons well.

Byrch inhaled the fragrance of her hair and nuzzled his chin against her brow. There was a heaviness in his chest, and he knew sleep would not find him this night. He should go back to his own bed, try to put her out of his mind. But he couldn't bring himself to leave her. If this was all he could have of her, if he could never have her love, it would have to be enough. Because without her, he would die.

Chapter Twenty-Six

Callie's spirits rose and strengthened as spring became the first wonderful days of summer. Edward's flower garden bloomed, and his vegetable patch was lush and green. The first sweet peas had already been picked, and another row was growing for the cool weather of autumn. Callie assigned herself the task of weeding and harvesting the bright blooms to decorate the townhouse. Edward watched her from the kitchen window as she bent over to dig in the soil. Women, he knew, didn't like to get dirt under their fingernails, but when he'd offered her gardening gloves, Callie had shunned them. She wanted to feel the rich, black earth between her fingers, she'd said. At times Edward was a bit disgruntled with her success in his garden. His rows of vegetables had never looked so neat, so orderly. And try as he might, he could never keep his garden free from weeds, not the way Miss Callie could.

He watched her now as she dropped to her knees, her garden basket beside her. Her movements were slow, sure, and deft as she plucked here and patted there. What magic did she have in her fingers to make the plants so green and lush, seeming to grow directly beneath her touch? He had choked back a laugh when Miss Callie had told Mr. Kenyon at dinner that she talked and sang to the plants. Mr. Kenyon had winked roguishly at Edward and forced a laugh that wasn't reflected in his eyes. Edward had to admit that having a woman in the house made all the difference. A house with two men in it smelled like a house with two men, plus a bit of furniture polish.

Callie's presence was welcomed. Edward enjoyed her company for a cup of tea in the afternoons. She insisted they lunch together at the kitchen table. In the beginning he was a bit ill at ease, but he soon came to look forward to her company. She made her presence known in other ways too, taking over some of his more loathsome chores. She was an expert at ironing, and he gladly surrendered the task of Byrch's shirts to her. It freed him for other more important interests: perfecting his chess game.

Edward finished up the luncheon dishes and hung up the towel to dry. If Mr. Kenyon had his way, a marriage was in the offing. Soon, Edward knew, he'd be drying the dishes with fancy embroidered towels instead of the plain white ones he used. Some things a man just knew. He decided he didn't mind. The kitchen could use a little color. He had watched a transformation in the house as, little by little, a woman's touch was added here and there. There were subtle little changes: a pot of herbs on the window sill, a geranium with sixteen giant blooms in a crock by the sink. The kitchen curtains were whiter and stiffer, definitely an improvement over his limp, tied-back coverings. Callie had hung greenery from the exposed beams; it was pleasant to look at and smelled woodsy. He couldn't remember how or when these little touches appeared. One day they weren't there, and the next they were. It was that simple. Like Miss Callie herself. And, if his eyesight wasn't failing him, his copper-bottomed pots sparkled, and he'd even go so far as to wager a full month's salary that the piece of needlework she was stitching would eventually add up to a cushion for his rocker.

Edward liked Miss Callie. She wasn't one of those complicated, vain women that Mr. Kenyon sometimes brought home. She didn't hide behind her hands or giggle, and neither did she assume a haughty, imperious attitude. Callie had a mind and used it. She wasn't shy about voicing her opinions, and on more than one occasion, he had seen Mr. Kenyon at a loss for words when her cool, calm logic had backed him into a corner. There was no pretense about Miss Callie. He hoped Mr. Kenyon was smart enough not to let her slip through his fingers this time.

Edward was grateful that Miss Callie was coming out of her grief slowly but surely. Her eyes no longer harbored that haunted expression. Her smiles were warm and genuine, and she was taking on a new life for herself. He was also aware of a new restlessness. She wanted to be busy, she needed to be busy, and the few homemaking chores she managed to wrest from him were not enough for her. When her gardening was finished, she would come in, wash up, and then sit on the back terrace to read the morning paper. Then she would usually go for a walk. She never said where she was going, but on the days he saw her take flowers from the garden, he knew her destination was the cemetery behind St. Matthew's Mission Church. He did notice, thankfully, that of late her trips were less frequent. She was coming to terms with her loss. He hoped that in some small way he was helping her.

Callie completed her weeding. She looked approvingly at the neat rows she tended so lovingly. Edward approved, she could tell. They'd already harvested a small crop of sugar peas, and the green beans would be next. The leaf lettuce was yielding enough each day for a small salad, and she could hardly wait for the first cucumbers. The summer squash and green onions were interspersed between rows of root vegetables to be stored through the winter. She hadn't realized how much she had learned from Lena and Hugh about raising and storing fresh produce. She liked to sit and look at the garden, imagining she could actually watch it grow before her very eyes. It was such perfect weather: warm golden days and light rain at night.

She liked this small, walled garden. The white iron bench that Edward had painted was perfect beneath the shade of the plum tree. She liked everything about the house on St. Luke's Place. Callie knew she was recovering from Rory's death. She still thought about him; she still ached for him, but somehow she knew she would survive. It was time to begin thinking about her life and what she would do with it. After being a mother, taking care of Rory and Hugh and carrying the responsibility of survival, Callie felt there was no meaning in these halcyon days spent waiting for Byrch's return from the paper.

Their arrangement seemed to have created a kind of armed truce. Only pleasantries were exchanged, their conversations deepening only on neutral ground. Only Byrch could ever fill the emptiness Rory had left in her heart. She loved him, of that she had no doubt, and she longed to let go of the terror that if she reached out for happiness, it would be snatched away. But that was a foregone conclusion, Callie needed to keep reminding herself. There was no future for herself and Byrch. They had made an agreement, a bargain. Three months, he'd told her, and she could consider her debt paid. It was something she didn't care to think about, and she wasn't certain whether it was because she had agreed to be his whore or that at the end of that time she would walk out of his life forever. The pang she felt at the thought of leaving Byrch was almost crippling in its intensity.

Callie carefully dipped some rain water from the barrel, washed her dirty hands, and wiped them on the towel Edward provided. She stored away her gardening tools in the box beside the back steps. Now for a cool glass of lemonade and the newspaper. She was interested in the latest news and especially in Byrch's editorials. How hungrily she read the words and remembered the topical events to discuss them at dinner. Often she mentally composed an article, comparing it to the one in the *Clarion*. Once or twice she had even found the nerve to put her views on paper and had showed her work to Edward. He'd read them with amazement, appreciating her choice of words and the slant she gave to the story. As Edward's approval increased, she became more and more creative, until one day Edward declared she wrote every bit as well as some of the reporters on the *Clarion* and that Byrch would be hard pressed to tell the difference if her story was anonymously submitted for his approval. Callie had glowed all day from Edward's praise.

Callie settled herself in the padded wicker chair on the flagstone terrace. It was a beautiful day, and she considered walking to the cemetery to place flowers on Rory's and Hugh's graves. But somehow it was too nice a day for cemeteries. She loved summer and its sweet smelling nights and the warm rain dancing on the slate roof.

Picking up the morning copy of the *Clarion*, she felt a part of the newspaper. Byrch had brought her down to the offices and showed her around, and she'd loved every minute. She felt herself in tune with the roar of the presses and the hustle-bustle and the general hubbub. She adored young Jimmy Riley, who she knew was smitten with her. For such a young man, he had a sharp, keen mind, which she appreciated.

Byrch had told her how Jimmy had started with the paper as a newsboy and progressed to copy boy. Now the redheaded, freckled young man was called upon to put his talents to use with his sketches, which were a notable part of the *Clarion*, and often he published a lead story. At times Callie felt guilty about trading on the young man's infatuation to glean as much information about the newspaper business as he would tell her.

Callie's eyes narrowed as she read a boldly headlined article on the front page. Another newsboy had been beaten and robbed, his papers slashed. He was the fifth newsboy so far to be injured.

Byrch must be livid, Callie thought. These were his boys, and she knew he suspected one of the rival papers retaliating against his support of a typesetters' labor union. The *Clarion-Observer* was doing its best to find the guilty parties, all to no avail. Jimmy Riley, once a newsboy himself, called the men behind these acts "sharks." Byrch, more vocal on the subject, referred to them as "bastards." And all because Byrch was one-hundred percent behind the National Typographical Union. Trouble had been brewing ever since the New York Printers Union was represented at the National Convention of Printers in December of 1850, but nothing so violent as these recent incidents.

Callie felt tears sting her eyes as she read about the newsboy's injuries. A broken shoulder, cuts and abrasions, and head injuries. Cracked ribs and a shoe lost in the scuffle. That was a touch from Jimmy Riley, she was sure of it. Make the reader sympathetic. Child gets beaten and loses shoe as he tries to fight off his attackers in defense of his job. How the child's family must feel was something with which Callie could identify. In most cases a newsboy's money helped his family to stay alive. Food and clothing, the necessities of life, provided by an eight-year-old child.

Someone should talk to the parents of the boys and write a story on how they felt. A follow-up with comments from the other boys would add more meat. Strong measures were called for, and a brief column on the front page wasn't going to help Byrch stop the beatings. People had to rally to a cause; their heartstrings had to be tugged.

Callie sat turning the information over and over in her mind, exploring different approaches to the story. The plight of the *Clarion*'s newsboys pushed all other thoughts from her mind. On impulse, she dropped the paper and ran up to her room, rummaging in the depths of her dresser drawer for her pad of paper and the articles she had written. Sitting cross-legged on her bed, she read and reread what she'd written, looking for flaws and contradictions, judging the quick, crackling style she had adopted from reading other reporters, especially Byrch. In her opinion, her work was every bit as good as what appeared in the *Clarion* day after day. Byrch had recently been directing his editorials to political issues, especially labor unions. It seemed a lifetime ago since he'd put his men to drawing stories of the human condition within the city, to describing and reforming the plights of the immigrant. It also seemed to Callie that there was a sorry absence of human-interest stories; most of the articles simply reported the news and events.

If a writer took cold, hard facts and added the human element, the story would carry weight and impact. She could do it. She knew she could. Would Byrch give her a chance? Not likely. Convention stood in her way. Women were simply not hired as newspaper reporters; the female contribution to journalism was relegated to the poetry corner on the last page or the society column. Besides, it was obvious that Byrch considered her only talents to be those of the oldest profession, and when their arrangement came to an end, she would be out of his life forever. His house and his newspaper would be off limits.

Callie dressed with great care, hurrying to be ready before Byrch came home from the paper. She brushed her hair to a sheen, lifting it from the back of her neck the way he liked, looping it into a loose knot, while allowing wispy curls to escape onto her brow and in front of her ears. From the cherry armoire she selected one of the dresses Byrch had commissioned for her. This one was a lightweight fabric of lilac silk organza with a fitted bodice and sheer puffed sleeves. The neckline was inset with ivory lace, which was repeated into an apron effect in the front and gathered into tiered ruffles in back. She'd never worn it, but when she first showed it to him, she'd seen the glow in his eyes. Ivory slippers, white hose held with pale blue garters, and a thin ribbon tied at her throat. She diminished the glow on her face by a sparing application of rice powder and touched pomade to her lips.

When Byrch arrived home, she met him at the door, and he caught her up in his arms. "You're a breath of fresh air," he told her, making her twirl to show off her dress. "You're beautiful, and I want to show you off. Why don't I take you out for dinner?"

Callie's spirits soared. She was well-aware of the difficulties down at the paper, and he must be exhausted with worry and outrage, but he wanted to take her out and show her off. It seemed so long since she'd been out of the house that she was eager for it.

While Byrch was upstairs cleaning up, Callie went into the kitchen to break the news to Edward. The man would have every right to be angry that his carefully prepared dinner would go unappreciated. Instead Edward broke into a wide, toothy grin. "Don't you worry, Miss Callie, there's nothing that won't keep for tomorrow. And you look so pretty, it's no wonder Mr. Kenyon wants to show you off."

Callie glowed with Edward's praise. "At least let me help you clear the kitchen," she told him apologetically. "It's the least I can do."

"Not at all. I won't hear of you chancing a spill on your dress," he told her. "I've already had my dinner, so I think I'll go over to Dr. Jameson's and see if Anatole is busy tonight. I think I've got a new chess move that'll set his teeth on edge." Edward winked. "Now you just go out and sit in the parlor, and I'll go upstairs and hurry Mr. Kenyon."

Byrch came downstairs resplendent in light gray slacks and coat, set off by an emerald-green waistcoat and sparkling white stock. Edward had shined his boots to a gleam, and the modest diamond cuff links winked in the early evening light. He almost took her breath away as he held the shawl Edward had handed him and wrapped it around her shoulders, bending his head to nip at the tender flesh where her neck met shoulder. For an instant she allowed herself to lean back against him, reveling in the feel of his lean, hard length against her. It had been nearly a week since he'd come to her room, and she missed him terribly in spite of herself.

The carriage waited outside, and Byrch sat beside Callie while they drove through the city's streets. "I've been in New York nearly two years, and I've yet to see the city," Callie said. "It's so big and so busy, and I'm always amazed at your familiarity with it."

"I've lived here most of my life," he told her, "I should know it." His answer was terse, a direct contradiction in mood to what it had been when he'd arrived home. "I'm sorry, Callie. I didn't mean to be sharp. You must have read about what's happening to my newsboys. Forgive me?"

"Forgiven. Where are we going?"

"To a little place I know where there's music and candlelight, and I think you'll like it. The cuisine is French, and their wines are superb."

The little restaurant was just as Byrch described it, and the service was impeccable. Throughout dinner, Byrch and Callie kept to the terms of their truce, talking about ideas and events and never letting the subject become personal. Feelings and emotions were too guarded and too vulnerable to discuss openly.

Over dessert, Callie sensed that Byrch was becoming more and more distracted. She put her elbows on the table and leaned toward him. "You're thinking about the boys, aren't you?"

"Yes," he answered somberly, pushing his plate away. "I'm

sorry, Callie. I wanted to make this evening especially pleasant for you."

"Don't apologize, Byrch. I read the paper today; I know what you're up against."

"Wait until you read tomorrow's paper," he said harshly. "Three more boys attacked early this morning, and one of them is in critical condition. Seven years old. Seven goddamned years old! I have every man I can spare out looking for some lead, some clue. I'd give anything if I didn't have to go off to Cincinnati day after tomorrow, but there's no help for it. I'm one of three representatives from the New York Association selected to attend the National Typographical Convention. This could be a breakthrough for labor unions throughout the country, and I believe in it. Politically it could be quite advantageous to me when I launch my campaign. Still I wish to blazes I didn't have to go and leave the paper just now."

"Won't Kevin Darcy look after things for you?"

"Kevin Darcy is a fool! I'd sooner trust Jimmy Riley's baby brother with the *Clarion* than trust Kevin. But he does own a share of the paper, and my hands are tied. Kevin sees the *Clarion* as a hobby, a distraction from his social activities rather than a responsibility. I go away, he plays publisher, I come back and clean up after him." Byrch scowled.

"Is there anything I can do?"

Byrch smiled, his eyes softening, "Yes," he told her, reaching to touch her hand, "just be here when I get back."

Callie's eyes widened in surprise, and she was about to ask him why he thought she might not be, but the waiter arrived at that moment, and the opportunity was lost.

It was quite late when Byrch and Callie left the little restaurant, and although she knew he must be tired from his long and troubled day at the *Clarion*, he suggested a ride through the city along the river drive. The streets were blanketed with that thin, early summer haze that drifts in low swirls near the pavement and creates haloes around the lamplights. The sound of the horse's hoofs on the cobbles seemed muffled as they wended through the quiet avenues. They felt a sense of isolation, far from other people and their busy lives, and it drew them closer.

Byrch wrapped his arm around Callie, tipping her head to rest against his shoulder. He breathed the fragrance of her hair and relished the feel of her against him. He regretted that he had given voice to his concerns for the paperboys and Kevin Darcy. He hadn't wanted to spoil this evening for her. He should have been more attentive, more courtly. Next time, he promised himself. He would do better next time.

Callie rested her head against Byrch's shoulder, aware of the way their thighs were pressed close together. She was glad he'd confided his problems at the paper; it made her feel closer to him, more involved in his life. They had been themselves tonight, talking about things that mattered instead of light, meaningless subjects. Sighing, she pressed her cheek against the fabric of his coat. He would come to her tonight and take her into his arms to make love to her. And she would be there, waiting for him.

The horse clopped along Riverside Drive in the still, early morning hours. Byrch tapped on the bulkhead above him and signaled for the driver to stop in the lane that followed the river's edge. "Would you like to walk, Callie?"

Smiling her acceptance, he helped her out of the carriage and took her hand, leading her along the path under the trees that lined the parkway. Benches lined the path overlooking the water. The wispy mists hung close to the water's edge, but the moon high overhead cast its silvery radiance to light their way.

"I remember that park in Dublin where you took your brothers and sisters," he murmured. "It overlooked the water too. I remember thinking you were like a little fairy godmother looking after the little ones."

Callie laughed softly, deep and throaty, so different from the lilting, girlish sound she'd made when she was just sixteen. Byrch wondered if she knew how enthralling the sound of her laughter could be. "That was Florham Park," she told him. "And I wasn't much of a fairy godmother to let little Billy get away from me that way. If you hadn't come along, the Lord only knows how I'd have gotten him out through that cellar window."

"You would have gotten him out. You were quite an enterprising young lady, if I remember correctly." He punctuated his statement with a squeeze of his hand.

"Enterprising, perhaps, but a young lady? I doubt it. I was hardly more than a street urchin, brash and willful. Little wonder Mum sent me off to America. It took Mrs. Powers and all her strength to make a lady out of me. At times I wondered if it was more painful and frustrating to her or to me."

"You really were a little rapscallion," Byrch agreed, laughing softly, some part of himself melancholy for that little lost girl with the wide summer-blue eyes and defiant, upturned nose. "It seems so long ago, doesn't it? So much has happened since then."

"Hmmm. A lifetime," Callie agreed.

They walked almost to the end of the parkway before turning back toward the carriage. They reminisced and laughed and shared those silly little things that are the joy of long-time friends. They felt connected to one another, whole and complete. It was like old times, before the talk of debts and strange arrangements and uncertainties.

Callie sighed with contentment as Byrch climbed into the carriage beside her. This evening had been perfect. Especially this quiet walk along the river. She had no apprehension about enjoying this time between them. They had been as old friends, enjoying one another. That kind of happiness was allowed to her, she decided. It was the other, the commitment, that she feared. The fates that directed her life had never been so kind or forgiving that she could risk reaching out for happiness with Byrch. For now, she would live with the arrangement, and if she secretly treasured each little memory of this time with him, knowing it must come to an inevitable end, she could not be blamed.

On the ride home, the carriage turned onto lower Broadway, only blocks away from the *Clarion*. Callie was nestled in Byrch's arms, luxuriating in her contentment, feeling his lips brush occasionally across her brow. Suddenly, she became aware of a change in his relaxed posture. There was a tightening of the muscles in his shoulder and a contraction in the hardness of his thigh. Taking his arm from around her, he jolted forward and rapped on the bulkhead above him to alert the driver. "Stop at the next corner, George!"

Puzzled, Callie peered out the window through the mists to what had caught his attention. Beneath a lamppost a young boy was hunkered down, working with a bundle of the morning edition of newspapers. One of Byrch's newsboys? "What time is it?" she asked. "What's that boy doing out on the corner this time of night?"

"Shhh!" Byrch cautioned. "It's not that time of night. It's closer to morning. There are only so many delivery wagons, and the boys have to be out early to meet their delivery of papers. Right now he's setting up for the early trade of vendors and factory workers," he whispered.

"But what's wrong?" Callie asked, alarmed.

"I think I saw something, and I only want to check on it. You stay here in the carriage. George will watch over you."

By the time the carriage had pulled over to the next corner, Byrch was in the street, hugging the walls of the buildings, keeping to the shadows. Callie watched him move, sensing his alertness. She knew there was danger. Unable to sit in the safety of the carriage a minute longer, she slid cautiously down to the street, following the course Byrch had set for himself. Ahead of her, Byrch had reached the corner, and she saw him press himself against the brick wall of a building, standing frozen and alert. When she was almost beside him, he turned, gesturing for her to go back, anger glittering in his eyes.

Callie shook her head, ignoring his command. She could hear voices from just around the corner. The mists swirled close to the street, making it wet and reflective. "This ain't your corner anymore, kid! Get moving unless you wanna end up like some of your friends!" It was a man's voice, thick with an Irish brogue and somehow distantly familiar to Callie.

"This here's my corner," a child's voice protested bravely. "Whyn't cha leave me alone? I didn't do nothin'."

"That's right, and you ain't gonna do nothin'. Not here, anyhow," a second man's voice challenged. "Now get on with you, or somebody's gonna get hurt! Show your face here again, and it'll be the last time. Understand?"

Callie heard the sound of papers rustling, and an instant later she saw the bundle thrown into the street, scattering about like leaves before an autumn wind. Her first thought was for the newsboy. Feisty as he was, he had to be frightened being muscled by two grown men.

"Empty your pockets, lad, and get on your way!"

It was then that Byrch moved. He was around the side of the building as though he'd been shot from a cannon. His fists were raised and ready.

The next few minutes seemed the longest of Callie's life as she watched in astonishment: fists were flying, grunts of pain filled the still night air as Byrch met his adversaries in the darkness. The newsboy cowered against the building, watching wide-eyed. Callie reached for him, bringing him out of harm's way. She told him to run for a policeman, fast as he could run. Without a word, the boy was off, quicker than lightning; Callie hoped he would get back in time. Byrch might be fighting for his life. These men were criminals.

Byrch had hold of one of the men, grabbing him by the shirtfront, bloodying his nose with his other fist. The other thug was lifting himself from the ground, coming around behind Byrch.

"Behind you!" Callie shouted, lurching forward ready to defend the rear. She threw herself at the man, fists pummeling ineffectively, but buying Byrch the time he needed. As one man tumbled to the ground, Byrch swung on the other, but not before Callie was thrown against the brick wall, sliding to the ground in a daze.

The fight continued. Callie skittered away from advancing feet and grunting men. Byrch's face was bloodied, and his coat was torn. The fighting was terrible. The men's movements were slowing, becoming sluggish, yet still they battled, landing blows, dodging others. Callie wanted to cover her eyes, block her ears, but she stared in fascination, feeling each blow that landed on Byrch as though she'd suffered it herself. Where was the boy? Where were the police? Was that a whistle she heard in the distance?

Behind her, footsteps. Quickly Callie turned, expecting another thug coming to help his friends. It was George, Byrch's driver. The old man immediately sized up the situation and went to the downed man who was just lifting himself from the ground. Something glinted in the lamplight, and George stepped hard on the man's arm. Callie heard a curse of pain. She saw that George was holding a pistol that he'd taken from the man.

"Help him, George!" she pleaded. "Help Byrch!"

"Mr. Kenyon's doing all right, miss. Give him a chance to finish the job."

True to George's word, Byrch backed the man against the wall, sending a final blow to his gut and another to his jaw. Callie saw him crumple like dead wood, sliding against the wall to fall to the ground. Byrch stopped to catch his breath, taking huge gulps of air, his chest heaving with the effort. His face was bloody, his knuckles raw. He staggered over to George and hauled the man he was holding to his feet, mercilessly dragging him alongside his cohort and pinning him to the wall. Police whistles sounded in the distance, coming closer now.

Callie went to Byrch, her first thought to inspect his injuries, but the familiar face of the man pinned to the wall stopped her.

"Patrick!" Callie gasped hoarsely. "Patrick Thatcher!"

Byrch glanced at Callie, one eye already swollen, his lip cut and bleeding. "Know him, Callie?" he gasped, still breathless.

"Byrch, this is Patrick Thatcher, or at least that's who he was when I first met him and his family in Liverpool. Remember Beth, my friend who jumped off the pier with her baby rather than deny her husband a chance at his dream? This is the man she did it for." Callie's eyes measured Patrick, clear and level, watching him squirm under her scrutiny. "He was going to shoot you, Byrch. George took the pistol away from him."

For a long, sad moment, Callie stared at Patrick. He was still handsome, but there was cruelty in his eyes and about his mouth that hadn't been there when Beth was alive. "Tell me, Patrick, was this your dream? Was this why Beth and Paddy died? My God, some of those newsboys are no older than Paddy would be."

Patrick turned his head, unwilling to face her. "I don't know what you're talkin' about. I wasn't doin' nothin'." He issued a gasp when Byrch bounced him against the wall.

"Who hired you, Thatcher," Byrch demanded. "Who's paying you?"

Slowly Patrick turned his head to peer at Callie. "You look like you did all right for yourself," he sneered. "Dressed in fancy clothes, all done up real pretty. What would you know about goin' hungry, about suffering, losing somebody you love?"

Callie turned her head, shoulders slumping. Byrch waited for her to tell Thatcher that she knew about hunger, about losing a child. Instead she stood there, still as death. Then in a deadly voice she asked, "Who's paying you, Patrick? Who do you work for?"

"Myself. Pat Thatcher works for no man! I've got an association of newsboys, and they pay me to protect them and their territory. When I knew the *Clarion* was standing behind the union, I branched out a little."

Callie thought she'd be sick. The sounds of running feet broke the stillness as two uniformed policemen rounded the corner, followed by the little newsboy.

After Patrick and his friend had been taken away, Callie and Byrch stood on the corner, watching the sunlight the morning sky. "You come down to the paper later this afternoon and get your reward for being so quick in getting the police," Byrch said, clapping little Kenneth O'Toole on the shoulder. "And don't worry about your papers. We'll handle all that at the *Clarion*."

"Aren't you going to say thank you to Mr. Kenyon?" Callie prompted.

"Mr. Kenyon? The real Mr. Kenyon? Jeez! Wait'll I tell the fellas! Am I really gonna get a reward?"

"You bet," Byrch laughed, wincing with the pain to his cut and swollen lips. "You just come and see me, and I'll take care of it myself."

"Can't we go down there now and get it?" the boy asked eagerly "It ain't every day I get a reward."

"Not now, son. Get on home. I said I'll see you later."

"You won't forget?"

"I won't forget." Byrch threw his arm around Callie and began walking to where George waited in the carriage.

"Hey, Mr. Kenyon. Where you goin' now?"

"Home! To get my reward!" Byrch called over his shoulder, giving Callie a squeeze and smiling softly into her eyes.

By the time George brought them home in the carriage, Edward was already awake and had started the morning coffee. The wonderfully rich aroma wafted through the kitchen as Callie led Byrch into the house. Edward's eyes widened in shock. "What will I do with the both of you?" he asked, shaking his head, helping Byrch up the stairs. "I'll never get used to the sight of you two bringing each other home much the worse for wear. What did you do to him, Miss Callie?"

"Edward, you're worse than a fishwife. I swear, if I even *think* you're laughing at me, I'll send you back to the jungle where I found you!" Byrch grumbled.

Callie tried to hide her smile. "Bring him to his bedroom, Edward. I'll go in and run a tub for him. Did you turn on the gas jet this morning so there'll be hot water?"

"Yes, Miss Callie." In truth, when he'd gone in to light the water heater earlier, he hadn't been surprised to find Byrch's bed empty, simply assuming that his employer was visiting Miss Callie.

"After you get him undressed, I'll be needing some salve and bandages. He's got a nasty bump on the head, and how his pretty nose isn't broken, I'll never know. Perhaps you'd better send for Dr. Jameson and have him take a look."

A loud howl of protest echoed through the hall. "You'll do no such thing! Just remember who pays your wages, Edward. I'll be fine, I will! I won't have the both of you clucking over me like a pair of maiden aunts. Am I clear?"

"Yes, sir, Mr. Kenyon," Edward assured him, leading him down the hall to his bedroom.

"Two old maiden aunts, is it?" Callie quipped. "We'll hold off on Dr. Jameson until this afternoon, but if you're not feeling better, we'll have to say you're out of your head and do what we think is best. Get his shoes off, Edward. I'll see to the bath."

Callie went through Byrch's room to the bath, turning on the tap and testing the water temperature. A hot bath would do Byrch a world of good; otherwise he'd be stiff and sore for days. She gathered additional towels from the linen closet and set them out near the tub. A few moments later she went back to Byrch and found him sitting on the edge of his bed, draped in a towel. "Where's Edward?"

A sly grin spread over Byrch's face until he winced from his split lip. "I sent him downstairs. I told him I didn't need him."

"Oh, you did, did you? And who do you think is going to help you into that tub. You look as though you can hardly stand on your own two feet." Now, in the clear light of morning, she could see the extent of Byrch's injuries. His left eye was swollen, a bloody abrasion marked his cheekbone, his lip was split, and his hands and knuckles bruised and swollen.

"Oh, I thought I might have an old maiden aunt around here who'd take pity on me."

Callie raised a suspicious eyebrow. "Well, let's get on with it." She moved over to him, helping him to his feet to lead him to the bath.

Callie had told herself she wouldn't look, but the temptation was too great. She'd never seen a man like this, in such personal surroundings. Byrch's body had become as familiar to her as her own during these past weeks, but she'd never seen him so unguarded, so natural. Now she admired the smooth line of his broad back and the heaviness of the muscles in his upper arm. His legs were long, straight, well-muscled, and defined. And his buttocks rode high and round and firm.

Byrch sank into the tub and looked at her. "Why, Callie, you're blushing!"

Angry that he'd noticed, she denied it, declaring it was the heat of the room that flushed her cheeks. "I'm going to change out of this dress. I'm afraid it's ruined," she told him, showing him the rent in the skirt and the stains from being pushed against the rough brick wall. "I'm certain Aggie didn't design this dress with a street brawl in mind. I'll just be a minute."

"When you come back, why don't you join me? There's room enough for two?" His devilish smile, combined with his black eye and swollen cheeks, made him look laughable.

"If you could see yourself, Byrch, you wouldn't think yourself so irresistible! How will you explain your condition when you go to Cincinnati?"

"Let me worry about that." The fight, while it had bruised him, had also been exhilarating. He didn't suppose she'd understand that, but a man would have no trouble knowing how he felt. There was something primal about a fight. Something ancient. Now that the fight was over, it was time to drag his woman off to his cave.

A few minutes later Callie returned, kneeling beside the tub and soaping a washcloth to scrub his back. At her touch, Byrch sighed with contentment. Her attentions went to his neck and shoulders, swathing his chest. "You're getting the sleeves of your robe wet. Why don't you take it off?"

"You're the one who's supposed to get the bath, not me!" she protested, but there was a heat in her eyes and her hands lingered on his chest.

"I don't see how you can properly bathe me unless you come in here with me."

"When a man gives a dog a bath, does he climb in with the dog?"

"That's very unkind of you, Callie," he teased, grasping her hand and smoothing it beneath the surface of the water along the flat of his stomach.

"Surely there are some things you can wash yourself!"

"Surely," he murmured, bringing his mouth so very close to her ear, sending chills up her spine. "But you see, I know your abilities, and you've spoiled me." Turning, he undid the sash of her robe and pulled it off her shoulders. She was naked except for her nightgown. "Hmmm," he nuzzled the flesh of her neck, "were you planning on going to bed?"

"Ye . . . yes," she stammered.

"And whose bed did you plan to sleep in, sweeting?"

"My own," she breathed, turning her face to kiss him softly, careful of his bruised mouth.

"And did you plan to sleep alone?" His hand found the curve of her breast and discovered the rosy pink crest stiffening beneath his palm.

"Plans change," she whispered, turning full into his arms, sliding her hands around his back, excited by the feel of his wet, soap-slicked skin.

She felt him lift her, sliding her over the edge of the porcelain tub, bringing her, nightgown and all, into his lap. His arms were strong and hard around her, keeping her from struggling out of his embrace. Her nightgown was soaked, the thin cotton fabric revealing her as though she wore nothing. "Keep still, sweeting. You're like a scalded cat. Don't you know by now that I'd never hurt you?"

He turned her about to face him. She was a pretty picture, with her hair askew and hanging in long ringlets about her face and her wet nightgown clinging to her breasts. "First of all, we don't want you to catch cold," he told her, mimicking her maiden aunt tone of voice and pulling her nightgown over her head.

Embarrassed and excited at the same time, Callie crossed her arms over her naked breasts and slid down into the steaming water.

Byrch pretended indifference as he soaped the washcloth and began lathering her shoulders and arms. Soap bubbles decorated her throat and chest like frothy jewels. Meticulously he washed each finger and hand, smoothing upward on her arms. Callie luxuriated in the sensation, excited by the intimacy. Lifting one of her legs, he tickled the soles of her feet and lathered her legs, dipping under the water and stroking up her thighs to where they met her body.

The warm water and the methodical massage brought Callie to a state of careless pleasure. She allowed him access to her breasts, to the curve of her back, to the roundness of her bottom. She closed her eyes against those tiger eyes watching her every reaction, his hands returning again and again to those places that seemed to bring her the most pleasure.

"My turn," she told him, her voice low and throaty. With the same care and gentleness, she lathered his body, working from shoulders to chest and beyond. When her hand grazed near the lower belly, she heard him gasp with anticipation before he took the washcloth away from her and declared that the water was growing too cool. But the heat in his eyes and the huskiness of his voice told her there were other reasons he wanted to leave the bath.

Byrch and Callie spent the rest of the day in bed, making love, sleeping, and making love again. Edward discreetly left two trays in the hall outside their respective bedrooms. But they ate together in Byrch's bed and made love again, holding each other long into the night.

It was difficult for Callie to believe it was morning when the sun shone through the draperies. Byrch was already up and about. "What are you doing?" she asked.

"Packing, sweeting. I leave for Cincinnati this morning on the ten o'clock train."

"This morning? But you said day after tomorrow . . ."

Byrch quirked a dark brow. "Yes, and that's what today is. When I told you that, it wasn't morning yet. Yesterday we spent the entire day in bed, and here it is morning again."

"I'll get up and have breakfast with you."

"No time. I've got an errand to run first, and then I'll catch my train. Go back to sleep, it's still too early to be up and about."

Callie watched him rummage through his dresser, pulling out shirts and selecting waistcoats from the armoire. She was still filled with delicious sensations, and in spite of herself, her eyes closed in sleep. She stirred beneath the feather-light touch of his lips to her cheeks. She purposely kept her eyes closed, pretending sleep. She couldn't bear to see Byrch leave, even for a short time. She was already feeling the loss. She had to keep reminding herself that this was a temporary situation. The time would soon come when she would have to leave him. The fight with Patrick Thatcher and the sudden appearance of a pistol served as a reminder to her that she was only courting disaster if she stepped out of her place and reached for this happiness.

Chapter Twenty-Seven

After a long, luxurious bath, Callie dressed for the day, selecting a soft, gray linen dress trimmed with black braid. The bodice was simply cut, following her slim figure, and there was a rib-hugging overjacket with wide lapels and frogged closing. The jacket was trimmed with the black braid, as were the seams of the six-gored skirt. Callie added neat black gloves, kid shoes, and a small hat in the same gray styled with a snap brim made feminine by the addition of a black velvet ribbon and gossamer veiling. Her hair was drawn up into a soft puff, wispy ringlets falling near her cheeks and at her temples. The mirror told her she looked as stylish as any Fifth Avenue socialite.

Downstairs in the kitchen, she found Edward beginning to prepare a tray. "Oh, Miss Callie! How pretty you look!" Edward approved of her costume, but it was the glow in her cheeks and the soft expression around her mouth and in her eyes that he was really admiring. "I was about to bring you a tray."

"I'd rather have coffee here with you," she told him, seating herself at the kitchen table.

Edward transferred the cup and plate of breakfast rolls from the tray to the table. "Going out this morning, Miss Callie?"

Callie spooned sugar into her coffee. "It looked like such a nice day I thought I would, but I've got to confess, I have nowhere to go."

"Well, perhaps you might save me an errand," Edward offered. "Mr. Kenyon left an envelope with me to bring to the paper for someone named Kenneth O'Toole. He said he would have seen to it himself yesterday, only he was busy nursing his wounds."

Callie's face flushed, but there was nothing in Edward's face that could be taken as a judgment for spending the entire day in bed with Byrch.

"Kenneth O'Toole? Oh, yes," she said, beaming, "the little newsboy! I'll be glad to take it down to the *Clarion* for you, Edward." Now she had somewhere to go. She loved the *Clarion* with its frantic energy and the sound of the presses roaring in the background so that everyone had to raise their voices a pitch or two. She saw Edward's questioning glance. "Didn't Byrch tell you about Kenneth O'Toole, and what happened the other night?"

Edward shook his head. "No, I'm afraid there wasn't time to converse with Mr. Kenyon. Was it Mr. O'Toole who's responsible for Mr. Kenyon's injuries?"

"Well, pour yourself a cup of coffee, Edward, and sit down. Wait until you hear!" Callie related their experiences, leaving out no detail, even telling him about Patrick Thatcher.

Edward listened in rapt attention, cheering Byrch's boldness, becoming quiet when Callie told him how she knew Patrick Thatcher, and laughing when she described the little newsboy's suspicion that Byrch would cheat him out of his reward. Wiping tears of laughter from his eyes, Edward said, "Miss Callie, you've got a way with words. You made me feel as though I were there! I guess that's what's in the envelope for little Master O'Toole. It's his reward, and I'll bet he's haunting the front desk waiting for it!"

"I'll bet. But didn't you read any of this in the *Clarion*, Edward?"

"No, miss. How could I? The only reporter on the scene was Mr. Kenyon, and he never wrote the story." He was quick to see the sudden speculation in Callie's blue eyes. "Now, Miss Callie, don't do anything you'll be sorry for," he warned.

Dusting crumbs from her hands and pulling on her gloves, Callie asked for the envelope. "We can't keep little Kenneth waiting, can we, Edward? Don't bother going up to the corner for a cab, I think I'll walk to the *Clarion*."

"Yes, miss. But let me give you some cash in case you'd like to do a little shopping." He stood, going to the jar over the sink and extracting several dollars and change.

Callie dropped the money into her purse without counting it. She was eager to get to the paper and deliver the reward into the hands of the littlest hero, and she found herself already structuring sentences in her mind. Edward was usually right about most things, but he was wrong to think that Byrch was the *only* reporter on the scene.

Callie walked through the doors of the *Clarion-Observer*. If only this could be her world. The sound, the bustle, the smell of raw paper and printer's ink. This strange, wonderful, noisy place was a world unto its own. At the end of her arrangement with Byrch, Callie knew she would need something to fill her loss, to occupy her mind and make demands on her talents. Something that would involve her totally. Her dreams of being a contributing writer for a newspaper seemed real and obtainably close just being here where it all happened.

Callie garnered a few stares of admiration from the seasoned reporters and more than one whistle of approval from the audacious copy boys. She held her good humor, smiling, waving to show she wasn't offended. They all liked her, she knew, and being squired on Byrch's arm certainly hadn't hurt. It was here on these presses that Byrch had published the account of her immigration. He had made a subscription in her name and had mailed it to the island when she worked for the Powers family, and she had read every issue. Even Hugh had brought her the day-old paper back from McGovern's. Callie felt as though she personally knew the reporters whose names appeared at the head of the articles. She was familiar with the shops and businesses that advertised.

Sighing, Callie realized that Byrch would never approve of her becoming a part of this paper, especially after their arrangement was over. He wouldn't want to have her around, and it wasn't his policy to hire women.

"How are you today, Jimmy?" Callie asked, pushing aside her aspirations to greet young Riley, who manned the front desk.

"Miss Callie! I'm fine. What brings you down to the *Clarion*?" Jimmy's freckles seemed to multiply with the deepening flush on his face when she smiled at him, almost matching the red of his hair.

"I've brought an envelope for Master Kenneth O'Toole."

"You mean that little kid who keeps coming in here asking after Mr. Kenyon?"

Callie laughed. "The one and the same. He's expecting his reward for valor, and I suspect he won't be cheated of it."

"Reward?" Jimmy's face narrowed into lines of inquiry.

"You don't know, do you? You don't know Byrch caught the men behind the beatings of the *Clarion's* newsboys."

"Worse than beatings." Jimmy frowned. "One of the kids died yesterday."

Callie was stricken. Patrick had done this.

Jimmy quickly went to her side. "Are you all right, Miss Callie? Maybe you should have a seat in Mr. Kenyon's office?"

Callie gulped, nodding her head. She felt her knees buckle under her. Patrick was a murderer, and his victim was a little boy. A little boy like Rory would have been. She allowed herself to be led into Byrch's office and sat in the deep chair behind his desk. Jimmy rushed out and brought her a glass of water.

When she'd regained her composure, she began to tell Jimmy about the events of the other night and then stopped in mid-sentence. "Jimmy, Mr. Kenyon wasn't the only reporter on the scene that night. I was there too. And since he didn't bother to write it, it wouldn't be as though I was stealing his thunder, now would it?"

"Reporter? You, Miss Callie?"

"Yes, me. Or at least I hope to be." Callie's eyes were already scanning the desktop for pen, ink, and paper. "Jimmy, you give me an hour, and I'll have that story ready for publication."

"I . . . I don't know . . ."

"That's right, you don't know anything. No one will have to know I wrote it . . . I'll use a pen name. C. James. That's what the byline will read, C. James," she repeated, liking the sound of it.

Jimmy's doubts were revealed in the grim line of his mouth and the creases over his eyes. "Listen, Jimmy, if it's not any good when I'm finished, then it won't be printed. But it's going to be good!" She was reaching for paper and pen, dipping the nib into the inkwell.

It took her longer than she thought, but two-and-a-half hours later, the story was ready. She sailed out of Byrch's office and dropped the pages on Jimmy's desk, watching him carefully as he read it. She studied his face: sympathy for the newsboys, disgust for the criminals, admiration for Byrch, and laughter for her vivid description of Kenneth O'Toole, the littlest hero. When he finally looked up, there was a new light in Jimmy's eyes—respect and admiration.

"I'll say one thing for you, C. James, you sure can write!"

Callie was so happy she wanted to crow. "That's just your opinion, Jimmy, and I'm sure you're too kind. Why don't you just sneak that into editorial, and then we'll go have lunch. My treat."

Jimmy Riley took Callie to a little coffeehouse on the next corner. He ordered two ham sandwiches, coffee, and pie. Theirs was a celebratory mood as they ate and talked, speculating on whether or not her story would pass the stringent requirements of the editorial department.

"If I know anything, Miss Callie, it's that you did a real fine piece of work and the news is hot! It's going to be in the next edition, you mark my words!"

Callie hoped Jimmy wasn't overestimating her talents just because he was a bit smitten with her.

"You know, you shouldn't stop there. There's a whole follow-up line," Jimmy said. "Mr. Kenyon always says no story is ever told until it's told to the finish."

"You mean follow up on little Kennth O'Toole, tell about his family and what he wants to be when he grows up and what he's going to do with his reward? And then there's the other boys, how they're getting along, and the story about the murdered newsboy." Callie's voice was bubbling with excitement. "And don't forget about that Newsboys' Association Patrick Thatcher talked about. As a reader, I'd want to know how it affected other boys, the ones who paid out for that so-called protection."

"You've got it, Miss Callie. A real nose for news!"

Callie laughed. "Now you sound like Byrch Kenyon."

Still, the idea excited her. And with Byrch away in Ohio, it was the perfect opportunity. "Jimmy, what's on your agenda today? Can you come with me? I'd like to interview those boys, meet their families. You know most of them, don't you? It would be a great help. I don't know how willing they'd be to talk to a woman who claims to be a reporter. And since I don't officially work for the *Clarion*, but you do, it wouldn't be a lie to say we're from the paper."

Jimmy groaned. "Miss Callie, you've got a lot to learn. Reporters will do anything for a good story, and lying is the least of it." But Callie's enthusiasm was contagious, and Jimmy willingly agreed. "I have a few things to do at the paper, and I'll have to let the copy desk know I'll be gone. Why don't you wait here and finish your coffee, and I'll be back in no time."

When Jimmy returned, he brought her a list of the newsboys who had been beaten or threatened, and their addresses. Hailing a cab, Jimmy and Callie were on their way to the home of Petey Smith, the little boy who lay in serious condition at the city hospital.

Callie swallowed hard when the front door of the dark, second-floor tenement opened. She felt for a moment as though she were looking at her own mother. Petey's mother had the same weary eyes, the same drawn look. The front of her apron was clutched in both hands as she stared at the couple on her doorstep. The weary, frightened eyes told Callie the woman was expecting to see someone from the hospital telling her that Petey was gone. The lump in Callie's throat made it impossible for her to speak. She reached out a hand and touched the woman's shoulder. It was Jimmy who blurted out the reason for their visit. The relief on the woman's face was instantaneous.

Ellen Smith invited them into a clean, shabby parlor. Callie accepted the offer of tea, knowing that Mrs. Smith needed to do something. She was back in minutes with what Callie knew were her best dishes. "Tell us what happened to Petey. Was he able to talk to you?"

"There's not much to be telling you, ma'am. I didn't want Petey out there selling papers, but his oldest brother convinced me it was all right. I have eight mouths to feed, ma'am, and it takes a bit of money in these hard times." Callie knew how hard Mrs. Smith worked, and that the reason she wasn't at the hospital this minute was probably the piece work she did, turning and stitching the shirt collars that were stacked near the treadle sewing machine. "Petey liked it," she continued, "and was so pleased that every once in a while some of the fine gents tipped him a few pennies for his perky smile and easy wit. He's only seven, ma'am, still a baby. My man died three years ago, and we've been living hand to mouth ever since." She dabbed at her eyes, her face full of guilt for sending her son out on the streets to help provide for the family. Callie moved off the chair and dropped to her knees. She gathered the woman close, pretending it was Peggy she was comforting. Jimmy looked away to hide his feelings.

"Did Petey know the man who beat him up? Did he say anything about a Newsboys' Association?" Callie asked.

"Ma'am, Petey never said a word. He's hurt bad. Those bastards—excuse my language, but that's what they are—beat him up and left him to die. They stole his money and destroyed his papers. He's just a baby," the woman sobbed. Callie held her close, stroking her back. Jimmy blew his nose lustily.

"Someone from the paper will be by to speak with you and

to . . . to leave you some money. We'll do right by Petey, won't we, Jimmy? This will help for now." Callie took a bill from her reticule.

Rash promises like this one could mean trouble, Jimmy thought. He wasn't sure of the paper's policy on something like this. He knew if he was the managing editor, he would take care of Petey and his family. Byrch Kenyon was something else. What the hell, he had already thrown caution to the winds, so why was he quibbling about the paper's money now? "Absolutely," he agreed. He could only be fired once. Callie would put in a good word for him with Mr. Kenyon.

Ellen Smith clung to Callie for a moment. "I know what you must be feeling," Callie whispered. "I promise you, I'll do everything I can for Petey and the others. Thank you for the tea."

"We didn't learn anything," Jimmy said in dismay as they left the shabby building.

"That's true. But I wanted to see Petey's mother. I wanted to see what she looked like and to find out how she felt so I can write about her and Petey. I can't write something if I don't know about it, now can I?"

"Where to now?" Jimmy asked.

Callie swallowed hard. "We're going to Timmy Jacobs's house, the newsboy who died. I'd give anything if we didn't have to go, but we do. You are going to have to say something to the parents in behalf of the paper. Say and offer whatever you think is right. I'll talk to Byrch when he gets back. Be fair, Jimmy. From there we're going to the hospital to see Petey."

A stoop-shouldered man, bent from years of hard work, stood by the open door of the Jacobs's flat. He was dressed in a stiff blue suit and an even stiffer white shirt. Callie knew the suit and tie would be what he'd be buried in when his time came. Jimmy shook hands with the man, and Callie nodded. She didn't want to be here. It was too soon. Too soon to have to go through this emotional turmoil. But she knew the devil and the hounds of hell on her heels couldn't have stopped her from walking into the Jacobs's front parlor. The small coffin and lighted candles almost made her turn and run. A small woman dressed in a heavy black dress sat on a wooden kitchen chair. Her hands were knotted in her lap as she twisted and untwisted a pleat of her skirt. She reminded Callie of a blackbird who has lost its courage to fly. Callie forced herself to stare at the small boy in the coffin. Blood roared in her veins, and her heart threatened to leap from her chest as she stared down at the small form. How still. Never to breathe again. Never to speak to his parents, never to laugh, to cry, to play again. He hadn't even lived, this child. His life was over even before he had a chance to find out what life was all about, and Patrick Thatcher had done this. Callie whispered to Jimmy, "You speak with Mr. Jacobs, and I'll talk to his wife."

It took Callie five minutes to realize the woman sitting on the chair wasn't hearing a word she said. She was in a world of her own, locked in tight with her grief. There was nothing she could do right now, but later, after the funeral, she would come back and talk to Mrs. Jacobs. She was startled when the woman turned and stared at her with vague eyes. "Doesn't Timmy look nice in his suit? He wore it for his First Holy Communion. His father was so proud of him. He's just sleeping, you know." Callie stared down at the woman and wanted to cry for her, to shed tears she knew the woman couldn't shed. She touched her lightly and fled the room. Outside, she took great lungfuls of air. Jimmy watched her, his eyes full of concern. He remembered the tiny body of her son that he'd brought to Byrch Kenyon's house. Why had she tortured herself by coming here?

"Are you all right, Callie?"

"I'm fine, Jimmy. Let's go to the hospital while I still have my courage."

Until she sat back in the carriage and closed her eyes, Callie hadn't realized how draining the experience of the past day had been. She had handled it all with only a few bad moments. Now if she could just get through the next half hour or so, she knew she would be all right.

Jimmy drew a deep sigh. It had been a long day. Now that it was drawing to a close, his worries started flooding back. He should stop by the paper before he went home and see what news there was. Here he was, out all day cavorting with Miss Callie as though he owned the paper. He was going to hear about it, he was sure of it. And all those promises he had made on behalf of the paper and Byrch Kenyon. A groan of dismay escaped him. Callie ignored her companion as she struggled with her own deep, dark thoughts.

The hospital ward was crowded with every bed filled. A cheerful nurse said that Petey Smith was at the end of the first row. "He's improved today, thank the good Lord. Please don't excite or upset him. There's a nurse with him now. One of Petey's brothers just left to take the family the good news that Petey will be fine."

Jimmy was so elated at the news, one would have thought little Petey Smith was his own brother.

Petey Smith lay propped up in a nest of pillows. His small face was black and blue, and one bright blue eye was almost closed. Hair the color of ripe cornsilk drooped over his bandages. "You look like a pirate, young man," Callie teased. "Here, I brought you a present from Mr. Byrch Kenyon." Callie held out a picture book to the little boy and watched his good eye widen in stunned pleasure. "I'm Callie James, and this is Jimmy Riley. We're from the *Clarion-Observer*. We just visited with your mum this afternoon. She's been very worried about you. We were all worried."

"I tried to save the papers, but the men were too big. I kicked one of them. Will you tell Mr. Byrch I did that?"

"Of course we will," Callie said gently. "He's going to be very proud of you."

"They took all my money and even my three pennies tip that Mr. Snyder always gives me on a Friday." Petey seemed eager to talk. "I'm saving those pennies for Mum's birthday. I still have a lot to go, and her birthday is in two weeks. Mum won't mind, but *I* mind," the child said fiercely.

"Can you remember anything else, Petey?" Callie asked. "Did you ever see those men before? Did they ever ask you to join their association?"

Petey blinked. "Yeah! One of those men came around about a month ago, and he said there was some kinda club I had to join. Only he wanted money, and I told him I didn't want no club and didn't want to pay no money. Then he said somethin' about not bein' so snotty and that he was gonna see to it that I didn't have any papers even if I could sell them. I don't know what he was talkin' about. Do you?"

Callie reached out to brush Petey's sandy hair off his brow. "Yes, Petey, I think I do. You're a real hero. We're going to write about you in the newspaper. Won't that make your mum proud?"

Petey shook his head. "Not as proud as if I gave her a shawl for her birthday. Mum says birthdays are for children, but I heard her tell my sister Josephine that she never in her whole life got a present for her birthday. That's why I wanted to get her a special present."

"In two weeks, is it?" Callie asked. Petey nodded. Jimmy winced. Another rash promise from the *Clarion-Observer*. He was going to have to start writing down all the obligations the paper had acquired in one short day. He knew in his gut that Petey's mother was going to have a shawl for her birthday, compliments of Callie and the *Clarion-Observer*. He wondered why he felt so good spending other people's money.

On the fifth day Jimmy made his usual late-night call to pick up Callie's column for the next day. His eyes were merry and full of life. He had something to say and was having a hard time keeping it to himself.

"Tell me. Tell me before your burst," Callie cried.

"Our sales have almost doubled since you started writing your column. People have stopped in as they're walking by to tell us how much they like what you wrote. Parents, grandparents, you name it, they've been in to see us. And here's your mail. People have been writing to thank you for bringing all this out in the open. Mr. Kenyon's cousin, Kevin Darcy, is having an unholy fit, but there isn't a thing he can do. What's important is the profit-and-loss sheet. That's the only thing he understands. Needless to say, no one but me and Edward knows that C. James is you. By the way, there are two letters here that came hand-delivered to the papers. I didn't open them, but," he grinned, "I know who they're from, and I think I know what they say."

"What? Tell me what?" Callie demanded. Never in her life had she gotten mail from anyone but her mother. Now she had a whole sack, plus two very important letters.

"Open them and read for yourself. You wouldn't want me to be spoiling the surprise now, would you?"

Callie ripped at the envelopes one after the other. She quickly read both letters. Tossing them in the air, she squealed in delight and danced around the kitchen. "They're job offers. Real job offers. One of them is offering to pay me twice what the *Clarion-Observer* is paying me. The other one said I could name my own price. Edward! Did you hear that! How much am I making?"

Edward looked at her with surprise. "You did it for nothing!"

"That's right, I did. Well, that's going to stop right now. What am I worth, Jimmy? The truth now. What would twice my salary be? I can't believe this! This has got to be the second-most wonderful thing that's ever happened to me." Edward smirked, and Callie laughed outright. Jimmy looked gleeful and as happy as Callie.

"You wouldn't leave the paper, would you?" Jimmy asked anxiously.

"It depends on how much you're paying her," Edward said craftily.

"But we aren't paying her anything."

"My point exactly, young man. Tomorrow you will return here in the early morning hours with your best offer. Miss Callie and I will confer, but I feel you should know that twice whatever it is sounds most attractive."

"Edward, Mr. Kenyon is the only one who can make that kind of decision."

"You're wrong. Mr. Kenyon's cousin, Kevin Darcy, is now actively running the paper, is that not correct?" At Jimmy's nervous nod, Edward continued. "Then I think it would behoove the *Clarion-Observer* to make a substantial offer before Mr. Kenyon returns. That way we could possibly avoid a lot of problems that might tend to surface upon his return."

"You mean like him not liking it that Callie is working on the paper, her being a woman and all?"

"That is correct," Edward said haughtily. "He would also have to think twice and long and hard before he dismissed her. I think you should take those two letters with you when you return to the paper. I want them returned to Miss Callie tomorrow morning. Do we understand one another, young man?"

"Perfectly." Jimmy grimaced. "Mr. Darcy isn't going to like this."

"We really don't care much about his state of mind. What we're concerned with here at the moment is that Miss Callie take the best offer."

"But, Edward, I couldn't work for a rival paper," Callie exclaimed.

"Of course, you can. A job is a job. Their money is every bit as good as the *Clarion-Observer's* money. Those are the two best papers in the city. Horace Greeley and *The New York Times*! Good Lord, think of it!"

The minute Jimmy left, Edward slumped down on his rocking chair. "I'm glad he's gone. I couldn't have kept that up too much longer."

"Do you think it's a good idea, Edward? Truly, I mean? Byrch is going to explode when he returns."

"It's called having an ace in the hole, Miss Callie. If Mr. Kenyon is adamant about you not working for his paper, then you have choices and options to draw from."

Callie pondered his words and nodded. "I do hope that the *Clarion* hires me. I really don't want to go somewhere else to work. It's what is going to be best for me in the end, though. You're absolutely right, Edward."

"Well, now that that's settled, why don't we have a cup of tea with some brandy before we retire for the night?"

"No thanks, Edward. I just want to go to my room and think about all this and read some of these letters. You don't mind, do you?"

Mind? Thank God that was what she wanted to do. Now he could take the brandy bottle into his room and slurp till his heart was content or till he forgot that *he* was the fine hand behind the two job offers. He was also going to have to do some praying that neither Callie nor Jimmy nor Mr. Kenyon ever found out he was the one who wrote the letters. Sometimes, like now, it didn't pay to think too much.

"Very astute of you, Miss Callie, to know when to call it a day. I think I might just do the same thing myself. Enjoy all your letters, you deserve them."

Callie threw her arms around his neck and hugged him tight. "I'm so happy, Edward. Imagine, Horace Greeley himself taking notice of what I wrote! I think this is one of the greatest moments of my life."

One of the greatest moments of her life indeed. Good God, this could be one of the worst moments of his life if anyone found out that he had written those letters.

Jimmy timed his arrival to coincide with breakfast. He sat down and fluffed out his napkin. "I did it. I convinced Mr. Darcy that you were going to be one of our best reporters. What he can't get through his head is why you want to keep your anonymity. It is peculiar that you, presuming you were a man, wouldn't be working at the paper. It was the two letters, though, that clinched the deal. Mr. Darcy said, and this is a direct quote, 'If he's good enough for Greeley, he's got to be good enough for us.' You're on the payroll as of today. Your salary is fifteen dollars a week. Are you happy?"

"Fifteen dollars? Edward, what do you think? Thirty dollars sounds so much better."

"Take it, take it!" Edward stammered. "You can work your way up to thirty dollars. Keep doing good work and then ask for a raise. Don't forget, those two letters will give you all the bargaining power you'll need later. Stay with the paper that has been good to you."

"Edward's right. I accept."

Edward thought he was going to faint with relief. Now all he had to do was get the letters back before Byrch Kenyon recognized his handwriting. In the meantime, a word of warning wouldn't hurt. "Miss Callie, I don't want to interfere in your business, but I wouldn't show those letters to Mr. Kenyon. It's enough that Jimmy and I saw them, not to mention the others at the paper. It would be like rubbing salt in an open wound."

"As usual, you're absolutely right. It's settled then. Tell me, Jimmy, what else did Byrch's cousin have to say? Am I to do the kind of articles I've been doing?"

"That's what he wants. And I have a message for you from Petey Smith's older brother. He said to tell you he is going to stop by and see you because he has something you might be interested in. I rather think it may have something to do with an idea for another article."

"That's wonderful. Now all we have to worry about is Byrch's return. It should be today or tomorrow at the latest." Her announcement brought instant glumness to the table. Jimmy made his excuses, and Edward almost ran to his room. Callie stared after them. Men could certainly be peculiar. Well, she couldn't worry about that now. Now she had other, more important things to think about. Like her article for tomorrow's paper.

Shortly after the noon hour Joey Smith arrived, his face a mixture of shyness and gratitude. Callie tried to put him at ease by offering him lemonade and cookies. She was going to have to speak to Edward; the cookie supply was dangerously low.

"I want to thank you, ma'am, you and the gentleman for what you did for all of us, me brother Petey in particular. We all got our fingers crossed that the streets are a safe place for us to work now, 'specially for the little kids like me brother. Me Mum was that pleased with the shawl that Petey handed over to her. The kid told Mum it was from the both of us. Now ain't that somethin'?" Joey shifted from one foot to the other and lowered his head shyly, refusing to meet Callie's smiling gaze.

"Hrumph," Edward snorted inelegantly from his position in the kitchen. "Another conquest."

"It certainly is," Callie agreed. "Is there something on your mind, Joey, something you want to talk to me about?"

"Yes, ma'am, there is. Working the corners like we do, we hear bits and pieces of talk that comes our way. Jimmy Riley told us to keep our eyes and ears open, and if we heard something that could be wrote in the paper, we would get a tip. I got somethin' you might be wantin' to hear. Petey heard it first, and then I asked around, quiet like, if you know what I mean. I think we're on to somethin'."

What was the lad saying about the b'hoys? Now what could be of interest about firemen? Edward continued to listen, knowing Callie was taking notes, and he could always ask her later. What made his ears perk up was her next, almost off-handed question. Now what was she up to? His round eyes got rounder as he listened in awe. Where did she get her ideas? Mr. Kenyon was going to be in rare form when he heard this one.

"I think it would work. We could try it on a trial basis. I thought that after your first two-hour rush in the morning, you and the boys could try it out and see what kind of results you get. I would wager there might be some tips at the end of the week. Home delivery of the paper would be such a luxury. What do you think, Joey?" Callie asked anxiously.

"It might work, ma'am. I'll give it a try."

Edward marched into the parlor with a laden tray. This heavy discussion called for refreshments. Never let it be said that Miss Callie entertained without serving refreshments.

"I couldn't help overhearing the discussion. Might I make a suggestion, Miss Callie?" At her nod he rushed on. "I think you should alert the other boys to your plan so they can move right into the areas you want before the other papers get the . . . the jump on you."

"Edward, that's good thinking. Will you talk it up, Joey? Of course, you will. The paper might be willing to add some money each week to your wages. If I were running the paper, I know I would give it serious thought. Eat your cookies, Joey, they're delicious."

"Would you be minding if I took one for Petey? He's partial to sweets."

"Good heavens, no. Edward, a sack please. By the way, I looked in the crock, and the cookies are down at the bottom. We best make arrangements to make some more."

"'We best make arrangements to make some more,'" Edward mimicked Callie as he went in search of a sack. How generous she was. Now that he had time to think clearly, he could seriously say she was the most generous person he had ever met when it came to other people's money and talents. In spite of himself, he laughed.

Conversation was brisk when Edward returned with the cookies for Joey. He began to pour the lemonade just as Joey made his announcement. "Mr. Kenyon is back, and things are in an uproar down at the paper. I had to go pick up some extras to work Petey's corner, and he said hello to me. He was carrying a satchel, and he didn't look pleased with what was going on."

"Edward, the lemonade is going all over the floor. The glass is full," Callie said sharply. "Why are you pouring the lemonade all over the floor?"

"Because I'm watching you squash that raisin cookie, that's why," Edward said nervously.

Callie looked down at her hands. "That's . . . that's interesting. Isn't that interesting, Edward? That Mr. Kenyon is back? That's what I mean, is interesting. Very interesting. Don't you find that—"

"If you say that one more time, I shall resign," Edward snapped.

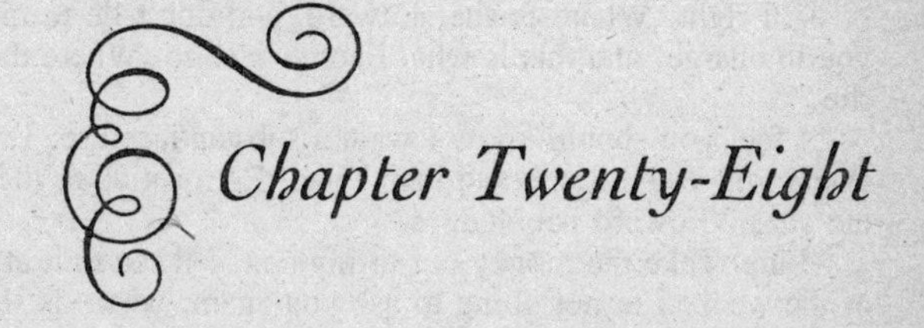

Chapter Twenty-Eight

After seeing Joey out, Edward fetched a wet rag and started to clean up the floor. "You have never seen Mr. Kenyon angry, have you?"

Callie shook her head.

Edward gave her a pitying look and retreated to the kitchen.

Callie washed her hands in hot soapy water. "I think I'll work in the garden for a while. If . . . if Byrch arrives, send him out."

"All right," Edward muttered as he started banging pots and pans. He might as well get on with his job. Dinner had to be cooked, and cookies had to be baked. He also had to take the towels off the line and fold them. He felt like a middle-aged housewife who was angry at her circumstances. He straightened his shoulders. It was time to ask for a raise. That's what he would do, just as soon as Mr. Kenyon stepped foot in the kitchen. A sizable raise. A healthy raise. One that would keep him comfortable. He certainly did deserve a raise. He was a slave to this kitchen and this house. He had to put a stop to this.

It was four-thirty by the kitchen clock when the front door slammed loudly. Edward jumped a foot. His eyes rolled back in his head. He thought he could feel the floorboards shake beneath his feet. The storm entered the kitchen, wild and untamed. "Where the hell is she?"

"I want a raise. I have to insist, Mr. Kenyon," Edward said haughtily.

"All right. Where is she, Edward, and don't lie to me. I left you in charge, and this is what I come back to. Where the hell is she?"

"I feel you should know I want a substantial raise. I'm worth every cent you pay me and then some. Retroactive to the first of the year," Edward babbled.

"Fine. Take the money out of my box. I'll see to it at the end of the week. I'm not going to ask you again, where is she?"

"Miss Callie? Why, I do believe she's working in the garden. Shall I call her for you?"

"I'll damn well call her myself. I won't put up with this . . . this . . ."

"Insubordination?" Edward offered.

"Exactly. Give a woman an inch, and she takes a yard. Well, she better have some damn good explanations."

Callie heard Byrch through the open window. Her back stiffened. Quickly she stuffed her gardening tools in the basket at her side and got to her feet. "Byrch."

"What've you got to say for yourself, *C. James*?" Byrch's voice was so cold and harsh that Callie shivered in the bright sunshine. "I want an explanation, and I want it now."

"Why? What have I done that's so terrible? Why are you shouting at me?"

"Don't try putting me on the defensive," Byrch snapped.

"I'm not sorry, Byrch. I don't feel that I did anything wrong. I was a definite asset to your paper for the short time you were gone. I know you're angry, but if you stop and think for a minute you'll realize that only good came from it."

Byrch stared at Callie for a long time. Her gaze was direct and unblinking. She was going to take a stand on what she had just said. He could feel it in his bones. The hot rush of anger coursing through him couldn't be held in check. "I won't have it," Byrch thundered.

"I suppose you think I'm only good for one thing, is that it? If I'm such a waste and amount to nothing, why did Horace Greeley offer me a job? Why did another paper say I could name my own salary, and why did your paper hire me?"

"That's going to be remedied immediately. I'm firing you."

"You can't fire me because you didn't hire me. Who do you think you are to tell me you're going to fire me? I did it for you, for the paper, and yes, I did it for myself too. I wanted to see if I could do it, and I did it. How can you find fault with it? I can't just sit here and pretend to enjoy our . . . our arrangement. I can't do that. I think you owe me an apology. No, I *demand* an apology."

The blue eyes were blazing. Byrch swallowed hard. It wasn't supposed to be happening like this. She should have been pleading with him to understand, crying really. Telling him she was sorry. Falling into his arms. Instead *she* was angry, angry at him. And she wanted an apology in the bargain.

"An apology!" Byrch roared so loud that Edward dropped his wooden spoon.

"Yes, damn you, an apology. Until such time as you can tell me what it is that is really upsetting you, I have nothing further to discuss."

"We have plenty to discuss. Come here," Byrch said, reaching for her arm to draw her to him. Callie nimbly sidesteped him and started up the garden path to the house. Byrch trailed behind her.

Just before she stormed into the house, Callie turned to face Byrch, willing herself not to be intimidated by his glower. "If you want to fire me, go ahead. I'll go to work for Mr. Greeley!"

Byrch felt as though he had been kicked in the stomach by a mule, an angry, ill-tempered mule with sharp hoofs. Leave. She was talking about leaving again. He couldn't let her see what this was doing to him.

She looked so damn beautiful standing there with that strange, defiant yet exhilarated look on her face. He couldn't permit her to call his bluff. At best he could keep her a few weeks while he tried to come up with some plan to keep her permanently at his side. "Oh, no you won't. We have an agreement, and until it's paid in full, you don't step out of this house, is that understood? Payment in full. I don't care if the paper is paying you *fifty* dollars a week! When I say your debt is paid is the day you leave here, not one minute before. Do we understand one another?"

A miracle, that's what she had been expecting. If not a miracle then perhaps a pat on the head. Some kind words. Was that too much to expect? How was it possible for him to hate her so much? No matter what he did, no matter what he said, she could never hate him. It was such an impossible situation. She was selling herself to him. Paying off her debt. He must despise her, but did he have to humiliate her in the bargain? Her back stiffened at his harsh, insulting tone. "Very well, Mr. Kenyon. Believe me when I tell you the three months can't end soon enough for me. I'm warning you now, don't interfere with my job." Without another word, Callie ran into the house and up the stairs to her room. Byrch shuddered with the sound of the slamming door.

Edward was reminded of a thunderbolt when Byrch stormed through the kitchen. He'd never seen his face as black with rage as it was now. What had happened out there in the garden? As if he didn't know. He rolled his dark eyes and stirred the pot that didn't need stirring. He consoled himself with the fact that even in paradise it rained from time to time.

Callie paced the floor in her room, wringing her hands and swiping at the tears that gathered in her eyes and dripped down her cheeks. She blew her nose lustily twice, and still she cried. Byrch wasn't just cold, he was cruel. How could he be so selfish that he would keep her here a virtual prisoner and force her to give up her new job? That's what she got for stepping out of her place. She was paying now, a price that was exorbitantly high. And in the bargain he was making a fool of her, or at least trying to make a fool of her. How could he belittle what she had done when the others had praised her? Horace Greeley himself had written her and offered a job. He was trying to rob her of everything. Three months. Three long months was what she had to deal with, and then she could leave. Just the thought of packing and leaving brought on a fresh wave of tears. Damn Byrch Kenyon. Damn Byrch Kenyon to hell.

There was a war going on, and while Edward did his best to remain neutral, he found it hard going. He adored Miss Callie, probably would have laid down his life for the young woman, but he was torn with his feelings for Mr. Kenyon. He literally owed the man his life. The armed truce was getting on his nerves. He hated hostility of any kind, and this morning at breakfast the hostility had been thicker than ever. Not for the world would he attempt to offer advice to either Mr. Kenyon or Miss Callie. His tampering days were over and done with.

It was mid-morning when the doorbell rang. Edward frowned. He wasn't expecting anyone, and he knew that if Miss Callie was expecting a visitor, she would have alerted him. An uneasy feeling settled in his stomach when he opened the door. "Mrs. Darcy! Please, come in."

"I didn't come here to see my cousin. Is Miss James in? Tell her I'm here, Edward, and please inform her that I don't have much time."

"Yes, ma'am," Edward said, showing her into the front parlor. He didn't like this. The look on the lady's face boded ill, and since she asked for Callie, it was a wise assumption that Miss Callie was going to be the recipient.

"Mrs. Darcy? Edward, are you sure she asked for me? What can she possibly want?" Seeing no answers in Edward's face, she laid aside her paper and pencil and followed him down to the parlor. One look at Bridget's face was all she needed to know something was wrong.

"Miss James. You look well. Sit down," she commanded. Callie sat hurriedly, her eyes full of questions.

"I'm not going to mince words with you, young woman. I'm going to come straight to the point. Your living here in this house with my cousin without benefit of clergy is causing tongues to wag. Just in case you don't understand what I'm talking about, let me clarify myself. People are talking. Your living here is causing a scandal, and it's hurting Byrch. You're ruining any chance he has to enter politics. Surely you can see that, can't you?"

Callie sat staring at Byrch's cousin, a dumbfounded look on her face.

"People are discussing your background, or lack of it. And let me tell you they have been most charitable up to this point. It won't get better, it can only get worse. If you have any feeling for my cousin, leave this house. You aren't helping him, you're hurting him. Why, just yesterday Kevin told me he wouldn't go to the next political meeting unless you were gone from this house. He can't hold his head up anymore. I find it rather difficult myself," Bridget said cruelly.

"I . . . I didn't . . . what I mean is, I had no idea . . ." Callie whispered.

"I figured as much. When you spend all your time doing what you do, I suppose there isn't much time to worry about what the other people think. If you have any real feelings for Byrch, you'll leave as soon as possible. Everyone, with the exception of Jasper Powers, is afraid to back Byrch because of you and the scandal that will ensue. Do you understand what I'm saying?"

"Yes, Mrs. Darcy, I understand."

"For some reason I thought you would put up a fight."

"I only want what's best for Byrch," Callie managed in a stricken voice.

"If that's true, then see to it that you heed my advice. Good day, Miss James."

"Goodbye, Mrs. Darcy." Callie managed to choke out the words before fleeing upstairs.

Edward sat down on his rocker with a loud thump. By God, there were some people who should have been strangled at birth, and Mrs. Darcy was one of them. Instinct told him not to go to Miss Callie. She wouldn't want him to see the shame she was feeling. He had to respect that. Tonight was going to be a hellish circus. He wondered how much luck he would have if he asked for the evening off.

Callie sat down on the edge of the bed, her hands clasped tightly in her lap. It seemed that the world was closing in on her from all sides. Never once in all the time she had been here had she thought about Byrch's political career and how she might be harming it. She could see the truth in Bridget's words. But if it was true, why was Byrch so insistent on making her uphold her end of the bargain? Didn't he care? Surely he wouldn't sacrifice his political ambitions just to make her miserable. Edward. Why hadn't Edward said something? Because it wasn't his place to say anything. Why did she have so many problems? Why couldn't she see beyond the end of her nose?

Now there was no choice; she had to leave, bargain or no bargain. The thought was so horrendous she threw herself across the bed and sobbed.

In the hallway Edward opened the linen-closet door and stared with unseeing eyes at the contents. Only his ears picked up the heart-rending sobs coming through the closed door. There was nothing to do and nothing to say. He had never felt so helpless in his entire life.

Exhausted with her crying, Callie washed her face at the washstand in the corner. How puffy her eyes looked. It didn't make any difference what she looked like. Who would care if she spent the entire day wailing her head off? No one. Oh, Mum, I wish you were here.

Maybe she should write a letter to her mother. She had to work on her column, but how could she when she had all this misery on her mind? She should also start packing so she could leave as soon as possible. How long would that take? Fifteen minutes. The question was, should she leave before or after Byrch came home.

Her heart told her she needed to see him one more time. Her head told her she had a bargain to uphold. But that was all before Bridget's visit and her cruel accusations.

She was leaving, that's all there was to it. And as long as she was leaving, she might as well change jobs. Thirty dollars was a lot better than fifteen if she was going to support herself. For the life of her she couldn't remember if it was Horace Greeley who offered the thirty dollars or the other newspaper. She would ask Edward; he would remember. She could always count on Edward.

Oh, Byrch, what happened to us? If only I didn't love you so. Her face flamed. She didn't know loving someone could hurt so terribly. True, she had been hurt by Rossiter, but it was nothing compared to the pain she was suffering now.

Drawers slammed, and doors banged as Callie dragged out her clothes. She hated them now, hated them because Bridget had helped her select them and Byrch had paid for them. Choice was the one thing she didn't have right now. It was either take the clothes or go naked. Clothes covered shame and guilt; she would take the clothes.

Tired of staring into the linen closet, Edward turned to head back down the stairs when the first sounds of slamming drawers jarred his ears. He recognized the sounds. She was leaving. Perhaps he should knock on her door and talk to her. But what good would it do? Mrs. Darcy was a busybody of the first order, but she did have a point. It was the way she had gone about it that was all wrong. There wasn't a thing he could say to Miss Callie. Whatever she did now was going to be strictly her decision and Mr. Kenyon's.

Edward puttered in the kitchen all afternoon, burning his finger on the hot handle of a pot, spilling freshly shelled peas all over his clean floor, and baking a cake that listed so far to one side that no amount of frosting could help. He chucked the cake, along with his dustpan full of peas, in the trash and set about making himself a cup of tea, lacing it liberally with brandy. It bothered him little that his employer might take him to task for drinking on the job. At times a man needed something a little stronger than tea to get through a trying time. He needed a little rest. The leg of lamb was roasting nicely, as were the potatoes. He had the situation in hand. Still, he felt guilty as he sat down to enjoy his tea. He felt even more guilty when he felt a light hand on his shoulder.

"Miss Callie, I guess I must have dozed off. Is everything all right?" Poor thing, her eyes were red-rimmed, and he knew that no powder in the world could cover the bruised circles beneath her eyes. She was dressed in a fawn-colored afternoon dress with copper-colored ruching at the neck and sleeves. She looked, Edward decided, every inch a sophisticated woman of the world. She appeared calm; there was no noticeable trembling in her hands as she set about making herself a cup of tea. Too calm was Edward's first thought. Too controlled.

"Don't get up, Edward. The lamb and potatoes are fine. I checked on them. I'm making you a cup of tea. I see that yours has grown cold. You barely touched it."

"Thank you, Miss Callie."

"Edward, which paper was it that offered me twice my salary? For the life of me, I can't remember. I do hope it was Mr. Greeley. I'm going to be leaving here as soon as possible, and I'm going to take the job that pays the most money."

Edward swallowed hard, his lunch working its way up to his throat. "I do believe it was the other paper, not Mr. Greeley. Is that wise, Miss Callie? I don't mean to pry into your affairs, but it would seem to me that you are doing so well now it would be a shame to disturb what is almost a perfect situation for you. You could lose readership with another paper. And another paper might not be as kind to you as the *Clarion*. I do hope you have given this matter a lot of thought. Money, contrary to belief, is not the answer to everything."

"In this case it is," Callie said bitterly. "I'm going to check it out first thing tomorrow morning. I wish someone had told me more about Byrch's political aspirations. I didn't think. I don't know why it never occurred to me that this situation could harm him politically. I suppose I thought that it was so far down the road that I would be long gone before he ever ran for any kind of office. I'm not knowledgeable about the ins and outs of politics. I see now that a person has to be groomed and free of any kind of scandal before he enters the political wing. Already I've hurt him."

Edward accepted her criticism. "Miss Callie, it's not, nor has it ever been, my place to discuss Mr. Kenyon's affairs with anyone. I hope you understand that and don't take it personally."

"I do understand, Edward. You have your place, and I have mine. The problem is you stayed within your boundaries and I stepped out of mine. It seems to be a problem I have."

"Miss Callie, I think you're viewing this situation too personally." If he could just keep talking and keep her talking, perhaps some idea would blossom in his head with regard to the damnable letters. "I will say this to you. Mr. Kenyon is a very wise, astute newspaperman. Politically he's a novice, but he's learning. Why don't you trust him to know what he's about? Making radical changes like you're contemplating right now might hurt him even more. I do hope you plan to discuss this with him. Listen to his point of view and then make your decision. Are you packed?"

"Yes," Callie muttered over the rim of her cup. "I think I will go out to the garden. Don't send Byrch out. I'll talk to him after dinner. There's no sense riling him up before he eats. You know how he gets indigestion if something upsets him. I don't mean that I'll upset him . . . yes, that's exactly what I mean . . . we'll wait. We'll wait, Edward," Callie said firmly.

"Very well, Miss Callie. Your shasta daisies are beautiful. I just happened to notice the lavender ones this morning. You do have a way with the garden."

A pity I don't have a way with people, Callie thought. This would be her last walk in the garden, her last meal in the house on St. Luke's Place, her last everything as far as this chapter of her life was concerned. Perhaps she should spend the time writing to Peggy. Another dumb letter from her dumb daughter in America. What advice would Peggy give her? She wished she knew.

Dinner to get through. Byrch loved lamb. Byrch loved food. Byrch loved flowers and her vegetables. Byrch loved Edward and this house. Byrch loved everything but her. Why? Was she so ugly? Was she so— She whirled and headed back up the garden path, her heels clicking on the flagstone walkway that she had weeded the day before. No blade of grass would dare to creep between the stones. The curving walkway had never been so neat, so well trimmed. It looked like something out of a picture book, Edward had said.

Callie fought back the tears as she stared around at the colorful garden. She was proud of it. She was proud of her job at the paper What Edward said was true, the paper had been good to her; they had given her a job when she needed it most. But to stay on and be in contact with Byrch was more than she could bear. If only she could make a clean break and still work for the paper. She would have to find a way, that's all there was to it.

As she neared the back porch of the house, she sensed that Byrch was home. She felt unseen eyes on her. Did Edward discuss her with Byrch? Would Edward remember his place and not discuss what they talked about earlier? Maybe it would be better if Byrch knew what she was planning. This way—no, that was wrong, he shouldn't know. Surprise would be on her side. It would give her an edge when it came to dealing with Byrch. She couldn't allow him to browbeat her, to snap and snarl as he always did.

Dinner was grim. Byrch found the delicious food sticking in his throat. Something was brewing, something he wasn't going to like, he could feel it in his bones. One look at Edward's pitying face convinced him that all hell was about to break loose. Callie looked overly dressed, like she was going some place special. Normally she wore light colors, "daytime wear" she called it. She was definitely dressed up, and she looked stunningly beautiful. Perhaps she was a little pale, but other than that he knew he had never seen a more beautiful woman in his life. And she was his. Almost. Temporarily. Goddamn it, she wasn't his. That was the problem. He knew he would sell his soul to the devil if she would just raise her head and smile at him. He would probably curl up and die if she said she loved him.

Over coffee in the living room Callie squared her shoulders and stared straight at Byrch. "I have to talk to you, Byrch. It's important."

Here it comes, he thought. It was going to be awesome. He could feel his hands close into fists. Callie noticed the movement and swallowed hard.

"Your cousin, Mrs. Darcy, was here to see me this morning." There, that was a start. Her voice was firm, almost emotionless. She was stating facts, cold, hard facts that didn't matter to her. "She said my being here was going to hurt you politically. She said I was an embarrassment to you and people were starting to talk. She was quite blunt about her opinions of me and what I was doing to you and how if I stayed here it would only hurt you. She's right Byrch. It's my fault, I didn't know you were so far ahead in your . . . in your political aspirations. It simply never occurred to me. I suppose I thought your making the switch from the newspaper business to politics was so far down the road that . . . what I mean is I thought I would be long gone before you decided to enter . . . it was my mistake," Callie said flatly.

"You make a lot of those, don't you?" Byrch said just as tonelessly.

For a moment Callie had difficulty understanding Byrch's words. When she finally comprehended the meaning, she flushed a rosy crimson.

Byrch stared at Callie's flushed face. "Hrumph," he snorted. So, he was right, he was her biggest mistake, and now she thought she found her out in his cousin Bridget. Damn Bridget. One of these days he was going to wring her fat neck and laugh while he was doing it.

"To my regret, yes," Callie said coolly. How arrogant he was, how cold he could be. It was almost as if he had known what she was going to say, as if he and Bridget had arranged her little meeting this morning. Nothing surprised her anymore where this man was concerned. He had the power to hurt her, and each verbal thrust wounded her to the quick. "So I'll be leaving here in the morning. I plan to speak with Mr. Greeley about his job offer. You won't have to concern yourself about me any longer."

Byrch's stomach churned, and the clenched fists wanted to beat out at something. "Aren't you forgetting something? We have an agreement, and your time isn't up yet. A bargain is a bargain."

She wouldn't cry. She refused to give him that satisfaction. A bargain, that's what he considered her, a damn bargain. "I'm prepared to give you all the money I have saved. I'll be earning more, twice what I'm earning now, if I decide to take Mr. Greeley's offer." Lord, she hadn't meant her voice to come out so desperate-sounding. How much money was the question. How much was a roll in the bedcovers worth? Would he insult her and put a price on it? Her teeth were clenched so tight she thought her jaw would crack.

Bile rose in Byrch's throat. Damn woman, she had all the answers. Well, she could answer him till hell froze over and he still wouldn't let her go. Not now, not tomorrow, never. "You don't have enough money to pay me, and we were all over that ground. The precedent has been set; we're not dealing with money."

Callie shuddered. Such hatred was more than she could bear. "Are you saying my money isn't good enough but my body is?" she managed to whisper.

"That's about the size of it, but don't get any ideas that you're something special. It's more convenient this way." The minute the words were out of his mouth, Byrch wanted to strangle himself. How could he have said such a mean, hateful thing to the woman he loved with his heart and soul? There must be a devil in him somewhere. A devil was making him do this. If Father Muldoon could hear him now, he wouldn't bother to have him say a penance, he'd order him sent straight to hell with no stops at purgatory on the way. He hated himself as he watched Callie for her next move, her next reply.

"Are you saying you won't permit me to move out of this house tomorrow?" Callie asked. She refused to think about his words and their meaning, for it she did, she would fall apart right in front of him.

"You've already ruined my reputation, so what does it matter now? And don't for one minute think that Greeley is going to hire you. When he finds out you're a woman, he'll send you packing. So will that other paper you keep harping on. It's only because of my stupid cousin that you have any job at all. Another thing, no matter what anyone else has told you, I do have the power to fire you. Believe that. I've been generous with you, but not any longer. You're fired!"

"What?"

"You heard me, you're fired. No more columns. No more anything. You can go upstairs and get ready. I'll be up shortly."

Hot, scorching anger raced up Callie's spine and spread out through her veins. "You can go to hell, Byrch Kenyon!" Callie sputtered. Enough was enough. He couldn't fire her. By God, her job was all she had left.

Byrch knew he had gone too far as soon as the words were out of his mouth. He stood by helplessly as Callie sprang to life. "You will not do this to me, do you hear? I will not allow it. It's true, we have a bargain, and I'll honor my end, but that's all I'll honor. No more, do you hear?"

Before he could answer, Callie upended his favorite chair. In her frustration and fury she toppled the end tables, sending crystal figurines scattering into thousands of shards. Books seemed to have a life of their own as they took flight to land every which way. The tubs of greenery were suddenly without blooms and looked like beheaded seedlings.

Byrch backed off a step and bumped into a trembling Edward. Both men inched their way into the dining room as Callie stalked them. "Do I or don't I have a job?" she demanded hoarsely.

Byrch finally found his tongue. By God, she was a hell cat. How could he have forgotten? "You just increased your debt to me. Now it's six months. You're in no condition to discuss anything right now. Do as I say and go to your room."

"Sir, may I remind you that silence is sometimes the better part of valor," Edward whispered.

"No!" Callie shouted. "Not till you answer me. Do I have a job or don't I?"

"Sir?" Edward pleaded as he noticed Callie gaining on them. Behind him was the dining-room wall.

Sobs tore at Callie's throat. "I hate you, Byrch Kenyon. I hate you and will always hate you!"

"All right, all right," Byrch said, attempting to soothe her. This was what he had been afraid of for a long time. She had finally exploded. How ironic that it had to be over a job. This job meant more to her than he ever could. He motioned for Edward to back up toward the kitchen. He followed slowly, his eyes on Callie. He watched her out of the corner of his eye. When she sat down on the one chair left standing, he changed direction and headed toward her. "You're upset. Why don't you go upstairs and take a nice warm bath. It will calm you." His voice was not unkind.

Callie stared about the parlor and couldn't believe the havoc she had created. She would not apologize. He had driven her to this. "Six months, you said." Her eyes were hollow, her voice lifeless.

"That doesn't hold anymore. Now that you've ruined my reputation, I have to give some thought to myself. Marriage is the only answer. I'll arrange all the details. A week from Sunday, we'll have Father Muldoon marry us here in this house. There's no other solution, so don't try to come up with reasons why you can't or don't want to or whatever. This is the way it is."

"Marry you! You must be insane! I'll be in your debt forever if I agree to marry you."

"It seems like a fair price for ruining my reputation. I have to start all over again, build up good will, charm the ladies, make friends of their husbands, do a little backscratching. I wouldn't have to do all that if it hadn't been for you. Take it or leave it." Byrch waited, hardly daring to breathe. What was she going to say? Surely she didn't truly mean she hated him. Even if she did hate him, he would still have her. Maybe she was right, and he was insane. It didn't matter. All that mattered was that she didn't get away from him again.

"Perhaps I am insane, sweeting," he said sadly, "but I really don't see any help for it. Your reputation and mine are already compromised, and I'm afraid my political chances are ruined. But if you were my wife, people would quickly forget. You say you hate me, Callie," he said persuasively, "but I never thought you'd want to hurt me this way."

Callie glared at him through tear-filled eyes. This was wrong, all wrong, Byrch realized. He'd just asked the woman he loved to marry him and was prepared to use force to get her to accept. Love was supposed to be gentle, kind, not a contest of wills and rejection. But when he thought about life without her, he was ready to take any risks, fight for her if he must, but he could never lose her.

"I . . . I never meant to hurt you, Byrch. This has all been your own doing. I really don't see how you can expect us to marry. Haven't we hurt each other enough?"

Assuming an arrogant air, afraid he would find himself begging at her feet, Byrch answered, "Apparently not, sweeting. But then no one ever said marriages were made in heaven, and ours certainly will not be. It's simply a matter of convenience. I will have saved my reputation, and you will have saved your position at the paper. Something we both want, isn't it?"

"Yes . . . I mean, no!" Her head ached, and she was having difficulty following this conversation. "I mean, of course my reputation is valuable to me . . ." Her thoughts were being choked off by her emotions. The man she loved had just said she must marry him and she should be happy. But it was that very happiness that she feared. What right had she, an impoverished Irish girl, to marry one of the most influential men in New York?

"Good, it's settled then," Byrch said, not quite daring to breathe a sigh of relief.

"No! It's not settled," she protested. "You've compromised me, used me! And all that has to come to an end. I've got to respect myself again. You can have your marriage, but I won't be your wife. You've pushed me too far, Byrch. Also, I will continue at the paper. Your word!"

"What do you mean I'll have the marriage, but you won't be my wife?" Ice was flowing through his veins as he anticipated her answer.

"Exactly that. I will not share your bed."

"You aren't in any position to make demands."

"I am now. Either we agree right now, this minute, or I leave this house. You can't keep me here against my will. I'll forget about my debt to you. I'll leave here, I mean it."

It was a new tone, a new determination. Byrch recognized the threat and consequences if he didn't agree. If he had to do it, he would. He couldn't let her go.

"Agreed. There will be no strings, no commitments by either of us."

"Put it in writing, and I might believe you," Callie snapped as she turned on her heel to leave the room.

"Son of a bitch!" Byrch fumed. He kicked at the overturned chair. "Edward!" he bellowed, "get in here and clean up this goddamn mess. But first fetch me a drink. Now!"

"This is a goddamn glass, Edward," Byrch complained as he downed the plum brandy in one swallow.

Righting the upturned chair, Edward turned to his employer. "You asked for a drink. Am I to understand you wish the entire bottle?"

"Yes, damn it, I wish the entire bottle. Your friend's work is going to keep you busy for a while."

It was going to be one of *those* nights, Edward could feel it in his bones. From time to time, out of the corner of his eye, Edward checked the level in the bottle of brandy. He decided it was time to make coffee. The room was put to rights, all the broke glass and debris swept up and in the trash. He did have to admire the lady's style. He never thought she had it in her to get so angry. Evidently Mr. Kenyon had also misjudged her. Even a dog would lash out if backed against a wall, he told himself.

When Edward set the coffee tray down, Byrch peered at it owlishly. "You don't think I'm drinking *that*, do you?"

"Actually, sir, I thought I might join you. The coffee is for me. Of course, if you'd like some, I'd be more than glad to pour you a cup. You do like my coffee. As a matter of fact, you always said my freshly ground coffee was the best in the state of New York."

"Shut up, Edward, and drink your coffee."

"Very good, sir," Edward said, clamping his lips together.

"I've had nothing but aggravation and heartache since she arrived here. I guess you know that. I did everything, and still it wasn't enough. I would bleed for her if I could. What does she do? How does she repay me? I'll tell you how," Byrch said, leaning forward in his chair. "She gets a job at the paper. *My* paper. People are actually saying—why, my God, they are starting to say she writes as well as I do! Can you believe that, Edward? Everything is C. James. C. James this, C. James that. I'm sick of it. I wonder what they would think if they knew C. James just wrecked my parlor. We should put that in the paper tomorrow and teach her a lesson. By God, did you see her attack me?" Byrch shuddered as he recalled the scene.

"I knew her when she was this high," Byrch went on, holding out his hand at some invisible line. "She was a child then. I helped her. I'm always helping her. Every time she gets in trouble, I help her and this is the thanks I get." More brandy found its way to his mouth.

"Sir, it's getting late, and you have to be at the paper early. You told me earlier to wake you at six."

Byrch's head rolled backward, and a silly smirk settled on his face. "Tell me, Edward, old friend, just how late is late? If late is early in the morning, I won't have to go to bed, and you won't have to worry about waking me up." His tone turned crafty. "Are you trying to tell me something?"

"Why no, sir, I was just reminding you of the time."

"Edward, you are the goddamnedest, most perfect person I ever met. My cousin Bridget would kill for you. Imagine that? What did I do wrong, Edward?"

"Miss Callie is going through a trying time, Mr. Kenyon. Patience, I believe, is the answer."

Byrch snorted as he peered drunkenly at the black man across from him. "I'm drunk, and I don't believe you. How can you be sober and say such a thing? Patience has been my middle name. What did it get me?"

"What was it you expected, sir?"

"Expected?" The question seemed to confuse him. Edward watched as his employer tried to focus his gaze. "I expected . . . some appreciation. Some goddamn appreciation. I did a lot for her. You can't deny that, Edward. A hell of a lot. She doesn't respect me. And," he yelped, jabbing a limp finger at Edward, "she ruined my reputation. What do you have to say to that?"

"I'm sure she appreciates you, sir. Have your shirts ever been ironed so well? Who do you think made this house into a nice home? Not me. All I do is make it smell like furniture polish. Who hangs up the towels in the bathroom? Miss Callie, that's who."

Byrch's eyes widened. "Does she really hang up the towels?"

"Yes, sir. And you have her to thank for the lovely garden with all the fresh vegetables and the beautiful flowers. I would certainly consider that appreciation. Are you certain you don't want to retire for the night and continue this discussion in the morning? It's past midnight."

"Get me a piece of paper and a pencil. Miss C. James wants me to write something for her . . . what time did you say it was?"

"Past midnight. We can all use the sleep."

"The paper first, Edward. I can't go to sleep till I write the damn letter. She wants a letter. I ask her to marry me, and she wants a letter."

Byrch applied pencil to paper and scratched furiously. "There, it's finished. See that, what do you think?"

Edward stared at the blank piece of paper that held only Byrch's signature. "It's your name, sir. I thought you said you were writing a letter."

"I can't remember what she wanted on the damn letter, so I signed my name, and she can fill in the rest."

"That's very clever of you, sir. I'm sure Miss Callie will think of something."

'She always thinks of something. I'm going to give it to her now. I've done my best. My very best. I would get more attention and respect from a cat. Why don't we have a cat, Edward?"

"Why . . . why . . . I suppose it's because you never asked for one."

"Tomorrow I want you to get me a cat, a yellow one. One that's soft and cuddly. A man has to have something to warm his bed!"

Byrch climbed the stairs holding the paper aloft. She wanted a letter, well, by God, she was going to get a letter. Right now. And he was going to watch her write it so he could know what it was he had signed.

He tried the doorknob and found it locked. A locked door! Maybe she was doing something only women do, and he wasn't supposed to know about. He'd be courteous and knock. When he received no reply, he kicked at the door. "Callie, open this door."

"Go away. I don't want to talk to you. You're going to wake Edward."

"Edward is still awake. Open the door."

"It's too late. We'll talk in the morning."

"I have the letter you wanted me to write. Right here in my hand."

"Slip it under the door," Callie said frigidly.

"I will not. Open that door, or I'll kick it down. This is my house, and I don't like locked doors. Who are you afraid of?"

"You."

"Me?"

"Go away."

"I live here. This is my house. I don't have to go away. You said you wanted your letter. Well, here it is."

Byrch backed up several steps and lashed out with his foot.

When it made contact with the door, he swore viciously. He tried a second time. Just at the moment of impact, Callie opened the door, and Byrch toppled into the room at a dead run, landing smack in the middle of the bed. Callie stood by the door, seething. He was right—it was his house, and it was his bed too. But they'd agreed to a new arrangement this evening.

"Come here. I want you. I want you now." He was completely sober; suddenly he realized Callie sensed the change in him and felt frightened.

"I think you should go back to your room," she said. "We made an arrangement this evening. I said I would marry you, and there would be no strings. You sleep in your room, and I sleep in mine."

"I'm afraid that doesn't hold at the moment. You see, this is now. Our marriage won't take place for over a week. Until that time we have a bargain. True or false?" He hated the way her shoulders slumped in the dim light from the corridor. Why couldn't she love him? Why was she fighting him? How had he ever agreed to a no-strings marriage? Before this was all over, he would make her love him or die in the attempt. Maybe that was his answer. He would die, and then she would grieve. But could he even be certain of that?

"Get out of my room," Callie told him with deadly calm. "I've had quite enough of you for one day."

Byrch sprawled on the bed, a smile breaking on his lips. She looked so comical, standing there in her nightdress, the backlight from the hall penetrating the thin material to outline each sweet curve of her body in complete contradiction to the glare in her eyes and the command of her voice.

"What are you laughing at?" she demanded.

"If you could just see yourself all puffed up like a little bantam hen, clucking away that the sky is falling!" He laughed again, infuriatingly.

"Get out of my bed, you great oaf!" Callie challenged him, her hands knotted into fists, ready to strike if she must. This was simply too much. First his cruelty, and now his derision.

Byrch avoided her by rolling to the far side of the bed, tumbling out over the edge. His foot caught the edge of the bedstand, setting the softly glowing oil lamp to rocking wildly, erratic shadows flying about the room.

Callie gasped. The lamp! Before she could warn him, she saw it tip. She rushed to the far side of the bed, already pulling covers to staunch the expected flames. It was too soon after the fire in

Shantytown, and her fears were still vivid and tangible. She didn't even realize that Byrch was sitting on the floor, the lamp safe in his hands.

It was a full moment after he'd replaced the lamp that he realized her terror of fire. She was standing before him, eyes wild with horror. Byrch took her into his arms to ease her shudders. Callie leaned against him, knowing only that nothing must happen to this man who meant so much to her.

Callie felt so small, so vulnerable in Byrch's arms; his feelings of protectiveness rose. He lifted her chin, bringing his mouth to hers, drawing from her a kiss that was hesitant and poignant, doubting that she would welcome it but beyond denying himself. The answering pressure of her mouth spurred him to further boldness.

Byrch took her to the bed, lying down beside her, taking her into his arms once again. He was aware of the slimness of her waist beneath his hands and of the twin mounds of her breasts against his chest. Was it possible she was unaware of the effect she had on him? "Sweeting," he murmured against her mouth, reluctant to break the contact between them, "I want to love you. I only want to love you."

Callie heard his words and felt their impact. How she wished he meant that he loved her instead of just wanting to make love. But her need for him sang in her blood, and she was helpless to deny herself the strength of his arms and the feel of his body on hers. Plowing her fingers into his wealth of dark hair, she initiated an intimate kiss, exploring the recesses of his sweet, brandied mouth, wordlessly telling him that if he would have her, then he must take her.

"Callie," he groaned, feeling the mounting tension in his loins, wanting to rediscover their passion, "you haven't heard a word I've said."

"Yes, yes, I heard," she whispered, searching the soft interior of his lips, pressing herself against him in welcome.

Byrch's breath caught in his throat. She was adorable, this woman-child, one moment aloof and angry, and the next earthy and impulsive, but she was always beautiful. Breaking their embrace, he rose from the bed and closed the door, locking it. "The only time I want you to lock your door," he told her huskily, "is when I'm on the other side of it, with you." Beneath her heated gaze, he stripped off his garments, standing proud and naked before her. Slowly her fiery gaze slid along his body, heavy-lidded and excited with passion, her mouth parting with invitation. Still watching him, she sat up and stripped off her nightdress, feeling the cool night air strike her flesh, making her hungry for his warm and intimate touch. She slid from the bed and opened her arms to him, wrapping herself against him. He heard her quick, indrawn breath as his masculinity pressed hard into the softness of her lower belly and his hands caressed the smooth roundness of her bottom.

Callie was overwhelmed by the sensation of standing naked in his arms. Her hands caressed the play of muscles in his back. Her thighs pressed against his, marveling at his height, the lean, hard strength of him. She could hear his heart thudding against her cheek.

His mouth captured hers hungrily, desperately trying to satiate his need for her. Their hands explored each other, softly caressing rediscovering each sweetly remembered curve and hollow.

Byrch lifted her onto the bed, lying down beside her and leaning over to kiss her neck, tasting the delicate perfume of her earlobe, the gently curving sweep of her throat down to the valley between her breasts. His hungers found the complexities of her, the slimness of her waist, the turn of her hip, the rising fullness of her breasts. His lips lingered where he could find and give pleasure.

Callie bent and twisted in his arms, yielding up to him and aiding him in his discoverings. Her hands found the smoothness of his back, the firm hardness of his arms, the softness of his chest hair. She tenderly nipped at the slope between shoulder and neck burrowing downward to the hollow under his arm. She was headily aware of the quiver of delight that rippled through him.

Byrch's hands worshipped her, his lips adored her, carrying her into a world beyond reality to a place of passion and desire known only to lovers. His arms encircled her, drawing her tightly against him, reveling in the soft yielding of each curve against his solid length.

She wove her hands through the dark ruffles of his hair, pulling him down to her breast, arching her back, and murmuring a whispered entreaty. He lavished kisses on her breasts, his tongue trailing little concentric circles around the crest before taking the tip full into his mouth. He heard her gasp, felt the writhing of her hips against him. She opened her legs, trapping his thigh between them, clenching rhythmically against it.

In the yellow light from the lamp, her skin took on a sheen, pale ivory against the burnished gold of the bedcovers. She twisted her head away from him, her lips parted, the tip of her tongue visible as it pointed outward, as though tasting a rare delicacy. He knew the sudden need that throbbed through her; he was captivated by her uninhibited way of loving. He had found a woman who possessed a depth of passion to equal his own, a woman unafraid to reveal her desires and pursue her pleasures. Just to see her, to watch her, was an erotic thrill that heightened his senses and brought a new urgency to his passions.

Her mouth tempted him, invited his kiss, the explorations of his tongue. She returned his kisses, opening her lips, inviting him to enter. Straining against him, her body rose and fell, desperately seeking to fill their mutual need.

Byrch turned over on his back, bringing her with him, his thickly muscled thigh still locked between hers. She lifted herself, tipping her head backward, offering him the hollow at the base of her throat and the fullness of her breasts. She brushed against the column of his neck, the ridge of his shoulders, arching upward again to increase the pressure of his thigh against her center. Her nipples grazed the fine furring on his chest and roused an exquisite tension in her lower belly.

His skin seemed to come alive beneath her touch and her lips, and she was ever more aware and needful of his throbbing expectancy, hard and hungry between them. Her eyes met his as he gazed up at her; she saw his lips tighten in a grimace of constraint as he fought to bridle his passion. Following her instincts, seeking only to satisfy their mounting passions, she straddled him, using her hand to bring him into her, gasping and sighing as his length filled her and created a new and different hunger that lay deep within. Supporting herself on her knees, she rode him, moving against him, bringing him together with her to the height of their desires. Her eyes were locked on his face, and he gazed up at her with wonder. He could see that this was a new experience for her by the astonishment in her eyes and the intake of her breath. His hands held her hips, directing her in her motions, lifting his haunches to help her find the friction between them that she craved. Her hair tumbled over her face, thick and unruly, and there was a feline litheness to her body, slender and strong, supple and graceful. She rotated against him, drawing the hunger and tenseness from his loins. Her body was offered to his hands, and she brought her hungry mouth to his. Together they found what they had sought, each sharing with the other, knowing that only in each other would they find everything they would ever need.

A gentle summer rain beat against the windows, seeming to isolate the lovers from the world outside as they lay in each other's arms, breaths warm and humid against each other's face. Byrch smoothed the tumble of dark hair back from Callie's face, burying his lips into the back of her neck. He heard her sigh of contentment, felt her relax in his embrace. He would sleep here with her tonight. He wanted to sleep here every night, but he knew he would not ask. If this was all he could have of her, it would have to be enough.

Chapter Twenty-nine

A message was hand-delivered to the house on St. Luke's Place, asking Callie out to dinner. Byrch must have felt extra prompting was necessary because he added that it was Edward's night off.

Callie held the note, biting her lips. This was the first communication she'd had with Byrch in two days, ever since the night he'd barged into her room. As though by mutual consent, they'd avoided one another at breakfast, and she'd eaten solitary dinners because of his evening social engagements. Despite the fact they'd somehow ended in each other's arms, their truce was nevertheless very real and constrained.

She hated this distance and guardedness between them and resolved that tonight she would make the evening pleasant. Byrch seemed to be holding true to his word and wasn't interfering with her work at the *Clarion*. In her heart, she knew she had no right to ask for more. If they could be civil to one another, even be friends and respect one another's work, it would be enough. Callie breathed a long sigh. She mustn't admit, even to herself, that she wanted more, much more.

Promptly at seven, Callie heard his footstep on the front stairs. She went to the door and opened it before he could insert his key in the lock. He seemed surprised to find her opening the door for him, and he stepped into the small vestibule, filling it with his bulk. Then he scowled. "Is that the way you always open the door? Just swing it open to any riffraff who climbs the front steps?"

"You're the first riffraff to arrive," Callie retorted. "Actually I saw you through the window." She tried a white lie, not wanting to admit to him that she recognized his footsteps and would know them from any others. "I'm not new to the city, and living in Shantytown certainly increased my instinct for caution."

"I don't like it when you're alone in the house. I worry." Then his face broke into a wreath of smiles. "I see you've accepted my dinner invitation." His eyes traveled the length of her, admiring the sapphire-blue dress that made her skin almost luminescent and deepened the color of her eyes. His arms ached to reach out and hold her, to crush her against him, but he was certain she wouldn't allow it. Trying to ignore the delicious scent of her cologne, he offered her a glass of sherry to drink while she waited for him to change.

"I'd rather wait until we can enjoy it together," she told him. "Just hurry, I'm starved!"

When Byrch reappeared in the parlor he smelled of the spicy cologne Callie liked. He was dressed smartly in a dark blue coat and trousers with a lighter shade for his satin waistcoat. He held his impeccably brushed gray beaver hat. She felt as though her heart would melt when he presented her with a nosegay of violets he'd carried home secreted inside a folded copy of the *Clarion*.

In the carriage, Callie sat beside Byrch, keeping up her end of the conversation, but always conscious of the way his knee jounced against hers. "Where are we going?" she asked, trying to focus her attention on the evening instead of the feelings stirring within her.

"I thought we'd go to Downing's on Broad Street. Have you ever eaten oysters?"

Callie wrinkled her nose. "No, but Jasper Powers was quite fond of them, and Lena used to shuck them in the kitchen and serve them on the half-shell. I used to watch him swallow them down in one gulp."

"Well, don't worry, sweeting, there are many ways to enjoy them without eating them raw. Just how adventurous are you?"

Callie stuck her chin in the air in that adorable way he loved. "I'm an adventurous sort, Mr. Kenyon."

"Yes, I know," Byrch said mockingly. "And since you've admitted you're a modern woman, I'm pleased to take you to your first oyster house." At Callie's questioning look, he laughed. "Don't worry, Downing's is not a waterfront cellar notorious for its criminal element. It's a respectable establishment that draws a regular patronage from the nearby banks and customs house."

During the ride to Broad Street, Byrch regaled Callie with stories about street arabs and newsboys. "There's a whole element of society you know little about, Callie, and since you've decided to form a close association with our newsboys and dealers, you should know some of their habits. There's a place over on Spruce Street, not too far from the *Herald*'s offices, called Butter-cake Dick's. That's where most of our boys go." Byrch told her about the all-night coffeeshop and the army of sharp-faced adolescents who gathered there every night, hoarse from newshawking, to consume a "butter-cake," a peculiar sort of biscuit with a lump of butter in its center, and a cup of coffee, bitter and black, for only three cents. He described how the newsboys' demigods, ex-newsboys who had somehow scrounged and saved enough to become newsdealers, often graced the premises, commandeering the scratched, beaten tables, puffing on cheap cigars, and turning the air blue with oaths and tales of lust and riches. The newsdealers in turn idolized the Olympian b'hoys, those red-flanneled volunteer firemen who came in stinking and reeking from a fire and bragging about their derring-do.

Downing's on Broad Street was as respectable as Byrch had promised and was the very model of comfort and prosperity. Callie was impressed with the mirrored arcades, damask curtains, fine carpets, and shimmering chandeliers. Mr. Downing, a tall, white-haired Negro, welcomed ladies in the company of their husbands or escorts, and tempted their appetites with elaborate dishes of scalloped oysters, oyster pie, fish with oyster sauce, and an unusual specialty of poached turkey stuffed with oysters. A flautist and a fiddler played popular tunes and sea chanties and created a background for the good food and quiet conversation. Waiters wearing snowy white aprons served at the tables while Downing officiated as host.

The food was exquisitely prepared and served on Luxembourg china with bone-handled flatware and sparkling crystal glasses. Byrch tempted Callie to sample the ale, which was the perfect beverage with deep-fried oysters. Together they enjoyed the poached turkey, served in paper thin slices placed over mounds of stuffing. Over coffee, Callie introduced her idea about home delivery of the *Clarion-Observer*.

"Think of it, Byrch!" Her eyes glowed with enthusiasm. "People will be able to have the *Clarion* over breakfast."

"Callie, I hate to dash your hopes, but the *Clarion* is an early paper. People already have it before breakfast."

"Only the people you know, Byrch. The ones rich enough to have a servant who goes out to the corner each morning to buy it for them. I'm talking about working people, housewives who watch the ads looking for sales. They'd be able to plan their days, and they won't be missing a bargain because they had to wait for their husbands to bring the paper home at suppertime. It'll be a boon for your advertisers, Byrch. Women will be able to plan ahead—"

"Whoa! I concede, you've got a point." Byrch stared into his coffeecup while Callie waited to hear his thoughts. Finally he lifted his head, smiling directly into her eyes, and she felt her heart skip a beat. "It could work very well. The *Clarion* is certainly out early enough to allow for home delivery. The newsdealers deliver stacks of papers to various corners, and they could just as well deliver to the homes of our boys. Another thought occurred to me. We notice a dip in our sales during the winter months because the newsboys are in school. Home delivery might help that."

"It can work, Byrch. The boys agreed to give it a try, and you can advertise home delivery right in the *Clarion*. It will take some time to organize routes, but it can be done."

"We've talked about it down at the paper, but it didn't seem feasible. The main argument was that people might not pay for their papers."

Callie frowned. "Yes, I've thought of that, and I hate to think of the boys taking the loss. But people are basically honest, and besides, we'll be getting off to a slow start. If there's a risk, it will be a small one."

"You've convinced me, Callie. The more readers, the more advertisers, the more the *Clarion* will grow. But there's a hitch. Someone will have to organize the routes, monitor the boys, do a bit of troubleshooting if needed. Someone close to the boys. I'm assuming you're that someone, is that right?" At Callie's nod of agreement, Byrch continued. "Will you be able to handle all of that? Your column and the boys and their money?"

"I'd like to try, Byrch. I believe the boys will accept me."

"The newsboys are very important to the paper. I wish we could pay them more than we do. They're the backbone of the industry; they get the product out to the public. Jimmy Riley told me about the Jacobs family. The *Clarion* paid the bills and sent the family a sum of money to help out a bit. I wish it could have been more. The day is coming, I'm certain, when we'll be able to have benefits like insurance for everyone connected with the paper."

"You mean the Typographical Union?"

"Exactly. That's why the idea of a labor union is met so negatively. It will only be the first among many."

"Next thing you know, there'll be a union for women. Some day we might even get to vote!" she laughed.

"Now you *are* being silly. But I suspect that day will dawn. Especially with firebrands like Callie James MacDuff marking the path."

It was past midnight when Byrch and Callie left Downing's. They lingered long over snifters of brandy while they enjoyed the entertainment the establishment offered. On the ride back to the house Callie wasn't surprised that he didn't suggest another ride along the river. Tomorrow was a business day.

Byrch dismissed George and the carriage for the night, adding that he intended to walk to the paper in the morning and wouldn't need the carriage until the following afternoon. They let themselves into the house quietly so as not to disturb Edward. After dousing the lights in the parlor, they climbed the stairs side by side. The touch of his hand on her elbow was light, and yet there was a possessiveness about it.

Would it always be this way between them? she wondered. She lived in his house, had slept in his bed, wept in his arms, and she knew she'd been closer and more intimate with him than she'd ever been with anyone else. His touch should be familiar, expected, yet he had this effect on her, searing her flesh with a touch, awakening her passions with his nearness, igniting her senses with a caress.

On the third floor, just outside her bedroom, Byrch stopped outside the door, twirling his hat in his hands. "It was a wonderful evening, Callie. We should do it more often."

"Yes." She managed to speak past the lump in her throat, hovering in the doorway, standing so close to him she could see the shadows his thicket of lashes cast in those exciting tiger eyes.

"Well, I suppose you should be getting to bed, it's quite late."

Callie nodded, unable to speak, wanting to throw herself into his arms. His breath felt warm and tender against her cheek. Had she moved closer or had he?

"Would you like me to light your lamp?" he asked, seeming to have difficulty keeping his tone light and even.

Callie moved from the doorway into her room, admitting him entrance. She watched him cross the room to the bedtable to light the lamp. Unbidden, even unaware, she moved across the room and into his embrace, offering her mouth for his kiss. She was mesmerized by the deliberate slowness of his hands as he undressed her and by the intimacy of his voice as he expressed her loveliness. Callie felt as though she would melt and become a part of him as his fingers found the laces of her corset and the ripe fullness of her breasts beneath her thin camisole.

Taking her cue from him, she worked on the buttons of his shirt, untied his cravat, and followed the path with her lips, tasting the freshness of his skin and inhaling his clean, masculine scent. He explored her shoulders and the long sweep of her back, his lips savoring the curve of her neck and the valley between her breasts. Callie felt herself yielding up to him, unaware of the existence of a world beyond the span of his arms and the touch of his lips.

One by one her garments fell to the floor, leaving her naked and lovely, accessible to his hands, his eyes, and his mouth.

His touch was gentle on her skin. He moved his mouth over her own, drawing sweetly, penetrating her lips with the soft, teasing touches of his tongue. He lifted her easily and placed her on her bed.

In the dim light of the lamp, Callie's eyes followed each movement of his hands as he disrobed. She saw the play of muscles beneath the flesh of his back, saw the flatness of his belly and the power of his thighs. But it was on his manhood, somehow so hard and so vulnerable at the same time, that her gaze was focused. She opened her arms to him, drawing him into her soft embrace, filling a need only he could create in her.

Byrch was impatient for her, needing her, feeling as though he could never satiate her desire for her. He wanted to plunge into her, feel her draw him deeply into the center, and yet he wanted to explore and seek, awaken her to his love. Callie was a woman who answered a gentle touch, a slow and steady progression of her own desires.

The lamplight illuminated her against the stark whiteness of the sheets, lending her a golden hue that glistened on the curve of her cheek and the planes and valleys of her body. Soft, dark curls bloomed on the mound of her sex, and he knew an unquenchable need to feel the smoothness of her inner thighs beneath his lips and to explore those regions that were so vulnerable to his touch.

Callie's hands traced the breadth of his shoulders, the slimness of his hips. Her fingers tangled in the furring of his chest, and she arched her body at his obvious desire for her. His caresses were gentle yet stirring; his kisses soft yet demanding. His hands slipped to her haunches, lifting her, holding her. Throwing back her head, she leaned into this new and sensual caress, raking her fingers through his thick, wavy hair, bending, lifting her legs to open herself to his greedy mouth. Her world spun around her, and nothing seemed to exist except his thirsty lips and her vulnerable flesh.

He held her tenderly, staving off his own satisfaction, while she climbed down from the clouds to smile up at him. He smoothed back the tumble of hair from her forehead, whispering, "You're beautiful, so beautiful." And he made her feel beautiful, and she wanted to fill this yearning within her to take him deeply inside her. She fit her curves against the hard planes of his body, shivering with anticipation when his thighs slipped smoothly between her own and he lowered himself onto her, sensing her urgency that he take her quickly, fill her with himself.

She enveloped him with her warmth, holding him prisoner within her. The long, slow strokes of his hips became more urgent, hot and flaring, quickening into driving thrusts as she matched his rhythm, arching herself to meet him. She breathed his name as she found her own release, locking her legs around him, urging him to his finish.

Long into the night they held each other, their closeness and caresses speaking eloquently of the love that neither could admit with words in the full light of day.

Callie awakened the next morning, her head still filled with dreams of Byrch. She rolled over, her hands reaching to find him. But he was already gone. She could hear the water running in the bath down the hall. Sighing, Callie snuggled under the sheets. She felt a rush of emotion thinking of last night, and she knew she had to stifle it. Last night was just part of their arrangement. She couldn't let it mean more than it was or cloud it with her emotions. Byrch was being nicer, not so mocking and cynical. He seemed to be trying as hard as she was to be polite and not to let things get out of hand.

Marriage to Byrch in another week. It was enough to make her weak in the knees. A no-strings marriage. How could she possibly honor that when all she had to do was look at Byrch and her determination dissolved?

On his way downstairs, Byrch peeked into Callie's room to find her still asleep. He recognized a small seed of hope somewhere within him. Patience. Time. After they were married, he'd wear her down and convince her, somehow, that the two of them were meant for one another. Time.

Chapter Thirty

allie stood beside Byrch in the parlor, listening to Father Mul-
oon intone a prayer to bless this marriage. Marriage! She still
ouldn't believe Byrch was actually making her go through with
is.

Kevin and Bridget Darcy acted as witnesses at Byrch's insist-
nce, their faces constrained and disapproving. Callie had had no
y in the matter. Byrch seemed determined that his new wife
ould enjoy immediate acceptance, even though he realized the
arcys only participated because their social ambitions prevented
em from refusing. After all, Byrch could be the future mayor
f New York City.

The pronouncement was made. They were man and wife before
e eyes of God and the world. Father Muldoon beamed and even
issed the bride. Byrch heaved a mighty sigh of relief, so loud that
dward shot him a warning glance. He hadn't realized how tense
'd been until the marriage was a *fait accompli*. He'd been certain
omething would go awry and that Callie would never be his.

Edward served a luscious luncheon—succulent little finger
ndwiches, cold wine, and a festive three-tiered wedding cake
the centerpiece for the elegantly appointed table. Kevin toasted

the bride and groom, and Bridget pretended to smile at Calli but her eyes were cold with speculation as she lifted her glas

Callie forced a smile and cringed inwardly at what Bridg must be thinking. The woman's eyes were suffused with suspici and speculation. How could she know this wasn't a marriage ma in heaven unless Byrch had confided the details to her? The sudde thought was so degrading that Callie felt faint and sick to h stomach.

After lunch, Bridget and Kevin left, offering their wishes f a long and happy life, their words ringing in Callie's ears eve after the door closed behind them.

Edward carried the dishes out to the kitchen and heaved mighty sigh. He was becoming as nervous as an old woman wi thirteen grandchildren underfoot.

"What shall we do?" Byrch asked, taking Callie's hand in hi

"Do?" She stared at him, not understanding. She withdrew h hand from his, remembering her suspicions that he'd confide intimacies to Bridget.

"Yes, do. You vetoed the idea of a honeymoon in Saratog Springs. Everyone at the paper thinks I'm going on a honeymoo That includes you too, sweeting. You won't have your colum to write for another ten days, and I cleared my desk yesterday

"I . . . I didn't . . . I mean . . ."

"You haven't given it any thought since this is a marriage name only? I almost understand that. You could sit in the parlo I could retire to my den. We could both annoy Edward, or w could go to our respective rooms." Byrch had to regain contr of himself. He was a bridegroom, for God's sake, and his bri didn't give a damn about him! "All right then, if you can't pla days ahead, what shall we do with the rest of the day? You're a dressed up. I'm all dressed up. Might I say you look lovel sweeting? Even Bridget thought so and was green-eyed with jea ousy."

The idea of Bridget green with jealousy pleased Callie, an she didn't notice Byrch's arm slipping around her waist. "Byrc I hope you aren't too disappointed about our not going to Saratog I just didn't want to be around all those people in such a popul resort." It was very close to the truth. Being around other coupl celebrating their honeymoons would create a romantic atmospher Byrch would only have to look at her, and she would succum to him, she knew she would.

"I am disappointed, Callie. I understand how you feel, b

ɔmetimes a new atmosphere can give you a better perspective bout things—things like your life, mine, our life together. But certainly have no intention of insisting that you do anything you on't want to do." He removed his hand from her waist, his voice ɔol and distant.

"Is that another way of saying you're already regretting this arriage and the bargain we made?"

"No, damn it, that's not what I'm saying at all. Why do you lways have to look for hidden motives in everything I say or do? Vhy can't you just accept me for what I am? I offered a trip, a oneymoon trip. You declined, for whatever silly reasons you ave, for whatever excuse, and that's the end of if. Now if you on't mind, I think I'll go to my study and read the paper, that ;, unless you want to read it first."

"No, you go ahead. I think I'll write a letter to my mother. 'ertainly she'll want to hear of my wedding."

"And of course, you have so much to tell her. You'd better et on with it, all those interesting details will take hours," Byrch napped.

Now what had she done? "You see, you're doing it again. 'here's no reason for you to take such a tone with me. Why houldn't I write my mother? It was your idea we get married,) save your reputation, remember?" Callie said stonily. Reading ie paper. On her wedding day he was going to read the paper. nd just what was she supposed to do? She had no columns to rite for another ten days. She'd be damned if she would work ı the garden on her wedding day. Edward wouldn't want her uttering around his kitchen. She'd already taken a bath. That ɛft a nap. Imagine taking a nap, alone, on her wedding day. 'ears stung her eyes. Was this to be the rest of her life? "Read our damn paper and see if I care!" Callie sniffed as she gathered er skirts in her hand to start the climb up the long staircase.

Byrch wished he were a child so he could throw himself on ıe floor and kick and scream. What did she want from him? 'ouldn't she see his agony? Did she hate their agreement so much he was now going to write all the nasty details to her mother? ord help him, all he wanted to do was love her, take care of her, nd be the father of her children. Was that so damn much to ask? 3y God, it wasn't. He had been almost sure she would agree to ıe honeymoon trip to Saratoga. Perhaps that was wrong. He houldn't have used the word honeymoon. A trip. An excursion) a new place is what he should have said. He had been so sure

he could win her over, being with her twenty-four hours a day
People simply did not live like this!

Byrch rubbed at his throbbing temples as he spread out th
paper. The words were blurred, indistinct, as he tried to focus o
one of the columns. Was all of this a mistake? Was it going t
get better, or would it get worse? If only he knew. Perhaps h
should send Callie back to Ireland, settle a sum of money on he
and never see her again. That's what he should do. She wa
miserable living with him, and now that he had forced this un
wanted marriage on her, she would withdraw from him even more
How in the living hell had he allowed himself to be placed in suc
a predicament? Because he loved her, heart and soul. He kne
now that his love wasn't returned; he should simply cut his losse
and try to live his life without Callie.

Byrch lifted his gaze to the ceiling. What the hell was she doin
up there? Crying her eyes out? Crying because she made a terribl
mistake and didn't know how to rectify it? He snorted at th
implausible idea. Callie was tough.

Tossing down the paper, Byrch bounded up the stairs. Witho
ceremony he threw open the door, surprised that it wasn't locke
He felt mystified when he saw that she wasn't crying or writing
her mother, but staring out the window. In a brisk, businesslike ton
he made his announcement. "Starting tomorrow morning, I'm goin
to show you New York. If you're going to work on my paper, you'
going to be the best goddamn reporter there is, next to me. I wa
you downstairs and ready at eight-thirty sharp. This is how we'
going to spend our honeymoon. I think I should tell you that whi
I was downstairs, I had a second thought, and that was to settle
sum of money on you and send you back to Ireland."

"What?" Callie gasped hardly believing the words she wa
hearing. Send her back? Give her money and send her back? "
don't understand. Why would you send me back? You were th
one who wanted to get married. If you were thinking of sendin
me back, why did you marry me?" Good Lord, surely this shiver
quaking voice wasn't hers.

"I've been known to be a fool at times, and that was or
of those times. My eyes are open now. But keep it in mind.

"But that's a . . . a threat," Callie said in a hushed whispe
Surely that wasn't what he meant. One look at Byrch's face tol
her that was exactly what he meant. Now that she was marrie
to him he could do whatever he pleased, and if it pleased him
send her back to Dublin, he would do it. She ached with the nee

to cry, but instead she stiffened her back and composed her face. "I'll be ready."

"Good. I'll see you in the morning. I won't be here for dinner, so don't wait for me."

Not for the world would she ask him where he was going.

The least she could do was ask him where he was going, Byrch thought. He could come up with some kind of lie. A long walk in the park, he could feed the pigeons; he could watch the children playing. Hell, there were any number of things a newly married man could do if his wife wanted no part of him.

Settling herself at her small desk, Callie picked up her pen to finish the letter to her mother:

> . . . and so, Mum, things are certainly different from what I expected. I'm so mixed up. Nothing seems to be going right for me. No matter what I do, it doesn't seem to be right. I've been thinking a lot about returning to Ireland. Do you think that's a good idea, Mum? I would have a little money, and if we were careful, I could get some kind of housework and we'd all be together again. I'm married, but I'm not married, Mum. I don't know what to feel about that. I can't take much more. I'm afraid to do or say anything for fear it will be the wrong thing. Byrch wanted to go to Saratoga Springs for a honeymoon. I said I didn't want to go, but, Mum, I want to go. I have a long time yet before I can get back to work on the paper; I have to wait for the honeymoon to be over before I can start writing my columns again. If I haven't learned anything else, Mum, I've learned that I can't step out of my place again. Every time I reach out for happiness, for what I want, it's taken away from me in the most terrible way.
>
> I don't have anything to do right now, so I'm going to take another bath in that bathtub I told you about. Did you ever hear of anyone who took two baths in one day? I think I might be doing a lot of that in the days to come.
>
> This is the first letter I've written since I became Callie Kenyon four hours ago. Does that sound nice, Mum? Write to me, Mum, I need to hear from you. I need someone who loves me.
>
> Your daughter,
> Callie

* * *

Byrch walked aimlessly for over an hour. He was unaware of the chattering, scampering children who raced past him chasing a kite on a long string. He paid no notice to an angry bumblebee that buzzed directly over his head, and he completely ignored a stray dog that yipped at his heels. Once he looked overhead as he neared a street corner to see where he was. He continued his aimless walk, his hands thrust deep in his pockets. His mind buzzed as angrily as the bee circling his head. Was there such a thing as backing oneself into a corner? If there was, that was exactly what he had done. Whatever in the world possessed him to threaten Callie with sending her back to Ireland? His stomach heaved when he realized that in the end that might be the best decision for both of them.

A small boy in tattered knickers raced past Byrch, almost knocking him off balance. The quick sidestep he took to get out of the child's way forced his dark thoughts from his mind. A moment later he heard his name called. "Oooh-hoo, Byrch."

"Flanna! I didn't realize where I was for the moment. Beautiful day, isn't it?"

"There won't be many more like this one, so you better enjoy it," Flanna trilled. "Aren't you a little far from home, Byrch?" Setting her basket of flowers on the low brick wall, she watched Byrch expectantly.

"I had something on my mind, and I find it helps to clear the cobwebs if I walk and think things through. Have you found that to be true?"

"For me, it's working in the garden. During the winter months I work in the greenhouse. My dear, departed husband had it built for me. I do so like earthy things, all manner of earthy things," Flanna said.

"I do too." Christ, what was he doing here carrying on this stupid conversation with Flanna Beauchamp? Because you have nothing better to do, an inner voice answered.

"If you aren't going anywhere in particular, why don't you come in and join me in a cup of tea. Or something stronger if you prefer. I was just about to go in and fix myself a cup. It's been a long day." She waited for Byrch's reply.

Hell, why not? He certainly had nothing better to do. Flanna could be entertaining when she wanted to be, and he had always found her amusing. Since he'd first met her and her parents at Bridget's dinner party, Flanna had married a rich but elderly man.

She was recently widowed and had resumed her maiden name, knowing it was more influential than her married name of Skaggs.

"I'll pass on the tea but take you up on some brandy if you have it."

"If I have it?" Flanna cooed. "Simon left me a well-stocked bar. You name it, and I have it, right down to Simon's grandmother's best crystal." Her laugh tinkled, and Byrch thought it was one of the most pleasant sounds he had heard in a long time. Yes, Flanna could be entertaining.

Byrch walked around the low stone wall and marveled at the colorful blooms in the wide expanse of green velvety lawn. It was every bit as pretty as Callie's garden. He watched as Flanna stripped off her gloves and slipped one arm through the basket and her other arm through his. He didn't know why, but he thought the moves were the most seductive he had ever seen. Jesus, she must make a real production out of taking off her clothes, he thought.

He liked the sound of the black silk dress rustling about her feet as they walked around to the back door. Not everyone could wear black the way Flanna wore it. White skin, ebony hair, and then the black dress. It could do things to a man.

Flanna settled Byrch in a small sitting room off the main parlor. "Now you sit there and put your feet up. You look tense, Byrch. Relax. I'll be back in a minute." She was as good as her word, returning in moments with his drink on a silver tray. She excused herself a second time to get her tea. It was a pleasant room, light and cheery, much like Flanna herself. Colorful prints dotted the walls, and the furniture was low and comfortable. A man's room. It must have been Simon's room, he decided. A man could fall asleep in a chair like this and wake without being stiff and cranky. He liked it. He had to remember to ask her where she got it.

Flanna settled herself across from him, her skirt hiked to show trim ankles. "So tell me, Byrch, how are things at the paper?"

"Good. Very good as a matter of fact." He had to keep his mind as well as his eyes off the slow moving ankle. "Circulation is up. We have a new reporter that is getting to the heart of things. Home delivery is going to be available soon. Good. Very good."

"I'm glad to hear that," Flanna said lightly over the rim of her teacup. "What was it that was on your mind that you had to work out by walking? Perhaps I can help. I'm a good listener. Simon said I was the best listener he ever knew. Simon always said things like that. I do miss having a man to fuss over."

"You'll marry again someday. Some lucky man will sweep you off your feet."

"I wish I could count on that," Flanna laughed. "He would have to be a pretty special man for me to give up what I have now. A very special man, someone like . . . you perhaps," Flanna teased lightly.

Byrch almost choked on the fiery brandy. Flanna was off her chair in a minute, thumping him on the back and pouring another glass, urging Byrch to drink quickly. "It won't kill you, it will help. Drink," she said authoritatively. Byrch drank. "There now, you see, I was right. Don't slump so. I'll just massage your neck and shoulders, and you'll feel better in a minute. I used to do this for Simon all the time."

"Simon sure must have been a lucky devil," Byrch muttered as he felt the long slim fingers work at his neck. "Hmmm, that does feel good."

Flanna's tinkling laugh seemed to circle the room. "Why do you think poor Simon died? Lord, he was only sixty-two. I just killed him with love and devotion."

And that's not all, Byrch thought to himself. "Keep that up, Flanna, and I'll go to sleep on you."

"Would that be so terrible? I have seventeen rooms in this house. Of course, people would talk. Drink your brandy and relax. Let yourself go and enjoy what I'm doing. This is the best medicine for headaches or any kind of problem. Body contact. Your body, my fingers," Flanna said wickedly. Byrch could feel his eyes getting heavier and heavier as Flanna crooned to him, all the while working on his neck and shoulder muscles. He could tell when Flanna withdrew and took her place across from him. One sleepy eye opened. All that black and all that creamy white skin. She suddenly reminded him of a vulture, a hungry vulture, as she stared at him across her teacup.

Flanna sat late into the night, sipping cup after cup of tea as she watched Byrch sleep. He was a handsome devil. She could do worse. With her money and his newspaper she could stand this town on its ear. But first she would have to find out a little more about the young woman rumored to be living in his house. Bridget would know. Bridget would tell all.

Flanna sat facing the small onyx clock on the mantel. It read 3:15 in the morning. Byrch had slept for nearly eight hours. Poor man, he must be exhausted. It would be a shame to wake him.

When she noticed that he was stirring, she slumped a little lower in her chair and closed her eyes.

"Flanna! Flanna, wake up. Good God, what time is it?" Byrch asked anxiously.

"Good heavens, Byrch, you startled me. Didn't anyone ever tell you not to shout at a sleeping person? I think it's around three in the morning. Why don't you let me bed you down for the night?"

"Thanks, but no thanks," Byrch grinned boyishly. "Thank you for the brandy and your company."

"It was my pleasure, Byrch." She tried to hide her disappointment.

Outside in the cool night air Byrch felt befuddled. He hadn't had that much to drink. It must have been the relaxing massage Flanna gave him. He walked on, and soon found himself in the Darcys' block. Oh, Jesus, that couldn't be Bridget. Surely that wasn't Bridget standing on the front porch in her night clothes, waiting for her dog to piddle.

"Byrch!" she shrieked. "Byrch! Is something wrong? What are you doing at this end of town at this time of night?" Her eyes narrowed suddenly when she noticed the direction he was coming from. Could he have gone to Flanna Beauchamp's house? On his wedding night?

"Will you shut the hell up, Bridget. You'll be waking up the entire neighborhood, not to mention Kevin and the children. What are *you* doing up at this time of night?"

"This fool dog had to go out. Who does she nudge when she wants to be let out? Not Kevin, I can tell you. Me, no matter what time of the day or night. I don't have to explain anything to you, Byrch. It's you who have some explaining to do. Just what are you doing at this time of night on the day you got married?"

"That's none of your business, Bridget," Byrch said, stalking off into the night.

Of all the goddamn miserable, rotten luck, this was the worst. By tomorrow everyone in town would know that he had been seen near Flanna Beauchamp's house at three o'clock in the morning. Knowing Bridget, she would probably up the time to four o'clock, and she wouldn't fail to mention that it was on his wedding day. If Callie got wind of the gossip she would be humiliated beyond belief. Byrch groaned aloud as he made his way down the darkened streets. Not that she would care. He winced when he thought of what Edward would say. Perhaps he should try to beat all the gossips to the punch and tell both Edward and Callie where he'd been, make a joke ou of it if he could. He could just picture the disdainful look on Ed-ward's face and the white, stricken one on Callie's. He felt as though he'd been dunked in boiling water as he rounded the corner onto St. Luke's Place. He wasn't surprised to see a light shining in his kitchen. Edward often waited up, dozing in his rocker by the fire place with the new yellow cat on his lap.

Edward looked pointedly at the kitchen clock and frowned hi disapproval as he got up from the rocker. The yellow cat scampered away, probably to nestle between the two pillows on his bed Byrch thought.

Callie crept out of bed and walked on tiptoe down the hall She knew Byrch hadn't been home since he left late in the after-noon. All night she had lain awake. The tears had long since dried on her cheeks, and her eyes felt achy. Should she or shouldn' she creep down the dark stairway and listen at the kitchen door' She knew that Byrch would be talking to Edward. Were they discussing her or what he had done since he left? She had to know She strained to hear.

"I don't know, Edward. I suppose I was more tired than realized with the strain of the wedding and all. I can hardly believe it myself. And then to have Bridget see me at this hour of the night coming from Flanna Beauchamp's. By tomorrow it will be all over town."

"I don't think there's too much cause for worry, sir. Mr. Darcy is a man, and he does control Mrs. Darcy, or am I wrong?"

"Kevin never controlled anything in his life, least of all his wife. No one, but no one, controls her tongue. I'm afraid I'm in for it, Edward. What bothers me is what Callie is going to think." He sighed heavily. "I think I'll turn in. It was nice of you to wait up for me, Edward. You don't have to do that, you know."

"Someone had to sit with the cat," Edward said tartly as he made his way to his room. For one brief moment he thought his eyes were playing tricks on him. He thought he saw something flutter at the kitchen doorway. It was probably the yellow cat trying to make up its mind if it should stay downstairs or go upstairs.

Callie raced upstairs. She wanted to slam the door and then kick it. She fought the urge to scream like a banshee. Instead she locked her door and flung herself across the bed. She buried her face in the pillow and sobbed.

All night she had lain awake. All night she tortured herself with impossible dreams. The least he could have done was to make an attempt to see her, to . . . to . . . he should have tried. If he could threaten to knock her door down once, why couldn't he do it a second time? No, oh, no, he goes out to see, what was her name and . . . and . . . tomorrow everyone in town was going to know what he did. Bridget would see to it. How was she going to hold her head up? How was she going to face Byrch in the morning and behave as though she knew nothing? Better yet how was Byrch going to be able to face her? People would start to stare, pitying her. Edward was going to feel sorry for her and offer her tea, his answer to everything. She was a fool. She didn't need Byrch Kenyon to rub salt in her wounds. Why couldn't she just be a fool by herself? "Damn you, Byrch Kenyon," she sobbed into the pillow. "Damn you to hell!"

Byrch stood outside Callie's door, the yellow cat purring against his ankles. With a grimace he bent down and picked up the small cat. The animal instantly recognized warmth and comfort and snuggled against his chest. Callie could purr like a kitten when she was contented. He groaned when he remembered how she had snuggled down into the cradle of his arm, her head against his chest. She made small little sounds of pleasure as she drifted off to sleep. "Get the hell out of here," Byrch snapped at the startled cat as he sat it down on the floor. The cat mewed in fright and immediately piddled on the floor. Byrch looked at the puddle with disgust. They had to get rid of that cat. Whose idea had it been in the first place?

The morning sun was filtering through the curtains before Callie found sleep. When she finally awakened, a glance at the clock on the mantel told her it was nearly ten-thirty. Ten-thirty! She'd promised to be dressed and ready two hours ago! Then she remembered. He hadn't come home until the wee hours of the morning and was probably too exhausted to show her the city. Callie smacked her pillow and suppressed a scream of rage. How could he? Last night had been their wedding night! He had spent the night with another woman, humiliating his wife before the eyes of the world. Callie knew she was overreacting to a situation she herself had helped to create, but it was better to feel outrage than this stab of pain at wanting him so.

She couldn't resist the temptation to peek in on Byrch. Opening her door a crack, she peered out. The yellow cat was snoozing peacefully outside Byrch's door. So he was still in there. Crossing the hall, she stepped over the cat, opened the door, and peeked into the dim room. The scent of his cologne and tobacco greeted

her. Byrch was sprawled across his bed, fully dressed. How coul
he? How could he sleep like this? Didn't he care about her at al
And was that slight smile that played on his mouth because h
was dreaming of that woman?

Callie quietly closed his door before her hands clenched int
fists. If she had a penny's worth of courage, she'd trot right i
there and hit him! The force of the imagined blow, the thoug
of her fist pounding into that smug, self-satisfied face was almo
a reality. He'd probably sleep the day away and recover his streng
to go to that woman again tonight. He would. She knew he woul
Like hell he would! Callie stomped into her room and tore throug
her armoire to select a dress. Undergarments, stockings, shoes–
he said he was going to take her out and show her New Yor
and that was exactly what he'd do. She'd have him walking an
talking and wear him down the best she could. With any bit
luck, even if he did go to Flanna what's-her-name, he wouldn
be worth the wear and tear on the sheets!

Byrch had seen the door open silently. Edward? Callie? Th
cat couldn't reach the doorknob. In the dim light, through slitte
eyes, he caught a glimpse of a nightdress. Pretending to be aslee
he waited, hardly daring to breathe. Would she come in? Hi
world was tilting when he considered the possibilities. Perhap
she was sorry to have enforced such restrictions on their marriage
Perhaps she needed him as much as he needed her. How long wa
she going to stand there looking at him? She couldn't know abou
last night, could she? And besides, what was there to know excep
that he'd risked her credibility as his wife and her pride as
woman? Byrch felt his throat working convulsively; he knew h
could not forgive himself so easily. When the door closed wit
Callie on the far side of it, he rolled over onto his stomach an
slammed his fist into the pillow. If she hadn't known anythin
before, she certainly would have her suspicions now! He'd ju
realized that he was sprawled across the bed, fully clothed, sti
dressed in his wedding suit!

Dressed to go out, Callie descended the stairs, holding u
the hem of her sheer yellow and blue-striped dress. It was full
skirted and showed off her tiny waist to an advantage; it wa
perfect for a late summer day. The aroma of coffee met he
when she reached the bottom of the stairs. She heard Edwar
rattling pots and pans. Taking a deep breath and steeling hersel
against the anticipated pity in Edward's eyes, she walked throug
the parlor and dining room into the kitchen. "Good morning
Edward."

Edward was fully dressed in his pin-striped trousers and black coat. His shirt and stock were dazzling white against his mahogany skin. "Good morning, Miss Callie. My, don't you look lovely this morning! That pale shade of yellow is wonderful against your dark hair." The only thing Callie could perceive in Edward's dark eyes was friendship. Bless him. "Coffee's ready. What would you like for breakfast?"

"Anything. Coffee first. Edward, I'd like you to go upstairs and awaken Mr. Kenyon. Only don't tell him I've just come downstairs. Would you do that for me?"

"Anything for you, Miss Callie," Edward smiled.

"I don't want you to lie, but it isn't necessary to tell him just how recently I've come down. Understand?"

Edward nodded as he left the kitchen to awaken his employer.

Callie took her coffee cup to the back door and looked out at the garden. The morning was still cool, and the dew sparkled in the sunshine like jewels in a golden setting. It was a new day, bright and shiny as a penny. A new day could be a new beginning, she told herself, a new start. She brought her cup to her lips. She'd die before she mentioned last night or asked her husband where he'd spent their wedding night. Callie sipped her coffee, suddenly feeling terribly sorry for herself. How could today be a new beginning? Byrch had broken her door down once before, but he hadn't even made the effort last night. He should at least have tried and given her that much satisfaction!

Edward cleared away the breakfast dishes silently. Everyone was silent this morning. Byrch sat drinking his coffee. Miss Callie sat opposite him, her hands folded demurely in her lap. While she might appear quietly poised to an unfamiliar eye, Edward knew she was hurt and angry. He knew, beyond doubt, that she was aware of where Byrch had spent the night.

Byrch eyed Callie over the rim of his coffee cup. It was going to be a long day. Lord, he was dragging. Despite the sleep he'd had at Flanna's, he was exhausted just from worry alone. Women could be the death of a man. By God, this was his honeymoon, and he was going to enjoy it if it killed them both. Forcing a lighthearted tone into his voice, he smiled. "I'm ready if you are, sweeting."

Something that pretended to be a smile tugged at Callie's mouth while her eyes burned with anger. "Yes, I'm ready," was all she managed to say as she too rose from the table.

Edward shook his head. This was not the stuff of romance and honeymoons. They should take the cat along with them so they'd both have someone to talk to. Edward resolved, as he found himself doing often of late, that he wouldn't take sides. After all, Byrch was his friend as well as his employer, and Miss Callie was good and kind and generous, appreciative of his every deed. How could he side with one and betray the other?

In the carriage Byrch started the conversation. He made his tone as light and as conversational as possible. This was going to be a pleasant day. "The way I see it, Callie, if you're going to compete with reporters who have been born and bred here, you're going to have to know New York as well as they do. That might seem like an impossible task, but you have young eyes, eyes that are newer, fresher, unjaded. You can look at the city and the people in it with a slant that is yours alone."

Callie watched Byrch as he talked. How pleasant he was being. She wanted to reach out and touch him, but restrained herself. "Thank you, Byrch, for what you just said. I appreciate your trying to help me."

My God, didn't she know he would lay down and die for her? Nice. She thought he was being nice to her. He told her little stories as he pointed out different sights. Callie was amused at his tone and the way he could poke fun at himself as he related his experiences. Her eyes were bright and eager, and she loved listening to him. She asked few questions, absorbing everything he said like a sponge.

"That's Delmonico's restaurant," Byrch pointed as their carriage wended its way past Broadway and Chambers Street. "Lorenzo Delmonico felt that the establishment on Beaver Street was too far downtown to attract the fashionable trade, so he opened another restaurant here. It's on the site of the notorious Colt murder." He watched her eyes widen, knowing she would demand all the details.

"It was back in 1841. Samuel Adams, a printer, arrived at the Broadway-Chamber Street office of John Colt, who was an accountant and a professor of ornamental penmanship, to collect on a bill. Mr. Adams offended Mr. Colt, and they began to fight. Mr. Colt managed to brain Mr. Adams with a hammer. What's remarkable is that Colt then nailed Adams into a box and had a cartman haul it off to the docks where it was transferred to the hold of a boat bound for Brazil. But there was a certain lady of questionable reputation who had a score to even with Mr. Colt. It was because she went to the authorities that the body was recovered at the very last moment and Mr. Colt was sent to the gallows."

"How awful," Callie said breathlessly. A delicious shiver ran down her spine. She inched a little closer to Byrch, her eyes wide as she waited for his next words. Byrch noticed her slight movement and moved closer himself so that their bodies were now touching. Callie didn't draw away. He made his tone somber and yet wicked as he continued with his story.

"Four hours before Colt's execution, however, he was granted a last, sentimental wish and was married in his cell to a Miss Caroline Henshaw. This was particularly surprising since the woman who reported Colt's misdeed in the first place bore a remarkable resemblance to Miss Henshaw. Everyone was amazed by the groom's high spirits. This became more understandable when two hours later an elaborate plot for his escape became evident. It involved the substitution of a corpse and the burning of the jail's cupola. It all came off without a hitch. Colt's fate remains a mystery to this day."

"How wonderful!" Callie said, clapping her hands. "I do so love happy endings."

Byrch's gaze locked with Callie's. "I'm partial to happy endings myself. So we do have something in common after all. I was beginning to get worried there for a while."

Byrch and Callie went on exploring New York with verve and enthusiasm. Through Callie, Byrch was seeing it all as if for the first time. Callie almost wept with joy when he pointed out the miniature Egyptian pyramid near the Forty-second Street Reservoir.

"This is a popular place on Sundays. Sometimes it takes on a carnival atmosphere. We can come back some Sunday if you would like," Byrch offered.

"Oh, could we? I would love that."

"It gets a bit frantic. They have what they call sandwich-board men, who are walking advertisements. Everyone has something to sell, and this is the place to do it. I brought Edward here one Sunday, and I thought he was going to die from excitement. He's never been back. The one thing you have to buy when you come is a bag of Hoarhound Drops." The carriage clattered along for a few minutes before Byrch spoke again.

"That's the Crystal Palace," he pointed out. "Look across the street to the Observatory. It's twenty-seven stories high and has a 'vertical railway' or steam elevator. I can't tell you how many people came here during the World's Fair. That's what made it so famous. That and the ice-cream parlor. Let's stop and get some."

"Can we really?" Callie asked in wide-eyed wonder. "I would love that, Byrch."

Goddamn it, why couldn't she smile and get excited over *him*? Why did it take a thing or a place?

Byrch watched Callie savor every mouthful of the delicious ice cream. Some of her barriers seemed to be lowering a little. She was smiling at him warmly now. She had even touched his arm as they walked into the ice-cream parlor. Patience, that was what he needed.

The balance of the day was spent touring with Byrch explaining and Callie listening.

"Did you know that the Metropolitan and the St. Nicholas are among the most magnificent hotels in the world? And," Byrch said dramatically, "the Metropolitan boasts twelve miles of water and gas pipes, cloth napkins with every meal, and impeccable service. I've eaten there many times, and it's an experience to remember. Would you like to dine there one day this week?"

"Would I? Of course, I would. How grand, Byrch. Do you mean it?" Callie gripped his arm and snuggled next to him. Byrch's eyes almost rolled back in his head. He'd move them both there if that was what she wanted, never mind just going for dinner.

"The St. Nicholas Hotel gives the Metropolitan a bit of competition. I'll take you there, too. It's the epitome of luxury. Bridget and Kevin prefer it. The interior is an absolute symphony of beveled mirrors, cut glass, marble, and bronze. Bridget positively drools when she goes there. She told me that the gold brocade draperies cost forty-five dollars a yard. Bridget impresses easily. The place is known for social climbers, international adventurers, and professional beauties. It's too damn busy for me. I'm sure you're going to love it."

"I'll probably like the Metropolitan, the way you do. I think our tastes run alike, don't you, Byrch? Besides, I'm not Bridget."

"Thank God," Byrch said reverently. Like him. She said they had like tastes. He would never understand, even if he lived to be a hundred, how he could love her so much and she . . . and she . . . He shouldn't be thinking about that now. He was making small inroads today. Better not to spoil things with hasty remarks and negative thinking.

For contrast, Byrch took Callie into neighborhoods where the ommon man lived and traded. A particular favorite of Callie's as the East Side. She proclaimed that it was like a bazaar out the Arabian Nights. She was intrigued by the crush of people, e running, shouting children, the cries of the street vendors awking their wares—pickle vendors with their rolling vats of our cucumbers, sweet gherkins, and sour green tomatoes; can- ymen tempting the tongue with licorice sticks, fudge, chocolate, nd the ever popular Hoarhound Drops. Carts were piled high ith fruits and vegetables, and from bakery trucks came the elicious aroma of rolls and bread and scrumptious cookies.

A community of Jews lived along Allan and Hester Streets. Vomen wearing black shawls over their heads argued and bar- ained for knishes and sweet potatoes and chickens and geese. Vater dripped from the melted ice of fish carts, and a man peddled ot ears of corn from a vat set onto wheels. And as always Byrch as at her side, watching her with merriment.

As the sun started to set, Byrch announced that it was time to eturn home. Callie was relieved. She was going to enjoy lying her bed tonight, thinking about everything she had seen and lt during the long day. She nodded gratefully and leaned her ead back on the carriage cushion. "I had a marvelous day, Byrch. hank you so much for taking me. I can't wait to write to my other and tell her all about it."

"It was my pleasure, Callie. You made me see things I never w before. I enjoyed the outing as much as you did." Without inking, Byrch put his arm around her shoulder and drew her ose. At first Callie stiffened. Then she relaxed and laid her head gainst his arm. How good he felt. How wonderful he smelled. was all right, just for a while. For the moment. When they eached the house on St. Luke's Place, things would return to ormal. She would go to her room; Byrch would go to his study. hey would meet downstairs for dinner an hour later after they eshened up, and then they would go back to their separate rooms. or now, this small luxury of being close to Byrch was all right.

The rest of the honeymoon week passed in a blur for Callie. he long days were filled with exciting, wonderful places to visit. ender, small, intimate moments with Byrch were something to easure alone at night after all the lights were out. Not once, by ok or deed, did he try to approach her when they returned to e house. He seemed to change, just as she had, into a cool, oof person she barely knew. If only she could reach out to him, ask him to come to her room, tell him what she felt. She couldn't. She couldn't take that chance, that risk, ever again.

She was sorry to see the week end in many ways, but glad that she could finally sit down and write in earnest. She was now a working woman, being paid a salary, and she had to do her best. It was all she had left. Her work.

Chapter Thirty-One

Loretta Cummings hung up the dish towel to dry and set about making a pot of tea for herself. This was her favorite time of day, this short respite before Jasper came home. It was her time to sit down, have a cup of tea, prop up her plump legs, and daydream just a little.

She had been so happy since Jasper and she had moved out of the Benedict Hotel near Wall Street and come to live in this modest house with its own garden and back terrace. Jasper complained that it was so far uptown it was almost like living in the country, but Loretta knew he was happy here too; he'd told her. Her relationship with Jasper almost spanned a decade—the happiest ten years of her life—and it mattered not a whit to her that they weren't married. Marriages didn't guarantee love. Not the kind of love she shared with Jasper.

"Loretta!" she heard the front door slam and his familiar footsteps in the parlor.

"In the kitchen, Jasper," she called, a worried frown creasing her forehead. Home at this hour of the day! Something must be wrong. He came into the kitchen, filling the door with his bulk. He was a handsome man, white-haired and rosy-cheeked, and since she'd been watching his diet, he had lost inches from h girth. She rushed to him. "Is something wrong? Are you all right?

The concern on Loretta's face pleased Jasper. It did a ma good to know that he was important to someone, but he hurrie reassure her. "I'm fine, really. I just came home because I nee to talk to you. I need to hear some of your good common sense. He took her into his arms and hugged her, kissing her smoot cheek and inhaling the fragrance of her cologne. "Sit down, drin your tea, and I'll do the talking."

"Here, you have the tea," she insisted. "I'll make myself a other cup, the water is still hot."

Jasper accepted gratefully. Loretta was the most unselfish woma in the world, and it was his lucky day when he'd found her. Whi she busied herself with the kettle, he watched the sway of h generous hips and smiled at the strands of silver that were a pearing amidst her ash-blond curls. He loved this buxom woma whose smile could turn his world right side up. She sat down the table opposite him and waited for him to speak.

"Did you read the *Clarion* today?" he asked her.

"I was about to look through it now. Why? Is there somethi in it I should know?"

"I want you to read a particular article and tell me what yo think. It's by that reporter, C. James. We've talked of him befor You mentioned to me that there's something different about t man's writing. I want you to read this and tell me if you ca decide what it is."

Loretta read the article slowly, making certain nothing escap her. "I still feel it, Jasper, but I don't know what it is. It certain is a heart-tugger, isn't it? That poor soul who lost her dressmaki business. And what about those families who lost everything the fire? Sometimes I find myself crying over Mr. James's ar cles."

"I think I know what it is that's different," Jasper said quietl "Take another look, Loretta. Isn't there something you recogniz A style, the way the words are put together? The emotions?"

Loretta allowed her eyes to travel from the paper back to Jaspe "Of course! C. James is a woman! Is that what you're trying tell me? Imagine, a woman working for a newspaper. It's wo derful! But of course, it's supposed to be a secret since she isr using her full name."

"I think so. I think C. James is Callie James, Mary's compa ion. I've been so remiss, Loretta. I always thought the world that girl, and I've wanted to go and see her since Byrch told n he was staying at his house. I feel worse now that he's married ier. But I couldn't bring myself to do it. Not after that scene with Rossiter when he told me I had a grandson and that he'd died in fire in Shantytown, of all places. I had a grandson and didn't now it. I wasn't allowed to mourn for my own grandson. I can't nderstand why Callie didn't come to me for help. I'll never nderstand that as long as I live."

Loretta stood and moved to Jasper's side, touching his shoulder omfortingly. "You shouldn't blame the girl, darling. You have o think of the position she was in at the time. Remember what our wife said and did. You can't blame the girl for something hat was Rossiter's fault and your wife's. It pains me to say this, arling, but it's true. From everything you've told me, Callie ames was a good girl caught up in something she couldn't handle. he was only a child."

"I know you're right, but it doesn't make it any easier to bear. here are days when I think of nothing else. I have to make it ight for her. I have to make what my son did right for that voman."

"Rossiter is a man now, Jasper. You can't do everything for im. He has to take responsibility for his actions. I don't want ou being upset. Has something happened that you haven't told ne?"

"Yes, of course, something happened. Something always hapens when Rossiter is in town. I thought I'd seen the last of him or some time to come, but it appears now that his mother has ent him packing. He came to see me today. As usual, we had a errible row. You would not have been proud of me, Loretta." here was such humility in his voice that Loretta's heart turned ver.

"Whatever you did, you did for a reason. I don't want to hear uch things from you, Jasper. You are the kindest, gentlest man n the whole world. Now tell me what happened."

"Rossiter came to me for money. I gave him some. Not a lot, ut enough for him to get by. He talked a lot, babbled would be nore like it. He kept talking about his son and Callie. He talked lot about Callie. He's obsessed with her. When I asked him vhat he needed money for, he said to buy more art supplies. He's oing to have a show in some gallery. He said he hated coming o me for money and offered to pay me back when he got on his eet. Seeing his son for the first time that way was a terrible blow o him. I tried to understand. In some ways I do. Callie must have oved my son very much. Pride, Loretta, is such a terrible sin."

"Is there more, Jasper?"

"A little. Rossiter brought two of his paintings to show me. They were so breathtaking I can't believe he painted them. I was shocked almost out of my shoes. I'm no art critic, but I've seen enough to know that what he did was very good. He brought a painting he did of the boy. Loretta, it was the most beautiful painting I've ever seen. What a lovely child our Rory was. What a man he could have been. I offered to buy the painting from him, but he wouldn't part with it. I offered him a thousand dollars, Loretta, and he still wouldn't sell it to me. He said there wasn't enough money in the whole world to pay for that picture. That I have to respect. I only wish Callie could see it."

"What did you say to him, Jasper?"

"I told him to go back to his painting. I told him that time would heal his wounds or at least scar them over so he can get on with his life. I believe that. Look at me. Look what you've done for me, my dear."

Loretta patted his hand and then reached for it and took it in her own. "What did I do except love you the way you deserve to be loved?"

"For all my life I will be grateful to you. I love you the way a man is supposed to love a woman. We're so good together, like two old shoes. I don't mean to imply that you're old, Loretta," Jasper added hastily.

"Darling man, I know exactly what you meant. The day you have to start explaining things to me is the day we're going to be in trouble."

"I don't deserve you," Jasper said fondly. "I want you to become friends with Callie. She's like a daughter to me, or was. There's nothing in this world I wouldn't do for her. I want you to feel the same way. And with Byrch entering politics, she's going to need a good friend, like you, Loretta. Sooner or later Byrch will invite us to his house for a dinner party now that the political camp is heating up. I don't want to intrude on them until they both feel ready for us. We do take some getting used to, don't we, my dear?"

Loretta snuggled closer to Jasper to show her agreement.

"I just know the two of you will be great friends. I just know it," Jasper said.

"Then we will be," Loretta answered. She would make friends with a baboon if it would make Jasper happy. She knew she was going to like Callie Kenyon. She liked her as C. James, and now that she knew exactly who she was, she would like her even more.

* * *

The warm, lazy days of June and July gave way to the dog ays of August. The heat was blistering and the front pages of ie newspapers echoed the general outcry for rain. The house on t. Luke's Place was blissfully cool if she drew the drapes against ie early morning sun. By afternoon, Edward opened the backdoor :ading to her garden and lifted the parlor windows, and a pleasant reeze cooled her as she worked at the desk in Byrch's study. It 'as usually late afternoon when Byrch returned home, and in rder to be ready for him she awakened early to work on her olumns and organize the home-delivery project.

Since the first excitement over the victimizing of the *Clarion*'s ewsboys, Callie's column had dealt mostly with the sights and ories she and Byrch had discovered during their explorations. Iore often than not, her sharp eye and innate sympathy led her ttention to the conditions of the poor and the injustices they iffered. She exposed the fact that chickens, meats, and in general ll food stuffs were more expensive among the immigrant poor n the East Side than in fashionable neighborhoods. She was iidway through a series decrying the exploitation of the working omen who conducted cottage industries in their homes while nding to the needs of their children. Wages for piece work and :wing were considerably lower for the woman who was unable go out to the shops or factories to accomplish the work she did her own home. "These women have no recourse but to accept wer wages for identical work and are the victims not only of ieir circumstances but also of the workshop managements who rey upon them," Callie wrote. Several examples to back her atements were published along with the names of the companies well as their owners. She also praised those few places who :ld to fair business practices. But it was to the children running ie streets and begging on corners that Callie's eye most frequently irned.

Callie had embarked upon a campaign to aid the plight of the iildren, and since her dealings with the newsboys for the home-:livery project, she realized how many of them were homeless id without any adult direction in their lives. She wrote about em, telling their stories in a straightforward tone tempered with 'mpathy. Through her efforts, a Mr. Charles Brace contacted her rough Byrch. Mr. Brace's chief interest was children. He had unded an organization known as the Children's Aid Society and id already accomplished a great deal. The society's first effort as to establish a workshop on Wooster Street where the boys could earn an honest penny at useful work, but Brace told Calli that the idea was proving to be a failure because of competitio from private firms.

It was Callie's column that turned his attention to the plight o the newsboys of the city, ". . . those homeless, reckless, jolly band of street arabs who are shrewd beyond their years but also ene getic, persevering, and not without their instincts for honor an manliness."

Byrch, Callie, and Charles Brace were directing their energie to finding a loft and fitting it up as a dormitory for the boys charging them a token price for bed and breakfast and offerin free baths. They believed they would be able to open the doo for the first time next spring, and they intended to call it th Newsboys' Lodging House. Mr. Brace was so optimistic that h was already planning an industrial school for girls, evening trad schools, and Sunday meetings. He was even looking into the ide of placing children in good homes out West.

On a particularly hot day in late August, Callie sat at the des watching the soft, white curtain billow in the humid draft. Sh felt hot and sticky and longed for a leisurely bath in Byrch's tub She dabbed at her brow and neck and then stared at the long lin of numbers in her home-delivery ledger. She was irritated by th heat.

On second thought irritation was too mild a word. Hurt, angry wounded, was more like it. Powerful emotions. What in the nam of God would she do without her work? Work had to be the greate comfort known to man or woman. But work was done during th day to make the hours pass swiftly. It was the night hours, th dark hours, that deviled Callie. It seemed to her as soon as th sun set and dinner was over, Byrch dressed and went out— political meetings, he said. Political meetings that Flanna Bea champ attended—sometimes alone, sometimes in the compan of one Phillip Horn, her frequent escort. Or so Bridget said whe she wanted to press the thorn a little deeper into Callie's sid And always she heard him come in during the wee hours of th morning. At times she swore she could smell perfume, but whe she tried mentioning it discreetly to Edward, he would tell her was the scent of the posies in the downstairs hallway that wafte upward. She had never mentioned it a second time. She nev mentioned a lot of things, like the way she ached and longed f Byrch to knock on her door. She would have settled for a bit kick, and scratch with her losing the fight. Anything but this apathy she was living through.

What good was success if you didn't have someone you loved to share it with? What did it matter that half of New York City talked about C. James and her fascinating articles? What did that do for her during the long, lonely nights? She lost count of the times she had tiptoed across the hall and stood, poised to knock, and always at the last minute changed her mind. They had a bargain, a bargain she had insisted upon. Byrch was obeying it to the letter.

Sometimes during the long nights, especially toward early morning, Callie would wake from a sound sleep, drenched with perspiration. Her first thought was always, had Byrch made love to another woman? Her jealousy was consuming her, threatening to destroy her, and yet she could do nothing: She had made the rules.

What did Flanna Beauchamp look like? Crafty questioning of Edward produced few results. A beautiful, well-groomed lady was all Edward volunteered. It was like pulling teeth, but Callie managed to extract the fact that Flanna was knowledgeable about politics. And rumor had it that she had her eye on being a political wife. It didn't matter who the politician was, as long as he was likely to move up the ladder to the governorship.

Bridget had been only too helpful in describing Flanna's wardrobe and the contents of her house, plus what she imagined was in her bank account. And she always ended her description with "Flanna can have her choice of suitors; men just seem to drop at her feet."

After Bridget's hateful visits Callie always felt like a wet rag that wouldn't dry. Inevitably she would take a bath and change her clothes, but even that didn't make her feel better. Callie Kenyon. Flanna Beauchamp. Callie sounded like a cat's name. Flanna sounded worldly and sophisticated. Beautiful even. If Edward said she was beautiful, then she must indeed be a gorgeous, ravishing creature while she, Callie, was plain and ordinary with a plain, ordinary name that sounded as though it belonged to a cat.

Just how fond of Flanna was Byrch? She wished she knew. She wished she knew a lot of things. Did Byrch like her white skin? Bridget said it was like alabaster. Did he compare Callie with Flanna? She didn't want to know. Suddenly she remembered Bridget saying that Flanna had dropped her married name. What was it? Oh, yes. Skaggs. Callie burst into laughter, the sound delightful, even to her own ears. There was nothing worldly or glamorous about the name Flanna Skaggs.

The presses—massive tons of iron and steel in the basement floors of the *Clarion-Observer*—thundered and roared, making the whole building vibrate, including the boards beneath Byrch's feet. He leaned on his desk, reading letters and notes that were a direct result of Callie's column describing the fire on McDowell Street. Some people wrote in praise of C. James's social conscience; others were outraged by her description of the two local fire companies who responded to the alarm but who were busy fighting one another rather than the greedy flames that had robbed families of their homes and shopowners of their livelihoods. Some of the letters called for reform; others, from fire commissioners, denied that b'hoys would ever forget their duties.

There was a knock on Byrch's office door. "Come!" It was Jimmy Riley.

"This just came for you, Mr. Kenyon." He carried a large flat package wrapped in brown paper. A white envelope was attached to the cord wound around all four sides.

"Hmmm? Bring it here." Byrch took the package, testing its weight and giving it a shake. He couldn't imagine what it contained. He dismissed Jimmy before he took out his pocket knife and cut the string. Disengaging the envelope, he opened it and found a note. It was scrawled in a bold hand. "Read your wedding announcement in the paper. Give this to Callie along with my love. Rossiter."

Byrch frowned and tore at the heavy brown paper. It was a painting. Standing it against his desk, he stared down at it. It was Callie's son. Rory.

For a very long time Byrch stared at the likeness. There was no mistaking the child he had held in his arms on the night of the fire in Shantytown. Rory's sweet little face must have been imprinted on Rossiter's memory for him to have painted him with such detail. Byrch was overwhelmed. There was love and pathos in every brush stroke. The colors were muted, as though seen through a dream. The boy's hair was golden, curling softly about his head and onto his peach-round cheeks. Rossiter's imagination had given the child life; the boy's blue eyes looked out at the world in wonder, and there was something of Callie there in the lift of the chin and the direct level gaze.

Byrch could have wept for what Callie had lost, but he knew in his heart that Rossiter's generosity would bring her great joy.

She would have a piece of the past; she would have something that was Rory. What a magnificent child he would have been, Byrch mourned. Being Callie's son, how could Rory have been anything less?

Edward worked all day in the kitchen. Dinner parties did not perturb him in the least. As a matter of fact, he loved showing off his culinary expertise and having the ladies plead for his recipes. Tonight would be no exception with his capons stuffed with wild rice. It wasn't the capon or the rice but the herbs and spices he used that made the fowl so memorable. Late-summer vegetables in a salad would be perfect. Ruby beets seasoned and marinated for hours were sure to bring at least three requests for the recipe. The tiny pearl-white potatoes smothered in butter and fresh chives were one of Miss Callie's favorites. He stopped his chopping for a moment and stared out the kitchen window. Tonight was going to be the first time Miss Callie set eyes on the ravishing Flanna Beauchamp. Would there be fireworks? What ever possessed Mr. Kenyon to invite her? One never put a dog and a cat in the same pen. He sighed wearily. Mr. Kenyon had so much to learn when it came to women. He supposed the main reason Flanna Beauchamp was dining with them was because Phillip Horn was her escort; or was it the other way around? He wasn't sure.

Mrs. Beauchamp was a lady. Everyone said so. A beautiful widow. An unbidden thought raced through his head. Black widow spider. Mrs. Beauchamp always dressed in black. Surely her mourning period was long over. He didn't know all that much about women's clothes. He did like color, he knew that. Black was for death and crows. He liked the way Miss Callie dressed. Perhaps Mrs. Beauchamp favored black because it made her skin more noticeable. She did make a startling first impression. More than once he had seen Mr. Kenyan favor her with a long, thoughtful look. But that was before Miss Callie arrived.

He wondered what Miss Callie was going to wear. Was it his place to go to the study and tell her that the other ladies would be dressed to the "nines" as Mr. Kenyon was fond of saying? Maybe he could manage to work it into the conversation in an offhanded way. It would be up to Miss Callie to pick up on his cue. That's what he would do. He would fix her a nice cool glass of lemonade along with some raisin-filled cookies. She would appreciate it as dinner was a good two hours away.

Edward knocked softly on the door of the study. It was half-open and he wasn't in the least surprised to see Callie sitting with her head propped in her hands, daydreaming. She looked up and smiled. "How nice of you, Edward. How did you know I was just thinking about coming out for a snack?"

Edward preened. He did do things right, no one could say he didn't. "Since dinner is going to be late this evening I thought you could use a little refreshment. It's a hot day, isn't it?"

"I suppose we should enjoy it. There can't be that many more left before fall gets here. How are the preparations for dinner coming? Is there anything I can do to help you?"

"Not a thing, Miss Callie. Do you plan on working much longer?"

"No, I'm about finished. I thought I'd take a nice long soak before Byrch gets home. He does leave the bathroom an untidy mess, and I like to get in there before him. Then I'll dress and just wait in the parlor. I'm very anxious to see Jasper Powers again."

"What will you be wearing this evening, Miss Callie?" Edward asked nonchalantly.

"I really hadn't decided. Probably the gray silk."

Crows and doves, Edward thought. No gray for Miss Callie!

"Miss Callie, might I make a suggestion?" At her nod, he continued "Mr. Kenyon admires you in the emerald silk, and it does wonderful things for your eyes. Even Mrs. Darcy complimented you on your choice. The people coming to dinner have never seen you in that particular gown, whereas you wear the gray one quite often."

"I thought that the neckline . . . what I mean is, it seems as though it might be out of . . . if you say so, Edward."

"When one has assets it is best to—how shall I say it—let it be known. Miss Callie, you have lovely assets."

"Thank you, Edward. I do want to look my best . . . for many reasons. It will be the green silk."

"Very good, Miss Callie. I'll be back for the dishes later." It was so easy. He often wondered if he was wasting his time being a servant. Surely there was room for him in politics. Wasn't that what politicians did? Make suggestions and let other people follow through? It was a pity the world wasn't ready for a black politician. Some day, perhaps in his time, but he rather doubted it.

Callie dressed carefully for the party. She was anxious for many different reasons. She was going to be seeing Jasper Powers for the first time since leaving the house on Todt Hill. She was eager to meet the dear man again. Then there was Flanna Beauchamp How right Edward was. The gray silk would have made her look like a soft gray mourning dove. In the emerald silk she felt regal, even elegant. What's more she felt confident and able to hold her own.

Edward stepped into the parlor to check on things. "Tell me again, Edward, who's going to be here tonight? My mind is absolutely blank," Callie said. "I don't know why I'm so nervous. I hope I can keep their names straight."

"Miss Callie, I'm confident you will be most charming. The guest list includes Mr. Phillip Horn, a possible candidate for assemblyman from New York City. Mr. Horn will be escorting Mrs. Beauchamp. Mr. and Mrs. Jason Webster, very nice people by the way, who are ready and able to contribute generously to Mr. Kenyon's campaign. Mr. Jasper Powers and Mrs. Loretta Cummings. Erskin Taylor and Devon Whitany will complete the seating. Then of course there will be yourself and Mr. Kenyon."

Callie paced the long, narrow parlor, her fingers touching familiar objects. Byrch's chair near the hearth, his pipe stand on the nearby table. At a sound behind her, Callie turned to find Byrch watching her. "You look so right standing there, Callie," he told her, his voice vibrant with warmth.

Callie laughed to ease the moment. "You always see me here," she teased.

"That's not what I meant, and you know it." He was across the room in two strides, taking her hands in his. "You belong here, you know that, don't you? You belong here in my arms," he dared, gathering her close, bending his head to place his lips at the sensitive point beneath her ear. He felt her stiffen in his embrace for just an instant until she leaned against him. The door knocker tapped against the brass plate, destroying the moment.

"Damn!" Byrch swore softly, his thick dark brows drawing together in annoyance. Unwilling to release her from his touch, he held her hand as he took her to the door with him, his eyes promising to pick up where he'd left off, later when they were alone. Callie felt herself shiver with expectation. Perhaps. . . .

"Jasper, you're a sight for sore eyes!" Byrch exclaimed as he slapped the older man on the back. "Loretta, I'm so glad you could come. There's someone I want you to meet."

Jasper turned and immediately saw Callie. Tears gathered in his eyes as she moved forward to greet him, intending to offer her hand, but Jasper would have none of it. His arms were around her, hugging her close, somehow touching the past and those remembered with love in this contact with her. He whispered quiet words of welcome and regret. "You don't know how often I've wanted to come to see you. I would like to think it was out of respect for your wishes, but it was cowardice to a degree on my part. You're lovely. I knew you would be." With his arm still around Callie's shoulders, he turned her to face Loretta.

"Loretta, this is Callie James Kenyon. Callie, this is the lady who has made my life complete. I hope you will come to know one another and become friends."

For a brief instant Callie was uncertain of what she should do. When uncertain, always do what the heart wants. It was Callie's turn to wrap the buxom woman in a warm embrace. Neither woman could see the wide smiles on the men's faces, so intent were they with their first meeting. Callie knew in an instant that this woman was warm, soft, and comfortable.

Byrch stood by like a proud new father while his two favorite people fussed over Callie and welcomed her. He was proud of her too. Like all men, he took full credit for her being what she was. Not all the time, just in good moments, like this one. It was a pleasant, congenial gathering as the other guests arrived. The women were included in the conversation and not ignored as women so often were at dinner parties. Jasper was amused at the admiring glances the men bestowed on Callie. He was aware, as was everyone else, of Byrch's scowls when the admiration threatened to get out of hand, but he ignored the undercurrent of hostility until Loretta whispered in his ear. From that moment on Jasper sat up straighter, his hearing and eyesight sharpened. Flanna Beauchamp, a lovely woman, was flirting outrageously with Byrch, who appeared to be enjoying it immensely. Callie was not.

"I think, dear heart, that there is going to be trouble in paradise," Loretta managed to whisper softly in Jasper's ear. "I think one of us had best take matters in hand. You're going to have to snare that seductress away from Byrch. Do it, Jasper. She won't be able to resist you, and for another thing she knows of your political clout."

Jasper sighed heavily. What she was asking him to do was tantamount to playing the gigolo. But if Loretta wanted it, he would do it. He would do it for her and for Callie. He couldn't bear to see the wounded look in Callie's eyes as she tried to keep up with the sophisticated Flanna.

"Callie, I'm just an old lady, but I do remember what it was like to be young. Enjoy Devon's attention," Loretta advised.

"A little discreet flirting never hurt anyone," she whispered to

Callie. "Keeps a man on his toes. If it looks as though Byrch will take a seizure, I'll intervene. But isn't Devon a dashing man?"

Unmindful of the circumstances, Loretta could not understand what was going on between Byrch and Callie. They were newlyweds and obviously perfect for one another, but something was amiss.

Callie smiled and turned her attention to Devon Whitany. It had been a long time since a man had paid such obvious attention to her. "Power" was the word that came to Callie's mind. Devon Whitany was a powerful man. A man who worked behind the scenes to get what he wanted. He had wealth and charm—a devilish combination. Seated beside Devon during dinner, Callie found herself engaged in a sparkling conversation with him. She liked the way his dark eyes flashed at her.

Seated across from Callie and Flanna, Byrch somehow became the target of Flanna's questions, one after the other. He had to smile and answer or be considered rude by his other guests. Conversation was soft and muted. Each time his gaze went to Callie, she was deep in conversation with Devon Whitany. Phillip Horn, Flanna's escort, appeared to be annoyed. Another problem. Christ, the one thing he didn't need was a jealous suitor after him, especially Phillip Horn. Damn Flanna. Was she doing it on purpose? Why? It was obvious that the others were aware of it. Every chance Jasper got, he jumped into the conversation. Loretta, usually a quiet woman, was talking nonstop with Phillip to try to ease the situation.

Callie was angry. Byrch was humiliating her in front of his friends. She felt like crying and leaving the table. Instead, she glanced at Loretta, who nodded slightly and winked. Callie swallowed hard and turned her attention to Devon Whitany. It wasn't long before everyone at the table was more than aware of the effect Callie was having on Devon, and they seemed to find it amusing. Everyone except Byrch. Damn! He liked Devon, even admired him. They had shared a close friendship for some time now and reflected one another's views. Now here was Devon, sitting at his table, eating his food, and making cow eyes at his woman! Jealousy ripped at Byrch's insides, and he could hardly keep his mind on the conversation. He'd only felt this way once before, at Callie's eighteenth birthday party when Rossiter had come home. If he'd acted on his impulses at that time, perhaps Callie would have been spared all that suffering. The primal animal in him stirred, pawing, hungry for blood. He wanted to take Devon by the throat and rip it out. When he was aware of Edward's firm touch on his shoulder as he prepared to pour the wine, Byrch could feel himself snatch back his control. He had almost made a complete ass of himself!

She was enjoying it! Callie was actually flirting with Devon, encouraging those flashing dark looks and that whispered conversation. Devon was leaning toward Callie, leaning too damn close, and where was his left hand? In his lap, or patting Callie's knee? There wasn't much Byrch didn't know about flirting and making a woman silly over him, but he'd never applied those practiced arts to Callie. And now here she was, smiling up at Devon and enjoying the man's sloe-eyed attentions.

Once during dinner Callie glanced at Byrch, meeting his gaze. Her smile was so warm and so intimate, Byrch nearly slid from his chair. Loretta met Jasper's glance over the rim of her wineglass. Things were working out. Tonight would be one of those nights. or at least that was what Jasper interpreted the look to mean. After all this time, Loretta could still get his pulses pumping with one of those heavy-lidded glances.

Callie found herself joining in the praise of Edward's fine dinner. He took the compliments graciously and smiled at Loretta when she asked for his recipe for peach torte. For this lady he would list *all* the ingredients. A man like Jasper Powers deserved the best, and he knew Loretta would whip up his torte with tender hands and serve it with love.

After dinner the men retreated to the back terrace, Flanna in their wake. The women stood by in wide-eyed wonder at the sight of the voluptuous woman being included in "political man talk." Callie was furious. Loretta made soothing noises as did Mrs. Webster. Their looks seemed to say that if Mrs. Beauchamp wanted to make a fool of herself, let her. They certainly knew their place,and who wanted to be surrounded by clouds of cigar smoke? Callie seethed inwardly as she made small talk with the women. Flanna out there with all those men. What was she saying that was so important? Why was *she* included? There was certainly nothing manly about Flanna. Was she standing next to Byrch? And Devon, where was he? With the men, of course. Damnation!

"Don't mind so much, my dear. It means nothing," Loretta whispered, confident in Jasper's powers. If anyone could thwart Flanna Beauchamp, it was Jasper. Callie felt better knowing the older woman was on her side.

An hour-and-a-half later Callie thought she would scream. Loretta looked as if she felt the same way. Ellen Webster was discussing cookie recipes and dress patterns. Just when Callie thought she couldn't stand it another minute, the men trooped back into ɪe room. Loretta smiled when she noticed Flanna walking with asper, her arm linked through his. Dear Jasper. Dear, dear Jasper. ,oretta wanted to tell Callie not to worry, that Jasper had things ell in hand. There was no time unfortunately, as everyone started ılking at once.

The party was over. Standing next to Byrch in the foyer, Callie ouldn't help but be aware of Devon Whitany's speculative, sen-ual gaze. Callie gave herself up to the embraces of Jasper and oretta, promising to get together with the older woman in the oming week. She shook hands with Phillip Horn and Erskin aylor. Devon, it would seem, deliberately waited so he'd be last ı line. He shook hands with Byrch in a businesslike way and ngered over Callie's hand.

"I'd like to invite you to lunch with me if your husband permits . There are so many topics we barely touched on in our discus-ion." He swung around to meet Brych's gaze. "Surely you won't bject."

Callie smiled to herself. Good. She was so glad that Devon's quest was being heard by Flanna and Phillip Horn. A nasty devil erched on her shoulder and prodded her on as she sought a suitable ply. "That's so true, Devon. I'm rather busy this week, but if ou care to come by next week, I'm sure I can manage it. Byrch on't object, will you, darling?" Callie asked coolly, her green yes defying him to utter one word.

Devon was it? Byrch snarled inwardly. By God, he'd soon put stop to that. Making an ass out of him in his own house! "Of ourse not, Devon. Callie is a modern woman. She does as she leases, which leaves me to do pretty much what I please." Callie lmost gasped aloud.

Edward, who was busily clearing the table, almost choked at ıe conversation that was filtering back to him. What was the ıatter with the two of them?

Devon Whitany smiled urbanely. "You can count on it. Good ight all."

"I'll look forward to it," Callie cooed.

Devon's sleepy-eyed gaze widened suddenly, and then the lids wered again. Next to Byrch, Callie thought him the most at-active man she had ever met.

For the second time in as many minutes Byrch wanted to put is fist through the man's handsome face. He speculated on what evon would look like without his teeth; the vision made him ıicker as he closed the door. He turned to Callie. "Don't you

dare, ever again, act like a common tart in my house, do you he
me?" he bellowed.

Callie backed off a step and then another. "Don't you ever da
to talk to me in that tone of voice again. Do you hear me?" Call
defied him.

"I'll talk to you any way I damn well please. This is my hou
and you're my wife. Or did you forget?"

"Not for a minute. You seem to be the one who has forgotte
that you're married. I'm not deaf, dumb, and blind, you kno
You've humiliated me for the last time. Flanna Beauchamp, is i
Well, you can have her and her money and her political ambition
You can take her and her black dresses and make a damn scarecro
out of her for all I care. You tell me to get rid of my black rag
and then you throw yourself at the very thing you say you hat
Get out of my way, Byrch Kenyon, before I kick you where t
beautiful Flanna will suffer. Shut up, Byrch, I don't want to he
another word. Get out of my way before I say things I'll regr
later."

"Now just a damn minute," Byrch thundered.

"Shut up, Byrch," Callie repeated. She'd had enough for o
night. She was halfway up the stairs when Byrch shouted aft
her, "You'll only go to lunch with Devon Whitany over my dea
body."

"I suppose that can be arranged," Callie said coolly. Inside h
room she threw the bolt and let the tears flow. Devon Whita
be damned. He was nothing more than a conceited ass. When a
if he did call, she would be sure Edward told him she wasn
home. She had behaved foolishly. Jealously and foolishly. Wou
she never learn? Where was all this going to end?

Edward winced and almost dropped the stack of dinner dish
when Callie slammed her door shut. He waited a moment, h
head cocked to the side for the sound of Mr. Kenyon's door. Wh
the sound reverberated downstairs, he almost jumped out of h
skin. Another one of those nights. He had no idea what was goi
to happen next. Mr. Kenyon could act like a bull when he wante
Miss Callie could be a pure vixen. "This time I think she we
too far," he muttered to the empty kitchen.

Byrch stormed up and down his room. What the goddamn he
did she think she was doing? How could she humiliate him li
that in front of his friends—his political friends? Because s
doesn't care about you, that's how, some wayward inner voi
responded. He should go across the hall, knock the damn do
down, and pull her across the hall by her hair. That's what

should do. By God, they were married, and she made a date to have lunch with one of the handsomest men in New York. His teeth clamped shut, and his mouth was a grim, tight white line as he punched out the overstuffed chair, swept his dresser clean, lashed out at the little yellow cat who slept between his pillows. The thin leather of his evening shoe split right across the top when he kicked at the raised hearth. Searing pain shot up his foot into his leg and thigh. He ignored the pain. It was nothing to compare to the pain in his heart. How cruel she was. Until this evening he had no idea her hatred was so intense.

He stormed about the room a second time, pausing at the window to stare out at the lovely night. He jerked at his tie and removed his evening clothes, dropping them on the floor at his feet. The yellow cat immediately took it as a signal to make a bed and sleep. He scuttled over to the pile of clothing and curled up for the evening. Byrch flung himself on top of the spread on his bed and knew that if he were a woman, he would cry. Instead he had to cover up his feelings and pretend nothing mattered. Take it all in his stride. Well, he couldn't. He had done everything humanly possible to make Callie love him. It just wasn't meant to be. He knew that now. Tomorrow he would go down to the harbor and book passage for her back to Ireland. It was best for both of them. The heartache would heal—eventually. Callie would be back home, and he would move ahead with his political career. It was best. He would settle a sum of money on her, give her the painting of Rory to take with her, and continue to send her money until she got herself settled or married again. He almost gagged at the thought. After all, she was his wife. He couldn't simply send her back without seeing to her welfare.

He should have given her the painting of her son the day it arrived at his office. He didn't know why he hadn't. Probably because he didn't want to see the pain in her eyes when she saw it. It had never been his intention to keep it from her altogether. He would book her passage tomorrow and give her the painting at the same time. He would make arrangements at the bank for her financial welfare. A clean break, once and for all. Normal people, intelligent people didn't live like this. At least he couldn't.

Chapter Thirty-Tw

Edward set about making breakfast, pancakes and plump pink sausages. He squeezed some fresh oranges and set things to righ at the table. While the sausages simmered, he set up his ironing board by the kitchen window and checked his iron to be sure i was just right. It was best to keep busy and not think about wha went on the night before. Who knew what would happen at break-fast? He shuddered when he remembered the way Mr. Kenyon had slammed his door. Edward felt finality when he heard it.

Soft stirrings from overhead could be heard. Were both of then up, or was it just Mr. Kenyon? It was a bit early. He himself ha risen an hour earlier than usual because ironing took so much time

Edward was reminded of a black thundercloud when Byrcl walked into the kitchen.

Byrch stopped in his tracks. He was surprised that Edward wa up so early. His plan had been to make himself some coffee an be out of the house before either Callie or Edward wakened. No only was Edward up, but he was ironing. Something frilly wit lace and bows. "If you tell me I'm not paying you enough tha you have to take in ironing, I'll boot your tail right out of here, Byrch snarled.

"Sir! This is Miss Callie's. What it is, is . . . you know damned well what it is, Mr. Kenyon."

"It looks like a petticoat to me."

"Well, you're wrong. It's a camisole," Edward said huffily as he tried to smooth down the tiny pleats in the bodice.

Byrch stretched his neck to see what his houseman was doing. "You're going to burn your fingers, Edward. What the hell are you doing?"

"Miss Callie is very fussy about her . . . about her unmentionables. They have to be ironed just so."

"For Christ's sake, are you telling me you've been doing Callie's ironing? Why doesn't it get sent out to a laundress?" Byrch smacked his forehead. "Now I understand why we haven't had a decent meal around here. Except when I give a dinner party. You do her ironing, you tend her garden, you cook special food for her, and don't tell me you don't. I can see it on your face. Guilt. You're as guilty as sin. And after *I* gave you a raise. When was the last time you changed the sheets on my bed? Aha! Weeks, I'll wager." Byrch exaggerated wildly. "Dust. Dust everywhere! Admit it! By God, Edward, this is beyond belief. No wonder she has all the time in the world to do her articles. Why do I put up with you?"

"Because, Mr. Kenyon, I am indispensable, as you well know. And I do not neglect your needs."

"I don't need any advice from you, Edward. I'm doing nothing wrong. I have the situation under control. It's just a matter of time until I decide to . . . to get her to come around. Ha, if you think you're busy now, what do you think it will be like if she stops working and has children?" Now why had he said that?

"I have considered that, sir. We will take in a laundress and a personal maid for Miss Callie. Of course, you will want only the best for her. You promised that the night you . . . er, ah . . . consumed your brandy."

"The same night I agreed to that stupid raise, right?"

"Yes, sir."

"I have another bone to pick with you, Edward. You have to get rid of that goddamn cat. Why in the world you ever brought a cat here is something I'll never know. This morning there were puddles on the floor in my room and a mess on the stairs. The house is going to stink to high heavens soon. Get rid of it!"

"Why should I get rid of it? You're the one who told me to get it in the first place. I said we didn't need a cat, and you said we did. You said you wanted to cuddle it on cold winter nights.

You certainly are difficult of late. Aren't things going well wit Miss Callie?" There was a knowing look on Edward's face tha set Byrch's teeth to rattling.

"Damnation!" Byrch fumed. "I don't remember telling you t get a cat. I suppose that was the same night I gave you the rais and promised to hire a personal maid and laundress. I'm not mad of money, you know."

"I know what I heard," Edward said, finishing off the last plea on the lacy camisole. "I have never gone against your orders, nov have I?"

"When you go upstairs to deliver Callie's unmentionables, de liver the cat, too. Let her tend to it for a while. Just get it the he out of my sight."

"Very well, sir, if that's the way you feel about it. Winter wi be here in a few months. Don't think I'm going out and gettin another cat. I actually had to pay a dollar for the poor thing."

"I'll give you the damn dollar. Get rid of it! By tomorrow! Byrch roared as he made his way out the backdoor, the yellov cat on his heels.

Edward always felt slightly foolish when he carried Callie' hand laundry upstairs. He could have it sent out, but doing thing for her pleased him. She was always grateful for anything he did

"Miss Callie, I brought your laundry," Edward called throug the door. "It's in this basket, right here. This other basket is gift from Mr. Kenyon. He told me to make sure I got it to yo first thing this morning."

Callie's eyes widened. "A present for me! How wonderful What is it, Edward? Quick, let me see it!"

Edward did his best to compose his face. He felt like such sneak. And just wait till he tried to describe the look on Mis Callie's face.

"Edward, it's a cat. Why would Byrch send me his cat? Wh is he giving it to me?" Callie asked suspiciously. "Oh, I see neither you nor Byrch has been able to train it, so you're givin it to me."

She always was as quick and bright as himself. Almost, tha is, Edward thought.

"I can't take it back, Miss Callie. Mr. Kenyon would be wounde to the quick."

"He's going to be wounded some place else if—never min Tell Byrch I thank him from the bottom of my heart. I'll hav something to cuddle this winter when it's cold and lonely. He'll understand."

"I doubt it," Edward mumbled as he turned to leave.

"Edward, wait a moment. I want to show you something." Quickly Callie ripped and shredded a day-old newspaper that lay on the table by her bed. She lifted her laundry from the basket and dumped the scraps of paper inside. Gently she lifted the yellow cat out of its basket and put it in the laundry basket on top of the papers. Edward watched in amazement as the cat pawed and scratched, then squatted down and did what it had to do. Callie smiled. "There are some things *you don't know*, Edward. Thanks for everything."

It was mid-morning when Callie finally decided to go downstairs in search of something to eat. She couldn't hide in her room all day, what was the point? Earlier she'd heard Byrch in the bathroom and heard him thundering down the stairs. She knew he was in a vile mood and was tempted to ask Edward if he'd said anything about last night, but changed her mind. It wasn't fair to Edward to ask him questions or expect him to take sides.

She deliberately waited until now to go to the kitchen, knowing Edward would be at the market. A note in a small neat handwriting told her there were freshly baked cinnamon rolls and sausages in the warming oven. The coffee was freshly brewed. Last night Callie thought she'd never be able to eat again. All night long she'd tossed and turned with a sick stomach that wasn't the result of Edward's delicious cooking but of her nerves and the confrontation with Byrch. She was appalled now at what she'd done: flirting with Devon while rejecting Byrch. She was a fool not to recognize that Byrch was at his breaking point. After last night he was probably beyond caring what happened. She'd made a fool of both of them.

Callie tidied up the kitchen and went to Byrch's study to start her article or at least to outline it. Last night Ellen Webster had told them of a little theatre group that was forming on the East Side and had also mentioned a women's cooperative in that neighborhood. Callie was fascinated to hear about the cooperative group. The women had formed a day-care center for children of working mothers and were now involved in wholesale buying of groceries to pass the savings on to their members. Tomorrow Callie would go out there and interview the women; it would make a revealing and informative article.

She was getting a late start today and would have to work extra hard to have it ready for deadline before the end of the week Work was a blessing, she'd decided. She could submerge hersel in it and become so involved that the hurt would be forgotten fo the moment. Sometimes it actually worked that way, like the da after their wedding when Byrch had spent the night with Flanna She resolved not to cry. Not anymore. All of this was her ow doing. All of it. Right from that first grocery basket to this.

It was late in the afternoon when Callie penciled in her las word. She'd made a list of pertinent questions to ask at the co operative and an outline of the approach she wanted her article t take.

On the third floor, in her bedroom, Callie found an envelop on her dressing table. She recognized the handwriting immedi ately; it was from Peggy. Callie picked up the letter and held for a moment. If there was one thing she needed right now, it wa her mother.

It was a short letter, hastily written. Estimating the timespa since she'd written Peg, Callie realized it must have been sent ou by return mail. Perhaps something was wrong. She read the firs paragraph and sighed with relief. Everything was fine, everyon was well. Her eyes returned again and again to those loving phrase that told her how much she was loved and missed. It was the las part of Peggy's letter that stunned Callie. Peggy wrote:

> Callie James Kenyon, I couldn't believe my eyes when I read your last letter. Why would you be wanting to come back here when everything you want and love is right there with you? How can you be telling me you stepped out of your place and that you're being punished for reaching out for happiness and love? As if God would ever do that to one of His own children. I know you, child, you are my own flesh and blood, my Callie, and so near my heart. You think you have done something wrong. Loving is never wrong, don't you remember me telling you that? Your place, Callandre James Kenyon, is there at your husband's side. That is where you belong . . ."

Callie blew her nose lustily. The truth in Peggy's letter throbbe in her heart. She believed, she had to believe, because it wa something she wanted more than life itself.

Oh, Mum, if I could only see you, talk to you. She thoug of Flanna Beauchamp and Byrch. Perhaps it was already too lat What to do? How to do it?

She heard movements in the room across the hall. Byrch? She almost flew to the door, racing across the hall. She had so much to tell him, so much to explain!

Edward, not Byrch, was there, selecting a shirt from the drawer and placing it on the bed along with an evening suit and Byrch's evening slippers. "Ah, Miss Callie, finished with work on your article, I see. Mr. Riley is downstairs waiting for Mr. Kenyon's evening clothes. Needless to say, Mr. Kenyon won't be home for dinner."

Byrch wouldn't be home. A change of clothes. That meant a late night, a very late night. She wanted to ask Edward if he knew where Byrch was going. It was certainly permissible for a wife to ask, wasn't it? The words stuck to her tongue. Sensing her confusion and dismay, Edward volunteered that he believed there was a dinner at a club scheduled for this evening. "I believe it's at the Masonic Lodge, Miss Callie."

Callie's anxiety was obvious in her eyes and in the trembling of her hands. Something was wrong, Edward knew. "Did you find the letter from Ireland on your dresser?" he asked as he added dark, thin stockings to the assortment of Byrch's clothes.

"Hmmm? Oh, yes, thank you, Edward."

"And everything is all right with your family?"

"Yes, yes. Just fine."

Callie's distraction worried Edward. He did like to be on top of things, but it wasn't his place to ask. Perhaps she would confide in him. He waited, deliberately prolonging his attention to the suit of clothes he was preparing for Byrch. "If there's anything I can do . . ." But when he looked up, Callie was gone.

Later, after leaving an untouched dinner, Callie wandered out to the back terrace. She was still there when Edward was ready to go up to bed.

"Miss Callie, I'm afraid I'm going to have to insist you come indoors. It is a beautiful evening, but it's damp out, and you'll catch cold or get rheumatism or worse. Mr. Kenyon would never forgive me. Come along now and I'll see you upstairs."

Callie stared up at Edward in the dim yellow light filtering through the kitchen door. He was right, she was chilled. Lord, how long had she been sitting here? It felt like forever. Her movements were stiff and somewhat awkward when she finally got to her feet. She looked straight at Edward. "You're wrong, you know. Not only would he forgive you, but he wouldn't care."

Callie was halfway up the stairs before Edward figured out what she had been talking about. Dismay was etched on his face as he turned down all the lights, leaving a dim lamp burning in the kitchen for Mr. Kenyon. It was way past his bedtime now, but he wasn't going to be able to sleep. Miss Callie was pacing overhead. He could hear her. Mr. Kenyon was out cavorting or doing something even worse. Didn't anyone sleep anymore? What had happened to the old placid life he used to lead?

Twice during the long night, Callie got up to walk to her door and peer across the hall. Byrch's door was wide open, his bed made and untouched. The last time she looked, it was five-thirty. He had spent the entire night away from home.

Pearly gray streaks of dawn crept into her room just as her eyes closed. She was up two hours later and downstairs. Edward informed her that Mr. Kenyon had been home and gone again. Tonight was going to be another late night; he said not to hold up dinner. Callie knew what it meant: Byrch was avoiding her.

The day dragged on for Callie. She couldn't seem to concentrate on anything. She still hadn't gone to interview the women at the cooperative on the East Side, but she couldn't muster the enthusiasm and interest. Nothing seemed to matter. Nothing except Byrch.

She knew she must look terrible. Too much worrying and not enough sleep. Thinking perhaps a hot bath and a nap would improve her spirits as well as her appearance, she climbed the stairs to the third floor and walked down the narrow, carpeted hall to the linen closet next to Byrch's room. The door was open, everything within neat and orderly. She seemed to be drawn into the room, feeling his presence among his belongings. It seemed a lifetime since she'd been here, with him, in his bed, in his arms. But that was another time. Daylight filtered through the curtains, puddling on the shiny desktop that was cleared of all papers except an envelope. That was so unlike Byrch. Usually his desk here and at the *Clarion* was a holocaust of confusion that only he could sort, knowing exactly where everything was and where to find it. Now it was as tidy as though he intended never to write on it again. Something about the envelope was familiar, disturbingly familiar. Once she'd owned an envelope just that size with the red slash and masthead of the Cunard Steamship Line. She touched it uneasily, picked it up, and looked inside. It was a passage ticket, cabin class, to Ireland, and the name Callandre Kenyon was printed in the corner.

Dear God! He'd done it! He *was* sending her back to Ireland. He'd threatened it and now had followed through. He was sending her away. Quickly Callie looked for the date. September 3, 1853.

Less than a week away! Callie squeezed her eyes shut. It was only twelve days short of four years since she'd boarded the *Yorkshire* to come to America. Four short years, yet it was a lifetime.

It was six o'clock in the evening, and the Angelus Bells were ringing as she passed St. Matthew's Mission Church. She followed the narrow path that led behind the church into the small cemetery. The tender grass that grew on Rory's grave would soon be ravaged by the harshness of winter. The little headstone that Byrch had erected stood beside Hugh's, and the flowers she'd brought last week were dried and dead and colorless, just like her heart. She'd come to say goodbye, and in many ways it was more final than the day she had watched the tiny coffin lowered into the ground.

Byrch heard the Angelus Bells as he let himself into the house and went through to the kitchen. There was no sign of Edward and no preparations for dinner. Byrch's heart leaped to his throat. Something was wrong. "Edward! Edward!"

"Yes, sir?" came the response as Edward poked his head out of the pantry. "I thought you said you wouldn't be home for dinner. Something wrong, sir?"

"You're damn right, something's wrong, and it's been wrong from the beginning. I took care of the matter yesterday. Things will either right themselves, or I'll die trying. You've my word on that," Byrch declared angrily, but Edward noticed a strange huskiness to his tone.

"About dinner?"

"Nothing for me, Edward. I just came home to take a bath. I have a meeting at Jasper Powers this evening. I shouldn't be all that late. I slept on a damn cot at the paper last night. I haven't worked this hard since I first became a reporter. I must be getting old, Edward. I could take this pace and the hours and never miss them before. I ache. I hurt. I feel as though I'm bleeding inside, and there isn't a bandage big enough to stop the flow of blood."

"Perhaps you need a vacation, sir?"

"That's exactly what I need—a long one."

"Shall I draw your bath?"

"I would appreciate it," Byrch said wearily. "By the way, how's the cat?"

"Never better, sir. I finally figured out the problem. You see, all you have to do is shred up some old papers, put them in a basket or box, and that's where the cat . . . that's where he does his business. No more puddles."

"I knew you'd get the hang of it."

"Actually, sir, it was Miss Callie who told me what to do. It seems they had many cats back in Ireland. I found it absolutely remarkable."

"Remarkable," Byrch repeated as he shed his clothes.

"I'll take these clothes downstairs to be pressed and lay out fresh ones on the bed. Enjoy your bath, sir."

"I wish I could, but I have only thirty minutes to bathe, shave, dress, and be at Jasper's house. If there's one thing that man hates, it's tardiness."

Edward bent down to pick up Byrch's clothing. Beneath the jacket lay a white envelope. Edward laid it on the dresser and thought he was going to faint when he noticed where it was from. He didn't feel at all guilty when he looked inside. One ticket to Ireland. He felt as though he had been kicked in his stomach. And in a way he had. Poor Miss Callie. He wondered if she knew. It would certainly explain a lot of things.

Downstairs in the laundry room Edward laid Byrch's clothing over the ironing board. For some reason he didn't feel like pressing the suit now. Tomorrow would be plenty of time. And if not then, then the day after or the day after that. He was angry. For the first time since coming to the house on St. Luke's Place he was angry. Gut angry. He would have sold his soul to the devil to be able to smash something. Something valuable and priceless. So valuable and priceless that he could spend years atoning for his temper. Instead he went back to the kitchen and poured some coffee. He settled himself in the rocker by the hearth and looked for the yellow cat. If ever there was a time to need that cat, this was it. It was nowhere in sight.

Byrch strode through the kitchen. "Don't wait up for me, Edward. Make sure Callie eats her dinner. I know she just diddles with it when I'm not here. And tell her to tighten up tomorrow's article. She's using too many words to get her point across."

"Yes, sir, I'll tell her," Edward said smoothly. He supposed he should have gotten up off the chair, but he didn't feel like it. He felt dismay course through him. He was taking sides. Careful as he'd always been not to do that, he had just done it. He was on Callie's side.

Things would never be the same without her. Never.

Byrch was no sooner gone than Callie came up the back walkway. Edward could hear her heels clicking on the flagstones.

"I'm glad you're back, Miss Callie. I've been waiting for you You just missed Mr. Kenyon."

"I did! But I thought you said he wasn't coming home for dinner."

Edward turned his head. He couldn't bear to see such naked feeling in the woman's face. Damn Byrch Kenyon. "He said he had to go to a meeting at Mr. Powers's house and for me to make sure you ate your dinner."

There was a strange lump in Edward's throat as he watched the young woman walk out of his kitchen. Her shoulders slumped the minute she thought she was out of his sight. Edward could see her hands go to her eyes to brush at the tears. Frantically Edward looked around for something to smash. He picked up his coffee cup and flung it into the fireplace. Instead of smashing to pieces, it was a clean, two-piece break. I'm just not the violent-type, he thought fretfully.

Callie lay like a stone in her bed. She was beyond the point of tears. This must be very like being dead, she thought. Byrch was sending her back so he could get on with his life and erase the mistakes they'd both made. She would never see him again, never hear his voice again. She knew she couldn't leave this way. She wanted more, needed more. Memories. She needed one last memory. Just once she wanted to go into his arms, free and unafraid. Even though she would know it was for the last time, she wanted to be in his arms, pour out her love for him with each touch, each kiss, instead of holding it back and regretting it later. Just once, she told herself. Only once. If he would have her, just for a little while. In her heart, it would be a very special goodbye.

Callie slid from her bed and padded across the hall. Her throat constricted when she looked in on Byrch. He was sleeping peacefully, the little yellow cat snuggled beside him. A smile tugged the corner of her mouth. A cat to sleep with when she should have been there, taking her place at his side and encouraging him to love her, instead of pushing him away because she was too afraid to reach out for happiness. She brushed impatiently at the tears in her eyes.

The moon had arched the night sky, and its silvery glow was penetrating the darkness of the room. Silently Callie slipped her nightdress over her head and slipped beneath the covers beside him. *This* was her place—beside him. He could send her away, but she would always know where she belonged, here at his side. This is where I begin and end, she thought, here with Byrch.

"Byrch," she whispered softly, touching her hand to his naked chest.

At the sound of his name, he awakened instantly. The anguish and joy in his voice when he called her name went unheard by Callie, who lay beside him rigidly, ready to run if he rejected her. When his arms opened to enfold her, she almost sobbed with relief.

The feel of him in her arms, the touch of his hand in her hair were so precious to her, and Callie wanted to engrave each detail upon her heart. Leaving him would be a kind of dying, a forever loss, and it was looming out there, beyond this world his arms could create.

She looked down at him in the silvery pale light. Byrch gazed up at her wonderingly, seeing something in her eyes she had never revealed to him before. It was as though she were trying to commit him to memory. He could not go beyond that thought, for her lips were caressing his, and her hands cupped his face, and his joy was so great that he would not allow speculation to rob him of it. Their hands reached for one another, softly touching, sweetly caressing: hair, lips. Rediscovering the wonders, they found those intimate, beautiful differences that made them unique. The curve of a lip, the hollow of a shoulder, the soft velvet of an earlobe. They were like children, discovering new and glorious wonders.

Callie's hands sought the flesh of his back and luxuriated in his warmth. Her kisses followed the lines of his neck and shoulder and she was aware of a shudder of delight rippling through him. A tear rained on her cheek, and he kissed it away. His hands slid down her body, adoring her, worshipping her, feeling the love she offered, and allowing it to light the shadows of his heart.

Callie offered herself to him, willing that he should take her. She wanted to lose herself in him, but she must remember and cherish this time, this last time, when he would take her to those mysterious heights where passion defied the fates and love was heaven's gift to the world.

Callie dragged herself from sleep and realized immediately that she was alone. Byrch was gone. She'd been too late, and it was over after all. Last night in his arms, she'd had one vague moment of hope when she heard him whisper her name. For one moment she'd believed there was love. Turning her face into his pillow she was aware of his scent combined with the spicy soap he liked. Tears would not come, only a keening wail of incredible loss.

Byrch entered the kitchen to find Edward busy at the stove

"Morning, Edward!" he greeted cheerfully, "coffee smells delicious."

"It's delicious every morning," Edward said tonelessly, not bothering to turn and face Byrch. He kept his back turned, his shoulders square and rigid. His temper was exhibited only by the clatter of a pan on the black stovetop.

"Something bothering you, Edward?" Byrch asked, picking up a piece of toast and biting into it. "Delicious toast, Edward!"

"It's delicious every morning!" Edward swung about, only a little startled to find Byrch still wearing his robe. Overlooking the fact that his employer was not dressed and ready to leave for the office, Edward burst into his rehearsed speech."Mr. Kenyon, I'm giving my notice. I don't want to work here any longer, and I don't want you for my friend any longer." Once said, Edward turned back to the bacon sizzling in the pan.

Byrch's mouth dropped open in amazement. "Leaving? Why?" Then one brow raised cynically. "Oh, I understand. Daniel Jameson has finally lured you away."

"No, sir. I simply cannot associate myself with a man who . . . who . . ."

"Spit it out," Byrch said nastily, realizing that Edward wasn't just plying him for another raise but was deadly serious. "What do you mean you don't want me for a friend?"

"Exactly that, Mr. Kenyon. It's not my place to interfere, but I cannot associate myself with any man who would treat a sweet person like Miss Callie as though she were so much baggage to be shipped here and there. In short, Mr. Kenyon, I saw the ticket to Ireland you purchased."

It took Byrch a full moment to comprehend the import of Edward's grievance. When he did, he laughed aloud.

"It may be a laughing matter to you, Mr. Kenyon, but not to me. I also remember how you said these difficulties between you and Miss Callie would be remedied shortly. How can you be so heartless? Don't you know that woman loves you?" Edward blurted, realizing he was beyond the bounds of the employer-employee relationship and not caring.

"I know," Byrch smiled, satisfied.

"You know, and yet you can cast your own wife out of your house—"

"Easy, Edward. Pour us some coffee, and let me tell you something. First, there are *two* tickets to Ireland, one for Callie and one for me. And when I said the difficulties between Callie and myself were soon to be remedied, I meant I was taking her back to visit her mother, who I hoped would talk some sense into her. It was my last hope. My only hope. Why do you think I've been working night and day? Just to settle things at the *Clarion* so I could take the time."

Edward offered Byrch the warmest and brightest of smiles. "Now hurry up, Edward, and get a tray ready for Callie. I want to bring it up to her before she awakens."

That was when Edward comprehended Byrch's dressing gown, noticing a glimpse of bare leg and chest. It would seem Mr. Kenyon had at last done something right.

Callie arose from Byrch's bed and slipped into the nightdress that had fallen to the floor last night. Last night she had crept beside him, expecting rejection and finding his arms opened to her. She had wanted a last memory, and he had given it to her. At least she would have that. That and something more. Just a little something that she could touch and hold and remember.

Brushing tears away, she crossed the room to his armoire. Byrch wouldn't miss a shirt, just one shirt, something he'd worn close to his skin, something that was a part of him.

Her hands roamed among the carefully hung clothes when her gaze dropped lower, catching a glimpse of something. Parting the garments, separating them to look against the back of the closet, what she saw took her breath away. It was a portrait. Her own Rory's sweet face looked out at her.

Hands shaking, Callie gently withdrew the painting. The initials RP spoke to her from the lower right-hand corner. Rossiter. Rossiter had painted this . . . this tribute to their son.

Callie carried the portrait in front of the windows, allowing the early morning light to give life to the painting. It was as though Rory had been captured on canvas, and if she reached out, she would feel him warm beneath her hand. She propped the painting against the bed and sank down before it, huge crystal tears rolling down her cheeks.

When Byrch returned to the room, that was how he found her. Placing the breakfast tray on his desk, he hurried toward her. She looked so fragile, so vulnerable, he was almost afraid to touch her, believing she would shatter into a million fragments. "Callie!" he choked. When she looked up at him, instead of the misery and grief he expected to see, there was a kind of relief, an acceptance, and she smiled through her tears.

Byrch crouched down beside her, taking her into his arms, feeling her precious weight against him as they both gazed at Rory's likeness. He cradled her with his arms as though she were a small child. He did not speak, yet offered her his companionship, his love.

Callie was totally aware of Byrch. She felt his caring touch, the tenderness of his lips resting against her brow, and his silent comprehension of her feelings. She had never loved him more than at this moment.

After a long while, Byrch said softly, "Rossiter had it sent to my office and told me to give it to you with his love."

Callie nodded. "Byrch, I've been so wrong. After the fire I could only think about what had been taken from me. I've been clinging to that loss, that hurt, afraid to love again. Afraid to love you, Byrch, because I was afraid to lose you. I thought losing Rory was my punishment. But I see now I was wrong. Rory was a gift. If only for such a little time, he was still a gift, a blessing. Just as you've been a blessing, but I've been too blind to see."

Byrch's arms tightened about her. Her words were soft, and as always when she was feeling great emotion, the gentle flavor of Ireland could be heard.

"I can leave you now, Byrch, without bitterness. I'll always remember what I've lost, but I'll also remember it with love."

"I'll never let you leave me, never!" he murmured, burying his lips against the hollow beneath her ear. "Don't you know how I love you? How I've always loved you?"

"But the ticket. To Ireland."

"Snoops. The both of you. You and Edward," he growled. "There was an irregularity with mine, I had to bring it back to be changed. That's why you saw only one ticket. Did you really think I'd ever let you leave me? Never, Callie. You're a part of me, part of my body, my heart!"

Byrch turned her in his arms, looking down at her. "Say you love me, Callie James Kenyon. Say it and show me. I've needed to hear it for such a very long time."

Callie whispered the words he longed to hear. Her eyes were bright and clear, unclouded by the fears and apprehensions that had haunted her. She would face life again, with courage and valor. She had the world now and the stars in their heavens. She had it all. Byrch loved her, and her heart was free to love again.

About the Author

For the past nine years, Mary Kuczkir and Roberta Anderson have pooled their energies, talents, and imaginations to write twenty-two books, all of which have been successfully published under their carefully chosen pen name ("Fern" for the plastic tree in Mary's living room that resembles a fern; "Michaels" after her husband and son). They are the authors of many best-selling historical romances, including *Captive Innocence* and *Tender Warrior*.

"Are we rich, successful authors and shrewd businesswomen?" the New Jersey duo ask. "You bet we are! We never stop learning. It's what we do best. Each day we work harder to perfect our craft and to write the best book possible. But, we're still wives, mothers (Mary is a grandmother), cooks, nurses, gardeners, and chauffeurs. When people ask who we are, we say we're Mary and Roberta. Fern Michaels is what we do, not who we are."